© 2022 Independer
(bookisbn.org.uk)
Publication date: 27/
ISBN: **978-1-80068-5**
Author: Phil Burdett
Email: philburd1@yahoo.co.uk
Website: www.philburdett.com
Please direct all enquiries to the author.

Cover artwork by John Bulley

Phil Burdett is a singer/songwriter & poet. He was born
in Bexleyheath, Kent, in 1961. He has been writing &
recording many poems & albums of music for nearly
four decades. He currently lives in Westcliff-on-Sea,
Essex. He is the author of two books of poetry. This is
his first prose work.
.
Also available at www.philburdett.com by Phil Burdett:

RHYMING VODKA WITH KAFKA
(Poems & Prose 1977-2018)

THE POOR RIVER LOST ITS MIND
(82 poems)

All persons depicted herein are unreal

MALEDICTUS

A psychotropic memoir

by

Phil Burdett

...this is for Phil Pavling, guru & benefactor, for his enduring sceptical patience...

PART 1

REWIND

"At the time I could no more believe my eyes than I can now trust my memory."

W. G. Sebald

"I want to be with those who know secret things or else alone."

Rainer Maria Rilke

May it worry heaven – an infant as yet unvoiced & dismal/cute - the big people have swept leaves into a trembling heap by the tool shed & plumped up his mat & placed him in a patch of quivery sunlit grass at the end of the long garden – his bear called bear sits propped against a bottle of sticky warm milk – small nervous birds with tiny, polished, vibrating eyes open wooden beaks to song - melismatic peals of fresh white melody tickle the buttery summerfat breeze – loud sirens & church bells in Lilliput – thoughts only for the bright shapes waved across his eyes – or brisk noises & sensations, brief tastes of sugar – plink goes the piano that is not yet a word but is called plink because that is what they say – try a word for the sun – lelow – but it is not that, it is white as purest snow, mother, white as ghosts

crushed rusks & gloopy milk dribble onto bibs & blankets that return cleansed by an unseen magic - & no dreams at night but miles of cavernous sleep dragging him as the lullaby melody lingers toward a raggle-taggle gypsy who busies himself building a slow light toward dawn

is it a mistake to base a story on a dream? – dreams are liquid - surely the voyage is long & solid earth would be a more dependable anchor – after all there was nothing other than the world to reckon with

or twinkling little stars – just pinpricks in a threat of gloom - how he wondered what you were – if you were a promise of light elsewhere - so high up above the world – something reachable, within the grasp of his probing fingers – valuable, a diamond in the sky, twinkle, twinkle - how he wonders

*

breaking out of mama's blues - the forgetting of her breast & nursing crook of arm – reading stories to him that become familiar to his heart - a vague religiosity beginning to adhere – a shapely altar & fragrant incense & look, look at the bright marble, how smooth - & look, look the window is made up of sunlit motley shards that depict a man draped over an intersection of beams – crux of hate

oh! oh! - but mother, see the tears, he is hurting! – look, look at the blood slithering down the polished glass in gullies of frozen pain, an instructive pain endured for the good of us all – for us all, they said, but how can this be? – codify these beliefs for me, mother, father! - rid me of doubts! – smother them with faith & certainties – everything had names but they took them away - mother, father, where are they? - & where now their cooing assurances?

here he stands & grows fat at the altar muse & yet, despite temptations, cannot bring himself to worship pain - The Great Teacher – for too long he thinks of the suffering of others in these cold, biblical terms – a world out of reach, helpless, the thick leathery cover, the transparent pages congealing with dark wisdom within

*

so onward, steady, goes the drip of life, the wounds & the slow sufferance of malign voices – this vision of a certain outcome far off, a vouchsafed punishment, this world of wrong moves & torn trousers versus 'there's a good boy' – they speak down as if addressing a dog

perhaps he is a dog

it cannot be that this dumb show is how the heaven of his infancy should be defined unless there is an unforgivable cruelty gnawing at the heart of all he is, a cruelty hidden from him behind soft toys & bright coloured blocks – he is nevertheless gently urged to deify each experience without judgement – he has a choice of gods & prophets – or the choice of none

it cannot be – we must return & start again – hang the tree with new fruit, start afresh – where best to begin? – begin with the voices – universal, sudden as winter, the stubbly & perfumed faces crowding above the pram soothing & bruised - reeking of smoke & muttering riddles of an arcane wisdom

sometimes they use no words, just garbled noises of what in other contemplative circumstances, could be construed as encouragement – thus it was that early he experienced waves of disillusion – lights flickering only to dim – the brightness of the primal palette merging to thick mediocrity – the world made a paste of his visions – there were no angels in the branches & even the sun borrowed clouds from nowhere – there was nothing to do but wait & watch as the early years fizzled & sputtered – perhaps the fireworks came later

*

on holiday then, without herald or ritual, he is guiding a vintage pedal car around a street map with unrequited care & precision – his highway code observed, the other cars mounting fantasy kerbs, parking in the driveway of the pretend fire station – prime the mine

or by the coast, bouncing, beautifully out of control, on a trampoline that smells of new carpet & laughing for no reason at each random soar & plunge - above him the sky peels yellow-tinged clouds from a blue dome like nurses slowly removing a plaster from a wound – below the sky's indifferent moods he is engaged in the falsity, the ritual deceptions, quietly announcing himself to an indifferent universe that seems bent on chaos & a blind trust in its longevity

*

here I am

*

return me to that magical time, he thought – a peculiar & dismal thought, nostalgic leanings budding too soon surely? – take me, he pleaded, back along the short path a way, where the lyrical bloom of secretly overheard conversation was seemingly forever sweet – & where, above the cot burbling, moony faces hung in vague pastel blobs – to weekends in the wide, green park where the soil was damp & rich with history – earthworms cut by the gardener's hoe – beetles & woodlice foraging like diminutive tanks across the divots of turf

there was a road – Devonshire Road – that he must never cross alone - & yet he remembers crossing this forbidden borderline holding the hand of his father - but sadly nothing more of the journey survives nor its purpose – perhaps it was a detour before the park – he used to watch his father there as he sat smoking, his rich tobacco teasing, by the lake & gleefully picked wild berries that squashed pleasingly between his stained fingers – spreading the blue juice across his cheeks like woad – crying in strangulated gasps as his finger grew a bulb of blood from a jealous guardian thorn – the bees in blossoms crawling, the dogs chasing ducks by the murky pond - see this all now as clear as day as if it has somehow been replicated on a screen

& yes though all our histories, no matter the outcome, unquestionably hold a blind reverence for youth, the now is always indecisive, the present always worried, doubtful – the past mysteriously twinkling, fixed & unimpeachable – but the source of the light it offers is never quite discernible –

memory chooses melancholy, it chooses to hang its cloak of sorrows upon such trivial recollections of contentment

it cannot be known what vital events were dissolved in these unrecorded hours – the long dead years can only live on through ink & parchment, film & photograph – memory can be tricked, it is gullible & bends to any favoured suitor – dark passages of memorial weight, the chink of sun from a door ajar – what lies beyond? – nudge it wider with a push of recall & there is that garden, the fence, the gate off its hinge – prime the mine

& in a misty, smeared greenhouse, a balding, stooped man in a pale blue shirt, yellow cravat & cardigan, your father sprinkling tomato plants with a tin watering can for eternity

*

Newtown Baby grew plump of cheek & his mind sharpened its focus on the small things - he was learning his noises through noises made by others - for all memories that are old, trusted, that hoard every button of enlightenment for savouring late in life or love, are best understood by small details that can be easily overlooked – it is the stamp of learning & is the only news he needs – those are ducks & these are geese – later there are swans – learn their names & the names of their colours – say them out loud with your voice – add it to the voice of others – there are shadows in the bushes that will not speak quite yet, but in time will be the only voice you hear – a shimmering rainbow rises in the mind & in time mother, father, brothers, friends all begin to amalgamate, begin to merge - their praise for his early, giggling smiles became part of the truth he needed to know – time receding now, time is already preparing to forget you – the stabilising wheels have gone from your bicycle & - if stared at long enough - the hands of all clocks are visibly turning – I is becoming He – milk teeth, baby hair – the closing shift of the skull's continents – need to get tough, little man, toughen up – sticks & stones will break your bones

*

he dreams of water & wets the bed with dandelion wine – he sputters & shrieks as the bathwater tumbles over his head to wash free the shampoo bubbles – the suds swirling around the impassive yellow duck & the flotilla of tossed boats that refuse to sink beneath the vast roll of warm waves that break on no far shore – the comforting smell of towels cooking on the radiator – the forbidden night behind the frosted glass – socks pulled over little piggies going to market – the thrill of breathless anticipation of the delayed tickling scuttle of watery fingers, laughter held in, almost hurting his damp ribs
    & there is a river tide constant in everything, sensed at first in the blood of a body gently forming, that seeks an open sea - & the single life of any curious creature is defined by the widening span of this siren, estuarine drift
    & as night descends from nowhere, the moon is pointed out to him – can you see his face? – look closer, colder, it seemed, but not in any way threatening - a cool sister to the sun, a casually hung lantern – he found the moon obedient to his wishes, an icon in which to confide – yes, it was the daylight that always disturbed him more with everything demanding to be observed, boastful shapes in stark light – above it all the fierce sun, too cruel to approach, no heart beating at its core – no yellow there, just a relentless, harsh, deepening, unwatchable whiteness

*

hickory dickory dock *(gently bounce baby to the beat)* –
time passing in ticks & chimes - up the clock ran the mouse
(run your fingers from your baby's toes to their chin) – *again
a delicious anticipation, a nascent fear of crawling life* - the
clock striking one *(clap once)* – *hit the beer bottle with your
pen & hear the decades it will steal* – *the mouse descending
(...now run your fingers down to your baby's toes...)*
     hickory dickory dockery tickety tock

*

& once, once only, a puppet show – Mr. Punch dragged
across a rectangle of black space atop a gaudy, candy-striped
booth – he we alds a truncheon that harmlessly batters wife
& baby, policeman & crocodile – the rolling madhouse
dream of a Lord Of Misrule, a French trickster – sand soft
beneath him, an ice-lolly dripping blue flowers on his white
sock – the surge of evil children's laughter – he is happy in
this nightmare of dada violence – chubby proto-Ubu,
darkening in fierce sunlight – the big people distant watching
– they are not permitted entry to this cathartic theatre of
cruelty – they smile approvingly as their angels clap each
blow – Punch's shrill voice narrating the brutality, kazooing
blades of justification, the reasoning of psychosis, tyranny –
candy stripes, that dark mouth of horror, passion play

*

his young eyes feeding a younger brain with just enough
– a spoonful of time – a liminal sense of place – somewhere
to return to - gilded by summers, slowed by the weight of
years until each moment is a burnished gleam in the mind
representing a determination of a lost halcyon anarchy – a
few shapes & names, this is all he needs – give him the mist
above a reeking pond distilled – Christmases approaching,

10

blue lights draped over a silver tree that grew from glittered parcels containing train sets, Meccano cranes, cars, buses, chocolates with arcane layers - their exotic, distant names like those of foreign towns - classic milk - purple and silver, peppermint créme crunch - green with silver, hazelnut swirl - pink with silver, classic caramel - light blue with silver, caramel deluxe - orange with brown, hazelnut créme crisp orange with silver, vanilla nougat - cream with brown, white raspberry - silver with pink - say twice their holy names - the rustling foil of discovery, catechism of sugar

*

god was certainly here, in this heaven on earth, if only making himself manifest at the year's end - he sat astride a chariot pulled across the sky by reindeer - he saw no reason to intervene day to day - his gifts meant that you were a good boy - good boy, again, like you were his dog - dog spelled backwards is god - Danny Coates had told him that trick like a dirty secret one day out on mud hill - it seemed important, the sweet strangeness of the juxtaposed words, the delicious trick of language - he stored it away

Santa was the honeyed threat - slavishly he forced his disciples' bowed heads to sleep each eve of his returning - The Newtown Infant complied happily - Christmases, for now, were held dearly in his memory, yet despite this, or perhaps because of this, he later grew sad at the onset of tinsel & enforced cheer that suffused the ever-lengthening prelude to the turkey & paper hats, broken toys & pent-up weeping - yet the ides of a better, purer yuletide remained steadfast in a bubble of time, a gently shaken snowglobe of cryogenic unreality, almost mystical in its ignorance of love

good memories, good feelings, tidings - Wenceslas duly looked out at angels heralding the day, starless nights silent as snowfall - yet slowly they too merged, slithering into a drift of one giant Christmas – stripped of innocence they became mere templates of half-forgotten pleasures – being allowed to stay up late with the big people – watching them they burn slim brown cigars & drink small glasses of dark pungent liquid – the television, incomprehensible now, where once Baloo scratched his itch with a tree & Dumbo sneezed & his ears grew big – the television screen stayed alive for longer & grew crueller by the hour - now cars crashed & explosions thrilled the streets of cities – mother, father, uncles & aunts - all talking differently in new languages over cold turkey, ham, their red faces bulge in the baubles – the tree glistening with no presents left beneath it & the paper crowns on their heads all torn & tired like a joke re-told – prime that mine

& yes this change was only the herald of changes yet to come - flashes of soon-to-be-lost time, already they began – already he feels a desire to go back, way back - until the world is everywhere, replete with mystery & he is tiny & helpless again – the rocking motion, side to side as he is wheeled to the shop on the corner & looming over the lip of his pram that towering clock splitting the sky with a gasp

*

& after the move to the new town came the magical day he was left marvellously alone in the big house, creeping into the big room, the chest of drawers, mordant by the billowing curtains – this mirror, mother's mirror – the first he remembered, reflecting his inquisitive gaze – the dresser with its laced doily, metallic, ornate bowl of tissues folded, fake jewellery, unpolished ersatz rubies set in a basket of tarnished fool's gold, flimsy, dull diamonds like the harbour lights of a foreign shore – she will never see the real thing, the real glister - & in the airing cupboard, tangled around the padded boiler, father's wine-making contraptions – essence of sloe, dandelion & berries of the Essex fields – bell-jars with grey froth gathered at their rabid mouths, tall green bottles of leisurely distilled country walks, pipes, corks, valves, the alchemic blueprint of a dreamy life of alcohol laid bare – the dark lair of a mad scientist seeking the stoned wonderland of the perfect cocktail of mythology – tunnel of trodden grapes - root to the branches of escape soon spreading – the open window allowing the sounds of his own future to drift through the net cotton drapes, refined – sour smell, cheap scent from years ago – the furniture had its own music, far-off, almost out of earshot – singing of time & the fathomless grace of abandoned houses

*

& there was always so much to hear - each new sound exploded in his head, utterly indistinguishable from the thing it described – apple, ball, cat, dog, eye, fox, girl, hat, ink, jigsaw, kite...onward in sing-song, to omega & to alpha return – Pavlovian bursts of voice – Mama points at...BUS! – what's that now?...CAR! - ding goes the bell & sick on his bib – laughing, loose in this unexpected kingdom where even the season's changes are witnessed in incremental motions of temperature & odour – springtime flowers a portent of the coming time of holidays - of warm sand & lush green grass – then, in turn, as you glance away for just a second it seems, worn & weary leaves fluttering to patchy dust - radiant mosaics that have imperceptibly spread over the meadows & fields littered now with conkers, acorns – before another winding of the clock & before the peculiar darkening of each evening as the light guiding his play is absorbed, the circle begins again

he must be cautious - in the clock's full measure he will glean a true sense of the time passed – he looked up from his book at the clock in the hallway that had the pendulum encased behind glass below its face – time, chime – the past filling up behind him, the future, for now, keeping its counsel – the present rhyme – time, chime – if things rhyme then it means something more – a connection somewhere outside the understanding – hear things others cannot hear – this is exciting, somewhere new to visit, to explore, to conquer – he began to dream of the Park Of Fumes as yet unvisited but waiting, beckoning

*

Park Of Fumes, yes – preferably autumn, proud to proclaim its message of death & victorious at its finest hour – Newtown Baby finds his future body reclined on the hillside overlooking his verdant realm – Brooke House nods sleepily in concrete meditation as it watches the misted geometry of a flat roof & cracked flagstone poetry – he loafs idly, plucks an unblown dandelion, pregnant & trembling, dim grey clutch of pappus awaiting a wasted wish – there are office workers doing push-ups on the trim-trac exercise circuit – they assume complex positions of worship on the wooden plinths & groan to nothing – they are a couple, it seems, they kiss - man & wife or boss & typist – their unborn immaculate embryos rehearse a bleat in her gut – spores murmur in his testicles – her womb sighs under the threat of a million luckless eggs – it is not yet time – there is little the season has to say – words drifted from factories to the West & the town from the East - the wind rises, the no-nonsense ketchup North in its breath, he clutches the stem, squeezing the milky sap & rolling it between his finger & thumb – a few hasty seeds escape the nest too soon – apomixes & exile, grip the tide, carry me home – he blows, the way a baby blows out five candles on a cake – more dandelions elsewhere soon, up along the way a little – his children – he swigs from the sticky neck of the Sherry bottle – Christmas,

14

instant, unstoppable – it is not quite that time, he thinks, he is premature, it is late September, the second coming of these lion's teeth & the tinsel is not yet up in the dry heavy windows

*

& yet still that first Christmas was a revelatory moment & one so astonishing that he felt his mind stretching to embrace the surprise – because each stage of learning, every faltering step, is an initiation into a new cult – the lure of mystery – he would gain the heavy keys to the next forbidden chamber, a path to a place that existed much nearer to the mysteries of the big world, an invitation to whatever cabalistic ceremonies they observed in their grown-up houses

& gradually - as springtime once more burns the snow & in the mind of every child the melting forms a pattern - events that once appeared to occur at random are now revealed as a simple cyclical process – he is becoming the, hopefully benign, deity of his newly acknowledged realm – a false god though, it must be said, decked in off-cuts, curtain raiment with a crown of gold tissue paper – no disciple or heretic - a piece of string gathered up & looped into a mock halo, & always in the background the shift from winter to spring, the mud hill, snow melting to the underlying soil, his Calvary

*

& when they put him to sleep with stories of castles & princesses, ogres & knights – it is not nightmares but their secrets that disturb him - it is what they do with themselves in his closed hours of slumber that reels him in – yes, one day the key will be his – the adult realm will be opened up to him – this banishment to the exile of night would be revealed as a cosmic joke, a ritual test - one day there will be the sound of his laughter in the big room - with a full moon through the curtain – one day he won't have to sleep

*

& so he claimed another breath & learned more names for colours - for it was the colours that were feeding his curiosity first & seemed to hold the secrets of this forbidden world – it was important, apparently, to learn the words, to let them know that the lock has been picked – the pupil has cracked the code

the toy typewriter he had been given one year tapped & clacked – the fed paper absorbing all the shapes of letters, the air of finality, authority, how they changed, became strident, when rendered in upper case – the dents in the paper, slight fades in the letters here & there that aged each document in a pleasing way – he once typed a row of Ls & drew a road beneath them so, magically, they suddenly became lamp-posts – pictorial, the letters were endlessly curious & told tales about the whole of time

yes & numbers too, though they were more troublesome - their arcane taboos & incestuous relations – he liked the 5s & 3s best – how the 7 turned its back to the stout cheerful 8, looking back at its past – they too spoke with a deep voice, but they needed letters in order to be heard & would always therefore, in his mind, be inferior

bold & gaudy, the curves & dashes tumbled pin-bright in happy books with stiff musty hardboard covers – he covered these books with strips of wallpaper for protection – glue peeled from his fingers like old snakeskin

there was no forewarning to these tales, no real advice as to which of them were best – he merely chose one for random reasons - perhaps the colour of the cover or the pictures accompanying the words, maybe the way the words were spaced on the page – he read to himself, lips moving slightly – yet he could hear the sounds rise from the printed page - a feral yet silenced music, understood bar by bar - each instrument slowly becoming lyrical

& yes gradually he began collecting the best stories & binding them in a book of the heart – his personal Bible, Mabinogi - his Gita & Sutra – memorised for reference & to bring comfort in harder times ahead – each new lesson enriching the store – learning to live with less of the world, the shrinking outer world, the lessening love

*

& the miracles of discovery were beginning to manifest themselves in peculiar ways – that late-afternoon, waiting for his friend to walk home with him from infant school – he must have been six or seven years old – he stood down the hall from the cavernous assembly room - & there, previously un-noticed, under the coat-hooks, was a small wooden bookcase in which new arrivals to the library were first stowed – he had a few minutes to spare whilst his friend chatted to a group of older boys he did not know, so he idly perused the titles, tilting his head so as to read the various spines – he chose one entitled 'The Giving Tree' & opened it randomly at about the middle – a small crumpled piece of lined paper fell out to the floor – at first he thought it was a leaf - he picked it up & with difficulty peeled it apart, it seemed to be damp & gave off a smoky odour, this led him to think that it must be freshly placed there as it was raining now heavily outside – the writing was bad, cramped & shivery letters with exaggerated loops & all in lower case '...it's not a dream, sail on...'

uncomprehendingly he read it twice with furrowed brow & was about to put it back when Mr. Evans' booming voice echoed down the corridor & he wasn't meant to touch the books without asking so he quickly stuffed the note in his jacket pocket & put the book back on the shelf

& unfailingly - for all these days of wonder - book after magical book would continue to appear on these shelves - no more messages though - a copy of Treasure Island had a piece of string that had served somebody as a bookmark & there were a few scraps of blank paper or folded invoices but nothing as strange & tantalising as that first discovery

still, he loved each new title, these new blessed scriptures without provenance - & it became evident that the worlds saved within the refuges of these tales were not like his world - the children depicted verso & recto - or on the stiff covers - were not like his friends - they carried brilliant balloons in bouquets & owned cute, red dogs that bounced gleefully after them across high-grassed pastures of perpetual summers - dogs that exuded loyalty, with lolling tongues & ears perked to each hedgerow rustle, each exclamation of intent

& these unblinking children, they never grew bored or old - they just stared with expressionless black eyes at him - eyes like the tiny singing birds back in the garden, back when he learned their song, their colours ¬ he tried to imagine these children as his friends, as he took a tiny step & tumbled with them - yes, tumbling is the only word for the way these children were falling - skinned knees tumbling & tumbling through cartoon trees & down rich, pliant hillsides - no scuffed, mudded grass here - the dog in barkless pursuit

there was always a dog - dogs added a gentle warmth to the misadventures of children - cats were wiser, depicted in high places of cool observance, trees, rooftops, often in silhouette, silent & always black, often omens or thrilling harbingers of bad luck, danger - yes, dogs tumbled in an irrepressible now - cats came later

18

& there was forever a river at the bottom of the hill & they would roll right up to its edge laughing & laughing – dreams, kaleidoscopic in the cotton-flavoured zephyrs, softly caressing their sticky brows – a cow moos in a field of tall grass, its stringy whiplash tail swishing through the midges' mad dance – the sky is eternal powder paint & ice cream – farmers lean across thick stiles & chew on briar pipes sending smoke-signals to paradise

& there was no doubt permitted in this Eden, never a crack in this forever, because there can be no allowance for doubt in such primal, vital rushes of joy – just another perfect moment to set next to the last – a buttercup reflecting under the chin – the girls in witchy circles with their odd, warm smell & big eyes winking up – there seemed to be more girls now – tying knots & braids in each other's hair, making dolls speak with alien voices & turning daisy-chains into bracelets with their whispered alchemy – he watched them like a sentinel watched an enemy camp newly positioned on an overlooking hill – he sensed that he did not need to do anything or say anything – things would even out in their own way – he must be patient – girls were cats, they waited - it was their move

*

some days – cloudy days, brittle with the expectancy of a coming rain - he often wondered if he was a character in somebody else's story – had become entangled somehow - was there someone right now watching his adventures? – it seemed unlikely but the feeling persisted that his story was being read aloud by an unseen author – there was no paranoia or fear in this curious sentiment - he had no sense of being observed – heard no calling to rescues or mysteries – for many summer months this aura of unreality had tinged his playtime with troubled musings – it only dissipated with

the tail of the cooling summer's dissolve as the leaves began
turning brown

   he sat on the hard chair in the empty classroom – the
shelf was high but he used the little set of steps – the books
were heavy but he was not surprised – these were big people
books – they were stronger, able to lift more stories – these
pages must sag under the weight of important words – he
would just glance – the glossy sheen, pictures, pictures of
paintings – the text was muddy, not many words
recognizable – women with frilly necks to their dresses,
horses in a dull field, not much to excite him here – then he
turned a page & there, facing him, was a startling image– a
dark island, a boat approaching with a figure in white – the
trees were so tall, the man, he thought it was a man, so tiny –
it made him a little afraid, like the ghost stories his father
read – yet he could not tear his eyes away – he knew that he
never wanted to go to this island but simultaneously felt
himself nearing it, he could put his hand in the icy water as
the boat drew closer to the rock – he looked at the words
next to the picture – Isle of the Dead - Arnold Böcklin –
the dead what? – he studied the words as if they would
give up more information if he re-read them – Arnold –
the man who cut the hedges by the school fields was
called Arnold – he tried hard to think of him painting this
picture, but all he could see was him painting fields,
horses perhaps – brighter colours, no shadow
   he stared again at the artist's second name, looked at
the curious two dots above the O – he looked at the next
page, then the next, then flicked through them stopping at
where the weight of the glossy leaves naturally opened – a
woman, long hair, laying back in a pond with a white
dress, her face crying but no tears – dots of white flowers

in a darkened, lush surround – why was she crying? – why does the cruel old painter not help her? – she will be wet, cold probably, he pictures her laying in the sun to dry her clothes – she is not sad, the hair touched by the warm wind – the painter begins a new canvas

then he heard a door open down the corridor, Mr. Evans – panic gripped him, hurriedly putting the book back, pushing it tight into the gap, he held his breath, strolled as nonchalantly as he could out into the hallway just as the tall figure entered – sorry I forgot my bag, sir – ok, run along – a lie, he had lied, why?

it had been exhilarating – he felt his heart in his chest pumping – the strong smell of tobacco as he passed the dark teacher – the clean burst of air as he exited the main door, bright colours, the blue playground & green field – he looked to see if Arnold the hedge-cutter was working today but there was no sign of him – the trees, thickly-leaved, dark – the tiny boat, the cold water – hair flowing like a gold river - Arnold cutting the stray branches – painting their likeness, brush in hand, beret, don't say the T – be-ray – like the way that painter was dressed in the 'A is for Artist' book, striped jumper, palette in one hand, brush poised – he could feel his hand drag in the water as the boat got closer – the tall trees, heavy book, glossy, the black leaves tight, the dead what?

*

no dog god – no god in the dog – the dog has no – too many bad things in the world – lots of sad things - he had soon concluded that there was not a soul beyond the sky to watch him dumpty tumble from every humpty wall – not even in summer when the sky was everywhere – he watched godless dogs scamper happily, he read his books, calmed his worries with the sweet drift of familiar words – he read of king's horses, king's men & he held them in his mind where they did his bidding – freed from the story – he would, in his cheerfully bewildered head, send Alice on adventures with Owls & Pussycats, off to fight Sinbad & Biffo the Bear, all in his own wonderland of reinvention – they would meet aliens, giant spiders, battle with dinosaurs & evil Orientals in pyramid hats - all desperately trying to put the broken numbers & tongue-twisted words back together again – enchanted words like abracadabras – unwords of unreason, employed to say the forbidden unknown out loud – the golden hair of princesses – the lady in the pond – castles, no god dog peering down in judgement

    & each night these re-told stories tricked him to sleep - every morning was a new page & it gradually dawned that seeing everything for the first time was like learning a language – a mandrake root clambering the tree of wonder, whose own deep root was the very stem of all belief – belief in that witchy sorcery – speech bubbles – knots of problems opening a gift with a tug on the right thread - he went to bed to mend his head, with vinegar and brown paper – mending his head for ever more – breathing in the glossy pages of each newly opened book as deep as a first kiss – sweet leaves, wisdom, it smelled of mown grass, of life – the syrupy, love-lettery dust blown from an attic trunk – leaves could be green when alive on a tree then brown as they fall then grey as they crumble – isle of the dead leaves – that's what – the boat was taking the leaves to die

    it felt good to know this – that he had solved the puzzle of the missing word – felt very good

*

    all around him the wild life pulsing & yet he knew innately that this universe was dimming – replacing flesh with dust hour on hour - it took years for the colours to lose their sheen, colours erasing outlines, their subtle dominance over form – & it seemed for an age everything still sang with light, exemplified in aromatic flowers of many hues that burned his eyes with a beauty that dared his fingers to touch – fear of winter, grey season

but this too had faded, & as the winter no-god slowly became his favoured muse, he had begun to turn his fascination to the logical schemes that he felt resided behind all complex mechanisms – engines, clockwork, the innards of broken radios – he longed to comprehend the vernacular of diodes, ohms, levers, pistons - beautiful, mysterious words that hinted at explanations of power, progress – he became engulfed in the strange language, the irrefutable precision of machinery

he recalled the cine-films his father had taken – the projector whirring to beam out the slides of bright lands, foreign landscapes – or the magical transparencies, little squares of nothing, framed like pictures - each new setting startling him as it clunked into view – each slide an ensnared moment in its own cage, rushing forward in separate, frozen stages as if seen from a train window – & he took them in - though the pictures had no interest - it was the clumsy, cold, mechanical nature of the viewing process that he loved – he knew that at unexpected intervals in the future such images would resurface like dolphins in the surf of history – he was gloriously in their thrall – he could not stop them – the same way he could not, though unsuperstitious, stop from thinking that a black cat passing before him was somehow an omen for bad things to come – both good & evil had ways & means to leave inexplicable   footprints in the fresh snow

*

23

yet there was no real mystery to it all, his teachers said -
just problems to solve, all with known resolutions – a tacit
nod & wink to formalities & rituals – machinery served the
world, it was a force for good – radios burbled & purred -
the television flashed & giggled – he secretly looked behind
it one day to see if the source of this magic lantern was
visible - the label on the dusty back-cover, he recalls - with a
hot breath rising from the grill – valves & solemn ranks of
wiring untouchable in electric shadow – it was clear that the
charades it provided were believable primarily because it
required no effort to believe them – he was happy, this too
was an illusion – content to not understand the cheery
figures manipulating dolls & bears on the screen – the sung
stories & harmless pratfalls – his comics similarly deceived
his reason, albeit in a pleasant, almost conspiratorial, way -
preferring Dennis The Menace to the softy Walter though
he knew he was naughty & got the whack of the slipper –
looking up from the page he eyed his father in his slippers
warily

& yes in a strange way he realised that these characters,
these mad stories, would always be with him – that he was
hoarding these dormant creatures in the nest of his soul
until they were kissed awake by the alchemic lurch of
chance connections – if he stored them up behind his eyes
then one day they will return to sing, play, dance & cry again
– how wonderful!

*

& it was all his own, this strange trip, unbidden, a period
of mental drift – he followed every talking rabbit recklessly
down the deepest holes, drank every odd potion blithely not
understanding or even caring about the effects, reeling in the
dizzying overload of surreality, taken high up into the storm

- so there were two worlds, real & surreal - he felt at home in both

yet there blossomed within him an awareness that these worlds were separated by a chalk line that this steady rain of unreason could occasionally dissolve - parables, fables, mythologies - all of these seemingly invincible comic heroes - were they vulnerable too? - would the dim hours of October Tuesdays claim their sheen?

when reading, as the real world slid away, he began wondering why they were so powerful - these daubs, these crudely drawn heroes - Plug of the Bash Street schoolyard, his name forever locked in the outlines of his mis-shapen skull - scaring the bullies with an ever new unfeasible contortion of his rubber face - they were archetypes of a lost design, cave-paintings reborn as turbulent recurring dreams - jammy handprints of wisdom - smiles of cats that were all that remained of their curiosity - they seemed more real than his friends

on & on, down the rabbit hole he slid & the opening of a curled leaf reveals a caterpillar that wriggled, took colour & burst into gaudy flight - turn the eager pages & brand new adventures begin - Minnie the Minx, The Rebellious Bash Street Kids, The Philosophical Numskulls, The Affable Roger the Dodger, The Elusive Billy Whizz, Tricky Dicky - though motionless on a page, caged in their tiny boxes, seemed to glide & swarm across the paper - he would first look closely at their expressions, then read the bubble of text to hear, in the mind's own voice, the words they said - cool magic - the tripwire over which each toddler falls headfirst into comprehension

*

the voice of his mind - whose?

*

25

& if mother & father stare more & more out of the net-curtained bay window then it is of no concern to him – they await the wakening from their dream while his has just begun - as long as they continue to provide these frequent delightful surprises, toys, books – more of everything, bring it all! – then all this paradise would never change

he loved the cars, the road-mat, the steering wheel on a plunger that turned the back door window into a windscreen - & most of all he liked the tape recorder he got one white, crisp & even Christmas – the next gift unwrapped, a five-pack of blank cassettes – he marvelled, feeling the serious weight of this elegant, solid machine - pushing it close to the radio as it was playing the top twenty countdown – he recorded himself, voice squeaky & not like the one he heard in the real world - he recorded people, the big people – his father saying the word '...helloooo...' in a gruff, spooky voice

& yes when it snowed his feet would tingle & ache from sledging down the mud hill – the snowballs flew & the girl from the other road built a tiny snowman & begged her mother for a carrot for its nose – snapped twigs for arms & two wheels from Danny Coates' busted fire engine for his eyes – remember how she was bundled in a fake fur coat with red wellingtons – he frowned when she stuck her tongue out at him – he recorded her singing a song he did not know - the best bit was pressing the key to play back – RWD – if the tape unspooled he gently tweaked it back with a pencil

the front-room fire had fake coals glowing & the dust when it burned smelled of the past & the frown of things dissolving – when he looked out of the frosty window the people passing by were like outlines, the drawing of Pooh & Piglet hand in hand – he amassed cassettes like rows of books on his bedside cabinet - all his music was labelled, capital letters carefully drawn on thin-lined stickers – the hinges of the cassette case always broke – the bedroom floor was full of these plastic nodules – he felt them beneath his feet at night before sleep & they always reminded him of catchy songs, of beach shells, stones

the radio was harder to control, it faded, blustered & became confused – the recorded things were better – he reached a stage of proficiency whereby he could go back to the exact point in a recording that he wanted to hear – a song seeped into his essential core, he memorised the chart positions - the voice of the DJ reciting the litany of titles like holy scripture was a vital part – radio voices were holy - they would fill the air at the click of a button – it was a time machine full of melodies – a magical factory canning the can of sweet, glamorous wizardry

& his dad said hello forever until one day the tape wore thin & snapped – he remembered the frightening silence – he sat staring at it unable to comprehend the loss – where did the music, the voices go? – he stared out the window for a longer time than usual – the chains of the swing had been wrapped around the frame again – the snow was melting

*

a sailor went to sea, sea, sea, to see what he could see, see, see – dream sailor, dreaming of sailing, no matter where – no fear of the hurtling wind & walls of dark water – ever forward, reeling, searching for sunken treasure & glimpses of a better adventure - but all that he could see, see, see was

*

a dream, a dream that will tell him that all of this time of wild, happy turmoil has a reason – he first knew of its weight one morning – suddenly waking with a gulp of air & for an instant still only seeing vague images, shapes that had steered his floating night

yes & in this dream a vast ship is loading with busy crew & cargo, setting course for a distant land – a galleon, built to drift forward endlessly through temporal seas – respecting no physical chains of cause, it rolls impossibly across land & through the hollows of mountains & hills - immense in scale & portentous of import – vast sails billow, the deck wood shiny, the scattering ropes & calls of the men as they haul, biceps bulging, trunks & bales across the dockside air – the year is unimportant but there is a sense of antiquity – there is a grandeur in the ship's great age, a respect due to her stately frame - a galleon, a schooner – these were words that fitted the bill, words he had learned from pirate pages – relics of a lost language, they lend a heft to the vision of such vessels – each night he sees it – big as a city - it is moored in the East India docks of his father's London, shivering in a clinging mist – he sees the gulls dance around the newly painted masts – he sees how, with only the slightest inclination, the sails tense & suck breath into their lungs – he feels the maddening pursuits of the north winds – but most clearly of all he sees the crew – steadfast, weather-beaten souls, trudging steadily up the creaking, knotted gangplank – he will come to know them like long lost kin - all the old prodigals - their faces, mirror-bright & yet reflecting nothing – each facial twitch imitating his uneasy nocturnal trembling

so it comes to pass that the outline dissolves – fantasies have invaded the real world under cover of sleep – from now on his storybook grows obscure, for it travels by hurried river & steady sea - each word tangling with another in the rocking hull as it breaks new waves - & all who are to inhabit these tales, written in his heart, in his impending book of lies, are gathering here - they are all of his own

making, would not exist without him - clambering aboard in
single file with easy tread
    all except one - the one that is not exactly missing & yet
not really here - occasionally audible yet never visible - a
trick of the ear, something almost eavesdropped, an almost,
a perhaps - a solitary word scarce made out, whispered from
the gust through a cracked skirting's timber - usually
uttering one yawning, open word, a vowel loose on the
clustering shadow - too indistinct to demand a reply - that is
spoken only by His voice & he knows of its worth without
ever asking, trusts it without questioning
    & tho' this conjured boat, this apparition, is never
really there, the crew are still duty-bound to its passage -
diligently, up the plank they stride, to the rich oak deck
scrubbed shiny like the floor of a school gymnasium on the
first day of term - first & eager always, a creature the image
of himself through tender years, he hears the melody of
each called name & owns it from that moment - his name a
part of this voyage's manifest - Newtown Baby, he becomes
it, embodies it, there & then - fresh as love, gurgling, milk-
toothed & rosy - he is preternatural - the forming voice of
an emerging new stretch of language - volatile as ill-mixed
gases - vibrant as a struck tuning fork - a quivering needle
facing true north, a churn of winch & pulley from the
dockside - cries of stevedore & common labourers - all of
this his fantasy replayed nightly to a baby of the new town's
dream & consequently his tale must be the first to be told

*

    a scrapbook of loose polaroids - sequential - his heart
creating a linear story to connect them - images born from
chemicals interacting - pattern recognition - strung on an
invisible line of thread blowing gently n the breeze -
picturing the picture - visiting the old sweetshop dead centre

in a canopied row – chemist, off-licence, barbers, then his treasured palace of sweets, haberdasher's, bookies & lastly the grocer's market by the subway entrance – the door had a little bell, ting-kling - succulent, nauseous air, smile of the confectioner, slight, wary - The Sour-Faced Newtown Baby purses his lips & scans the colourful delights beneath the perspex lids – dusty jelly babies, sherbet, electricity on a blue-blooded tongue, snaky coils of licquorice, chocolate tool-kits & coated banana foam – the packs of footballer's cards scented with bubble-gum – savers, doubles, swaps for the playground bartering – they are more precious than money, the currency of a dying faith – saintly names printed beneath their icons, Perryman, Beale, Chivers, Gilzean, his team – just needing Jennings & Knowles for the full set – card-stiff pages of bad haircuts & awkward mugshot smirks – home, he would spread them on the rug by the three-bar fire & marvel – after securing the new batch of beloved favourites with paste, he sorts through the remaining rogue's gallery of mystics & villains of other rival teams – Hurst, Stepney, Chopper Harris, Fiery Bremner & St. John – he would walk, hands deep in a red, chequered, fur-collared coat, blue & white striped scarf knotted at his Adam's apple, across the concrete bridge to the park football on Sundays – distant church on a hill embracing the slow cloud's lambent shadows - bags of sponges & ointments – the shivering players cupping sneaky half-time cigarettes & cut oranges sucked & thrown to the slimy grass by the white touchline – groundsmen, flat-capped, pushing the white lines around the muddy rectangle, blob of penalty-spot, bereft of the last vestige of green – jigsaw cracks in the baked, crumbling islands between the cankerous iron goal frames

dark, oily netting, a fisherman's snag – onion bag – gathered with the corner-flags at dusk & stashed in the silent, wooden hut at the haunted field's edge – mesh, stashed – the words were cousins none of this to be forgotten, merely mislaid – a small, unexceptional trunk in a somnolent attic – its key found by happy accident in a search for something he believed to be more interesting

yet every glance can trigger a newly plucked chord on the soul's harp - every day rescued is a tear welling but not yet fallen – the sound of a kicked leather ball drags him back to this innocence of play – pick a side, pick a colour – white plays blue – shrill whistle, begin

*

& on the way back home to moist, slow-roasting meat & lugubrious gravy, a tinny voice suddenly, through a speaker, up there, on the builder's ladder – the sound waves transmitted into forgetful air – they swam around his face turned skyward & percolated in his frozen ears

"...good fucking morning citizens of this inflated, ill-fated little blue ball - it is a Tuesday - if you are an observer of the Gregorian calendar that is - & I'm your host outside of Time itself, Miles Ducat, here with the latest wireless-driven gust of causal phenomena to help you distract yourself from the low-grade grind of the everyday machine – today's year is '66 so here comes your headlines & deadlines, folks – stop the presses - the aliens aren't here yet & there's a river of fire in the heart of the desert & guess what? your parents & the government were right about everything after all – Ringo is the sexiest Beatle & Freewheeling Dylan still walks a windy Volkswagen street with his folksy girlfriend forever – Nobby dancing, the orange ball in the onion bag six times – Bobby hoist the golden prize aloft – however sadly, due to poor visibility & severe winter conditions, the spectacle that is the twelfth Elfstedentocht skating tour in the Netherlands is a fiasco – Sylvia Plath suicides in sad old London – aw, I'm just making it up now – this is a secret channel remember,

31

just for YOU baby...weather, the big thaw begins, first frost-free day since the recent wintry weeks began – Philby gets his safe asylum in a government flat in Moscow – another child goes missing in guilt-ridden Manchester – an update comin' on Einstein's Relativity Theory, you see? The time doesn't matter here, we go our merry way & all of history is a concertina – play whatever tune you will – Michelle by The Fab Four - we'll bring that to you after the weather forecast at the top of the hour – close your eyes & we're back in the first year of the yet to be swung sixties – only a lonely decade ago, time-travellers – but hey now, let's have some music now to soothe the beasts in your rotten, Jehovah-forsaken, collective souls - here's Connie Francis..."

*

the bottom of the deep blue sea, sea, sea

*

in obedient hush, in file behind Newtown Baby, the crew padded slowly across the deck of the dream ship - close behind & jaunty of step, possessed of an easy touch of sallow confidence that had yet to be stained by the bitterness, the arrogance, of his sadder, later years, stands The Lonely Troubadour idly strumming a mandolin – from his back pocket a flute protrudes – below deck other instruments sweeten in his cabin of many-colours – a willing pupil of history, he seeks the corners of the world where indulgencies can be found & misdemeanours are seeded - made fertile in strange soil – clear eyed, ebullient, his firm jawbone hidden in brazen, rude flesh – there glistens in his eye a star the light of which, though it could be just a nascent teardrop, he will be drawn toward as truly as a moth gathers itself to fire – his mouth clamped tight on a rakish cigarette betrays a slight smirk of gallantry, a sureness, a resolve – he is to be trusted as an anchorage in the teeth of the dark, unknown storms to come – a bulb of heart, healthy but blackening in mousy chambers of cheap smoke – breathe this foul dock worker's air gladly, me-hearties, for beyond the ship's rail there be strong liquor & petrol fumes by way of chaser – ask a child of the city, any city – but don't ask The Troubadour, he fears everything & feeds on the fears he engenders in others - converting them to the energy of song – blue eyes slightly askance, paling to a shimmering grey in winter light – over time his secret music has made him unimpeachable, heartsick & aloof – the world spins below him on his string, merely another planet, dull to the touch of his bare feet - he is only an outline, a rough preliminary sketch – still a follower, supplicant to the true prophet, the unblemished mystic – his future incarnation - the wily drunken ghost that calls his enemies friends & calls himself Captain

*

Captain Rehab they had christened him, the old wild salts of the ocean, telling fables of many drunken hours in bleak saloons the wide world over – now he barely touched a drop, save for a touch of heavy spirit when the night stretched its paws or a different rain fell – he cared little for how they prattled their legends or whatever legend they chose to call him - his real name, the name his mother wished upon him, was long lost, way back, like a cigarette tossed from a rainy car window – he knew the name, though, like he knew the voice of dusk, fearing both

Newtown Baby slumbering on, twisting with the wind through his dream's taut sails – he tries to focus upon the Captain's face, to bring it closer in his fertile night-watch - & Lo! - there he stands, feet splayed, almost silhouetted against the gloomy recesses of the wharves - forever at the beginning & end of his life's never-ending cycles - peacock proud at the top of the boarding plank piping aboard his former selves - he stares wildly out over their heads as they bow beneath his gaze, afraid to catch the eye of this grisly titan, the icy, calm embodiment of their fate - a rainy face hanging beneath a battered, dusty hat of Whitman - leather biker trousers scuffed & ripped - cocksure & steely of soul - the persuasive appearance of one who has travelled every contour & latitude, seen it well, conquered it all & twice over - a honeycomb of badges decorate the lapels of his tunic - one for every mad campaign, strip-show & funeral attended - badges of every shape & size, he collects them in lieu of memory, as pirates notch their kills on masts - he slides a gloved hand into his shirt, Napoleonic in profile but twice the height & girth, a fever-dream of Napoleon fashioned in rough oils of nightmare by his sleeping, fearful enemies - though he is prone to lapsing into brooding, melancholic fugs, his pride ekes from the sweat-silvered creases of a face hewn in oak - from his pocket peeks a blue telescope & on his breast a battered silver watch-chain - thus both vision & time are harnessed - when angered he is insatiable, his voice demands attention like a squall of wiry feedback from a dropped guitar - he puffs out his chest, lights a green clay pipe stuffed tight with the wild skunkweed of the shaman & takes his place behind the solid, wooden wheel - his cockney bones of coral, his pearly mince-pies - why sail out when what you seek is behind you? - full fathom five their harbour lies like submerged houses awaiting a mermaid's pillage - in the streets of downtown Atlantis the bell for last orders rings - ding-dong - hark! - now he hears them — ding-dong - the seahorse bartenders hourly ring his knell - the abstract jellyfish plot their Miro course through planes of drab colour - hereafter all is fluid, a feather on a river, flux of possibility & charm - the wheel tested, gripped fast &

wrenched slightly to gauge its resistance – he is both his own
destination & a prince in exile – the last human that poor
Newtown Baby will become – the last eyes through which
his soul will see the dimming world – the end of his dream
yet to begin - ah, me

*

& what was the source of this recurring dream & the
immense sadness of it? – a few dramatic pictures in nautical
storybooks? – the glimpse of new roads, unchartered water?
– the deeper worries that daily bloomed like black roses in
his verdant, Elysian fields? – he let them play out, these
fairy-tales – each night he took a deep breath before closing
his eyes to the window framing a tree-streaked moon, before
his ears closed to the downstairs chatter of the television &
the ticking heartbeat of the hall clock, its patience, its soft
muted tolling – he would always wake up safe on dry ground
– the waves, slow in their sure determination, receding as he
dressed & steeled his soul to the glimmer of a fresh morning
– many hours to go before he set sail again into the
dissolving line, smeared chalk in rain – hopscotch without
numbers, stones falling on the empty flagstones - & he gives
himself willingly once more to the dream as it unfurls its vast
tapestry – the lady lays down in the dark water – a store of
dead leaves in the hull - the sun now balanced at last, rising
in the mists of the Thames, the dock placid & morbid with
the grievances of cranes as they swivel to the day's first task –
the crew aboard, Captain Rehab closes his eyes, consults his
heavy book of maps & breathes in the madness of distant
tides – he knows the powers that ache behind the eyes of
each of his shipmates - these are not shanghai-plucked
landlubbers, unsalted & sunblessed shunners of Neptune's
druggy wiles – no, they will chew on stinking tobacco cud &
brag old yarns with the hint of kelp on their breath, fingers

35

raw from snake-slip of rope – their guts steady as a spirit-level through each forthcoming wild pitch & spiralling wave – though each of them, man & boy, are legendary & locked in their capsule of suspended doubt, they nevertheless hold the dust of all ages with respect - they know too well that forgotten remains & live embers alike hold fast to a soul in transit & render each dusty handful thereof sacred – they are sifting the holy dirt for old friends & unborn foes – it is dust that is the crumbled flesh of the dead – a dust that they seek to tamp down & yet yearn to rekindle – they never asked to be remembered thus – they know too well that they are stowaways on a fabricated galleon fashioned from the vivid air of a child's fancy, sending postcards from their points of vanishing – they require no grail, no promise of revenge - no impertinent whale haunts these surly Ahabs - for none of them shall e'er grow older than they are right now, fixed in amber - nor do they recall how first their fates converged & all of them came to exist at the whim of time played out by this Captain

listen now, as he sleeps them into being - as already the first disparate shanties begin to coalesce - listen, for it will be the collective voices of this crew that will chorus the unholy fables from here on in – voices mingling to one constant mantra – a softly breathed curse stretched & spun like a web across generations

*

turn the telescope slow across our chartered course - I am having a visible day - today, I can be observed – twelve years old perhaps, no older - so be it - the streets of the new town are damp & when I reach the playground it is a minefield of puddles that dance with reflected clouds scudding across the colourless sky – yes, the other children can see me today, see my face, in which can be discerned my uncertain mood – they can see my expression as it shifts to another more sombre than the last

a pigeon gargles on the guttering of the headmaster's roof – the white bulb hanging between grey curtains – the noise of the bouncing ball – two sweets have wriggled free of their wrappers in my blazer pocket & are sucking at my slow fingers – sticky peppermint cream in silver foil – once inside the hallway there is a galaxy of rich smells – floor-polish, chalkdust & cloves – a constant murmur as of disturbed birds, an unceasing percussion of feet on wood – I know instinctively that these things will remain with me more than the myriad successes & failures of the day – the teacher's dry lessons are rendered null - everything that is said to me is being erased – the blackboard wet from a damp sponge – the dust of words now haunt the air – the chalk is put back into the wooden box with the sliding lid – I breathe in the atomized powder & wait for the bell to ring – Arnold, or somebody nearing the end of their life's maze, has swept the leaves from the playing fields into fluttery, neat mounds & the wind is hiding - safe behind the poorly-built wall of the bike shed upon which, in felt pen or soft chalk, are written the loves & hates of a hundred fleeting puberties - – the leaves are motionless & curled like the hands of supplicants – it is only when autumn appears that the bad voice once more springs from the mind like a geyser – it seems to become more strident in this breeze from the classroom window, to relish the change in the colours of the trees - yellow to green to reddish-brown, then stiffening to a crackling laughter that swims on the eddies of coming Christmas – it is then that the guilt settles on the heart – a morbid guilt felt keenly by these wastrels, knowing they wasted their innocence - as a billionaire burnt money to light a cigar – I tilt toward that open window's breath - the heavy, buttery voice of that guilt, sickly & strange – the worst voice of all that chatters without purpose or resolution – it speaks of things we, the young, should not hear - it is urgent, persuasive - gluey phlegm in its throat like the crack of an accidental snail-shell underfoot

Newtown Baby sat on the school steps, three down from the top, & thought about how his mind still carried the confusions of past days even in this tranquillity - he tried to find the right word, the correct answer - he let his meditations snuggle down like blossom, no longer restless in the eddies of the wind's surging - if dust could speak, then it would sound like this, he thought - perhaps, he thought, there is something to be learned from dust in all this hurtling world of duty & play

*

a cardboard shoebox with air-holes bored in the lid so the caterpillars could breathe as they grazed the tired lettuce & stalked the tufts of grass & dock leaves he had plucked from his father's lawn - his father now, behind the smeared glass of his greenhouse - pruning the meagre tomato plants & moistening seeds in their beds with judicious drops from a small metal watering can

later in life, when walking in rich woodlands, the odours of that hour came to him - as if time had chosen its essences raw - a freshly opened pouch of tobacco - the smell that lingered in an empty tea caddy - biscuit crumbs on a window ledge - yes, it floated into his daydreams when he himself was surrounded by children running, laughing - the old man in the greenhouse, shirt white, black tie tucked into cardigan - he, for now, merely observed - but there was, even without him understanding why, something permanent, something that lingered, something that something wanted him to record about the tableau before him - my father, he thought, my father hoses the lettuce in a tray with water - he looked at the word 'hoses' in the

38

sentence he had written – where did that come from? – he had used that little, beaten-up watering can – his father watered the lettuce with a tin watering-can – that was not right, somehow – how? – he tried a few more versions but each time it was this first coining that resonated – he left it as it was, this was *his* language, *his* way of remembering – hoses – it conveyed how he felt despite containing a distortion, a lie – his father had coiled the hose around a bracket on the greenhouse door & it was a vital part of the scene he was describing – why describe it? – there was something about the sound & the shape of the phrase – for the first time he had created a fiction, with its own set of secrets - first egotism, first cryptic code, first poem - he smiled curiously & underlined it with his thick pencil – this was a moment of dust, a clue withheld from the rest of the world, this was something he owned

*

yet they came out of that dust, these grinning children, through streets of three-wheeled shopping trolleys, trampled cigarette packets & torn, wet packaging, bright striped & malodorous

on & on & on – blue smoke from the old chimneys that stayed in the mind long after the sad houses crumbled – stodgy, squat buildings of porridge-coloured granite with bulging floral curtains in bay windows – the little pyramids of attic rooms that once stretched across the view from the omniscient church on the weary hill - now only uneven squares of   flat rooves divided the ribbons of potholed streets – their geometric certainty, rigid perspectives, narrowing the eye, better to focus upon distant pools of rain reflecting the oblongs of the dull municipal huts

buses rumble by, Lowry queues of downcast ciphers – buses that wear their destinations on revolving legends

above the sweep of thick wipers – the drivers milling at the depot café, milky-eyed, offering only cantankerous snarls & rippling conspiracies of football & workday politics
    yet the dusty children still head north – the true point of escape – zeal for exodus, their intuition as guide, freshly decked in their battle-dress of choice - fluffy chins, leather, perfumes & face-paint - their clutched, sweaty tickets to the promise of rides on a timeless circuit kept tight in their fist

*

    I heard you speak of childhood – a lost one, perhaps? – yours?

*

    above the school, almost painted on the crowing heavens, The Church Of Santa Claus – chocolate-box haven of Saint Nick, after whom the school was named – harvest festivals, with sniggering blasphemies secretly shared through frowning gauzed windows of blue & orange shards – ache of holy splinter – dead-meat gasps - Old Serious Jesus high, bloodless on his perch – outside the sanctum, a dour silence in the creased fields of mown grass – single file, up the crunching pathway through the tombstone guard of honour – the double-file pilgrimage swells to an impatient swarm as late neckties are bullet-knotted around grimy spit-washed throats & almost tucked beneath inky collars
    after the service is mumbled & duly ignored they return to the profane schoolroom once again - they skip through swung gates into the slate-blue playground, chalk symbols from forgotten games – devilish pentagrams – geometry of Beezelbub - etched in Aztec vectors by gods of hockey & netball – like windsocks the limp baskets hang torn atop rusting poles – the guttering above the headmaster's room

40

that leaked forever, clogged with bird-nest & thrown mud –
above, a sky full of dark gods drips slender ropes of blue
rain, as a shrill bell slices the yawl of voices & the birds stop
singing
    into damp queues of last year's friends, & quickly now,
because of the coming weather – pulling anoraks over slimy
hair in the big reverberating hall - cathedral air of heavy
polish, holier than the old church – the threat of being
summoned in assembly gags the throat of the settling rows
of untucked children – nose-fingering in wan beams through
chalky dust windows arched – the morning lecture, litany of
accomplishments & disappointments, more dust for history
to devour – Newtown Baby watched the cold child-breath
that everlastingly hangs & swims & is only rendered invisible
by sunrays, curl around the beams of the dirty ceiling –
forgotten balloons from the school party sag, withered on
crooked nail by the door's frosted fanlight – the immutable
stage curtain always not quite drawn - showing a vaulting
horse & two brooms leant awkwardly against a rickety
stepladder, a bright yellow wall with a red bicycle leaning –
this hall whose scope in imagination swells - where atonal
school musicals rang out – morning prayer,

ourfatherwhoartinheaven
hallowedbethynameinkingdomcome

    a hundred cheese & onion voices intone – the damp
smell of woollen sweaters & bubblegum – the gentle creak
of woody oak beams, the moist haunting of air tight with
angelic surveillance & stale choir-breath lingering after
countless sermons – that bicycle

thywillbedoneonearth
asitisinheavengiveusthisday

fat piano fingers, the closed piano – opened for hymnal
– unsure of the tune but all voices have that monk's lilt – the
sad falling from grace notes – yellow wall

ourdailybread&forgiveusourtrespasses
mumblemumbletrespassmumble

the many school musicals enacted here – understated,
monotone renderings – Guys & Dolls he did – a gangster in
an over-sized, blue, pin-striped suit – the summer-cream &
ghost's egg for make-up, it creased in his old-young squint –
the roaring lights sweating down on Brylcreemed slicks of
quivering guys & glamourous cheeks of rose-petalled dolls –
stubby gangsters slapping racing form & the mystic names of
the litany – Paul Revere, Equipoise, Epitaph – Harry The
Horse right here – masters & sons of the distant painted sky
of America – hoof-heavy steps of mobsters & clerics -
formerly shy classmates now wise, cracked actors in balloon
suits – toy machine guns, plaintive voices shrivelling in the
unfamiliar ocean of notes, that plink of prison piano as they
sing, sing, sing out their getaway hearts - Brando-cherubic,
Sinatra-tonal, grinding out quacks of sweet-hewn, unbroken
song - to chime over garbled twists of rimshot rhythms, the
piano, yes, always, always the cumbersome rumble of ivory
– counterpointless fingering of black notes, a collision of
anomalies, accidentals

forthineisthekingdomthepower
&thegloryforever&ever

the red bicycle, yellow wall – the assembly had dimmed
to a low-lit soup of shadows & murmurs – a broth of
indistinct sentences from which the ear could spoon its new
path, its chosen obsession – words could be anything –
Newtown Baby stared at the red bicycle & browsed the

yellowing pages of childish croons - once the questions are
understood the answers begin to fall into place, the only
frame was the rules of his own making, it was his beautiful
conundrum, they were his astounding words, they just need
to be fitted in, tiny corpse-words, buried in soft paper with
his digging pen

*

amen – let it be, an eternity of summer days ago – the
tribal mercenaries fled the school gates chased by a clanging
bell – they escaped the dark school for a forever world of
eternal, joyously mindless, knee-skinning holiday - porch
tiles hot, the old mud hill baked, a rough pudding of caked
sod to roll down & down in coughing, pig-pen dust – all the
plotted conflicts in the trees & bushes - dry squawks of boy
soldiers – twig guns & his best pal, Al Coates – stoic actor,
playing the head of the bad guys, the Kommandant Coates –
he had turned up one day in a real tin hat, borrowed under
sworn oath from his older brother's motorbike - Germanic
& terrifying, it glinted its unforgiving authority in the Nazi
sun
Newtown Baby had been a sniper high in 'the war tree'
– an easy to climb, leafy hideout that became almost a
second home all that generous summer long – the very top
was accessible & offered a panoramic view across the play
area through the camouflaging greenery of summer leaves –
the enemy would usually approach from the west, scuttling
between the thick bushes that ran along the cycle path &
approaching the tree from behind the swings – every day it
was somebody's turn to die – every day we, the fallen, rose
anew
those burlap, sackcloth days - unspooling with no record
of ever really passing – as if they were ready-made ghost
memories, already being scrapbooked & their hours

43

lengthened by magnets of a longing, far, far off in a distant time – days almost ripe to be forgotten, now rescued again – spirited away from that immense hall of slow learning – away from the sound of hushed teachers flitting down the polished, squeaking aisles as outside the winter rain fell on the prison gates – a low prayer for the bad results, the frowning report-cards, the failed crop, is learned by rote & recited & the pitter-patter roof applauded with the last Spring rain – the brassy release of old music, old costume - grandad-suited in end of term derangement - almost drunkenness, a happy drift of the last easy lessons, the kind of delirium that precedes the throes of the bottle's oblivion – the mood was flexible, ready for the heartaches & rushes, ready to be flattened by the ballast of apathy or sharpened by ambitious knives – stirring the pot of warm days, a warty, witchy brew, waiting on that holy hill to begin the slow slide down

*

& here we are, sailing serenely through the supposedly treacherous waters of puberty with rocks thrown down upon the deck from all sides – here, the weather is relentless, a squall of susurrated menaces, both far out at sea & ashore – but the mood of the crew is light – shanties & ballads break out & collapse to mumbled memory - slowly their clothes darken & tighten – as if they were transparent maps draped over a continental shift, delineating the skeletal longitudes of their search – they drifted easily in a benign providence

there is a radio in every skull yet the music they listen to is tame – it whistles through their life leaving no trace of melody – they shuffle through vampire evenings in which every conversation is stalked, hunted down, in order to be drained of lifeblood – sucked dry, to be spat out with the flavourless gobbets of chewed gum, on the paving stones

44

these miniature plastic sculptures are the pale, twisted, gnarly embodiments of their discarded opinions – resentful nubs of petulance, precursors to the satisfaction of the cigarette - each popped bubble from a girl's mouth releasing the ectoplasm of boredom

who among them looks the oldest? – singing, come buy my wondrous taboos! – but there is nothing that really stops their progress – no police or ship's warden - their daily rebellions are petty & confined to the vagaries of nominal friendships in continual flux – life is ordered, considered, rejecting the old for new – the drug they seek is stimulating not palliative – heads full of rivers running wild, a rolling cerebral avalanche of disinterested silt – every so often one brave soul breaks out, he senses that every task or action has consequence, is not innocent of a possible underlying ill-intent – & he hears an inner voice, previously unknown to him, hissing to be careful, think before you play – he is confused by these burgeoning tendrils of guilt now rooting through the soil of his green world – he is not alone now, his steps are counted by other fingers & by other scales his heart's weight is measured – he is considered, accounted, he is judged

*

judged! - yes & soon there will come a certain rhythm that will be irresistible – see that boy swig that bottle of sweet stolen cider – see another flick that wave of gelatinous hair from his brow – shiftily hanging by the fountain in nervous packs & tapping their metronomic forefingers to the pulse of something imperceptibly rising – it is a forbidden music they have been longing for – sleek, oiled nights are spent fine-tuning bursts of anger through a transistor radio's crackling pop - eavesdropping on the anthems the long, broken, sad old caravans of migrants & refugees from the distant sonic

battlegrounds were peddling – the dense, erotic threat of
morning coffee brewing – radios talking but never listening –
eventually tuning the dial to other planets where growling
fuzzbombs throw flinty sparks in acoustic shadows

*

& his father would call upstairs when the beat reached its
terminal intensity – for crying out loud, are you bloody
deaf? – so much dependent on crying out loud – he
wondered what that desperate phrase meant – it had a
strange compulsion, a sense of some deep truth at the core
of its apparent vacuity – he tried it on his friends, they
laughed – he did not know why they laughed – how could
you not cry out loud? – cry inwardly, a far-off, muffled howl
like a wolf or the coyotes in the westerns – occasionally he
would say it to himself to see if he could see the humour or
the meaning – it was just some words, though, a string of
words that may as well have been wooden beads for all the
wisdom they allowed – he turned the volume down for ten
minutes then increased it incrementally until his father cried
out loud once more

*

at this time of growth, becoming, love recoils - knowing
that resentment is the only required fuel - the punk flowers
emerging in steel & whimpering ink - steel pre-fabulous
schoolhouses that they occupied like prisoners-of-war or
mathematicians trying to decipher codes – the fading
teachers scratched their signs & equations on the squeaking
board to no avail – they had lost their allure, these mysteries
would never be fathomed – the class floated like a boat in
autumnal mist through the yawning days with bleak stares &
detentions spacing out the hours – spit-ball paper arcing in

46

the bored air – minds slowly ebbing to family dinners - meat pie, mashed potato alps overlooking gravy lakes, the black bubbling lava brawny under a limp crust, peas bobbing like drowning sailors, primary wads of jelly dancing in willow-pattern bowls of chequered ice-cream – then the news, the soap fables & tomorrow's brave new world – Sunday is the worst of all – a dreary slithering cavalcade of church pews & fast-talking old film stock punctuated for one glorious hour by football – watch it as if it is happening now – yesterdays spent oblivious to time - if you don't want to know the score look away now

    & every teatime was a Sunday all of its own – church-heavy & respectful - all the time knowing that elsewhere in beautiful, spartan bedsits the smell of sweat from jobcentre queues & the estate boys with vinegary Christmas aftershaves climbed the corporate step-ladders to nowhere – their slick moneymaking plots turning in time to bile in the throats of freshmen, the poor graduates fumbling in the trenches for footholds – like kids playing war – do ye want to come out & play war? – you know someone was always the first to die – clutching a heart-wound as he rolls down old boot hill – or fell like a plugged Comanche from The War Tree

*

    on & on & on – ride on, young whelps of war! - their mettle winter-hardened & cascading downward on a man-made sledge over readymade inclines – laughing – pure smiles under rednose & clownish cheeks – it used to sting like hell to stare & he had to stare until he reached the bottom or crashed sideways laughing halfway down – always the slide down, down - scooping icy slush into his ruby red wellington boots as he slid

*

& when did you learn all that you know now? - try & remember the colours before you learned their names - do you? - black is the first colour then a kind of blue - can't say it, yellow - leh-yo, or lelow like hello - sharp colour, too risky & blinding - yes & remember how the lelow chalky girls always used to covertly draw their skipping pentagrams - hopscotch enigmas - the rolling pebbles landing three times on six - taking the left hand path or the right - the dichotomy solved by the luck of the stone - clap clap clapclappity-clap go their soft hands to the impossible counterpoint of their chanting - *Malleus Maleficarum* - arcane knowledge, don't ever ask - hear their song, frog & newt's eye, they will reel interminably across his years like a pot-stirring hag's vicious omens

*

a sudden joy remembered from a quiet station bench- Newtown Baby - learning the tricks of a cassette player - click - muddy music forlorn, crushed - click, hold down to record - whirr back in time & click again - unruly spools of tape spilling out like intestines - ridged pencil hopeless & the blunt, clumsy screwdriver too thick - all is corrugated, lost - click - forlorn it left him & crushed & denuded & silent
the early pop songs' sirens reaching the shoreline of Newtown Baby without touching his inner ear
no doubt lost to history now - geography too - we are contemporary in our pleasures, never noticing each fad as it dissolves - as well to try & bite candy floss - the songs had a yellow tinge, they drifted into his life through cracks in the weather, the summer-strung hiatuses - music was all music was & unlike children gathered no dust, had no enemy

*

dusty children yes – whooping & honking like wild geese chasing small dogs up the inclines of a mud hill, staring out across the ersatz parkland to the industrial rectangles & the mysterious stout bulb of the Ford spring-onion water tower – chasing small dogs back down the inclines of a mud hill – out of the dust, always grinning – on small-screens, after the cartoons, mobs hurled bricks in grey rain in a land called North

friends whose names are now unimportant, friends that are forgotten like mud scraped from boots, or snow melting by a two-bar fire from stiffened gloves – cold as the wheezy nothingness lurking below our brittle sanity - whither the snows of yonder old sledging hills? - in winter hoary, in summer beautifully bronzed but always the well tramped-down domain, wet & glutting the drainpipes with ice - the sledge runners divulging roiled grass & worms torn asunder ne'er to repair despite the stares of a scrum of willing eyes – thought you said they live on as two worms, Jenny? – serpent eat thy tail & shed all claim to mortality

yet it is this plain mound of greasy mud & charmless grassy clumps that he remembers most of his early gathering places - a ceaseless freewheeling go-kart of memory, still to the same old calamity blithely trundling – nobody at the bottom of the hill to arrest the progress – nobody waving as he clutches the handlebars, stolen from an outsized bike, for all he's worth - the shuddering wheels cling to a crucifix axle – Mackay following on his old bicycle madly – shreds of trouser-bottoms savaged in the oily chain – feet push the pedal that in turn turns the wheels – turning away from that summer of mad treasures - treasures that somewhere still burn brilliantly - a votive candle, piously replenished, for it is saved, vital, holy

*

49

remember, remember & remember it all - everything &
nothing could be relevant - so his eyes constantly scoured
the waking hours for signs - he felt a constant anxiety to
gather up in the little wicker basket of his heart the small
things that helped thrust each minute into the clutching year
- he roamed evening streets of the nondescript town with
his, fiercely partisan but benign, gang members - stern-faced
regiments of cowardly soldiers with that brethren bond that
combatants have - siege-headed, all for one & one for all -
yowled surnames served their purpose, names attached to
the soul with the fixative of trust - Mackay, Tremain - faces
that will always stay young & mud-smeared - they were
reliant on the comradely oath - sardonic, fresh faced
warriors in an underground struggle against adulthood -
against sugar & spice & all things that girls & their limericks
& jingles threatened - sauntering the late evening roads
these comrades marked their territory, their school jackets
emblazoned with the sewn badges of dull yellow in imitation
of past gold - incomprehensible imagery & tired Latin -
discoloured with the filth from their wars - other schools
beware - the absurdly proud schoolmasters may as well have
issued fatigues, billy-cans & tin helmets
    Newtown Baby sighed an ancient, moaning sigh, even
then - deeply knowing, yes, even way back then, that this
was to be the only dominion in which his reign would gain
purchase - & how these potholed, asymmetrical plains
would slowly erode any wish for adventure latent within
him- it would sate the craving for any conflict or journey for
epochs hence - he often stood atop Mud Hill gazing past
the dull greens & browns of the Park Of Fumes out to the
muted boxes & stately chimneys of the factories out on the
industrial site - with his tired eyes he could see the defeated
rubble of histories, in his mind's eye, cities yet unexplored,
laid waste by unknowable atrocities that he had obliviously,

puzzlingly outlived – did something, some part of him endure from older years? – the question was unsettling but constant, like a river rolling under a distracted city

yes & sometimes when drowsily walking through the new-town's peripheral woodland a certain mad purpose would grip his heart – a sense that perhaps there is a reason to fix these pretty hours in memory - because one day they will be useful as well as decorative, serving as a temporary balm to an inconsolable misery as yet mysterious & distant – the streets, shops, churches, all whispering of their mortality, of their passive surrender to change

scuttling with his rattle of street mice under the subways that led to the factories – inexplicably but appropriately festooned with murals of animals, dinosaurs - that, one day, would put his pretty daydreams into a mortar & grind them to ash – haunted, those dinosaur, animal subways - where pre-teenagers were already kissing awkwardly with hands deep in insouciant pockets – love with a backdrop of wild beasts & extinction – they learned the lessons of a lessening love, not in a classroom, but nervous, in cinema queues - rendezvous kept, eyes downcast – one day a princess will come by here &

& what?

*

whither the stick-gun-clutching, second-hand, khaki campaigns in greening boughs of luxurious War-Trees? – these performances already partly forgotten now that the real circus has come to life – shaken awake from narcissistic dreams – what is the use of playing? - in the mirror behind your bristly face a new clown stares – cue the music, 'cos every fool knows that all comedians go to heaven & all musicians go to hell – especially those black, head-hung-low dudes that adorned the blues & jazz record sleeves in

51

smoky, knife-cut silhouettes nursing the sweet horn's curve
& bell – louche boys, fat with jazz urges, stopping time in the
finger-clicking street – freeze-frame - looking sideways at
girls, follow their skinned knees as they clamber up trees &
who knows what goes on behind abandoned garages? - pull
down your pants for a penny chew & lift up your skirt for a
sherbert-dip – go on, ask her in your borrowed bad-man
voice – hear that voice now, listen – serpentine sibilants hiss
like the wind through falling wings of angels - Adam bribes
Eve in the garden out of earshot of their master's command
– bribery of first lust – confessionals & guilt rouge their
cheeks – sin alive in the godless playground as the church of
ice-cream chimes on every street

*

& yes, each gang had their territory mapped out –
unwritten treaties drew the borders in crayon - Newtown
Baby & his acolytes used to hang around the parking area
behind his parents' house – a row of private garages -
pudding-leather footballs rebounding thunderously from
their ridged steel doors – mercy shown to no swot with his
Walter-soft head in a fusty book - chary mercy to the weak
for they have inherited this infertile earth – you pursue the
lost things, the hidden rules, the supposed wisdoms that still
will not save a single pleading breath – there is no joy in
your searching mind & the commandments are homemade
& malleable - oh, don't dive like the goalkeepers dive
because the concrete is unforgiving – climb every lamp-post
but only so far – reel in the joy a little
    & the faceless local council, in their inscrutable wisdom,
declared that the new, new town must have green spaces,
where grass meets water & the trees curve – darkling landfill
mounds & the imported wildlife – the high-stepping, stately
bird's evening regatta – & even though he knew it was all a

sham - it still opened infinitesimal windows in Newtown Baby's heart - he was willing to believe this plastic beauty providing it was the scene of his changing - it would all fade soon leaving only the impression of grandeur

another day another swig of cider & the weekend coming on strong - Mackay lacklustre - throwing pebbles at the keep off the island sign - the low gossip of homeward traffic - the rushes & grasses at the contoured, arcing shore - all his words were unwritten, forgotten mostly now - laid eggs of conversation fertilised by alienation - one day, through poetry, hatching in the unwitting mind years later - he had become the town & the town was like a train, eager to leave the station, waiting for the signal

& above it all the church of Santa Claus - black as tar on the bleary hill - peel off layers of unquestioning devotion - gnaw at the sap-moist flesh of the white truth laid bare - church song mute & bells never rung - the party-hat spire rudely points at god

stare from the bedroom window at nothing changing - the boxy modern houses, the tailored patches of garden - even the white sky hung above it all like a tarpaulin, unchanged for all eternity - the starlight never circling - ancient clustered sprays of night foam, focusing the prisms of your idling hours - the weak light, dead for centuries - postcards from a mythic, sunken island - yet with each sip these inanimate ciphers replenished - the boredom began to sing

the realisation dawning that alcohol is the key - the twist in the Moebius strip - one side, one boundary curve - the illusion of progress - through its devious twists he will travel, through the morning fog, to the fading sun of opening hour - they would live as ghosts that passed through the concrete of life - they vowed to drink longer, louder & spend every holy bursting night sanctified & stoned under the garrulous starlight, forever questioning the silent ghosts that wafted from their futures – palsied revenants, blue-white, the ominous thunder in sanguine dreams

& he used to see ghosts all the time back then, mostly up by the old church of Santa Claus - dissolving, splintering opaque forms awaiting the transparency of heaven – these were real figures to him, becoming mist to set themselves drifting free, hearts stilled in the shock of an abrupt unbeing – or ribald old saints back for another bash at the sinner's gong – destined to fail again, to flop back underground to the sniggering worms - was it such a saint that this young/old man's memory missed? – it was as if his whole life so far was an act of pointless waiting, expectation – false Godots up on the hill – here comes nobody, arms akimbo, anticipating a flatulent kiss – breathing the dead sky in a walking blur of dreary hallucination

there will always be ghosts, he believed secretly, there will always be an England – for her history is the future – the myths of hidden bloodshed – the carnage of victory & pillage – he needed to immerse himself in the huge belly laugh of its misbegotten past & drive out its demons – by accident of birth a patriot - yet aware how, beneath his feet, the soil disintegrates & slides into - that ultimate goal - the patient sea

*

ah, joy! – back then he could get lost in bright mazes of innumerable joys - & whither the day guided him so then his feet followed – all the while observant of how the girls played with the girls – the boys, serious, sullenly watching – as the rain made whispers in the thin trees by the bridge in the park

& how the chimes of the ice-cream van united the warring gangs like a summons to peace – ears pricking at its first bell & all football matches or wars halted - scrambling home to search for pocket money in school trousers or deep in the biscuit-crumbed ravines of the sofa - listen, how those angular bells expand as the van weaves toward your heart - the happy parallel to Larkin's mordant ultimatum - all streets, in time, visited - in time all faces reflected in the sliding window of dog-eared stickers declaring lollies & ices in faded hues - Fabs, Popeyes, Oysters, Wafers, Choc-Ices, Zooms, Lemon-ices, or the luxurious & almost sinful Mivvis - bright as a quick fragment of chilled rainbow - the shadows thrown by the whipped cream machine - the van vibrating, warm to the touch - in which the shapeless, dark, hirsute man, easing the turd of cream from the silver tube perfectly every time, speaks soft vowels of broken Italy - his voice dripping lemon-ice through his Mediterranean burr - he leaned over the counter beaming at the cupped hands full of silver & copper or reaching into a mysterious cave to clutch a spray of milk pop-ices - tear-frosted with a waxy taste

a religious silence descends as the crew devour their spoils - almost unwilling to ruin the spiral of vanilla already sliding down the wafer to his fingers - Newtown Baby rapt as he slowly licked it to a pyramid as the cone cracked, oozed - later the garden & the radio perched on the sill of the open kitchen window - watching father as he taped up the handles of his bike - or tanning stones as he watered the flaky roses & sprigs of daisied grass

Newtown Baby scrabbled for enough coin - never enough - sometimes his father would give him a five pound note to buy a tub-full & - in the fenced off summer garden beneath the hung washing - he watched him shovel migraine scoops of snowy ice-cream into glasses of bubbly cream soda

*

55

after school the juniors would mingle - in cool dusk,
descending slow, sparrows whistle & blackbirds caw - their
sharp klaxon note mingling with yelps of children tangling
themselves in the climbing frames - drowsy minds aching in
lost fogs, the six hulking stone chess pieces out back of the
house, visible through the net curtain of his bedroom
window - their pretend Stonehenge – druids drawn there as
evening beckoned, the dripping cornets smudging like
candles over pudgy fingers gripping – the weakening sun
holding close a promise of nightfall unwinking in an orange
cloud-bed - behind the houses, beyond the garages, the
chess statues' immobile stone held their mystery whilst
snagging the loose hems of cheap grey school trousers –
each monolith a violence of compacted pebbles – the
concrete of here & now that will not stir & skins blue-pink
knees & elbows – plump fruity orbs of P.E. bags adorned
with wiry epistles, rude biro declarations of love – stitched
from old curtains or leftover remnants by mother - they
hang inverted, sweat-soured Mussolinis in the tieless
afterschool rapture - a heart, crude in chalk, on the redbrick
wall – Jenny's name pierced with a crooked arrow – his bag
of leafy design, mocked by his classmates – but he liked it &
welcomed the mocking

*

joy is not a word overused in adulthood - where did it go
& again who cares? - is that your question? - I do...I care –
he is I – was I – he speaks to me in old age – me, here, now
– beyond even Old Captain Rehab's span – the joy is weary,
the children are beginning to disagree - they bicker like
hungry starlings – some want a change, are changelings –
others sense a safety, an exile in the park's bucolic man-
carved greenery – soon they speak in tongues across a great
divide - the piss Christ & St. Augustine arguing over dead art

56

but all too soon the crippled claw of times foretold
throws a malodorous duvet over such crayon mornings – yes
& soon the sunlit bliss is a piss-yellow saviour drowning not
waving

he read a book on Egypt from the school library & was
duly entranced – so much more than a tall tale, these old
ways, bright colours, pictograms unknown – it bred in him a
love for codes, rune & sigil, the desire for an alchemy that
could set an ancient fire to the teacher's parched, chalky
mathematics – the twisty algebra foreboding – these were
graffiti auguries of a different, distant conflict – mummified
curses that suggest, cajole – eye over pyramid, silent sphinx

it became a relief to read elsewhere – to escape the four
walls bedecked in crayon artworks & glittery angels & find a
less-travelled path - yes & soon will come the day when his
education becomes a means to a dull end, a preparation for
the big life beyond the gates - drag of learning, the weighty
sackfuls of potato books over neanderthal shoulders – aged,
burdened, inconsolable, drooped – wayfaring pilgrims in
pursuit of unwanted knowledge on the guilty homeward
path – he would find his own chalk & write on the wiped
slate in quicker, portentous colours

*

homework began the decline, or detentions to copy out
the mantras of obedience – exams, the knowledge beaten
into ploughshares – reams of rote scrawled in the crook of a
billion inky arms - three pages of illustrated Egypt &
captions stolen from an encyclopaedia – plus, minus &
division – two chapters of musty Hardy, the candied
precisions of Yeats - or Lear & his slouch toward madness
on the foolish heath – from madness he proceeds to lunch –
Tupperware box clouding, milk & two custard creams &
half a Mars Bar solid from the fridge like the geological

strata of a chocolate epoch – work half done before a last dive out the darkening door for late football - or war-gaming - or careful cars pushed through mud – time before dark, time yet – soon the dark will be what calls you out further – soon hairy skin & nervous heart – across new, endless playgrounds of an inexplicable & thrilling lawlessness – passing adults who all know the terrible algebra & do trigonometry in their balding heads for fun - & have jobs in the suited, booted city - & all the useless children of the dole generation left standing in gaunt relief against the dystopian backdrops of scribbled stone – unthrown punches twitching in thrusted pockets – sour blotches for frowning mouths - ragged twists of bled colour in grey slushy roads

*

one autumn day, one brackish lake of an autumn day, he found a fly, dead & husked by the rays of the sun, on the classroom window sill – he poked it with a wary finger – this, he mused, is irretrievable - Janus shows his other face at last – & speaks hesitantly of bad things, worries, sadness to come - yet never changing that measured tone of voice – benison to omen - that voice that must remain, constant in narration, insistent, throughout life – it rises in the chalkdust from numbers that these professors squeak on to the pristine ache of the board - smiling fives & beak-nosed sevens – the confounding vectors & venns that lord over the wastelands of learning – dead flies wherever he looked now – collected in webs or piling up on window sills, they could no longer be unseen – they were the big lesson beyond all other schooling & forever outlined the blueprint of his nascent philosophy – every dry husk a full stop to sentences that brook no argument & play mean god with the very existence of god

*

    & Captain Rehab grips the ship's wheel a little tighter –
the docksides growing smaller as the huge vessel dragged
away - saddening in smoke from the warehouse fires that
line the shore - peering through the elegant shadings
masking the gentle lapping of waves - he lights his pipe &
conjures his hermetic childhood one last time – torn images
repressed in a photo-frame – wreaths of quelled mirages –
he knows the vast mass of the ship beneath him as it eases
from the dockside in aching degrees, imperceptible inches –
knowing that soon it will be gone forever & given up to that
rushing grave of deep loss – his heart is barely in the game -
a threadbare pump that thuds in a cage of old rib-bones - a
tired lover knocking on the door of his beloved – it has
weathered pain worse than mere memories allow – what
could childhood possibly have left in its leafy bag to scare
him with? - still he will recall it all now & will duly weep a
little later over its litany of desolate trials – wash it in rum &
swilled ale

    & although he begs his better nature to go easy on the
detail & not to let this burden of years lessen the authority of
the mind –he prays yet louder to nowhere & no god duly
answers - still, his very essence craves a respite, a relenting
mercy, an amnesiac drift into seas of passing doubt,
cleansing & rekindling – a sense of drift but a drift with a
purpose, a vocation undisclosed

    but no, once more the bitter remembrances rise in
blood-red fog – through the fissures in his resolve they
slither despite eyes screwed shut - you would think the
rivers of tears had by now long dissolved these poison pills –
in time, he would finally fashion a moat around those
haunted rooms of the past in which envy lurks & where
anarchy, twisting the meat of the heart, is mistaken for the

last, faint palpitations of hope – futureless, it is all he can know, these intimations of the past

& here they come, sure as sorrow – old trysts, devotions, embarrassing liasons, love-letters & goodbye notes hastily scrawled - pored over for long sleepless nights – in his rootless mind, as he steers this ship gently through the yielding waters, one by one the unrequited lovers gang up & threaten to violate his peace

the first unbroken heart always the wickedest, the easiest to regret – & yes, yes now he remembers – remembers it all - how she wrapped small fingers around a red handbag & - lunchtimes, twice a week - could be seen plaiting wicker baskets in the extra class – tiptoed at the window he burned inside for her black hair bobbed & green eyes concentrating on tricky loop & weave – her dextrous fingers are bony worms eating at the pulp of his raw lust

& he is back there, entirely, all at once, in that remembered palace of doubt - at the window, unseen, he watches her, & watches his younger self watching her - swallowing his rampant heartbeats that drummed a thousand longing words – heartbeats drenched in lunar motives – it is too late now to stop the fall from dignity upon which love insists – all the reticence of old age rendered useless as the recollection plays out like before, as it ever will on this ship of disremembering - he is there now, young again & manacled by that very youth he sought as freedom

list! – whimpers of bitter joy still escape the Captain's lips - as through the miasmas of time he eyes the only love he truly craved - here she was & remains, unchanged - framed forever in mullioned orbs - this voyeuristic, yellow gaze of a child – flitting from pane to pane, trying to find flat glass for a clearer view - for every blue reflected distortion ruins the contours of the angel – it is a shy heaven she inhabits, unknowing & beatific, allowing no suitor's gaze –

she is a beautifully posited question with no response, his first examination, his last prayer

*

& he wanted her to see, but don't see, no, don't turn or look up, just let me, let me forever watch & be watched, let no heathen prise the forgiveness from her grasp, let down your hair Rapunzel, I scale these citadel walls, O god in heaven let it be me that...
that what?

*

white on black departed - feathers soft on skeletons - warm words free in the twilight music room where Newtown Baby mouths silently the lyric to the stories yet unwritten – the sliver of oily disc plops to the revolving mat & revolves, the stylus arm swings jerkily then drops in turn to light the flame
me shell marbell – song day monkey vontray bee end on song – the old radiogram rectangular & voguish on the swirl-pattern carpet in his brother's room – spindle drop - kerlick - one splat disc on top of last & somewhere this scratch appeared – electricity & danger now floods in to the repeated groove – Newtown Baby grew to fear this song like a repressed guilt – strange world of broken silences, sound not sound – unsound – it drags the crow of omens 'cross the moon - black on white departed – white stylus arm too quick - black disc wrong speed – uneven, unequal, unsound - beware of the tigers – beware of the closed eyes that bring her into the picture that the soft melody evokes - *I love you, I love you, I looooove you...*

*

o god how he loved her - god, no less, loved her too - words fell over themselves in his mind in their eagerness to be thought - the trance that she induced by each motion of her head thrilled & moved him beyond the edge of tears - how long did he spy on her as she weaved her little baskets? - forever, perhaps, for he still looks on her now, the Captain sad in recollections, unblemished in memory - unspoiled in the kaleidoscopic window - he did not care who loved her before or after, though he would not want her to have to endure a love less than his - & often he dreamed her into a convent or outcast on a remote island & it shocked him how he hoped for her loneliness - how religious his nightly contemplations of her became - how even the Sunday, slow churches on his lone walks reminded him of her quietude - deepening walks to unpopulated old parts of town where his head became a kind of temple to his mad devotions - the sculpted breasts of angels in the crazed arches - bat-flapping heartbeats in the vaulting domes of his skull - snakes of doubt whispering across the atrium looking for unmoored graves

she is constant, running through his body as a hunted animal screams through a hushed forest - still the old Captain sinks deeper to the vision, back in time, he inhales the window as if her scent would pass through it by force of will - he vows never to forget this - never to blink for fear that he would miss a moment - to love her for all his life was his secular prayer each night, the mantra spinning the wheel of their shared destinies - Newtown Baby saw her every night before troubled sleep in his here & now, his there & then

but the old Captain sees it in the gript, useless eye of the mirror - like the specks on the dream ocean before him now, though he knew them to be passing ships, he yet willed them to wave, to acknowledge his ardour, his voyage -

longing for that first time, that glance that demands a million others, when there seemed no barrier between happiness & eternity

*

& then she was gone

*

& days began to shrink as shallow pools of life gathered in the gutters of dull roads & pretended to be more than reflections upon death, more than just his increasingly downcast gaze looking blankly at things & storing them, labelled, away in the relevant drawer with the dust, the pencil shavings & erasers – an unexaminable life that worried at his sleeve, like a tetchy infant it demanded wilder conversations & new colours – childish innocence gave way to an oblique, entropic sloth hung with ignorance – all his friends slowed imperceptibly as if a film reel was losing its power – friends who had been the rough surfaces that keened the day's blade when dullness reigned - whose marmalade fingers sought a hand with which to entwine – on some dark days such as these he saw the immense skies frown & heard the thrum of traffic murmuring secrets or threats, depending on his humour, & their voice made him able to pick out the spots of joy, the little blessings, meagre fare but vital too & he began to see a different set of possibilities & gradually lightened his heart, using the darkness to appreciate the cracks of light &, for a while, carried his burdens & cares lightly for the first time
but there were still days of disillusionment, days when the torpor of his imposed routines won out over any rehearsed enthusiasms & as the daily perils manifested themselves in tiny, almost undetected defeats – fear grew

like a permafrost creeping - bristling in palpitations & goose-flesh - rising to a phantom crossing his future tomb - as this misconstrued life, this incomprehensible journey unravelled - it was a beast that he could no longer control & inevitably, as in his favourite story of that time, Frankenstein's handiwork rose & began to stagger

*

Newtown Baby, saddening, at last spurned the wisdom of the big people & flitted through his own day-shadows – flitted through calendars that no longer held the future captive, his casual diaries were not ever vouchsafed the mettle of his love – the pages remained vague, idly doodled - ink-stained, tarnished & yet somehow, to him, beautiful as a book of hours

& in time his rebirth became known - & the Newtown Baby Troubadour is awkwardly paraded around bewildered classrooms to perform like a freak show for the snot-sniffing inmates – soft nylon strum & pluck – Amazing Grace as a hesitant instrumental – *sotto voce* grunts from behind upturned, graffiti desks – he remembered being transfixed before them all by the inkwells & pencil-cases, exercise books & multi-coloured pens – he trilled his baby gospel uncomprehendingly - how sweet the sound in memory failing – a wretch unsaved, once found now lost to a blighted, secular sorcery – once all-seeing now colour-blind & in debt to the woodcuts of old magic, the lithographic spheres – his graceless, amazed notes melt & suspend in the stifling broth of a labyrinth of gravy-coloured hallways

*

& moving slowly - inching fist over fist up the scholastic rope-ladder – the lessons grew less lovely - ritual reigned over magic – every subject was physical education - run, jump, throw, compete, compete, win & win again – to come second is to lose – the bullet-headed teacher, pommel-horse as a lectern, reading the sprint times out with sadistic relish - or wonky-faced Mr. Josephs with his Yorkshire puddings of verbal alchemy sliding from his distorted mouth amid suppressed laughter – a constant baiting, kept just below the simmering lid during the weekly physics & chemistry classes – Old Wonky Josephs limped & lisped – spit flying from his distorted lips - he glared at each slight tittering & involuntary squeal – & piled on his cluttered desk the heavy books full of curious, incomprehensible symbols, arcane & destined to be forever inscrutable – incantations represented by graphs, runes & algebraic streams of hexen consciousness – the dark codex of an deep odious well – mystical calculus was constantly scrawled on a smeared blackboard & wiped clean with a swoop of the duster before it could be even vaguely comprehended – the answers left as hanging motes in chalky air – Josephs' fist pounding on the desk to command yet more amused attention – he raged inwardly & probably drank alone in mordant pub snugs for Dutch courage & weak solace - a portly, unkempt bastion of quiet ridicule - blubber of Ubu, pens peeking from a breast pocket – where did he run to after it all became too much? – the residents of more merciless cities await – somewhere hence, his shade still drifts through a reflective hour

The Bored Troubadour knew these equations would never truly scare his sleep – a tune that had stuck – tinny, transistor-brittle, from an early passing window flung – it seethed in his shiftless brain - he watched her, front desk, not laughing with the others, not looking up from the text until Old Josephs drawled his next languid *ko-an*

The Zazen Troubadour waited & hoped - he didn't know much about history, less about biology – but he did know that he loved her & if she had just said that she loved

him too – why then! – what a wonderful, wonderful world it
would have been

*

Frankenstein walking now, the audience tense with
suppressed terror – why do you recall the dust from the
school projectors so vividly still? – even the grim pedagogic
air in the old cine-room – the floating accumulation of
cinematic powders cannot fill his lungs with new language –
projected motes of illuminated horror – the teacher wipes
the board & rolls down the screen – the top marksman, the
star-child, the giver of milk – only he will be honoured to
operate the projector – it is wheeled from the cupboard like
a birthday cake

*

& came the sacred day that his father deemed him old
enough for a tour of London, father's old haunts, Oldtown
Baby's kingdom – the family did not go on many outings
together, the occasional holiday abroad – they had taken him
a few times up to Southend for a kiss-me-quick day out with
sandwiches wrapped in foil & flasks of tea for the beach –
but this was a real expedition, just himself & father, they had
hardly been anywhere just the two of them – perhaps to the
park when he was younger, he couldn't recall – & yet here
they were, setting out from a waving mother at the netted
window to the station & right away there was the excitement
of awaiting the train on the opposite platform – they were
not going to the sea – they barely talked all the journey, his
father muttering mainly about the change in the passing
fields – he described the huge east-end docks, the cranes &
the pigeons of Trafalgar Square – a promised tip up the
monument – there was a monument tube station! –

Newtown Baby's head could not contain the idea of the tube & had no idea what The Monument may be but it was all thrilling beyond words – the fields coasted & fused under pylons shifting their perspectives in a delicate ballet – open green squares subtly gave way to warehouses & stockyards, wooden pallets stacked in awkward piles, oil drums & things bulging under tarpaulin in the service areas of unnamed factories - twisting pipework in gunmetal shades emitting white steam – finally, after dragging slowly out of Stepney East, the buildings loomed taller – smoky houses & glimpses of connecting streets – shops, flats with hanging baskets of blue flowers slid by giving a tease of urban everyday life – workmen digging up the road, here for a flashing frame then gone & rolling easy into the next slide

Newtown Baby's heart almost stopped when the train suddenly plunged into the tunnel before Fenchurch Street Terminus & emerged, creaking & complaining, in a gush of excitable clatter as it subtly traversed the points, out into Fenchurch Street Station, vast, all-encompassing, lurid as a bright new dream

*

the commuters – a wash of hate across their faces fixed – dirt smeared on the huge station clock that beat to the rhythm of their workward trudge

*

after the trip from Tower Hill, the great ivy-clad edifice of the outer wall still impossibly huge in his mind, they travelled a few stops to Monument tube station, up a heavy iron staircase & out into the noisy groan of the capital morning – the prosaic, solitary Doric column stood before them dead centre at the end of the street – Oldtown Baby told him it commemorated The Great Fire – this he recalled vaguely from a history lesson at school & at the time had wondered why it was something people needed to remember – fire, root of fear – exothermic release - carbon dioxide, water vapour, oxygen & nitrogen, all is alchemical – the traits of the pyromaniac that our mean monkey minds never quite outgrew

climbing the steps to the monument, clinging to the big hand of his father - for maybe the first & last time, now he thought about it – he sensed, as they ascended step by careful step, a growing emptiness behind the old stone walls, a decrease in pressure, subtle yet unmissable – on reaching the top he dared not step away from the safety of the solid structure of the tower – beyond the laughably flimsy iron railings huge old London spread itself shamelessly like a painter's hired whore – domes, spires & steepling brickwork nestling in shinier swathes of metal & other angular multi-coloured blocks, all infested with worming strips of scuttling cars, maggots rifling a huge dead beast – the sun choosing where it landed, green patches & mud-brown clumps of woodland – his vertigo receding slightly now, he focused on the grey strip of the river snaking into a mess of hazy nothing in middle-distance – he imagined being one of the myriad dots on its bland silver ribbon – a mote of history ignored by the metropolitan thrall – he felt a calming subservience to its gravitational tug & ebb, as if he could swim through the colourless air between – he was in a place knowing neither progress nor inertia, no crow's flight, no circuitry – where all moved yet evinced a motionlessness both trapped in hours & transcendental – if there were ever such things as angels, he supposed, they would glide these eddies far above the hurt – mute guardians of a coughing planet who, via its burden of joys & exaltation of all sadness, welcomed the sentence that this judgemental water bestowed – he thought of the last time he may have held a

parental hand – his mother this time – on the jetty jutting
from the beach just past the pier – warm estuary wind,
unusual for September, brushed his closed eyelids tickling
the lashes – behind him the coast exhaled a breath of chip-
fat & candyfloss – the gaseous flotsam of toffee apple
choked the airstreams – jingling amusement arcades, bells &
klaxons from the fairground rides

& yes he gazed out now across all the yearning boroughs
of a mutating city &, letting go of his father's grip, took out a
pen & wrote two bold words on the back of his now useless
Laindon to London train ticket that he had secretly kept -
perhaps as a souvenir for a vague scrapbook he planned to
compile or his school project

the biro wobbled in his hand, the wind & his fear of
heights was all-consuming but the resulting legend was more
or less decipherable

sea/me

& once more closing his eyes, he was again back there
on the jetty - he had picked up a tatty feather discarded from
a weatherworn gull – he tucked it into the band of his cheap
straw hat that he had bought with his pocket money – he
had walked around nervously at first, aware of the odd stare
from amused passers-by, the feather, it felt good in his hat,
he thought - & he remembered how later that day it had
blown out into the sea whilst he waved from the pier at a
tanker bound for the refinery – he was not sad, he
understood the feather could not be kept too long

opening his eyes wide - back on the impossibly high
monument tower - he sneaked a look at his father to ensure
that his attention was distracted by his own tall thoughts &
tossed the used ticket over the edge on a sudden whim – he
had expected it to fall, yet it swam magically upward on a
capricious draft & butterflied out into the panoramic space

& - only when it was almost invisible - began descending, flittering, spinning down & down toward its unknown destination - somewhere amid the tangled Cubist planes of the dappled rooftops & funky Mondrian roadway boogies & woogies - he thought of it as a message in a bottle, unsigned - his unanswerable cryptic quiz to a crazed world viewed from his heady idea of heaven - a simple declaration of unity - sea, me - a poem to the vacuum, an ode to rhyme if not reason - his first unpublished juvenilia, set free as a bird, far from dull lessons in the school of dust, it was a poem that learned to fly & belonged now to the wind's caprices & the city's roar

*

school of dust, yes - a grey mass of children that crouched in scarred fields, a prison of ancient heavy thought wherein the burden of learning was something to be carried stoically, no matter how weighty - but London had seized the innate gladness in him - he must lose the dry knowledge of musty classrooms & find language in life that soars - that could be etched like his poem on a falling page - his friends & family seemed rooted, their ambitions stopped at the gates of dreary factories, their thoughts weighted by routine & commonplace chores - Newtown Baby realised that this was too much luggage to take with him on his glorious trip - he realised it deeply, impulsively - sickening his gut with the force of a divine revelation - standing in a field beyond the sprawling town, he was filled in an instant of revelation with the sense of voyage

& in his still-recurring dream aboard the nocturnal ship the Captain, remembering every detail of history, tenses his tattooed biceps as the past kisses his heart - musing on that first London visit, musing on the new town's uninspiring clumps of houses & mock green spaces - he remembers it

70

vividly & dramatically – how the wheat stretched to trees huddled & dark beneath the hovering, fuzzy vista of the distant town – recalled how, transfixed, he chewed a plucked spear of grass & felt the sap sour on his tongue – the memory breaks silent water, the sleepless black nights of insomnia a receding trauma – the sirens of a police car mingling with the garrulous song of birds – there are many insects underfoot & he can imagine well their busy lives, their fastidious diligence & attention to survival – he watches a ladybird scuttle on his shirt sleeve – it is a hot, diffused summer of voiceless tall trees & the branches sport sweet colours – rich greens, sweet yellows, reddish browns – & yes a new song swims in his head & will not sink – Love Grows Where My Rosemary Goes it says – it is like a madrigal against the pastoral backdrop – it is the first true melody, outside the trance of Michelle, that adheres to his pliant mind – his eyes narrow further with the recollection of a sweet girl's many faces – again they whirl & chant, throwing hopscotch stones & turning ropes & rhyming nonsense – their skirts of bright colours lift in the centrifugal stirrings – he has forgotten his watch he got for his birthday & is outside of time – he thinks of school & it seems disconnected, flimsy & ridiculous – the lecturing & dreary succession of rote boredoms – he pictures the school, tries to fix it somewhere in this glorious summer's light – but it is winter's building now, blocked to passions & terminally retentive - drifting to archaeology, as cathedrals fade in those swimming Monet washes to the sombre hues of a museum – he knows it is Tuesday & time for English & Thomas Hardy's rustic nuances, bonnets & manners – words that cry silently in grammar's cages & die therein unloved – he was tired, tired of wasting time on these nothings, these bland conformities – training his wild thoughts on characters imprisoned by typeset – tired of looking up during a lesson

71

to see rows of dim heads full of playtime trawling the useless, shrivelled pages

the school faded, there was to be no further education wrought by hammer & nail – it was time to peek behind the blackboard – to stretch the symmetry of accepted fears – the school became the old school & no longer mattered - it is way back there now & ill-defined, like the brief imaginings that an author discards - a ghostly house in a story

& from that moment onward the morning register called his name unanswered – he never heard the resigned, almost imperceptible sigh as the bored teacher marked him absent once more

it was only another Tuesday in the huge old world as time shrugs & passes – the future was a sea welcoming his stream, letting go of a past moulded from the clay of voices, with one voice resonating in the swirl

it is Tuesday but there is no time

*

& Les Gray sang in a band called Mud

see him as he turns, with hips swinging out of time, the number 1 on his gaudy drape lit by studio spotlights – or Mickey Finn, head down in the groove as the grinding elf Bolan pouts & grins

at the age of five you can do the jive

the coo-coo-ca-choo-choo train ain't no mystery train

sneery boys eye up the wallflower girls draped around the social edgelands of the school disco – come on & dance, why don't you wanna dance? - hold me close, don't let me go – come on boys, feel the noise - young heartbreakers to yourself be true – all caught up in the tender crap & it's magic says the pilot, knowing that heaven misses another angel – knowing the psalms of innocent pop

worlds collide on the small Grundig portable TV screen scrolling in the corner, under a floral lamp, surrounded by dying pot-plants, the images of urban decay flicker & spit – rediffusion, the spread signals fuse & meld – a stern-faced old newscaster belies his staid air with a red bow-tie - he intones like a monk over pictures of rubbish stacked high in the foetid streets of the big smoke
a rat is tracked by the camera's gleeful eye
Old Lady London waves at him from a tarnished carriage under the moon of lost love – & there are stars in the sky but nobody looks up for fear of missing the swirling constellations of the brilliant tubes that glow like warden's scanners from the convulsive shop windows of the damp high streets – there are a million devices, a trillion pin-pricks of stardust – yet nothing living at their nucleus but the dim spark of our failures & petty victories – no god, no dog star, no electric messiah, only atoms as empty as the heart of progress - amen

*

& so he slipped away from it all, as a parting ship slips its moorings - across the ersatz fields to the library – to grab a clutch of books hard & soft – to drink in the skittery thoughts ingrained in the earthy ink – avoiding the frown of the lady filing cards behind the desk piled high with wise old words – sparked & fired by these forbidden books, his heart flashing after dreams driven by these blots of ancient hieroglyphic confidences – old words, infidel scars, dripped on holy creamy pages that turned to blood on snow in his blessed night-streets - or grew damp from the pavement, soft ebb through the lined pages, an emergent pigment of the slow, invisible rain
he absorbed the sentences, the learning process was underhand, unwitting phrases entered the soft skull as new

music – he read diligently – sly Kafka, wry Vonnegut, the innocence of Brautigan, Barthelme's mysterious vignettes, then through the open gate beckoned Camus & Sartre pulling on the beard of Tolstoy – all their astutely whispered propagandas became glorious truths in his widening head - truths to be retold & upgraded in the excited dining hall next day with Mackay – smell of luncheon meat, custard, syrup & tupperware – sidestepping the teacher's eyes whose chalky lessons he had gleefully bunked – especially Mr. Evans, big eyebrows & patrician's regalia, frightening the hallway with giant footsteps – or cruel old Davis, physically educated, shinning up a burning rope, the plimsoll whiff of torture

*

& how once, & once only, the bigger boys ganged against him on his way home - prostrate in the tangled, thorny scrub after the bully's push & sour laughter in his ears, Newtown Baby cried a little – realising he was face down, frustrated by unattainable revenge, among dead leaves once again – dank odours of earthen worm & wood mulch – he rolled on to his back as the bully's laugh faded - the sky bright blue taunting through the black forked branches – he lay for a while biting back the phlegm & bitter snot – bully boys are cowards, the teacher said – they live in fear of being found out - rugby shirt sweating in their homemade cave – now it was his time – the last time, he told himself – no harm done really, muddy knees, grazed elbow, a few thorns in soft skin stuck - his mocking shoulder bag, leaf-patterned, slightly torn at the hem – he recalled mother sewing it in secret for the first day of school – setting off in royal blue jumper & grey shorts, white shirt & blue/white striped tie – little man growing too fast to hold a mother's love - he had entered the school like a witch summoned to trial, shiny floor waxed & dusty bookshelves as yet terrifying, undiscovered - rooms big as a palace & tall windowed, plastic seated – & yet all the mystery soon evaporated in a familiar boredom – no matter how superb the cathedral, how glorious the hymnal, if god is absent it is but a warehouse for stale ideas & learning - untroubled by the catalyst of discovery – all this he had found to be the case – there was no way of stretching the years spent in endless, identical classes anymore – the hours concertinaing between two bells

   & anyway the beautiful library owned his heart now – the school slithered down his memory into a gloopy swamp of unrequited numbers & geometry – the faces of his friends in turn slowly grew to reflect their academic disappointments – he alone had found the well – here were tales that provoked a million questions - a sick marshland of proud failings that he nurtured & developed in a feral mind – the mad things he gleaned from these forbidden books gave a lie to the lifeless curriculum that his friends daily endured– he ran the fingers of his mind over sculptures of Hepworth found by chance in a magazine – bitten apples, bulbous lyres of warmth – even the perplexing language of the criticism made his very heart drunk with the mystery of it all

   those poor bored kids, blind on a conveyor belt of sanctioned intelligence, conflating a parade of impenetrable writers into one giant, inaccessible, mythic ogre – was this act of sacrilege executed purposefully to deny their individuality, or was it subliminal, some kind of unconscious totem-making? - an unbeliever's tilt at the sacred – in darkest realms of heaven all fire is profane – silence best – the deed always pure, blasphemy only possible with the holy word

   & yes, in the beginning all of life was Shakespearean, monolithic, carried forth on torrents of oily sentences – but now he wanted words that would rend the garments of the saints – a disembodied brain is all he was, random particles making random memories, choosing which ones to discard

& which to cling to, the tiny deaths & matted heartbreaks –
all the stretched canvas waiting to be spoiled, make of them
strange icons or rip them up & make shoulder bags to swing
as he stalked the Rimbaud highways & hitched the Cassady
trucks on the roads to somewhere, anywhere but here –
Boltzmann brain – feel it pull down the church, chop up the
dry old cross for kindling, throw the Buddha on the fire for
warmth – Newtown Baby Brain had let go of the wrinkled
red balloons of belief & was glad - let them drift & dream
dull dreams – he would make his skull a laboratory for
magicians, an alchemist's cave - he would serve an
apprenticeship as the ink-fingered visionaries spidered their
cunning words across an unruly page – a secular mystic, his
laboratory the rolling path, as he concocted new sleepy
demons & stoned philosophies, fashioning a world of his
own design, as a warlock blends his hallucinogenic soups

the first sips of alcohol confirmed this magic to be real -
he would drink deep & regret nothing - until a sound, not
unlike countless voices whispering in an immeasurable hall,
begins to burden the air – a song of himself – innate & sweet
of melody – a song that he would spend his whole life trying
to sing - it would be heard in the chimes of the ice-cream
van, in the school bell of freedom at three o'clock – the lazy,
sublime counterpoint playing beneath the dirges of routine –
a fantasy-maiden's voice, drifting her notes down from
carefully constructed castles - hovering, unseen by the world,
misted above the far-off beckoning distances – it would ring
true even in the creaking ropes of this ship of foolishness
slow turning in the vigorous swipe of Mother Thames – out
on the maddening streets, in the perfectly deranged city, he
would build his temple of music that would keep his secret
safe, pure - a protective aura of reverberation & yet urgent,
as if each speck of time must be used up, the drug of
solitude in its thrall – every cheating word to be unrhymed,

made wild - for all things born of such a will were imperative
- & heavy deeds had yet to be done & soon

the fig had been offered & accepted - the snake curled
in the thicket & let out a satisfied hiss - Newtown Baby
slithered from the skin already unsheathing in his wake - &
on a bright screen, emerging from an already receding wash
of shadow puppetry, The Lonely Troubadour opened his
eyes as if for the first time - the damp, unsteady legs of a
hesitant new foal struggling to support him - that holy
Tuesday in bright fields above the new town - he stared
above it at a cloudless heaven & vowed never to lose this
feeling of indestructibility again

*

the Captain opened his eyes, many decades hence,
gripped tighter the straining wheel & breathed deeply as he
saw the river rolling beneath

now a pause in the captain's log - a momentary lull
before another draining blast of storm begins - ashore some
trees have fallen, roof-tiles lay cracked in the road - the
women sing again now the rain has stopped & blown leaves
are gathered drying against a wall - for now, the dust sleeps
- hugging the earth close - a reflex born more out of
hysteria than any true longing

a log can be both a detailed record or cut lumber, as in
woods and forests - words can mean anything you like, as
can dust - some see the gathered breath of centuries -
others the ash of love

*

& he used to frequent the swimming baths, dutifully &
slowly doing his six lengths with a pause at each length's end
to feel the surge in his muscles & watch the water calming to

77

reveal his red trunks, pale legs, enjoying their bald, floating weightlessness – the antiseptic, leachy catch of chlorine in the throat – the warming sun through the huge banks of windows that looked out across the park to the town

yes & afterwards he would buy a can of cream soda from the vending machine & sit in the blue plastic spectator's seats to watch the swimmers glide up & down up & down the cool Hockney shards of fractured blue - & one day – remember? - there was a leaf floating in the deep end – how did it get there? - blown in the door & trodden through? – however it got there it was hypnotic, he could not take his gaze from it – it was the punctum of his snapshot hour - the swimmers brushed it aside but still it bobbed & danced – immaculate green raft – a mysterious island verdant in the cool blue shimmer – as if it had fallen fresh from an overhanging bough

& The Troubadour remembered – remembered the taste of cream soda, leaving a delicious vanilla breath in his mouth – the chlorine rising – the strange, sunlit leaf dodging the divers & old women treading water – buffeted by the bursts of bubbles from the grill – contented leaf – at play, no desire to be rescued – he wanted to pluck it from the gentle drift of human traffic & press it between the pages of a book of poetry & let it be a smiling surprise for a browsing customer in a dusty bookshop – toss it to the north-wind's eddies from the monument - or set it free in a river to hurry seaward or be sunk by children's stones dropped from a low, Summer bridge

he remembered, remembered

cream soda – chlorine – sunlight on blue – green leaf – it was a good day – he had felt energized by the vigorous exercise & gone for a walk across the bright park – the trees were lush & in full feather – the leaves, he thought, looked sad, like tethered farmyard creatures – or like those solitary horses he'd seen chained to a gatepost at the roadside he gazed up through the branches fixing his still-watery eyes upon the clear sky – it had never been so clear – it was immaculate, a temple shorn of angels, an ocean to which all the universe's leaves were falling

*

or watching transfixed as a small child blows bubbles carefully from a circle soapy-dipped, a fraction of love like those inexplicably sad images caught in the zoetrope's frantic blink – beautiful orbs, oily, domes of pure light, they float wildly upward to joyous disintegration – kisses popped to hushed air, lemon-breathed

& a day of drunken larks, from the Basement In The Bubbly Sky staggering with the miscreants talking, arguing, embracing for no reason – heading alone later to The Waggon pub by the cinema – more drinks, a few shots before the dreary bell - & he stumbles the steps down like a puppy, one by one, each harder than the last until he is beneath the shelter of Brooke House, out of the beginning rain – again it was the ill-sensed shifting of water seeking release – be it pissing against one of the building's thick, elephantine legs or blue streams further below the crust of the world – his eyes already juggling motes of blurred morning – amoebic blotches, split & congeal – tides in his veins awaiting the currents of early coffee – tidal shimmers in the puddles blooming on pavements – this rain felt friendly, soothing his arid skin – a returning rain, spat to heaven by far off oceans & dribbling back to earth to mollify his frustrations – Newtown Baby contemplated the intermittent splashes falling from the jagged concrete above him – bulky grey, bulky grey as the sky beyond it, a poultice lain across the throbbing cloud mass

& yes it was at that innocent moment that he heard the music for the first time – a cosmic purr of sound that defied notation, spurned all rhythmic or tonal analyses – worrying his inner ear with shy gifts of melody, spirals of ethnic turbulence driving its core – hypnotic blips on a radar scope, • he first felt each pulse in his temples – he was a receiver of alien communications, a disc reverberating to the percussion of distant entities – mists of an implosive star - & he knew, then, somehow, that it came from a sense of exile, a zone of sad leavetaking – it was the uncharted score at the root of the river's exhilaration – an answering chorale to his nag of perplexed interrogation - love's impossibility, love's lessening orison – the question-mark moon ascending, ghosted, behind the cloud's greasy windowpane – a moon of rain, dropping beads of light on lumpen, parched soil – making the ugly duckling town beautiful - pock-marked puddles, acne of hidden creeks not yet forgotten – it is surely their velvety babble that multiplies & rises in a contemplative hour such as this – when the night streets are skinned & everything is dragged through red ink, lava-lamp, barber's pole – oil & feathered bruises – blood-rags for the raw necks of shavers – swish of razor, careless & keen – Sweeney's dead – *tod und verlust* – yet the lost lusts sang lustily once more – dead as folklore yet still it all sang, flowed like the wine that fills the goblet of the evening heavens – flowed, yes & came together in confluence & chanted a valedictory anthem, a dormant river's final sigh before eternity

*

punk flowers – shining black, blacker still than the night for which they refused to close – a stoic menace of rawhide & whipped flesh - slimy black roots pushing supplicant tendrils up, upward beyond the redbrick dowdiness of The Newborn Lonely Troubadour's town - up through the cracked paving beneath the squat housing complexes & storage units of bleak beauty - as they surface, blinking &

stretching with these biblical, black petals - aghast at their reflections, they reveal their icy grey hearts in all they say & do – uninviting, grey hearts under confused badges of leathery, creased revolt – a new rose that refused to grow where his Rosemary goes – damned new roses given to new loves though no love is evinced

walking the winding stretch of paved sand from his parent's house to the concrete chunks of the town centre, he listened for omens in the January evening - Sweet Jane's twisty intro, like smoke & flick-knives, shards of guitar wrenched from a bedroom window as the web of net curtain swells - even though the shocks have receded, even though the Germolene-coated plasters have been quick-ripped from punctured skin & the rumble of solemn, unemployed hours are quelled to a soothing background muzak, restoring the antiseptic calm

& even though this calm is really a balloon, strange, floating high above the country of the mind, nothing, it was important to aver, really mattered – he learned to love the misunderstanding of poetry as opposed to the rigid, obvious logic of history – he allowed weeds into the garden of Eden – knowing that these things too will drift & all the faces of old school friends will gradually lose their definition, like outsider's sketches made in rehab time by drying drunks – soaked harbingers of philosophic rust, praying to nothing but a pastel sky on grumbly amen corners littered with cans & kebab-meat

*

The Lonely Troubadour paused on the street as the light drained from the day - muscly, choking motorbikes cruised by with PVC-clad dreamers astride, anger & light reflected in polished chrome - black animal-skin – sweating biker-boots on invisible black ice, a tiny arctic escarpment to

the partially frozen gutter's flow – his giant steps heading
nowhere over that smouldering hole in sweet, first-month
snow that his casually tossed cigarette had made - & he
notices - startled by the impatience of traffic - the pigeon
breaking for heaven & burbling menacingly at the screech of
tyres - & he knows all at once the fear that they sense, the
rising blood in their eyes
    pigeon ascending – the throaty laughter of its wings - oh
to ditch this world just so! - to be gone in a flap of grey at
last, in a momentary burst & flutter of panicked wings – he
sees how their easy flight turns them slowly into toys - he
watches them rise as the rooftops burp & drowse across the
sombre miles that the clutch of habit too soon forgets
    sad rain, old tiled rooftops in winter hold the saddest
rain – please tell me of a friend you lost once, long ago, long
lost & gone – that is the sadness that would venerate this rain
– you had friends I trust?

                        *

    & he is growing still, sinews tautening beneath bracing
skin – a subtle shallowing of breath & sharpening of features
– beginning to be afraid of different monsters – beginning to
hear one voice freestanding among the hub-bub of his
comrades' clamour
    sour, seventeen & leisurely as that tired old rain - The
Lonely Troubadour stood – a grounded toy, soft-boned, in
a phobic street, his fire unlit & safe in luddite ignorance,
wrapped & coddled – absolutely nothing to do & his head a
happy balloon of ashen children's breath – in awe of the
pigeons' throbbing & gargling threats - blood in their glassy,
heroic eyes - not looking up
    & their eyes are a reliquary of sorts – collector's glass
protecting caught butterflies – cognisant of nothing earthly -
slowly murdering the sky's trick questions with numb waves

of random flight – pleasingly letting the inertia of heaven erode the slow watercolour of day, globes of undiluted paint dripping from canvas to floor

*

& nightly, more & more, he feels the steely strings of a guitar against his fingertips – a world of noise waiting to pour – he knows that he must earn the gift - his skin is a rocky coast, it tenses and hones with every onslaught of a new sonic breaker – with every song growling louder from the transistor radio he kept in his inside pocket – the aerial sticky with the sap of a boiled sweet – listening, as darkness fell he soaked up the transmissions of anger from the distant city – every rule broken felt like a chain being cut from his legs - each novel musical experience, though brief as a mayfly's thought, rewarding him over & over with trophies to reflect his growing reputation, his standing among peers – he sensed that he was evolving - bled dry of his childhood nectar, diaphanous, serene as a marble Buddha – feeling as if his induction to this world beyond his friends is nearing a kind of climax - that the next phase of his voyage is ready to be taken – it is a new feeling, a victory of sorts - he steps up in his gown like a wizard & accepts the prize

*

dissolute, the caravan of tired souls – from the den of the market trader's beery revelry out into a warm spring night – have you got the bottles? - yes, ruby port, Fonseca, the old man won it in a raffle at Christmas & will never touch it - also a half of brandy, Three Barrels it's called – enough then, with the six real ales swilling in their guts chasing the meagre fare of crisps & peanuts they made unsteady progress across the roundabout to the park the gravel path crunched beneath their steady footfall in blue night hush – birdwatcher's hides & the anachronistic shapes of reconstructed cottages loomed in middle distance adding flavour to their timeless ruminations - they bickered as to how far out across the landfill site they would go to find the perfect spot to drink & dream – far enough to feel the dislocation required for thoughts & words that, by their nature, would only thrive for this one night, this flash of now – the distance a lone bugle note could travel – the carry of a hearty peasant's yell - who was among them the gentle man?

there had been talk all week of the planned march against the community charge that had been recently enforced by Thatcher's government – placards stencilled, slogans of great urban wit devised - gallows were being constructed at Tyburn in anticipation of grand heresies & seditionist plots - there would be alcohol, music & a sense of comradeship among the broad divisions of motley youth – the streets would ring to the cries of the just – rag-seller mixed with lay priest in this most fervent cause enjoined – there were rumours that the king would meet them halfway with concessions & amnesties – The Clash were to headline the rally in the park

they felt the sprung grass giving way & the soil solid beneath, the sullen mass of waste from a billion emptied dustcarts grumbling like an angry history beneath them

never had any of these three unwise boys taken in such copious quantities or in such varied forms – by the time they had wandered far out of Pitsea town toward the landfill site, under the throb & fizz of the vaulting pylons that stretched lazily into far darkness, they had diverged from their initial close trajectory by a good few yards – so too his fellow traveller's minds gradually grew disinterested by the static hum of the other's prattle & in turn fell to self-reflection - each now innately sensing an understated, introverted mood, an attitude to the pilgrimage that pertained to their own varying degrees of melancholy – a mood that would perhaps later result in a kind of singular epiphany

for now the air was sombre &, to their left, Pitsea station menaced the vast curdling skies with its huge ebony slabs as they neared the park gate

the path they walked had formerly been called Marsh Road but had been re-baptised late in life as Wat Tyler Way

'...the peasants, they march again...who cares? – they know their fate...'

muttered Mackay as they passed the road sign

& yes the Troubadour & the third Nameless Pilgrim walked resolutely up the path ahead in lengthening shadows until eventually this silent unknown companion also slid unnoticed into the growing darkness behind him

& as soon as their nervous chatter had subsided to a surprisingly rich quiet, something felt wrong in the Troubadour's head – it was hard to pin down - a fickle sensation, a touch of being startled at its edge - the crack of twigs beneath the hoof of a foal, dry exhalations of a wintry fire

& all at once the unnerving impression of being lifted as if he were borne upon a palanquin in some eastern parade – he made a gesture as if to hurry their step – to his left a horse, white as the moon, snorted in the gloom of a mud field - his companions were so far back that it seemed they were no longer of the same corporeal sphere, had evolved beyond themselves to a state approaching the atemporal – who goes there? – Aufhocker! Boo hag! Skin-walker, show thyself! – choose Pitsen or Pitsea! – his head swam with burning knowledge, his eyes scoured the rough darkness ahead for imagined terrors

then, in the wash of blue-black, in mid-horizon, he could finally make out the lights of the refinery winking & blurred – The Troubadour thought of New York & its promissory skyline that had evoked so many wild ambitions in the hearts of exiles – his head reeled as he dropped himself against a mound of warm earth & swigged from the brandy, its fire catching his breath & forcing a cool intake of night air into his chest

*

home, late, almost 5.a.m. - strumming the badly-tuned guitar with rhythms born in the first breath of ash & spirit, the cool air of a transfigured night rushes through his fumbled chords - a glass has been removed from the frame & the photograph stands naked - now all senses are assailed

yes, the smeared, dusty glass once reflecting two curious faces - two shapes - the younger self staring glibly out at his current incarnation – it was never going to be too long a time before these mirages would conspire

outside, dawn shakes dew from its feathers - a toffee sky broiling ugly in the east – hushed threats of a shower, not a full, incapacitating rain but that awkward mizzle bad poets love – such rain that only thirsty nomads would ever crave

The Lonely Troubadour yawns & the suddenly old new town yawns in reflex into blue shuttered mornings – they are both stretching limbs past the spring – he will forego sleep – sleep can be postponed, it is the moon's ally

he will spend his daylight hours awake, a custom that remained throughout his life

*

that afternoon, as if by magic, a wan sunlight, which caresses the wintery town into an austere beauty, emerges – he sits with a can of shandy by the mother & child statue under the shadow of Brooke House, teetering as ever above him on its four granite legs – the statue is resonant, almost mystical, this morning - it squats fat in a fountain of slush &

86

cigarette butts – a fountain ghosted with dew, solid, a monument left intact after a tyrant is overthrown – he squints to make out the carved shapes, what they tell him, their intentions, good or other – he takes out a notebook & describes the sculpted figures

a dark grey mother clutching an impassive cherubim
around the fountain nothing dances

nobody walking by emerges from the general veneer of disinterest that engulfs the early shoppers as they cruise the malls – blank slate, steely eye & pram-grip – chain-smoking corner-hangers gibbering their rancid eavesdroppings – they are frozen, faltering on the cliff-edge of sculpture with no reason to plunge to beauty - the statue cannot speak to them – & what is more there is not one among them likely to care a jot for her as she holds aloft, as if in sacrifice to the gods of commerce, her stone child

he has friends now, supposedly has things to do, places to be - but he spends a disproportionate amount of his time alone there, on the dead fountains edge, watching the masses slip toward the hungry ditch – his friends go about their day elsewhere - they hang decadently in the sordid playgrounds of pubs that beckon their thirst - after pissing the week's grant up a wall they will show remorse again, perhaps – but in the new town the regretful, hungover state is sadly the commonplace – there will be no clarity or reconciliation attempted, the cheap alcohol firing up their anarchist heads & then sneakily depriving them of a will to rebel

in his mind they are all similar – the boys especially – the girls differ in a few ways – closing his eyes he tries to think back to parties or pubs that gaggles of them had attended - the slate stares of bone-coloured girls, skinny as skipping rope – or sullen odalisques, mordant in repose, with stilton veins on fat chalky legs – stood in chattering droves in the chill, smoky doorways of saloon bars – their vivid silhouettes etched against the sacred, ritual jewellery of winter – their halted dreams, by day secured in overcast office blocks, by night dissolved in vodka chasers – the town cares not one bit - & her morbid pastel shopfronts softly mirror the town's inertia under striped awnings – these girls, they would take over his world, he thought, if he was not •careful – they were plotting his downfall with the lure of lust – they wink & laugh as they file in suspicious droves to the toilet to share information, draw up new plans for the next assault – talking hex at the moony god as they touch up their lipstick

*

& as his friends faded into this existential mist - some of them succumbed to the wriggling bait of these females & slowly darkened their garments accordingly – they became martyrs to a vague cause - sacrificial, hung on crosses high above the town - they writhe in delicious paroxysms of pain - these crucified sinners, trying vainly to embrace their captors – black crosses on white stone walls - their misguided early marriages tightening their minds into constantly clenching fists of distress – The Lonesome Troubadour pondered his misogyny as it hovered at the edge of a more satisfying misanthropy - why do people need others?, he thought - at night he lay on his bed in his parent's house & wondered if his life would ever amount to anything beyond a critique of the unreasonable – he listened at the night window for signs - was that a saint he saw one night walking back from town yelling implorations in the park of fumes? – or a crow, fattened by imagination, serenading silence with his one caustic note?

he spent long nights with Mackay, his trusted partner in sardonic misery, fuelled by Triple Vintage cider from the local off licence, composing hilarious fake religious rituals on the sacred bench by the lake in The Park Of Fumes – one night - after his friend had wandered away singing across the dark grass - he decided to read everything that he had jotted down in his notebook over the year – he read aloud, as if he had a rapt audience, the expectant hush confirming the spell he believed he wove – it was a confessional, a cleansing, an imprecation to the shifting squirrels & rats snuffling in the burnt-out shed by the lake, the frowning ducks pondered, the breeze muttered through the tall reeds – all was lost

yes, lost - down in the park of fumes those holy nights with cackling Mackay – green cider bottle, triple of vintage & ye bought it with sweating pennies, being the tallest & voice lowered – across the bridge of wintry concrete where no angels sighed nor dwelled – though their minds unravelled, it was liberating & he felt alive – thought tripped on thought on the gravel path down to the false lake - to be false lake poets, windy & dull-watered – entranced by the mysterious forever in the night stars - pointing out the ploughs, bears & myriad elusive explosions – swirling in freed fantasies, stuck in cider-webs, gazing through Greek mythological windows – old Andromeda nursing the raptures – mother, sing your own praises – prettier Queen than the deep nymphs – shine on – nymphs whined to bold Poseidon – a new monster cometh to annihilate her kingdom – shine on, up there with a eunuch Cetus, spayed dog of war

& always, if the spiral of golden contemplation became too much, he could glimpse sideways from the sky to Mackay & beyond - to the nameless one - & be reassured that he too was lost in these arcane reveries - alternately blown through the vast freedom of limitless space & chained to a rock face by the colossal ogre of an imagined threat –

the petty workday grind washed away – as the cider &
smoke galvanised their conversations they became as alert as
prisoners awaiting the gallows – a plot of freedom, ready to
flee to the hills – so often staring up to the improbable
endlessness of milky black – naming the specks of light
anew, dedicating a constellation to the soul night at the
Winged Horse public house – another for The Owl &
Pussycat pub
   & in dotage, only their owly, catnip dreams pushed
gently out into the black waters on a beautiful pea-green
skyboat – nursery rhymes will return when the time comes
to be saddened by such trivia – when stars no longer twinkle
but burn up – when all the king's men cannot repair their
hearts – when cartoons bring tears

                              *

   but your star, Newtown Baby, your star was always going
to be Andromeda – inverted & fascist/holy

                              *

   & slowly, but inevitably, the little adventures outside the
town's Perspex bubble became more fervent & numerous –
dipping an elbow into the near boiling water of the big city
pot – on the westbound train, pulling into West Horndon
station – The Troubadour was accustomed to its usual
deserted platform – its air of a subtle abandonment – of
careful, diligent maintenance, perhaps by remnants of the
railway past that secretly, under cover of night, swept floors,
tended flower-baskets, straightened waiting-room chairs,
repainted tired sills & brushed cigarette stubs into the sidings
– thus was preserved this illusion of functionality when in
truth no soul ever alighted here

however, on this still spring morning, as the train slowed, he saw, perfectly framed in the carriage window, a vicar & a tall black woman in a brightly coloured wrap standing a foot apart at the dead centre of the platform

they looked up the track in opposite directions - motionless for a few seconds - & then the vicar sneezed, making the woman start & place one long-fingered hand to her breast – then she began to laugh, a tinkling, melodious sound that, though muffled by the glass of the train window, still left a delightful glow in its gentle subsiding wake – & then the train pulled away & the little *tableau vivant* slid sideways, stage right, into the mysterious wings of obscurity forever

*

numbed to slavery – childish in ambition but suffused with the need to grasp the adult's coin – he loafed at leisure – but in the fullness of time The Workshy Troubadour sadly dips his toe into the murky, threatening pool of employment – he waited for the van – it was early, nobody sane awake – he thought of the refinery where he had secured a job as a cleaner – it loomed in his brow & furrows creased his contemplative stare - gunmetal huddled under bulge of sulphur - on the shoreline, the journey of the dawdling Thames, visible from this squall of mud, the other side, as far as the booming gunpowder plot at Shoebury – the white, rusting van through Stanford-le-Hope to the Alphaville of Coryton's petroleum necropolis

& so it came to pass, many years ago, way back on a porch-swing of the temporal plane, an eager new recruit to the industrial cleaners' weary clan puts sandwiches & duffel coat in his labelled locker & dons a third-hand, soiled yellow waterproof - Lonely Troubadour in sad diesel-drenched overalls is baggy of mind & shapelessly clad – first making tea & moving bins, later jet-washing stones by the already stonewashed jetty – a cool spray blows back, pricking his wind-burnished cheeks – the tanning stones in sun calmly drying – he thinks of his father, the watering can, Summer heat, the past childhood hangs heavy in his hot days of innocent toil – he spends lost hours at the science-fiction outskirts of the refinery – he lounges on a steam pipe, reading Philip K. Dick novels, one after another, until he has read them all – then Zelazny, Asimov, Heinlein, Van Vogt – or awaiting the morning parade of dismal, hefty ships rolling Londonward upriver – inhaling their raucous hoots & bellows – the gulls lunge & break the starbursts of sunglint from distant Kentish rooftops – sailors flipping half-eaten breakfasts into the intermingling waves – the birds descend in hopeful swarms, but not one morsel can be salvaged from that impatient, uncaring surge - *is all that they see, or seem to see, all that I see?* - *or a delusion too?* – he daily writes these epistles to the gulls, smug in solitary majesty, high in the sky – at first light they are down, bickering with the Canada geese for discarded crusts – much later, in the full morning glow, they swoop high, compensated in their natural dominion, they cruise in comfort, assuredly among allies - crisp & white against this metallic, blue-grey dawn

Johnathan Livingston Troubadour is watching, with momentary thoughts rendered null by the broil of uneasy happenstance – his food cycle disturbed, his mood ruined by his troubled hungering, a soul edgy with truncated dreams – he watches the swirling water from the jetty - the tender cascades confer, chuntering their travel plans – a penny saved each day to conquer their seamless geography – a reluctant duty enriches his chaste gazes, hollers from the oily-overalled louts of the pump-house gang, bright eyes sparkling – in wonder they watch these perfect white birds gambol in circles above – far out beyond the water, over mud, gravel, den & furrow, they glide – deep above the agitated psyche of the imprisoned harbours, the workmen watching & sweeping as they dance - how they tiptoe through the silenced air! - from first gleam of day they slip easy betwixt salty, wet fingers of breeze – sun-crested - & tumble in unison to the profound throb of the sea – sharp, yellow beaks stark against the fluffy smoothed whitecaps - they are drifted clouds of a summer's imagining

under the jetty's wooden trellis, in cawing throngs they hatch their avian strategies in rowdy code – a terrifying sound like a child imitating distant thunder

The Oily Troubadour sat by the pump-house & chewed a reed of rare grass – revelling in the physicality of his job, the adult thrill of becoming tired – & his current favourite harshness was a winter spent labouring on the tank farm – circumnavigating the fat, stumps of gas-metal tubes & pipes - unclogging gulleys solid with sheet ice & clay – old-time, real man's work – the feel of his foot on a dented shovel chilling despite the crushed woollen sports sock & steel-toed boot or, with a panoramic flourish, giving a severe poetic gaze to the pristine, sudden collapse of guttering snow

snow on snow on snow, fallen upon the bundles of rags with which the brawny contractors wiped their gloves - the anchors tying mist to earth – the estuary's frail plants, the naked, fragile sticks, shuddering in fright of north winds - yet still stalwart, sinuous in the blur of the estuary's ghostscape – a pillow for the drunken head of Hella - &, painted within its broad brushed span, The Stoic Troubadour in hard-hat steels his levelled eyes along a rusted conduit of metal at a jaunty angle to the curve of a gas-tank & sails a matchstick along its channel – squint, it is a world in microcosmic relativity – & he the Leviathan Heyerdahl of the scuttling rust-flakes pursuing the craft downriver, breathe deep, take pleasure in the strength of its fantasy – moss clumps are waystations, havens & harbours – disused quays jut from the cracked piping – tributaries await their rainfall in twists of holed metal - he watches as his matchstick Rai zigs & zags toward the abyss – Gulliver perspectives – a growing game keeping the mundanities of his hour slumbering beneath the net of joy

in the late shift he is dispatched, with his troop of fellow shapeshifters, to the Sulphur Recovery – a queue of broken pterodactylian eggs that render the sunlit skyline futuristic, dystopian – feeding his fertile Sci-Fi dreams - they disgorge their steam in heroic farts of crude petrol & - nose twitching in fetid air - the Troubadour watches as the sky displaces the fading patches of limpid pastel far above the salted shore's grasses as the gaggle of other contract workers see their own boredoms reflected in the idle vista - dumb as slapped fish they stand, in a shuffling, belching queue for old picks & shovels, as crafty chemicals permeate their sleepy pores - mundane egg of morning gone - a new stretch of day, the last hill before home time – the anticipation of alcohol is primordial – a sneaky feeling serpent-wrapped & suggestive of ancient truths undiscovered – the constant mental calendar turning, the promise of the weekend – days of stinking, damp heat with a yolky globule in white clouds peeping down – a day to flicker, for us to briefly see before it slithers into hungry evening – until the moon was formed, her underside burned – & soon a night to flash above us – broken white star-debris gathered in frenzied constellations - the stars of heaven, the same stars above the drunken park, so long ago, so long – they found echo in the lights beneath the swilling estuary that he saw some nights on the graveyard shift – all the time the scribbling of poetry & song, the relentless absorbing of stories, the rockets, the lurid covers, pale orange Martian cityscapes, light years of exploration, further planets, other solar regions, fantastic metal cities, angular, gleaming under three suns

The Troubadour, who always told himself he felt lonely in crowds, sits on a hard bench in the smoking hut & takes out his omelette sandwich, herby egg blob, protruding yellow from bleached, spongy bread – he chewed slowly & thought of his money earned, fat in his back Friday pocket – ten pounds for his keep to mother & the whole remaining plump wad to squander as he wished – in record shops, pubs, off licences & bookstalls – on mad trains to the madder shops in the big city, where leather jackets hang in biker queues above shiny brown Chelsea boots awaiting his small-town, Newtown limbs to fill them out & walk proud through the hick streets of his outgrown town – wages for sin – each sacred coin & note made unholy – an unspent nest-egg, greedily secured from last week's harvest, added to the hungering pot

to Camden, maybe – his new adult playground - shirts, panchromatic & billowing, in windows coloured by wild shards of psychedelic glass – acid-spiked robots slouching in their doorways – blasts of urbane metal exploding from the darkness beyond – The Freshman Troubadour hesitating as if the money earned by such soiled hands in such a distant, disparate place as Coryton refinery could never be legal tender there in the fertile spring of a Camden morning – he would watch the parade of goths, untouchable, moon-haunted – surely the transference of coin to till, a Beltane act in this season of witchy women, would grant him access to their underworld? – they slide the streets, silence forming a protective bubble around them - dripping menstrual seeds on the ancient earth – this realm of dusky faeries – the Pale Troubadour scratches rhymes in his notebook & is trapped between the resulting poles of harmony – great Roman birthing stones make up the walls that encase these nightflies - they winked at him as they passed through the magic doorways to abundant, fecund nightclubs – but he always left his last waltz for the missed train home – bottle in hand, by the lock, sending valentines to Boo on postcards of double-decker buses – abandoned by the Essex pull to slow-dance between twin fires of strobe light from the cars roaring over the bridge – the mysterious hobos supping from their varying bowls of shared grog - Morning Dew, Dictum's Ale or Merrybegot's Old Conceiver – reeling as the nocturnal pole-dancers discard rags of soiled clothing

The King Of The London Rain eyes his maybe queen – his Walkman pulses to 'Mefistofele' by Arrigo Bolto – & yes he too dances within himself, as captured in the memory, in slow cycles, descending in graceful spirals to a soulless den of patchouli fog, merciless sisters, Nephilim fields, Bauhaus slashed by Bowie-knife & Poe, he sighs, defeated, nihilistic, • his heart enflamed

but this all awaits – for now his daydream pops like an oily bubble

& so the Troubadour is reluctantly snapped back to his greasy diesel sandwich – he sniffs, unsure, & dips it quickly in the hot tomato soup from a tartan flask slow-poured

back in the tea-hut Madeleine the wise old tea lady will be drooping in smoky wan-light – longing for her last offering of homeward tea & chastened by aforethought, he stubs his crushed Sovereign against the meshed door of the smoke-cabin – the day done, king of nothing – O but what grand designs has he laid! – such brave chameleon dreams to impress the nymphs & - of course - his former self, Newtown Baby – this is the holy state he had dreamed of at school - deep, dead reasons unspoken – designs grand yet unseen - & now the thunder, now the lightning - the rain is bullets of steel tears – they shall meet after the long battles to come – Olden Captain, Bold Troubadour & Elfish Baby – three warlocks messing with the fabric of hours – in Bexley upon the heath – in the January fog in dirty, grey air - a shared reverie – a shiny new record yanked excitedly from its paper inner-sleeve – violence told in New York litanies, a tumbleweed of suicidal Elvis brogue spilled over clustered, grey windstorms of dusty synth - Newtown Baby listens & listens again - dream on, dream baby dream

*

& the jobs changed but the dream endured - but here & now & far from suicide's plough, he scrubs dull yellow stains from dull iron with rags in diesel drenched - two years hence - the same rags, same diesel - in a rebel's park - Wat Tyler's shade daily urging him to march anew - the tractors & farm machines dragged, astonished, from forgotten graves of Essex farms - on the wall of the barn where they worked a small blue transistor radio hung from a bent coat-hanger - it was tried every morning but never could be tuned to any station, a repository of white noise - a solid, cream-coloured portable radio, remember, with its aerial snapped, stuck to the thick workbench next to the vice - this worked very well, it serenaded a stilted airless space frozen in winter & stifling in summer - ill-lit by three hastily co-ordinated bulbs, their little cathedral of renewal stood, secluded, unenlightened in its scrubland meadow, resonant with yaps from the DJs of the pop apocalypse - Bates in his Smooth Motel of Our Song, Travis Fickle & his hirsute spinning flakes of corny pop, Saint Anthony of the Black Burn, who, like Ahab, lost his soul returning from the wailing sea - & worst of all, Stephen The Just, haughty jester to a world of housewive's tears in the dismal, velour-wallpapered afternoon of his life - to the beat of these horsemen's hooves the Troubadour thereby danced - on the ceiling, without feeling, as both Bee Gee & squeegee merged in his memory - Lionel Rich Tea dunked in cold funky coffee - the jokey banter with the irrepressibly cheerful chief mechanic was inanity made word, but passed many a dolorous hour - & forever & ever the radio roared & squawked its urgent demands - easy listening made difficult – somehow remaining alive through the reinventions of a coming storm – the DJs built their barricades of banality high – earwormy globs of weirdly popular song recurring down through politically symphonic days – easing the ache of graft & speeding the payday nearer – more careless coin to spend on song & wine – deranged golden suits & loaf-shaped hair, such high-level chic was not for the likes of The Troubadour, for he was the freak – hanging tougher after work with the politicos & mercurial bar queens of the Basement In The Sky – they will rock you with their frail certainties – champions & friends – or in the Commodore pub, flat & angular, nearly out of town, where thrice a staggering lady propositioned him by the hot dog stand on Stacey's Corner one tense & fevered night – he shied away, half-smiling - always half-something – oil-slick boys line the pale, wet roads – valleys of burger-grease, their casual hip talk, frank with vehemently expressed, badly thought-out opinions, echoed around the deserted car-parks & market-stall skeletons – fake bikers & gypsy-raggedy, prom-bouffanted molls queued for a detumescent dog in a bun, smeared with mustard like ochre fire so that it could be tasted at all – Johnny's Big Dog, that's the one that you want – Saturday night & they just got paid in kind, the red sauce dribbling down the lapels of their leathers

summer in the park of fumes by the lake on Sundays in slow waves of heat - & of course it will be like this always, always & forever - for how can it ever change? - summer nights in exile from the dank pubs & disco - kiss you all over to your own rhythm on fake drums – & yet, Troubadour, at the town's end, under a vague lunatic moon, who are you in essence? – chatting a wad of nonsense to a pre-Madonna in summer heat – deftly spinning your boy-web with one hand on your heart & the other clutching a polystyrene carton full of mayonnaised chips – baby roadkill lounging in a parking space on a moped built for two

hour of skunk, cars of lust – the shy lovers' melting grey
faces kiss vacantly in doner-kebab rain

*

ah shucks, ah phooey, but with what or who was he still
fed up? – too many whats, many whos
with all the new town's glassy reflected light – so why not
hop aboard an after-work train & spend a night wandering
the mad city with Boo?
& yes, yes she says immediately, of course, of course she
will, of course
so many rover-ticket rambles, all the thrills awaiting for
two destitute, bawdy bodhisattvas - delaying their blind
nirvana to gleefully help themselves to manna
discovering new haunted houses of joy each time - jerry-
built saxophone cathedrals in the crazed jazz kingdom of
shuffled tempo - or buskers running on empty, down brown
avenues of weary autumn oak - the endless lines of badly
parked cars
your best friend & her best girlfriend awestruck by neon
– heart-wild, pretending to be handsome – the sky too late
for dreaming
Boo suited London - bonny though she looked, in Wat
Tyler Park - a heartache waiting to croak - but here she
burns brighter, golden, like a sun queen – no more gravel
paths down to the estuary edge with a tape recorder - skirl of
old stones - beastly burdens that once gave you satisfaction
& nights spent together in black rainbow rooms – a rod for
your own back - these droning pipes in your heart, faces nod
& wink in your soul – slim chances in lanes of lovers
snagging jumpers on the jagged wood – she was a speck of
always in a never night - too much, too little, too late – The
Pious Troubadour self-righteously decided to kneel before
this angel - but don't bring a bouquet, she hates flowers –

just croon a little & swig the rum & with a little luck your wings will one day grow as your shifty sins slip-slide away – & your queen left dancing there, victorious, taking it all – all the furtive, dashboard-lit desires

they prepared for a shared quest, set before the mirror night - to end it drowning in tantrums, alcohol, guilt & love – they were unstoppable in their blustery youth as they rode, bareback, the thunderous circus horses of the night's serenades - born to run like the sandy river, to run until they see nothing but a void at the limits of the spectral city – nothing but old death there, in a dumb-show of sumptuous mimesis, standing & waiting, the old ferryman by the shore, with his bony fingers of fire & boat full of the phony embers of some extinguished Babylon – the ferryman reads from The Troubadour's tattered green notepad

O take me back, pale, imagined sea
aboard that boat that rolls
through crowded river dreams
let me meet my Captain – let his memories be forged
in our profane acts this evening
as we slide into whichever hell we find
time out of heart, time out of mind

& that time, out of their minds, Boo lounging on the sea-wall smoking his last cigarette, he stared past her from the adjacent bench, out to the deathly still January estuary - sails, buoys, red flags by the crow's stone where the city's reach finally gives up & rests

& what bound them to the span of wanton years? – the knowledge, the necessity, curiosity & endurance of every bland minute that promised a wilder hour – sliding through other people's timelines – dissolute & brief in retrospect but every understanding fully embraced as each slender moment shone

her red bicycle, the tring of the bell, the easy yellows,
browns & greens of the wandered wood – & yet he knew he
was sinking low as she rose higher – the slow parting finally
came when she met the sky & a mid-day sun was too bright
to stare down – a sky that, on certain days, when a daub of
pale blue bled through puffy white, touched a nerve in his
memory & pressed a sigh from his sputtering heart

yes & henceforth he would whole-heartedly toast her in
his lonelier alkie moments & laugh sadly at some bitter feud
long resolved – but ultimately she had gone & he knew it –
though he willed her into his sleep - board the dream-ship,
O angelus, always walking with him, talking with him, soul-
weary, drunk, always moving forward but never quite getting
home

*

yes & more & more he felt driven by the anger & light,
whisky, rum & the old faithful real ales, sturdy & amber as a
beacon of rescue or dark as a suicide's pond – clutching the
thick jug resting on the clean, solid benches in the pub
garden – his blown cigarette smoke embodying every ghost
of gossip

he kept his close friends guessing, second guessing, kept
them wary, as tense as a sailor's knot, tethered to his edifices
constructed of grand drunken conversations & fantastic
unlikely plans – but their sprawl of talking was only a hotel
they lived in - towering layers of rooms to let – where high
above a pinched light through drawn blinds reluctantly lights
a rug of ashes

the streets of the new town - prostrate chessboards
arranged in Haussman slabs of red-brick mediocrity - guided
these soulless pioneers to the call of a wilder land – a sweep
of future lit by a holy road that cut through the snags of a
thousand snowdrifts – strange connections were made

between seemingly incongruous things - he had cried real tears one night reading about Paris in '68, the Situationists & listening to Joni Mitchell's Blue - experienced an almost religious clarity when walking through the neon shopping mall with Tim Hardin singing in his Walkman headphones - the guitar humming warmer in the cold bright sterility

he was touched constantly by incongruous music - moved by the fact that all cities finally forget the mud beneath their feet - beaches paved over - but above all he was touched by any evocation of a river in song or story - it was the river that he wished for - the dream he hung on to, was it ever what it seemed? - impermanent river - at swim in no hour, that refreshed itself with each flash & rolled through every second of every song he loved

*

the love that loves to love the love - staring at the passing prams & buggies - astral months of idling, dole money dwindling with each smoky hangover - music filled his ears, a backdrop of jazz like a rolling scenery behind an actor, filled his love of the commonplace & - despite his oft-professed hatred of the town square - more & more he sat alone by the fountain of the mother & child just staring as the dumb parade passed- watching with him, the immobile mother, the rain dripping from her stony hair, the baby gazing, frozen in awe, into the eternity of her lifeless eyes - tableau & epiphany - &, when he succumbed to his growing will & eventually left the town for good, it was always the subliminal linear greys & rich, deep browns swamping the brilliant shopfront displays that first came to mind - the splodges of shopfront colour like badges on a school jacket - & it was always Brooke House, frowned in weary light, a disapproving headmaster, high over the square, that kindled his toughened respect - purest concrete in the soul - but,

lurking behind this façade of harmless modernity, he heard
a threat, a siren call to obedience – the dead pipedreams of
a rebel always crushed by the authority of the knuckle &
jackboot

*

he read the news with a growing fear – nails of fearsome,
driven words – sheet metal hammered into crushed pages –
the soothing bathos of the local newspapers – unrolled each
morning across café tables – snippets of arcane truth to talk
over & tall tales to partly ingest – weird old Albion's lush,
green folklore unspooling like a snagged tapestry – bleary,
first light, opinions formed on thin ice & coughed aloud
only to be screwed to silence again – the employment pages
– every bad job not good enough, the good ones telling him
that he wasn't good enough – the bad jobs telling the hourly
pittance, the unattainable jobs the annual haul – he dutifully
queued, hungover courtesy of the state, every, frowning,
rainy Wednesday morning at the unemployment offices by
the cinema – the dole office smokers sat reading the week-
old magazines in a soupy fug of indifference & piped muzak
– clutching his unlucky ticket he watched the ticking
numbers waiting for his summons – grim counter-clerks
shuffling through forms for hints of a secret life – a law to set
them free on default – chancery would be a fine thing – the
names, the numbers, the clock motionless above the water
cooler – the blue smoke dancing across the fly-caked neon
strip – the process, unfathomable & compulsory – the dim
acceptance of being stuck in a loop of misery – scraping the
bottom of a beer barrel for solace whilst, somewhere out
there, annualy compensated horsewhipping bastards gallop
through leaves in a rusty autumn field or point sports cars
down a curve of a Mediterranean road as the cobalt ocean
glistens in pointillist repose – fuck it all, fuck this dead town

sucked to a crude monochrome by this endless elephantine weather – fuck its chip-fat stench & laundrette culture – fuck the dusty buses with their sweaty, bilious drivers – & fuck you & me most of all for standing for it

he sits in a hard, brown, plastic moulded seat that fits no arse on earth - turns the pages of the old magazine kindly provided – adverts for suits, after-shave, watches, trinkets of fake gold – but the pictures, though bright & glossy to the touch, held no warmth – these were not real, angry, farting, pork-pie-eating people – they never peeled the wrapper from a late night kebab that nestled like sticky death in its pitta conch – never broke the tip of a stubby bookie's pencil – never had a burly lad yell his fruit & veg mantra in the striped awning market place early

no, whoever these mannequins were, they were beyond this dystopian mire – never queuing in never rainy hamlets – busy copulating & populating an ersatz arcadia

gloss & perdition – the rows & rows of porcelain-perfect ⋅smiles advertising glistering necklaces, hideous bracelets, all for the look-at-me, look-how-rich - plunder from a dead king's tomb

& yes The Plundered Troubadour wondered wanly if there would ever be a reason, outside of a funeral, when he would wear a suit & tie

& as the dole year wore on, more & more faces joined the throng of tired disciples, trudging in the rain up the wet cinema steps - every queue leading to another longer, slower queue that led in turn to the end of the first – as reluctantly, lost in their heart's brooding mist & thoughtless as goldfish, they staggered ever onward back around the block to the beginning – to another form to fill, another monotonous voice spilling schemes & numbers that even they barely understood - *please note that what you're entitled to depends on your exact circumstances - make sure the information that you put in is correct*

comply – tick the box that you live in – identify yourself
– own your coming failure – grow up & sit down – here's
your comfy slippers – it's a nice little flat, really - nice little
television with all the shit soap operas & bad news you need
– yes, here's your life, pal – a dog turd rolled in hundreds &
thousands – it's really a chocolate éclair mate, take a bite –
Majorca looks nice, I'll do some overtime – maybe get a bar
job in the evenings – must sort the garden one day – some
decking, bit of trellis work around the chrysanthemums – I
could get a cat, company for when I'm older – intransigent
beetroot jar lids surely will be the bathetic cause of my first
coronary - put a little bit away in the Nationwide account to
pay for my box & epitaph – here lies Johnny No Cunt -
born & died whenever – did fuck all

any benefit you get will depend, among other things,
upon contributions paid (or credited) to you in the tax year
before the benefit year (starting on the first Sunday in
January) in which your claim starts. For example, if you have
paid standard-rate contributions on earnings of at least £750
in the tax year beginning 6 april 1977 you will normally be
able to qualify for full-rate benefit for claims commencing in
the year from 7 january 1979. If your contributions were on
earnings between £375 and £749 you may qualify for
reduced-rate benefit. Subsequent spells of either incapacity
or unemployment are, however, linked if .the gap between
them is not more than 13 weeks. If your claim links with an
earlier one it will be decided on the basis of the same tax-
year as the earlier one was.- go to section 3

three cigarettes in the queue – told to come back in ten
minutes to room 4b – outside for some respite, coming up
for air, The Troubadour plucks a dandelion bravely
struggled through the paving & blows it, watching the seeds
fly – make a wish, he thinks, where do I start – wish I had a
million wishes – return to room 4b to be told to go to room
2b – or not, he thinks - nod politely, scream inwardly, fill

105

out their poxy form, agree to fill shelves with beans for sod all an hour, push the swing doors, breathe deep the late morning air, collect your pennies, buy fags, do not pass go, head for pub - repeat

*

so it is ordained, so it came to pass - back into the government funded funny farm - back with the hipsters & beautiful losers - see them hang by the fountain, on the steps by Brooke House, or mooching bleary through the mall, these awry, wry, teenage Newtown Turks, that ocean of unrequited lust - barely re-treading old burlap dreams that impend & dampen in an early, winter shadow - they are as inconsequential as the mist on the pond - rising each morning out of blind duty & nightly falling with a sorrowful grace gone astray - denied at heaven's gate, plummeting like bad angels with a million reasons to forget - & The Troubadour was made to feel that he was among them - the sneering discarded dreamers - never saying out loud what was meant to be said - never quite re-telling the rolling tale of his petty troubles, that rush of urgencies that flooded his lowland thoughts only last night - o last night! - it had all seemed so clear then, so articulate - yet now his tongue lolls & his comrades look bored, so he falls silent, points his dripping nose at the paving stones & waits out the playtime before reality bites again & he can join the appropriate queue

*

the old man sat alone most Sundays on the same bench in The Park Of Fumes - one day The Troubadour asked him why he looked so sad - the old man replied that he had once, when a young man, read a story about a fisherman that had wrestled with a large fish & that fish had dragged his little boat far from shore – he had eventually won the battle & secured the creature to the side of his vessel but on the way home sharks had gradually devoured his catch until there was nothing left – Newtown Baby thought the story funny but did not let his amusement show out of pity for the old man who was visibly moved as he recounted it – in the awkward silence afterwards the old man had patted him on the shoulder & said

'...I wish he'd never caught it...wish he'd just let it go...'

later that evening Newtown Baby tried to write a poem about the old man, using a clickety, little typewriter he had been given for Christmas, but the incoherent, vague lines he tapped out disappointed him – they lay dead on the paper, bereft of any of the meaningful sadness that the old man had so obviously felt – he clacked a few times randomly with eyes shut – an awkward army of mostly nonsensical words appeared – gwqhxmoo & lhjsdvfkk – he left them at the poem's end, an epitaph to his failed voice

then, with eyes open, wrote his own name & address – it looked more absurd than the poem – he wrote Once Upon A Time There Was An Old Man On A Bench – clickety-clack, the keys kicked high like the legs of a chorus line in a seedy strip bar – the poem grew longer, it was no longer his – it discarded its luggage, smoked a cigarette, got drunk – then it took a train to the coast & swam away from him beneath the white ocean surf

*

a drunken day, London mostly, that's where he started, the museum, a gallery, pubs, can't recall exactly, he had nodded off on the last train - he had slept all night on the seaside station – shaking with the cold when he awoke & remembering nothing of how he had travelled the thirty miles or so - past his stop - to the coast - his mind remained comfortably subdued, vague, in a deliberate way, a way that suppresses bad memories, Valium calm, shaky hands pushed through matted, gritty hair - eventually he opened his eyes fully & something definite, a sliver of remembrance, slowly drifted into his head like oil swims through water

a dream he had, many times, as a child, of a figure stood beneath a gas lamp on a foggy street that beckoned him as if eager to confide a terrible secret - he had never dared to walk toward him - the first night he had woken up suddenly - drenched in nervous night sweats - he calmed himself by reflecting on the image of the figure, how it posed no threat, how it would be easy to walk right up to it & discover its secret intent - in this simple way he hoped to dispel the inexplicable anxiety that the dream engendered in him - make it meaningless enough to vanish - & yet stubbornly the dream recurred - each time the figure more frenzied in its motioning - night after night he stood frozen, unable to obey its imprecations - until the dreams stopped abruptly on the eve of Christmas in his sixteenth year - his coming of age - sixteen spins around the bored sun, searching for a house he felt sure was his own - a rock that could not be eroded - but there was no safe house - & each inhabited year was a temporary, prefabricated hut on this motel planet, a bleak, cavernous, un-heatable shed decorated to look like home

he had thought no more of the dream - but now, once more, it flooded back to intrude upon his starless nights - it had re-appeared a few times in his early childhood years - then a brief hiatus until his teens - nothing had altered, no development in the story - again just the beckoning figure & curious air of urgent, yet not sinister, intent - the last recurrence happened in a stupor, after a fierce afternoon session of casually mixed liquor listening to old blues on a furry radiogram in a girl's flat (who?) - he remembered Lightning Hopkins grumbling over rough-plucked catgut -

he knew in the dream that the black ghostly figure was a picture- he knew it was a shadow – he had never heard him talk but had seen him – there was nothing that old black ghost could do this time – worrying his head with these graveyard songs & tales of damnation

but this time, in the dream, he went further – pursuing the beckoning devil down the street until it abruptly sprang into an alley that The Troubadour knew to be a dead end – he dived after it but the figure had gone (of course!) – & in this developing dream he had walked back down the road to where he had first seen him & curiously the old gas lamp under which he had stood was now bright neon & modern as tomorrow – he recalibrated the events - a figure that beckons yet retreats into shadow – an ancient light that remains so only when the figure is present – such are the games the subconscious plays, he thought – the desire for danger, the hallucinatory magic of illumination – Jung nibbled at his soul – his waking hours were a respite from the turbulent, archetypal sea of night

he hated the futility of the dream & it had disturbed him then no less than now – the feeling he had on awakening was not fear or frustration, rather one of an intensely devastating loss, as if a parent or beloved friend had suddenly died – it was such a vivid sentiment that he always drove it quickly from his thoughts – but no matter how he tried the same sense of abandonment crept over everything his brain put in the way – he found two cigarettes in a crushed packet in his top pocket & lit one gratefully

he wondered - as he stretched the uncomfortable night from his muscles on the station platform - if the dream was an omen of some kind, could somehow be deciphered – he had a notion that maybe something good, something useful could be divined from it, despite the seemingly random & unnerving nature of the dream's narrative – he sought a blanket of reason to throw over the fantasy – he had read somewhere that a juxtaposition of opposites formed a good part of the, still hazy, science of interpreting the sleeping mind & The Lonely young Troubadour, not understanding the loss he felt & yet undaunted, proceeded to fashion an explanation in the soggy morass of his morning brain

perhaps the figure represented his dull, wasteful life so far? – the sombre hues of the dream alley were certainly akin to the shadows in which he hid his failures – maybe the neon light was a signal that the future was there, waiting, illumined by its progressive glow that banished the old gas-lit past, the twilight conspiracies & folklore, to the shady alleys – the cigarette was helping & he warmed to the theme – he considered that change was the message, transformation – that perhaps he now stood teetering at a precipice – casting aside a cloak, with eyes full of a certain sunrise ahead, he must be prepared to execute a mighty dive into a canyon of welcoming light – he closed his eyes again & could almost sense a warmth seeping into his wintry skin as though the dregs of every bottle he had drained had suffused his heart anew – gaslighting meant deception, he thought – the dream was making him drunk again – he needed to refresh a glass or two – fill his conviction with the proof of raw spirit – he knew the fire & how to light it - Comrade, Socialist Alcohol! - Brother Illusion! – the revolt begins on my returning to the fold! - wait for me in every doorway of every bar – together we shall rise! – hold fast, I'm coming home!

*

yet despite his shaky attempt at psychic exorcism, all day the memory of the dream drove away the more pleasant recollections – the topmost cream of his daylight reveries – & the more his anxieties festered in his every casual thought, the more that he felt a new thirst, almost divine in its purity - a need of strong alcohol, rum, whisky – tequila drenched in ice, sour lemon smiles behind a frown – or maybe (he was near the sea after all) buy a few cans & half a bottle of cheap firewater? – yes, a stroll down to the absurdity of the stony beach - seashells - the slow, eerie, silent prance of herons – they always reminded him of clergymen – get a wave of ozone in the lungs, breathe in the agitated breeze off the water – feel resurgent, moistened by salted atoms, the soft sand underfoot, the pebbles crunchy, stained, soaked in a fine spray of miracles – see the mysterious ships sailing for elsewhere, or dead islands invisible to all but the lost – where the dwindling words of sea-bound fishermen crow in the flat, cold air – a rustling zoo of possibilities trembling in his heart – a paper plane made of a poem launched at the full sky, a song picked out of the early lamps across the estuary, their notes muted only by the staves of slow trade-winds – yes, he needed to see the stranger people that infested the early hours – see their haphazard limbs & hear the language formed by their bruised synapses – walk with them, talk with them as they stumble, fumbling toward godlessness – he needed to embrace an unbelief, which to the strong-minded is a kind of abandonment in itself, an ecstasy, perhaps, even a form of redemption

& the old pier-master may be there, his shrunken trophy skull nodding, drained of hurt, bone certain, guarding the nothingness beyond the estuary head, who dreamt nightly of his own wild oceans – he needed to speak with returning seadogs, shipwrecked wanderers, itinerants that were now cursed to remain landlocked sailors with the vast tides still bleaching their bones

yes & one day perhaps, when finally captain of his own voyage, The Sea-Drunk.Troubadour may be vouchsafed the reason why the sea drags all these saddened hearts to those, faraway, once-upon-a-timeless sands – know the oceanic voices, why it hisses like Eden's reptilian cackle – how it recalls the sound of a needle placed indelicately in a spiral groove & a loudspeaker sizzling like an egg hatching – daydreams of the wider waters birthing him, he felt his life to come already mapped, in vinyl discs & sleeves – liner notes & discographies like treasure maps – several likely spots of discovery marked with an X

thirty three revolutions happening per minute – a constant changing of the guard, the veterans of the sanguine, hippy wars nudging the unborn to their tombstones – each one a corrupt voice chorusing from a high pale horse – The Troubadour felt it all as a promise, a huge sea of possibility - & he was but a novice deckhand – the waves were high but the adventure was far too thrilling to dismiss, the sea's call too strong - & yes, he thought, he was willing to drown himself in that gigantic voice – its velvet horror & shifting colours – blue, white, blood-red, black – cod-mariner cowboys, custodians of the country tune - riding the fantasy of a supple, piebald sea-horse steed across a spring-lit stretch of dusty prairie – ten-gallon hat waved high in a sham, star-studded rodeo - while back in the dusty bowl of the failed harvest the sad old blues stayed at home, with no hay in the stable – the neigh & whinny from a cluster of night horses, dark, incomparable in their melancholic mean - a merry-go-round of apocalyptic chargers revolving through shaking fields of time with their child jockeys clinging for dear life to their painted necks – the whole show a part of the tragicomic, circus fairground of music history – a history of movement, a lexicon of change – & there she is, icicle-thin Captain Smith, an iceberg-bound ship, dreaming of horses, horses, horses, horses – a white mane capping the rolling wave - the flail of a snipered bird – burdened white men wailing the mouldy, beaten poetry of ageless slaves

*

112

"...heeey pop pickers, Miles here – yes siree, 'tis good old Mr. Ducat, the bad cat that loves ya back – & I gotta tell you people I have blood in my fuckin' EYES about this pigeon weather, man – fuck this news – IT'S THE - & lemme tell y'all this now, right now - goddamn it people – I'm sayin' it's the METEOROLOGICAL EQUIVALENT OF fuckin' NOVELS - WRITTEN BY SOME (I dunno) WAR VETS – or some Tom Wolfe kind of shitty-old-pity-me-getting-old crappy SADNESS – (pause) – riddle me this now - how many books do I have to carry in my peeking pocket? – how many formless stanzas of Ken Patchen do I have to re-illustrate with my Rorscharch inkwell HEART? – (pause) - sorry for shouting, dudes – sorry for a lot of shit that only this holy radio station can ever, ever, ever, EVer dial you up – y'know I'm getting this stuff from the source, people – there's a message comin' through me & I ain't responsible for NONE of this shit – now then, tell me sisters – tell me from your lonesome little musky tepee - will you all still love me tomorrow? – really? – 'cos only father TIME - & a four-part harmony jingle - will tell - out there across the suburbs we got virgins debasing their choir practise to massage the egos of DJs - oh man oh man – this is the money shot & moonshot, right here, honey – the ultimate hand reaching beyond earth's chickenshit boundaries, the blessed beak of GOD pecking the red dirt & hoping for some dropped corn, y'dig? – get himself some bindweed to poke around in, maybe – we gotta pause this reciTATION for some STATION identifiCATION – hey now, the weather's a million degrees in the south & there's snow on your tits anywhere north of Brentford high street, but Amster's dam is cool as a penguin's pocket, sister - so clad yourself up like a fucking eskimo, Joe - or go raw bollock naked my friends, because...because...because...fuck it, it's Wednesday, people – all you Gregorian calendar fans - & music is the food of lust so play on, brothers & sisters – may the laughing god *bless the soul of that everlovin' pious plutocracy that daily screw us blind, amen – fuck the universe & all who sail within her rotting hulk – it is nearing three in the godforsaken morning – the witches have fell asleep face-down in a cauldron of wholefood broth – the devil is puttin' on his bicycle-clips so let us not deny even the fallen Light Of The Morning his last request – so then, comrades - until next time or the last time, have a groovy life my old muckers, my old suckers & from me to y'all, to ease your bumpy highway to hell, here's Edison Lighthouse..."*

*

radios blare from way above – anonymous disembodied voices thrill & calm – the stack of singles, the coloured sleeve – each one chosen by holy decree to sing out across the drear streets of Babylon – words from high, the floor-spots of heaven – the dead impresarios peering down at the empty stages, a third of their light diminished to the point of complete darkness for a third of a day – as it was foretold – The Prophet Troubadour kept his counsel & moved his silent pen - it was time to describe all he can describe – to draw, in the stony sand, with eyes closed, an automatic portrait of himself – time to leave the dreams behind – the great ship had never been there - the strange figure beneath the gaslight had never been there – the basket-weaver angel had not been there - he, himself, until now, had never been there – born into the lurch of sunlight after hungrily supping in the womb of night – now forceps tugged him seaward & he must respond with poetry – if it was written that the Captain at the wheel of his past was to be the sole warder of his future dreams then let it be so by analogy alone – no reality, no trauma

(...down the street a short way, a child, no more than seven, under an old lamp post, hesitant – he needs

114

guidance, he is lost perhaps – the Troubadour beckons him
but he does not respond – just closes his eyes sadly...)

normally, early each morning, when he is finally
released from the dreaming, the radio beside his bed reels
off the calm, enigmatic inventory of the shipping forecast in
low, intimate tones – at his window the first light of the new
day is bleeding from the east above the dim houses

but this morning is different - the empty, cold station is
an unpleasant reminder of his recent drunken failures – the
bench bruises his lower back – there are two empty bottles
& a few chips in greasy paper at his feet - above his head, a
lone gull describes a parabola in languorous, musical, snowy
stanzas – he stamps out the fizzing stub of cigarette – red
roof of the signal box - auguries of blood, riot of change, the
paling ochre pages of past imperfections, hoof-beats muffled
in snow, the broken wing

*

later, down at the beach, after falling asleep again by the
windbreaker – after a sleep cleansed & dreamless - rising,
fresh with seagull laughter & tingle of sea-skin, from a sea-
weedy flagstone pillow, The Eternal Lonely Troubadour
stared from the stony sandbanks at the cryptic, fluctuating
nothings of the breaking day

in the distance, through shrugs of fog, he saw the old
jetty, loosed from the grasping fingers of retreating surf,
jutting from the trickling hourglass shore, it stalked the
estuary on limpet-caked legs of tanned wood & iron –
ghostly wafts of its odour assailed him – it was poised,
primed in its insect diligence – rippling the dry air, pithy,
centipedal – the brash ozone filled his flaring nostrils with
the dynamic urgency of hot bitumen

carefully now, stepping soft along the rim of tide –
though awash himself with deeper tides no less powerful -

The Lonely Troubadour, freeing underfoot the noise from the trodden pebbly sands, pondered these reassuring voices that he trusted – the haunting wind, the rain, the ocean – the occasional gasp of bristling electric air before a storm – & most of all that same, loyal voice that spoke only to him – outside comprehension – beyond skin

*

& somewhere beyond his understanding, on the bigger sea of his subconscious sleep, onward in the dream the great vessel rolled – out of the East India Dock – the cranes throwing shadows across the deck as the Captain watched his sibling crew scrubbing the old wood & scuttling here & there, hauling coils of rope, the stirrings of hummed shanties oozing from their souls with the growing swell beneath the prow – gleaming with a worker's perspiration in the morning's last bitter mists – & even when the dreamer wakes the dream remains at full sail, gliding on the billowing surf & leaving a wake of agitated, roiling essences – on past the sandwich-chewing early-risers cross-legged on the quaysides beneath the heavy warehouses' shade – a dolorous low hoot of the klaxon echoes through the timbered spaces between each cavernous hall – spaces ripe for murder, intrigue & a hundred dubious transactions – where deep in the past, old jack tar's rummy songs hailed the coming of twilight – cut-price Brandos smoking on layabout bales – the connivances of the grifters, the guiltless shirkers – they spin their yarns outside the world of the sea – the sinister river gossiped their rumourous conversations to the listening sky above the dark city – these ships are implacable, unrelenting as glaciers as they dredge secrets with each ploughing lurch through the crested surf
under the acquiescent arms of Tower Bridge she rumbled – her sails breadth stretching to pluck the apple of

116

a risen sun – the estuary ripples lend a shifted scent the open sea & the whiff of her breast regales the Captain's inhalation & his lungs well with recognition – like his brothers before the mast, the hint of ice-bitten sea-breath stirred in him as an old song kindles memory – there was no thought given to the voyage as a whole, just the seconds by seconds passing, the tip of the tiller in correction here & there, here & there a dry kelp laugh to greet a seagull's questioning bark – a slow seeping into the ritual until at one with its majesty – feeling the sensuous tickle of fish willingly diverging before the prow's insistence – becoming in a way ennobled by nature's touch, effortless in a slow, dipping forward nod toward that reward, that ultimate & blinding freedom of open water

his ship was cloaked in time, this much of her destiny he knew, dream-washed – it had seen the dark, slender barges toted by mystic lightermen slide unruffled to the wharves with cargos of spice, coffee, tea, an unheard of contraband torn from the distant pillaged coasts – the stevedores steady watch, the gangs swinging their hooked hands, clawing the hessian pillows of treasure from ship to shore with easy rhythms – the songs played out as light on the swell, dawn notes, soft, reverent

& caught in the grand design, from his solitary vantage point on the great shore the Troubadour could feel the immense weight, the full might of his approaching adventure – the world behind him, no forms, no queues, no humanity-clogged, smoky roads churning with the directionless funk of cars

& he knew his ship was in safe hands & that the history he was busy making was a fragment of a bigger memory locked in that wild Captain's brow forever

*

117

startled to work by an April daybreak - as callous & unambiguous as any quick star - he walks, effervescent, amid the bellowing winds - blithe, near a seashore in a sad dream, he is troubled by urgent things, burst & scuttle of worried crab, a dog splashing & barking happy in receding tides - his mind, once becalmed, now anguished by the world's stupid energy - he mops his brow with his soiled sleeve - holding fast within his fisted hand specks of some crumbled leaf rescued from atop the tomb of a sickly autumn past - the memento moribund - things go downhill, the day darkens - a pall descends on both weather & mood

he meets, clowns, villains, he meets the medicine show stranger, as cold as a dagger, with his potions, fables and capsules - but the Troubadour, drunk as time, is oddly spooked by a sudden dread & retreats without partaking - the green glassy bottles & tiny phials tight in the wooden grip of oak shelving under covered wagon - where did he pick up that leaf?

he decides to act, to write a missive to no god in a red, narrow-lined notebook, with cover ripped - he tries out his sermon on the rocky promontory

"...dear life...I want no quackery or placebo - no part in the drama - just plant my feet in the clay & let me grow - wired & beleaguered - for these wasted days are leaving me factory numb - get me to the country station & out to the forest lands - the smoke, the stars and the rum - help me inhale deep of the scent of that soil I know - let me, with this inhaled breath, reel in the harvest, let brothers in industry fetch the beer barrel from the old Plotland house - fetch it whether it be full or drained - for we can always let it replenish itself with these October storms - it's always best to wash your dusty hair in autumn rain, there is no feeling that surpasses it - set your feet firm, prepare for that forged road - once a far ocean beckoned from that hill of my old green innocence & now I begin to fashion an answer to the call..."

sighing, he screwed up the remaining unread pages & tossed them to the mercy of the wind & sea & remembers a brief holiday with Boo up in Wales – suddenly, for no reason, remembering, why?

because in dreams Boo walks with her tipsy, moody old Troubadour of golden, olden times – rising in elfin Welsh ascending hallucinations - from a tent in fallow farmland to the bridge at Anglesey where silent, other-worldly breaths of dovecote charms were passed – the dovecote was cool, damp – they had sat there for a long time drinking, talking & in the lengthening pauses between their chatter, silence expanded – a hush like a stretched cord between two conch shells, connecting two ghost oceans – compressed toll of holy bells - perhaps the very bells they heard ring out across London that day, just more absorbed white noise now, a texture in the symphony - thin, metallic purity of the Welsh air

& they had never heard such thunder that rolled in that night, the same god drumming yet here the biblical heft, the judgemental ache of sonorities, cleaved the cowering valleys like the dissuasive voice of Thor - & he read her his poetry, flowery odes to the gulfs between mountains, bad Clare & musty Thomas, it was as if the staid grandeur of the rich land would permit no other style – or from his book of American Verse, stained, stodgy, impossibly small font, well-thumbed – germs of old haunted neural passageways spreading out from the past, spores of continuity, seeded word bombs

yes & in Celtic daydreams they saw the imprecise smudge of a village approaching them – shifting cubes & sun-streaked colour fields tumbling over the toothed contours until, before they knew it, they were embraced by its, at first, suspicious, moonstruck inhabitants – farm, chickens, an incongruous & improbably red wheelbarrow - a kindly milkman spoke in Welsh to a small spaniel – the impenetrable beer in the sun-streaked old pub – quiet on quiet with livestock lowing – a bottomless bowl of peanuts, barman reading the menu, a book of spells – the white yard with a Morris Minor minus one back wheel & rusting sleepily in the rare warmth – wheelbarrow, where was that poem? – who was it? - Welsh Canine Wheelbarrow - the next pub along the way looked open but was only selling eggs so the Troubadour lit a cigar & watched the squirrels tie themselves in figures of eight around the flaccid branches of a sycamore tree – time refused to pass – the sky spread out in jigsaw blue – it had all been so perfect but he wanted the imperfections back, he wanted the precipice of hope

up ahead, off the curving road, four chickens trot & peck, dappled in a thick, brown, immortal lane

*

& yes, at times he almost believed that he was everyman – from crouched cave dweller to bristling brigadier – king, admiral, pope & shaman

& yes he rehearsed these vivid visions nightly, these solemn prophecies that foretold of hundreds & thousands of somnolent humans moving simultaneously & constantly through time, down their chosen missionary roads, across old seas, circling in convection spirals that forever return, depart & return again to no home

& always by means of the sea - the sea, our blood sister since prehistoric times – the first voyagers, blind knots of .ingenuity, setting forth on rafts & reeds & rugged canoes – vast cauterized areas of smouldering forest behind them, their camp razed – The Troubadour walked with them, feeling their primitive wounds - sadness, deepening in him - for the marriage of man to fertile soil has lost its fever & disappointed, farms strung like factories across the close-shaven fields that hum with technology, silver in green against disapproving red skies – the union with earth now sundered, divorced by an affair with open sea – still the dangerous earth throws up its warning signs – in remorseless rapids of crawling lava – spiralling ballets of whirling dust – photographic evidence emerges – cadmium street scenes of horse & bonnet - the grey legs of pioneers as they bathe in stout rain barrels

America's immense gravity, tugging, remorselessly at the sky - somewhere echoes of nowhere bullets fizzing off dry leather saddles, spinning, rodeo dancing 'cross the Great Virgin Wheatbowls Of The American Plains – cracks & fissures reopen & close - & somewhere, here, in the great reckoning – in the groaning wreckage of caustic Albion – set adrift with the nudge of a calloused, perfidious, fatherly hand, sailors clamp their decaying teeth in braver winds – to seed & rummage her blighted water is their quest – a tribe in sullied name, shaking their shamed identities – seeking new home, tribal, forgetful, all kinfolks gather close & learn to mistrust history – stood high on that Welsh farmland, late at night, Boo snoring in the battered tent, whisky singing to her strangled dreams, he swam in wonder – further & further back he goes, to follow hunter-gatherer diasporas – from beginning to end, from Orinocos & Constantinoples he searches beyond the myriad exotics chosen for history textbooks & celluloid pillages – he recalls his lessons, musty class ringing with Egypt, pharaohs, golden vistas, ancient hieroglyphic shores – he remembers crouching by the school pond in a trance of macrocosmic glory – ear to earth like a pagan - launching matchstick-masted reed boats with his toy soldiers aboard – a last, lost hope in their sorry sailor hearts

& yes they are now all old-timey seafarers, salty piss & shoddy smears of bitumen to proof their sails against the fates – sun high in a cry-baby heaven – plip, the plap of drops feeding the tiny pacific breakers

& of course, as the sun sinks through the old blue
depths, he spies across the lilypad choke of drab water –
there! look! - his once true love sitting in lotus aspect, with
the meticulous poise of a Vermeer cipher, weaving her
basket for eternity – she is beautiful, implacable, not sharing
the slightest glance – blue eyes, no heart, freckled tan, gone

*

& so it was that hourly the sea drew him near, Newtown
Baby, out of dust he came & yet now grown he hears
Mother Ocean for the first time wailing to his Troubadour
heart – spooling her endless great poem – birthing the
loneliness of the questing in his breast – listen to the wave-
song, listen to these things she says, close your eyes, stand
next to her & hear – hushabye it croons - ssh, sssh now
  & tell me of what do these tidings speak? – as in plash &
suck they whisper still, constant pleadings – an urge to
sleep? – then slumber now if hushabye they say
  through recession & succession the secrecy slowly begins
once more, so it does, so it does – a sentiment of sad losses
– sensations, victories so close & smilingly savoured that
they seem smug somehow – passed on in pieces guarded by
shimmering stones, a washed out hourglass, slip of supped
grog, rope-burns shown like tattoos, silhouettes shaped of
flashed distanced figures, sentinels showing the door to his
sly enemies in visions – sing & sing again those blessed songs
that ye never once whispered or purred – encore, says the
gull – a pause like the trapped song before a final wave
breaks – effervescent, whistly hissing the sad unpublished
scores & scriptures these blushing sessions shadow

*

or

a picnic up at the bluebell park – the town lay peaceful
at the feet of the gently sloping green hills – clumps of dark
trees in twisting lines grow silently over fencepost & stile –
sheep living their sheepish lives, cows happily chew nothing
& release long, solitary yawns of pain to the sky – he watches
as she sets the gingham table cloth, sandwiches, ham, pickle,
cheese – Tupperware tubs of crisp salad – he is sure that
this is how a thousand summers will unfold – the thick blue
sky smudged with white rainless cloud – the horse nods &
sniggers – a bee passes like a tiny electric razor – he reaches
up to where the Frisbee stuck between two branches &
plucks a leaf to remember it all by – the Frisbee falls of its
own accord – press the leaf between poems

   & later, as the fleshy evening rubs nervously against the
embarrassed sky, as they walk slow down the long hill -
cider-yawning, ladybird bright – they cup hand to ear to
almost hear, faintly, in the safe, distant panic of the town, the
tedious arguments of the petulant cars, scurrying homeward,
rats on a river of tin

*

erdgeist - guts of the dirt – he can sense it beneath the
paving stones of this North London street – wet, cloying
grunts of earth's revenge

   Lonely Troubadour picks at the Guardian crossword as
a pigeon picks at a fallen chip – immaculate conceptions -
resolutions are but a viper in the rug of his consciousness –
he awaits Boo – pure virgin's nemesis - who is crossing the
busy road with her borrowed twenty pounds – his soul
companion - who in some ancient myths bore the children
of revolutions past & sustained St. Giles on her leprous milk
– & who, under the influence of Benedictine, was known to

have taken slings & arrows in the cause of her saints – blind to failure & heart of rich oak – creature of rare passion & peace - & yes he wrote it all down with intent to fashion a short story – mythos, erdgeist, underground seepage of ancient ills, Boo as saviour of the sainted thouroughfares, hearty cheers, wooden wheel & hoof-clatter – daguerrotypic images blister through the fabric, lyric cartoons of Hogarth misery, tree spirits glimpsed by an earthly child – paw-prints, clues, snow of doubt melting – blood-spots on white, like those he saw drift – translucent moths – across his hungover morning gaze – perhaps they were bequeathed by time, memorials, kindling logs for a sleepy fire, bone-chip, meat of poetry – the erdgeist stirring, woken by his empathy – these brief sallies into the city were no longer enough – a truth was being whispered, a summons to chaos posted on the river's tongue

& what if the real was unreal & contrary-wise? – what if the old curse yet strode these mosaic islands unheeded? – a multiversal leakage, absurdity poking through the stage curtain – there is a mist shrouding the gate of heaven – race of immortals, the heavy ghosts of Celtic past – Ireland's muddy birthing pool – & yes all that remains now are the skitter flicks of animation, the strips of mythic colour in comic-books & they shine like pearls in the illuminated letters of books of hours – Disney debased, Hannah-Barbaric – all dreams die therein – squashed face of tomcat, concertina of bulldog, electrocutions, torture, the severing of limbs, rolling pins, frying-pans, catlflap slammed & snap of mousetrap – yet they rise again to die another day – it is the human animal that never owns this antic foreverworld – this parallel world is lost piece by piece, replaced by our mad sanity, our parched duty - The Troubadour mused, alcohol clearing the misted gate, the hallucinatory promise of a deeper key beckoned – erdgeist stirring, he was par-blind, a tease of angel in his mind's branches, colour-blind in a psychedelic realm

café quiet, radiant in chrome, the sheen of wiped surfaces reflecting an age-old mirage, an encouragement of afternoon sun - tipsy as a faun, delicate path through waiting traffic, she has bought a book of Blake, he fetches from his shoulder-bag a Beano annual & they read to each other, Gnasher snarls red menaces to the Angel innocent, Biffo bear, aloof, to Jerusalem, momentarily, chained

*

Miles Ducat, DJ for the evening in the Basement In The Sky, selects, from a neat stack next to the ragged mound of vinyl records, the first dose of curative song & smiles weirdly - lighting a cigarette he inhales the clean, nourishing smoke & triumphantly holds aloft Dub Housing by Pere Ubu – he leans to the microphone

"...night-print & hollowed out ghost-places - dense in the scratched cardboard square like Nosferatu fitfully dreaming a Rorscharch ink-print – the cracked pipe steam from Ohio factories – where clanking behemoth anvils reverberate in disused minds – let the blurting, fatted, Arbuckled swaggerer croak at us & yelp like gangster's tyres escaping in anthill mobster Fords & as we piss away our paradise – the fix is in, the celebrated feud of the angels has been established - the grand mischievous sprite & other attendant demons have been cast into torment eternal..."

he lets the squiggly bedlam of the first track interrupt his patter & lights a Slim Panatella with practiced ease

yes, & old age flagrantly grins at The Troubadour as he listened – an ever-watchful Captain – it looms large even in the cold stare of his accumulated fears - the ghastly relics of castles in the air lurk - (look! even there) - in the folds of skin on the microwaved milk congealing in the bedside cup -

125

for many little petty grave-robbing details can combine to dig up some overlooked act of *lèse-majesté* – some bullet-riddled corpse of youth - a distraction, music, no more - a rough & ready amnesia that seeped into Newtown Baby's senses & slowly faded to the barest ache of recall as The Troubadour slowly evolved – the tiniest element set the wheels of curiosity turning - his cigarette ash on a rainy grave perhaps, a slam of a door twice & a key turning, crow's feet & mascara, morsels of burnt paper falling from a bonfire in a garden - the tiny curled worms black and writhing - no more

but there were elemental images to which his ageing soul seemed to cling desperately – the sea & its complex & overwhelming histories, attendant rain & cloud shadow, the sisters of moon & tide, it was clear he would never know the final chapter of its vast biography

& the music – once pretty melodies to learn on the soft strings of a Spanish guitar, now the factions & suggestions hidden beneath are making him mad, making him believe in the prospect of madness – a madness that, troublingly, was preferable to the muted colours of his day to day existence – it presented a world outside the world - & it all seemed to resonate outward from the distant capital, which he saw in his mind's eye as a radio tower rising above a hectic miasma of clubs, bars & slippery tiled cafes – where old men set fire to sugar sachets in tin ashtrays & talk of revolution – the waitress smokes in her break by the door that opens to a street full of city rain – a city that always wakes up to noise – trying to remember itself

*

& yes do you remember? - waking who knows where - after whatever chain of disasters born of bad philosophies & fashioned in drunken trances – that time, looking out of a jammed window to a cemetery – priest hushing the shadows behind the tombstones - the grey queues of marble & granite awaiting the parade of the unlucky living – the trees dancing in brown wool – swallowing the watery light dripping from the dawn – the serious red buses, frowning, muttering, loomed in the gloaming – remembering, he had somehow gone to London yesterday – red buses, they growled up the wet road past the graves – overtaking workmen carrying their satchels of sandwiches & flasks of tea – the birds remained silent in stark branches until the rhythmic chunter of the buses' engines had passed beneath – only then chorusing their freedom to the blotchy sky of drizzle & fug – do you remember? – a room, a bed, lumpy & the heavy eiderdown with its hideous pattern – something familiar assails his ear - the shipping forecast, the radio he had left on all night beside his bed - Viking, Forties, Dogger, Sole & Bailey – mud-banks & hollows somewhere far away - absorbing the radar blips & giving faint echo – Land's End, St. David's Head – brown fug of cemetery voice, breathless in the studio vacuum – steady lists of unknown worlds, man's voice, sensible, suited, hair-parted - he imagined it worming from the tombs through the bleak rain - Lough Foyle, Carlingford Lough – dry words for distant seas – the warm poultice for a bruise of coming storm-clouds - the rhythm of this litany of ridiculous names stayed in his head, wrapped in tatters of sleep – the words had become tidal, inevitable - Ardnamurchan Point, Cape Wrath – a short fable in a secret language, word broth, the poem of distance & the threat of danger – diluted psalm essence – Channel Light Vessel, Machrihanish - the window's tapping rain blurring the graves, stretching parcels of death

two old ladies putting damp flowers on the shiny marble – the sea boiling in their souls, in torment - it rises to sob a few approved tears that are unheralded in the soft, wet air – the buses are still murmurous, grumbling, soft wet red through the roadside stone & shrub, weaving & lurching with chugs of dark gears – still the endless far off voices, Dogger, Fisher German Byte – the lone, sad Dachshund sniffing the distant stench of the netted catch – the hint of doom in the old ladies' curdled perfume – they wring prayers out of their creased hands – Humber, Thames, south-east veering south-west – handkerchief from handbag to wipe the rain-tears – poor old so & so he was a good man, he had his faults but who hasn't? – there is no time passing, the clouds gilded with a promise of relief – the workmen will clock in & put their half- finished newspapers safe in their lockers – the old women will shuffle to catch the bus back to the high street, perhaps tea & a scone in the bakers - thundery showers, moderate, good, occasionally poor

*

yes & exactly how lost can a solitary soul get? – The Troubadour outgrowing his present - living is dying in this cornucopia of small fish – this constant rebelling against the big pond grew so wearying – there is an ocean out there at the end of a long, lonely track – the names may not be as exotic but they are attainable & elsewhere

so pass quickly on through - Laindon, West Horndon, Upminster, Barking, Stepney East, Fenchurch Street – reel off a different litany, stations of the cross – misery line, way of sweet sorrows, his *Via Crucis* – his shining Calvary looming on a communist hill

here, locked in this open prison, all he can do is quietly flounder – he is already feeling his mind drifting sluggishly backwards through his brief map of days – stilted time, maudlin pride, the cruel happy anger of the pubs the only respite – he was a boxer on the ropes, the architectural hubris of the new town his assailant – meekly offering his chin to a terminal punch – the red brick walls returning his thrown ambitions like a tennis ball rebounding - newly rouged girl/women, counting off the numbers of years, as skipping ropes swung in terrifying arcs & hands were slapped together to curt, primal rhymes - he had dreamed beyond it all, there was a universe of wilder wind to navigate, he had seen the maddened sea & returned to the village & it was no longer enough

*

so the stranger boys nervously gravitated toward the seedier cultural havens, pubs that were empty by day - the heavy red-brick spleen of the streets, the concrete harmony, the damp monster of sound collage, dense fleshy music stuck with rusted pins - the stacked, oak barrels behind the bar of the Basement In The Sky - a twist of lemony anguish in the dead hearts of all the rebellious clientele, the pallor of the grave in the skin of long-terminated idols - dreams resting in peace as the wars raged, endless, above ground - this haven for undiscovered failures - looking to history for answers to unspecified questions - art students, bleating angst for cubist Gertie & looking in the cracked glass at Sapphic servant Alice - back through time & snug in the broody nest of their own Rue Des Flores - knowing it was only a clique, a gossiping cynosure of adolescent fear - listening in council flats of grim decay to angular songs through crackly speakers & taking in by day sharp portraits of the town comprised of panicked collisions of cones & cylinders - a moveable, inedible feast for colour-blind eyes - the text dense, the illustrations faded, turning the pages, caravans of daubers & smudgers flick by as pianos rattled triplets of assonance in the blue storm of ancient corridors - posters hang on the off-white walls of the stairwell, then as now - the barmaid yanks the brown liquid from the pump - for her rose is not a rose here - this sterile, overspill town still hiding virginal wendy-houses behind the fig-leaves of Plotland allotment & heritage - this beery, brassy town of truncated horns & reverb screams - where brown grass offers up protests in the thin clay gaps - change is as good as a resurrection - *mutis mutandis* - in the chip shops, shoe shops & card shops sickly aromas merge - leather & sunflower oil, paper glue & boot polish - & the whole town mixes in the head a gloopy mess of young perfumes that ooze through the wrinkles of The Troubadour's grimace as the grave chuckles like rolled dice in his conversations

a few rebels make a move, taking impromptu days off from their dull jobs on temptress sunny mornings – trying to train their hearts to flee - fishing trips out in the country when no red phone box meant no contacts - & yet the elemental things remain, base sensations are still unhooked - as if the wires of communication have been severed, the threat of finality earthing the telegraph fields – the cocked head of paused birds – the modern church, with its Christ tangled in a vortex of futurist javelins, sits empty by the blind garden - & in the chapel of contemplation, radio static skitters where once melodious voices of the dearly beloved sang out their pious reassurances – now the fields smell more of tractor than of horse - roads ring with invisible vehicles that give out a siren to warn of their coming – ice-cream vans turning into Black Marias - they move through the street in flat, micro-tonal, misty shapes emitting a low throb, like wine glasses softly rubbed - it seemed to The Troubadour that all protest, every dissenting question, was being muffled by the baffles of the padded town - it is so easy just to coast in these blithe, fractal days – the beer is watery after a sip of rum & the roses look fake since the concrete flowered

*

130

books, sweating quietly –nervous in the gaunt library, like bewildered priests at a Stockhausen lecture – in a blue plastic chair The Bewildering Troubadour frowning, inhaling the book-breath of literary pirates & plunderers - their spices & garlicky knowledge - all of them dangerous & so much more thrilled with life & strung with pearls of understanding – yes, he is in the right place this morning, sat in this blue plastic seat by the table of clumsily piled children's books - he calmly watches the town slip behind rain through the window – that grey pencil rain, stealthy, uninhabitable – tapping the shoulders of land-locked toilers with unbearable reminders of the distant sea – he sat, watching through the windows, all morning - tall, blue, tinted windows, the surrounding frames have poster-paint pictures each child has signed – mummy, daddy, school, Darren 5, Emily 8, Colin 7 & a half, thick crayon skies hang over felt-pen houses with deep green lawns & red fences, the brilliant yellow suns burning, perfectly round, in the top corner throwing no shadows

finally he shuffles, with his carefully selected books, through the rank subway under the roundabout - old graffiti words seep through the re-painted, chipped subway tiles in echoing peals of desperate love – Jim & Sally forever – I heart Alex - the voices of town planners, suspended in time, creep into the stale air, brown suits, grey shirts, black shoes, white-boards, list of possibilities, coffee, biscuits

"...do we have a name for the town yet?...'

"...yes, we're going with that first choice, it's a derivative of some old farmer, sense of the past, bit of history to lend it charm – same with the surrounding countryside, bucolic, add hill to old hill & there you are..."

same old tapestry snag - domesday knit & purl - when Adam delved & Eve span - unsettling, the voices interrupted the colours of his reveries – demolished the crayon houses - he shook the empty exchange from his soul with a shudder

131

& walked out of the subway's astonished mouth, gratefully
gulping the damp breeze
    at the bus stop, the subdued, moist flushes of the shops
sniggered behind him – an old woman, waiting for the bus
home, two lumpen shopping bags & a red umbrella –
mouth gaping in a rictus of unfathomable astonishment –
subway to her failing mind, dazed by the hurtling seasons –
her purple coat buttoned to a throttled neck – in a dance of
drips from the awnings her gristly dog mopes unleashed –
she will soon be safe, back within her old four walls & sepia
church-prints - she will only purse her unkissed lips to sip
the gentle steam from her boiling tea – & from her one true
window, four workmen slave in silhouette on a rooftop
opposite - they swing muscled limbs against an ice-cream sky
– arms rising, falling, like oiled machinery – they play out
their reparations to a backlit stack of chimneys stretching to
infinity – puppet-men, cut from black paper – they wreathe
petals from the still darkness beneath the seagull's cry –
oubliettes of tarmacadam & grease – they are night- insects,
hallowed wraiths made of absences & vacuums, working
toward a thankless nonentity – dust-devils, imploding stars

*

    The Newtown Troubadour. loose in the baby new-town
– the paving stones ill-fitted & clunking as he walked, each
step a drum-tap intro to the song of the multitude – mind
not right, unkind - the glum metal lampposts defaced with
love's trysts – their casing burst open & fuse exposed - & up
above these avenues of tapering antennae pastel flags hang
limp as grand-maternal skirts, unshaken by the gusts of
words & crude art scratched into their torsos – inert, stupid,
they stare down through phases of dry heat, greaseproof
paper distortions – exoskeletal shopping trolleys rolling
slow through Sunday's savage lines, roof & awning - jigsaw

foliage, maggot-pecked - tree, metal, leaf, the disfigured grey stone beyond it all – in limp curves of air, the sky, slithery strips of polythene, a dishonest blue sham of its mother liquid, is smeared across damp white paper by an eager child - random hypnotic glyphs dripped over the baize, gelid falsities of the park & high overhead mysterious offices, pinstriped conversations churn in the biscuit-dunked, weak tea world of the typewriter & crucified ego – polystyrene cups of lukewarm soup, pens nervously peering from breast pockets of white collared shirts, the stymied grace of occluded endeavour blurs the image like reeking incense

"...now then, she is a prize little princess & no mistake! - what shall we call her? - the old pram meat & mewling ingrate..."

"Chloe's a pretty name - Julie at number 32 - you know, Dave's Julie – with the Volvo? - called theirs Chloe..."

sour yellow dandelions guarded the greenhouse skirting, it was the year he begged for a pet - he drags a last clutch of unfiltered smoke & stubs his crushed corduroy dog-end in the lid of a jam jar upturned

"...we called the tortoise Elvis - painted his name across the shell & dad said it looked like ancient scrabble squares - we laughed & sometimes sat in striped deckchairs with ice-cream cones..."

bad sprouts evilly grinning – furtive, mushy carrots hidden beneath clumps of good-hearted mashed potato – & yes he likes sprouts now – ah but how the big people were cunning – how their plans for him had played out down the years, exploding randomly like forgotten landmines after a war - on the lawn - our treasured plot, our green allowance - between split, rotting fence-work & broken trellis - or spectral with sparklers in bonfire smoke-light – the frozen time, the caged memories stuck tight to semi-detached walls - rectangular sepulchres for the undead, candle-haunted in streets without footsteps, the browning paving slabs clinging loose with clay borders squeezing out from their entombment

& sure of the constant threat of pubs, the easy dissolving hour – making Faustian deals of borrowed coinage - sure that Lucifer works the night pulleys - his puppets jerk at the cold, blind shopfront displays - no pulse, dead town, grey wind & Elvis the cryptodyral remnant of a sad clan, lone survivor, born old, plodding away from the next comet's apocalypse, he chews the existential lettuce leaf & lumbers to eternity through the fresh-mown lawn

"...where do you fancy this year?"

"...up to you my dear, all fine by me – somewhere warm though eh? – no bloody caravans this year eh? - old Murray in personnel says Malta's nice..."

"...what's wrong with the bloody Isle Of Wight? - your mother burns easy remember, that weekend break in where was it?..."

blood dry on infidel walls – baked clay totems

"Murray, you know, wife just had a baby..."

solemnity of bricks – piled in dust of revolutions

"...grandma won't fly at her age – her veins..."

destinations, the click of airport timetables

"...there's always Ventnor, that blue B&B with the hanging baskets..."

The Troubadour is suspended by a thread, low fruit, a pendulum halted by stuck cogs – the day slowly pushing him to the cheer of a foamy jug, he could taste it – ten cigarettes, three pages unblemished in the notebook, five pounds & thirty pence - enough

*

it doesn't seem to get any better, 5 a.m. – awake despite the tug to sleep that stale headaches employ – he dresses in the same outfit from the previous blur of night – walks to the yawning newsagent - he buys a can of ginger beer to wet his throat & the wind calls him - his name written in breath - scowling through the icy shards of stoned, staring windows - through the letters that the lost women of the past never sent - vultures circling high as their ghosts put on his overcoat - meet me at Brooke House or under the lollipop clock that's wrong, always wrong - or in the bland, cataleptic parks between factories - heavy ground so bodied by the county's red clay, paved over - hopscotch courses dissolving in blue rain – scratch the thin surface & the old soil festers beneath, death-warm & worm-sucked – mythically swollen with deep-rooted, boneless Pocahontas – an obsolete doyenne, reborn & rejected anew as an exotic Miracle-Queen of the Bata estates – The Troubadour spat, ugly twist of coffee-strafed phlegm - his brain was clogged with patches of desolation – spilled tar on a white beach – his river of thought still carried seeds of ideas & schemes of escape but they struggled to surface through glutinous pools of lily-pad & spawn

he pictures an hour-glass to reassure himself, an old trick, & time gently slips from bulb to bulb as he turns it over & over in his head – renewal, the sack of recollections swung over a blistered shoulder – bulges of mad bracken & the exhausted stench of mouldering fruit – crab-apples from an Eden tree, inedible – the new ocean crystalline, already wriggling with the impending droves – he knows he is beaten, etiolated – he knows he cannot face work today - so he wanders to the westbound train that drags him to the sea, to watch the waves, as always – the waves are adamant, beautiful & present him with no argument – he could spend a healing hour just fixing on the old dull heave of time as the longstanding routine of the fatigued tides gently lessened his panic

but he doesn't need the peace, not today – no, he will drink venomous, mysterious ales in the pubs of the seafront crawl – there are pool games & jukeboxes, over which hangs a fog of raw smoke as hustlers argue bets & promises through their cigarettes - it was a mistake to come here – darkness will fall again before he knows it & soon there are night-rats in the car-park of the discotheques, shouting at skinny girls & hailing taxis in shambolic queues by the burger stall – squirt, gasp of air, ketchup over mustard - his chin is growing stubbly & his unkempt clothes are already betraying the clipped, polished order necessary for the daily trek to oblivion that employment offers – his sense of purpose fell apart, a victim of the stalking night's scattered hours

he oversleeps the following morning, bruised eyes widening at the sight of the lying clock – fuck it, slap the alarm shut, there are other jobs, the dole lurks with its grimy envelope of ready cash – waking at ten, rubbing a sore, bristly chin, he is gripped by the desire for cleanliness - he wants a close shave to snick his quieted morning skin to sharp focus – it is still night in his daytime head – the sun & moon are conspiring sisters – cackling witch laughter – an invisible shout in an alley

& yes everything is sorcery, magic seeps under the beermats & claws at his whisky chasers - already Clubland Whores & Tarot Snakes are again queueing for the chugging parade of predatory taxis - & if he looks up at the canopy of space beyond the bedroom window – cloudless & white this morning, burnished, feathery - he sees flapping ghosts of his wages soaring in chevrons on broken wings to the void – money doesn't matter but pretends to matter much - & by closing his eyes he is already there, moonlit, eastbound train long gone, tracks & platform silent – his bed a bench of splinters & nails

*

136

& these were the peripheral fears, the dimly lit suburbs of the mind – the repository where somehow his affairs of dishonour are forgotten – schizophrenic portraits, an arc of delusion, the trajectory of a tossed stone across a foggy pond – he is the mistake unmade by entropic dissolution – a reveller left behind – & the dawn's a long-lost darling promising a golden road to sweet, crimson night, brother of dishonest toil, sly sister weekend – The Troubadour has stepped from one routine to another – from prosperous to dissolute – but he cares not, he knows the game is fixed – he has been walking now far too long through a mess of lost opportunities to expect a winning hand – nothing clings, no love or loss of dignity ever adheres - stumbling to the outskirts of a city he barely knows, looking for her still in swarms of blood-hot faces rubbed across the night – the eternal companion, sisterly comrade-in-arms - where did she go? – even her name has escaped - perhaps she skated away one winter on interlacing slivers down the river - past the lowing dockyard klaxon - fresh from the end of graves – a new Pocahontas, buried there to form the skeleton of a Troubadour nation – & perhaps the Good Captain spied her bobbing raft as it passed his prow – in the tangled eddies of the morning's half remembering

*

cold, cold the steel bench of the new town – colder still the thought of it decades hence – arms hugging himself in a hurting wind – hugging tight as if he loved himself – raw cheeks puffed against a steady hail that bursts in a thousand tiny detonations on his Safeway carrier bag keeping his night library dry

he thinks of her now as then – years the only marker – a surge of involuntary disgust almost making him yell out loud in the busy market square – stifle, swallow eventually calm again, deflated by the inevitability of the daily impositions, he sinks into his sodden coat like a weary turtle & sleeps to try & paint himself back to her warm forgiveness – his breath, as he sinks lower, imitates her loyal nocturnal pulse – they slept under that building, block of flats – Brooke House? – nearby a statue, mirthless in wet fog - a dark grey mother clutching an impassive cherubim – half a warm can of souring cider

Brooke House, yes - or else – if the rain had abated - by that dead winter fountain's rim - Mark loves Deb in magic marker scrawled - as indelible as the Woolworth's sign – a passing fidelity, a brief encountered passion, gets burned on the tit of a nude stone mother, astride which the dull child, stony hair frozen, frost haloed, sits aghast – peeing quiet rivulets of acid rain down his mother's flanks - her thrown back head, captured defiant in a diva fit – January icicles extend her Ophelian locks in spectral braids - wintering in that old real season of sledges & frothing, frostbitten toes – a realm of white dust where something ancient is celebrated – where the sudden gust disconcerts the flags above the spiky church of glass – flags, they weren't there yesterday – baby bunting – the upper classes must be giving the peasantry the gift of another parasite – these pennants are muted tongues - keeping sniggering secrets of royal babies, or coming circuses - Olympiads & World Cup losses - circuses to distract from the authentic pain of the humdrum tapping of workaday hailstones on the tented roof

he despises flags, bunting, the sport's-day loudspeakers, fetes & trestle-table bric-a-brac – cheap porcelain country-houses, sheepdogs & parasol women with tilted bonnet - & always the string of flags, flags, flags – cheery triangles signifying nothing, teased by the guilty wind on drooping rope above it all - limp strange-fruit corpses – gaunt, pallid dishcloths awaiting the suds & eddies - taut, tremulous, then bursting open, proud as blood – risen phoenixes from the sad collapse of mourning restored - fluttering in the whittling rain as red bricks tan to russet in the car spray - crimson & yellow leaves scumble the beige stone floors in the busy service yards – carved maps where the rain has rested on wet plastic tubs, behind which sloth-children drape jumpers on bike racks & thrill to the taunting of lip-stuck punk girls on boyfriends' laps, chubby arses in leather casually sat – they are fashionably bleak, horny as church cats – gothic under Brooke House's gut, milling around the broken lift – they are classical, a tableau of decadence & revolt - & in Hammer horror echoes, on a snatched fag-break, a janitor whistles something of Christmas in the stunned tinsel & bellying, baubled ache of the bright chrome mall – but The Hermetic Troubadour is insulated from their blind electricity - absent in music – the dream-world's dance - walking & pretending to get lost in the psychogeographic swim of slushy new town backstreets – his headphones are telling him lies - friendly fire, that something is happening here, unclear as to what exactly, but there's an armed man over there so be aware & nobody lives here anyhow in this well-lit box of heirlooms on spindly-tree crescent, where sweet wine from the Algarve rots in the cabinet of fathers & the Aldertons snip at their paranoiac neighbours' prying hedges – whilst The Bowdens polish the BSA's exhaust & shine the tank & the kids, why the kids they all smile from their duffle-coats under white-wood porches - abducted waifs in Super-8 – their parents at work, they bunk school – the office waits for them all, the rusting syntax of futile, nihilistic conversations threatening their very sanity with the pointlessness of the soul, of time – nothing worth the stretch of recall, a palace of dry phrases palsied, shifted by tremors, a clutch of life choked by the drought, desiccated minds of blown sand

"...did you see the game?"

soft drizzle on cardboard sounds like a frog – new-town
edgeland, shrub & pallet – sheds crammed with corroded,
arthritic lawnmowers, blunted & rusted hoes, bait-boxes of
slow-dying maggots, claw-hammers, rough chisels, husks of
summer-burnt flies – browning windows barely masking a
fused dichotomy of protestant labour & allotment zen
"...never offside, never...fucking linesman was ten yards
behind the play..."
fish not biting – pecking the mossy film of reflections
under the brown heavens - Sunday football whistles from
the distant park - mother reads the cackling columns & mint
sauce congeals in the blue-hooped egg cup
& yes, some of England's wizened, old glory is forever
nurtured here – brushing sideways its bootblack curls – The
Dumb Men Of Blighty shaving mechanically in toothpaste
mirrors, their women grow old & tangle strands of thick
wool in endless Fairisle patterns – & yes, there is a sickness
that threatens a catastrophe, a premature demise – they feed
on palliatives, nudges from the music of their young – while
grandmothers cast their bingo runes – lives lived Ambre-
Solaired & Parma Violated
& yes of course he knows that this universe is not his,
the rewards are all way out of his reach & dislocated by time,
grubbily elite – yet he kids himself that he could have it all if
he so chooses – own the clattering typewriters, the churning
calendars punctuated by arrowheads, weekends highlighted
in yellow - all those creamy skins preening to their holy
mirrors – the fantasies of deckchairs, gift-shops & towel-
draped sun-loungers – creaking hammocks bulging under a
beery sag of sweating out-patients in paradise – all the
holidaying militia, the drab barren miles of calcified flesh
no, not for him this nervous, waiting-room life – this
surface vulnerability – why dwell on the meaningless details
when bigger things threaten the hush – the office window,
factory door, the tease of vivid air - & January lays a strip of

dull snow over centrally heated lofts - blue slates, steaming air-vents, antiseptic tides dragged over the bald, grumbling shell of earth – a quaking crust beneath which his fellow renegades will wait – impatiently staving off judgement day coffins – snipering their drunk chances at the last bell's call to arms – accustomed to the gunshots from a never-ending war that become a clock's ominous ticking – the incoming bombers, symphonic wail of siren & the bullet's ricochet yelps – a stirring timpani of distant explosions & the throaty growls of labouring tanks – all the old beautiful conflicts that lie dormant at the back of conservative minds – The War-Ravaged Troubadour lights a stolen cigarette & listens to his cornered voices fill the spaces under the vaulted glass above the bus station – he listens & takes his guerrilla orders in the backstreet acoustic shadow – noting down his shell-shocked fragments of reason in spidery lines of tired poetry

but already the patriot's doubt sniffs the fear in our nape - the pores pucker to feel the stiffening hairs firming a knotted grip in the voicings of the throat - shifting away from our recollected visions as we blather of ageing

until one slow, fly-blown weekend the change occurs - he's in town, paying rent two months overdue, & a deeply magical transformation detonates in the counterculture – something happening here – he stops, hey, what is that sound? – he has reached another summit, the only way is down to the valley to make base-camp & scour the tea-leaves for the wisest move - already flowers adorn the hair of his comrades – already they march to a curious new rhythm – the streets are stiff with placards that in tall stencilled script describe our dear leader's failings – the talk is of revenge, whispers of unpaid dues, murky articulations, dense slang, alien & abbreviated are urging the fired masses to pulse like a clenched fist in the dirty streets - & sure enough the hackles tremble, the brim quivers with an overflow of repugnance – let out the cry! - *venceremos!* – the time is

now, sudden comrades! – accidental brethren! – we must
fight!

*

but it is soon Sunday – there are no late buses & the beer
garden has a bloody kids' area – they've painted over the
graffiti in the bus shelter & it is all of a sudden evening – a
stilled, morphine evening of lamps dimming beyond the
cropped lawns of perception – a strained evening of tea,
sponge cake, doilies – two cats are in the cushions & mother
strips her torn hair from the brush – the rebellion has
inevitably been turned into cartoons on the television &
overlaid with velvet voices on the safe radio news – the town
is deserted, dustmen sweeping beer cans into sacks – on the
stone rim of the mother & child fountain a crow caws at the
silence – The Troubadour is a soldier without a war, he
stares up through the crossing branches of a bare tree – a
blunt cicatrix against the upturned palm of a dull sky – &
there is a habitual futility tugging like gravity at his blue
mood – a sense of an uneasy truce soon coming – he is not
a specialist, a required recruit, he is just a knowing soldier
destined to be unknown – he will fill no plinth with his
statuary reminder – no, the battle has been pledged without
him &, out there on the cutting edge, in the bombed-out
avenues of London, already the places at the barricades
have been taken

*

Boo spreads across two barstools & digs the waves of
mutilated surfing roses flowing from the ratty speaker by her
ear – Link Wray, linking rays of west-coast fuzzy sunlight,
needles in the roar of his raging, altruistic scree – Boo nods
distractedly, it is easy to surf through her hair with your eyes

– head tilted back & creamy, blushed swell of cheek – her
nose breathing smoke to a distant island shore
   & does she ever think about that time they took their
raw devotion to the boisterous seafront & cracked open the
door to the Liberty Belle? - the jukebox playing shades of
fallen angel's wings & suicides - it was tantamount to hearing
the uplifting chords of their own private rhapsody – or
riding wild in the Gypsy Shamanic Rover with the Mystic
Ricardo - out to festival beers in the speckled, henpecked
peripheries – & was it really like the stories said? - yes it was
- that same shamanic native un-American who careened
whisky-blind through southern towns & fields, foraging for
soups made from hedgerow & earthly magic – heathens,
they fled from imagined ghosts – in the cracked rear-view
mirror there was nothing chasing - & yes they were chasing
in turn the nothingness that enticed them – Mystic Ricardo,
goatee wild & black hair tied with coloured braids of wool -
he knew every sound that pierced a campfire night, the
malevolent communications of hidden birds swooping from
invisible branches, animating the limbs of haunting
Tarkovsky trees at daylight's first ember – gipsy strange, he
clutched the big steering-wheel with a single gloved hand,
leather grip, talking non-stop on every raised subject, a word
enough to trigger reams of grunted twists of poetry -
knowing the names of every tiny petal of each wilted spear
of grass – a friend to staunch riverbanks & straying brook
alike, the lapping giggles ceasing as he bent his knee to drink
down from his cupped paws their cool, blended, trickle of
silences – a waft of scented air pointing him to tracks of
badger & fox – Boo & the Old Newtown Baby had been set
free with this raggle-taggle remnant of Essex folklore – all
that summer mad they followed his pure, messianic
benevolence onward through draughts of rawest ciders &
berries - fixed flat tyres & watched him swear at the
stuttering motor, oil-caked, brutal - until finally, as learned

143

prodigals, they washed up back in Newtown – pure, cleansed by the damp truth of soil, babes no more – eyes closed, she was now, head back – was she on that road again? – & yes Miles Ducat was DJing, as ever, the night they got back & unwashed burst into the Basement In The Sky – they ordered two Abbot Ale's & a round of rum

& as if reading their minds Miles grins & riffles the stacked vinyl – triumphantly selects his prey & sets needle to groove, loosing Astral Weeks on their fleeing thoughts like friendly dogs romping the tall hay

& yellow leaves of grass moved in their hearts with the weightlessness and sovereignty that the leisurely drifting mantras necessitated – arrangements swam, pretended to fire, caught unawares by those old jazz sidemen prophets finding their feet in this new land of Celtic exile – tentatively they plucked & stirred the snare, these holy players, they slid with the slim slow rhythm & were as nervously curious as the unblemished planet they explored – the wild, red-haired tongue-talker, caged in a booth, erecting a frustrating fence of wiry guitar - with mystic ease the skittering brushes lick the smears of drums - the tobacco-stained, perpetual, Dylanic hug of a fat, black, fatback mother bass swooping beneath the yowl of a Whitman child & rough ridden, edgy as foreign gossip

at the head of the stairwell tousled youths & greased bikers punch the stuck buttons of the cigarette machine & curse the ancient deities with fishy tankard breath – distant, downstairs, a mandolin is strummed & the churn of Uilleann pipes above the rabble can be heard snaking, adding a sly authenticity to the brew – pipes of the raised elbow – how easy the grease of inspiration slithering in their throats - & windows darken unnoticed in time & the neon bulbs make the chromes & silvers glint to life under the gaudy optics – small glasses follow their parent flagons to tables, many-circled & smeared by the piss daubs of the

Fauvist hoi polloi – the carpet, a squashed shrubland of ashen contours, gives up sprays of dust motes as Nurse Plimsoll & Dr. Marten scrape past the stub-leg chairs & rested handbags in search of a respite from the dance

Miles grins & recites beat poetry through the crackly, dying shreds of feedback from his cheap microphone & yea these acolytes, brim-filled with stale bitters, edged warily through punk's first blooming, they saw the paramount minds of a blank generation devastated by apathy & skunk weed & wrote nothing down – peckish & hilarious when naked, dragging themselves through the stale, white-bread streets of the new-town at noon looking for a tranquil Guinness - seraph-headed Miles – lording over his heaven on earth, gurning high from the stolen plinth of the almighty – his soul aflame for the antediluvian, ghastly union of the pipe's blare - to the lustrous farting roman candle in the cogs of sunlight hours – takes Astral weakly from the decks & places Trout Mask Replica on a startled turntable – moonlit with Vermouth, he holds this new lamp aloft - & the rust knows cowards & the bus rolls back to the coast where the limits of the world reside, as deemed just by no god & bad train timetables

The No-Good Troubadour Boyo, attracted, perhaps by the possibility of gleaning further arcane threads of learning, leaned in on the conversations of the late-arriving Mackay, who chewed his north-eastern vowels, rendering everyday words & phrases hilarious by their very utterance – they garbled lusty jokes & misunderstood philosophy until the bell rang dry & the cows came home

but of all the strange twists of language that swirled about The Celtic Troubadour's folksy head, it was the Irish tongue that licked his ear the best – the broth of paddies frequented the quieter hours of the pub's week & he soon latched himself on to their Sunday lunchtime sessions – for then it was their little cabal's plotting house, a surrogate church in lieu of salvation – jackets dark & dusty, suit trousers not quite matching, fly-buttons only occasionally fastened, off-white pressed shirts open at a hairy neck – they were stereotypical & proud of it – cartoon Celts, grotesque & wondrous, the flood of ale & whisky pouring into their paunches equalled only by the torrent of unlikely fables endlessly burping out of their ruby, wet mouths – three middle-aged wise men, Frank Kavanagh, winking braggart & sage, Mighty Mick O'Bride, womanizer & petty warrior of minor political causes & Tom Maher, poet & famed last-bell balladeer – soupy boys of broth, ebullient pages torn from a wobbly almanac of the Auld Country – they distrusted every customer but heartily welcomed them to their table for the admission price of a pint of livener or a swiftly chasing shot of warmth – they dragged the low-life culture of Dublin through any English bar they graced & increased the cultural quotient of any local lore - their very voices made drinking to excess not merely pleasurable but a necessity – listen to them, it matters not which character speaks, for they are an unholy triad, a linguistic roller-derby of overlapping legends - three mouths with a single mind, fuelled by stacked-up gas & expertly rolled cigarette smoke – all bar-staff & bootleg bookies cheer at their stumbling entrance – any loose coin, unwanted for frivolous revelry, is sure to be put to work on an ill-favoured nag

the bar darkened with the skirt of a passing cloud & they paused to roll new loose-lipped cigarettes & plot a new twist to their conversations

"...it'll be a bloody fine Tuesday when ye get these fuckin' bets on, Mickey – I got a fiver burning holes in my pocket for that three-legged shitebag runnin' in the three-thirty at Redcar – Christ alive what time is it already...?"

"...half two – I'll put it on when this place shuts – you'd be better off wastin' it on another round than throwin' it at a bloody crippled horse..."

"...you can lead a horse to whisky..."
the *bon mot* hung in the smoky air unresolved, alas
"...what's she rustled up for dinner, roast of pork would
suit me - nice bit of cracklin' - can't top that, I tell ye..."
on they blathered & dithered - each fable, tall tale, each
invention, concoction, quotation & tortured dialectic, every
twisted song & false memory were at swim these unholy
Sundays & the flotsam of it all sloshed around The
Troubadour's skull - by now a lake of spirits embittered
under a lager sun - all the long afternoon - hours afterwards
deliciously dragged out, processions of spun controversies,
scribbled poems & eventually a wolfed, re-heated dinner,
the weeds of corny rhymes festered until they bloomed
again as night flowers on the decks of his waiting dream ship
old Dublin postcards he had found in an elasticated
batch on the Newtown Market - when that city was rife with
gossiping genius & bawdy reverence - horses, always the
moping horses - & trundled metal barrels glinting in weak
sun - but it would never again grow new, a time lost, yet it
fired his fantasies of escape & was the only depiction the
Troubadour had of that home to his lunchtime cabal, his
merry thieves of time - he often fancied that they slipped
through a portal & slept right there within the postcard's thin
frame, until the first barman's bell dragged them to their
Sabbath & shamed confessional - take this tenner, here, get
us a good round in to get us going - here's one for ye, what's
the difference between a long-distance runner & a randy
chef? - one goes for a pant in the country... & yes you shall
dissolve to a muzzy sepia, the boys' pranking grins outside
the snug's shady windows, bold porter, gluey sawdust like
your morningtime mouth - sleep it off & wake to the reek of
frying pig & duck eggs - slowly grease the bloody pan &
swallow hard - get it down, the fat will stop ye disappearing,
there's bugger-all of you minus the hair-shirt on your back -
because a fat man is a happy man, it makes the bass voice

boom, an echo-chamber the old gut is, I'm tellin' ye – three-thirty, Redcar – it's a copper-bottomed dead cert – I'm tellin' ye, would I lie? – brimstone-ruddy face punched by fists of ancient double chasers – those death's birds tweeting in a wheat-field mind – his eyebrows, two settings, vague dismay & mock-surprise – lift a lazy buttock for a slithering fart like a released balloon & sew a fuckin' button on that, Tom – chorus of disapproval & held noses – barmaid mutters, filthy bastard & there's uproar & shy/merry swigs as Frank leans conspiratorially to the severe barmaid beckoning her ear & whispers in deepening brogue to enhance the effect

"...I made dat wit' my bum..."

two feet from the unfolding action but a million light-years elsewhere, Tom Maher, poet, who had begun the day with a few in The Bull before arriving, was lost to all methods of communication except that of, the tongue-tied versifier's last bastion, mighty mother song – an awkward, strangulated melody struggled to part his bubbly lips, tinged ochre by slumbered, forgotten roll-ups

"...the bells jingle-jangle...ba-bum-tum diddle dangle..."

a motley mixture of tunes ensued, curiously worded, segued, threatening Molly Malone at all corners but sideswiping Clare To Here & Dublin In The Rare Old Times before landing belly first in Carrickfergus – at a loss for the second verse of whatever it was that troubled him, he fell silent in deep Behan musings, a dark frown hiding his memory's desperate search for the lyric

though by far the quietest of the crew Tom Maher was The Honorary Irish Troubadour's favourite – gentle odour of Sligo mud, Brut & bomb-dust, radical madrigals of peat & ember – forever misquoting the lost legends of literature & song – adding his own dishevelled philosophies to their heft

& yes he once memorably refashioned Under Ben Bulben so comprehensively it stood alone as a work of abstract genius – W.C. Yeats, Mickey had christened him –

148

written on the cubicle wall in felt-tip to give those in the
know a smile - wobbly rebel songs & children's rhymes alike
got lost in translation, but he still recalled a little of the old
tongue & could reel off a few fine sacred lines before the
terminal dram hit his synapses, with a sound like a drunk
pissing on a fuse-box - yet his native warmth found a true
voice in song & his song was one song - a song of pride,
which he attacked anew each time with an unshakeable self-
knowledge & chortling abandon, the key set by the strong G
major of the closing bell
    he was in addition a sly purveyor of awful jokes that
morphed his countenance from rugged melancholy to that
of a mischievous child that had been caught swearing by a
nun & repressing giggles outside the headmaster's study -
indeed, he remained constantly teetering on the edge of an
infectious, leavening laughter, yet, in half his moods, he
could be stoic as an Easter Island statue - a changeling,
perhaps, but at all times solid in the service of his call to the
opening bar
    you rarely got just a pint when he was flush & he spent
the builder's hot coin with the eagerness of a condemned
man - a downy-haired, falling saint in ruined trousers - bless
his bones & we'll see him in a certain heaven if he can
scrabble a tip for St. Pete - he had, like his friends, seen the
abuse & ribaldry of the London circuit back in the sixties &
could still be a safe guide through some of her seedier
nooks - his heart may be stony to the prospects put before
his ailing years but it will soften at the dab of a Teacher's
with one cube of ice - don't want to drown it - look what it
did to the Titanic, darlin' - wink, cluck of tongue on the
roof of his mouth - a conductor's tap of a baton & the
orchestra commences - morbid fugue over ragged streets,
cobblestones, the fiery braziers smouldering - all this in his
bedraggled dream that nightly squeezed behind those baby
blues way, way after closing

*

up and down the city road, in and out The Eagle

*

Captain's moods, manifold - elsewise & elsewhere, he
steers through fog inside & outside his skull - the ship obeys
beneath his stance like a faithful sheep-dog, coiled to spring
at the slightest cluck of tongue - 'twas thusly Old Rusty
Rehab sailed, normally with eyes downcast, but occasionally
gripped with a fierce pride, staring mad over a tensile billow
of wave & spume - his shade now freed for a brief vignette
outside the dream, as is his wont - Captain Rehab finger-
combs a salted beard, he is, of course, unseen, in the low,
backseat of a drowsy homeward car - he who excess
deemed superfluous now sits amid the detritus & tatters -
boring holes of meaning through the skulls of the pliant
youths in front with deep, echoing, cadaverous eyes - high as
an autumn bee, his mind a clutch of sparking loose wires set
fast in spilt pizza-topping - he had sat up all night chain-
smoking in the somnolent, grizzling hours of darkness
listening to phantasms of the sub-ether, absconded night
horses, galloping across the static on his radio, seemingly
living in a fertile, uncanny darkness, the kind that nests
inbetween wintry, new-town flats - dark birds slap their deft
wings, buoyant, across the peaks of the wet, snake-scaled
rooftops, weaving between aitches of spindly aerials - the
sudden, still sight of a crow-shape menaces, tilt-headed, mad
of eye
   & yes The Crazed Captain is wired, contemplating the
paranormal chirrups of avian jazz
   the night horses, yes - they ghosted the whizzing scenery
from the car window & there, in a slow-descended mist, they

gallop, sure steps increasing in ominous momentum – blue-grey, lithe & snorting, flanks of bitumen steaming white – Old Rehab winces as their dread hooves ring on asphalt – seething into the wisps with snorts, whinnies & matted manes trailing

such visions could only belong to the far shore of Lethe, by god – cerebral haunch of sweat & shine – harbingers of a long-blackened hope – Captain Rehab drove them onward through his clammy mind, urging them to waver & perchance fall at a brush of fence or hedgerow – but no, onward yet they grunted – churning the devoted fields under the eternal wires & pylons – becoming death beneath the arching, sepulchral tree-clouds of an ominous dawn, unseen, more undetected than he, they disappeared through suburban lawns to stir the dogs cowering in kennels behind the black yonder ridge of the unlit far houses

*

& yes & yes - saintly, lunar Boo, who disappeared & swept up the debris of a sinuous midlands university with her melancholic hazel eyes restless – setting the modern dances of her sniggering tragedy loose among the vulturing old dons of pedagogic confrontation – yet she came through unscathed & dutifully taught the learned bullshit to creamy new heads - who were promptly expelled from her classes for uncaring & falling too easy in mercenary love - or shouting boorish, Jewish limericks from the skylights of the Ginsberg Memorial Needle (closed Fridays) – or whatever & ever

but for the here & beery now she opens her bleary eyes again - &, getting a tad weary himself now, Mr. Miles D.J. Ducat Esq. puts on a cassette of old B.B.C. sound effects & slumps beside his records under the desecrated parapet of god to craftily smoke his remaining leaves of grass - as sirens, tractors, drills, riots & seagulls fill the room & drunks bawl disapprovals that grin like lullabies to his baby's yielding, unclosed skull – he is scared of churchy women with loaves of grey hair & is more alone than eternity – he had watched as the Newtown Baby turned to Troubadour, like a slow fade in a bad film – & he watches him now with the jaundiced viewpoint of a minor artist – he is part of his own show, his own dream - playing louder music & telling people what louder music he plays – a perfect equation, both perception & the thing perceived

yes & now ambulances hurtle through every street in search of mortality, a cortege of singing, white coffins ever nearing, in hollowed air, the raven-shaded pit – the immortal youth, watch them speed by, hear the mock of the sirens' Doppler & absorb it like a shock of new art - or a glitzy commercial for hair spray – for all is music is vibration to the ears of the deaf

Deaf Miles Ducat speaks into the microphone - low, unintelligible - no doubt many truisms, the late calmatives of familiarity – authoritarian, inducer of awe, he is the last blue line of concord, a fascist jukebox, drumming up the dregs - the angry voices of policemen shouting at a demonstration, easily discernible from those raised in protest – he is no man & all humanity, the unbelieving dog – before him a wasteland of staves & quavers, wrought poetry & idly smashed toilets - Prufrock of Ages – higher than the world above the last-ordered strays - he echoes in paraphrase the clairvoyant's last words – fuck off, ladies, fuck off

*

& so it came to pass, so it was written, the weeks folded into tightly-woven days, fuelled by the delicate pouring of uncommon music into the Troubadour's ears – be it from tiny buds of headphones, the militant ends of the radio dial

152

or Miles Ducat's vast stacks of speakers – the music of the street & spheres, astral planes & things burrowing below the surface now late emergent – words strung over lusts & loves, lost like spider's webs in a shower of hail – notes catching, sticky on the stems of truth, without ever truly resolving - sinews, bass pulse, the squawk of sensuality – it was the constant backdrop, the landscape painted by minions awaiting the master's decisive first brushstroke – The Troubadour sang inside his monochrome cocoon & flexed his stifled, gaudy wings

& Tom Maher, a poet, no doubt singing inwardly too, dolefully stares into his own stare as he shaves his ashen face, scraping the reluctant blood to the surface of his cheeks - dousing the cold tap water across his closed eyes – his best terrible suit, no tie, chest-hairs peeking over the clean white shirt – meeting The Troubadour at the station, at once observing his beret pulled level in the awkward style of the English flat cap – his mind baguetted & reeked of onions – for an hour the jokes & teasing were relentless

"...oo la la, monsieur, tres chic I'm sure – but we ain't goin' to the frog quarter, pal – I'll show you the pissed-up Paddy quarter, London's streets of green..."

two stubby tickets punched, their coats flap in stiff wind, the station deserted & bare but for two party balloons & a suspicious tabby cat skulking behind an upturned porter's trolley – Tom Maher, poetically rolls two careful cigarettes for the train – rolling out the carriage creaks, the time eked out in poetry, murmuring song, hipflask swigs of bravado, Celtic breath shared – breathe deep of the whisky & drink the moist tobacco down – ring the bells of Old Holborn – the clangour of West Horndon station flies past in a hurry to get nowhere – Upminster, Barking, fragments of calm – theatre tableaus with Uncle Vanyas & Vladimirs stood by battered suitcases – another universe's dulled hour flashing in a gleam born of the train's brief pausing – two bites of a

153

doorstep slab, cheese & pickle – crumbs brushed from knees to the fag-butt floor – disembarking, two failed fellows ill-met – pushing through the commuters, stark, burnt shades of waiting, new brooms propped against litter-bins, small heap of swept debris & dust, the furniture of transience – a swift, early one in The Fenchurch then out into the burst of London streets, failed bard & nascent minstrel - tipsy fellaheen - Christmas nearing, a sprinkling of hell's illuminations in the seasonal windows of shops, pubs – even the news boy has a Santa beard – glitter, the devil's dandruff, death smell at a christening, blood singing in mottled veins – up the tube line to Camden

"...there's this bookshop ye have to see..."

winding, wobbly, through the scurrying druggies, the thin market stalls draped in tie-dye & gothic night, cloth of heaven, star-spattered, red bulbs & lava-lamping eerie shifts of colour – jugglers & bellowing itinerants, a sudden dive past two American tourists (...honey, is that Dingwaaall's...?) - & Tom's inside the curtain, a book to hand – with his free hand he sweeps the arc encompassing the racks of bulging books, all unheard, none new - pulp, paperbacked portals, archways lined with postcards from vague cities, bridges over rivers, marijuana leaves & tacky wish-you-were-heres – on the yellowing wall above the chain-smoking owner a set of prints decayed like heiroglyphics in a greeny haze – washes of post-impressionist angles, bilious broadsheets & scrolls from times of civil unrest, Sacco & Vanzetti, a chilled rope in a damp courtyard, exercise at dawn, hiss of the final chair

The Tacky Troubadour devoured a slow row of titles – Marlowe/Faustus, Berryman's Collected Verse, A Season In Hell, The Bridge – one shelf higher, closer to god, Krapp's Last Tape, A Short History Of Decay, Somnium, In Search Of The Miraculous – a makeshift shelf between two pillars of a connecting arch is pregnant with slim comics, volumes of verse & chapbooks, xeroxed, bleak punk literature that stuck to the fingers & smeared under the gaze – great literature, penny bloody-awfuls, moonstruck hippie blather, spidery anarchist stanzas of never-come-the-revolutionary zealots – a full, pugnacious heart in every misbegotten page – brief outline on the back cover, tantalising biography drawn in a few sentences – born at blah, schooled at the university of blah, worked three years teaching blah blah in some blah city, died of drink & blah – there's your leather-bound tombstone & gold-leaf eulogy, there's your brief footprint in the indifferent age's dust

a winding staircase down to Religion, Philosophy, Essays – bright pastel colours of the children's section by the door – a brown teddy bear stapled to the wall above by its eviscerated paw - Five Go Down, Alice's trip, Grimm & canny old Aesop bookending in dull russet, frowning disapproval – dead words buried in coffins – the eyes of Tom Maher, a living poet, his mouth, nicotined, half smirking, frowns at turning pages – searching his pockets for spare change but there's no change there – he would sell his boots & walk home barefoot for a copy of The Quare Fellow or The Life Of Whitman illustrated – he calls out across the reverential silence

"...hold your hour & have another...let's go for a livener in the Hawley..."

the rest of the day whizzed by in a bright, sunlit blur of limericks & misquoted genius – there once was a Paddy called Behan, who wrote up the shite he was seein', he drank the whole world & frightened the girls...with, alas, no punchline forthcoming – upon the Hawley toilet wall a crude figure with unlikely limbs & a disproportionate cock & balls was drawn – art imitates literature – there once was a po-face called Burroughs, who told of our dreadful tomorrows, he lead a wild life & shot dead his wife, which was only the start of his sorrows – trying the thick Benedictine from the heavy green bottle, a major discovery, those fecking monks must have been off their tits all the time, the table lurching like a ship's deck, awful urinals down which lemon cubes of sickly freshener were chased by the ever darkening poet's piss

where do the scribblers all go when they die? - The Captain, thoughtful in the dream ship's old wheelhouse scratches a drying nib listlessly across the logbook - the window shows dusk but it is barely mid-morning, twilight in his wearying mind - old Tom, dead now for sure - who knew him other than I? - I knew, is that enough? - did he get the word poet carved under his name? - who shovelled him under? - are there glorious drunks still being maintained in closing hours on his sweet behalf? - are there carnations withering weekly on his slab? - if not then see that it is so – warm soul's flame eager to be known - don't allow the prudish rushes & sea-bed grass to cover his name now that he has sunk so deep

there's a sea full of them - all the sad old drowners

Tom has a serious expression on his third return from the gents, fly button unemployed, shirt awry & tucked in his peeling belt at the arse - he has fresh penned a poetic original composed on life's most rewarding seat - he reads with one finger aloft

> I'm burning up my days in drink
> & in between I try & think
> Of other journeys, better paths
> But one more sip & I have to laugh
> I'll fuck off when they bolt the door
> & leave this poem on the floor

The Burning Troubadour pockets the slip of foolscap & clinks drinks with Tom Maher, chink - they blink at the beautiful punk girls & flick-knife sharp cool kid giving them the rehearsed casual glance from the pool table - love, O hairless love, croons wistful Tom & - paling suddenly in a wad of gay sunbeams - shuffles to the cubicle in time to just miss the bowl - the love that loves the love

*

dear anyone left, today I'm invisible again & glad of it – the faces of old artists through cracked sepia that line my wall above the fridge, they all break my heart – there is a robin trilling jazz flute improvisations on a chocolate branch of traced icing & I am skating toward the broken shards of new year – trailing cloud-torn December behind me in the stony, wretched wind like an orphans blouse

*

the Dole-Sick Troubadour's new job at the shiny airport awaited – he would sort screws & components for aeroplane seats into small polythene sacks & deposit them in their corresponding plastic trays on the grey, gunmetal, heavy-bolted shelves
or another time was it? –he could not say – all of time now pungent shards of iced recall in the gradual pooling of a wintered creek – the jobs roll by in shifts of grey & sickly green - working at his father's place of labour, pulling faulty televisions from a construction line – a rolling rubber river of dreary fizzing static screens – lost faces picking at diodes & reading the daily blues in folded papers – tears bulge behind lifeless eyes – crosswords unfinished
The Troubadour pounces
'...let the dog see the rabbit...now then, six down - & drums grunt strangely in the daily grind...5, 3 & 5 letters, third letter U fourth letter of last word N...'
& elsewhere & anytime again, some new hell, another bleak house, another graceless warehouse of the damned,

operating a machine that potted yoghurt – a machine that functioned far beyond his understanding, that clanked & Heath Robinsoned & smelled of sour babies & cat-sick

mostly though he thought of his first job after school, when physical toil was still a vague reward – the huge oil refinery out on the estuary - too young, he was, but they took him on – sweet sixteen & never been pissed - there was simply no time, no time – flung into the chlorinated deep end of the grown up gene pools - back at mother's house - somehow it was never father's – prepares lunch at some ungodly hour, sweat-drenched in no sleep – a van to catch in twenty minutes at the roundabout in town – a big journey for a small world

other jobs come & go – the kitchen of a bakery shop – The Troubadour pushed fingers and thumbs into the pie's pastry, lava-hot from the oven, forming a series of hollows around the rim to cool the mudslide meat & napalm jam – in his mother's kitchen once more he prepared for the ghastly day ahead – he stared out at the early, dew-wet lawn – he thought of his dead tortoise - the rain had stopped & the slow, treacle of song that began to trickle from the radio coincided with a sudden dry, yellow sheaf of sunlight gently widening across the blue linoleum – now a blast from the past, for a listener's birthday, happy birthday, have a great day - this song makes him sad always – *that was The Beatles there & Michelle of course* - tortoise, supernatural being – pray may he rest his mortal pie-crust – tortoise ascending to the pearly gates – can't come in without a soul I'm sorry – do their ghosts leave the hard shell behind? – do bells toll for thee? - me shell mar-bell

or yes waking up even earlier for the morning shift at the refinery – sitting in the front room with a coffee & cigarette steaming in his shaky hands - the bookcase & lamp were shadowy, underlit by the eerie radiance from the television, sound turned way down – they sleep still upstairs – family, strange word - broodily silent he sits on the rough settee in a shifting landscape of light and dark – a phobic, censored darkness - not dread of darkness itself, but fear of its grave potential - or imagining clusters of envisaged menaces that have been secretly buried by the darkness – faces, masked & cryptic – the dark of pre-workday mornings is like an engine, threaded with the wires of nature's unknowable disdain

slug to the kitchen to make toast – that easy friend to the waking hour - he glanced at the clock on the mantelpiece in the adjacent dining room as he spread the butter thickly, evenly over the compliant slices of white bread & placed two wedges of garlic sausage on the one less-buttered - 4.30! – Old Father Time himself would curse him for getting up so fucking early

what a fucking job! – cleaning bloody pipes in a refinery, Jesus Chiming Christ...

even the old faithless Crombie overcoat is distressed by rank smoke from a hundred unloved cigarettes – distressed like a returning soldier

& wrapping it around his shoulders it chills and taunts him with last night's bitter air - one wriggly arm mistakenly inserted into the mysteriously torn inner lining, its easy egress annoyingly frustrated at the snot-blemished cuff - & so a curse, sigh, then try, try again - successful at the third attempt & now utterly engulfed in the swathes of cold coat-skin, simultaneously euphoric yet flustered, he fastens the two lower remaining buttons - scarf, red, twice around the neck & plaited in front - tucking it into the coat causes, he observes, a ridged, ugly bulge – duly untuck

& out he goes, out into the why-aren't-you-sleeping air - walking slow, unenthusiastically, on through the boxy houses & piebald, scrubby lawns – past the bakery café where soon, unbeknownst to him now, he will work - the taste of grained bread warm through the kitchen's slatted vent – the first rays

159

of margarine sun spreading, like saluting arms of tomorrow's perpetual embrace, he strolls, hands in pockets, into the paling dimness further

on the way to work in the dank Transit Van he gazed up at the old church as the demolition crew scurried about like insects devouring a weary prey - the cold of dawn forgotten for now, recalled as something lost - its light somehow now interred within his chest, soft gentle panting of dawn-light, cough of risen sun - the old ruined church glowered down whilst they stopped at the lights - The Troubadour glowered back, get gone, Old No God Boyo has no place in his working world - he heaved a shrug of cold defiance at the building's agony - he later imagines what kind of rank ancient preaching still hung in that disturbed space - house of a wild priest - saddened by his tethers of scripture - the words, he imagines, floating strange across the room & out of the window - or through the crumbling walls & on, eternally on, even perhaps drifting through the heads of his congregation - they will not know who speaks these words to them - it is just a solitary, joyless voice, ill-omened - sweating in their thoughts as they sleep or crawl to their godless work - but they will hear him - yes, past the half-drawn blinds & triple-locked, suburban caves, past your temporal carelessness, the dark words flitting, nomadic, migratory - this priest is danger made flesh, dis-ordained & loaded with the babel chime of the undiscovered scrolls - yes, The Lay-Troubadour thought, that is how he wished his sermons to be absorbed - a text hotwired, jimmying the doors of perception, for god is the subliminal, memory's ghost, the unheard scream

*

peace - finally it breaks - lingering, near to the ground, over the booms of steel on steel - it is weakening into the washed-out blues & yellows of an almost holy day - kalick-kalack, kalick-kalack - there are spiritual tourist-guides - glamorous & thrilling modes of transport yet none suited Captain Rehab as well as his great ship, the backseats of lost cars, or best of all, a train - when still not quite emergent, a young Troubadour at heart, he would buy a rover ticket granting transit across all of the city - chosen at a whim with no terminus or appointment to cloud the rapt journey - for the spirit of the train is never youthful, not free to squirm backroads & wood lanes ridged by hoof print - a bird, not quite a crow, crushed in the fast lane as he once crossed a motorway at night, its body a collage of ants & tyre-prints, the indelible evil of the mind's scrapbook - random people he followed, they are welded to routine, in thrall to vinegary urban Albion - now, as an old ghost in his own past's dream, having boarded his beast of choice without ticket or money - his omniscience a cloak of invisibility - every & nowhere - he lights his pipe & coughs twice - then clanks the window down & flinches at the frightened, desperate wind - weeps at specks of once gentle rain now angered & thrown at his eyes, a hail of infinitesimal swords, high on the sap of hurtling spores he reels like a seed in the quick, blurred greenery & greedily, in camera-shutter blinks of his eyes, devours the lingering dismembered spires of flashing churches - the shock of stations & tunnels rattling by in spilled blocks of Braque & whirls of Klee - then back to bracken & clay, nostrils packed with the retch of dark soil - from eastern coastline to the western plains of outer London by rail, by rail - passing through faux-viaducts, flyovers with peeping cars glued in jams, making connections & hopeless associations

this gospel chain, veining the flesh of England, a one-way slow curvature toward giddy god - not a lobby in which time must quicken - nor palace of heartless splendour & dismal opulence - a tunnel of lost love heading back, to the no-one

home that a hobo never clearly recalls – his belongings in a
small hold-all by his feet, sandwiches of luncheon meat &
celery - a mouthful of warm lemonade - his carriage
exclusive, a mobile headquarters - furniture, fittings built by
mythic artisans, the exotic dead, lost craftsmen of the
unread prefaces to history books – this clash of steel, clash
of two unlucky sevens, rolled on this consecrated string of
dim pearl carriages taking him to cloud nine
    along the way freight & staff are offloaded, set free to trip
through towns & cities & flit across grazing lands – delivering
the post, the bills, the love letters, the birthday surprises – it
seemed   an   affirmation   of   a   divine   intelligence,   all
dimensions confirmed by the pre-eminent saviour – his
memory was fading & he knew it would end up dying, after
all his trouble taken, after all his kvetching – he held up his
heart full of bad stories & god blessed everything else - for
on these fixed rails death itself journeys – light & with a
poised scythe – four stoic horses tethered somewhere out in
those browning meadows – white chickens peck at corn
flung as dice across pentagram farmyards, here & gone
forever – & the parade of stations only serves to strengthen
these glory-bound rails, hold them clutched like the strings
of two dancing kites – blessing their parallels & sunbeam
flashes with a smile through a winking window & porter's
cap badges that glint & spangle from toasted platforms –
always the same things, suitcases, trolleys, stacks of
newspapers knotted with string – the pigeon affirming the
dropped crust – different suits & flowery frocks full of
different people with different souls – chubby, red-cheeked
businessmen with burst bags of gut flap, spastic with Sunday
beef & gelid minds of gravy – speak-your-weight machines
hint at the future – breathe in your stomach 'til it aches &
haul it up on the cyclops & hear the sci-fi robot voice – the
truth-sayer, who, with the authority of the great mechanised
unknown, guesses your gravity - I Speak Your Weight – &

yes from the faint past the message crackles through the quiet loudspeaker, defeated by the roar of a hundred, white-hot, metallic wheels passing – the next train will always be arriving – the distance availing not - clockwork devices that attempt to imitate our brains' pointless circuitry - devilish appliances with which we measure trust & by which we steer the course of our wayward faith – capsules of commuter meat, meandering through dry water towers & mildewed signal boxes, with a capped ghost figure wrenching the beer-pump levers & switches - wagons to divert into sidings of bindweed & mouse-shit – the grand gauges of the switch-points' puppetry & the grand design unseen within the controller's play – endless journeys for any or no reason but travel itself – but all tracks lead to the capital

, & the hobos, tramps, down & outs, are all gradually appearing now, or being noticed more, perhaps – slunk in doorways, abandoned houses, rooting for deadly chicken in the bins, murmuring their humiliating mantras like monks shuffling past a prayer-wheel – some could order whisky in six languages, argue Neitzsche with a professor – yet chance & fate has deemed they wait for brass raindrops to fall blind to a corduroy hat – the pity eats at their bones – the cold, the misfortune, the pure unreason of a world hurtling away from them in bright shards, leaving a brown & grey world of stolen milk & damp clothing – yes & some were old sea-drunks, washed up on the concrete, who awoke with a gasp to find the sea too far

others shuddered nightly with some hidden calumny forever unspoken – elsewhere their mothers, fathers, sisters, brothers all held the tiniest scrap of hallowed remembrance of them in their busy heads – or mouldered in graves, shot clean of the care due to it all – & a callous night awaits the fall of the last of daylight's soldiers, holding its nose before mopping up the last stragglers like vomit – their faces, twice aged – spider webs & padlocks in their eyes – it is a new sweet plague metastasising beneath the towns & cities – pagan, chthonic & primal – it rises, a wave of revulsion slow-turning at the point of revolt – they huddle around greedy fires & silently stew – heads moving only to occasionally glance mordantly at the passing trains

*

humble, yet potent, these journeys tickled the sleeping imaginations of a thousand adolescent notebooks – journals in bedside cabinets, stained with kebab-juice & pale ale – these burgeoning punk flowers, exotic creatures, their bawdy antics fostered by these old tin engines – the Northern Line to Camden, hear the metal rush of sound first, then their bored faces glooming out of the yawn of a tunnel toward sleepy groves of onion-breathed commuters – or on the hinterland, where underground meets the wide, scratchy scrub plains of Essex – here chug the diesel pug-noses, tiny eyes & sturdy, leviathan physique, hauling nameless tubes of noxious, skull-boned gases - or high windowed boxcars like taunts from the Belsen mist

& yes, it haunted the cycle of a bored child's mind to fathom what kind of monster made such clatter, echo & swish – the fine old steam trains trailing white spools of smoke through cowboy plains in library mornings – 'horses of iron' sayeth the Red man, wise – their truths taken at face-value, their suns a shining pool in heaven behind the last mountain – wounded in the knee by the strings of harrowing Fords – boot hill & last stand – rusted old hulks poaching in a white desert sun – their whistles were the last phantom, telephonic scream of a consumed age – the big-hearted groan of a dying beast - another distressed blub & whimper among many, it sadly seems – one last croak & whisper then & into ambiguity the train evaporates – the natives bow their noble heads, at last defeated, to the sand – their souls are impenetrable, their children named after the first creatures seen in this grand spiritual design - like the ricochets of bullets fired in a far off past – dull algebra of motorcars – the sum of a thousand journeys adds up only to its terminus - the terminus into which their mythic metal horse pulled - with the worn out bodies of the last of their warriors boxed in tow - freight of ignominy, heavier than horses yet soon dispersed, dwindling to nothing like steam in a thirsty western sky

from Latin & disturbed dust it roared – '*trahere*' - pull, draw - jaded by a heavy morning heat – the sleepy creak of carriage rattles westbound now on two steel rows of cast metal – an opera of shrill mouse-brakes – scraggy fields, brown, untended, slither by the half-cracked window – 'press to pull down' etched on satisfied metal – the view is restricted but relentless - a vision of damp rolling wildness that causes an axe-sharp mind, such as old Newtown Baby's, to break glass in the event of its lingering emergency – then cometh the small rivulets, the unstoppable creeks, blindly heading gleefully nowhere – under the hulks of burned cars – *viva el revolucion siempre* – mini-protests of graffiti swathe the rows of blind garage lock-ups – tags of the narcissistic undead, the zombie bored – they declared themselves alive by fiat, night by night in spray-paint hisses - a tangle of mediocrities & disquieting lusts, their mode of liberty – yet from the sublime rhythms of the constant trains, they sense that this liberty is confined to an unchanging track & that these rails will never own the boundless freedom of seagulls – motionless yet sliding the coarse, fishy air - from where the far-northern Humber rolls down through mad Albion - through Mondrian geographies of farm & grain silo, to where the poplars sway by leafy, racy cricket greens & on to the swelling of the city

leaving these villages with their rows of polished Sunday cars in gravel driveways – sun beaming & morris-dancing &

the distant man on the hill hunts like a sprightly imp, escorts his sleepy sheepish rovers in silent triumph – O Anglia! – how thy frowning grill apes my sorrows!

*

he nods away sleep as the train gathers a slow, lumbering momentum, ticking through tilted curves – an intricate lacy confusion of treetops & directionless avenues – then entering the kingdom of the great gasometers – a tinplate fez-farm - skeletal, shivering stripped in gauzy mist - The Troubadour always loved the gasometers & was always surprised by them, as if somehow they could not exist in the imagination & were destined to be remembered only on sight – yet they always fascinated him – from out of leaking ethers of time they suddenly bloom into view – foursquare, solid, unmoored like the rotting, severed limbs of a monstrous pachyderm, quiet, measured & swollen with a guilty, Oedipal air

dear me, I'm packing up my kitbag & I'm never going home again – afraid of forests, alleyways full of hissy tomcats, virgin wolves - ready to go, for the righteous patrician has extended his kingdom & seeks after my soul – London, turn again

time enough for that

for here & now, in The Lonely Troubadour's kitbag of melting thoughts, the gasometers fade & become melancholic auguries once more – sentinels, wise to the city's sense of sanctum – old disused battleships, stoic & wry, cautionary preludes hewn from stone necessities – the cubist realm of memory – nearby houses, shops, churches, betting-emporia fade to translucence - tracing paper, chalk after rain

& yes, it appears that this world is only real when dictated to him by the motion of the carriage – as if his heart

166

obeyed the train's sluggish tempos, the conductor's baton, the wheel-rims' tick & lurch

& then the blithe assurance of London, emerging from the shrapnel hedgerows – skyline of stumpy, nibbled pencils – the brutish tablets of bleak house stone & threadbare, needling spires – sheer, monstrous walls of ice, mocking your image as you pass by - criss-crossed in red biro, each cordon a snug hive of money - a grub-nest sated, languishing fat against an iron sky – great constructs made tall enough to scare, made of glass so as to reflect the less fortunate back on themselves – & yes in their mirror-ball facades chained aeroplanes play at freedom, each full of sweating, sunburnt tourists, cling-filmed chicken & duty-free cologne - scraping the gaunt skies, scattering birds & at their apex, with a last lurch, sinking like space-junk into the growling metropolitan net of runways spidering out from the arrivals lounge where, nearby, the train waits, purring

& on arrival, as the train slows to kiss the pout of buffers, every scenic morsel is filed in the memory – the blue, chipped fence & muddy child fingerprinting the kitchen hallway, treading colourful dog-shit through the lounge – every portrait unchanging on a facade of brown & beige – the coming city sucks the train through a tunnel, going down, way down, straight to hell, my boys – two sets of hoofmarks on a private road - a bakery, no time to smell the womb-scented rolls slid from the oven - a barbershop, with mirrored customer flicking through a magazine whilst the owner sweeps the dead hair - or a grey funeral procession moving away to the distance, so many people – he had collected them, labelled the boxes he had made for them, each night, nose pressed to the kitchen floor in stupor, reliving the journey – in the security of a toy world, amniotic, a willing submission to a soft trick of mind – must hold on now, just for a few years more – must remain unwilling to admit the fantasy is unreal – he is transported

167

back, every time, riding the train-set on chequered, pastel linoleum – ahead lies the real city, yes - but every night it must always be packed away by No-God

*

& where o where is his no-god now? - whither the great emancipator? – the devious plot twister - reading a whodunit with the last pages torn out – forever wrapped in flags of rage & the grand black standard of anarchy - naysaying the hopelessness no more – protesting any ridiculous consensus – dismissing even the likelihood of authority - the folks by the folks for the folks - confinement of the enemy
   & yes perhaps the furtive awareness of a cowed populace should only be encouraged to a fixed point of delirium then snuffed out – there is always the sea, television & art to tickle the peasantry under the arm, revive the stale bread & spark the old cruel circus, the Troubadour mused as he read his latest book – a less than comprehensive history of modern art
   sheen of academia's gloss – canapes, crucified monkeys, faint odour of the clique
   so to end then, in Eden - it was only last spring he felt that first stab of joy again – sun can cuddle the most brutish mood to mellowing – as daffodils groaned upward from the choked roundabout verges & his eyes began to ache without the shade of his protective sunglasses - fall slow away then, turning pages of two decades & await rebirth & salubrious budding – Bliss Of Eden – it's ok Boo, there's no chewing gum in your wildwood hair – oh Mackay! Mackay! - I'm all mouthwash & razorcuts again! – out here in this messed up timeline - diurnal, weekly, eternally – a mere four dead seasons is all we yearly get - Calpol, Speed, Acid & Beta-Blockers – then Christmas drinks & before you know it it's Calpol again - his heroes passed through many stages &

births & you know them not - he that dwells out of sight of crowds - from the wings - only he knows them all — ragbaghavad of geetars strum before a backcloth of ashes – he learns many enigmas that have mystified the passions in all empires, most austere of which is that of self-adoration, ego – fleet inner arguments that are disproportionate to their vehemence – a febrile mind that is host to detective novels & fantastic bildungsroman in which the proud roman buildings of youth bleed to defective crumbled hovels of his dotage - from the very early evening of olden times, of all doors of perception, the most ajar is the one that leads to his vision's ghost – the dying of the night - as the foundation of all we experience - famine & fraudulence – a heart full of dirt exchanged for bullion – cartoon characters, some good & others evil, the evil ones are thrilling but the good ones win out in the end – so it's better to be good? – he hears a voice elevated, above all other, higher than joy or lightning – he is singing of the theology dormant deep inside the past — the hurricane lantern of pragmatism - prepared for storms-a-comin' with their whispering tornadoes where weepy valedictions & brass maledictions abound – new forms, suggestions & methods slowly begin to ameliorate his creativity - experimentation, juxtapositioning, the seeping of one solid thought with an arbitrary experience – our bliss of Eden split by lightning - curses, foiled again

*

& yes something is changing around them, these city boys, freshmen of the main drags & dives – yet up there in the big smoke old Carlisle still meets Dean Street in bitter Soho gloom & January is killing the hobohemians with no juice for the fights yet to come & wherever the hell the Newtown Baby, Captain & crazy, dumb-struck Troubadour got to be today for sure it ain't on no earthbound, mis-drawn map

   no, only the sky and their minds are open - the old house of cards that held their hopes & plans is collapsing & there's no way onward & certainly no way back - their youthful bird of paradise has piss on its shoes - something changing - so be it, alright, ok

*

   spring flitted by once more & was duly astonished & obligingly melted the frost - its fingers cleaved the easy shadows like butter - veils of cotton wool & pinpricks of stars nightly opened their long-perished eyes - the days were sticky honey, fermented wine bubbling, urgent & cloud-tipped in warming, hoppy sheds - in the teenage nooks acid, whisky, rum & cider bleed across a printed page in patchwork stains of rebellion - all hail the holy summer we shall eternally waste - because youth has no wristwatch & sunshine cannot be tied to a tree - the likes of us never see winter, Boo - that realm of whitened, scarred hillscapes, dark early bus stops & coughing smoke vented from engines - days of marble & epitaph - crows peripheral in blurred trees - let it sail, sail away to hell & tenderness with the slow fall of blossom & the still russet lanes of grey-washed, caustic Albion - where at long last lay-priests of pain are preaching with The Captain watching quietly in his mirror, whose tale is yet to be closed - he has yet to err on the side of truth or falsity, those sly old parentheses - waiting to catch a glimpse of his own history as he departs for a different now

   & The Troubadour & Boo, on another sojourn to the capital witness a strange & portentous sight - Degory Priest, a most anarchic & untutored cleric, teetering, uneasy with strong drink, atop the roof of a Ford Anglia, without tax or insurance, on the pagan bow of Putney Bridge, his

imprecations defiling the astral plane with specks of atheist
vomit – he frowns at passing hippies that are mockingly
waving & hooting from a floral-painted Morris van - he farts
magnificently & gazes through the misted morning fauna
across a city he deplores & distrusts - blows village green
snot into a cricket-white handkerchief & yells – hear him -
out there on the edge of vanity & loss – hear him as he
testifies now! – reading from his scrappy red notebook in a
voice that cracks in concordance with his ashen gullet & the
coming ripeness of his vestigial lusts
    The Troubadour was transfixed

*

    widening his arc of reading, often choosing a book
merely for its title or cover, in strangest dens, the secretive
nature of permanently suspicious bookstall proprietors –
frequently sold a dud, always managing to scrape a little gold
from the pages, even if it had been the property of a fool –
mining, sieve-brained, tiny holes catching the biggest tale,
dust of dross falling to the skull's basement – many arid
purchases, yet there were flashes in the river that were not
mere tricks of moon – shaken into his ever-open notebooks
to be recycled on whisky typewriters weeks hence – mythic
bulletins - Kurt Schwitters dying soon after building a crazed
weltschmerz wall up at fusty Windemere – the mudslingers
& holy drippers - unschooled savagery of Motherwell,
Clyfford Still & his ripped swathes of fake landscape – all
can be stirred, added to the stew – mix it in – keep reading
& filter the scum – build huge ugly jewellery from the
unpolished gemstones
    on the train journey up to the city he had turned to the
discarded magazine left by a fellow traveller on the seat
opposite – a supplement to the Times – *all news is a bloody
supplement to the times* – an article on Cortez, a depiction

in ink - comic-caped & overlooking the plains of death - *una mala voz canta a través de la llanura* - he ponders buying a biography of the wretch - what's on the following page? - a retrospective assessment of William Burroughs - hmm save for later, he stuffs it freshly torn into his jacket's inner pocket along with a travel article about Aix-en-Provence - the fresh William Burroughs cut deep into his little finger at the knuckle - sharp paper cuts deep - blood ceremony, for the love of a friend - after the bombs fell silent at Pearl Harbour he joined the fray - his eyes speed-reading the bones of the text - blah Cezanne blah, Mont Saint-Victoire blah - he bled all the way to Stepney East cursing each fresh black drip - his pale-blue handkerchief an atrocity

all books welcome then, yes - all that information to be filtered & sorted - links & exchanges which fused at points in time - his slant on the evidence will make personal each curated fact - he chose to absorb the language of the critic also - affirm their authority when helpful, deny when a burden to his ready understanding - at times he felt it was important - that it called to him to plunge into the cesspit of the academic life - tweedy, Meerschaum-pointed thoughts that he shook his head to be rid of

no, the outside world always seemed more appetizing, more alive with possibility - he would wander, not quite a *naïf,* more as a labourer in the harsh factory of chimera & magic - no drunk priest preordained to solve the great blueprint of life himself - no, too, to the idiot spirit that has genuinely but pointlessly loved & is happy for it - yes though to the jilted groom that never forgets, there's a real story he can claw on to - the lost girl he drives mad but truly worships - the belief of reconciliation clung to, until the slam of church door & sweeping up of confetti, the tossed unclaimed bouquets he thought of marriage & shuddered – took out his notebook, familiarly red with a pale coffee-cup ring, & scribbled hurriedly

as the sunflower's acne-pocked face
revolves to track her false dropping idol
through drear skies burning
from the moment his blurry visage
strafes a sky of hope
to when he plunges into that pissy pool
of sallow dead sun beyond
a sugarcandy shitheap at dusk
so shall the forsaken grip
the misty paw of their chosen one
the same fierce look which they bear when crossed
ah but they bleat as stuck poets!
t'was morningtide & ruin was in the air
as was the stale breath of pioneers
run from the Romeo church, Juliet
turn again, turn again
there are no flowers worth saving

*

yes, turn again O thwarted prodigal of the new town – Penny-Poor Troubadour, with your leaf-patterned sack swinging from a pole balanced across your left shoulder on the road to somewhere, perhaps anywhere – though the stout-bellied cattle of the east London hinterlands may frown, lowing in the wilful light of a Tuesday's dawning – you are now ready to take a seat at the big table where the game of chance is played out - though the table is stacked with fake coin & the other players hide their gazes of ill-intent under stout, wide brimmed hats – on occasion, to go back home again, though you already feel the capital is your

173

true home - but to never forget that it is the province of doubt that you are trespassing – he had read many stories that conspired to inform him that you cannot, in fact, go home again – that the universe speeds away from you daily - you must expand your horizons with the pioneers & ride the cosmic bulge & any revisiting of old vomit is just hours wasted in nostalgia, all for a trust in some selective memories of brief, possibly even illusory happiness

he was, he concluded, finally & unequivocally, bored of traipsing these ancient ruins of the new-town – & one day, weighted down with the ballast of frustrated exile, he had been led, by his reliable subconscious dream guide, through the tiled subways once more to the Park Of Fumes – ever unchanging, the lake was there, man-made & it still retained its falsified prettiness despite, or perhaps because of, the grey town sulking in the near distance – there's nothing as pleasurable than being willingly deceived, he thought – he thought of the bottles of bad cider & purloined whisky that he & Mackay had swigged here - & the old man who had told him about the sea story, surely he had not been there for years now? – dead probably, or confined somewhere, being sadly brought his pills & porridge, nightly stabbed with needles full of calmative depressants

so here he was, on that hard, cool bench, where as a Newtown Baby he had sat years ago – awash in the longing of changes - on his faithful bench that had supported mad conversations & solitary scribblings of desperate poetry & song - & he looked sorrowfully at the pointless water – he had hoped that there would be some kind of revelation, a splinter of witchcraft beneath the fingernail of mundanity, but the lake gave up nothing other than its cursory parade of ripples as the squawking moorhens landed – a conversation came to him in halting fervour – had it happened between them? – young & old interacting?

'...why are you not here?...'

174

'...I'm ancient, melancholic - I have other places to be...'

'...well, in that case my position is clear - I suppose I'm meant to say now that, let's see, how about this...I am young, optimistic but prey to doubt, faithlessness...is that how you see me?...'

'...that is how it is...we are time-traveling, some forward, some back - the tide creates that illusion, study the tides - water has many tricks - you are too young...'

'...do you live nearby?...'

'...always...'

'...I'd like to write a song for you, about you I mean...do you mind?...'

'...I'd be disappointed in you if you didn't...'

a half-smile, retracted quickly - then

'...tell me the first line...'

'...ancient sad one, he lay in wait for death - the shallow breath...no more, it's gone - it can't really be finished - in a way it should go on forever - I'll try & remember it all - I can bring it next time...'

'...enough for now...take your time with it - things change - perhaps you should wait 'til you're older, old as me, then we can make the words sing together...'

'...you'll be dead though, surely? - it won't take long, I write quickly, like to get the impressions down instinctively - melodies too, they come to me all the time...'

'...imagine waiting years before you picked up a pen & guitar - imagine the store of energy amassed - the song would explode on the page!...'

'...I have time...I'm too young, remember?...'

'...you are young *and* you remember - that may change...'

'...I will write it down, I won't forget...'

'...for now you write your words on the tides - the tide will remember all you have forgotten - you will find the likes of me easily in pub corners or at café tables – we will talk as we talk now then move on – once I immersed myself in nature – bathed myself in the neon of many cities – certain people stood apart from the incoherently mumbly, unhappy crowds – ambling aimlessly, trying to avoid any choice, any destination - but they had to stop somewhere in time – their destination found them soon enough – the wilds of nature are no different – paths hewn through forests are the same as rush hour traffic – whether psychogeographical or psychopastoral – destinations always await in ambush for the refugee's heart - you see a stranger man & you follow – perhaps their eccentricities attract you – they are nagging at your brain like a crossword clue – their name on your lips unuttered – you become a disciple to their voyage – then, you lose the thread, become distracted, trees, tall buildings, street names, they all blur into a mass – you find yourself – to your dismay – somewhere – I have done this forever – forward, back, through a thousand names – it is wearisome, yes, but preferable to standing still, in one place – taking root, for that is death...'

'...I don't...I'm not sure I...'

"... don't think, close your eyes - now, picture in your mind a desert – one charred black tree & a red house with four windows, three lit with a yellow light one closed off by a blue Venetian blind – can you see it...?"

"...hold on...yes, yes I see it..."

"...good – now, hold that image tightly in your head & slowly count down from ten to zero never losing concentration on the image, don't allow any aspect of it to fade – & when you reach zero I want you to open your eyes suddenly & say the first word that comes into your head – don't think about it until you mentally say the word 'zero' to yourself & then blurt it out, ok...?" - the Troubadour silently nodded, the strange picture floating like a shimmering hallucination behind his eyelids - "...right...ready, go!..."

ten, nine, eight, seven, six, five, four, red house, burnt tree, three, yellow, blue Venetian, two, one, zero...'

"..."

no word came

"...you are not ready – no matter - try again another time...the epiphany should be instantaneous – no matter, it will come..."

the traffic noise from the main road to the east drifted through the fabric of the unsettling contours of the park – whale music from the obscurity of a faraway sea – he thought of the day his father had taken him to the end of the pier & pointed out the buoys, yellow, orange, bobbing in the swell – he had said that they were dragon's eggs & it was bad luck if you saw one hatch – he had only partly believed it but it stayed with him as he stared beyond the pier railing to the tumult that slowed in distance to a velveteen gloss – whales do not attack, they open their huge mouths & feed on the coming surge – legions of krill, tiny fish, the urgent lives – all are absorbed – a vast god made flesh, an unassailable religion inexorably pulsing forward, forward

the wind from the estuary had made his eyes heavy & watery, salt-stung – a day out, they had brought sandwiches, cheese, thin ham with thickly sliced tomato – how real, vivid, the lunch seemed, he thought – how ridiculously incongruous they tasted after the saline rush & spume of a crashed wave – his father hummed a tune – what was it? – the song had disappeared now though, it was too late

the moorhen flapped & took off clumsily from the relaxing water - he was back at the lake now & could no longer remember – he opened his eyes, he had closed them for just long enough for the word 'river' to appear in his mind – the years behind him seemed to be awash with future days – the light had dimmed to an extent where the darker outlines of the trees that distorted in the lake became more, lucid, fresh he had almost expected the world to have changed entirely, a place where ghosts & memory were afforded a more prominent importance, in a sense, the park's low-grade mystery was the last thing he expected to see but, of course, the park was still there - the old man, however, had gone

*

a flinch - augenblick
shufti of foresight
or backward squint?
Father Time's not telling

*

there's white boy soul, there's Hall & Oates, surreal, sub-Burroughs stabs at Todd Rundgren descending minors – who gives a fuck, right?...no question mark necessary – she's long gone – poor girl - & yes already those feelings of excitement he had experienced are gnawed at by a rising sickness - born of nostalgia for the very comforts he is fleeing – turn twice & carry on - toward the city's Fat Roman Swell Of Industry & the old burdensome heritage – from peasant burial-mounds to royal bloodshed – where the hangman at the execution dockside awaits the next poor Martial's Dance – know the darkness of the city's voice – know the satanic mills & easy truths told with bad intent - & know too, despite the city's grandeur, that fool's gold reeks under every quick, brown leather footstep of her damned souls, crushing their emptying days with the burden of temporary promises, shiny tall buildings & soup kitchens for the romantically destitute

late, late & later The Destitute Troubadour sits after the last bell - on the wharf by the twilight yearning swab of the estuary's dense flickering – the lights of the refinery winking & blurring in fat distances of shimmering greys – listening to whatever last song the jukebox offers – (it tells him she's so fine, O sweet lord of mine) – he thinks of pylons stretching across the tired miles of Essex & the wretched messages they support - & he needs to grasp those yawning, cat's cradling wires, carrying wine-breath odes to tired lovers & sing it like a merciless angel, in Celestial Morse Code, tapped throughout eternities to her bedside – lay low, close to the wharf's chilled concrete – the river can flow backwards for you Canute Troubadour, take you all the way to a new spirit in a jangling city – so yes, lay low, look at the madness of stars reflected & keep the river beside you, taunting your exit by its slow, westward flow to the sea – a sea that lies in wait like a trawler's dragged netting, to tangle in the propeller of your childish fantasies – faith in dreams is lost & yet the dreamy ship is still sailing, all the while its sad murmur running a sleepy commentary to your answering heart – it will pass him as he heads for the capital, pass under the weight of dream, whilst he sits in cafes, bars, wanders down side-alleys with dead names – peers into shadows suspiciously cloaking alleyways leading to vitality, a spark, the guts of the matter – to become one of those swift shadows that only the vagabond's eyes catch, flitting, brief patches of a sweeter, lighter dusk against the mordant walls of night

closing your eyes now, the wind blows a gift of oil & gull droppings off the water - breathe deeply & allow a last fond thought of your bed, your music, your home, the bells of a thousand churches chiming, their beckoning song swings through your head & bids you heartily to drink

PART 2

PLAY

"What we perceive as the present
is the vivid fringe of memory tinged with anticipation."

Alfred Whitehead

"If you want to lose your faith, make friends with a priest."

George Gurdjieff

Once upon a wilder time a solemn, distracted soul could often times be seen in pubs & cafes at choice locations all over the city – blackening, yellow teeth biting the biro & sporadically scribbling pledges in the margins of newspapers strewn across the table before him – the obsession of the cryptic – the insoluble riddles of life – their thrall became so marked that, for a time, his whole life took on the enigmatic nature of a puzzle - & with life, as in the puzzle, he felt the same niggling curiosity about its ultimate solution – he was convinced beyond all argument that somewhere lost in the babble of language there were subtle clues as to the meaning of these, apparently directionless, travels & stuttering short-cuts down blind cul-de-sacs that had comprised his twenty years on earth thus far

this misfortunate boy, already way past his formative years yet teetering precariously on the cusp of a more serious stage of manhood, became slowly more & more absorbed with the complexities of his heretofore shallow & crude understandings of life's process

barefoot he stood beside a busy stream, flashing blue & grey through the unperturbed rocks & over the beautiful polished pebbles - he dipped a toe & felt the aching cold, then plunged both feet in the flow &, though the water soaked the rolled cuffs of his work jeans, he stood for a minute, wincing happily at the delicious pain, before returning to the warm, grassy bank

then, slowly, he stepped into the stream a second time & where once the wavelets plashing his goose-bump calves were chill, uninviting, now it almost burned his skin – the flow ardent with the intensity of a thousand possibilities

his heart raced & everything before his gaze seemed to offer up new chances – Hyde Park spread her arms & welcomed him to his first summer's day resident in the city

– & he felt his feet drying on soft grass, a swan effortlessly drifting & pecking up the thrown crust from his ham sandwich – his heart was set upon becoming another chapter in the book of this metropolis, at least a new ghost in the shifting map, the streets & subsumed waterways forming his veins, the gnarly buildings & lost statuary warting through his fraying skin – he felt newly emboldened by the knowledge that he was the hesitant captain of his ship & right now there were few tweaks of the wheel required – he put on his socks over still damp feet, swung his satchel over his shoulder & headed for Marble Arch tube

*

The Pubcorner Wizard sat in a fog of possibilities, the bar reassuringly nearby – the sly window looking out on the street to check the incomers – red woollen hat pulled down to the cusp of his eyebrows – newspaper spread on a damp, but not dirty, table – a respectable clutter – his cigarettes & pouch of tobacco open, available – a pen for the book of puzzles or daily Guardian crossword – his approachable demeanour a net to the passing familiars who cannot resist pondering in comradeship the odd clue, the niceties of a juicy, cryptic code deduced – but The Pubcorner Wizard hunts down conversation like a hovering owl – slowly he reels them in like a wily Ahab, then harpoons them with his chosen manifesto of the day
"...now, look at those lads by the jukebox...pubs are full of bored kids – same as forever, pal – it's just how it was, y'know? – I'll tell ye, the big secret is to rumble their lack of guts, their wilful blithe spirit, inspiring – feed off their boredom – use their apathy as your muse – their job is to fill ashtrays with crushed roll-ups & make eye contact with barmaids – we have a greater purpose, true – but our ultimate purpose remains the sweet fulfilment of our own

private absurdist agendas – declare it! - we are also a level better at drunkenness, you & I – we smoke in more definitive ways using the old style – y'know - gestural sleight of hand, shall we say - to convey our disdain – these are not the words of a sorry man, my friend – oh no, these are useful insights into your urban survival – we never ever let our beer go flat – temperature is important - bitter warm, cider cold - there's always foam on the returned jug – study the foam, it is a meditation some mornings – you can make out a thousand faces, clouds, swans, dragons..."

he pauses to relight his Marlboro with a brusque fizz of match – the window checked with a sideways glance, he draws a cat's face & two doodled signs of infinity in the margins by the cartoons

"...never sit near a plant pot, it could be wired for sound – there are secret cabals out there, believe me, who hang on our every fuckin' word – I may be an agent, how would you know? - for the government, I mean - though this shit goes way beyond that - the illusionists are among us – they're everywhere & invisible – unshaven, consequential – don't think they're above suicide or murder – they crave your dreams 'cos they lost theirs – they can't find themselves in big cities – always on the outskirts y'know? – hinterlands - their heads are full of the dreams you waste – want my advice, son?

he pauses for effect, raising a mildewed finger

"...don't ever put your money on a three-legged horse..."

& he laughs a good bellyful of ale laugh & wipes a pearl from his drippy snout with a motley suit-jacket sleeve

"...I'm full time in this game, son – don't you worry your empty head 'bout that – I'll be here when you've pissed off down your own little avenue of disappointments – I'll be here when you come back with your tail between your legs & I'll be the first to laugh & buy you a pint – here, any ideas on this? 6 down, 11 letters – 'bring down curse upon man

183

before speech' - third letter L - ah, what would I do with my life without beer & word games? - rhetorical, that - sometimes I recalibrate the old philosophies, that passes the hours, Swedenborg this week, now there's a rum old fucker - from flying machines to faith alone - some days you can walk down Frith Street & wave his books about & five or six people will engage you in an argument - other days I piss my trousers to get attention - really want my advice, pal? - do the laundry like an artist & paint like a dustman - we are war babies, all of us - the hallway bulb in our mansion has blown - there are bus tickets in the gutters of Dalston Junction with our poems sketched on the back - we fatten up so as not to have to go out at Christmas - good food, puddings, pies & cabbage - cooked well but still crisp - an unopened jar of olives in every larder - if you turn off the telly you can hear the mice roaring in the air-vent - never keep old wallpaper up when ye move in anywhere new - paint your walls red & green, lots of eyes everywhere to remind you of death - put on Coltrane records & write a story about animals learning to talk - sing a song in a language you don't understand & play an instrument you haven't learned - think sideways, never hold back a fart & burn photographs of the rain..."

*

the Troubadour stared down Tottenham Court Road & the recent upheavals flooded in - so long ago it was - last week - another lifetime - how he returned to origin with barely a backward glance - & let it be told how the escape was made - though his heart now belonged to Boo, a runner just like him, a coward & hero bound together by doubts - she had met him in The Park Of Fumes - the new town's blotch of green - that fake Arcadia where they ran together in heavy patchouli jumpers of gaudy colours - spinning in tandem through quarrelsome nights of outlaw dances – she clung to him as he clung to her – as if nothing else needed to be held so tight – first love – careless love - would you Adam & Eve it

then, later, in a hidden corner of history where myths conspire, once upon an unspecified time, on a bench by the edge of Leinster Road park, near a school at the swollen heart of this unspeakable overspill town in the hinterlands of Essex, sits, sat, or will sit the most abject & unholy trinity of men ever to be caught burning a bridge – they reside in one body for this one time only – it is the eve of their tripartite separation – a severance from each other & also from the town, where they felt constricted, lost & where, they felt, their past was being rewritten against their will – he, they, are mad drunk as a sailor on the last day of shore leave with a broken tattooed heart on his chest – bless the salty no-god, bless ye too O Melancholy Dion

in truth it's not really a park at all, more a greenish-brown, tussocky oversight with proud, rusting metal goalposts without nets - a choked, muddy, arid cough thrown out of the old red brick lungs of this chilled & benighted new-town – a town without change, or the purpose required to change – a town where someone pressed pause & forgot about it – & somewhere outside it all, the murk of unloved fields stretch beyond the horizon & paradise & hell are but a train ticket away

they are contemplating a slatted wooden bench, scarred with obscenities – they check for dampness & gingerly sit, judges at a tribunal, sombre - before them, souring through cider breath, lays an expanse of bored grass - an accidental field, somehow not yet concreted over – an untended gap between graves

& it is deeply late, after the pub has long closed – a holy hour often visited by wastrels – & for this one night only, Captain Rehab, Lonely Troubadour & Newtown Baby share a body – the body in turn shares stolen, flat lemonade & two reeking chicken kebabs steaming dreadfully under a cloud-lidded moon – a storm has been predicted, gales, lightning, relentless rain, but for now the sky is a bliss of stars & shy wisps of cloud – their talk is of escape, having all, in their way, broken free - free of the very school that now looms in bleak, chain-link security behind them – the science labs, weirdly still illuminated, with books & test-tubes stashed in fake-wood cupboards –neon thief-light seeps through the bars of an iron fence on the playground's outskirts – they sigh, old school tales reeling in their head, as the welcome anaesthetising effect of the alcohol lazily segues into a dull ache behind the eyes & - for one glittery hour – they sense a collective goal – exile, escape – that bursting seed planted by their communal dream urged to bloom – they take long draughts of a shared joint – its smoke painting the future in swirling vapours above the lazy line of silhouetted, charcoal trees

it is the passing of rites between three ages – they are ready to shed old skin & let the breeze dry their sticky wings – in the distant hills dim thuds that could be their heartbeats – they feel almost human – the town grumbles, a pall of low outlines - someone is burying something in cover of darkness – gravedigger's eyes flashing - yet that falling dank soil that they sense is perhaps only alcohol hiding the old pain - that cloying morass that once slowed the changing mind is now becoming the fertile ground that their imagination first sought - a suppressed world of phantasms & wild plans wrapped in a balm of suspended belief - as if to give voice to such a dream would burst it, like a soap-bubble, allowing the air of heaven to seep into the skull with her ghost stars, dark wine & phases of lunatic moon - until the gateway of delusion closes again, finally, sinking in upon itself - leaving chem-trails smeared across a blue waking hour

Lonely Troubadour slumps & sadly recalls, in this rare tranquillity broken only by the shouts of homeward youths, walking down to the water at Leigh by the estuary & vowing heroically to drink enough ale to rekindle the fire in the belly of his song - alas, a futile task - for the very angels that swim in the frothing glass at first pouring, that send hopeful gasps upward through the murk, dissolving the hurt with fresh surges of empowering, arcane knowledge, are in reality the self-same devils in league against him - the blast of rum is powerful, a rich detonation in the head - but the strength it instils only lasts 'til the opening of the pub door homeward & the steely knife of that first sheet of cold air - 'til that cruel moment the door slams behind him & a lock clunks - securing bottles of dreams away once more - & where are your comrades now? - these seemingly immortal soldiers, fevered missionaries, where now their bright plans & their shimmering ideals? - their sunny dreams, it is slowly revealed, also fade with the blind, incontrovertible drift of autumn time - a life lived on the island between two bells - opening time, closing time - alarm clock & factory home-time chimes - & what - lost in the clamour of the orgy - appeared to be liberty, was just another open prison he felt duty-bound to never leave

now, The Prisoner Troubadour knew that the playful god that decrees all twists of tale & writhing plot would never allow such a fertile situation to go unresolved - it is clear that a harbinger of hope is required - a Jimmy Priest for the dry alkie denizens - the pub-flies, waking at a sudden cry, only to sink once again & snore on cushions of their folded arms - yes, a saviour is called for, a ray of light - somebody drenched in a bibulous authority that commands respect from the whisky-sodden masses, yet carefree - a friendly alien bringing news from the sci-fi future

*

187

& lo, it came to pass – the saviour cometh, the iceman cometh – down from the big city to save their souls – his mind ruined by bad acid & expensive dreams, locked deep in a loop of hallucinatory decay – there, emerging from the tangled thorn bush near the hissy road, staggers old Degory Priest– a mythic wastrel, a psychedelic charlatan – he zips up his clerical trousers & farts – frowning as he reels and slides about the mudded green, occasionally dipping in & out of the black shapes of vague shrubs – The Troubadour gazes in awed rapture as this uneasy priest stands bellowing like a moose on a bench & squats to fart again into the echoing bins - look ye all upon my works & marvel!

this surely is a man blessed by a religion I can follow – I wager for sure he knows all the latest songs & dance crazes – knows too, the secret word that will finally unlock a girl's heartbreak – & most of all knows that you know he knows you know

running after him across the stodgy grass like a child would follow Jesus or a murderer, the Lonely Disciple Troubadour imitates the priest's every wild gait, he laughs & sighs, aches, sings along with each bawdy verse – words that he never thought he knew – they cavort arm in arm & kick their legs out in comic rapture – pausing just to be swigging from the bottomless flask the priest produced from his long cloak, like a magic trick, with a flourish – the Troubadour spins one last time & finally, exhausted, drops to his knees in the soft earth & cries

the priest sits next to him with a thump - he lights his last cigarette, bent as a cranefly's leg – recites the lord's prayer as rewritten by Lawrence Ferlinghetti – he whispered that he had learned it by heart from the lips of Jesus himself - & it was credible to The Troubadour in that moment – for his language bloomed in the Troubadour's muzzy-bright skull – his stories held the magic close, blew fumes of indignant sorrow, an insular, amorphous philosophy ventilated by ragged snatches of song, the torrent of absurd logic mixed with the autumnal cigarette smoke was entrancing – the holy breath from sleepy tramps fresh risen in the shade of dustbins – leaving, like ale, a sweet glimpse of romantic foolishness on the tongue – the priest's first sermon

"...the drink failed, dear barman, so bring another – honeyed sweat the odour from her hair - sweet childish cigarettes, the taste on her lips – we cry at the story's beginning for we know not the catastrophe that the last chapter brings..."

another damp explosion from his bony arse delivered with a grimace – the priest continues

"...drink! - O my captains! - for it is a joy such as felt on a child's Christmas morn to be drunk beyond the reach of do-gooding angels – verily a most inspiring & chance alchemy is loosened in the soul - songs flap through the jukebox mind – firework language rips through the roiling blood – a checklist of divine believers - Temptations, Jan & Dean, Chris Montez, Beach Boys, Wreckless Eric, Buzzcocks – let us worship forever these unstoppable, imagined waves of sound, dancing & surfing across the whole wide world of romantic fiction! – true romance & true fiction – not the sleazy nodding winking syntax weekly shovelled in-between the old ladies' magazine covers – let the suburban mythic rise..."

& yes, out of nowhere, in a caravanserai of thoughts, the Lonely Troubadour plucks a satori fruit - he recalls stealing sherbet-dabs from the pick 'n' mix counter when the owner turned to put on his glasses before serving – a criminal, baby-faced killer - & he smiles, despite himself

& observing this scene from the realm of the real sci-fi future, as a ghost, back on the bench, Captain Rehab has seen this waxen smile before

way back when it was

& he approaches him slowly & puts a consoling arm about the Troubadour's shoulders – here I am

meanwhile, flat on his back now & silent at last, Degory Priest gawps at the sky as if it were a broken television & between mouthfuls of the Troubadour's cold, leathery kebab, broods voicelessly on his plan for their escape

*

& The Troubadour smiled that waxen smile again – out of the sleeping pub, street fresh with resonant rain, each puddle giving the gift of soft neon back to the stars - & he wandered for hours, somehow finding his way to the station – nimbly he jumps the untended barrier & staggers down, down, down the halted escalator & stumbles into the yawn of the last train's sliding doors – carriage empty – beer cans, burger cartons, a stiletto shoe – after a lull of brief sleep he awakes with a jolt as the train emerges into half-light, half-dusk, indeterminable & planetary – the electric worm clears its throat with a wheeze &, chugging through the slow tick of dung-coloured suburbs, lurches westward on sparking rails – hedges, walls & gardens slide by, children's swings fashioned from rope & tyre, melancholy & still, breathless laundry drooped over yellow clotheslines – his head swims sweetly & his feet tap to a maddening rhythm that doubles the backbeat of the train's clickety hum – he clutches the book he had borrowed from the priest – a short history of decay – he flicks through the pages, tobacco tinted & sticky with the night's dog-eared, beery paste – who carved these granite words? - random twilight thinkers, Felicity of Epigones – who was Epigones? – who was Felicity? – more golden dross to learn, another inhalation of mind – the words made little sense & his eyes throbbed with misunderstanding – an occult childhood in Transylvania, was that right? – brief biography - he put the book down with the last glanced titles

in his head & closed his eyes – arrogance of prayer –
lypemania – besotted whisky-blind hermit in a Paris grotto -
quousque eadem? - he wrestled with these cryptic phrases
as the train gathered speed, the knots briefly untying,
tantalising, until a tired shriek of melancholy brakes finally
sent him deeper into his dreamless, bloodsucking cave

*

next morning, by way of respite, in the city's despite, he
found his boots walking into Seething Lane, his favoured
thoroughfare by name alone – there, clutched to the bosom
of the past, the tiny church of Saint Olave, patron of the
Nordic legacies, London Bridge warrior, a secretive faith
shop, blind pig of belief, verdant with its little scrap of
garden – all the city hub-bub fading, just his Walkman
turned low down – Jimmy Webb, taped by anon, junk shop
cassette discovery, serendipity of far Wichita's native
wisdom – pylons again stretch far in his mind as soon as his
saintly arse hits the bench in the church garden & his
hungover eyes are shut – & when, as the second verse
begins, he re-opens them, a thousand motes are flickering
that he first mistakes for some hallucinatory residue left over
from an old lysergic episode, or haunted specks from the
great fire of London – maybe they were the microscopic
shrapnel of German bombs – ah no, alas, they are only
seeds from an accidentally kicked dandelion, ripened &
urgently trusting in no coming wind – The Windy
Troubadour sees a cluster of them by his battered boot &
kicks anew – a host ascends, floating high, catching
whichever haphazard currents are passing, purposeful gusts
to which they can hitch their blind trust – he watches them
sail & smiles a smile he saved for just such a circumstance
church garden, Seething Lane, hangover easing, seed-
flight, headphones fat with a song of longing

he senses a slight but sweet regret that slowly dissipates with the dandelion's diaspora, upward silently, a floating congregation seeking out a universal sermon in the godless metropolis – god speed, he thinks, & may you land in fertile soil

*

The Universal Troubadour picks up his mandolin & strums a few bars of The Night Has A Thousand Eyes - gnats rodeo the tiny horse winds around the bedside lamp though it is dead, bulb blown, still in twilight they reel, the atoms of thought, microcosmic, exigent

ugly, they are, close-up under microscopes – ugly like all things are when made bigger – & what of the still more miniscule creatures beyond our thought? – existing only to chew & fuck or split - or whatever hideous way the bastards proliferate – silently they live on your face in their countless disfigured millions – each of us a secret universe of mauled tics - this is the way the minds of prisoners change – small details are magnified until everything is ugly - until one day, whether by a violent act of defiance, guns blazing, or stealthy tunnelling with stolen cutlery, that promise you once upon a time made to yourself rolls around & the glorious breakout is secured

*

to the city, then - the capital– only there among the slick-backed & greased could the last vestiges of Newtown Cry-Baby be squashed by new memories, renewed by vengeance – here a Troubadour outlaw could really preen & scowl - an artless, suburban fox loose in the polyglot metropolitan hen-house - rolling his hoodlum cigarettes in chrome-countered cafes - tobacco dust & creased Rizlas in his lap

the mandolin chords are growing stale – folk to punk –
the city always demands that the volume be turned up full -
yet the minstrel is still tired – tired of what, he is not sure –
no doubt something formless, distorted & disappointed –
burps of anger, masturbatory images dragged up as evidence
for life's grand design - mindfarts in gelatine – freeze-frame
explosions

'...I don't want to die here...' – he wails & thrashes a
medieval power-chord to the ostrich night

he had left the new town the following day - swearing he
would return only to run madly amok - with a machine gun
spraying the sleepy mall with the bullets of his adventures

*

Early Troubadour walking slow – buys a Daily Mirror at
the miserable kiosk, thin radio scratching at the disinterested
air – incoming ear buzz of woollen, misanthropic, swaddled
mumbles from beneath a red turban – icy thanks dribble to
stony ground as Wizzard sing in Spector chambers – The
Troubadour tries, but fails, to see his baby jiving & pops a
polo mint into his dry mouth – lights a cigarette & pushes
the inky news into his shoulder bag – tune in his head now,
stuck – read the headline but now can't remember it – old
news already – Grub Street still grubby & street-smart –
unwithered it glowers - in the morning gales of bad omens
they scrape their busy nibs across the yellow foolscap –
suicide notes promising lurid revelations & attendant guilt –
church-doorway gossip – old lady breath, peppermint-
haunted – hobo blankets will tomorrow be lined with their
salacious sonnets & hack haikus – a weathervane unrequired
in a north wind of no change in which no answers blow –
two teenagers in black plimsolls idly kick a tennis ball
against the shuttered shopfront – everything bolsters the
backbeat – pretty woman, entrancing, intriguing, hair

tangling in the steady gust from the alley, a detail of the universe that she cooly ignores through tinted glasses – her skirts may dance but they dance alone – see my baby – & yes Wallflower Troubadour sucks the last smoke from his cigarette & rehearses for her an unspoken greeting – but she passes quickly through his lost chance – his jacket jives in the wizard wind, flapping in the wake of her disappearing promise – another brave morning in the heart of bright Albion – the old shops get painted up as if new – bread & jam turns to feta cheese & pitta – he feels the timeslip like a song that has escaped from a future radio – fat music dieting, squeezing into rattling speakers & earbuds – the whitewashed walls of the multi-story car-park are insulted by blots of jealous spray paint – perdition & the ambience of corrosion – rough sleepers strewn across disused tracks - Boho graveyards tainted, desecrated by jets of epitaphs & eulogies to one-trick poets – the perpetual motion of the wrecking ball – the desk-toy of the city troll high & safe above the folklore of a changeling street – '...I'm a genius!...' - cries a Mack Sennett tramp draining sour clots of old milk from a found carton – the underground is thick with wanted posters, the missing who want to be missed – rebellion, now a museum exhibit, is roped off & please don't touch - children file around it in awe like it is a pterodactyl, a mammoth – the milk-carton genius sleeps under last week's business supplement like faith slumbers under wafery leaves of a bible – above him a torn poster – come to sunny Southend-on-Sea – briny sea-wind agitates the corner flap

The Troubadour wets his salty thumb & turns to the TV page, creased by the cramped bag, specked by a brief rainfall – The Old Grey Whistle Test – different wizards, different jives – prog cartoons from a jerky Disney vault – he marks the programme with a tick - the rain stops & a sleepy sun focuses its reluctant gaze on the shaken, closing umbrellas – another unsung genius picks at the grimy, sweet bins behind the bakery - wild hair, grey, white, where dark almost blue - thick beard of the grizzled, unkempt anarchist - the cupped, soot-caked hand held to his broken mouth awaiting a cough dredged from his sparrow chest - he hacks, spits, chewing gum & oyster grit - he keeps his hand to his mouth - keenly anticipating the prospect of another assault of expectoration - he looks like he is holding an imaginary microphone, The Troubadour thinks - he looks like he is singing

*

Pubcorner Wizard waits like a landmine over a sullied, deadwood table in a heavy timbered pub of polite lunchtime commerce - Pimms & clinking glasses with lollipop stirrers - sickly perfumed secretaries quack & preen, getting the new boy from personnel drunk, putting flatulent soft rock on the jukebox - the barman turns it down & gets a ripple of applause

the Troubadour lights a cigarette & soon decides it is a one pint & go pub - not a soul he wants to know or bore - from under his arm the book falls - Songs Of Innocence - a small pocket edition he never puts in his pocket - a mild & understandable pretension given his age & shoe-size - the bookmark has separated from the book, oh shite, place lost - that bit he liked about night & father - Pubcorner Wizard spies the fallen bookmark & grunts - picks it up for him

"...fold the bloody page corners over to keep your place in books, don't listen to the fuckin' purists - I used to scribble on mine in a thick bookie's pencil - give somethin' back - I wrote 'BOLLOCKS' in the margin of Wordsworth's prelude - I wrote 'SEE ME AFTER SCHOOL' under Ginsberg's Howl & I wrote 'FINE LINES DO NOT ALLOW YE A FAVOURED INGRESS TO HEAVEN WHEN DICTATED BY A BUSTED FLUSH OF A

HEART' on the flyleaf of Appollinaire's bloody thing, what was it? – Alcohols? – how did I let that slip my mind? – it's all arse gravy & tit-wash anyways – there's philosophic truth to be found in a 1950s bus timetable if ye have an hour to waste & a thesis to fake – here, see if you can do this one with me, the last clue – 6 down, two words, both six letters - 'song of a season departing' – any ideas? – when in doubt ask a poet or a copper – I take it you're the former - if I get it I can win a hundred quid – that'll keep me in eggs & ham for a few weeks - & a few pints of the yellow stuff thrown in for good measure – I was one answer short yesterday – I knew it was a name but couldn't think – Mack Sennett – y'know, the silent director bloke - someone said that Stan Laurel drank in this pub once – might've been the landlord – love the silents, me – Stan & Ollie, two sweet old entertainers them – the French fuckin' loved 'em, y'know? - *clown et august* – that old caper – Chaplin too – they love puppets & mime as well – Chat Noir club's where it started – there's a boozer - funny cunts – used to be one that came in here – Claude, with his red umbrella & bicycle clips – used to drink Benedictine – ever drunk that? - like cough mixture after a tramp's pissed in it – he had a daughter that waitressed down in Soho somewhere – now, what was...? – Amandine, that's it – dead proud, he used to show off her photo, y'know? - pretty girl – absinthe, that's another one – mashes your soul that shite – that painting, who was it? - Degas...no... - one of them fuckers – used to have a print of it on my little table-top fridge at my old gaff down in Mornington Crescent – little fridge - where I kept my cider, back in the 60s that would've been – I was in the building game then – good earner – absinthe drinker, yeah - saw the print of it in a jumble sale in a chipped red frame - two miserable cunts, man & woman, at a table with a full glass of that green gloop in front of him – fucking dark, depressing as hell – it touches a nerve though – reminds me of the

Coach & Horses pub – same feel to it – a place where you go to forget shit & end up forgotten ha! - any road, all this blather about booze makes your gob dry up – mine's a cider with a bit of ice, ta pal, get yourself one being as you're buyin...."

forever on the train, way back when – eastward, westward ho – ho ho ho – there & back – home is there & back is a place where restless, open-ended thoughts dream of there & back again, repeat – & when you're there you dream of back until you wake up here again – the old yo-yo – The Troubadour dizzies, he feels that he is dissolving at the edges of his body – becoming the rain that slowly envelops the passing fields, flower-hung balconies, stacked damp pallets in builder's yards, the petroleum savour of labyrinthine pipe farms, the desolate ache of gasometers & sump-leak

the lock on the door is broken and the air hangs dustily in burnished slivers of leftover night & peeled tangerines – Yuletide tang, sorrow in there somewhere too - he returns to his stale bed and lights another cigarette – The Troubadour lounges, sating an inexplicable desire for the wispy curling of gentle smoke, burning leaves crushed inside a tube of paper that, perhaps, he muses, has been treated with a hint of exotic resin – they always did that at parties – sneaking a pinch of crumbled dope into the flapjacks – extra vodka in the punch – can't smell it – the bullet with your name on it that you never hear coming – these days he was smoking for pleasure rather than effect again, no longer suffering the wild disorder of his first craving – instead, responding to an ancient mechanism, a friendly fire that urged him to better cope with mortality – a cigarette is a temporarily closed mind, a necessary pause – its evils are postponed by a mystic, vague contemplation, thereby banishing any ugly notions of thick tar, retching, ash & bubbling coughs to the dispassionate outer edges of his thoughts – blah – drink is more profound - a considered addiction, a loser's choice - & therein lies its virtue – go into a pub – buy a bottle from the off-license – premeditated preferences made – smoking is not like that - it is a reflex when the mind is unengaged – bus stops, queues for the cinema – the hellish wash of slow mornings – write something down about this, he thinks, write it in smoke with a cough in the margin - notebook out, find a biro that isn't bleeding

throughout
thy contested epochs
of human priorities
contemplation & habit
endureth

whyfore this antiquity? – this blowsy, ragged Wardour Street English oft times verily 'tis spoken here by mine & thy good self O ego – all his suitcased notebooks stained with the drivel & drool of bloated wordery – philavery of the obscurantist - hideously furnished sentences – ormolu & chintz – quick brown dogs & lazy foxes, or whichever came first, leaping each other – puffery to inflate a terminally punctured tyre – high stuff gasping in thin air – another one, Christ there's no end – it will declutter in time

it is national poetry day.
for those
who like pretty words put in place

in a rational
& entirely ordered way
like those porcelain birds
seen on wallpapered walls
& other such balls
I suppose - Hooray

a grasp of need – a simple self-medicinal procedure, an intangible old convention, which breathes desperately on down through the polluted centuries – a deft murder of crow-speak, state-sponsored, despite the knowing smile of the victim - the empty prescription leaves a poltergeist in the abandoned church of the lungs - two left – borrow one off the priest when I see him later – nobody gives out free fags anymore – it's a harsh world

*

waking to a grey light – early again - irritated now - a 5 a.m. low-hung aeroplane grumbling across the heavens - somewhere a ridiculous dog barks – what was the name of that dog in Tom & Jerry? – that voice, a shovel moving gravel – blearily elsewhere in earshot something creaky opening, far off in the great not here, it rasps in the marshy silence growing beyond the curtained glass – Lonely Once More Troubadour lays back on the hard mattress & rolls his head to feel the cool pillow & sniff wraith-like enduring wisps of new laundry - he imagines the walk to the shop – the gummy pick'n'mix smell, sickly – the beautiful lines of fresh cigarette packets like a dwarf's library – in the shock of air, how he will softly breathe in controlled spasms to relish the plaintive, tremble of nosehairs, marimba vibrations of the lung – the exchange of pleasantries, the transfer of warm coin – a nod of assent, understanding – cigarettes, coffee, cereal

the sky looks ill - he thinks as he shuffles back - it is
bloodless, strained - he gives the planet thirty years & looks
at the backwards joke clock on the wall above the dresser -
five more desiccated hours until the bar re-opens - yawn, try
to burp without throwing up - easy forcing up of the old air
- dry cider, ash, pepperoni - "..holy trinity.." - his voice that
breaks across the traffic is unexpectedly desperate, a patient
given sudden oxygen, blunt old scissors cutting cardboard -
how did he ever leave his bedwarmth - get up, just do it,
swing the cosy legs out into the chill

The Troubadour methodically dressed for a longer
haul, he puts on his black overcoat & affecting a slightly
haughty, passive air looks upon the carefully selected debris
of his kingdom - a Kit-Kat has melted on a brown tablecloth
next to the local newspaper left open at the want-ads - he
switches on the radio - radio 3 - classical - Mahler or is it
Prokofiev? - he does not know - a song, it is - *lieder* do they
call it? - Mahler then? - no - he flails in his mind-den for
recognition without success - the strings rally & soar across
toast-crumbs & a buttery knife - perhaps Schubert - he
pretends to himself, even alone, that he cares - the burbling
radio gulps & fizzes as it retunes - the orchestra dissolving
like a tablet to a mess of carbonated, static laughter - the
big-bang's residue, gift that keeps giving - particles sizzling,
cosmic censure, old Chinese whispering in the rose-pattern
wallpaper like the aural deliriums he read about yesterday at
Degory's lair - opium dens, snakes, pigeons blabber & flub
in the roofbeams that are the floor of the flophouse above

he reaches for yet another cigarette - eyes falling with a
troubling ease upon the first troubling reminder of the day
just passed - words on a blotchy page of foolscap - fool's
cap? - don't try those games - mind not ready yet - some
pissed up poem mayhap? - no, prose it seems, O god,
serious I must've been - he picks up the sheet of wiry scrawl
& squints

200

"wanna be a member of the found generation...wanna be a black man pluckin' the diddley-bow - nailed to my bleached porch in the afterglow- hey! fuckface! you heading north? if not then what's it worth?..."

(remainder illegible)

eyeing coldly these late drunken words - how vital it had been to scratch them down - as if nothing else mattered in that forgotten instant - terrible hand he has when inebriated, barely able to shape the cramped letters, they spidered across the guidelines of the page like burnt tissue fallen from a bonfire - he spies another page of it on the fridge - this one torn from his red notebook, left open & smudged by leak of biro & blessed for good measure with a sobering coffee-ring halo - the words still drunk, they dance, or so he fancies - or are frozen unawares in the act of dancing - into contours, alchemical signs lost to the science of daybreak - subject matter leaps wildly, here, a fragment of The Fall, whose hexy album he sees now outside its cover on the floor, there, a messy stack of blues & folksy field hollers - conversations with the blues - he read that last week too, Pubcorner Wizard was it? - he'll ask me if it was his - it all fits & shits itself out eventually

he lays down face up on the bed again, momentarily dizzy - second time today, not even ten yet, christ - but just as the old dullness seemed to have permanently set in for the foreseeable morning, a different slice of his mind sparks & engages - & the first sharp fragments of his sour dreams seep gradually back to the light through their dry, corrugated swathes of reassuring countryside - that smeared morass of despondent quintessences with which sleep decorates its fearful chambers finally clearing just enough to recall some hideous morsel of the previous night's unravelling

the kernel of the dream he had focusing now, it slips through the walls of his skull like neutrinos & into the squeaky nylon pillow, plump as a slug, coverless - he had noted that lately the purpose, assuming there was one, of his recent dreams had become too slack, too imprecise to fire the words that he wished to speak – he was daily perturbed by the sense that all he has ever spoken of is being lost to time, wasted on a drunkard's wind

he saw it as a fairytale, his beloved swooning like a princess in another ogre's arms

The Troubadour Prince picked up the ruined notebook & idly flicked a page - there are more words yet, he squints anew

"...wanna be a miner, blackface and flask..."

this offering followed by another bleary line with only the word 'canary' surviving & a phone number, next to which the legend 'Martha' – lower case – then printed once more in the margin lengthwise, underlined presumably for emphasis, it yelped anew - 'MARTHA' - upper case, in a different ink & a crude drawing of a pair of breasts in failing biro – a speech bubble rising from the cleft betwixt the breasts declares

'...footfalls echo in the mammary...'

so many are the regrets of sailors too long away from home, feeding on the little failures that one lost night clings to - so many old temptations, suggestions - a vaguely familiar diary, another *aide-memoir* to provoke internal squeals of sudden reminiscence - yet these lines all own a universal desperation - they came from his desire to share himself – he was but an amanuensis to the prisoner's spirit that inhabited him, these were dictated lines, nothing else chose them - their opacity was as bleak & ultimately answerless as a quiet, dawn lake that gives no reply to the dying interrogations of the night's maddened wind then, all of a terrible sudden, the mirror in his bathroom fell with a sharp crash - he wandered in and stared, as a giraffe would stare at a ringing telephone, at the mosaic of splintered glass in the sink - his astonishment glared back at him from a kaleidoscope of reflected bad luck - well, he was having quite a morning

"...shittrrrrrr!..." - he growled

then, an agitated shuffle of bunioned feet outside the door, be-slippered on a musty carpet aged by her diligent years of stalking, her steadfast duty of repeated tramping – yes, the landlady is - & will probably forever be - carrying her boiled egg & charred fingers of toast back to her room where she will eternally watch the early news on the cream-coloured, scrolling screen of a tiny portable television – earthquakes & distant wars course into her eyes – pictures from what may as well be a far planet strained through the dubious medium of a twisted coat-hanger aerial

"...coffee..." he declared to himself sternly

to the paltry kitchen he mordantly trudged - the naked, unsheathed guitar, fat hips, hunched shoulders, sat like a Renoir whore by the fridge - he briefly fingered the four rusted strings, mentally dancing, albeit listlessly, to his own unwritten urges – Pere Ubu blaring dub architecture in his mind, last night, last night yes - flayed jazz drowned his notes with waves from the dirty street - he tried to glean some words, a trace of melody but was unable to follow the twisted bass lines snaking under the crocus-squall of vocal – he, defeated by the mental slippage, throws a sideways glance through the soiled, gauze-crossed window - the birth pangs of shops, milk bottles renewed, postman whistling a squib of a tune nobody can quite spit from the tip of their tongue - The Troubadour turns again to the angry scribbles on the pad by the sink - he says to himself in his aching head, think on this

*'...today I shall meet dreadful species of humankind –
yes & today - as a matter of course - vile, mendacious, vain,
morbid, rattling vessels · of humanity that bloat & shrink
according to dietary obsessions, shall duly obsess & blithely
pontificate, breathing repellent oaths in my face with their
reeking nicotined pant or...oh! some such etcetera - same
old same old - dragged mewling to this earthly paradise only
to push retro prams full of sheep-faced children against my
shins - all the while a virginal sun is cowering behind the
horizon & the wide sky awaiting her smock of clouds - what
am I to do? - everything happens out of sequence – all is
dislocation, atonal - everything happens out of time - I will
do the washing up later - maybe tomorrow, perhaps next
year - I will go past the record shop's window - I will
stupidly attempt to speak in French to the exchange student
that resides in the flat above said establishment if she is
smoking, as is often the case, on the step leading to her
doorway - "...bonjour! il fait toujours tres froid..." - & she
will grunt her good morning in curdled English or else
ignore me, save for a knifing look of disdain...'*

*"...ah, pourquoi sont les jeunes femmes etranges si sage
et suffisantes...? - porquoi en effet..."*

believe it, he mused, if all these ornaments, these brief
attractive juvenile fascinations – these intense, smoky, beery
young women that he still gawked at so dotingly were to
switch tracks tomorrow & true love should once again die
on the vine in the arms of weeping Aphrodite - Celtic
souvenirs from leprechauns vanishing – then he would be
forced back to the anarchic world of his putative comrades
once more – the blarney of that mad priest would still be
treasured - as this split second flash of time says it should –
The Troubadour had an augury of diminishing innocence,
let his good looks lose colour, what matter? - let the
cherished shambles of this church of no joy & no god hold
close each blustery yearning of his spirit song – a zen mind,

he sought, luxuriantly still – aleph-mem-nun – concentrate on the sacred breakfast - in the name of the further sun & wholemeal toast

    he searched the unspeakable cupboard beneath the sink for a dustpan & brush to sweep up his shattered face

*

The Troubadour regularly practised defiance, on a whim he would test the snap of wind with a wetted forefinger - & often he drank in the mad priest's church, too often brazenly at the altar but mostly in the dry, booky pews – Degory drank too but affected a clerical dismay nonetheless – on the best of nights they both got aboard the unholy rollercoaster, swigging hipflask nips of lightning, reading desultory passages from the thin biblical leaves – once he stood, drunk, at the old chapel doorway ripping out page after page & sending them flittering into the strong Autumn winds that immediately reversed them back down the high street or sent them wildly gavotting high in the bleak, slate skies – back to no-god, return to sender

    or sleeping, all booze exhausted, occasionally by stealth having gained ingress, in the small, deserted sanctuary at crack of night, where one time, spooked by Lovecraft & Machen, he fancied he heard the names carved on every tombstone being listed by a revenant raconteur, each syllable coated in dark chocolate, counterpoint of church wind fluting through the mudslide flesh, solemn, bad harbinger tones - as names of the missing are listed by reporters after a disaster – he writhed & hummed his half-remembered nursery rhymes, throwing out desperate hymnals to banish these monotonous premonitions but to no avail - a sweet dread suffused his marrow, the gripped hand in a horror-show cinema - & yet part of him relished the roll-call of absent enemies, those whom he had at least outlasted – some nights he sat frozen in beauteous terror & waited until the last name had been uttered & for the voice to fall silent - before falling back with an exhalation to crash into mountainous sleep – the dawn's edgy glow already steeping the worn windows in their gaudy brew of glasswork, chipped & washed-out by the seas of time

old dealer priest, preaching to the silenced choir – the slain army of misfits tight in unconsecrated ground – where under dwells the leftover cold stew of guilty souls born of witchcraft & devil worship, freshly executed criminals, deaths achieved by suicide, Tyburn's treehouse of strangled sky dancers

& after a while the secrets of Degory's enthusiasms became evident - the confessional was where he kept his stash – in an old carved, gargoyled snuff-box he had found in the belfry cupboard – an old red rolling machine, steel case for large Rizlas, a sheet of blotters stained with a prepared LSD/water/alcohol solution, a half bottle of cheap brandy & a few vials of something Jimmy Red had given him one long night that they had spent blathering by Karl Marx's grave up at Highgate, trying to invoke Bolshevik demons to foster the coming light of morning's revolt – the colourless liquid, gloopy in an old-fashioned beaker corked with sullen lip, the contents of which the priest had tentatively tried once only & yes indeed such were the ferocious hypnagogic hallucinations he had endured on waking, once only – save that little caper for weirder times ahead, Jim lad – but he thrust it deep into his frock coat nevertheless

ah yes but mostly old Degory Priest talked to himself - & at length, facing a mirror or catatonic before shopfront glass - having no real congregation to speak of – most had scattered over time to dissemble hoary stories of his satanic methods & sleazy details of wildly prurient sermons – it was common knowledge among the local streetwise that hallucinogens fed his already wrecked imagination – the church had been condemned twice, bombed out in the war, crumbling to mother earth ever since – it was fine & dandy enough for Degory though – he brooked no breach of his sacred spaces & his small knot of pallid confessors served only to feed his store of guilt or furnish him with the latest medication currently in favour – his followers would follow their own shadows to the grave - their sins were plump & fertile as a cluster of grapes untrodden – his teeth stuttered excitement as he unfurled their debaucheries in his head, pausing to swig at the brandy & savour intently a particularly fevered anecdote from his store, he would cross their sweaty foreheads with rum & give them a dry Ritz biscuit by way of the body of god's lamb – all the while staring them out, curiously staring until they looked away – his countenance almost attained a kind of sanctified bliss at such times, much in the way a gorilla peers at a banana before its first bite – he was a Priest Of Pain, yes – The Troubadour had secretly renamed him - hangovers were his hell on earth, in lieu of a distant paradise yet to be reclaimed, he daily drowns in torment, he seemed to enjoy them, the cure for a hangover is plotting another, bite of the same dog returning – agenbite of indog – write that down

'...Atlantis, yea, there I will meet with you...'

he would wail, to nobody, from the reeking pulpit at dawn

'...from Hades & from above the mercy seat, from between the two cherubim which are upon the ark of the bitched testimony, the command shall be given! - are you unhappy? - are heavy burdens weighing you down? - do you feel that you cannot escape feelings of despair? - Christian, you are not alone!...'

The Priest Of Pain, yes – he had given The Troubadour a box of fat Cuban cigars out of nowhere one morning

'...a little token of my extreme...tastes of revolution & bearded tears...'

he lit one now, it burned with an intensity that was almost audible - he held it between his finger & thumb, palm cupped, the leery, dark smoke rising - rich hooks of brown tobacco, he coughs, these will last him forever, how many in box? - ten, Christ

The Cinematic Priest had spoken of his old dream of being a film star - they had disagreed on his choice of roles - the priest envisaged himself as Father Barry in On The Waterfront

'...some people think the crucifixion only took place on Calvary - boy, that had some nuts in it that little monologue - even as a kid I felt the punch of those words - blood sermon rising...'

'...but you would never have gone against the union, Degory, surely? - I see you more as Jean Massieu, the mad Dean in that Joan Of Arc thing - Dreyer was it? - no make up to hide your ugly mug, close ups unforgiving, black & white - yeah, that's you...'

The Passionate Priest smiled, shook his head & sighed at the quaint romance of his childhood fantasy - his pulpit was more ship's hold than burning cross, though the drama appealed, he had to admit - he closed his eyes & pictured his hero Karl Malden nudging hamming Artaud off his silver screen

two cats snore in swooning, spoony comfort in the nook of the shadowed pulpit, rats scuttle between the broken vase & the menorah, six candles lit, that he stole from a blind, Jewish pawnbroker

*

The Troubadour is troubled of heart & mind - smitten by some gothic, hipster girl - barmaid at the Elephant's Head, best jukebox for a mile either way up the Camden High Street's slithery drag - of course, she never uttered a word by way of encouragement, no - she just silently pulled the pump that drew that golden ale from the bottomless well that magically refuelled his nightly revelations – he rambled onward through a forest of anecdotes getting nowhere – testing her air with doomed flights of fanciful wit - but halting & reining in that ardent, wind-drunk kite-soul stretching ever starward – up, up, up through the massing clouds, the sleepy years the marinade of alcohol soaked – cigarettes counted, two left for the walk home – accosted by the Salvation Army, trawling the kerbs for their nightly soul harvest - temperance skirts of a motherly girth spread wide in gun-metallic grey – targeting the battleship anarchists, bullet & bombproof – faces meekly upturned, god-lit, toward the sky under the spread legs of history - following each fold ever upward & we'll say no more, new money clanking in the shaken tin, black boots & hats of traffic warden authority, stiff brim - neat greying hair cut around the ears – their souls aching to fly to join the gang in the bye & bye, sweet or otherwise – upward, yes, to the penitent face peeking like a beardy, beaten snare from Christ-laundered pleats – the ambition of the saved, a demonic drive toward rebellion thwarted – puncturing vanity & earthly pursuits, hollow the bold & stray no more – see the light in darkness shine, come follow the dry revolution – but a sinner sneaks in the Hawley for a devil's jar - put the big burping bottle down only when I'm dead – here's my marker for a beery-breathed gaggle of sinners guaranteed – stag parties hunting down their last catch - the groom's in a gutter & the wedding's off again

yes, yes & all those tenebrous nights chasing the chaser in the sleazy respectability of the Lock Tavern - romantic swigs of Havana rum reeling around the ringing fountain of pinball bells – the barmaid reminding The Romantic Troubadour of Eliza Doolittle – gargled vowels & rinsed consonants, touch of market barrow mud about the lacy bootsole – he a lost waif, she two years above and blossoming in holy, Victorian, tight-corseted repression – or Penelope Pitstop, with The Moustachioed Sinner Troubadour, tight-crotched & pillowed in writhing dreams, snickering mutt & goggles steamed up as the engine drops out of the car before the finishing line every time – yes, Camden Lock, it is late, almost late enough to be getting early – The By Now Lamenting Troubadour strumming the imaginary strings in his head & scribbling the screed of the weary disenchanted sailor – witchy air & baleful moon – wolf music, mother red-capped – gah, fuck it, even this water is eager to get somewhere, to enjoin a bigger, speedier flow – all the fables it drowns in passing are offered like sacrifices to the waiting sea – he sat watching the canal drift across the rippling moon

& he thought suddenly of oil on guttered water & his old job at the refinery – how that reeking van kidnapped him every week-day morning at 4.a.m – it coughed & rumbled through the refinery gates into another world – those big tankers brooding by the quay, thrilling, pregnant with travel – the drab stone roadways traversing the plant, where thick, lagged pipes tracked the gravel trench kerb sides & listless men in grey or orange oilskins carried toolboxes on narrow paths to the low, arched huts of green metal - stewing over glutinous tea, daydreams of repair, renewal – all wishing someone was just fixing them up & re-plastering their cracked hearts

& though still a Newtown Baby back then, he was stepping from the van with the confidence of a changeling, picking every little piece of himself up – joining the rebel congregation in the smoking huts – the silent, oily crew lighting their Marlboros by pressing them to the glowing electric gauze – a last puff to keep their frozen boots trudging on the weed-strewn tracks leading to the last station in this golden dawn - someone perhaps by his side –

210

someone whose name he is already forgetting – merely an occasional acquaintance who had as much self-respect & belief in their calling as he – hardy, physically adept & not afraid of black soil on their hands - but most of all filled with hope, caring about time & not a slave to the hours – one of the born toilers, workers, the lumpen proletariat archetype – it was this band of unmerry men he felt himself flowing toward – slog through the chores at hand & it's off to the last orders to swig a little anaesthetic to keep us laughing at the drowning of the day – for we're all standing at a station with tattered, attic suitcases - packed with nostalgic keepsakes accumulated on the path to exaltation – Chaplinesque, that poem he read, suitcase & twirl of majorette cane, Crane, yes, cane with an R, slapstick tumbler from the stern into the propeller wash, farewell wave as he goes – I'm off to that by & by where a Labour sun is shining, all consciousness risen - subtle, bitter or underhand, motor churn, petrol burn – seeking The Holy Mechanic to repair the the flapping fanbelt, the sputtering plug, the timeworn workings of the heart's worn engine

& yes these freedom walks in the realm of old soaks who stayed the course & stood their round, these baby paces in rebel's footsteps, where the sour wine tasted sweetest & a bell of pleasure rang with the simplest recalling of worthy toil - it was as if he were a prisoner newly rehabilitated & reminiscing about the old lag years – do ye remember, remember in the tea-hut the grey overalls hang on the bright red hooks – remember how that Newtown Baby told himself to keep a tight grip on his magic world - because he knew that way above the refinery steam an invisible horde of drunken angels watched over his every blunder - for if they drop his heart - or accidentally mislay some little essential component - he knows, he knows the crusher will be waiting – yes, this analogy worked, he convinced himself, tipping the barrel of old metal strips into the colliding, unbreakable jaws

- a broken heart is indeed like an old engine - allowed to gather rust & be casually thrown away before any thought of restoration - but today he must work - today he is half-sheltered from the obstinate rain in the leaky pump-house - he scrawled his false conclusions & vague resolutions into his diesel-stained notebook - & when the sun nervously swam from a drizzly, retreating cloud, he swung a bitumen-encrusted shovel over an aching, bruised shoulder & set his stern face northward - onward, to the tank farm, to hell with the pump-house! - a Mayakovsky line of angular worker-ants file into the van once more - empty your head of poetry, comrade, go tell it to the tax office - here is your task, unchosen - just believe us that for these next eight hours you are born to shift these creaking wedges of solid crude oil from frozen gullies & diesel-wash these spindly pipes & wheels, here's your pay dangling from that thread, go chase the carrot now, you can almost smell it, it smells of saloon bars & record shops & hollow, gas-ring mornings

there was respite, of course, jobs that he favoured - again the river intervened in his slow headway - the quay where the vast tankers hummed immobile in choppy, eager tides - the rumble of foreign voices, hoots & horns - all being scrawled into those old stained notebooks & typed out as bad poetry back in the perfect obscurity of his ill-lit bedroom - on a slow, calm pilgrimage - after a long day's work at the refinery his bones felt brittle, his hair stank of oil & sulphur - dragging Mackay & cider down to the mystic park of fumes to drink petrol unrefined into vestal, holy wine, steam-pipe Ubu piss to a blissful vinyl hiss - under transformational dove-light of an ascendant moon & gravel purring under booted tread - scattering his anger at the falling of the hours - already deeply sensing the wasted coming stretch - his head span full circle, heart hurt by Triple Vintage cider there by the Berryman-saddened concrete bridge - two inseparables, listening to a mix-tape down by the ersatz lake – a small Philips tape recorder regurgitating their choices – he slips easy into a world where images tangle in the mind's eye – where youthful & stubborn Dada hearts still danced to old Jarry's wail – Ubu bootleg, before they exploded – the factory buzz, repetition, strained through a mesh of struck iron – a clang of anvil tone by fat old suit of Crocus rapped - as white specks fly from steel, the stars divulge a pattern to his fortune – a hazy path between the now & his point of vanishing – the Melody Maker, NME, Sounds – forbidden pleasures, gnostic scriptures - foretelling bars & books & feelings yet to grow – a prophet in his country past – taking another swig of hipflask brandy & a rip of stolen joint & they float on a slow hot air balloon of other people's imagination – rising way over the stilled lake & out across the industrial estate's white chimneys – above the Ford onion-shaped water tower - a libertine rising – breathing in words, always the incessant language that nags to be voiced – using the blues, the old phrases & psalms, to dig out a recipe for just a taste - to feed the caprices of love, O careless love

or Sunday, Sunday - pigeon rain taps his grey window as the tide of radio refocuses itself – bush-wire music – washing across the beach, a wake from the good ship Caroline – O Caroline no - a melancholy loss of consciousness, a deep cave wherein one tired conga taps – remembering that gold-leaf London day with Boo - he sees his honeying mind skating down a winter terrace – Walker & Walkman – shared headphones on the train - Montague sapphire – loneliness, together in loneliness, the cross to bear & the cloak they wore – the old sun behind a cloud forever – Boo in hippy skirt, red boots – music thick from dread speakers dusted with ash - kaftan notes curling like campfire smoke around a softly pink bulb of lantern failing

& ashen the dawn window, brighter now - smoked ash a-tumbling to the sofa's beige tundra - fat strings thrilled with

213

kindled wonder – soaring violins – chased by cellos that may flood his eyes & find a way to slide along the black ice of his frostbitten soul - cutting him to the crazy paving marrow - & as it fades upward it will kiss the rising helium moon to leave him as just a smile, Cheshire cat gone – smiling & digging out rhymes from his head of Essex clay with a shameless pen

*

or Saturday morning & he's just got badly paid again – sparse, green grass of giro cheque – wages of sin to take to the iniquitous city – thrill of Tottenham Court Road subway emerging wild to sneak unseen past Centre Point & guilty as a leper through St. Giles & environs, back again, retrace the traces, down an innocent street off the main drag to flap through the hearty racks of records - rough trader shining a light – if this music had a smell it would be wet rain steaming from these dogs of independence that scour & flick the vinyl in heavy judgemental greatcoats – not breathing or looking up – pause to hold a swelling map or a stinking toy – buzzing cocks, Prag Veccing the slaughtered puppies of undertonic bass-kicks, charged by volts from Berlin cabarets, squinted at through mascara slits of gilmoured eyes, wheels spinning in ruts & death-row damned forever – com-sat cherubim hang from the ceiling fan, circling the earth after the fall, Cortina trap & dancing dead with residents & presidents – a minute over Tokyo, one o'clock, the clock ticks, ticks toxic – see more & read about it – *c'est la chute et la ville brûle* – prising open cardboard Xeroxed sleeves, appearing, proliferating, bands splitting like amoebas day on day – driven by those throbbing surrender notes from the hostage suburban sprawl - postcards from a Celtic Tweedom – princesses trilling plainsongs of protest that spoke of freedom from a Kafka castle – the churning

214

rhythm slinking into urban psyches & geographies – reds striking the blues & rioter's dustbin shields glint white in long shot summers – under the brutal Westway, in sepia anger, bovine coppers & copper-coloured troops of jarring sevens clashed –psychotropic eddies in the last gang smoke of Brixton – who's side are you on? – wedged betwixt red miner threats, clutching beautiful banners of crimson arrows & sooted faces flecked with the stoked, riverine heart's crimson confluence with scything, hammered colours of revolt – neck-split acoustic third-hand guitars – anti-poetic, axing through the pole supporting the taxman's bragging black flag – smoky air full of rocks & Molotov's cut-price concoction – milk bottles shake on the stained doorsteps of the curtained, frightened, twitching old

for this is youthful, the colossal & it is carved by sweet leviathans in marble – a new sacred text for ages hence to peruse, develop & discuss – heroin journalists scrawl the definitive articles, dismissing a blind dinosaur faith at its genesis – mad, bare-chested wordysmiths - worthy & arm in arm with charmed violent women in jet eyeliner & exhausted rags of love – the north will rise again – faraway in factory shadows, by brewery canals in thin, ochre rain, heads talk of suicide & dream of babies bouncing & this heat broiling the blues into a story of the ink-fingered news – Elvis on the moon & not dead but bespectacled & little white niggering the swinging sister rays & bored Oswalds & deadest of the Kennedys in the crawling Ruby gun club of the U.S of A – no cure for the soft boys & subhuman lads, insane & in league with psychedelic, whitewashed bunny-men all disappearing down echoing holes trying to get back to the secret garden of Adamite anti-christmas & where it was 'all about his mate anyhow' – a snake king forever crawls – big apple bitten & shy – hell is a void destroyed by monstrous garage hands & flaxen boyish Mao-bands of four – dolls hewn from the bitten apple – talcum-powdered &

pistol-whipped by Dirty Harry blondes – games of chance dictated by the shadows & the sweet ass of angelic upstartled little Indians – tenemental dubhoused in alternative tepees or polystyrene bondaged in search of an identity – mole-kids burrowing into the sub-cultures & no-go-zones - out where the huge city of tiny bookshop lights never sleeps – motor-skulled & naked acidic bikers pack lunches & radical chicks, Chairman Maoing the backscratchers – many ages hence – Verlaine – freed from pissy little wish-list anarchists, left bored in their spectacular situations of the cross – he renounces his name and stirs a Mark E. lunar stew of sirloin Blake & thoughts of dressing like fops (think what we could do!) – yank hacks drawl like greaser Bogarts in trash-can alley grime - lest he forget, banging on from rusty carburettor dung-heaps on spider typewriters in nightfly, lonesome, spacehopper offices – lest we forget the old horse poem-smith - pissing in abandoned factories & ghostly dancing with one hand waving free – free, yes & dreaming of Ethiopian heat - highly sassy in dead head-dress & cloaks of teardrops in heart-breaking colour-blind hues – spun out of minds on bad rocks to African radio waves - jahfaraway & blood in their eyes, not looking up – reed boats & velvet notes – foxhole, Warhol who is your guardian angel – Bowie-knifed by the sun queen bitch at the junction of Campbell's & Plastic - Oh No - & inevitably the popular, explosive street art falls like nuclear rain from the conveyor belt to your unsafe euro-sceptic homes underground – rotten & vicious hits from flowers of old romancers – never mind the bobby-sox & moonbeamed genies docking at the gay station bar – where smoking bones, blips on the radar of love & fires in buildings fill the meatheads of the boondock winter-lands – and the thin man clutching his Zimmer-frame on the road to glory still gladhands the punks & dead beats & fizzles with a Lightning Hopkins thunder - & somewhere lost in there, The Joe-Schmo Troubadour is no go, badly reviewed & on the brink of holy, he gets driven to the old fart's home in the college to waste vinyl & taste Jesus on the mainline of a lazy train – that no fun train humming through the stations of the dross – long gone the wild mercury & no backward glances - once upon a time Old Rehab looked so fine and threw super tramps a dime to prime the pump for the Damascene changes to come - & he swore by the generation's voiceover – solid dictums from speeding hipsters in the twilight of the radon-lit cities – mourning their passing one too many times & positively forthright in frightening streets – the streak of speeding headlamps strung out tight like nerves – crawling from big pink windows with basic songs on secret tapes - & there ain't no Citizen Kane on the bayou – time is almost up, baby blue – maybe it's all over now, Boo – maybe the bloody tracks left in the arm of the law will give us away –he saw, he saw - two policemen kissing on a raw graffiti wall – he saw, he saw – tough guys hammering the smiths in the palaces of odium – he heard Americana bleating from the transatlantic womb – rapid, high movements in sleepy Athenian temples – thousands of folk maniacs & merchants of menace greet their heroes across the Atlantic void – Hey Jack! Hey Mark! – the fuckfaces walk & dribble their bliss into stardom - from the slack-jawed multitude of pulpy independents & blurred riders staring at their Oxford brogues shiny in Cambridge footlights – nibbly little woodland creatures fresh from the Tolkien forests of drowsy academe – squinting like matching moles at the bright lights & downtown enemies & snake-oiled makers of melody so willingly charmed - mystery chains of thought – the druggies dealt music on the corner of dirty Alexis & Barrelhouse – those malcontent ultra-voices droning from bad brains - masterplans dictated to phones permanently connected to the telegraphic hours – unromantic & ultimately unaltered, clubbed with Byronic glee into peg-legged, submissive postures – garlic-repelled &

eyelashes batted by the gothic misery sisters - merciless &
cryptic, locked in long-closed mines of Kohl - pastel,
warbling birds fluttering on television-screens that no longer
scare grandmothers - revolt rendered uninventive by
necessity, they disgorge their weekly hundred hairstyles &
Gretschy, kvetching rickety-backed, scratchy notes from
speakers once torn by howling wolves - meanwhile, out in
the unsound edge-worlds of suburban mythology, the kids
are alright - happy-jamming with post-mods - teddy bears
out on a brand-new picnic - scooting & skating through dark
parking bays & targeting the chromosomal with their broken
strings & arrows - killing every jest with a leathery, cramped
style that ruins the shiny birthday & poops the party -back
to alpha, beta on a clean blackboard in the concrete canvas
of the urban jungles that vine & root through old rural
stretches of ambient land - frustrated towns, fists of
nowhere, the overspill of Cockney into the plots of land
cackled at by the river's cruel surge - the Germanic view
from our house to the bow-wowing, diamond dog-eared,
pages that flap through a backstreet - new-town ink, strange
stories & hi-rise kingdoms of the blind drunk, all loom over
flooded market squares & paddle through glum underwater
moonlight as it bounces like skimmed coins across
polythene lakes - thumb the sleeves, savour the coloured
vinyl of your memories O Newtown Baby Blue - no more
strip-mining his soul to be closer to the populace's shifting
image as it peers from metal boxes & tower-blocked,
brutalised slabs of grisly throbbing, porridge-grey brick -
homes made of darkness, the slash of curtain through which
they squeal like fingered horns - market stalls where they
gasp like momentarily excited tourists, fish-mouthed,
cameras clicking -communist collective, New Yorkshire
states of mind - floating on smoky ghosts of Ludd & bloody
revolutions - going down a dusty road feeling bad, to
smudge the stub noses of the stiffs, the cold, cold hearts of

company men – gullible travellers, priests of torture, replete with the food of beserker lay preachers – poets wait to find their age, quieted, until a stockbroker seethes all is not well – ah, Newtown Baby blue, the old dandelion wisher himself – eyes peeled, nose twitching, mouth chewing long-gone gum – one fine day to be watching over it all from his ancestral home over a pot of scouse & blarney bubbling – too many records, too much music – the heart can only beat so much – there is an essence rare, a pure sap to be distilled

the records fall back to lean luxuriously against the serried racks - he approaches the long gone, gum-chewing assistant leaning with foot up on a beer-crate full of unpriced vinyl – a Dickensian wraith, Cramps T-shirt, torn leather waistcoat & shot-blasted dreads

"...is the new Fall single out yet...?"

"...that'll be tomorrow, now..." – disinterested Irish mutter, not looking up – ah well, more beer money - The Troubadour nods &, turning almost militaristically on Cuban heel & toe, swans into the hot flood of Hanway Street's gelatinous scree, absorbed into its breast as if he belonged – across the busy road, unnoticed, the ghost of a someone, half-remembered, smearing butter on crumpets, hot, then Marmite – it's a whore's tampon, a blood-smear of memory, in drink's gleeful grip the blasphemies bloom – smear of yeast, grow something then, I dare ye – the red of the streetlamp pesters the colour, the gullible fake butter slithers & slides – dough the meat, dough of thighs, calves – drip on, sinner, get your sodden exoskeleton home

*

police helicopters circling – something's happened – the probabilities were endless, the world keeps spilling her surprises – most likely just another myoclonic jerk found himself stuck in Father Time's itchy sleep pattern – let him rot in his mistaken identity - & in the street outside the Polar Bear pub a dumb cat chases nothing in grey rain – speech-bubbles from the doorway float up, up - their debauched assertions skim idly across the cloth- ears of the tapering consumer cruise – parade & motorcade, endeth, thy soul wearies – turn your eyes & there! – no there! - an old pisshead with an ill-fitting prosthetic leg hauls his sagging, bundled carcass up a side street - slugging through a stage-set of drained tin cans, spilled burger-juices & soiled newsprint, yelling as he points to his distressed gait – his wooden limb is a poem only the vulgar would write – be braver than him, try – he shouts, of course, for nobody is half-listening

"...I went to Venezuela, I think it was, wherever & those Dago islands, with Margaret in the locker, underneath the page three bird...the fuckin' bitch whore...all around the world all at once...now look...'

he gestures at his stump with a withering look suspended between pleading & contempt

'...pollarded in me prime!...Jesus what a fuckin' shit-show! – no-one gives a fuck, tellin you all – my bloody leg out there in the fuckin' Atlantic, floatin', every fish havin' a nibble – but we survived it – we got back home, for better or worse – now, see 'em salute the guns, the artillery - & we're last in the fuckin' carnival – I saw their nervous saluters, the young sailors, embarrassed – cunts – hope the intake of that breath that they sucked down in shock was their last...give me five pence & I'll buy you their bloody soul – twenty quid & I'll buy youse all a pint – can't say fairer..."

but he was a ghost too & dutifully took his leave through a dusty stretch of alley wall

The Corporeal Troubadour, The Material Priest, they swam in the thought that made him, they think these ghosts up separately, but they come to the same vision - two heads as one – the holy man fades & tires first for once - was seen to blink, even – he slumped exhausted on a discarded sofa &

a ginger cat mewls & scampers, chicken bone in maw – hiss, grrr, come & take it if you want it – I'm a feral thing, no soul to brag about – what have ye both to barter with? – what smells you got there that I ain't sniffed? – get away! – I've snaffled better than ye both down by the oily wharves – get on your knees – for my feline, throwaway prayer's all ye deserve – wwwvooooowl, howooowl – & that's just the overture & prelude – enough, methinks, to sink your timorous boats – if you listen, carefully now, you may hear a church bell – often mistaken for a heartbeat – that's your poetry, your hapless sermonising – that clang, dissolving like piss in a sozzled gutter – run with the rats for they seek the same prey – you think you're better, think on – cats, that is all we are & need to be – know your place, human filth – feed us occasionally with your myths, the catnip of your begging bowl

& with that the cat's one sermon was done – a talking cat, an anomaly – another spectre? – perhaps

*

& yes the daily office-rats maraud the eager cluster of winding Soho lanes – refugees from the clack of typewriters – suits that elsewhere denote a mark of authority, verve, respectability, here become furtive, sordid – pornographic cowards devoted to magazine racks & brown doorways of fetid repute, dimly-peopled by stained coats with ludicrously out-sized corduroy trousers held loosely in place by broken belts - & the junkies, lifeless as mannequins, stewing in cagoules & drainpipe jeans – cod-eyeing the window displays – women's fashion, perfumed handkerchiefs, modelled by ample odalisques in glossy leather-draped windows – sneaky whipped creamy arse & slap of thigh - Blakean angel up the escalator pursued – sex seller, pedestrian at night, bicyclist in the daylight hours, the proprietor is scrubbed & pumice-stoned, his ruddy skin chafes under pleated jeans of a militant, distressed flare, he balks at a passing prostitute in violent red micro-skirt & yellow fishnets – dreams of being a minnow for her trawl, dreams of waking on ash-strewn sheets in a third-floor bedsit - with her smoking naked whilst waiting for the toast to pop

but The Furtive Troubadour is growing uneasy inside this crush of powdered glamour, this hushabye kingdom of unasked questions - coven of whiches & street-whys - this bad choice factory – he sees it as it is - a jungle full of snares, mantraps – a whirlpool of flushed water that has a dismal afternoon of Monday rain at the heart of its dark disorder – an uncertain radio, signalling constantly unheard distress – on pillar & pole the fuses hiss - fractured rebellions are slyly hinted at by anonymous fliers - brand new disobeyed orders smoking up from the old furnace of burned literature that didn't suit the cause – so it goes, north side of the despairing industrial cavalcade - wastepipe & hinterworld – stolen kisses in the T.S. Eliot Memorial Toilets – all the anarchists are Italian, they hunt in swarthy packs, bristling & dragged by crestfallen visions of their immaculate, alabaster mothers - Durutti-Fruti - en route to an eternal twenty four hour long party in broken, crooked houses – brownstone, tall steps to the porch - transported brick by brick straight from New York

The Old City Troubadour sniffs at a tempting, vague marijuana breeze – dreading the lack of control he feels rising – it could lead to meeting Captain Rehab uptown with his vibes & Babylonian, double-zero shades tilted back – the undulations of reggae bubbling from echoing crypts & stalled cars - slyly robbing the smouldering spear from his hands - the clock ticks again & apes the sub-woof – dub-marine beeps & pops from strict, deepened roots – head-swim to bass-mental parties upriver, uptown – ebony glamour of the soul literature – brawny, collie weeded &

222

corn-breaded – O pointed star of misty miracles that tickles at his words with feathered wisdom – the solutions of all those maddened professors destroyed in exploded time – the hint of an eminence gris-gris - he must surely scratch the very source with his periscope eyeballing above the sweeping Thames – above it all the helicopters buzz like a swat of disturbed wasps in venerable cloaks of cloud – The Troubadour is centre of scrutiny just for doing nothing suspicious - he hides his notebook so as not to be mistaken for a cop

we must look like a lab experiment
rats on acid, see how they run

Boo lurked by that window two years ago – there she lurks still, perhaps - she's drunk, tired, miles from home - don't upset her

*

on throwing wide the window of the squat, a boisterous dawn broke upon his sluggish, yet curious, senses like newly unsealed coffee - *who's a clever boy so grown-up in the huge city?* - the seventies were grinding to an end, the clangour of musical insurrection was being boxed in radios for safe-keeping & this hillside-green boy is no longer caught in a sixties Kodak hue

ah but squint one eye & is that a make-believe, pirate version of Newtown Baby there, way back in the distance, bisecting a flat-lining horizon lately crossed? – his daily excursions now, out where the cemetery statues of the outer regions of the metropolis untouched by the turmoil were both nemesis & guardian angel, were becoming more frequent - as if by pushing outward from the molten core he would be afforded a better view of its coming implosion

223

he had spent a troubled night dreaming of his former, hazy, childhood self – the rebirth pangs unheeded for years – sores he thought long healed wept anew

ah, Troubadour! – that old talcum dried on your new-bathed shins – holiday havens in rich, warm island winds – that caravan & chalet site – way back - there was a pretend roadway, a circuit you navigated with solemn dexterity in a toy car of ornate antiquity – or face pressed close to earth by dunes – perfect place to push your cars through – lemon-ice & oysters on the way to the trampolines – the big people safe in their deckchairs reading about the world they left behind in vast sheets of flapping news – do you remember? – they will take you to your first pub but you sit outside – brought crisps & lemonade with two straws candy-striped - & later succulent orbs of slimy chicken in a sweating basket of tanned, dusted chips – remembering the beermats, the lettered ashtrays - & how it was all a foretelling of this dissolute life, a premonition of how the universe deals out her plenty in differing shades of fortune – watching himself grow, watching his mind fill up, cloudy sentinels waited in the shadows to wink & sell to him their enticing machinations - a figure secreted behind a withering tree bearing a solitary fig – snakes that charm beyond the realms of possibility – the voice of unreason cackles low & is mistaken for thunder – it follows your dream home, that lurid laughter – god moved in incomprehensible ways & his anger was fearful & born of your fear, nourished by it – now of course these days he remains at a wary remove, he was no god without a care, but a kind of prisoner's transcendent outward calm, a calm that belied the required inner distress, became his replacement for true tranquillity – it was a tether to reality & it mimicked the bond that tied soul & body so strangely together

& lurking in the shade of sleep was always the big dream that, as time passed & dreaming lost the sheen of mystery, meant little other than escape, transcendence – torn pages from a book of changes reeled wildly in the dream & years later the text kept changing – all through his first schooling, the new floor-wax smell assimilated & imposing metal lockers duly assigned – following the class down for lessons by the fusty pond because it is too nice, too nice to be indoors, now the sun is jelly & ice-cream in the super-8, sunspot, dappling, tree-shadowed corner of the school field & why does he still try to remember those mosquitos fizzing & darting through the swirl of olive vapours above the languorous twists of dark water – or the bubbly spit on tree bark & spawn of lily-pad frog – jar of newt, bulge of toad neck, spells & potions, the little net that trawled the pond was flimsy but reaped a million flashes of recollection

out by Highgate Cemetery again, he willed it to haunt him with its socialist spectres, for this was a morning of deepest remembering – not a shoddy nostalgia or mere rose-tinted wistfulness – more the hard focus of a ruthless camera, light flooding through an honest lens – he queasily convinced himself that he had done with the past, but the past was a jealous love not easily jilted – the city did its best to erode these pangs of recall but it took just one glimpse of the river to ignite once more the engine & set memory to dance

& yes, how, within the dream, on that first London night, his whole childhood danced – he left the nest a Troubadour, ready for everything hurtling his way, yet waking in the squat in that chill, first dawning he was still, at heart, a Newtown Baby – he had dreamt of the past that first night, vivid & suffused in oranges, yellows – the school, the pond again, why? – no answer as to the reason this stagnant cup of grim water should hold such a sway in his reveries – yet here he was again, loafing, as he unwraps his secretly saved luncheon meat sandwich from the foil & leans against a wrinkled, stout-bellied tree watching as the others squeal &

mumble & cry out loud as they launch lolly-stick torpedoes at paper boats & Stephanie – Stephanie! – nearly falls in – play-fighting, she is squirming deliciously away at the last second, but - ah! oh! - getting the edge of her shoe smeared with grim water – & there is again that piano music from a window of the schoolhouse, scales, warm drops of sound pushing through tightly-strung, motionless, marble heat – strict piano keys persuaded to sing with pudgy shapes of hesitant flesh – shield eyes, blotchy now, to hear third-man bells of an ice-cream van & there is a hole in his new jumper, just there – words rise from the class reading on the playfield near the hot sandpit – vivid behind his sleep, he feels those midsummer breezes drift through the golden hour of bliss – each gust twists around him & feels like a playful hug, something cuddling the brain, fusing synapses – close eyes, open eyes, sneak a quick look upward – let the words buoy you up through the warren of witch-finger branches & translucent green patchwork of bony leaves – like gravity had been temporarily reversed - drawn by a blister of glittery sun that melts the ever-lucid, cloud-smeared slab of infinite blue & surely never, ever, stops shining

the whole summer living inside of him - heavy eyes, aching even in slumber from its glow - as if pressed from behind by a wily force – remember how red blotches swam the rippling froth at the edge of the pond & always the startled sparrow bursting cannon-quick from the knotted trees – reed boats, poorly constructed, with flags of green leaves, collapsing & dissolving in the water like tiny misshapen skeleton hands - or bobbing triumphantly - or sinking slow on launching to cheers & laughter – & good, obedient basket-weaving Margaret has fashioned a mainsail from a lolly-wrapper

& yes 'Rocket' she named it, it was splendid & by far the best design of the armada

& there it goes, powered by the trade-winds in his blustery, nocturnal, London mind, proudly still barrelling through choppy cross-tides under the swooping giant mosquito helicopters

so the dream rolled on, relentless, throughout that first, heady capital night – that huge ship caressing the roll of surf as it headed seaward – his dream-state deducing a nirvana of subtle connections, the confluence of time & memory – slow ship of dreams, seemingly freed now, as he thought that he had freed himself from the past – yet now it came back, in full sail, to test his newfound fortitudes – his claims to be such a Troubadour On A Lonesome Road – all that old Dean Moriarty-farty shit he shovelled into himself – desperate to become the full-grown man, the big person – reassured by his ongoing creation of more recent memories that at least promised a slight change of perspective, a chill of dread that stirred when looking back – a twist of the kaleidoscope, a fish-eye lens – distortions of the grand illusory façade – images from his evolution, he knew & the dream taught him this much – that his revolution was cyclical, a constant rebirthing recurring in a hall of mirrors

& slowly a few previously unrecalled scraps entered his London reveries - ghosts through a wall, they announced themselves in shivery flickers by day & in thick cloaks & fedoras by night

he remembered the radiogram day, for example, when out in the Longhill Hills with the Night Country Medicine Man - a stranger, a shadowy character blown from the capital through the town by a shrug of wind - who opened his bag of cures to show him starlight shining above the quivering trees

& yes this traveller, this shoddy shaman, sold fantasies & chimeras for all the dawdling, rancorous hearts out prowling their cautious suburban map - Troubadour! - hear the

calling! – but once again it was a false revelation, only the
tune he had always longed to play
　　he vowed to change his name again that night & scribbled
a few contenders in a spirally notebook

The Plain Dealer
Ishmael
Johnny Firepockets
Old Maudit

　　there was a definite flavour of raw quackery, a wintry,
narcotic, glistening doubt about this so-called Medicine Man
though his ways were enticing – indeed, in some dreams he
showed up in a horse-drawn wagon of rattling potions & pills
– these blue ones to quell the tension of a love too long
pent-up – these red ones to flagrantly burst the bubbles of
your infancy – yet the townsfolk flocked to his meetings –
their curiosity drawing them closer, moths to his flaming
charm - what's in his bag? – I heard he's got three golden
pieces & a red silk robe for a princess - wishes & fairy-tales
for builders & navigators – I was told his mind is the mind
of a butcher, seeking roadkill & discarded hopes in the heart
of the city – ah, the eternal lure of the White Witch Hill –
there were notebooks in which to hide it all way

t'was a blotted square & it made fair all earth
in company good it switched our favours
& blended might with weakness
only to humble the former
he bade men tell him, who shall be my Captain?
the leader to drag me out
of this chemical fancy
be it a most evil fallen lord
or a promised insight in a dream
of Christos' very winding sheet

O never lead me to sobriety
& I will not touch another glass
or cigarette packet shall I open
until Londinium is my backdrop
O gleaners of half-truths – puppets of fate
grant me nothing better or worse
than that

& that meaningless poetry drove him on through days of bloated wordplay, necessity of experiment, writing things he barely understood because the poems he loved best he failed to understand – the only true, concomitant factor was the wired, wrought, mystical, coded language itself - letters, phrases & paragraphs & breathless, tortured stanzas all seemingly free for use & abuse

& some early London days, up by Highgate, as on the strange road outside the cemetery gates, sentry pigeons guarded a white sky, lined up on the roof & aerial of the small block of flats opposite, he became lost in the maze of Sunday tombs

& yes he remembered how the angular balconies on the red-brick estates had seemed to ache for a thousand Juliets – his late night wanderings, bottle of luck in his paw, his sad, drunken wail at her door – a tape-recorder his strummed lyre – the gorgeous shame of love – the crushed flowers in a doorway - no doubt these images, forged on the anvil of sparking words & associations, had guided his change, his re-christening, solidifying his present incarnation - but he was equally sure that that acid & rum-slashed night out in the Long Hill Hills with the Night Country Medicine Man had added its own sweet layer to his transformation – a pulled trigger of divinity – an illegal frisson edging his bewildered grope toward innovation

stone cold Marx, there he broods upon his gravy with a deep spooning scowl, the trees are becoming starker, or is another day failing to breathe? – he swigs the flask by way of answer & stumbles the long path to the whispering road

*

& so it was, autumn found a newly-fashioned anti-hero moping along the length of his once-favoured streets in the city & saddened by his loss of purpose - The Sorrowful Troubadour of Eternal Loneliness at last – such creatures sadden quickly & inevitably fall prey to the holy Pubcorner Wizard – that dweller in saloon darkness, spanner in the ghostly night machinery - to widen this wastrel's path toward glory – his kind of glory, abject & ruinous – for the wizard, another man of medicine, had spells too – portals flung open to curdling misunderstandings, invitations to myriad curiosities & enchantments – he awaited the searcher, the pilgrim – the sly pedestrian of backstreet pavements – the magi that sought to glean the mystic powers that he possessed - with which, so it is said, one can negate any unnecessary inclination toward rootless wandering – he wanted no simple tourist guide – a pirate's map of buried pleasure spread out before his hungry eye, a comprehensive *vade mecum* extolling the human race's diverse methods of ecstasy

The Troubadour got off the tube train at Romford & headed for The Lamb pub - The Wizard would be gleefully up for spending The Troubadour's busker coin on bad brandy, if he was in luck – preparations of tequila & smoke stiffened his resolve as he emerged from the subway into the writhing market

& lo it came to pass - by way of a fever dream – the events took a strange turn early - Pubcorner Wizard, in the guise of an archangel, had transformed that house of illicit spirits into a hostelry rife with odd incantations – a bazaar that swam with the bawdy market traders, sandy-haired,

230

tattooed denizens of the new silk roads – all engaged in varying degrees of gossipy half-conversations & The Wizard, cornered but not without weaponry, acting as courier to dream-states, he would shapeshift into anything & anyone that The Troubadour randomly chose to speak with – for example, The Teutonic Barmaid, in the form of a beautiful Rheinmädchen, spans the gossip of eternity shrunk to fit a minutes passing – one year for each of the hours on a bar-room clock above the gilded optics - at the conclusion of the tenure, The Drunken Angel will duly collect by way of compensation his offered coinage - snag his knowing mind in a dripping net of joy & whatever memories it contains shall forever be the property of the forgetful universe to do with as it will

eventually leaving, The Loquacious Troubadour is at last by chemicals sore diminished, eternally pathetic, vine-led & fate-driven, any road, no matter how perilous, open to his wandering – ill-chosen travel miscalculations & the subsequent hardships thereby formulating his ad-hoc vision for the day – he was an animal set loose on the world – idly fleecing his pockets - notebook, leaky pen, half-butts still smouldering, dusty sweets, no folding money, alas - saying to himself where *is it*? – he surely cannot have spent it all? – the rent gone – three weeks until the dole cheque – shit

later that evening he stood awhile, mock-heroic, satanic gaze, hazily Germanic, manically, in leather flapping, on the desolate lip of Westminster Bridge – *trauriger Mann auf einer Brücke* - waiting for an expressionist brush of history to depict his inexpressible urgency in oils – ah, be wary, Troubadour - for there will come a greater agonising hour of fog than this mere lost interlude - & only then shall he truly know, in his emptying heart, that the terrifying day of his soul's final obscurity is at hand & the only course back to any kind of Eden will be a mistier bridge, weakly fashioned from the Archangel's skeleton – a task that, at that late hour

& with such depleted energies, was surely beyond his powers of survival

& yes the old words can carry him just so far – the rest of the road is furnished by thought & thoughts were, in his present state, stuck in a quagmire of weed-smoke, beer & alchemical symbols

back in The Lamb, what seemed like centuries ago, having sent The Sad, Rambling Troubadour on his way with supplies for the trip, the wily Pubcorner Wizard spools his tobacco dust between the hammock folds of a rolling machine, crumbling the dry shag in twisted heaps, smoothing the thin papers, two per each magical creation – the spell of the lunchtime now broken by cruel jokes, limericks at a lost love's expense – a bawdy, sapless, shrunken history – a crapulous sailor's tale of deep treasure sieved for truth & wisdom in briny tides of strong, rich ale

they had spent their last expended minutes silently tossing peanuts at the chrome, grinning jukebox – *let's go for a little walk ba-dum ba-dum* – even his old faithful universe of song was issuing orders to march

& later yet, The Ancient Of Hours, under a loveless moon, out in the dirty street again - itinerant rats – glistening fur & shifty eyes, swift - hewn from the inner city slabs of Pisarro lights & Courbet darknesses – Pubcorner Shaman unsteady at the door of his bedsit – while The Troubadour wobbles in distant elsewhere – fumble for keys, that old drunkard's dance, in stoned & blasted incredulity – allowing himself a glance at his flaking, ink-caked fingers, so nimble once as they tamped down the curls of weed into the religiously folded, wafer-thin papers – lick shut – the need to wander without destination, eternally somewhere – The Wizard knew that wanderlust well – lack lustre strolling, a dim *flaneur* of a billion bastard highways –no street new enough to sate his itineracy – *wanna tell ya, that I love ya – walk & talk – under the moon* – onward to new pubs, new loves & redeeming barmaid angels *of love* - plenty out there, my benighted brother of bawd & belligerent beauty – let's go

*

a Fall gig, somewhere – beer spilled on his trousers – you've got beer on your trousers, mate – thanks – a cigarette that lasts forever – conspiratorial kick in the low-life toilets – the piss, green & curdled as it boils discarded tissues in the foamy drain – muted slates, slags masculine – pseudo-philosophers, the long-dead walking, bad man London, spectral, confidential – he has become a part of a ragged cult of failure – a good thing, he feels – afterwards, in the closing pub, two proto-grungy malignants eat spaghetti from a tin, one has cut his thumb – Degory thinks the man playing pool is the bass player – two pigeons dead in a foul road of burnt trees – clock, no hands, cigarette machine, only Players #6 – mind loosening, faulty wired, quasi-astral – there is nothing outside as far as they know – the world is enough without all this bloody heartbreak, let me sleep – The Troubadour tries to work out what he is missing – the old fear grips The Priest – something he's taken, try one of these – wash it down or spill – the beer thrown in the lavatory pan, cut out the middle man, cut out the sickly, morning bellyache - the night's dense shadows bleed into the froth of a faulty neon tube above the cemetery lounge – the barmaid's eyes bleed into her powdered cheek - the thumb bleeds through spaghetti juice to the ashtray floor

*

William Blake, cheesecloth & highbrow, son of dissenters & dissenting in turn – upturned eyes scour the bad-tempered gargoyles, the obnoxious granite grotesques above draper's emporiums & shy tobacconists – his thick-etched, inkwell mind unmade by angels – staggers on to Old Compton Street at nine of the morning – a herald of light from the low sun backlighting his pudgy frame – he waves at cherubim assailing his skull – he chants a catechism to himself, all coughed vowels & snake hiss – then vanishes as a lorry obscures him – the lorry delivers trays of sweet pastries to the Cafe Boheme outside of which sits, on a table under the awning & smoking a Lucky Strike dog-end saved from last night's revelry, the Troubadour of Loneliness – he greedily attracts the attention of the prettiest waitress & orders another coffee to serve as hostage whilst he nips to the newsagent for more smokes – on his return he sees that there is a gift of roll-up - made exquisitely with red liquorice paper – immaculate, uncreased - perched on the saucer of his cup – he accosts the girl as she re-emerges with a tray of aromatic Danish delicacies

"...excuse me, did you roll this for me?...." - he smiled, holding the cigarette up in between forefinger & thumb

"...yes, I saw you trying to light that squashed thing from your pocket – it's liquorice – very nice – not dodgy or anything ha ha...'

her laugh, wind-chime stroked on dappled tide

"...thank you, I have bought some more now though, there was no need...really..."

a trace of foreign accent she has, Italian, Spain maybe - looks Mediterranean too, olive skin

"...ah, keep it anyway...it will be an emergency..."

ay-mair-jon-see – French, southern though, the tan – Aix – Cezanne country – she has a nameplate on her waistcoat – keep smiling when she comes out – ask for sugar next time so I can see the badge, small writing

urban life, cafes, bars, the workplace – these are his new mythologies – lithographic revenants, regular people of the abyss depicted in stark, rich, confident lines - *if I ever saw an angel then I would paint one* – Courbet had it down – the

234

real thing as thing only - this notebook should be destroyed, underline that - Kafka had it down - Max lied to him - find a better Max - this bloody clue, should've bought the Guardian - Times always harder - not harder but you have to get used to the compiler's tricks - come on, 4 across - '...mad master wanders Northern Venice...' - anagram of Venice? - a painter I haven't heard of? - get away from it a while & it'll solve itself - back to the notebook - funny how a few lines drift into mind & it sets the whole bloody train rolling - that man last night talking about science fiction - Dick fan - big Dick fan eh? - god that was a puerile thing to say - said it though - no turning back - interested I was nonetheless - got into it about how the boffins were making such progress with computers that they reckon one day they will invent a robot that will make art, write books - I wondered if they could make a computer become religious? - it's all a kind of programming - ah yes, now I remember the conversation better - funny how the memory works, coffee, beauty, a fag, never lets you down - wanted to write something down last night - but did I? - he flicks through the notebook - can't find it - maybe I waited until sober - try a poem out of nothing - here goes - lots been done on the sci-fi thing - keep it straight

in the future
robots will write novels
computers will sing like operatic tenors
visionaries will drag ecstasy
from pocket calculators
& I will still sit alone
on wooden street corners
with my steam-powered love
& clockwork friends
telling the old time by the backstreets
by shadows on that tiny sundial

on my wrist
& you will be late
because there is no future
& late is beautiful

the waitress emerged with a neat stack of six chrome ashtrays – wiping the table with a yellow dishcloth before emptying the old one in a large red bin by the door – still smiling, bent over his table wiping – longer than necessary? – just his imagination – brief eye flirt – oh, nearly forgot – quick glance while her eyes are averted in case she thinks I'm ogling her two-buttons-open blouse – Amandine – a name like a time-machine – just whisper it & the future & past spring open

& it was all so simple then says the radio - back when every ride was just a ticket to the dance – all the way to London on trains full of suits & aftershave, ties & briefcases, husbands & wives & pens in breast pockets & lawnmowers in the garage & curtain rails to be fitted & new tea-towels with welcome to Rhyl scrawled on them & power steering & two weeks in Formentera & there's a good film on ITV at seven, darling - & Bob in accounts has had a heart attack, only 52, that's no age & who fed the cat? - did anyone feed the bloody cat?– all stewing on a train of mystery that spirits away the rural with its tired abracadabra & ushers in a shouting city full of new spells – amplified so as to demand attention – it roars in like a through train, as the door opens on dour, cavernous Fenchurch Street – opens on life

& the big smoky apple, it is not a behemoth, a leviathan - it is just a desperate city that the muses are tired of haunting, come on - made for gaudy animals & trying its howls out in a chamber of echoes – hear ye its sonorous pity, come on! - a mere store-bought, blood-red hat does not cut it here – your emotion dampens in her crying poetry rain, so come on!! - get your heart to that time out of mind, you will find it in lines of white powder that the streets will provide – the goddess of romance must at all times be protected - keep that flower alive that she gave you, each petal a tear, a pearl, an undersigned heartache – The Romantic Troubadour will wear his poverty crown with false pride & the main drag's river will not drown him yet - he pledges his time to burn brightly, to cleave to a longing for an indefinable liberty – yes, let him take you to London town, where bleached white neon gases surround you & what's that secret we've found? - let him whisk you away to the smoke & mirror pubs – let your hive of adolescent thoughts chase the honey around – there is something stirring in the cauldron of probability – near old Piccadilly, where the shiver-grey light dances - let him blow his cigar-smoke from the doorway of the Hawley Arms, recite Hart Crane poems from a bad memory atop a table full of empties in the Intrepid Fox or wherever, the lazy dog, whatever – or talk a bleary philosophy arm in arm with a tramp on Islington High Street in soft snow, that falls like the sanctified dandruff of our lilting landlord – & why not let him read the sanctimonious paving stone legends by the river's jagged edge as the Thames whispers by, unmoved by poetry or song – only the sneaky moon has the key to the tune to which she dances - let him kiss you deep in the merciless river, come on!!!

but these sleights of mind fade all too soon & - after pissing for an age, the visionary king has not emerged from the bushes – only the crack of an air-rifle & a low-droning motorbike, distant & feline, breaks the pooling of low silence

songs instructing, demanding that they be thought about before sleep is allowed & if the sandman is late when ye get to bed at some sad old 4.a.m. - & the punishing moon hurts the darkness & the ceiling is staring you down – then be sure there's nothing to pray for & nowhere to live but here &

bloody now – yes, for reverend ever amen - the high life is way out on the cutting edge, distanced from the shining city - he knows, yes, The Troubadour knows he's not lost – so don't fear the madness that blows like a storm at your door - at the sound of a phone ringing its fever takes hold, shaking his civic soul down to the raw meat – this is the hour that brightness fears most, & old poems fear more - though you try and turn the page it is still the song you sang before – insistent, unrelenting - your hands may play the sweetest tune but the essence of her remembered stare hits the key change or repeats her farewell as a corny refrain – it choruses through many wild nights of wintering rage, paling in time but still resonant, nestled under late sadness in a brandy glass - & though the sea may crash the cymbals on a beach far, far, somewhere away - he knows the unwritten score, yes, The Orchestrated Troubadour knows - though his reasons are of the low, mean kind & his words, his words are like these snowflakes, Boo, these dirty, crappy snowflakes that just disappear into the shiny street - melt soft to the touch on your stuck-out bulb of tongue

& she owns the keys to free her mind in her bones, does that shy/mad girl - ye walked her home, dismal/cute - will she echo the hymn that you wrote in blood for her? - or carry, for your comfort alone, a bad weight? - or will ye both, in dotage, rage at all the successful old schoolmates who may ride these trains right now, to a job that buys them a gilded palace of entropic security? – will you covet the fortunes of those that never threw loaded dice? – does their shit smell sweeter from your side of the fence?

no, a lifetime of running only gets you back to the start again - & so, through your one smeary window, stare hard at the sky – make shapes of the clouds lit by The Mothery Moon & hear the earth exhale noisily through pulmonary trees – The Sidereal Troubadour, hot with regret, standing at the junction of Dean Street & Romilly Street in a

beginning rain – begins again, mouthing zeros of breath with
his sighs hung like the apparition of her name

*

& morning comes & so what? - where's Amandine? – or
any long, dark waitress of the soul? – any Duchess Of
Infinite Last Orders? – close your throbbing eyes & there
she is & you watch her safely now - because you're not in
love or even lust – you imagine what it would take to want
her walking with you now – if she was breezily washing up
on the coast of sleep by a star-bright ocean clear - waltzing
the random strobe of spotlight snow – the world still singing
in response to your call, wraps you in feathery down when
you get cold – not like Boo, a drunkard's dream girl made
unreal by a sinking ship of dreams – almost remembering,
dismembering - as she plays the hero at a pub out in the
sticks - pool shots leave the table as she tries out all the stunt
shots - & look, see - the pool-table's cashbox has fallen open
- so yes, they treat themselves to destiny & scoop up
handfuls of the precious, illicit coins - then spend it at the
bar just like they never gave a fuck – three chasers, first one
to finish gets the spare – he smiled, dismembering the
unmemory – an unpolluted Mo Tucker drumbeat behind
rim-shot eyeballs pounding - veiling the grave-grass laughter,
the poor souls drowning, the guts, the brawls, the pissy-wet
jeans & mudded knees of it all – all gone, the beautiful now,
all gone the sad, sweet tune, gone way back without him – all
the way back to the endless way back when

*

out here, on the escarpment, on a whim, via tube & red
buses - everything is ordered, nudging toward a kind of
mild-mannered perfection - where the commuters ding-

dong the doorbells – hey honey, I'm home what's for dinner? – chops, two veg – lovely – naughty bottle of red in the larder – a film on TV – finish the crossword sleepily begun on the inbound morning train

here's one for you honeybun

3 down, 6 letters – '...a withering prize...'

third letter 'R'

yes & thoughtless & bible-heavy they witter on for hours, withering toward countless Christmases, through shifts of autumnal daylight that's saving nobody – they are dried leaves buried by shovelled snow - a ghost in every chimney & a lonesome drunk in old lover's lane

enter Renegade Troubadour & sidekick Degory Priest – a delirious, second-hand Bonnie & Clyde with their fortune, their sweet illegal stash - at the bar - ordering whisky with the growing queues of beer not for the taste just to get drunk quicker – it could be after-shave - sleepy barman never saw them whip the peanuts off the rack – two stale cheese & pickle rolls curling toward heaven in a sweating plastic greenhouse on the bar – if it's 11.57 & the morning's bitter, wounded by sleet & a place called home is sweating at the bottom of the next barrel & a pickled onion is the most beautiful thing in the universe then *que sera...*

& then they find a party, massed hipsters in a bloodless mist, actors, poets (...god help us, pal...) - & yea morningtide cometh slow, train duly missed, ages it took to get stoned from dreadful slivers of seedy crabgrass - & yes, if the phone starts ringing & won't stop ringing, no it won't stop ringing – undrunkenly pluck the undrunk happy wine from the Rheinland – tipsy it from its lonesome shelf & let your lazy minds merge in dance - that's the Glühwein talking fast & loose - smouldering - Scritti politicos & the ubiquitous Ubu shamble

The Hipster Priest is stoned or dead & so he grabs up his favourite hat – not too heavy, soft brim, straw maybe,

papier-mache could be – a hat built to tilt, for walking in the
sweet early sunshine that hasn't yet congealed to yesterday's
sultry dusted air - & yes, he finds himself by the dreary river
without trying, a subliminal search for the sea perhaps, with
a borrowed book by e.e.cummings that he'll never give back
'cos he ain't comin' back, Jack - & Troubadour you will be
blessed today with no pain, no nausea, physical or spiritual,
& through these tiny, tangled words, delineating your stream
of life in lower case, you may achieve the perfect mood to
goad a new day with optimism – he scans the easy text, gulps
the crooked lines down, resting anywhere - submerged in
the trickery & sentiment - as he searches for reasons not to
go to the ten o'clock pub – just walking with the poetry in
his head, again the old psychogeography & *derive* – those
old ghosty stalkers, those seekers of nothing via a deliberate
deed governed by the absence of a grander locus – he
denies, denies their ambiguity - every journey must take him
somewhere – let the unconscious lead him not astray but
home

    but suddenly the pub door is in front of him & open &
smoke drifts through dusty light from the window to the
snug – the old need for an ascension & decline – to drink
himself up the hill & all the way down again – let dead
romans count the years against whistling days -
MCMLXXIX in his head calendar but possibly later– year
of our invaders - drink 'til the cows come home - drunker
than thou – drink wrapped in wild polymathic talk – making
heavy connections from the cryptic swim of language –
polyglot alcoholism, drink 'til the baseball hall of fame
welcomes Willie Mays - 'til Russians make a thousand suns
shine underground - 'til the mashed potato's dead and gone
– 'til The Deer Hunter wins awards as the Chinese invade
Vietnam – 'til Mingus dies in a painted wheelchair of sad
jazz pastels as his disciple whales suicide on a ghosted beach
– 'til we almost lost Harrisburg & space junk falls like Icarus

unseen in far oceans – drink heartily & without fear, as he declares to all in earshot that the fucking politicians are all mistaken, all of them! - & how, about that good old human suffering eh? - & how the old masters are always proven right in the end – so swig the ale down 'til the clash of The Generations Of Sevens rings in your brand new Walkman – propose a distant toast as Sandinista rebels enter a mythic Managua – for we are a potent band of brothers strewn across the continents are we not? - & constantly scribbling shorthand pocketbook prompts for future bad poems

'...there a thousand Yankee suns under the desert...'

for these times are destined to replay again ages hence - on sepia reels in desecrated cinemas – they hang hard in his reminiscences & tremble in the damp, Ektochromatic air of exhausted summers – bless the endless sessions that keep him from sleep - & on his coat-tails but not quite in shadow, back at the slumbering party, Degory dances & dances that old, foolish glue wine boogie around the dead horses – his head full of The Troubadour's memories as retold by his late-night stand-in, his drunken doppleganger – how he set fire to marshmallows in a firework park of fumes – set fire to now, let the wise mother alcohol gut the dreaded threats of Christmas & its bilious Dickensian warmth & its sick, snowball pastes that heighten the sorrow – he had ranted of old Boo, how she cheats at Scrabble when he's looking away but he knew & did not say – sleeping out on the golf-course & play monopoly in fancy dress – she will cancel every taxi home – monopoly money for the basement, Sunday pubs of the frozen mind – to live in that foursquare world, the community chest dealing the dirt - no money, real or fake, to spend - as your tiny silver hat does the circuit of utilities, cheap dives – drift like an urchin past the grand hotels of the west-end – learning forfeit - in & out of jail to get the blood

242

money back - losing your house to some satanic landlords operating out of the Old Kent Road - & yes, there are secret parties in these houses, these Pentonville Road hostels – Degory had taken something awful & could barely talk – they blagged their way in by being drunker than the creep at the door & there was a traffic cone on the stairwell & somehow you found yourself in a late night bagel shop – that weird chewy bread & possibly cream cheese – you have never seen a bagel & carry it like a sacred relic back to the party's temple of scattered suspense & belief – the mornings never make sense of the night's primal urges - pray tell, why are there are dead flowers in the toaster? - you roll stoned into the kitchen on a trail of empty tins - a hipster man you recall inviting back from some numb pub has broken the tap, fell asleep on the table & lazily designed a poster – he mumbles his morning apologies & epiphanies – his mother was a jazz singer, he was thinking of moving back to Amsterdam, he had three grand in the Abbey National to travel through India but his dad is dying so he'll wait for the inheritance, his favourite song is Yakety-Yak – he has brought women with him that lurk & smoke through thick chewy lipstick smudges - woozy Benedictine angels, plotting train routes & evening rendezvous - leaning on the fridge holding hot coffee mugs in both gothic gloves cooling it with their soft breath – you're welcome – how many sugars? - liquorice cigarettes, again, where do they come from? - pre-rolled on a butter-dish & they tried to get you drunk again – don't tell Boo – where is Boo? – ah! she sleeps back in new-town suburbs with your guardian archangels, or under roses in the strange garden where floral tea-towels depicting tin-mines of Cornwall & sordid trousers of the night flap on a cat's cradle of orange plastic clotheslines – she is dreaming of green lakes & warm wine, crackling pork on heaving Sunday tables – she knows, Boo knows, that the only road to heaven means a whistle-stop in hell - buttons in your pocket – she knows they need a holy language to express the riverine undercurrents of cool whisky that make wretched confluence in the romantic's heart

& Degory meets him at the pub & they both try it all again, the wonder, the horror, but all they do is grumble in a furry storm like night dogs – steal eclairs from the bakery - have their cake and eat it & throw the wrapper out the door of the bartered homeward cab – try to breathe in the danger, find a new stupid law to break & throw your wages down a well – a figure watches, thorny head full of switches – they wave & shout at a girl with a broken stiletto heel - but she knows not what they love & anyway they are broken too

*

perhaps a light goes on in a distant city somewhere, not here – no, never here - where the roads become narrow, pages flap on by & The Backseat Troubadour sprawls in the rear-view glass, baiting Captain Rehab stout at the wheel – disabled & caned, it's brother vs. brother out there beneath an unforgiving firmament – on a tormented borderline that once was such a sweet horizon – they are carnival freaks, the parade of circus malcontents – the torches that they carry give off light more than they warm – the same light that throbs out of his TV – cold, unforgiving, fridge-light – not enough old love poems left to make a fire – his vast dreamboat once more set adrift in calmer seas – he selects a pillow of words on which he can rest his weary head – fumbling in his satchel he finds a book – snug as a hobgoblin in a pub-corner - & Larkin's spiky, brown-trousered company of snuffling mole-words burrow through the hull into his brain's saturated engine room – confident alcoholic arrows he thence fired - as the first sip of sweet banana milk passed his lips – he watched them rising to trace an arc in Whitsun skies – all the worries & doubt, all

commonplace trivialities are fading now as the rough
bedlinen warms to the familiar words that soar &, in
cracked, urban distances, plunge & bleed to rain

*

wakes, four a.m. - nothing quickens or slows in the tomb
of morning - he can hear the streetlamps so hushed is the
spooked road - the room is cluttered, aching, beautifully his
book of Ducasse's old chants, laid to rest on the graveyard
bookshelf, opened at the folded first page - he had re-read
the opening line many times & always late & tiredness always
bade him desist - ahead, another ruined day of vacant
December to seethe through - in which the promising
sputter of last month's firework dreams wither now to the
tap of spent, fallen sticks - he too, from a kind of heaven
fallen, without fire, cooling & falling to waste ground - his
plans were too sad to live - a last visit to the old home - a
day reading a newspaper in the fat cemetery of his good,
bad, old, new town - & so the world spins stupidly on & he
oblivious to it - as elsewhere poor Donny Hathaway falls
noiseless through bleak air - for now is the sad, sad winter
of Winterland's closing - & the once thankful deadheads all
discontent - punk flowers wilting fast - Johnny rots as Sid
slumps hissing in a sickening cell spitting suicide & seething,
slow stupid slugs writhe in his cerebrum - the extras return
to dud schlock & pub rock - as if every star, like those
thrilling rockets, is waiting to plummet & all wishes are
prohibited - Boo is back there, falling too perhaps, sleep &
gravity & rum - don't ever grow old, Boo - there is black ice
up on the tarmac at the destiny chicane - the ancient Norse
goddess Thatcher is coming & these pubs are putting ice in
the cider & selling crisps in strange flavours - outside, in
those threatening streets, vigorous, skinny bikes are chained
to our old dog-pissy lamp-posts & the last few mohicaned

kids lurk beneath tables in the Irish snug where a bald pug
growls & vampires are stealing the dominoes – where
lamenting, bronze-age vicars roam the arid halls of our hard-
won politic, stinking up the oratory – ah, Boo – where are
the cracks through which the sunlight shone? – write it all
down, may come in useful one day – there's room on that
old new-town diary he kept - torn page he used as a snot-rag
– he recalls writing it in dying red biro at the table by the
door in The Joker public house in fair Essex, that low
county - it tells him the truth plain, his once-bright thought

it's all gone to shit, boys
let's move to the city

*

Soho, a cautious insanity - a recovery of the senses after
last week's brutal onslaught - walking from the Cafe Sun
Luen – springtime – Lonely Troubadour greets each cipher,
each evanescent countenance hung atop a myriad of pastel
clothing, that drifts idly by with a look of practised disdain –
through unhealed scars of back alleys – past neon-sharp
storefronts with dazzling constellations of glistening,
pointless jewellery – in & out of mulchy bookshops, tight
with ripped spines & regiments of dinner-jacketed,
establishment penguins – Frith Street, the home-grown jazz
& Mozartian clavichords hang their forever changes on the
flaps of stained awnings – a week of vague wanderings, until,
waking dream suddenly burst, looking upward at a whim,
the cold, chipped street sign announced Wardour Street
ducking & diving in The Intrepid Fox – that gregarious
bitch saloon of little repute
The Recovering Troubadour & Degory Priest sit nursing
the nurses that are two Dictum Ales – the priest is restless –
he talks of Red Jimmy

"...Jimmy boy? - he had a brain, uh, problem? - ...some sort of tumour the quack says - or something or other fucked in there - they're doing all sorts of tests - he looks ok these days actually - he'll *be* ok...but there are questions, always questions old chum – the bastard council are pulling down old St Erkenwald's...you heard?..."

but the Troubadour was not hearing – the babble of a screen playing endless reels of old gangster films above the bar distracted & distressed him

"...why do they put this crap on...the TV I mean...in pubs? - I come up here to get away from that shit, y'know? - too much...I mean what are we here for, man? – in this bar I mean - could've gone to any pub in the city but no we chose...YOU chose...the Intrepid fucking Fox..."

"...it is indeed an immoral boozer – Joyce would disapprove...mouldy cheese behind the perspex over there though...he'd go for that...couple of copulating flies to give him a stiffy...they used to play old music hall tunes on a gramophone here once, Sundays...so the old dear in the newsagents told me...she's a bit batty though...I love the old vaudeville, was thinking that Reverend Vaudeville would be a good name...Reverend Harry Champion..."

"...moulded - I don't know if my childhood moulded me for anything, except growing up...here's Jim now..."

Jimmy Red was forty three years old & for a decade & a half of those years a London Underground man – the Troubadour thought he must have been called 'red' because of his significantly radical tenure as the Union representative (there were many juicy tales of insurrection & communistic late-night plotting with the cleaners) but later discovered, via a sneaky over-the shoulder look at his passport, that his second name was Redpath & perhaps that was the more prosaic reason – he certainly looked for all the world like a creature that resided under the streets - that wiry, earthy fragrance of a troll, dull flowers, caked roots – a blinking, astonished, photophobic animal – an emerging mole, bewildered by the surface of the world – his tightly rolled cigarette rarely lit – counting out coins with his grimy, yellowing fingers rather than breaking any banknote – he chewed gum constantly & from a distance seemed to be talking to himself – he would sing random lines from Pink Floyd songs in a sudden tremulous tenor – he had a Syd Barrett magazine cover framed in a hideous, gold frame purchased in a bucket-shop from which an amateur still-life had been ripped – he was surly, quiet but tolerant of jokes at his expense of which there were many – the Troubadour liked him, his sunken intelligence & always smiled when he used to see him striding, fists in jacket pocket, mouth churning, headed for the bookies on the corner – liked a bet, Jimmy Red – nothing silly, few quid here & there – he only took his risks when the whisky held him hostage

one glorious night, with forged passes, he got the priest & the Troubadour all the way out to the train depot after hours of nervous imbibing at the Junction pub near Upminster station – they had spent two deep, strange hours listening to him waxing lyrical on the beauty of the old rolling stock, third rail electrocutions, the foliage of railway sidings being the new hedgerows & a few tawdry ghost stories of haunted signal boxes & voices floating down the midnight tunnels

he ordered a pint of Guinness & a double gin with lemon, no ice & sat on a backwards facing chair with his arms crossed & proceeded to roll the first of many failing cigarettes – the three men slowly amassed the empties & filled the tin ashtrays, talking across each other's subjects & finding a level of prolix lucidity that normally only sick dreams can muster

all the while a pack of cards flashed across the beery table in bewildering rounds of rummy that grew in intensity the more the rules became twisted

"...you holding all the fucking eights there, I know it – don't give me that Clint Eastwood squint – you're the bloody ruin of this hand..."

"...snake & sacrificial offering - god gave blame to all the animals..."

"...why the long face Jim my lad? - as the barman said to the drunken donkey..."

"...a happy man has simply not heard the terrible news..."

"... ah Brecht! - my favourite wealthy anarchist...a wise quote, sir...*echt* Brecht – wily old Weill sweetening his word bombs...Christ but those krauts can be sour old cabbages, *nicht wahr?*..."

"...nasty crash at the Westway yesterday...saw it in the paper...a few dead, enough to tempt the bold print – gets the councillors off the front page for a while... "

"...yeah...doing eighty-five in a thirty mile an hour zone...two women died, her dog survived...all I saw was this Labrador at the wheel, officer..."

"...I haven't had a cunt all day drinkstable...whisky's a heart attack & Guinness is a stroke...here, old Lenny said you were rude to him the other night in the Polar Bear...what're ye doing in that shit-pit anyhow?..."

"...ah, I was bored with the cunt...so I put my snorkel on...just been swimming down by the Lea river...that shut him up...barman made me take it off..."

"...what's that ye writing Deg? – takin' notes for your next bully pulpit, heh heh...give it to 'em straight...all the right answers..."

"...ah, that's where you are mistaken, sir...the sermon isn't so much an answer as a series of terrified questions...if you want the real god's truth then watch old Film-Noirs on a rainy Wednesday afternoon – like those up there on the idiot tube - or read the obituaries – reminds me, I need to buy a new copy of the Eno album – you know, the one I use as background – where's the best record shop these days? – Jimmy boy, you're hip to the trip..."

"...Rocks Off is the best...Hanway Street, off Tottenham Court Road...bought the new Fall single there yesterday...the owner was telling me there's cheap digs in St. Giles...where the lepers are..."

"...leopards?..."

"...there was a woman in my congregation last year who cut her boyfriend's balls off for having an affair...so she said...I believed her, looked the sort - she had the intensity of the wronged..."

"...lepers you mong...there are no big cats in Centre Point last time I looked..."

"...he won't go to heaven with no bollocks...ain't that the word of scripture holy father?..."

"...I think the album's out next week...did you hear Dragnet? – fuckin' amazing album..."

"...no man whose testicles have been crushed or whose organ has been cut off may become a member of the Assembly of God...one of my favourite passages, I quote it often...tattoos don't cut it either...defilement, dear boy...how much do we understand of love? – there are more devils than angels in the back alleys of this city, I tell ye..."

"...they have a suggestion box at work...you know, ideas that can improve the day to day running of the trains or speed up the ticket offices etc...I suggested painting big smiley faces on the tube trains...imagine yer man waiting, bored, hungover, first thing...depressed at the prospect of eight hours in some poxy office...then out of the tunnel comes..."

."...Deuteronomy...some weird shit there is in that little masterpiece...of course, I generally deal in the more, uh, liberal readings of the texts...Gnostics, the lost word...old Plato had a few ideas...throw in a few pennyworth of the mystics & you begin to see what I..."

"...I saw a llama in Archway once...might've been a sheep...hadn't touched a single drink...all doubles..."

"...is this your paper, Degory?...can I do the crossword?...I forgot to buy one this morning..."

"...I have gone astray like a lost sheep...one of the psalms, I believe...I had a vision when I was travelling down in Mexico that time, did I ever tell you? – an old tribe of shamen...*curanderos* they call them...tied up with the Catholic church a lot of those fuckers...but these were sound - mostly good old boys dealin' out the grisly wisdom for a few pesos - but some go rogue with the peyote & stuff...I stuck to Tequila & a few mushrooms...all for entheogenic purposes you understand..."

"...what's that book you got there?...fucking poetry, I suppose.."

"...I took acid for the first time in a bluebell wood...it looked like it was on fire...blue flames, cool as you walked through them..."

"...8 across, three words, 5, 2 & 5 - '...to be free of sin, in Monaco?...' - come on Deg, this is up your bloody street..."

"...little blot on a paper square no bigger than that - the flower arranger, I called it...never seen a blue like it...making the mundane fascinating, all you can ask in fairness...a concrete flyover...the colours...wow wow wow...you should take it with friends, though, the first time - people you trust, in case it all goes fuckin' mad...spiders on the wall, talking fuckin' insects...had a bit of that...really fucks with your ears too...some music, Jesus... listened to a Can album ten times in a bloody row...different every fuckin' time...worse, mostly..."

"...it's not an anagram of Monaco...not used to the Times...prefer the Standard..."

"...bit of Floyd...can't beat Syd for tripping..."

"...whose shout?...I might have a Jameson...oh fuck, it's me ain't it?...crisps?...peanuts?..."

"...Castaneda, oh yes, that was my fuckin' bible in those days...Swedenborg & all that crew...balance the terror & the wonder...there's the fuckin' key right there..."

"...*trip to a mmm dragon...la la la...ghost tower...*"

"...old Mark E. Smith had a touch of Swedenborg in him - journal of dreams, write them all down & learn their lessons - the northern Daedelus with his own labyrinthine bull in a carrier bag - named a crater after the cunt, dark side of the moon though - see, Floyd again, it all runs together in the end, boys - Swedenborg was a different sack of ferrets though - buried in this very city too - psychic he was, scared the living shite out of the queen of Sweden y'know? - surviving life's about making good connections - which, funny enough, is the exact polar opposite goal of the London Underground - *we are, basically, because God is...-* & hey, while you're stood up get us two salt & vinegar...nuts get in my bloody fillings...who's that surly cunt at the bar...? - he's been starin' at me for three full minutes...I'll have a word on the way to the gents..."

*

"...*nobody recalls what caused the altercation but the self-styled priest had been heard outside the Intrepid Fox in Wardour Street raising his voice & using profane language shortly before the alleged assault...the victim, a Mr. Raine of Clerkenwell, sustained a fractured cheekbone & bruising to the upper arm resulting from three blows with a wooden cane...*"

*

Jimmy Red phoned, said they bailed the bloody priest &
only cautioned him because the feller never pressed charges
– doubtless on drugs himself, looked out of control –
speeding probably, or amyl – laying low for a few days no
doubt – coppers were laughing at all the old bloody gasbag
he gave them outside the pub door – bits of it floated
through the Troubadour's fuzzy mind now – he dutifully
wrote some of it down – Jimmy didn't care, just carried on
with his crossword & bought another round – & yes The
Troubadour checked his notebook as he sat outside the
Café Boheme, pleasingly simmering in a weak sunlight – no
Amandine today – what day is it anyway? – his neck was
sore from shaving – he stared at yesterday's word harvest

convergence of schisms – LIST ROADS –
vagabond in a cold church –
thou shalt sup thy ale
with grand old Swedenborg
in the society of heaven –
soft feet on gravel road
I am The hippest priest in this godforsaken city
in there sits a wild man of the tunnels
& a Grand Troubadour
created in his own image
both ancestor & descendent –
to mercy, pity, peace & love
he leaves his all too human form
Saturnalia, her rings brighten the vacuum
The vacuum cleaner between the fixed stars –
Polish the chain of being & nothingness –
I'm drunk on the blood of the prophet –
burning the candle at both ends in pale sunshine –
Urizen divided these streets –
made shamanic chaos of blind waters
turned the London rain into the channelled obedience

'...dogshit...' - he said softly, put the notebook face down
& lit his tatty, rank stub of cigar

*

dream days disturbed, needled by qualm & subterfuge,
barely refreshed by the niggling carnival of leaden episodes
that played out on the city's inexorable streets - an example,
Friday - a Krishna devotee sips warm orange juice on the
pavement outside the Slaughtered Lamb - a scruffy, grey dog
sniffs his tambourine - *tableau-vivant*

*

yet sometimes the streets seemed like magician's smoke
- a deliberate masking of something underhand - or a film
projected on a dirty sheet - some angry mornings he felt
that he could punch through it like it was a cinema screen -
the delusion was so vivid some days that he almost tried - a
big gaping tear in the fabric - ripped canvas, flakes of
cracked paint - revealing what? - earth, leaf-mulch, worms -
it was reassurance of a kind, the reassurance of a tether, an
anchor
why then was it that some days felt stable on their feet,
more securely roped down, anchored more than others? -
Tuesday mornings, or occasionally, like today, Thursdays
around eleven - especially at that kind of non-hour - a brief
lacuna of contemplative meditation before the urgency of
the day's plans kicked in - he always stopped wherever he
was at this time & listened for a signal- he panned his gaze
listlessly - The Pausing Troubadour viewed the familiar
shops & alleys, cars & bridges as if they were situated in a
vast basement - the habitually clouded & heavy sky above

him representing the real world that could surely be attained by an as yet undiscovered staircase – maybe that staircase was his subconscious destination – the thought, for some reason, dismayed him & he frowned – be friends with the world, he mused – make an effort toward communication – reach out

a small spaniel, stumpy tail motionless, passed by preceding its blithe owner – The Troubadour reached down slowly to engender trust in the beast, palm upturned in welcome – the dog reared, snarling & with a lunge nipped a slit into his palm with a snag-tooth – The Troubadour, heart galloping, examined the wound swiftly filling with black blood & noticed for the first time how his heart-line was unbroken in a strong articulated curve across the span of his hand – the dog's bite was a tributary to it, pooling where the line briefly doubled – the owner was profuse in apology – scolding the still growling dog with imprecations – it stood foursquare, trembling, coughing, momentarily subdued by the yank of the lead

all day long the bite ached – thrumming in his veins until he took his first sip of beer – it was an ache that set him apart from the humdrum swarm

*

The Troubadour stewed in the first groan of light & grovelled before god in lame desire for compassion – the hangover rolled to his eyes as he scoured beneath the bed for socks – dressed but unwashed & bristly of mind & chin, he greeted the wobbling solids of the day with a mild pleasure – a reassurance that everything was inconsequential & abstract – as unmoored as his ship of doubts felt – above a fish & chip shop a golden grinning whale mocked his sanity – the tube journey was a molten hell of after-shave, elbows & halitosis they say that you can't be alone in the city – they say a lot of things – the characters that passed him by were fictional creations – his own – they smiled or frowned according to his will – snatches of speech, overheard mutters, full of the old complaints or bright with some new enthusiasm – on this kind of stray morning he walked a lot, mile upon unknowable mile – the streets shifted through many ages, history whispered above betting shops & boarded-up pubs – dingy dens wherein the grease-haired gangsters were all old aristocracy & the spotty, bespectacled booksellers were escaped artists, old bargemen & cockney intelligentsia – with a head full of coiled snakes he scoured the solid side-streets for something wraithlike – he bought books from tatty stalls beneath railway arches - resentfully, with money that could have been wasted on beer – he passed frozen tableaus, parallel universes of eerie laundromats – a lurid, low-rent science-fiction fragment preserved only in passing, held in the aspic of melting remembrance – a statuary of the glanced instant - &, like statues, the images of women tugging soggy clothing from the mouth of those beautiful silver machines became ennobled, frozen like a captured truth in the demolished past – the rays of concentration bent around their loneliness like the light of Eden around a black hole

The Troubadour stood at the junction of Dean & Romilly Street as was, these days, his almost daily practice – a sense of ancient cholera hung in the incurable, congested air, a wan light that seeped like distilled gravy from a muddy bank of fat cloud - some people are like figures in time-lapse reels, registering as a singular permanence as the waft of traffic - both motorised & pedestrian - passes through them as streaks of mad light – unhurried angels, pale as corpses, they hold the anger of the city in their gaunt, incorruptible stares – a mechanic peeks from beneath a broken-down Ford Anglia, bonnet propped open – he glowers straight at

The Troubadour unwaveringly – a troubling, dank, oily garage mystique - overalls & clotted hair swept back off his forehead

a radio voice, tinny, speckled by static, leaching from the raw wound of an open window above a shop

"...it's five past the hour & you're listening to Radio Caroline...the nice chap that just brought my coffee says that the sea is still & there's not another ship in sight – yesterday I thought I saw a small craft near the horizon way in the distance but it had vanished by the time I'd got my binoculars – a couple of songs now, long tracks both of them...plenty of pretty noises that should take us up to the half hour...hope you're having a great day wherever you are out there...comin' up soon, Freebird by Lynyrd Skynyrd...but first up this is The Pink Fairies & Uncle Harry's Last Freakout..."

he stood unconsciously drinking in the two songs for ten minutes – balm where balm was inadmissible, a jug full of ridiculous love & a wasted empathy from the rotten world – folky, hipster of the dandy Soho yawn - regressing, a mighty baby of the oldest town - with the traffic noise & cinematic sweep of the pointed roofs adding their thrills in counterpoint to the throb of bass & snare – screech of tyre a bent guitar string through a London amplifier – the echo from the walls of the outskirts – squall of apocalyptic prayer – he thought of druids, white-clad in the drift of standing stones, lines & dusty stacks of vinyl records intertwined with large books of sheet music, old jazz, tablature & tadpoles on a winter wire - he thought of Red Jimmy repeatedly playing his Mick Farren & The Deviants album that always jumped at least five times per bloody side – in his present state of mind Freebird was an intruder, a long-winded tourist overstaying its welcome at an airport bar – the following Pink Fairies track suited the beginning drops of cool rain & the manic gurgling of kettles – it throbbed & murmured in

257

the deep aroma of hot leather & the luxurious stink rising from newly moistened drains – The Deviants were Red Jimmy's favourite band in the world – Mick Farren had frequented a few pubs near where Jimmy had lived in Ladbroke Grove – it was a good memory of bad rain – a deepening weather that yelled over feedback through a cloud of afro tangles – man-sweat & plimsoll perfume – The Troubadour looked up at the radio waves streaming from the window – beyond the sill the interior was dark, a vague hint of orange that could be a painting staining the barely visible wall to the right – a Mick Farren kind of Thursday morning, slower than the ensuing afternoon's clattering hours – The Troubadour blinked away a tiny fly from his stung eyeball - his fog of confusion showing no sign of clearing but he was becoming friends with its possibilities – he suddenly felt an urge to mix with an unknown crowd – a touristy smattering of inquisitive faces, colours of holidays, sweet air thick with fresh bread, pastries – Covent Garden, the pub with the balcony – jump-cut to the squeezed psychedelic toothpaste of the tube map – he sat on the train watching himself watching himself through the opposite window between stations – he got out at Leicester Square (he had a weird aversion to Covent Garden station, it brought on an inexplicable claustrophobic panic every time he risked it) – he had caught the last throes of the rush hour & in the lumbering hordes he felt outcast, unwashed, a refugee from the godly masses breathing polo-mint air in sanitized clothes – he stared down at the ankles of the person in front of him & trusted them to guide him to freedom - the escalator was inexplicably clear though & as he glided upward with eyes closed he fancied that he was an angel being readmitted to heaven, or an abductee rising on a beam to an alien craft – the metal pressed into his aching feet through his thin bootsoles – he strolled – a benign zombie - through the impossibly tight crowds, a thousand other incurious lives, to finally emerge into the spatial relief of the moderately-populated stalls of the market

the slow, steady men in stained grey coats delivering crates of vegetables to the stallholders – a compact, raw, earthbound aroma – stale mausoleum tug to the whirling sensory web – a touch of decay rising from the potatoes, swedes & turnips stacked in awkward mounds in the fake-grass bed's bright orange tufts – tomb food, dank root – dogbite – the crumbly stench of a rabid field of tubers entrenched – nocturnal, rich soil turned by a metal blade – pebble, horse-hoof & worm – dogbite, itching now – run some healing beer past the bloody thing, cure-all

he climbed the stairs to the Punch & Judy pub overlooking the square where the street theatre & magicians & buskers played to the holiday crowd – for free, pass the bucket, more silver than folded notes – he bought a Guinness perfectly poured, half inch of creamy top suspended over an unknowable darkness, no sham shamrock just a curled nipple where the tap dripped its last – he sat on the balcony & lit a Lucky Strike, his treat for the day, back to the cheaper brands tomorrow – juggler, magician, tall & in pancake white-face – comedic & of the Italian art – harlequin leotard brightly quartered – a few card-sharp malpractices, mute show of baton twirl & showy hand gestures – he is a remnant blown fresh from the jester caravans of the ancient London freak-shows – the silent secret whispered behind the muddy children's cupped hands

the balls looping hypnotically in the amazed air – he receives the pit-a-pat applause with a solemn bow & moves effortlessly to the next deception – hoops linking & unlinking in mesmeric sleights of his white gloves – opening his rouged mouth in mock astonishment a his sorcery – the children squeal & look up to their parents for explanation, for permission to be astounded – the inscrutable holy

Guinness sipped, moustache of soft foam – bird's-eye view of the free circus – head clearing, clouds broken by sliver of religious sunray – a man on stilts passes waving, level with The Troubadour's eyeline – a small mongrel barks at a unicyclist, the children laugh as the rider barks back louder

suddenly, as if recalling an old fear, The Troubadour was overwhelmed by the need to see the river – he gulped his Guinness down to a protesting stomach & as he exited, gulping back nausea, waved briefly at the barman – the stairs reeled before him in a gentle swim – he steadied himself on the top step, gripping the solidity of the handrail - dogbite, throb & nag – outside the pub he stood in the passing stream of miserable tourists & breathed deeply the needling air – the tube train journey to Embankment was mercifully quick & uncrowded – the ticket-office hurt his eyes & filled his ears with clamour

stepping gingerly from the doorway he sniffed the Thames – metallic seaweed, engine-oil, smack of fish-head & drowned pirates cut from the wharf's gallows - the morning air was devastating, chill & faithful to its duty of dissembling the river's humours - he found himself panting as he climbed the metallic steps to Embankment bridge – he guiltily tossed his meagre change into the tramp's enamel bowl – bless you pal – no problem – you are not real, the money is forged – a monopoly wad of fake prosperity – a liar's promise – beneath the pavement a billion coins mouldered – foolish gold – the fools buried with it still in their greedy fist

at the top of the steps he paused again, surveying the anarchy of the spreading metropolis – a relief map of greed & loss – tall towers, churches, the myriad warehouses & storerooms – febrile city of facades shimmering like mild epilepsy – his eyeballs shook, a tic worried at his eyebrow – the hangover shifting like tectonic plates beneath his mud skull – a discarded burger-box reeked under the bridge's

mesh of riveted metal – through the ghosts of meat brief
wafts of more delicate scents permeated – indifferent, limp
salad, tomato, lettuce, onion – then the sudden stench of the
florist's stand rising on an updraft almost making him heave
– Crysanthemum, he thought of the ridiculous word &
hated it – the spores lodging in his nasal hair like pods from
an alien future – below him a grimy lorry honked,
ponderous in a clumsy three-point turn – petulant traffic
heckled the hapless beast whose driver, fat & smoking a stub
of cigar, offered apologetic Zen-like hand gestures –
momentarily placated the pinched faces frowned, fingers
drumming the bakelite steering wheels – spongiform muses,
a collective gelatine dream of offices, desks in depressing
rows, walls of perforated beige – the shrill clatter of bells that
signal imprisonment & freedom in turn – the lorry driver
dreams of hitch-hikers & service-station pasties – the suits &
ties float above the mess behind glittering windows whilst he
ploughs a polluted furrow into the carnival of rats – the
traffic paused as if a child had tired of playing with them – a
screenshot of expectant faces frozen – rats always find the
river, the prayerful water subdues their fevers – valerian root
& sewer pipe artery – the tramp counts his windfall, he is
perfected by invisibility – circus soil, itinerant, the sadness of
a dead leaf blown through a deserted hallway - dogbite

*

Highgate cemetery at night – faint lights of London
through a risen mist – The Rising Troubadour holds the
wine bottle up to his eye & looks at the broad panorama
through its dark lens – panning to his left, it distorts a pale
statuette, to the right, a tree swells & looms in crisp, spidery
perspectives – he puts his hand on a stone cherubim's
buttock – swigs the red blood, tart, vinegary – *sang des anges*
– the stone cool, damp

"...come to life, why don't you?..."

Donatello – that bloody old chiseller – The Troubadour flounders in an impressionistic gauze – gummy webs fracture & stick across his forehead - uneasy, he sways under Rousseau vines, the old *gabelou* – weighted by the rush in his veins he slumps against a skewed headstone & farts – he checks his pocket for cigarettes – two left out of ten – dole tomorrow – the moving banquet begins anew – his eyes are too sad to hold the shy starlight meant for lovers – he hears a squeaking, creaking, sneaky sound – eek-a-mouse – or rat, god no - no, a bicycle, inexpertly ridden - approaching, unlit, dead ahead – he lights his Zippo to make himself visible – the darkness is the palpitating, smoked darkness of a closed book – his body pressed tight as milky vellum pages crammed into a bookcase – he was the contained mystery, a tale untold

"...who goes there?..."

no reply – the figure cycles past not five feet from him, blue macintosh & trilby hat – brief face of a comedy verger – no acknowledgement, can't have seen him – he traces the air with the Zippo flame in hope of flashback trails – residue of long-dead planets – above, right now, how many dead? – cycling at night – looked like that actor, what's his face? – Donald Sutherland – yes, Day Of The Locust – on telly, it was, last month – could be Hollywood down there right now if you squint – Hollywoodland, the sign a *de facto* cemetery of sorts, that poor bitch who jumped – Peg something? – jumped off the H – he could recall the death note verbatim, being something of a collector of last words - *I am afraid, I am a coward* – braver than me - *I am sorry for everything - if I had done this a long time ago, it would have saved a lot of pain* – something compelling about the last words – full stop & stop – H was the first breath of help – then no more voice forever – he knew Hancock's final note too – he knew about things that go wrong once too often – but ending it? –

child's coffin as sad as that – too little, too early, surely best to take every risk once denied by circumspect morality - become a tramp, stowaway on a ship, anything but *that* – better out of it sometimes though – sleep, the oblivion of the beer-glass, the unnatural high of a bag of sick glue, the whisky bottle's an oubliette – each to their own second-hand void – we all have our trapdoor of choice – food be damned, the escape hatch is hard gin, a cheap supermarket option - juniperilous

these trees swishing in a gathering wind, storm coming – he loved storms, to stay out & feel the vigorous, unyielding power of driven rain – the brief illumination of electricity, a shock of daylight, the bones of night laid bare – thousands of bones under him now – he swigged the last of the sour wine, pulling his coat up to cover his neck & rested his head on his hands clasped behind his head – wait for the thunder, the gradual menace of its lazy timpani – god's busy moving furniture, his dad used to say – dead planets, dead light - the mist has now vanished in the increasing wind – mist itself dead sea – his fake Hollywood twinkled falsely in clear view, he stared at the glistening yellowy glow – how each light has its own aura, little halos – listening, the chattery branches, the wind talking to the dry leaves scampering the gravel – swarming locust wingbeats underscoring the nod of sleep

the dream is thus prepared, patiently waiting the cue, the psychic nudge - the ship's nauseating lurch, the wheeze of spray across the deck, white flecks of foam – & Captain Rehab, way up there in his old sou'wester, wrenching the wheel back & forth – no rest until this beast passes, boys – the shore is a memory, lost to a Turner maelstrom of dense blue & cream, churning – a blackness like deep space beyond it all - though, yes, of course, out in the estuary widening, foggy bulbs marked the tragic shipwrecks & their inevitable ghosts – & his ship, that nightmare of doomed timber, is somewhere out there too, a clang of ship's bell,

whereupon the Captain's crew scuttle & yell – onward it
rolls through the phases of time, nodding sagely at each
breaker

& yes Old Rehab's nut-brown head creates its own
microclimate of thrilling weather-systems, the contours
expanding through the past – through unfolding stories –
whilst sunk beneath the prow the bones & bombs, sleeping
munitions, that drowned in the war - one wrong move & the
whole estuary blows – the rain easing a little, or is it the wind
that dropped? – shore line visible now through the lash of
wave spray

poems are formed of such tempests, these squalls of life
stuff – & years hence when remembering this night at the
mystic Highgate graveyard will his soul then tremble? – as it
floods back will he cower? - sensing from years ago, the
sudden violent change of wind direction that almost turned
his voyage over – remember – The Captain, eyes shut, back
there, himself once again to guide his past self through the
storm – time has a turning point, a pivot of recall - it all
started after the unlit cyclist passed by, just a few seconds
ago - a few distinct seconds as easily recalled as a colder year
of splintered wistfulness – The Troubadour shivered, it was
as if he had dragged the storm's anger behind him tonight –
as if he existed solely to trigger a chain of remembrance - the
poor girl went out for a hike below the big sign & found a
purse, a shoe, a jacket – she immediately looked down the
mountain & saw a woman's body – dead bones stepped out
for the last time into thin air from the vast H – the stars
hurtling upward, the thrash of trees, the leaves whipping the
soft flesh of her arms - *If I had done this a long time ago* –
the dim lights seem to hover above the now still water – &
she floats now above the Thames – the unknown star - & he
is further downriver again, look, there is the pier in the
distance – Yantlet, they call this area – the old barges used
to haul the tea, spices, whisky – sacks of plunder from

barbaric coasts – belly of the empire – tacking left to the north shore, follow the glinting lamps from the houses – a rustling sound that could almost be milk over cornflakes, he thinks of breakfast – always distractions, must concentrate - too late, he's hungry now, red wine leaves a yawn in the gut only bacon can mend – opening his sticky eyelids to thrill to a fresh gust of deathly air over the tranquillity of damp granite – the high waving grasses between all the dead ones - trying to warn him – what did Walt call it? – uncut hair – his long hair still cold & matted, his mind, cold & matted – he stood up & stretched his back, hearing the complaints of vertebrae – grind of knuckle on socket – the birds, silent or unnoticed 'til now, broke into a tentative melody up in the higher branches – his arms felt as heavy as lead, his whole body drugged, like he was carrying an ocean, the whole world's deepenings - as if the universe of water had, in its entirety, soaked into his wired, irritated skin, chosen his frail frame as its home

homeward then - hellish tube journey, sodden clothes & frozen flesh, train deserted - crushed beer tins & other night detritus rattling up & down with each lurch & swerve of the carriage - late, late returning, shuffling his delicate headache into the rebellious kitchen, so tired that he couldn't sleep – still up at five a.m. - the despair enlightened only at the heart of a lone candle lit – all around him the despair was inexplicably expressed in commonplace things – the indistinct washing draped on a red clothesline like tokens, emblems of all the lost uprisings – the kitchen top, grey mottled surface, knife smeared with Marmite hardening – he opened the cupboard, only three slices of white bread without the blue tinge of decay – on the sill a dry cactus & a half-potato in a saucer thriving on leaked rain, its alien feelers stretching tentatively into our planet's atmosphere - posters on the cupboard doors – footballers, Best, Perryman, Bonetti – Lenin with shades drawn on him in felt pen, Thatcher 'What's Wrong With Politics?' with 'this fucker' & an arrow pointing – Jerry Garcia strumming, Dylan with polka dot shirt, the framed front cover of 'Sniffin' Glue' magazine, the one with The Damned on it – & a ripped page from an art book about the miniature Tatlin Tower being constructed

from the piebald ceiling hung a dead bulb, over which his upward shadow was thrown – on the wall by the door a dartboard with one dart stuck in the bullseye & two more on the floor under it – the blinds that hid the morning's dim stirrings were crushed at the centre & ridged with dust – he lifted the middle two slats & peeked out at Mornington Crescent imperturbable in a milk-float serenity – a shy, colourless landscape, the downstairs of the mind

kjnnk – toast

the kettle, blackened at its bottom, begins its hoarse whistling on the gas ring – paid the bill this week then, Zac – a dark presence at the heart of the heat pipes' low grumbling – the commune's inspirational quote of the day on the fridge, stuck with a sliver of Gaffa-tape

"...if there's any hope for a revolution in America, it lies in getting Elvis Presley to become Che Guevara..."

he takes the carbon-scraped, margarine-heavy, toast into the front room where the dawn has been allowed to hang an eerie blue-grey blush – three mattresses on the floor separated by ashtrays, a terrible brown sofa, sundry empty bottles, squashed cans & torn newspapers – the floor, where visible, is either balding pools of old rugs from a time before the place became an unofficial squat, or tiles, chipped, dark crimson – photocopied fliers for meetings & gigs are piled on a large writing desk upon which a huge old typewriter & cheap plastic globe stood in ominous silhouette against the bay-window's backlight – two shelves held a line of ragged

books - Hesse, Pilger, Lovecraft, Marx, Barthes, Godwin –
anarchist Xeroxed pamphlets interspersed with yellowing
New Musical Expresses & Morning Stars

he lit a roll-up partly crushed in the biggest of the four
ashtrays – it was the last of the Moroccan poor Zac had until
Wednesday but so fucking what? – slowly the window
brightened pleasantly in gentle stages of stained yellow as the
room filled with the musky wisps of his liberated joint – he
cracked the window a little – weirdly, somebody was playing
music at this early hour, or had never stopped, perhaps –the
slow, steady drone & plodding groove of The Doors' L.A.
Woman wafted in & embellished the smoke with a cod-
mythic tinge - The Relaxed Immaculate Troubadour sat
back on the low, legless sofa & considered a stroll to the
market for a better breakfast – the Doors ended & after a
pause Neu's Hallogallo began - snaking into the cooling,
woozy room – the industrial 4/4 thud of motorik, bloodied
& insistent, a torture drip amplified, with an eastern swirl of
fat, spacy reversed guitar whining above it like the victim's
scream – wild party music for the krauts, he thought – the
flat next-door it came from – that fucking white Rasta freak-
head who was always in India for the winter, or Senegal –
skinny as a clothes-pole & his motoring head full of thick,
skunky weed & bad speed - the wired Rasta, what was his
name? – Piggy? Ziggy? Wiggy? – something iggy anyhow –
had slyly inducted The Eager Troubadour into his sprawling
world of foreign, enchanting sounds & esoteric literature
one long, stoned night back in his first week at the squat –
flicking through his wads of vinyl stacked on the bare stone
floor – Lee Perry, Sun Ra, Faust, MC5, The Monks, The
Residents, Kevin Coyne - & books of magic, theology,
theosophy & German history from The Grail Knight
Lohengrin to the mysticism behind the death of the failed
Nazi empire – together, in a soporific blur, they had
invented scenarios for a film that would never be made -

Hitler deep in bad thoughts on his favourite bench outside art school in the Meldemannstraße - Vienna flowering with brutal truths – a psychotic drama of art & analysis – Valhalla beckons but for now, the sadism postpones its strategies – the soundtrack would be culled from the crackly discs gently warping by the two-bar fire - corrupt landscapes of sickly schmaltz swept clean by ambient waves of grainy synths - apache pulse – a crystalline polished ostinato pricked by tribal hullabaloos & explosions – the Rasta had wanted to learn to paint but could never unlearn his schooling enough to express his abstract thoughts – he bought endless cheap canvases though, or painted over old still-lifes he found on the market – scratched scars of charcoal, gouache dribbles & faulty lines of chalk - expanding & contracting week on week - Malevich geometry & soulful trickles that strafed the canvases like napalm – nothing gelled, nothing pleased him - the slow brandy-drinking through the daytime increased, the fiery, amphetamine night hours distended – one night, after returning from a basement dub party in a foggy, blue fit, he trashed everything – screaming imprecations to a history of fallen gods, leaning from his window to inform the midnight world of his righteous fury – he wreaked a systematic purifying, a purgative havoc, upon all he had formerly held sacred – not a picture nor poem survived the onslaught – he could be heard sobbing for an hour before a bubbling stream of giggles slowly replaced the misery

& he had never painted or written a thing since that night – happy to merely look & listen - only his partly-burned journal conceals anything of his frustrations & nobody will now ever read that skittery scrawl should it be discovered after his time on earth has passed into dust

secretly, he had kept just one of his pictures, framed in a fake-wood rectangle, hung wonky on his bedroom wall, a lone refugee from the carnage – it was just a few intersecting coloured lines that hung from a conical form fringed by ghostly red powdery halos – he had written on the base of the frame in black ink

throw
my abstract darts
& pray
for a surprise

The Abstracted Troubadour slipped his thick Norwegian Army coat over his Paisley shirt & red jeans & set off to find food – mapless & undriven, unwaveringly without purpose – in search of the miraculous, for the clattering of metal poles, the chatter & bluff, the birth-pangs of the nascent market to eat greasy, fat, smoky bacon sandwiches &, thus sated, to head for the equally lubricious lair of the priest

*

the priest's shelves were hot from the lone radiator smothered behind the casing – its thin planks creaked with dry mysteries bound in cracked leather – red & black predominate, the pages' faded cream hidden like petticoats – The Troubadour perused the titles without interest – yet they comforted his mind in inexplicable ways, as if a poultice was being lain across the throb of a headache – he drank in the cryptic legends as a fish with mouth agape drank the wine of the idle sea – he let the sideways titles drift by - The Voice Of The Silence & Isis by H.P. Blavatsky, Meetings With Remarkable Men by G.I. Gurdjieff, Journey to Ixtlan by Carlos Castaneda, thick books on art, Expressionism, Dadaism, Pataphysics & Oriental Ceramics, Science Fiction compilations, Ghost Stories & Marvel comics, Zen & The Art Of Motorcycle Maintenance, Catcher In The Rye, Beckett's Poems, Yeats'

269

poems, Walden, The Beat Generation, The Lost
Generation, Pan & Hunger by Knut Hamsun – some he
had seen before in his myriad library wanderings but others
were temptingly obscure to him – some were intriguing by
title alone – Radical Chic & Mau Mauing The Flak Catchers
by Tom Wolfe, Tertium Organum by Ouspensky, he
selected one of the slighter volumes whose curious title had
attracted him - Les Chants De Maldoror authored by one
Comte de Lautréamont – he blew a cobweb from the
binding & took it back to one of the dusty pews to
investigate whilst the priest was rehearsing his sermon for
the Sabbath
"...ye know that ye can borrow any tome that takes your
fancy, boy...what've ye got there?..."
The Troubadour told him the title in a hesitant French
accent
"...ah mad Monsieur Ducasse! – old Maldoror is a man
after my own Ubu heart – morality be damned - *Plût au ciel
que le lecteur, enhardi et devenu momentanément féroce...*-
do you read French?..."
"...no...is it not translated?..."
"..that's the original version in the tongue of the poet
himself you have there – I have an English one somewhere,
I believe, in my study – you must try to read in the original,
boy – lots of beauty gets muddied in a poor paraphrase you
see? – I'll go & fetch you the English, stiff-upper-lip text ha!
– It isn't too awful to be fair..."
The Old English Troubadour flicked through the
incomprehensible pages – he pondered how strange the
concept of language – the loose tongues of babel – we
evolve on different rocks & talk a stranger's way – all related
though, tangled up in invasions & relations – soft French,
like cream cheese spread on the page – the German harsh,
a fishbone caught in the throat – he vowed to himself to one
day learn enough to read a novel in the original French – he

glanced at the text again – the title, the mad priest had conjured it from memory – more to him than meets the ear – if I could speak it fluently I'd be showing it off in every pub – the words coasted fruitlessly past his eyes like hieroglyphics on a pyramid wall – he looked at the cover again – a charcoal sketch of the back of a man's head with beetles crawling over it – Les Chants, that's songs isn't it? – Songs of – Mal means bad...or is it the name of the singer? – Maldoror – sad ring - all old books made him sad for some reason – like tombs of lost thoughts – grassed-over word graves – all by someone gone - me one day - old songs, ah! – me & my complicated shadows - a shadow proves you exist, have substance - they are the guilty stains of paradise into which it fell, bliss of Eden split by lightning – old words you belly-farted into a bemused being unasked - you have travelled great distances since then - yet there are still heavy miles to go - a long drag homeward to somebody you call 'me' - 'me again' not 'me at last' – look up to the sky for no bloody reason than some other book of spells told you to look there - & an old shaky aeroplane is rising above the forest - the engines build to a roar, the seat- belt sign winks into life - take off & ascent is smooth & below the calm earth receding, its Mondrian blocks of colour strafed by wires - wires hissing with phantom conversations, frenzied communications - just beyond the reach of your hearing - sleepwalking, you are, in wild air - soon the greens, blues, reds & yellows fade to lost memory - & grey & black are the shades of the last big room - & at a time when so many answers are needed from the sky only questions bloom in your mind - what was the purpose of this journey? - why are my fellow passengers so young? - so calm & unruffled as a Spring river - & from what source, a recoil from anger maybe, did the light pour? – how do they live without their safety-net prayers? - with no joy & with what idolatrous reverence?

.   like the bunked off work days with Boo – all the time under it all a sadness waiting to sprout – time & distances availing not – lion of youth roar no more - call him Ishmael no more, stretching a bleak mind across the spiritual haze, Yeats' lines & rest, long gone in the rosy crosshairs of theosophy – gone to mud, to Maud long gone meat & writing from the gravy – no longer trusting in the *poet maudit* of old – needing a new muse to poke the old embers– he used to stalk & talk improvised trash verse to seagulls – out by the estuary edge he was always struck dumb by the beauty of a yellow bicycle, rust-chipped & wheel-less, leaning against a bright red wall - & now he is almost self-righteous & full of modern architecture & the graffiti poems of broken toilets - so he would gather up his confused thoughts & head to the garish sweep of coast on the eastbound train, that shitty charabanc of loathing – the rattling, metal, on the borderline of a sagittal universe - the language, unsettling, glottal, chortling, reassuringly immortal, shuttling rhythm, cattle-trucking train – a dour packed lunch of processed ham sandwiches & your Summer trousers & unnatural comb – what's out of the window? - a parallel window, reeling the petrified images ever faster past your reflected face – isolated ghost houses, just one more solitary home & unvisited - to hand, a book of revelations, a portal of escape unused - a going away gift dreamed but unrealised – so then, pull down the window & smell the approaching sea – ozone high, transformative, rite of passage - Baby to Troubadour, Lonesome, up the chain to that ever patient, clued-up old Captain – singing that mumbly blues mortified by history – no matter, he is of the river now & the river, inaudibly voicing her aspirations, feels no wrench of conscience, no twinge of doubt nor disheartened ache of regret - for the moving waters own no misery – hopes too, stout little Spring-blossoms, propelled by moon-kicked, capricious tides, see them sail, sail away - as a mantra is rendered choral by the criss-cross of reel to reeling magnetic tape, time-lapsed voices piled up, begging, pleading, one more time - sing, my sea girls! – my loveless seaside girls - ice-cream siren girls of useless seas no more

sing, sea-bear, lingering moaning song of bear - & can you hear the sea in these words he sings? - sidle to the crash of ocean in our land of lost masks & sing of lessons learned, turn to the crowd & elucidate the sorrows - sing the seasons turning slow to ash succinct as promises of tomorrow – or sunlight blessed by memory's flashes - rust & carcass – used-up silver, brassy in the wash of hiss & gasp - trusting the blushed stones she carelessly erodes - sweet kiss & suck of salted centuries implode - they must, they must - restless shift of sands - our hands secure to the mast - we were, we are, we will be dust & dust alone drifting – so sly the sacred passions of the sea-bear soliloquy – seep through splashing dreams, slither with suspicious steps into your sighs, into your soul, sauntering with his ancient serenades - can you hear the waves? – list, listen the sea is here - the massed voices of the wistful sea chorus, here - hush, the sea-bear listens - hush, love, the sea is here - entice the old anguish from the past to shiver the timbers of the underclasses

time is a friendless train, each mile a stone unturned, the mossy rocks inertia reeks of winter's kill – no harbour, no shore, no tethered town of fisher-folk – just the slackening drift & nothing real except the window flashing - train in rain & hail – it's got to get to wherever you're going, it can go nowhere else – it is ending a journey at where you must be – don't be late – & he liked to read by rivers, or at the sea's first confusion out where the river ends – yes, he could get the train down to the coast – take some sandwiches, yes, wine – the city can grind you down – get some salty air back in the body – get out of the smoke for a bit

the priest was swearing viciously at a rat in the ruined vestry – taunting squeaks & vulgar threats echoing at a slight remove, as if in heaven, as reluctantly The Troubadour put the book back on the shelf & waited for The Most Reverend Degory Priest to return - & when he did, apologetically almost, he said

'...old Turkish shaman in a Chinatown café, always sat in the same seat or thereabouts, he told me - the world, it's fucked man, am telling you now this, the surface goes deep down, like a brain, tin circles small & smaller again - the dreams are well keeping, the keeping you understand? - well down, deeper we are all poets & priests, that much is nothing, we need our answers like we need the last gin, no? - need & want, they sleep in same bed but uneasy - don't drag them apart because both of them you need together...but don't listen to me listen to yourself, you idiot!!...' - pronounced id-eeeee-yot - all this speechifying pricked with a steely emphasis born of frustrated passion - he was a fool, said the priest - maybe read that back - a fool, Lear's - has there ever been a more useless statement? - fool's gold in a tumbler - sun through a bottle there's gold in them hills - bit of gin left, dirty glass, my dirt probably, no worse than another's - see if the day needs it, if the old juniper still bites - swig, epiphany

*

another fine London morning, Lord will they ever end? - the effortlessly relentless beat of the Damned's Neat, Neat, Neat had worked its hypnotic spell despite jumping twice & he felt, just about, re-energised enough to begin confronting the day's unharmonious arrangement of nebulous schemes, the chance psychopathologies & psychogeographies - the tube subway gaped, Hellbound Troubadour descending into the mathematical, evenly-tiled earth, he yawned, buying his all-day rover ticket from the capped, disinterested attendant with a well-practiced, sarcastic grimace - a pound noted,

274

platform full of petals on a shite-brown bough of bargain-basement haiku - playing moody Solitaire, not looking up, a Cezanne-shaped bloke arrives on the busy platform - a lost, drooping, moustachioed time-traveller under his heavy blue cap - the commuters stood in hushed dread - mute Kafka nonentities with nods & sniffling - giving nothing away, his badly dealt hand disguised by a Wyatt Earp smirk - hurried, bloody handkerchiefs pressed to dripping noses, bad news rolled tight & clamped under moistening armpits - awaiting the firing squad of rattling wheels to echo from the frown of the waiting tunnel

he boarded the train & sat reading a discarded, wretched newspaper, becoming strangely entranced by its shocks & banalities, carrying it through the connections all the way to Leicester Square - easy puzzle - except...damn, leaving one clue incomplete - 7 down, 9 letters third letter 'R', eighth letter 'E' - '...pioneer, endlessly hard drinker, in bouts...' - he got off still pondering, jogged up the stairs & out into the sudden blare of the perpetual traffic of infinite London's mid-morning thoroughfares - turning right in a pleasing, somnolent haze, dipping into the freshly opening Porcupine pub for a livener - two hurried pints of spurting, frothing newly-drawn ale & grabbing a fist of bar-top peanuts to sustain any energy thereby accrued - maybe jacket-potatoes later, butter-damp, softened, still reminded of their boiling - then out again to wander a while up & down the seethe & yelp of Charing Cross Road, past the ranks of bookshops with their heads bowed under the brims of awnings, niggling him with sweet memories of Olden Tom Maher, poet, his image quickly squashed by an intake of impatient car-fumes - the teasing wafts of Chinese aromas spicing the already dense air - after a bout of a few minutes empty dawdling he emerged into the square itself, the incongruous greenery a shock to the senses - of course, the pigeon lady was already there every morning at 8 a.m. - & then returning at 11 sharp - she sat on the step by the little arched fencing crunching up toast crumbs in her carrier bag as pigeons bubbled in the eaves of shops & jerked their tiny heads in anticipation - great flocks of them, for blocks, all gathered expectantly - perched precariously on the taut telephone wires strung over the boisterous streets - she is monumental, Rodin's vague Balzac mass, thick-coated, woollen & studious - a motley broth of diminished colours - dancing in her mind, but motionless, to her own sly jazz, pigeon rhythms, a low, green, fertile music - he had watched her many mornings - she always came - friendless, seemingly, but not unhappy necessarily - flinging the stale bread like a bride tossing a bouquet to the throng of bickering bridesmaids - she is mortally afflicted by her aged body, as eventually are we all, yet she has retained forever the incandescence of a road-spirit, a guardian of junctions - the impudent breeze passed quickly around her stout island - she is England's avatar as much as any - the cops smirk as they pass & cough into their gloves - one day, when she isn't there, the air will seem vacant, like a slammed gate

a lone fiddle-player sends arcs of melody across the Celtic distance - two Japanese tourists fussily assembled their lenses, screwing them on to their huge cameras - there was a sense that elsewhere, not too far away, something ingenious, something momentous was brewing, as if this were an island of frightened calm in a stirred pot of the city's worries - the wary eye of a social whirlpool - its focus, the pigeon lady, expressionless, emptying the last specks from her bag, the fiddle's tearful lowing, the clicking of shutters capturing the moment before the catastrophe of her leave-taking

The Troubadour watched, enthralled - harbinger, he thought suddenly & triumphantly filled in the last answer, placing the folded news into a burnt-out metal bin - fire, snag on which the metropolis continued to catch – old London, spectral, confidential, ashes & embers – roaring up in the hive mind, faces in the flames, words to be jotted down – it was a diary he kept, a journal of loose wires to be carefully disentangled after he had faded into the city's smeary palimpsest

lighting a rich Gauloise & inhaling the plume of a far, other city, he snapped himself back into the tempo of the passing day &, humming From Clare To Here, headed in the vague direction of Wardour Street – he looked up, the air dense, throbbing in his skull, storm on its way

*

& he found all barmaids beautiful – they were a muse to him, constantly, exquisite bookmarks slipped in-between the duller pages of life – usually new to the city, on a respite from college, at art school, piling up the pennies for a mad scheme overseas – they were rarely fixed to the job for long – as transient as the sad parade of fools they served

the lamps were a replica - archaic, brass shades - red bulbs where the candle should be - the barmaid never looked up until a customer approached the bar - beyond the curve of her shoulder, reflected in the bloated glass of the optics - the door blew open & a dance of leaves pirouetted around the floor – out there the busy universe purposefully stayed on its sober path whilst her bibulous crew drowned old troubles, imagined & actual, in these way-stations of doubt – ballet of flustered leaves, an autumnal *danse macabre* – a requiem of winds weeping through door jambs for London's grave sins

London, the people, yes – vanishing out here in the northernmost boondocks – urging the outskirts to reel, alive with the music on his pumping headset – crazy paving stepper - walkabout & trauma, the entropy of a sunset hour -

277

hear the night coming over the horizon - in a tangle of language, of jangled Fender guitars & mid-Atlantic brogue they wail, *gloria in excelsis* - yet that morning found him inglorious - the day's duvet crumpled at the foot of an arthritic night's pallet - nothing has been learned, no destination reached - church of fen, cross of king - saints with bloated pancreases & Peruvian bears abandoned & blithely labelled with love - creepy euro-tunnel visions of our coming Waterloo - blooded heads on poles, eyes rolled heavenward - flags & emblems - & old Rehab, on shore leave, smoking under the arch by the pallid terminus many years hence, was once a Newtown Babe, now a Tacky Troubadour & every second hung so slow as he growled through the fervent volatility of backstreets & slid down the snakes of lanes to taste the dwindling mix of flavours from the ventilator grates - grappled with the snakes of delirium, wept upon the ladders of window cleaners - treasuring the sips of smoky rum, a purloined snapshot between buses of a winter tree in Archway, a singular crow, itself the message he chose to disregard, caws its zeros to the vacant skyline

& though he tries so hard to refresh his love, these places are becoming death, where ye all have to go - the starry memories locked in the fool's gold paving stones - the resurrection of such memories becoming a guide to the next unsuspecting tourist - there were endless names scrawled everywhere, phone boxes, benches, stained in the breath left on kissed shop windows - within London herself there are sacred spaces that cling to treasure, hold more of her creepy quintessence - first time travellers may only pause, may only sniff, as the aroma drifts by - but the seasoned visitor is always captivated & feels each hair in his moustache tingle as if they were antennae thrilling to a new prey - lovers or enemies lurk around blind corners & deep in the ugly, bitumen-fat, bubbled-up shadows, in jetsam alleys of gun-smoke, where the updraft from a buried kitchen filters through the singed flue – old pages from diaries, newsprint, the fliers of dead anarchists & kids' church fete posters gather in her damp corners - blown carelessly, fed by flotsam winds, rotting as if abandoned there by time – they are startled on occasion, as if something certain is glimpsed through a vision of chaos – cut-up maps of streets blustered to jigsaw nonsense – this is the church of an unfrocked holy man – mouth bent to the flask & fragrant musky incense – his divided soul wildly dislocated in topographic uproar by an unseen, malevolent design - for design means owning both a plan & a motive - the outward design, in every sense of the word, of Degory Priest was that of something determined to be seen, to be emotionally & physically manifest – an immense growth on the world, visible from space due to its innate power – its aura of spiritual grief, its sheer unarguable base existence – his dragged cape's mauve, black sheen, his favoured tall stovepipe headwear – occasional fedoras & trilbies at a whim – the loping, impossibly unnatural gait seemingly of an equine construct, giraffes stepping over landmines – yet drugged, a film slowed to half speed from a stately gallop – tight neck of folded stone, fluted like carved columns or velour drapes, disappearing beneath a high crew neck or turtle gathering

the very sky itself seemed only there to redefine his presence – shamed into self-loathing by comparison it reddens as he emerges at dusk – out-of-date now, its vagaries of wilful, once-fashionable silks & strafed, tie-dye colours – there lay in his path nothing he feared & in his wake the city's eccentricities dulled & withered to the banal ditches of the forgotten realm – Degory hoisted his vulture-headed cane to his chin & grinned

*

279

All Hallow's eve, Samhain's dirty secret unleashed, the burning times begin – at the soul of the inflammable city, down by the Intrepid Fox's doorway, menace hung like a second-hand suit – some places in the city were forever doomed to be haunted by violence – Degory Priest ducks & dives, a quick peek into the Chinese kitchen, savage eyes return the overly casual glance, perspiring red meat, the swift fall of a thick metal blade – a vehemence, long-buried, now being disinterred by new anger, new colours – necessary violence, tugging the braids of the metropolis, remembered beyond any slight interval of peace, a murderous stone thrown into the bliss of pastoral beauty – throatier rang the local cries, they hang evil, sleepy hooks in the head – packages passed by hands trembling, the mumbled exhortation of the dealer – the junkie doubt – you got some? - or on a pathway once, beneath London Bridge, after standing drunkenly rocking on a pub table with The Troubadour declaiming stanzas & claiming Hart Crane as his inner ghost – waning, due to excesses, Degory fled, donning another poet's super-heroic cape – stealing the blood behind his gaze - & trying out a eulogy for the new morning of the city – Crane's wild lines tugged him onward - yes & how many dawns, pall from the Thames' nudged undulations? - the pigeons subservient waddle does not suffice – in plastic imitation of the mad birds' susurration, crisp-packets, terrified & aloft in the dawn currents of bleary light shall drop down & form an axle to his churning wheels – in colourless risen beams, discarding ashy spheres of turbulence, the OXO building high over the shackled, gravy browning tides like fake old Liberty – Degory thinks of jittery films of immigrants arriving at Ellis Island – wide prows disgorging the caps & bonnets, the suitcases of rags, panoramic flocks with eyes widened toward some hazy, discontinuous image never truly unveiled - but be quick to return again, Dick Whittington, to see the same delusions presaged to these contemporaneous eyes – legends passed down through seasons in a different hell

& he stalked the forbidden docklands, now rainy, now dying or dead – the last barges silently gliding past a glacial drift of tall buildings – through a moonlit gap, tall cranes in the distance swing empty hooks in measured arcs - look up, look upward always, if you want to learn, to know – the tacked, slate rooftops & the story-soaked stones take him back through time - then, with the sweeping curve of a stoned visionary, he abandons his eyes to the kaleidoscopic storm of sudden colour - as ghoulish as fogs wrapping the struggling tugs as they put out to sea – he sees them, crossing blank waves like a page being filled by numerals – spidery notes of old music unfinished, stashed like forgotten documents, away, away

& he spies The Lonely Troubadour searching for him, there, across the river by Embankment station in slow rain - avant-guardian, high-stepping in leather coat & cowboy boots, avoiding the enveloping dusklight as though these prying rays of eventide took too full a measure of him – & two score years hence he shall return, prodigal, indifferent, jaded – but for now he is a perpetual, youthful motion - & yet he suggests at some ancient gesture, some old calling, that is guiding him in his meandering – a lost path exhausted in that expressive, consequential stride - walking now against the sun then twice around the stone - once we were a crowd, a trinity - but now it's just Old Cap'n Rehab & his bubbled, fermented froth of souvenirs draining like phlegm down the chunky, mullioned mug of his memory - cheers, *salud*

& lo! out of some underground station scuttle, cabal or garret cometh the modern attic-dwellers - bedsitlamites - two-dimensional & proud of their blotchy pallor – the priest, of course, ignores them, cursing their souls for to quell their obnoxious disdain for vitality – he takes out his eyeglass & watches The Stealthy Troubadour as way up ahead he plods onward, whispering blistered poetry to his plimsolls & apologising to the voices of history from his parapets – on & off the tube – back on familiar turf, pausing, now, on the godless end of Dean Street – halted there momentarily, paisley shirt distended, as a piercing quip tumbles from the gobsmacked, nulled, daily procession of weighted office-parties humming around café tables – cowed, he scrambles for the sanctum of the Coach & Horses & blends to the relief of shadow at a neon bar in good time for misery hour – the beer tastes of petrol, the newly-opened cigarettes of base metal – the Crane book drops from his pocket as he retrieves his lighter - esteemed & quixotic Mr. Thames! - how thy swirling unions inhale the estuarine flavours still!

*

Hogarthian Universals – he invented his own street, the Troubadour, christening it Crosswalk Gin Lane – where babies burn while mother glugs the liquor of defeat – dirt & syphilitic sores on her legs - a barber has forsaken any duty to the complexity of life & stabs himself with narcotic pinpricks in the crumbling garret of his shop until his hatred lay sorely & fatally punctured like a balloon that once signified a child's joy – his barbering business bust because nobody can find the money in the streams of filth for a haircut or shave - & on the footstep, lower than the female who has let her little one drop to the greasy stones, a cadaverous leaflet-seller takes a break – or is conceivably dead of starvation, we don't know – fate hath thus pulled the plug on his warnings about the evils of intemperance – now a vast & imposing edifice rises like a brutal flower through the mud & rat-shit – it towers above the scurrying peasantry – rests for a century or two - & gathers them in again to nest in the squalor between those varicose legs in the shadow of her barren belly – St. Giles looks down, patron hallow to

282

beggars, blacksmiths, breast cancer, breast feeding, cancer patients, lowly cripples, Edinburgh (Scotland), epilepsy, noctiphobics, forests, hermits, horses, lepers, mental illness, outcasts, poor people, rams, spur makers & sterility - a holy helper - his bowl held out for the wailing condemned man on the way to Tyburn gallows - o hangman, hangman stay your hand awhile - first stage of cruelty, last breath of hope

yes & Tyburn brook & Westbourne river, listen now - how many boatloads of souls depend on your carriage? - & from these manifold underground highways of slick water great ambitious rivers roll - Hyde Park sabbatical - a book of poetry on the lap - hungover, dozy in a gentle sun - life studies, head full of Lepke's fate - it is the year of the rooster but the hour of the skunk - grandfatherly figures, malodorous, damp with history, regret - The Rooster Troubadour's warm hands on the warmer book - open the sleep-glued eyes - & yes he tries to distinguish the snakeskin Serpentine from the dowdy, maternal mist - an airborne perspiration, as if the earth was sweating out the poisons of the morning - children lob pebbles, the circling wavelets fan out from the motherly eye - genesis of birth-pang, nothing returns - the flow resettles & resumes its groggy trundling - awash in her milky displacements, the usual array of polythene bags, crushed cans, a trespassing drunkard's arbitrary wreckage bobbing above submarine calisthenics of supple weed

she emerged, astonished, from the brightening mist, a woman, aged but nimble, if a little over-cautious, of step - hippy, loose-knit shawl, soft red hat of medium brim, tinted rectangular sunglasses, a miasma of diaphanous scarves constantly being rearranged & folded around her neck - in reluctant tow, a small Pekinese dog, a more or less permanent scowl on its screwed-up face - tiny teeth bared, wet growl like a wasp under glass, no god in its grim stare - The Godless Troubadour smiles & she smiles at his smile &

performs a half-curtsey – she is Rosie & how do you do & she adjusts her rosy scarf – the dog's name is Santiago – seeing his raised eyebrow she explains that she is from Chile originally &, well, it's a little nod to the homeland, shall we say – she has no accent, words are enunciated in clipped, middle-class tones, Surrey, Middlesex, slight Slavic tinge perhaps – Sarajevo, she lived there too - the dog collapses on its side & she picks it up, holding it with one hand against her shoulder - she's met Magritte – she had learned to fire a pistol aged five & always dreamed of living in the world of the westerns that she so ardently adored - John Wayne, Gary Cooper, but 'Jimmy' Stewart was her favourite

'...Destry Rides Again...he was so handsome in that...my god...dear Marlene too...ah...'

she believed that the pyramids were built by aliens

'...I have a book...you must read it...'

& yes, she danced for a touring troupe when in her teens in downtown old Sarajevo

'...folk dances, you know, too many twirls, my clogs too tight for my fast moving feet...'

The Troubadour pointed to a rose brooch on her dress & asked if she got it because of her name

'...no, the brooch is named after *me*...' – a half-smile, then – '...there have been many times when I could not afford such things...I've lived in these bad places...during the war...cockroaches, bed-lice...now I can buy scarves & jewellery...things are better now...do you like my scarves?...blue is my favourite colour...it reminds me of the sea...'

& then, suddenly, as if she had just remembered it

'...I don't want to be forgotten...that's all...know a god is waiting...now, how about you?...what is your story?...'

The Troubadour told her of his meagre investigations into the world of song – at first enthusiastically - yet how could he explain these years of idle searching? – the ennui of a parched young life?

he proffered a few anecdotes, a few less ribald tales but it all seemed milky tea to her strong coffee life – she became sadder of a sudden, a wistful look

'...ah a world of song, it is beautiful what you do...we all try not to be inconsequential, I think...'

'...I will write you a song...you won't be forgotten...'

'...& him too...' - she pats the tiny dog's head - '...will he be in this song?...'

'...of course...thank you for your story...it's beautiful...'

Rosie smiled wanly & nodded & performed her odd half-curtsey &, without any reply, drifted away in her sea of scarves already blending back to disappearing in the misty park – just before finally turning her head away she let her smile collapse a little & The Troubadour felt a pang of melancholy the source of which, henceforth, he could never quite fathom, though he thought of it often

she will return to a book-lined room, fragrant with rose-petals, sandalwood & a slightly stale tang of her strange perfume, *L'Air du Temps* or *Hermes' Caleche* – & she will one night, perhaps this one, gracefully ascend to heaven & be greeted by her lost friends - they will huddle around, cheek-kisses, petting the dog, complimenting her hat, scarves, fragrance – & she will rekindle her tales around the fire of an indubitable god & the cool wind will carry the breath of them all out across the churchyard smoke – he is forming the song that she will inhabit as he walks, not 4/4 time, she is out of time like the river, jazz, folky, a hint of Balkan swing to the beat – a stir of shanty-wet cadences that are buffeted by the waves of her concentric fables, spreading shore-ward from the vortex of the tossed stone of memory – & she will breathe through his song, be heard in barrelhouse & folk hall, in a sad busker's dry harmonica wail – he must cling to her moment, fix it true

he had promised

The Troubadour stopped & looked up at the huge white buildings in the bright sun – Bayswater Road, the weight of July had burned away the mist now - he is short of breath, suddenly, a little overwhelmed - the shadows are long, distorting the relief of window frames, curves in the blush of reddening architecture – there was something about the solid stone against the darkening yellowy, blue & pale orange sky – what is it? – crimson emergent once more - he breathes in deeply & holds his breath for five seconds – through the doorway of Rosie's tales he felt like he had been transported to a different city – he closed his eyes for a full minute & then opened them – the clouds had crossed the sun & the light was draping silk stockings across the buildings' pale skin - he folds his notebook at the still-blank page & slips it into the bosom of his jacket – he lets a single clumsy teardrop laugh out loud & it is shy, embarrassed, thankfully unnoticed by the humourless throng of shirt-sleeved exiles that flooded the streets in droves from their airless cubicles

the train station was busy with the lunchtime rush-hour so he hailed a cab, an expense he would later bitterly regret, recent dole-cheque notwithstanding – Soho was beginning to wink at the dimming day when he got out of the back door & paid the driver – he saw himself reflected in the doorway of the murky Cafe Boheme – hair straggly, jeans patched, fake-suede jacket distressed, pocket slightly torn – behind his reflection in the glass a young woman stood motionless – a red hat removed, disappearing into yellow glints from the bottled sunshine of the optics, a brief glance before eyes downcast, fresh, young, tense cheek, twitching slightly – then gone - into the blur of street & cafe interior with nothing but the squabble of traffic & the hurdy-gurdy musical soup of a thirsty mid-day rush revving its engine

no slice of hope through which the vision could peer, no crease in the tumult where a silent sliver could gasp - as the amber light hovered & the pedestrians waited, straining at the leash, for the clang of swung door, the tinkling pour, chunks of ice, plip plash – cars slowing, all the crowd's eyes on the three bulbs - amber fades into red – the surge, the clamour, the glow bright in their heads like a Hallowe'en pumpkin, tearing at the skin of the coming nightmares, a pent-up repression of a thousand other amber lights, when will they turn? – turn they must

the Troubadour slid away through a familiar, welcoming, wooden door & ordered a pint of Guinness & a brandy – the old writer's seat was free & he collapsed into it – the Coach & Horses was empty, the crowds flooded in gay droves past the window – the bright sun gleaming from the shiny ashtray – he took out his notebook & spread it at the folded page – gold had dissolved, the hour was amber, waiting for the spark of green to catch fire

*

& Captain Rehab, dream-ship moored, revisited these havens & harbours too – he would often find his old self scribbling there - oft times, yes, lamenting the same passing changes - from his rock of routine, to which he ever more often clung – behind the sanctity of solitary chess & Guardian crossword, he sat unnoticed at the bar's curve – two worlds of confusion, two lives made one, the puzzle remains - intricate yet harmless problems solved in black & white certitudes

3 down, 10 letters - '...bad voices claim duet's ruined...' – no other clues intersect – a nameless delta of uncertain calling – he sets the chess pieces up at the corner table - & The Captain, never taking his eyes far from his former Troubadour self, shuffles a pawn between two squares & hesitates to play his imaginary opponent's next move – a freeze-frame, poised, pivotal, undecided – The Pubcorner

Wizard was always there or thereabouts of course & slid
into the vacant seat opposite - he observes the Captain's
move – frowns – The Captain smiles & the chequered
board haunts his eyes when he regards the street – the
Pubcorner Wizard stares into the Captain's gaze – black &
white, clattering rush of passers-by - a bleakly disturbing
parquet overlay to the bustle & grind – a grid over a
newsreel – The Pubcorner Wizard is mildly disturbed by
this reflection all day - he will later purchase a dogtooth
jacket in a Camden shop, unaware of its origin, its
wellspring running deep under this forgotten, short-lived
entr'acte – puzzled by the spontaneous purchase, he stows it
in a trunk by his bed - he will not wear it until he is much
older, despite always packing it up carefully whenever he
moved home

*

wrapped in red & blue scarves outside skeevy
Chinatown cafes in winter, reluctant to return to his dying
ship of dreams, Old Captain Rehab *san* – still on shore
leave from the old vessel listlessly at anchor in shallow
waters in The Drifting Troubadour's head - ever present
military long-coat warding off the elemental - as toy oriental
faces, serious, smoking long Cezanne pipes under hats
pointing to a remote, diffuse nirvana, drift by head down -
because all our ancestral pathways could be oriental – the
greasy chip paper of Shen Zhou – cinnamon-flavoured wave
of nausea off the Kanagawa coast – tightly knitted rows of
cafes - & the Pubcorner Wizard takes slow coffee here to
tamp down the morning furies – his heavy head burning
vanities – the cold soup in a blue ceramic bowl – the lemon
water & box of tissues – he observes the Captain morph
backwards & take minstrel form once more

& thus liberated The Oriental Troubadour departs, his head full of meetings with remarkable drunks, he is quickly walking now, deeply immersed in the task of solemn secular pilgrimage, to the garden behind St. Olave's church where unwanted daydreams of Gurdjieff are still permitted – a chance gardener, that could be the old charlatan himself, seeking his new moulds of other creations - & cheerless Ouspensky there too – watering the little square of meagre but overgrown garden – big lumberer, tiny face hung on huge head - retreat, retreat – the weary sunlight of a dying Cathay – land-grab of scorched mental terrain - liquefied mind full of rugs, eastern vessels full of winking solutions & resolutions for paths least trodden & always forgotten, only to be vivified in pictograms & half remembered again in Chinese whispers on the fragrant street of illuminations

he had bought his first copy of a creased, heavily notated Ulysses from a library sale – thin pages turned with licked forefinger & thumb – the stench of a smoulderous bong from outside the nearby dank Turkish café, ominously threatening language from an Ottoman gossip-nest nearby – musical nets of twigs – klezmer worms writhe on the brushed hooks of a soft carpet of low breeze - troubadour bait - but luckily before the chubby old Beezelbub lullabied his furry mumbles to this Grand Son Of Morning – before the pub of eternally changing knowledge was refurbished in faux-shrine, pearly-king hues & as he was a-leavin' to drag his sorry old pilgrim's bare feet through empty deserts for to kiss the mirage - mad old red citizen Jimmy Joyce's useless choices & shenanigans leapt from the library shelf, did a jig of joysprick & bucked on the yaw & roll of his own barnacled day-ship – goodbye fat fake – beware a Jah lie is coming – repent ye later in towns of night - & the big book of everything bade him in again to wake - stole his blooming, day-delirious, leaping, piss-tangy heart & Hellenized it –

fool's gold over mollified bronze – amen – let it be, the ultimate yes, ending at the beginning of the river's run

& was that the old shameless man himself he had seen? – or hellish shade thereof? – one night dark-coated against a Rezillos gig poster in Highbury under the stark, groaning elevated railway? – some days everyone could be anyone & here they come – history is always pushing dead pawns through the checkerboard streets – so, for sake of the story, there goes everyman Jim, quietly thrilled & in Bloom, a stately frumpwizard descending spiralling stairs to a hidden opioid bazaar with blue-grey moustache & wires crossed – Martello cylinders of the mordant buildings towering above his jitterbug mind - impassive – blocks of Picabian machine paint shifting in grinding masses – chocolate browns undulate in-between the grand glass of antiquity - churned fats, bulbs of buttery arms float in taut enamel bathtubs – laying cloak-and-dagger clues across a faded map of deep treasure holes – all the names changed, every country dragged back to its source in search of the unlikely navel, the womb words of forbidden fruit - & all his old words are lost now – all those wearisome old linguistic atoms blasted apart by a supernova of realism - at the centre of which the old master's flabby grin shines unknowing – shine of charlatan grinning – glaze of corner-torn clandestine photography burnt at the frame – Christmas card Santa – that dove by his side is more cruel to this poor Lonely Old Troubadour's sight now than the scholar's blackboard – that white whirl of junk numbers in black space – get in the bin with Jehovah & his trailing cubs & runts! – let this minstrel raise a glass to hell above in the yellow shards of World's End barlight – the manager echoing Ouspensky again in a swollen Modiglianian pointy-face of studied frowziness – bugger them all to Hades & back with their new universal models & intricate third-ear melodies – let them search for their own music at their own river's end – let their prosaic hearts lend credence to the bilious guts of song – they can bluster whilst this dawning troubadour downs bright beer & soaks his dark thoughts – the Pubcorner Wizard smokes his pipe & watches approvingly as, somewhat unsteadily at first, this emboldened Ulysses flourishes a soft hat on exeunt & staggers a few hundred yards down the knife-sharp street – gesticulating wild as he descends the escalator – the rubber gripping tight to his sticky palms - & boards the subterranean train - & as he drifted in & out of sleep, he thought of another frantic time, recent in memory, when The Priest had, from his wobbly pulpit, announced to a bored throng of alkies & homeless snorers

"...I could just teach the old ways by rote – blithely mutter the pith of psalms, the shaking litany of prayer cycles, the small talk of a polite god – I could prove once & for all that it's all bunk – all mere phatic communion, the grooming rituals of apes...my enemies torment me with their plots! - a supposed friend, lost to unreason now, plans a great book about our dwindling Kapital city – he has rechristened it, unleashed a metropolis of puppets & ghouls – Guignol – that's what he plans to be calling this dubious manuscript – however it rocks & rolls it is no brother to my brave town, my sweet old stormy sea of Roman ruins – let him blunder through his misnomer alleys & invent whomsoever he might – a curse be upon your head & may fire be set free in your spent pockets...it'll ne'er see the light of publication in my span..."

yes & earlier, he let this slide between his last sleepy blink, whilst deep in a dismayed study, from the pub's urine-doused corner, under the fitfully-allowed gleam from a bald streetlight of broken glass, The Unremarkable Lonely Troubadour had watched the last morsel of that wise old Homburg dip like a light-brown sun below the line of pavement & vanish to the underground of night-townsfolk - & he fell finally to unconsciousness convinced that he had witnessed the master word-tickler in his fading glory, he trod homeward, swords reversed, happy - albeit wracked with the threats of the vile priest's tangled reasoning, still cascading through his brothy young head like swilled Goulash

& yea! - praise be! - a different creature he is, to be sure, on arrival at Camden's fair town again the next sun-bright morning - settling his mind in meditative silence at the ticket machine - ineluctably the police poster floods into his wide eyes - it cautions him thusly - beware of pickpocket - & he is ready - like an incoming conductor of a nervously attendant orchestra, he taps his baton cane thrice on the guard's sentry box, pays his pound of flesh & walks out to the ghastly crowd, a limitless fraternity of bad authors, spilling like sewage on to the Chalk Farm Road - his mind set fair to contemplation, though, he remains impervious to provocation, a blueprint, fresh as a star - zen-flat, like linen

*

the secret, remain still, write as you think, think as you see, see how you feel

a drunk in a doorway clings on to the mother bottle, the gin teat - in drowned sleep, for only there is he blessed - *pietas* - therein his supernatural paint-box touches with deft colours the mute pleadings of his fantasies - he mumbles in reverence to an underground language that flows in the merciful wash of relief - see how the wiry words weave their dances? - all month he walked to & fro, fro & to - was downcast, unlovable - milkman be so kind as not to chirrup your banal airs & jigs if you should pass by this threshold slumberer - just put the milk beside him & slip away, a billion other brighter doorsteps are thirsty - among the syringe & bloodied tissues of a thousand shop doorways lay the real muses of bards - in repose, at peace, bound soon for eternity in their stained grey quilts yes & on the sick old Camden crawl The Troubadour would slowly encounter the cast of minor characters in his passionless play – writing about them, talking with them, drinking from their appalling flasks & unlabelled bottles, hoping that the regular sharing of their myriad fire-waters would bring their stories to life for him – see through their silent façade, demolish the stage-set & burn the unrealistic scenery that the world's words had built shakily around them – he believed that the more he made himself a willing co-conspirator in this unreal universe the more then these fake actors would be impelled to belch out a confession, sermon or a soliloquy to rouse their somnolent congregation

& they were all preachers really - po-faced at pulpits just like old Degory Priest – fine pub orator, indubitably, none better – yes, the wild words that his sleep imagined would take flight on his sixty-proof breath by day - perhaps he could sing the new song of a rechristened capital? – be a driver at the wheel of a new *savant-guard*, a Situationist priest, a tentative spirit-guide to a lost congregation of downcast geniuses, all who would be compelled to tell their stories - or leave it to chance, for some younger street-wise warrior to type the closing chapter as we, the passengers, struggle to think of the first – the priest was too vain to let his own glory be dissipated – he requires his downtrodden masses merely to hear him – but their stories are carried by rivers, rivers of whisky, gin, brandy, rum – rivers of piss & vinegar, the lost, unchartered rivers of the capital's buried past, Fillibrook, Fleet, Tyburn Brook, Old Counter's Creek

& yes, already their tale is flowing, out of the bright window, across the dusted, sun-bleached saloons & nothing god could conceive will e'er surpass it – a tale of redemption through the mystic word for which they all waited - on, eternally on, dark energy drifting through the heads of even old Degory in his diocese of neglected regions – carried upon a tide that tickled the bootsoles of the cycle of humanity that groaned through the city streets, running parallel with the tube trains into which they crammed their palsied meat – these sleepers, rough men & women for certain, but with that coarseness comes an edge that the nervous populace could never blunt with routine

& what of Degory? - all four walls & none at all, so resided his holy space – no dog-collar tying him to the sacrilegious temples of the modern world – everyman was his parishioner, the specks & motes making up that unwitting mass, those freethinking sailors on shore-leave from the oceans of monotony

The Troubadour pondered his acquaintance with the unholy man as he strolled & in his wistful way he found himself in the wrong street, lost, but pleasantly so – he, without pause, strolled on regardless until the environs became familiar again – he saw the 100 Club sign & knew where he had to go – his own bar, a secret haven that only the true faithless inhabited, he set off immediately with renewed zest

*

& so in the ornate shambles of Bradley's he sat, the dim-lit basement bar just off Tottenham Court Road, a dirty, brown Tuesday worries the streets through wired-up glass, frosted, above his head - he sniffs at the flawless bowl of Spanish brandy & sips as, after a medley of vague ballads & Mariachi, Dion's voice hits the air & vaults the ocean of his dolorous mood with melancholy at its heart - wafting over the rolling breakers of contemplation - eddied by angels in sharp silvery suits & snapping fingers still grimy-nailed from the Bronx - a lover who turned wanderer - forever seeking his rubies & roses, as that distant city's monochrome turned to flowers behind him unseen – flick-knife doo-wop, he slicks back his oily flop of hair & just gazes, dark-eyed, unaware, watches the new girl forever giving him the run-around at the horizon's vanishing point

    & nothing really matters right now but the brandy swilling Proust in his brain & Dion, magnificent, the hep, hep, hum-de-heddy heady nonsense chopping like a rotor in the wake of his voice – The Troubadour glowing, drinking it in, to add to the million other voices that will be unleashed when the boat finally sails & he passes through the gates or swims to the surface & expunges a sodden cry – a billion more lusty subterranean words - unheard since the first sad coin was dropped in a beery jukebox – for, especially in the hours before closing, this music becomes a force, owning the gravity of a Latin prayer – the barman is beatific, the jukebox is an altarpiece & the red bullfighting posters slowly all begin to come to life

*

    morning touched Degory Priest lightly on the forehead & he began, not yet awake, to mumble deep in his bedclothes – in comfortable disarray from the night's turmoil – the first language of the new-born day, steady stream of libretti that offered little by way of elucidation or instruction - serving more as a mantra, a soothing calmative, to offset the fearful moment his eyes jerked into life & greeted the fullness of morning in its true horrific colours – then he will sing, his voice will imperceptibly seep across the waking town, into kitchens & bedrooms that stealthily act out the leaden dramas of this breakfast hour - & they will barely know who sings these words to them as they sleep or crawl to their work – ah, but they will hear – yes & past the half-drawn blinds and triple-padlocked urban caves - past the twitchy net-curtains & the military hedgerows, past these immaculate emblems of their precision & carefulness, they stalk their guilty paths, thieves faking alibis as they leave prints along the felony trail – a dog may bark at nothing but silence in the mews & crescents - or a yawning cat, warmed in smudged sun-patches, will lick its perfect paw – the passing priest will startle & provoke – eyeing the wary cat, flick a cigarette butt & watch his head snap to the sparks flying upward – yes & that is how the priest wished his sermons to be absorbed – tiny detonations in moments of calm - eyes closed & palms downward on knees – hint of supplication – touch of reverence, then the struck, gasping flame

in his golden days he was Ahab at the pulpit – he would ride motorbikes into the midst of wedding services – crash the most dangerous parties – Red Jimmy recalled being at a warehouse dub party somewhere down on the docks & suddenly - rum-crazed & pious as Gabriel - Degory Priest swings through the window like a leather-clad Tarzan – black beanie for a halo & shattering glass his herald – he had a nose for debauched gatherings, always sensed celebration & misrule – his antennae twitched at every dance-step, backbeat - yet his coming was always unforeseen - for god, he preached, is the subliminal – the cry in the street – the lost lamb's wail - the unheard biker's scream

& yes Degory, Degory 'tis of thee I speak ye auld pig-priest - King Of The London Rain – never young & forever slung over hungover barstools – your haunted folkmares night by night, courtesy of stranger alcohols, purer than nails of holy thought driven in – he has stolen all that he has ever written & slyly disguised it in the cloak of psychedelics & ethanol– he breathes deep the cheap cigar's pungent stench, he is fully breakfasted now & in frock-coat & black skinny jeans – the day is grinding time to powder in the driven streets – weary shopkeepers creak open their metal shutters & pull up the blinds to reveal the day's bargains – chuntering snakes of children, uniformed & downcast, traipse the lollipop path to history, maths, geography, sciences & free milk & Mars bars melting in the dinner-hall heat – 'twas innocence of a kind, yet their plump heads too, in time, will feel the keener edges of the priest's foolish ramblings probing deeper

out in the church garden, warming to the days projected oddities, despite the head-pain & early hour, the delicate priest is perched on a stepladder of questionable security – he hammers a wooden sign to his house of worship

DEGORY PRIEST
LAY PREACHING
PSYCHOGEOGRAPHY
&
HYPNOGOGIC SUGGESTION
NEGOTIABLE RATES
BEGINNERS WELCOMED

he chants to the rhythm of each hammer blow in a high sing-song voice akin to that of dolls in cheap horror films

'... *Tit-u-lus Cru-cis* – *Tit-u-lus Cru-cis...*'

catholic residents eye him angrily from sleepy windows across the street

'...*Sen-a-tus Pop-u-lus Que Ro-ma-nus...*'

he pauses hammering to observe, with disdain, a small dog pissing nonchalantly up his failed olive tree

- "...rain over us...outside the dogs and sorcerers..."

he spits viciously at the dog which remains unmoved in its nirvana of uresis

"...begone, ye whore's cunt..."

a bent nail is hurled, the beast slinks to the gate & stares back at Degory Priest with a look of haughty, German Shepherdess, disdain - *die welt als das urteil anderer*

this is a day to spend below ground, he decides, a day only the glint of moonshine can redeem the journey to Bradley's subterranean bar takes the brooding unholy man past Centre Point & its salubrious ecosystem of down & out, needle-pricked, denizens, trapped creatures, ejected from the shock of life by some random social spasm, people of low esteem & yet often high minds that merely have been dragged down by undercurrents of an irrepressible skulduggery, an almost, at times, unnatural, mystical force – it is as if life has given them a reminding nudge to let them know that under the fake-tan, chrome & plastic surfaces a festering skin pustulates, a disease that no balm can assuage – they are residue of a social experiment & unthinking gentrification – ghosts of the very lepers that once inhabited this parish of ramshackle, tenement hives – their revenant ancestry crept from the same doorway of St. Giles In The Fields church, the old saint himself now their gloomy nominal patron – & it is here that his spiritual descendents still congregate - sunken eyes deep in scaly, wind-scrubbed faces, they mope the dead space under the brutal folly, itself abandoned to a faded expectation of pleasure & profit – it stands in bleak memorial, the haven to all that is phantom in the fractured city – its bedlamites huddle & shuffle in chill climate, they are faded flags of a lost island, bled white, bags of skin crawling to the suck of syringe, crushed in the illicit obscenity of their ruined nooks, spilling the milk, cracking mirrors for better luck – discarded mutant progeny, unused meat born of a thousand butchers, watchmakers, booksellers, belt-makers – rough traders in the sputum-strafed tubercular dust – pirates of doubt, doomed to wander the building-sites & edgelands between Bloomsbury & Soho's seedy vaults – the priest hurries by, one sneaky eye on their travails & the other on the cellar of boozy refuge that waits for his soul up ahead

The Leprous Troubadour is seen lounging by the steps that lead precipitously down to the dark bar, casually smoking & reading the liner-notes to a clutch of LPs recently harvested from Rocks Off record shop, esteemed purveyor of audio delights, sonic serendipity & olden, waxy ephemera

"...how goes it, old bean? - anything worth the trouble of listening?...I could do with some scuttlebutt - if gossip was beer I'd die of fecking thirst..."

"...hi Deg, old blues stuff mainly - Son House, Lightnin' Hopkins...got the new Wire one...Red Jimmy says it's shite though..."

they exchanged several similar pleasantries & opinions as they descended the chestnut-hued stairwell & entered the vivid, Christmas-bright bar that already smelled reassuringly of sweet liquors & unemptied ash-trays - the jukebox, softly chugging, whirring & buzzing in the darkling nook with no expectation of monetary reward, played an eternal mix of singles eclectically gleaned by the proprietor from market stalls or donated from the dubious collections of the clientele - yet despite the wildly diverse sources, the music strangely seemed to reflect the bar's innate ambiguity of mood - no note seemed out of kilter in the palace of its timeless nature - Herp Albert drifted his brassy parps of Tijuana as the first Tequila was ordered following two hefty jars of Tartan Ale - muted conversations loosening their already tenuous grip on accuracy & recall - Runaround Sue duly crackled into life - O melancholy Dion, how you feed these lamentations with bites of a bigger apple - it is listened to by the priest in awed silent reverie

the barman, a sweating grin of hirsute, Mediterranean ham, always greets the beginning strum of Robin Sarstedt's guitar with a nod of approval & a mumbled 'my favourite' - & where did ye go to my lovely sinners? - did you lose the will to pleasure like these dwellers of the hidden halls of cheap cigar smoke & thick, oily chasers? - & yes the three-strung Spanish guitar on the wall does its best to resonate with every bass line - the bullfighter of heroic pose winks at

the occasional Mariachi horn – & Degory Priest is floating to
the moon on the wings of wormy Mezcal– *con gusano* – he
is shedding the cocoon of any religious piety & the flap of
Mariposa night butterflies will alter the future if not broken
on the wheel of becoming – up ahead, destiny's converging
road, a ribbon of human dust scattered & shadowed under
darkest mountain ridges against a greeny-orange sky – the
jukebox is unforgiving, unstoppable, unrepentant - Minnie
mooches, Sonny's death letter officers croak & do not fear
the reaper – even The Crapulous Lunchtime Troubadour is
fizzing with politic & fixing for a quarrel – he engages with a
fat leech in a brown, ill-advised suit at the bar &, despite an
initial threat of serious dispute, it takes but four more grainy
ales to see them in a hugging détente – Billy Fury furious no
more, his jealousy waning halfway to a paradise regained too
early - & the fat man buys a round of evil rum that should
never shake quaking hands with no Mexican Tequila fire –
encouraged, he sits at their table & tells his damp tale of lost
marriage & a business off the Caledonian Road that went up
in flames for some bent insurance scam – he sells used cars
now, his soul a shell with no pearl, he smokes four of the
Priest's cigarettes & leaves on unsteady, bunioned feet to
seedily wait around somewhere to die – more Mexican
balladry soon soothes the disturbed air & the barman grins
another meaningless grin as the trumpets herald a creeping
dusk – *Volver, Volver,* the spicy croon of a desert throat –
Ranchera lilt – bleached sun deathly & never setting, until
the belch of Popocatepetl signals the last breath of the
Consul – his path snake-crossed, the other side of Eden –
The Lapsed Priest snorts at a joke he has told himself –
through a straw bubbling his beer like a childish milkshake –
snort of a bull's last throes, reddened arrows protruding like
sunken masts from his arched spine, he has the fatalistic
slouch of a doomed man waiting to be escorted by a clutch

of mysterious *hombres* to a single gunshot in volcanic rain –
a horse flees, silence, curtain

*

& yes The Recording Angel Troubadour clicks record
on the Philips tape machine in his bag & a C90 spools
slowly on low batteries & the microphone is muffled by the
denim dark – he wonders why he feels this urge to capture
wasted hours, a vain hope to reset the dying age & listen
back to their wan ruminations in the concrete validities of
morning, hoping to find a chance gem or two within – it was
an occasional fetish that, due to poor quality results, he
abandoned in favour of the good old reliable red notebook
scrawl – yet he often mused that, somewhere out in the sea
of time, his stained cassettes, labelled with only dates &
locations, would turn up in bargain-baskets of the charity
shops & in racks of mixtapes on scaffold-pole stalls, from
Bermondsey to Archway, a glorious hidden drunken history
to mystify all curious purchasers – a pure moment of frozen
revelry, ghost voices, field recordings, a lost Bohemian fart
that lingers still in the nostrils of all the future migrants &
exiled youth
    the bar door swings, another sad passenger clambers
aboard – they slip in unseen as if slithering from a mirror –
fresh from the end of a session in a nearby sunken hellhole
– the 100 Club or some such den of fools – the new stranger
drinks down two vodka doubles neat, puts on an army coat
he was carrying over his arm, wipes condensation from his
horn-rimmed glasses, bent, with sellotape covering one eye,
then, before the last gulp, replaces scarf & trilby hat – the
scene is film-noir directed - cut to close up of him pouring
pills from a bottle into a small cloth bag - return to mirror
shot of his wary expression - he adjusts hat, stands, puts the
bag in inside pocket & exits the door, his broad back still

reflected in the bar mirror – the row of upside-down bottles float like defeated angels around his departing frame – he is off to a bigger sleep but this old jukebox never sleeps – fed, unnecessarily, by constant coins from a couple of un-noticed Pubcorner Wizards' holy, holey pockets – its speaker offering up glam wizards of its own – incidents in ballparks & can you see his baby jiving as if the glamorous rock was still rolling down the seventies hill – mouthing the Dada words & the bed gets in his hair & give him back his dues, give him back his natural fucking comb – out where thought ends & lyric begins – junction of discovery & mope

& yes everyone coming down the street that you meet will all, in time, gravitate downward to these crepuscular, shabby bars with no trace of redemptive sunlight worrying them – outside, an abstract, cracked, distracted night has fallen, head over arse, over its untied shoelaces - but that is outside, always outside – if you don't believe the time then look at the stopped clock on the wall by the cigarette-burnt sombrero – a Sweep puppet is talking to a gothy-punk girl smoking dark roll-ups over a jealously cornered absinthe - close up of puppet – & the sad puppet puts an arm across its midriff & bows

& the town is full of mad Jacks, sons of Wolfman & Ironfoot – monsters of the London fog, their brown-bottled reciting of curses sweating through the demolished stone – gypsy vernacular, the syllables of malcontents – nebulous, vindictive & sated by the promise of a half-forgotten revenge – their dracular cackling ricochets the cat-gut burr behind blind windows of Denmark Street & find echo in the sad-lipped clowns back-flipping across the paving stones of Covent Garden – busker-musky & flat cap hungry for that held breath, renegade tinkle of silver – rookeries of the paddy poor & hovels of the faux-spiv millionaires who will pay you next Tuesday, see you next Tuesday & they forever never show & owe you a couple of unredeemable turncoat pints – desperation seeks a safe place to spill beer & lose the mind for an hour & basement bars fulfil that noble role – places wherein only arson & bestiality will get you banned – even then admission will be granted on your returning the following lunchtime – catch an eavesdropped whisper of old Jimmy Tomorrow, visiting angel, to refresh the belief in Harry Hope's clemency & to give the same old legends, the blarneying apologetics to thine host, their reprieve & get them served once more

The Stumblebum Troubadour & The Priest Of Night are leaving as the first bell clangs behind them – Sloop John B's weary chorus sidles by & as they stagger up the lighthouse stairs its expiring melody washes with them into the cold night air & a pellucid vision from recent history wafts through them –sick memories gone, more to come – torn photographs cast on a sea of time – the ghost speaks to The Troubadour only, yet the priest feels its chill - it was back at a party, top floor of Brooke House, the new-town spread out in front of him & Boo was gathering coins for a taxi - the early dawning light reaching over the rooftops' geometric blanks like boxes awaiting answers – on high, coming down, Sunday, call up The Captain ashore, no reply – the rooftops wet & softly burnished, valueless Scrabble tiles with nothing to say – call a cab, call a bloody cab - the soft asthmatic burr of a dialled telephone rolling back to zero

& the old dream sloop creaks through the ruins of waves past the crow-stone – they feel the lift as the surge passes below the hull – feel the animus of drowned regret in the bulge of ebb-tide – the taxi arrives, honks a horn - feel so broke up, I wanna go home

*

electronic funk, hi-hat like a mouse behind a skirting board, busy, snapping at a fat red rose of bass blossoming from an earthy wound

the car window gaping in astonishment at the maddened sound it releases – it has stopped reluctantly at the lights to offer this to the world – as if the urban emptiness needed a hymn, as if this repetitious thud & prickle was a prelude to a spoken wisdom

but no words came, just music

& he watched, amused, as the pedestrians at the crossing absent-mindedly tapped their nervous feet, slave to an internal reasoning, while at the same time frowning at the invasive rhythms, the nag of beat

they had not requested this song & it somehow angered them - perhaps there had previously been a quality to their silence, a masking serenity, but that had now been lost

the car pulls away at the first hint of green from amber, engine sputtering, raging – the calm settles again like a blanket drawn over a drowsy baby – the birds tentatively resume their meaningless choruses – they seem outdated, trying too hard, whirls of antique madrigals played too fast, terrified by the coming age of change

The Troubadour, by way of respite & contemplation, sits himself down with crossword & pint in the Hawley Arms' public house garden, a few benches, flower-baskets, broken step-ladder – in his stained notebook he scribbles rhymes for an unwanted song – a young lad, moon-face, spotty, NYC cap, discoloured T-shirt & stonewashed jeans – sits down at the opposite bench with a boom-box into which he places a cassette – he thumbs the play button & the same heavy funk music explodes, horn-drenched, raunchy, instrumental, punctured only by guttural chants – he stares at The Curious Troubadour & in a vaguely threatening manner enquires

"...is my music disturbing you, mate?..."

The Troubadour, undisturbable, replied, smilingly
"...not at all...it helps actually...turn it up if you want..."
the rain held off until mid-afternoon despite the radio's
threat – as soon as it began it abated, leaving only a thin, but
refreshing, sheen on the parched stones – The Troubadour,
fuelled by the exchange of musical views & the good ale of
his favourite pub, finished the last two answers of the
crossword, drained his glass, stubbed out his cigarette &
stepped out of the doorway between two Irishmen
drunkenly discussing the form over The Racing Post – green
breath & blarney-stoned – fortunate sons of the old soil –
counting their winnings before the race is won – the barman
waved at him as he doffed his hat on leaving
     he got the tube down to Leicester Square – he needed a
hard-nosed, polyglot setting, a back-burner pot of hard-core,
bubbling humanity on which to broil the tough mutton of
his thoughts – the train was heavy with polo-minted
languages & workday, office sweat – finally emerging from
the subway he saw, hesitantly wobbling astride a grey bicycle,
an old, Whitman-bearded Jew - jet-black, the spirals of
dense hair curling from under his Homburg's brim – his
orthodox, full, Guinness bulk, dragging dank shadows
beneath trailing train of his frock-coat - round, thin
spectacles, tortoise-shell frame, his determined stare straight
ahead – wanderer, satellite - forever circling his diminishing
home – The Troubadour felt uneasy watching him, he
should avert his eyes maybe – onward the vision cycled, a
storm-cloud drifting through the pastels of a tourist
landscape – thoughts of mortality, friends no longer with us
– an impression of sadnesses deepening until we are no
longer in touch with them – the weight accrued from ailing,
faithful pets, the famished earth's gasp, old rain
     The Gentile Troubadour gently bit into his crisp-crusted
cheese baguette – the sprinkling of diced onion stung his
nostrils – what was her name? - old leather book of wisdom

– cracked binding clinging to the holiness – candle-lit words on greaseproof leaves, warm as a bath of gumbo, lumpen, lugubrious – eyes led through the viscous text from first word to last, the path of decay – long merciless road – the Jew cycles past again in the opposite direction – blue-cheese legs pumping the pedals in a tight bandage of inelastic socks – travel as fast as the gout allows – one-way ticket once the rot sets in – no bus or donkey ride – every climbed mountain crumbling to a landslide behind him – he is an embodied threat of holy downpour - a swish of bat - spook-walker, blown like a glossy, brooding sleuth through the drizzly streets of Troubadour Soho

*

later, sorrowfully drunk, & the night sky is a chewed blackjack spat out by the dirty sun – a loaded gun beneath its cape – pistol shot of dawn concealed – The Glum Troubadour makes a gun of his forefinger & thumb & aimed at the skulking moon – pew, pew, pyoor – you're dead

but it was never alive – reflecting the stolen light, drained of all the sun's angry heat – in The Troubadour's mumbling gut a swim of bitter ale curdles

& his tape has unspooled three times & he's scared to press record anymore, there is nowhere to go & everything is stuck fast in vague promises of tomorrow – take it out on the past, burn the old news into the printed page – take it out on a windscreen wiper of a delivery van, bend it back – take it out by swigging from the defiant hipflask that gives the finger to a closing pub door – take it out on the Dumb Blameless Moon – fastest rum in the west - pew, pew, pyoor

& the constant urge to take flight, choose any random path, it billows in his sail & drags him leeward – the glance askew at a foreign voice – the serendipity of a found church

& the slow contemplation of its oppressive past – all events, all things adding their weight to that tug of bad dreams that are leading his flimsy hopes & wishes astray

*

Lonely Troubadour has returned to his cave & stares at a badly drawn impression of his face some vicious bastard has scrawled across a cracked mirror - spilled & crushed disasters of the recent lost evening abound - broken blood vessels chase elusive baubles & blurred phantoms beyond the sight – Lonely Troubadour's voice - hollowed in jaded monotone - issues from a tea-stained Philips tape recorder at the side of his bed resting on two telephone directories that rest in turn on a pine cabinet with no door

"...*quiet in here...saloon bar always better...same faces, it's like going to church for these lot...world of wonder, for me anyway...can't seem to get drunk enough tonight, beer ain't working...anyway I'll read it...it's raining so I came inside...written outside just now...(cough...sound of cigarette lighter)*

> *we were bound together*
> *while you were here*
> *- my last night -*
> *our last...*

it don't sound much when read out but I like it – get it in somewhere - it's for Boo I think but it's kind of an all-purpose sad valedictory really...this fucking tape is gonna unspool again I think...hang on...don't know if it's going to be a song or poem yet...for some reason it doesn't need any more to it, dunno...going to buy some fags...finally run out

*of those cigars that Deg gave me...end of me old cigar, end
of me old cigar...hurrah..."*

    he singsongs the last vaudeville phrase like a child – then
a deep silence ensues, then the tape is clicked to life again, a
few indistinguishable words against a raucous backdrop of
dub reggae, then click to a breathy silence broken eventually
by a light snoring like the careful farts of a bilious worm

    he could not recall what arcane purpose had initiated
the practice of constantly recording his drunken utterances
before retiring to bed, it was a kind of vainglorious tally, he
supposed, a nudge to memory

    this nocturnal recording habit occasionally irritated him
but more frequently the replayed litany of slurred speech –
sometimes not his own – a recording angelus that cheered &
admonished him in equal measure, certainly enough to
justify the effort of lugging the device from pub to pub

    let it be thy conscience's map – a pilgrim's journal – a
season in hell – his personal Voynich text – his Maldororian
song – insipid substitute for a confessional

    Lonely Troubadour yawned, then, having realised the
cassette was not going to reveal any more secrets of his
wanderings, snapped the off button & surveyed the visible
world, home – not home – the room had a dismal prospect
– it was no comfort that it was his unholy creation – in wan
rays sad old jetsam lay strewn – the sliver of escaped sunlight
breaks the monotony of a beige carpet - a bent book of
poems by Mayakovsky - crushed rainclouds of trousers on a
grey-white sky-rug – a fetid pizza box & thin, gnawed crust –
& outside, the nothingness is struggling to become light &
through his window early lamps still float dismally above the
sallow street - the topmost drawer of the oak tallboy is open
revealing a guitar-playing snoopy figure and two marbles,
one chipped – here I was, far away – he thinks - he sneezes -
black specks in the green gelid wavelet - god as ye flit here
and fairy there could ye ever see your way to smear a dreg of

dawn across the pane? - dimly he recalls a German woman from the recesses of the night before - is that why these ugly phrases keep drifting to the surface like drowned kittens? what terrible things did he say to the night? - did he talk to her of sorrow & piteous penury? O sainted John Of God have mercy on all the homeward utterances of pissheads!! - his saddened mind throttled the recollection - his yellowing fingers scrape the curtain, heavy, across the squeaky rail, revealing bitter light - that threatening glimmer that hints of an unwelcome dawn - unstubbed cigar

The Ghosted Troubadour allows the slow reminiscence to blossom - the act of sober remembrance is a delicate, painful process not unlike stepping barefoot through broken glass - he is, at once, simultaneously, in the future & past - his now, his presence, is dissolved - everything he touches can never be real, each thought is an omen or tainted by an ancient curse

flowers on the sill, he meant to buy a vase, the little things, the petty forgotten chores, these are the cancers that slowly eat at the bones of memory

the long walks homeward - the bark of echoing violence in foul-smelling tube stations - a brief hiatus, sounds of a party overspilling from a tenement yard - they offer swigs of whisky from sour bottles - Degory Priest throwing his arms wide & giving the Angelus - cheers & jeers - along the street a little way a busker busking spiky songs by the arched railing - these images floating downward in his clearing head - down through space but not time - & his last-night self falls through space but not time to that almost forgotten musical street

"...twelve bars & he's been drunk in all of them...a myth to bring it on home...the guzzly, galloping twelve holy bars of the blues..."

who is speaking? - best left unheard - unknown - his maddened liver pleading - wherefore do the wicked live? -

who speaks as the ur-voice of all half-remembered parties? - Job was it? - or just another voice saddened by the fickle moods of alcohol? - moth voices, teasing the bitter truth, close to the flame but no cigar

far off a cow flops dung in a field of rich grass soft speckled with daisies - a mouse-poor poet aches beyond the furze - a long way from John Clare to here - beyond the axe & rock of ages - his phantom remnant appears to the Troubadour behind closed eyes - pushing a heavy soul uphill - can a city ever be blessed? - sanctified by ancient words & song? - The Bloviating Priest, a psychotic pastor, alienates his flock with crazed shrieks & imprecations - gothic night descends - let the night terrify as in times long lapsed - nobody is scared of the dark anymore!

until dawn, the indulgent pacifier, returns - & outside in the street there is yet more memory to glean in yielding light, distanced by indifference, uninhabited - then, from nothing, a rabid milkman chews a whistled fragment of tired song - Love growing where his Rosemary is going - way outside the dreams of generations - his ambitions, his diminished hopes, are mauled - buzzed by the tics of bad memory - yoghurt, orange juice, silver & gold top, eggs - he is saying nothing about the world yet says it all & somewhere, everywhere, out there a poet writes under the looming weight of a disused factory - in eternal nowhere that same poet wanders the asylum fields from Essex to Northampton - guileless, a leaf blown along the Great North Road - as lonely as a summer thundercloud - cheerless tempest in the folds of his brain - he assumes the prodigal stance & sings of his coming deterioration - yes & nowhere, somewhere, everywhere the dogs bark like spectral punctuation - fridges & spin-dryers rot on the lawns - white goods of the bawdy dispossessed - the sober furies chase an Irishman down the heartless Camden High Street veering right to crash into the Hawley Arms public house -

& fads like Frisbees are hurled at leaping children - Rubik's cubes are furiously resolved – The Troubadour with his egg on toast, milky tea & orange juice turns the TV set on at the wall & on the lathering screen Mount St. Helens erupts, barely drawing a bored glance – yes & finally outside a pop star signs an autograph gladly, self-satisfied – the riches substantiated – his Holden Caulfield ramblings a blasphemous dilution of the original screed – raise high the roof-beam Old Salinger – they will hunt you down & test your worth – they gather like a posse, they seek the X that marks the spot – just one photo, just one line from the old hermits & we take it all in as manna – Salinger, found, but Paradise slipping, reporters accost him at his constitutional & in the end who it is becomes immaterial - an old man raging at a lens by a car – this occurs all in one blink of time – memory is a forgetful infant - or a pack of wild beasts & nobody remembers the dark as the builders stack the new bricks over sacred cemetery bones & continue to swing the demolition balls into the face of history

on the tape the silence is broken & The Late-Night Lonely Troubadour sneezes twice – chow! cha! bleeee-hu! - &, recovering, intones

"...all my dreams have come true & I don't like them anymore..."

& yea he turns the cassette tape over in the machine – fresh voids of hissy time therein to bleat – & a holy stone elsewhere rumbles back downhill & dusts the marbled relics of another poor god – he regards the pale window - raining a bit – he puts a Fall album back in its sleeve, wonders if Degory got home alright & turns to check his old leather coat still hangs on the iron hallway hook, dimly lit by fanlight

*

311

stepping sideways, deep in the morning, Degory pays his respects, for what they are worth, on a street, back by the seaside for a day, where the cumbersome, holy bulk of St. Erkenwald's is to be demolished - may it worry heaven - that huge warehouse of worship - in whose unyielding & vaulted regions of incense & eschatology all manner of kindly patchouli ghosts once scampered the dusted spaces, chanted in the booming hallways &, now freed, hover astonished in a frozen rapture

it is as if one day the very godhead had spoken to our lonesome traveller priest & told him that his yesteryears are but a collection of beautiful ruins & this sacred debris, for eternity, will be your church - the phantom machinery of heaven is always churning - the priest had chosen his derelict temple in London with care - he knew the power of sanctified ground, black massed cogs hauling wishes up to heaven - warehouses of the blind, tomb-thick with ash & marrow, ringing to the song of sulphurous priests' calumnies - once upon all time, pews shook with Christly oaths &, high above the shimmering zeros of angelic mouths, steeple bats applauded the dolorous, cyclic motifs of bells - there had been fire in the echo of sermons - or at least a sense of fire

The Priest Of Fire tried, in vain, to be awed beneath the cumulative embrace of the partly vanished west wall - he looked at the chipped gargoyles - the holy abstractions - the glazed cherubs swollen with the gas of mercy - no fire - look now at the bell-tower, that escape hatch, that valve to the celestial sea of music - crested white with seagull shit - as if crowned with all the conceded skin of a dropping moon

he felt nothing but a cosmic absence - paling ashes - reminders of fire - for it is fire alone that spits guilt in your drowsy ear & unleashes the heat of morning sun upon your sugared trances

312

& he longed for that unquenchable, steely heat of anger & light that he had first felt back in his formative years of wandering – when he had prayed for floods, a rain of poems, rinsing the homeward pilgrims clear of doubt – he took one last look at the old building, it could be a shopping mall, a grain silo, a brothel, & slowly headed through the godless streets to the train station

& from the haughty deck of the ship, years hence, Captain Rehab scowled back through time at this memory – lost at sea, a still point in the roil of waves – abashed, he faked a submarine prayer

"...I am home now yet my true home is far – indeed, as distant as was my gaze that sad embarking hour...be it crumbly old god-shop – pivot of a prayer wheel – aah, hush yer mouth – keep it under yer bloody cassock all that pious bias – 'tis nowt but scriptured drool & bible spit – penny for your demons out, out, out..."

under the leaky station awning the priest shivered as that sermon ran through his bones & it was not until the sentinel outpost buildings of London slid into view that he felt a hint of his old fire returning

*

The Leather-Clad Troubadour sullenly walks, whistling, to Mornington Crescent underground station & buys a day rover ticket – after two rainy, undemanding days the sun has begun to shine once more & he feels a vague sense of renewal as he takes the escalator down to the windy tunnels of cracked, cream tiling – the men in red overalls are busy changing the posters – mute Malevich negatives descending, framed in calm reflective oblongs - he finds their gentle nothings friendly, unquestioning

his train is dirty but empty except for a tall man in a drab overcoat with his face buried in a large book – quickly

313

glancing at the cover, the cod's-eye of the Troubadour sees its title 'The Legend Of Dimu Castle' – a large black square separating the title from the author - Luci St. Mead – *nom de plume*, the 'i' on the end a giveaway, Lucille? - even a male perhaps – a crafty little swap of gender to glean the feminine empathy – he can see her plainly in his cynic's mind - gothic-lit – rituals, bats & heroines – the old darkness in us all – why is this weirdo reading it? - bit old for all that gloom, he looks – he seems the sort that dandifies his days to conceal the squalor of his nocturnal hours – boho fleapit & tuppeny-rope joint – drunk dreams glued together by oily Vermouth & timeworn cigarettes smoked at late, insouciant bus-shelters

the weirdo got off at Embankment then on to the circle line & then – nearly lost him – changing again with the same purposeful step, quickening apace – at Earl's Court, with the Gumshoe Troubadour a little too eagerly behind him, the door failed at first to slide & then, still a few breathless yards behind his prey, finally emerging from Fulham Broadway out into the dappled street – The Troubadour lighting a cigarette as his pencil eyes, sharpening to focus, delineated the shapes & signs – the long-coated weirdo with book now lodged under his arm, bustling off down the street in the other direction from the one in which The Troubadour squinted – gnats circling in the oily, warm air, the whole street sweating hamburgers & popcorn – shops pin-bright in pastel shades – people, forever more people – angry parents dragging mewling kids – drivers mouthing curses behind tinted windscreens – red to amber to green & all the way back to stop

& suddenly a hipster in denim & leather cap smoking a licquorice roll-up - cool, leaning against a parking meter – partially visible title of book in pocket – 'Beneath The Underdog' – Charles something or other - poetry maybe? – The Nonpartisan Troubadour made his own book-title

314

visible as he slunk nonchalantly by – still 'Les chants de Maldoror' - & still unread past the first line or two – that will meet approval, he thinks, but the hipster affects not to notice & stares blithely up at the sky looking for other, more intriguing questions

a commotion - from nowhere a sweating man carries a sewing machine in a red cardboard box slowly across the zebra crossing – Singer, it says - behind him his wife shields from the hot sun beneath a flimsy pink umbrella

the hipster smiles at them, making them nervously smile back – Lonely Troubadour puts his book back into the inner lining of his poetic underdog's jacket & heads down the tube again – boarding the train & disembarking at Putney Bridge – he scrawled on the book's inner title page – *'I needed the river & the river always delivered...'*

the bench he favoured was delightfully empty & warmed by the sun so he sat in a poet's slouchy way & opened the book to the folded page – read past the first few lines, let the unnatural phrases just dazzle, remember how words used to bewitch by bewilderment? – he read slowly, arcane jazz twilights trawled his burnt mind in measured maelstroms of the printed buzz – may it worry heaven

he looks up at the passing water - a tailor's mannequin, half-clothed, caught in a small eddy between moored boats – expressionless & pure - *L'inconnue de la Thames* - or an unquiet Rusalka rising again with life-enhancing moistures & balms – the faceless undead of all rivers are left to swim – awkward & onward down broken canals – through time on unconcerned rivers they float, letting their old failures bring their collective minds together & provoke a new memory or two in his own - a handshake from the grave dripping fire & clammy baked earth – he finds himself sharply, unexpectedly recalling – why? – the combination of that floating ghost & his book of surrealist gobbledegook perhaps? – anyway he sees clear in his mind an old man limping through discarded rubbish on a shard of estuarine wet-land – why? – a pause to shiver –maybe these revelatory instants are the bookmarks in his unwritten biography – he writes

> *the fattening mosquitos of ideas, plans*
> *let his sad old body*
> *vampire their bothered blood*
> *roll the black skull dice*
> *'til the double seven bites*
> *now, lounging - nay loafing –*
> *nearby the very ribbon of water*
> *that will – past, present & future*
> *slither by all points*
> *to the Eastern depths*
> *in solitude of sorts...*

The Lonely Troubadour plucked the imaginary guitar that he kept locked in the closet of his mind & entered that quiet, make-believe room with a single chair dead centre – a shuttered, slatted window throwing a zebra print across a white stone floor, cool to his bare feet – freed from danger & myth, unafraid of werewolves & mermaids – with a straightforward military, rhythmic strum in a minor key he drums out an uncomplicated waltzing cadence - & with eyes tight shut pulls primitive, tranquil words from the red air – a brief musical interlude, abruptly to cease, he nevertheless feels placated but somewhat saddened too - & soon the nervous world is let in once more – his eyes, after the infant song's fading coda, slowly opening to the same, ever-changing waters – his ears tuned to hearing the same, diverse birds - they jitter & resonate in summery green clusters of puffed feathers, the traffic groans way beneath their trilling – the planes soar high above them, silver dots vanishing in blue

time had elapsed & the mannequin had freed itself &
had silently floated downriver towards the yet harsher song
of Essex & the open sea

*

metapataphysical – smearing the absurd with theosophy
– puppet theatres & confession booths – The Physical
Troubadour has lost his inner compass & washed up on an
unforeseen city square - the cassette spooling in his third ear
– the wind is wide open, as if in the backdraft of a gunshot –
he recognizes the territory & frowns at the reasons that may
have brought him here - Smithfield's burning grounds – time
has tricked the mind again to lure him this way – he had
forsaken the Thames for rivulets of greenish water coursing
the gutter, stuffy old death in the air – martyred Proddys &
Catholics alike – a butcher god's last will & testament –
another prelude to Lady Londinium's downfall – her liver,
lights & tripe gagging in the mouths of the reeking drains
where evolution's arrow stalled – giant blubbery dugongs
congeal & gloop against the sewer walls, thrum to the chants
of lynch-mobs in the streets above & the garbled screech of
the captive trains below - a handbill on a phone-box torn –
Jack Of All Trades – any job considered – no task too big or
small – neat handwriting, Upminster address & number – is
this Jack for real? – there must be an open hostelry nearby
in these thirsty streets - The Quick Brown Fox or The Lazy
Dog – pubs to men of all letters - watering-holes to
cognoscenti & cognomen alike – Jack Daniel's now
implanted in his body of thought
   *"...do not under any circumstances get drunk on wine,
which only leads to debauchery...instead, be filled with the
spirit...holy or otherwise..."*
lead on Ephesian prophet & let's dive in old Noah's
Wine Cellar on the way – for the jack has many meanings,

317

multiple aliases - jacks is a game – Springheel or London or Kerouac – whichever titillates the urban imp that dwells within the budding rebel, the cheeky urchin & buys them a one-way ticket to the underworld – see them now, these flibbertigibbets – carrion idealists, minor players that swing from the nooses of the gauche maverick's gallows mind - they hang in their head for but a season, disappearing like the erotica of Blake when their cheap work is done – the hunt is primed, beagle's hoot & the horn is roostering the cold air – the prey identified – they are doomed to be forever searching the lair of Jack Definitive, The Capitalised One

in a snatched blur of morning sleep, on a park bench in raw sun, a narrowing dream emerges - The Capital Troubadour sees a sign while strolling in familiar old Dean Street – spare room to let - & the synapses leap & arc – Bleaney, Austin Osman – the curtain, encouragingly, a few inches above the sill & through that gap he spies the mystic artist teetering along the borderline of his self-mythologies – flaxen, the hair of his gaunt maidens – pentagrams encase their forms – owls in the belfry brain - Beardsley & Bleaney exchange lurid gossip in the shadows thrown by his exile – to let or not to let – forty quid a month, no toilet inside – a radio brags the quiet news & football scores in a corner next to the impassive Narnia wardrobe – old wooden hangers, a shelf for shoes, a wire strung across the inside of the door for ties - he takes it – the blood money drops into a palm upturned that protrudes from behind a bedroom door

& the very next morning he wakes to see the park full of children – a ball rolls to his feet, a red ball – he kicks it & a red dog bounds after it

he dutifully checks his inner pocket but has forgotten his notebook – he never forgets his notebook – try to keep it all in mind somehow – link it like a daisy-chain – keep tabs on the metaphysics – Bleaney-meany-miny-mo – Austin Osman

318

spare room – these coral constellations that burgeon on the mind's damp reef - red dog, red ball

& Boo now sneaks into his thoughts – the real world disappearing too often, lately, down the whirlpool of flushing time - from Mud Hill, back there again, once & once only, but sweetly enough – their new town below spread like a *shtetl* - Jewish & deep in a flurry of snows that took the October rooftops by surprise – she loved the Chagall pictures in the dark gallery that time, those endless, furtive London street-walks – smoking her Silk Cut, he his cheap cigar, raggle-taggle sophisticates, berets askance, drunk on the merest passing waft of Parisian cigarettes in Chinatown's tangy, pork-fat, neon street markets - they plunged in mystic trance through thick, pasty, gouache skies & swam to undulations of fiddle & cranked organ - with her Irish hazelnut eyes half-closed – her eyes, yes, hazel & still authentic despite the ageing sundry dissolutions - & the early blushes of evening are sumptuously garbed in gowns of burgundy & orange – beyond the chimney stupor – beyond the buttery wall where her cherry red bicycle was propped

& that chorus, that siren factory whine that cleaved to Icarus' fatal wake – high above the mud tracks made by ancient wooden wheels still turning – they let their innocent eyes fall over the mute cross-stitching of gables that throb in fog, with a fathomless, peasant broth grumbling suspended above a peat fire

*

yes & The Dream Ship is waiting, tethered & impatient - but now the Captain has drunk his fill & looks further backward to the old main drag of the village old town, therein to spill his wits – this haunted fountain of the undertowns – comic stagger – pipe extinguished by rabid spittle - Leigh-on-Sea his monomythic garden of unearthly delights – it frantically clings on tight to the northern side of the estuary's waist where the momentarily tamed river Thames, in its dotage, prepares for the vast unknown open waters of the North Sea to the east – at low tide, the foreshore yields to alchemy & becomes a wide expanse of mud flats & snaking creeks broadening out towards the nurturing channel of the maternal flow - Yantlet Channel – looking back eastward to the winding Hadleigh way, that he had walked so many times in his youth, stretches into the distance chaperoned by grasses & streams – a solitary train clicks & clanks toward the water, from grimy London freed – leaning toward brightness, for Legra Town is a meadow of light - his dark thoughts lit again by its charm – the oblivious commuters, stretching their magazines & papers, lean back in their seats - unwanted, these useless chronicles flash by them – hilltop settlements, bawleys surf the ridges of the harbour – Lightermen, Peterboats & Smacks, sick of the sea, vomiting their shrimps, lobster, crab, seabass, haddock, cod, sole, mackerel, cockles, whelks, mussels & oysters on to the fish-breathing, shell-crackling sand, their bounty purged by the footprints of wharves – ghostly vessels, such as the one he commands plotting courses before disappearing - later primed to set sail - to venture forth & crush the armadas - or John Wesley's shade over there, smearing his method upon the bleached bibles of a white church – or the folksingers merry with mead, dragging their carcasses through this grand old saga unseen – their least thoughts blow by unheeded as The Captain heaves & balks - the olden words they held within themselves as they sang in chorus with the luminous night-sky & with the riotous waters surrounding – equal to, yet not more than, their collective joy – & yes The Captain, dreams of being at the wheel, in command again - he stumbles on along the lost byways of his stolen shore leave, way back when - through winding, tranquillizing alleys dwarfed by the stone-faced buildings' admonishing frowns – his tiny radio scratchily emits Tim Buckley's plaintive croon – until, of a sudden, as if in a fantasy, on wind-ripped Bell Wharf, appears a creature seemingly half bird, half woman, in profile, but with her face turned to the sea - to her feathered breast she clutches a harp sweetly strummed – her long black hair shining as it teases her pure white shoulder's curve – The Captain instantly falls through bottomless caverns of love – & knowing she has many names, gathered through all time & all born of tides, he addresses her as Ondine – she pauses, her strumming as if in consideration - then resumes with a sorrowful bowing of the head – what breed of beast is she? - an enchanted Moura perhaps, dead as white surf? – or his very own oceanid, here to please, granting him brief audience? – she takes the form of a bird only when on land, perhaps? – yet beneath the waves her fishtail swishes & she is Melusine, destined to wail & buck at the drag of stars – time is as time was & will forever be – his soul is chased by music from her zero mouth – high above her song a warbling moon, incandescent – yet the song he hears is his own - it takes effect at midday, in a windless harbour in a far city & ends only in the grave

Captain Rehab swigs from a crumpled can of bitterness & sails sadly onward once more, abandoning yet another pursuit of happiness, out toward the promise of unspent, lusting oceans – his ship leaking, his crew long dead - flesh rotting away, circled by the beasts of prey – this vision has been claimed by other more worthy suitors – long ago they stole her feathers for their vainglorious dreams – at first, her divine nature kept them alive, but, unable to bestow food upon her devotees, she died within them all – her poor tainted heartsick sailors - who starved to death but refused to ever renounce their love & depart

& so Captain Rehab is back, lurking outside the bar – he watches closely as the yawning mermaid works the coffee machine – Melusine now revealed as the temptress – Philo he is, clutching books made of cloud – she drifts through the tin tables polishing – he sees her on the CCTV – wherever she is – but she never sees him – the dull rain now falling on his dented hat the very sea she swam – syzygy of jesting Jesu – demiurge, lost creature that, outside his mad heart, should never have lived – her house, up on the hill of one light, by the church – visible from the wharf as he looks up through rusting ship's binoculars from out of the fading dream – through gravestones her window-light visible, black trees, mournful in twilight – sipping the heady wine of denied possibilities – in the glow she is raven-pelted, cruel in sharp beauty – he is back at the bar again & it slowly empties & she allows him a half-smile as she passes & drifts to the car-park – failing to love as he loves the love that never loved – he has nothing of her, no mandala, charm or souvenir – a photograph of a pet fish she sent – all time, in a clock she built from driftwood, is trapped forever – a bolted sea-shell clasps the stilled hands that shall never turn – he lies on the cool grass – he climbs the hill, sleeps outside her house, deep in the dark on a damp bench, midnight – the lilting music from the sails of the mystic boats below in inky pools – those bright boats that drifted sweetly in May sunlight are now jagged silhouettes swollen against the darkening, cobalt fishbowl beyond the landslide of streetlamps

keep her light – keeper of light – there on the shore of devotion's deepest water, sure of the yawning oceanic lure of devotion in his song – or on a stairway, descending, after the last bell – adrift on inner seas, breathing in deeply as waves of her dress wash by

*

322

a further memory near a different shore –Newtown
Baby & father's ghost, awaiting the ferry, the weather warm –
let it roll back into the soft part of your doubtful head – as
you put down that book of Whitman's whimsies – & pass
through a portal from the borough of Greenwich to the
borough of Newham - flood-tide below them – though time-
locked they are watched, of course, by time-slipping Captain
Rehab & with them he sees the shipping companies of
Woolwich loom to the north & the aching hulks of iron
drifting west via lighter & barge, the heights of London's
cubes & Hawksmoor spires & domes to the south and east
   The Captain & Lonely Troubadour - lost in ancient
lines, soon to be modernized, his father's phantom fades –
they will later see the shift of freight & cranes dip & pivot
over the containers as old bargemen scowl from the wharf-
side sands – fifty years from this captured time, & again they
will see them, as they build the backdrops to these
panoramas, through which this disparate multitude have
drifted & will drift again - the sun six hours high, opening
the songs of himself, they read together his balm of listed
treasures – yes, how warm it was back then – as Oldtown
Father leads the child up the creaking, mottled gangplank &
once more they hear the calmative throb & gulp of engines,
smell the metal, sweet like a tube station's bacon winds -
hundreds of new-born babies hence, their grandchildren too
will see them boarding & back through dulled time, in
flashes, their minds shall helplessly flicker – the discharge of
the ferry, seasick & vomiting grey on green-grey – &
forevermore behind its stern the glint of morning speckles
the muddy, bilious mushrooming of the river
   & yes the crowds at the quay stare out at them as they
drift - looking back through the countless years & across
streaming ripples, their keen eyes impenetrable as stones –
observers all, bewildered in their meaningless wheres &
sand-shifted nows - real-time availing little– it is a blink of

eternity, nothing more – yet without it the universe would vanish

& the sun glints from the handrail as churning water, that entity that never moves in lockstep with time, rolls & broils under the curved hull – seagulls haunt a sniff of troubled flavours above the measured orbit of the nodding prow – small children tossing crusts of sandwiches - silently snapped from their parabolas by scissoring beaks - or allowed to fall to the swell - only to be rescued & absorbed by a more expert or fortunate gliding swoop of white, balletic wings

hold fast this vista to your mind, Newtown Child – your blithe detachment permits you no reason for forgetting– snot wiped from his crusted nose with sleeve of dad's coat – two small boats pointed at with cries & jumps of joy - & you, Captain, face to face with all hours – hurtling scenes of past eras thrill through your blissed mind - veils of the western tracing-paper airs – the huge sun high, almost lost to a blur of haze, finds you in throes of doubt – the father stands at the rail - shoulders turned & tight squint – the north shore is reeled in, as if by an invisible tether, & the elusive features of the faces on the dock clarify – the manly smells & noises of the engine-room – industrial shards of sound like the metallic flutters of Varese – old steam·broiling with fresh steam & issuing from leaky joints & firehoses hanging limp like a row of dull cartoon elephant trunks awaiting buns

& on the approaching shore the crowd wait for their crowd to disembark, so many people, Newtown Baby had thought, yet they will all disappear down the well of ages, only to make way for a thousand, million more to plummet in turn – he had never thought before of how the land dies slower than its people – this scene would have been replicated down through the ages & would be replicated a hundred years hence – not much would have changed other than some minor technical differences, the machines & craft, but the people would be utterly gone – linked through the desire only to cross a river, a desire that harks back to prehistory – he had read the great man's poem of time, Brooklyn ferry the same as Woolwich, & rather than emphasising his own insignificance he had felt a part of a grander design, a necessary chain – he clutched the book to his breast now as he strode behind his ghostly father to the further shore

& Captain, O Captain - how inquisitive you are snooping from behind the future's curtains, my old neighbour! - the ferry moans its mournful dirge to you under the wide open eyes of god – am I to study nature forever? - to what end & for whom? - huge days are floating by during the simple contemplation of a leaf - hundreds traverse this river - work-heavy, sky-blown heads primed for belief– backs broken in toil - returning home to a nightmare stew of their trials & lusts – O Captain, you fled once at these omens - you, that from shore to shore rocked in bliss at each turn of the screw – you! – the multigenerational sailor, slumped by an old oak, now recalling in leisure such piquant first impressions – the past subsists on these wispy fuels, these dreamy philosophies – it is born of a wilful inertia born of repressed memories – choose your dream carefully – make thee a single golden hour distilled from the best light of the day - so compress the berry & see the juice run into your happy flask – quintessence of recollection - easier said than done – a mass of hopes packed tightly together to forge a brighter hope, forge a fine plan from scheme after slippery scheme – the ship is in smithereens in raging rapids, yourself a mere sliver in the rinse of decades – & yes, all these landlubbers you see now, crossing on your precious ferry, grinning & weeping across this swill of foul water, they will be nothing but pruned branches carried by the swell sadly retaining a fragmented sense of the ever-replenishing tree from which they fell - care nothing for modifications of fleeting fashion & quaint chance, a new season's wardrobe – it will only briefly disguise these new-born cadavers – yes, for ever onward rolls the eager river to the jaded sea, have no doubt – the river knows its destination, we vainly crave her other shore beyond which lies a dream – & we too will briefly feel her power, the short voyage from shore to shore - each astonishment dulled to diffidence by a subsequent thrill – but the sea is where all dreams renew, it is that gasping image your primal brain clings to – the security blanket that calms & submerges you in its folds

The Insecure Troubadour, head aching from following Whitman's winding map, needs a drink – a refreshing of his river, a clearing of the dams & locks - word-drunk, he will now seek sweeter wines to kill that familiar taste of decay – grasping nature's hand, in deference to the poet, picking sloes for fermentation & berries for nourishment, he orders a double gin & a bag of peanuts & raisins - his notebook will remain unheard 'til years hence

so be it

& yes, unheard, in times long flown, Newtown Baby hummed a tune that he will forget for forty years – poetic words from different rivers shall rudely awaken the sleeping portents & fire a song – Captain Rehab projects himself to return awhile - hums the tune 'neath his future oak & reads the secreted words at his leisure – his body prostrated, bathed in the husks of acorns hidden in un-raked heaps of rural leaves - & The Lonely Troubadour, stretching his aches against the hard slats of the pub-garden bench, allows pirate thoughts to invade – how did the brief traversing of the river mean so much? – the poem, the water's course, the ferry horn – it was as if some member of the presumed multitude of future passengers was looking back & writing a poem or song about a Troubadour who was writing about looking forward, whilst both reading poetry from the distant past that predicted both their courses of action - these tea-leaf stirrings are promising adventure, he thought –

pioneers, blue-bearded, drop-foot plodders with eyes full of silver - they too lived this river time - they too strained to see beyond this Woolwich shore - desperate poets praying for divine messages of consolation - sad poets bleating, needing desperately to be told their worth - to be reassured that this slice of eternity will soon be theirs to harvest - to believe their troubadour souls - & that the circle, sea to rain to river to sea again, shall remain unbroken

*

another dewy morning had somehow emerged from the depths of night & damp birds were startling to life in the dripping trees - it was the hour that nibbled at the sleepy houses - when milk-floats purr past the early driveways & gradually, warily, beautifully even, it began to rain in earnest - as if the droplets were born out of a need to cry down the upstart fires - the embers of hope

& yes London was watching the rain as slyly as a thief's peripheral glance - her cars grizzled in the wash that the drops laid like a cloak of mirrors over the skin of tarmac - & The Solitary, Dampened Troubadour stood peacefully outside the newsagent & lit a Red Band cigarette from the ashes of the previous stub, which he then flicked - with thumb over forefinger - expertly into the gulping drain - a good omen, he thought

the concrete surrounded him, the glass office frontage & canvas yanked over scaffolding - the awareness that they were rooted in him now, these edges, hard exteriors, these furious waves of slow traffic - he no longer lived back there by the restful sea - the call of the capital had reeled him in but the initial excitement had now begun to drift into a kind of hyper-vigilant nervousness - he knew that he had sated his hunger for tall buildings & mouldy stone histories - he had wearied of the stealthy creep of Ripper shadows in the

327

Whitechapel fog & Charlie Peace plotting his capers in a striped shaft of cell-light – the great fictional city where the new kissed the old, full lipped, & drank every backstreet hole in the wall dry – it had not let him down quite yet though & there was still enough thrill to offset the drag of days - & he genuinely felt most at home, not in his grubby squat, but in the sprawl of the crucial streets – the raw flesh of London gripped him still & his heart felt the tug of family in the clutches of her tentacles of mews & lanes

due to living at the squat, however, he had, for better or worse, shanghaied a new crew of lubbers & litigants – a mere catapulted stone's distance from the Camden drag, his digs mouldered in a constant dewy shroud of condensation laced with skunk weed – in winter his houseplants died & the windows froze – in summer the sunlight merely replaced the condensation with sweat & rendered the dense, heady air unbreathable without hallucinating – each had their tasks, the cosy routines were like a reassuring hug - plucking two milk bottles from the step – putting out the empty beer cans & burger cartons – feeding the weird Rasta neighbour's cat with a saucer of tuna fish each morning before it rewarded them by crapping in the window-box

yes & all things got paid for mysteriously & nobody seemed to own the bill – the morning ritual of buttering charred toast with a thick ornate steel knife, purchased from a market stall crate of pirated cutlery, was almost devotional in its silent holiness – & each morning he would stare out of the bay window & survey the grey streak of Eversholt Street, still winking awake, a Ford Anglia rusted forever at the far kerb, two schoolboys perpetually threw stones at the metal shutters of the unlet shop next to the grocers – each clang as religious as a church bell's tolling to a deaf god – he felt part of a story, like a novel's lull before a plot twist that disappoints – yet still he spurred himself on into each hour detecting in the slightest of shivers the delicious frisson subconsciously felt before an unexpected change – yet no change came

& the tale will unfurl in yet more complicated ways – old years, like old houses, will be demolished or vandalised in ruin, or bombed out in wars, only for their bricks & beams to be stripped & used to fashion years in the new style – memories are phantoms, mirages seen in the brick-dust risen from demolished years, they are the ashes mumbled to nothing by priests at the breach of the tomb - but old ghosts live on in the mortar & each new build will be plagued by a torment of past anguishes, disappointments – until it becomes a monstrous tower of babel – a house with too many voices, with one lone voice deeper, more resonant, than all others – & it sings to The Troubadour when he sleeps, a song of leaping distance, clear air & wild cloud, a song of a home lost - & he butters the black toast with his antique knife & stares from the sad arched windows of this liminal chamber of mordant utterances & he thinks of the countless houses he had seen rolling by the train windows when he used to ride the thrilling rails to the city way back when – all those portals to a world he cared little for but sensed to be traps & he would never be caught so easily, no – the awful sight of an occasional ashen face, staring out at the train, dreaming of change or escape – of being that hero that could someday get away, leap the wall, move on – they are suspended in half-life, he thought, not knowing that they could change the meaning of their life, their loves, he thought - & now he was that staring face, that grey expressionless robot that fervently prayed for the universe to sweep him away to excitement & adventure – he thought of the river, how he had always joked that it should flow toward London rather than away – he saw the commuters beginning to mass at the corner for the bus, others filing toward the tube subway to be swallowed into the city's gut & suddenly, astonishingly, he saw The Priest, a vision in black leather

329

trousers, cape & wonky dog-collar, bottle of rum in hand, shouting an obscenity-laden litany of arcane bullshit at the terrified throng as he weaved through them like a salmon heading, to spawn & expire, upstream

mid-day before he ventures out - The Changeling Troubadour picks up a muddied postcard from the road - it is addressed to the occupants of the first house in his street

Mum - having the best time, Van Gogh museum was great, going to explore more museums tomorrow & maybe go on a canal boat ride, how romantic eh? - see you soon, will call when we're at the airport, love, Jenny xxx

he turned it over to reveal a picture of a field of tulips stretching far into the flat distance under an impossibly azure heaven of airbrushed perfection

he looked at the pile of bin sacks upon which a small mongrel dog was pissing & then up at the lifeless sky of scudding clouds squeezed between the converging roofs of the houses - a thin, silver jet-liner eased through the mass of grey, slicing like a freshly sharpened blade through taut cloth

he put the postcard in his pocket & walked to the corner shop to get milk & cornflakes - he counted the coins in his hand - enough, after cigarettes

*

small mirror in a pub toilet - cross-hatched wires on a frosted glass again - tree shape trying to wave a greeting or a warning - music, music, bloody music

the cheap vagrants & speed-chewing litigants carousing & bellowing their petty complaints at a bored ceiling from which a glitter ball hung serene - with a silent room full of slack mouths reciting the words back at them - punk flowers, litany of bromide to litany of remorse - we are all prostitutes on the jukebox – on the jukebox we are family – blood drips from a vicious wound – punk flowers plucked, punk berries smeared across a broken car windscreen in Frith Street

& yes she smelled of jasmine, wore knee-high PVC boots in cool orange – fan-heater blown, small electric fire faulty, one bar of three glowing – o bondage up yours – fat creatures of the city swamp ooze by the old Café Boheme in Old Compton Street – he enjoys a moment of calm – for now, he has forgotten to remember all the bad things – Blake saw angels in the leaves, he saw polythene bags twisting like dervish ectoplasm – he stubbed Russian Cigarettes Of Dubious Origin in the chrome ashtray & flooded the street with imagined seas – walking past an old junk stall he saw a game of Subbuteo – discarded Christmas, outgrown the fun – face down close to the carpet, flicking the plastic players with his forefinger, their feet encased in a semi-sphere that returned them to their upright stance every time – suspension of belief, these hardy mafia victims that never squealed, never grassed – the fuzzy felt field & huge ball of innocent disbelief – the innocent could not snitch so they ended up with concrete wellington boots & were vanished, one more fish in the sleepy Thames

he was fascinated by her hair, shiny, shiny, shiny hair & leather boots – the music had a distinct edge of threat – they had put red bulbs in the back room of the pub – a local band, sub-Stranglers, poker-staring, finished their set with a song called 'Murder You' – vicious on the jukebox, she sidled up & was soft spoken, more velvet than leather – a rumour that someone was spiking the bar-top drinks, a girl in a studded dog-collar was freaking out in the toilets – The Troubadour felt fine, relaxed, if a little shimmery around the gin-blossoming edges – Leather Boots said her great-grandfather was a rabbi – the tall glass with a red cocktail & two fat straws – now Louie Louie, stuttering dances begin,

331

consisting of angry punk gestures, careful do not touch, the nervy embrace of a new decade – the barman says that it is like this every weekend, live bands, a rebellious jukebox, new box of unhappy weirdos – the barman grins, a day-glo yellow shirt with hate & war scrawled – a red cocktail half-drunk by the charity bucket - punk flowers, hit me

finally, in her room, she read freakish words from the Talmud & rang finger cymbals – there were records strewn across a fake eastern rug – when she passed out on the toilet he listened to songs on her old Dansette – load the disc & press PLAY – her dad had bequeathed it - it was like a toy, a Bauhaus relic – old rock & roll, a few new bands he had not heard of – yet another music unknown to him & for that reason weirdly alluring – like the indecipherable chants drifting from a found temple on a long pilgrimage – the thick slices of vinyl

he chose at random, Vince Taylor, The Television Personalities – he felt fine, Tanqueray gin, only a little bit - the unexplained raindrops ticked on the skylight – he was perfect, then, in this woozy nirvana, closing in upon an elemental state of joy – wide-armed, windblown on a precipice – ahead of him a slope descends through sunset cloud against a red sky – shepherd's delight, devil's wallpaper, beyond good & evil – there will be another time, another scene, let it play out – he played the Vince Taylor record again, then the Television Personalities twice more – there will be rain ticking on the skylight forever – he stole the dregs of gin, perhaps she stayed in the toilet or went to bed – carriage clock – raindrop - tick – tock – tick – tock – rain - drop – door click - sunshine tomorrow

*

one good day – new-town, summertime, remember? - & there was a leaf floating in the deep end of the swimming pool, yes – how did it get there? - blown in the door & trodden through – however it got there it was hypnotic, he could not take his gaze from it – the swimmers brushed it aside but still it bobbed & danced – immaculate green raft – a mysterious island, verdant in the cool blue shimmer, as if it had freshly fallen from an overhanging bough – yes, The Troubadour remembered – remembered the taste of that cream soda leaving a delicious vanilla breath in his mouth – the chlorine rising, tickling the throat – the sunlit leaf dodging the splashes, divers & old women treading water – buffeted by the bursts of bubbles from the grill – contented leaf, epicentre, at play, no desire to be rescued – he wanted to pluck it from the maelstrom of human traffic & press it between the pages of a book of poetry & let it be a smiling surprise for a browsing customer in a dusty bookshop – or set it free on a river to hurry seaward, or be sunk by children's stones dropped from a bridge – he remembered, remembered

cream soda fizzing – sharp chlorine grips the palate – sunlight on blue – green leaf – it was a good day – he had felt energized by the vigorous exercise & gone for a walk across the bright park – the trees were lush & in full feather – the leaves, he thought, looked sad, like tethered creatures, trapped in the sky – or like those solitary horses he saw, out by where the yearly circus set up, chained to a gatepost at the roadside – bright greens on rich blue, yellow gilded, a buttercup yellow

he gazed up through the confusion of branches, fixing upon the clear sky until it filled his eyes & he could no longer see the horizon to get a sense of up or down, just the branches, leaves & mostly sky, stretched across forever, until it became an ocean to which the leaves were falling

*

The Deserted Troubadour woke from ugly sleep with a start that registered in his eyes like a lightning bolt –a strange dream still gripped him, reality fragmented, real versus other real – he had been on a street in a strange city – chased by dogs - a glow above his reflected face in the glass door of the pawnbroker - was it his halo? – he had been expecting one for months now – in a field of daisies, he had no clothes, ashamed of his nakedness he had wrapped himself in the skins of animals that were drying on a fence at the edge of the field – he had walked to the city again, swaddled in peeled remnants of stolen coat-skins – slowly things focused & he was home – home - before his still-swimming, painful gaze, the dingy room resembled the pub in most aspects – stale air, sweat & smoke & after-shave - fragments of crisps & half-full plastic glasses of cheap, burping lager – the low thrum of indistinct, yet vaguely familiar, bass-heavy music – & he felt the shame, the sense of apology rising, without knowing what he had done wrong - probably something, to someone - he felt deserving of the headache, the lack of recall, he felt almost spiritual – he reproved himself by way of absolution in a few muttered oaths, the dawn confessional to his inner priest

he took a bite from a naan bread - Eucharist – he strummed a numb G on his guitar, hideously detuned & the stub of a cigarette still stuck on the end of one of the tangle of strings around the headstock - his guitar slept by day – it had the weary mien of a preoccupied, nocturnal creature – this squat was its burrow, its lair & the city was elsewhere, yet ever the vigilant warden – the music he played did not thrill him – this guitar killed no fascists – there was a cloud tightening in his mind, he thought of the awful blues band he had joined & it gripped his boredom like a vice – he thought of the city, sprawling out like a spilt beer across the sober suburban villages – he was a daisy drooping in a vase of leathery plants

& how many bleary mornings had he spent at the café up the road, shovelling crusted sugar into endless coffees? – & staring, staring at the sign in the shoe shop opposite – misery reborn as a dim-lit raft of commerce - every day, moccasins, half-price sale – it never changed – the cheap moccasins eternal

yet, like a series of *ko-ans,* these rituals, these repetitions & reductions served to granulate the deeper truths & as the walls shrank inward so the held breath of bad thoughts exhaled – poisonous mind-flowers ripe for the easy pluck - once more, the same thing as before & no changing it now – perhaps ever

Early Troubadour walking slow, footsteps timed to land between the throbs in his temples – he buys a Daily Mirror at the miserable kiosk – misanthropic, swaddled, woollen mumbles from beneath a red turban, Marxist beard – thanks dribble to stony ground as, from a tinny radio behind the sullen vendor, Wizzard sing from deep in Spector chambers – The Troubadour tries, but fails, to see his baby jiving & pops a polo mint into his dry mouth – lights a cigarette & pushes the folded news into his shoulder bag – tune in his head now, stuck – he read the headline but now, seconds later, can't remember it – old news – Grub Street grubby & street-smart – unwithered in the morning gales of bad omens & gossipy schlock, they dutifully scrape their busy nibs across the pale yellow foolscap – suicide notes promising endless lurid revelations & their attendant guilt – church-doorway tattlers – old lady breath, peppermint-haunted – pages & pages of newsprint, hobo blankets, lined with their hack haikus – weathervane unrequired in a north wind of no change & through which no answers ever blew

two teenagers in black plimsolls idly kick a tennis ball against the shuttered shopfront – everything bolsters the backbeat – pretty woman, entrancing, intriguing, hair tangling in the steady gust from the alley she ignores through tinted glasses – her skirts dance but they dance alone – see my baby

& The Wallflower Troubadour sucks the last smoke from his bent cigarette & rehearses an unspoken greeting – no chance, she passes quickly through his lost risk – his jacket jives in the wizard wind, flapping in the sighing wake of her unspoken, disappearing promise – another brave morning in the heart of bright Albion – the old shops get painted up as new – new fads to wear & eat, bread & jam turns to bland feta cheese & pitta – he feels the time-slip burgeoning, volume swelling like a song escaped from a future radio – voluptuous music forced to diet, squeezing itself into tiny rattling speakers & earbuds – the whitewashed walls daily insulted by blots of jealous spray paint – Boho graveyards tainted, desecrated by jets of epitaphs & eulogies to one-trick poets – perpetual motion of the wrecking ball, that desk-toy of the city trolls, high & safe above the folklore of a changeling street – 'I'm a genius' cries a tramp, draining sour clots of old milk from a found carton – & the underground is thick with wanted posters – rebellion, a museum exhibit, is roped off & delicate, please don't touch – & tonight the geniuses will sleep under last week's business supplement – like faith slumbers under the wafery leaves of a bible

The Wafery Troubadour sighs & sadly contemplates the sleeping mounds of humanity in the shop doorway - above their slumber a flapping, torn poster – COME TO SUNNY SOUTHEND-ON-SEA – briny sea-wind agitates the corner flap – The Troubadour wets his salty thumb & turns to the television listings, the page creased by the cramped bag, specked by a brief rainfall – The Old Grey Whistle Test, ten-thirty – whispers & cries, different wizards, different jives – the Prog cartoons from a jerky Disney vault

the rain stops & a sleepy sun focuses a reluctant gaze on the closing umbrellas – another lost genius picks at the bins behind the bakery – thin wild hair, grey, white - where dark, almost blue – thick beard of unkempt anarchist, the Troubadour decides he will let his own grow out – freak flag fly, rebel against the rebellious norm – deaf, dumb, blind & inert - a roll in the dirt with people hurting naked & blue – in shock – their hard, dead eyes followin' you - burnin' on through - the crimson curtain shaking at two o' clock wind - morning euphoria – the gut of the angelus dream

got no strings to make me walk - or make me talk – words broken into jigsaw – a homeless mind inhabiting the other where - push me around - feel somehow safer in here - the ventriloquist's voice is trusted - I just don't know if I can fake these old blue troubles no more, sittin' here on the step with an uncertain someone's unwanted beer, on this squalid, twilight shoreline of the passers-by

I'm older now, he says to nobody, can you remind me how we used to love? - of that glorious time, surely not so far back?

Old Maudit, still sailing on, with his sack full of dread & sadness & a brand new, bitter song – his tall tale true, his recital of woe, my *cantastoria*

the genius eyed him with a sneering contempt, the cupped grimy hand held a filthy roll-up to his black-lipped mouth awaiting a cough dredged from his sparrow chest – ssp-tttt! – flob of chewing gum & oyster grit – his hand still ready for another cough, eyes screwed shut - he looks like he is holding an imaginary microphone – he looks like he is singing

*

'...it's like a balloon being inflated in your head, boy...'

The Lonely Troubadour stared at the tiny grey blotter on his fingertip – stared doubtfully, shivers rising

& he frowned a frown of resolve – here goes

337

the priest's desecrated church was abandoned & cool with a late October air, the debris of religious jetsam was strewn across the dirty tiled floor – ruined hymn book pages, extinguished incense sticks, flyers urging people to embrace the coming rapture – he affected a nonchalant air &, eyes wide, placing the blotter on his tongue, swallowed it with an audible gulp

he idly inspected the walls – where one would expect icons & portraits of the saints, he was puzzled to discover torn posters of a distinctly secular nature – adverts for punk gigs, pictures of the Brooklyn Bridge, a damp-mottled, torn postcard depicting three nuns smoking in a guilty huddle – the joss-stick holder, wooden, carved vulture head - dusky sandalwood, peppery patchouli - he let his gaze wander upward past the rotting beams & saw five bright stars through a not inconsiderable hole in the arched roof – dim, red-faced biblical figures yellowing in chipped panels, a single light bulb, powered by a spaghetti tangle of illegal wiring, hanging from the centre beam like a suicide

'...no good body comes here at night, boy, I'll tell ye that...some of my best work has been done from midnight to dawn in this little sanctuary...witching hour...heh...'

the shadowy formless mass of Degory Preist climbed the seven steps to the altar & became illuminated by the torchlight & candle he had set up there earlier in the day

'...how long 'til it kicks in?...'

The Troubadour had expected the effects to be more or less instantaneous, like a swig of brandy on a cold night, but as yet there was no noticeable change other than his feet seemed colder - but that could be real, the earlier rain had leaked through his boots – the priest spoke from a zoetrope of shadows cast by the passing car headlamps through the gap in the stained glass

'...you'll learn soon enough...now shut yourself down & listen to the night...'

The Troubadour watched the priest intently & now gradually, through the murk & dust, he became visible again – transformed by creases of moon, his empurpled visage, a coarse relief map of his torments – a stippled, ochre tongue that voiced a hurt malevolence born of a bottomless shame – his pocket watch, the Troubadour had observed, had no hands – the denial of hours, a universe bereft of the focal urgings of any rite of passage – his sermon, if such it was, droned onward, pale echoes offered in desolate ricochets from the once sacred walls

"...the world ever in the throes of creation & collapse, the eternal nanosecond in which all our fleet appearances dwell – life, my old pals, my brethren, is a clifftop cemetery slowly toppling into a dead sea that welcomes the long-gathered bones with her wide arms – & we sigh, for after an eternity of chains even the abyss seems like liberty - the earth reimagines its shifting maps & we do what we can to stay where we are, with fixed borders that are illusions, claimed territories that imperceptibly change - in ultra-slow motion - until unrecognisable as our once sacred turf – the ache of the continental shifts belies all patriotism – what use is our god? - a worship of a body now dust..."

Red Jimmy lay in state across the front pew snoring – a king of nothing but the London rain, in pomp upon his catafalque of rotting wood

yet The Troubadour had the uneasy impression that he heard, in sleep, & what is more, understood every queer phrase & twisted sentence the old priest uttered – as he listened he realised that his snores were a perfect punctuation to the text – beef-notes, lordly, & as sonorous as the blare of a worried owl in a haunted barn – the priest raised the pitch of his oratory half an octave

"...blood of ancients floods us all! – you are acting out the consequences of the fools that preceded ye! – the dead body politic you worship moulders by the Samaritan's highway – where is your god now? – sulking in Neitzschian shadows, busking in the subways of Cioran, French-kissing Camus' mangled ghost!

the pilgrimage has been hijacked & taken to Cuba, brethren – I was on the march last week to the mass rally of misfits & mavericks, rebels & heretics & the holy words of our bright new evangels rang in my head – Strummer, Poly Styrene, I heard the clash of culture over raucous hymnal Telecasters

Bobby Dylan may have been bound for glory – me, I'm still cynical & hungover in my liberal bed - warning sirens, the police dredging the streets for dissidents – I sell the Morning Star to my flock & tell them to doubt it sometimes, be free with what is left of your will - we're on the last march now, people – join the agit-prop babies – '...*la propriété, c'est le vol!...*' sayeth old man Proudhon – in his black cloak of myth - bomb-chuckers, hurlers of rotting fruit - the fickle laughter in old alleys of the capital - Black Maria's on the hard-shoulder, smouldering, burnt-out & widowed

see now, all your houses are abandoned to the squatters – they are already heaving printing presses into mildewed basements as you stack your possessions in the removal van! – the book is being rewritten, friends, do not be afraid to get ink on your fingers, read the word while it is still wet!...'

the sweating priest lowered his head & calmed his voice to an almost croak, a pleading whisper, just enough

'...amen...please take a while to browse the literature that is available on the table in the nook by the door as you leave – we are a progressive church of eternal revolt - we are growing – we are serving the whole community without exemption – bring us your poor & needy, as that old French bitch statue proclaimed – Ellis island stewing with racism at her feet – read the works of the giants on whose shoulders we stand – out there you will discover Kropotkin's collected pamphlets, I stapled them together myself, Tolstoy's Slavery

340

Of Our Times, Malatesta – I aim to be the last megaphone voice you hear on the last free radio before the fall - an existential hipster priest - agitate, educate & organise – they cannot kill us all - we're still here...we're still here

& after the last march is done – the mood of the city will feel like the aftermath of a civil war – there be Popskull & O Be Joyful In The Still Acoustic Shadows & old sugary ruin in the dregs of winter wine - may your stone black heart be careful/callous, cool & cute – hardnosed, as stolen love drifts sadly back in time - the choked smell of gunpowder - the silence near a fervid battle hauntingly paused - yellow tinted soldier blue, rises only to collapse in the blooded ditch again - every rebel banner torn by angry fizzing metal – Old Father News takes pictures of them all – grim paparazzi reapers circling the maggoty meat – the widows wait in hope knitting scarves for the war effort as tattered years fold back revealing the dead-letters that they wrote

& like all the civil wars of history, English, American, Venusian – there is mortality & sentiment enough to make you gag – an innate short-term memory loss throws a shade across the brutality – until morning's unforgiving light once more disinters the carnage from tomb-stoned, shallow soil

we're on the last march, my brethren – amen, I say & enjoy the trip..."

Red Jimmy loosed a damp fart by way of parenthesis or hallelujah & the dim bulb winked its last, plunging the stealthy silence into an appropriate, if unwelcome, darkness

*

& once upon a different time, out lost in thoughtless ambling on the city's weird outskirts, this Troubadour he boarded the dream ship for just one hour – he stood at its prow, over his shoulder Old Captain Rehab stared down like an approving father

341

& The Approved Troubadour shut his eyes softly to hear the cars of the north & south circular whizz & fade, still out there beyond this façade of ocean, somewhere – & as dream mingled with reality for this one strange day only, in equal measure, he felt that his mind could fall one side or the other – time & memory fusing, the only true alchemy he ever realised – the strafing cars beeped in real life at the threshold of the ocean in his head - he let the murmur of their engines drown out the crew's ribald song & then vice-versa – both worlds possible, he alone to choose - & as sails thrash in pockets of angered wind & the decks split & stain, he knew it was a voyage born of a high north wind, the clear, infinite expanse before them the only destination possible – they were set fair to burst the curtain of a horizon

& the wind spoke soothingly through its bluster – listen to the wind's voice, always – as it blows through every dockside dive & speaks to those who wish to be carried high, away from their so-called homes, away to wherever they end up when she ceases her capricious squall

native's blood ye were bathed in - waters around ye – the scribe's lethargic muse doused within your crumbling heart – fix the roof of your soul – fasten tight the spirit's window for the pirate wind cometh to tell ye of the wild life ye spurned - as sure as hell he'll skin the last strip of pelt from ye bones – aye as sure as sailor's graves stalk the footsteps of the moon - know this - as sure as ye sit like monks in this murderer's bar & whores dance in heaven - I saw them! I saw! - they left us robes of stained linen that stank this boozing hole out for years - & ye hate poetry like ye fear death I know, I know

& I blew through the sails of Columbus' fair ship - the manifest reads like a hymnal – hail these folk here listed: Humility Cooper, Newtown Baby, Oceanus Hopkins, Lonely Troubadour, Walt Whitman, Wrestling Brewster, Captain Rehab, Myles Standish, Degory Priest – so gather

tight around my voice ye brave pioneers & clutch the rail -
before the last sombre shadow sways in on the sneaky tide -
but if ye never trust a word I wail again just grant me this -
'tis truth there is a blanket behind the stars & we shall draw
its dirty threads ever close - snug beneath our chins, in our
slow house, done with fearing - one day - yes sir, all done -
but a deeper darkness waits in silhouetted trees - vulture-
thick & snake-eyed - & before long a stolen yet merciful
forty winks shall open his dreams like a rose & damn these
cartoon pirates to their fate - they knew their course for
sure, as we set ours now - so let us be done with their wicked
bones - let there be no more talk now - only my voice in
your head from here to forever - board the dream-ship,
quick step - & raise up the sail - ye are tired & I know the
very soul of tiredness - feel it shrug aside your troubled
dervishes - sleep in my turbulent arms & dream here on in
lullaby of Northwind

dripping black honey from the hive mind of history into
the cave of your ear

so rock way back in your wicker café chair, Old Weary
Troubadour, & slowly return to earth with the lilt of the
blown river kissing each descending step to slumber

*

The Hungover Again Troubadour, deep-rooted, acid-
weary, suspicious as a dockside mongrel, sits in Bradley's
Bar - again & forever again - looking like the first line of a
bad song – the chords played in deep echo in his troubled
heart - *F#m to G#m* - with a broken time machine for a
brain & a cold bottle of thunder almost drained on the table
before him – the loose wires frothing in his pudding head,
that once used to flap & swish like a donkey tail dismissing
flies, now miserably hang like thrown spaghetti from a wall –
it is a head full of honeydew & fog - climate of coming

343

dread, elephant weather, heavy, bullish – *Gm back to E* – he is laden, his mood shattered to the point of a delirious happiness, a song works on itself in his wrung-out mind – drink curdling in his gut that only the strum of blues can quell

gunmetal morning, a blue week of misery stretches long – Tuesday alone was a thousand years - culminating in a weekend of lurid, boozy dismissals & fights – a wild-hearted reiteration of old prejudices – *Am7 to C* - no longer a grim, crisp-crunching, glucose-aided voyage to the dreamy dole queues that shit out the bad gossip & sweet hearsay about a factory hiring, a building site wanting new fetch-monkeys, or supermarkets with empty shelves awaiting your creativity & desire – *G to D, hammer on the little finger, top string* - the compassion of the community has passed away, he thought bitterly over another cloudy drag of Dictum's Ale – this bar of Bradley's is home to the secret poets, the failed, crushed authors seeking a library full of vanity publications - Lenny The Painter, Mick From The Tar Game - hiding the vodka beneath their donkey-jackets & hugging Crombies instead of eternally punching the unforgiving clock – tickety-tock & time's up - ah it's all gone to shite boys, it's the shock of the new that always comes to the proud Luddite old - but the tenderness of these working men, the holy collective, the spirit that their poor dead unionised fathers instilled still rang true

Degory Priest! – he explodes into the bar fresh from a swim in the fatherless Thames – he gleefully spies a likely, cowering benefactor in the readjusting gloom

"...Billy man, buy me a beer! - next Thursday I'll be in the Stagger Inn with pockets full of I.O.Us & twenty quid to last me a month – I'll see ye ok!..."

D back to Am – & he'll spin out the yarn again like a Speak-Your-Weight machine – pockets coughing with the dust – Billy answers in a reluctant affirmative - flat robotic

344

staccato, cheesecloth shirt & gruff nicotine burr – *E7 to Am*
– work is the curse & the peasant's song is still full of the
dumb old melancholy pride – some have known little else in
life, this nightly social is their true family not a mere respite
from the unquestioned toil – it rumbles like a river of grief
behind their sleep – threat of redundancy, the sack, nervous
picket lines & braziers stoked for warmth on cold mornings
– fuck the scabs, hefty rocks gathered to pelt their cabs –
blue shall forever be the colour of entitlement, red the
melody of resentment & cack-brown the relentless chords of
longing - listen, hear their voices in the dock-front pubs &
cheap backstreet bars across the shifting metropolis
    "...ah Degory! – buy me a chaser! - that's your old pal
Scargill on the telly..."
    & do they remember in these stolen moments their
flooded past, their wayward histories? - do they recall any
time when the reds beat down the blues? – when the heart
beating strong in the chest evinced a feeling of triumph? – a
time when the communal tendency endured? - *Dm, slow
regular flatpick* - but now the heart that once pumped blood
to this staggering mass has failed & there's nothing left but
right - & the good old sing-a-long way back when, when
    & way back, The Troubadour sat in this very seat in
which he now slumps - after the last march, after the flask of
rum & spliffs of the rally in the park – listening to Son
House & his letter of death – listening to Bert Jansch & his
needle of death – death flowed through his veins in
Shakespearian tumult – *yes & when he shall die, take him &
cut him out in little stars - & he will make the face of heaven
so fine* - after the bickering rebels had graded the long-dead
Russians' import & trustworthiness through drowned hours
over Polish vodkas – after the bored Lord mayor's show left
its trail of horseshit & streamers & police-aware tickertape –
after the party was done & red men with small twig-guns
shouted at the castle walls of the chortling rich – the middle-

class arses sat safe inside their coffin-shaped houses & European homes, where they sipped Christmas sherry & plugged their ears with muzak & scratchy boilerplate to mask the daily failures & threw another seasick, captain's log on the fire of history - *that all the world will be in love with night - & pay no worship to the garish sun* - The Troubadour nestled tight into his defiant mood of lazy mutiny, his union dues merging to deep southern blues & part way back again - amen

Carl Sandburg - a take-a-chance book of poetry for thirty pence from a Brick Lane bookstall - whose trenchant boom was the thunder that vivified the shifty sleep of The Lazy Rebel Troubadour's recent broken nights- & throw in a second-hand hardback Ulysses to boot - student scribble all down the margins but readable still - amen to that too & pray let the ultimate affirmatives abound, Molly Bloom & the wild poet's abandoned cares that shall serve as ignition to a billion cranky engines of the word - big fat amen swelling in his head

big fat yes, the people, yes

& now just the Troubadour, yes - sat ruined in this cabbage-coloured underground bar with nothing but a row of optics beckoning - & shadowy recollections of a wasted day beginning with flashes of virtue & ending in The Clash on the jukebox - once more, the chords in his head having failed, in his surly, lip-curled notebook he scribbles uncertain words - waiting, it will come from nowhere & return there - the slow glide of letters across the inner eye - as if there is an arcing gap between the alcohol & the brain's nerve-ends that is suddenly connected by a buzz of light - the rhythm is always close to hand, a footstep, a bird cawing, the tick of the bar clock - all seems to fall in time with the tommy-gun rhythm - *E7 played with vigour*

...by the time I get tomorrow

use that, he thinks – perhaps the sun will shine on his
face when he leaves the bar – the steep steps are beautiful,
caked with the palimpsest of alcoholic strata – spit, ash &
spilled beer – he pushes the pull door & sighs – try again in
the sweated air & his mind is gone from this chore of leaving
– leaving home, leaving bars, to never arrive at that far-flung
elsewhere, high on Sugar Candy Mountain, mad Cockaygne
running around his brain – nothing but raw fruit to eat but
there's all manner of spirit in fruit – the paradise may not
yet be lost
    he farts melodiously – a fanfare for the common man,
cries the priest – the barman calls him a filthy bastard & a
cowboy enters the bar stage left - the clock ticks louder, its
hands fly backwards & - in slow-motion – it explodes

*

bleh! - bleh-hu! - bleeeh-hu! - ah! - thrice sneezing in the
pollenated wind the priest, wiping his rheumy stare with an
unholy snotrag, blesses himself quietly without any authority,
as such, & tries to re-focus on the turgid soup of a Soho
mid-morning – he feels the touch of mystic poltergeists at
work in his threadbare soul, still slightly awry from last
night's infusions, he surveyed a world unhinged, a gunge of
inexactitudes synchronizing at the confluence of Dean Street
& Romilly – a Jew, long frock of darkness, exaggeration of
cossack headwear, passes on a coughing moped – two
indeterminate dogs bark stupidly at a rubber bone,
unthrown, unsqueaking – the disinterested sun is ageing the
skyline of jagged rooftops – a busker threads a new B string
through the tiny hole beneath the peg, his cap upturned on
the damp paving, only copper for his talent – a street
magician juggles, soft green imperfect spheres at first then an
array of multi-coloured batons – the chrome table flashes

347

between their revolving forms – Degory Priest, still reeling from the sneezes, listens – the busker pauses for half a cigarette that he then extinguishes on the sole of his boot – he strums a morbid A minor then a strident G7 – closing his eyes to the indifferent street he wails, the words floating in speech bubbles past the locked windows above the cafés' awnings – he is a lineman for the county, he trills, & has driven many roads – no you're not & no you fucking haven't, thinks the sceptical priest

high pollen count today, Degory dons his wrap-around sunglasses & loosens his greasy dog collar with his thumb & forefinger – he searches in the sun for clues, directives – his senses overloaded, mustn't lose the point of the day – calming his fevered head, assimilating the input – he attempts to fashion a sermon, to pluck the text from the shapes & colours – pulsating liquids of brain & gut – driven by this need, a desire to explain himself to a god in whom he has no faith – nothing made more sense the more he thought, so he stopped - perhaps the sermon must convey faith in something he needs – bit of backdoor thinking – a need more than he wants but he wants it for all time – more than eternity then, desire for the infinite – he frowns & attempts to light a well-chewed cigar – a lorry barks & grinds its gears – he sits at a cafe & orders a mug of tea – the mug is blue, chipped white rim – the teabag, thoughtfully left in so that his preferred strength of brew can be achieved, has burst – theatre of cruelty, forest of fallen fruit – he wishes for the cloth of heaven & asks the waitress for a light – she brings him seven matches in a charred box, three dead – he takes a confident swig of the disappointingly lukewarm brew & is rewarded by a mouthful of tealeaves – they swim like ants before his reluctant swallowing & nestle in his wrecked teeth – tickle, irritant spores – ble-huuuu! - fuck it - bleh! bbbleh-huuu! – he descends the tube station steps as if they were a ladder to Hades & gets on a train mercifully free of humanity – alighting at Tottenham Court Road he staggers the short distance to his favourite watering-hole, dog to old vomit, downstairs again, surely now nearing earth's core - it is bloody well hot enough that's for sure, gladdened by the shimmering, metallic gleam from bar & optics, he rests his sacred arse on a stool & orders a double Tequila to stem the flood of unruly statismospores & ease the accumulated traumas of too many vicious mornings - the barmaid greeted the familiar holy wanderer with a not uncheery grunt & playfully polished his shaved head with her bar-cloth - the fake lamps reflected his weary comic grimace in their bell-curve brass – little transparent red bulbs in imitation of sad candle or smirk of gaslight

'...my hair grows on the inside...'

he said wryly, sneaking a look into her chilled blue eyes

she forced a laugh, unamused, faraway – in the brassy lampshade's surface he saw the cowboy enter beyond her shoulder – the barmaid smiled genuinely at the cowboy & blew him a theatrical kiss - he sat heavy, imperiously, in the seat nearest the jukebox & took out the Times crossword, tapping his colossal boots on the metal foot-rail - his impenetrable brown Stetson, air-holes, roughened leather – uncompromising, like his sandstone features – overhead, beyond the ceiling, in the untamed street, chattering typewriters reverberated in the heads of office drones moping to their lunch hours - the cowboy was in his element, he relaxed in his skin like a sun-dulled lizard – The Pale Priest felt usurped - as if the vast weight of America's imperial past had occupied the bar's passive Iberian charm, a battleship off the coast, sabres rattled – the priest sank low in his seat, uneasy in the shadows he eyed him, he knew that it was now this effortlessly mellow yet ominous stranger's town to do with as he pleased

the waitress set a brandy chaser up & he drank it down in a tossed gulp – no money changed hands – Poor Degory, not prosperous by any stretch, felt a sudden need for music, a poignant soundtrack to this unsolicited Spaghetti Western – he went to the jukebox & stood at the cowboy's broad back, inhaling gently the aroma – copper, musk & vultures, salt & dry tobacco – he chose three songs to compliment his altered state – returning to his shady seat as Carole King reassured him that he was no longer friendless – The Cowboy smirked, lit a half-cigar - luxuriant, nebulous loops that vanished like spirits through the yellow ceiling - tobacco-dust apparitions of the far-flung parched prairies – his eyes were like prairies, unremitting & kin to murder

the song ended & Neil Young said to an old man that he was a lot like him – above, in the real world, morose lorries mithered at the traffic lights in the monochrome ghost of an unstoppable rain

The Cowboy hummed/whistled along to the bare tufts of Neil's dejected guitar that skidded on slippery, dazed molasses through the grubby air, finding the sunburned parts of the skin & inhabiting every arid pore – he opened the paper to the puzzle pages & he considered the last clue, chewing on the biro tip – letting the nib hover over the packed crossword tantalisingly, as if about to pounce on an answer – he muttered to himself

'...4 down, 8 letters - insubstantial plaster wound around top of a cut...'

he looks up at the ceiling, at his dissolving smoke rings – the barmaid coughs lightly into her cupped hand & polishes the bar top – Neil sings that he's a lot like she was

the cowboy croons along & the barmaid blushed as she wrung out the cloth in the steel sink – The Spectral Priest felt the delicious welling of a tear in his eye, despite himself, a tear not born of any recalled sadness, & all of a sudden he felt irretrievably older than the man Neil was whining about – again, alas, time had stopped – it was lunch hour forever – the emotionless jukebox whirred another disc & plopped it

350

flat on the rubber turntable – Scott Walker, himself born an angel, lugubrious in a mist of hissing damage, intoned like a monk the opening couplet – loneliness, capital L – the cloudy priest sank back in his chair & pulled his denim cloak up over his shoulders – he imagined the rain above him through the concrete – the roads, the pavements, the endless trudge of the people, the puddle's deepening shades of blue – he sipped his liver's nemesis gingerly, the slice of lemon bobbing, kissing his lips with its bitter acid, wondering, not without a wry hint of carelessness, if he would ever see the sunshine again

*

The Troubadour thinks back on the last march - he is seeing himself back there now, clearly, in his crystal ball of white rum, emerging from a gaggle of drunk women, on to a street mad with carnival & protest - the masses of excitable human flesh that thronged the city streets that day,-, reds striking the blues, he thought – positive arrows of anti-nazi lollipop banners jig the spaces above tousled summer hair – up ahead steel drums bubble on the cauldron of a flatbed truck toiling its way up the troubled route to the pulse of a collective steely dissent – further ahead in the park, beyond the nod of police horse & cackle of megaphonic urges, a huge stage , brightly adorned, is observed by six punks from their precarious roost in a creaking tree– thin electric guitars hiss over the assembly of anger & light

& there's a stone wall blooded with the bull-graffiti of comrades – tribal chants against the chancellor met with unfriendly fire – *slide up to barred A at 5th fret*

Degory Priest is there, of course, in full clerical garb & a red trilby - he rolls his third cigarette, sprinkling some sly Lebanese sorcery into the Old Virginia &, seeing The Troubadour lost, pointing the way to the frontline, a smile splitting his new wiry beard – he has sent some guy called Jeb up ahead to scout – they hitch a slow lift from another vague straggler called Nat – a nervy golem risen through the rank & file & leaning from a dilapidated green Bedford van among a forest of hirsute faces – patchouli & essence of oak – the Priest speaketh

"...been through the long street & past the picket line – saw Billy Brigg in Braxton, I mean Brixton...uh..."

he's at the mercy of the smoke & firewater now – his brain is mudlarking, unable to breathe - reeking proles of childish thought churn through the fast accumulating debris – undaunted, he continues his analysis

'...bloody truncheon-happy Old Bill moving them back, a dark blue wall of shifting menace – beak visors & action-man faces, expressionless – a crying gypsy woman & her son in a painted wagon bedecked with fake flowers, her beau swearing at the coppers & wanting to set the class war in motion – he vaulted the chicken-wire fence to escape with no regard for himself – bastards...'

back to doubled E, hammer on the 7th

the collective march had snaked its way through the city since about ten in the morning, with stragglers joining in & drunkards bailing out, it kept a steady number & momentum, chanting, singing, until it reached the festival park - & though it had a festival's celebratory feel there was definitely a sense of underlying tension – it was a party on a minefield - so many battlefields to come - red is the colour of blood & toil & red was everywhere – a flag under which the commoners stride - yet nothing of the mere commonplace is acceptable here - it is the wink & promise of the bizarre which electrifies these troops – a steel band, two clowns on stilts, a reggae DJ on a milk-float - heavy political frowns of the gritty north, oleaginous mine-fodder for the most part - sliming out of the sump of monochrome cities, towns, and villages – *a burst of deep F minor on ARP synth* – Degory Priest is struck from behind on the nape of his neck by some randomly hurled object - the conflict feels real now – his mouth full of bitten tongue, chomping down on savage words – leading The Troubadour reluctantly into battle – though neither's heart rallied under any flag – they established their camp as the warriors from the south – they were made welcome but with a slight air of suspicion hanging, for some saw them as lightweights, blinking one-eyed sovereigns from the country of the blind

& The Troubadour looks back as the last march rolled forward through time - taking cover & respite in pubs, busy, nervous landlords eyeing the refugees – slow, delectable pour of brown bubbly pint after the walking – old Degory Priest disappears to the toilets in conspiracy with a flat-capped dealer to score something sweet for the next push – the fat jukebox explodes with the opening bars of Sweet Home Alabama – a Scottish voice, thick with phlegm & revenge, gives a second-hand rebel yell

& The Troubadour rests his head on the wall & is time-slipped again to the American past – foggy ditches & cold, reddened meadows in the throes of civil war – yet the images are indistinct due to the ancient gun-smoke & the riots of the recent London past getting woven into the tapestry – musket-fire & tear gas – maybe the tab of acid is coming up, he thought – it was only a light trip, the Priest had said, he used to call them 'lunch breaks' - something to take the danger out of the day – the music curled a little at the edges – the Alabama riff with its twangs, plucks & pushes, warping in a confederate swim of crosses & stars - his slick thoughts ran together in confluence, where new mirages were forged – he tried writing it all down as it swam in his soupy head

The Bull run a raffle to pay for a van - the little stream of tributary marchers mixed with confederates sneaking down back alleys - one man in a wheelchair with blooded

stumps of fingers plays Love The One You're With on a three-string guitar – D with G hammered on – strum with fingers, tamping etc. - old school style – in an old barn two brutal military stills full of whisky – wounds dabbed with iodine & rotgut – the ridges in the distance rise through the gunpowder clouds above plains where buffalo roam, home on a range of monochrome fields in spring - North London is northern border – the north rising again - a stone is thrown & strikes the balls of a bluff copper – a sad little journalist scribbles in pub corner with the threat of a buttoned macintosh camera hidden – set the old anarchist wizard on him

Degory Priest's newly-acquired Yankee-Burger reeks in the beery air – a travelled man on many roads – now he drifts through this fantasy of conflict reeling through the Troubadour's laughing mind – they leave the pub & join the march again, Troubadour still scrawling barely legible hieroglyphics in the notebook

Poor Degory, he spent his whole general grant as a student to buy a trip to India – travelled 'cross America & took peyote with the Navajo roadmen so he always comes up shy & low after their seeping mantras slowed his blood

"...where the fuck..." - The Grinning Priest hazily asks – "...are we headed?..."

'...follow the fold, man...follow the fold...'

they enter another bar, shamrocks & leprechauns, shit-tourist Irish, Guinness looks ok though, great pint for when you're tripping, like drinking sweet glue – The Troubadour reads the word 'snug' printed backwards on the window & flashes to hooded rebels in smoked out streets – sombre news in 70s sepia, rubble & women in headscarves holding their kin close - greasy children throwing rocks & bottles of piss at a retreating phalanx of crouching police – he gazes at the march passing the window – faces shouting slogans through the backwards lettering – guns & anger – the image burned his eyes – they finished their beers & left after a catastrophic attempt at darts that, at least, had the barman in hysterical laughter

outside a *drang* precedes the slow *sturm* brewing in the stoned acoustic river of the angry chanting hordes – stink of sickly dope slowly fed back through the crowd, as if they were swimming upstream in its flow - impossibly distant, Billy Bragg barks & gurns his Clash-lite, nerdy threats from a crackling transistor radio-strength p.a. & ice-veined Rastas lurk in the wild sonic boom delay of a newsagent's doorway – head-swung club of bass housed in low dub – a long, dark smoke seedless & reasoning – ground out a batty-boy nation – vegetation for the people – in hock to the vanity of a waited-on man – *Emaj7 through big hall echo with reverb & delay* - standing over the whirr of radio dials showing the drop in pressure – the DJ toots on a fat J – may tell your ma – many natty fears in matted Camden lock – seen making not baldness on their head – mau-mauing the Thatcher flak with his lupine scowl – a cool white suit in Hammersmith – two heavens clashing in swords of brassy sunlight – a kid in a Santana T-shirt with the legend 'ARE SHIT' scrawled beneath with black felt-pen pisses against the stately edifice of Barclays Bank

'...a serious blow to the reactionary forces, the walls are tumbling...'

saith the priest with a grin of pure malice, wide-eyed, amphetamine stare, Troubadour can't quite meet that stare, always looking beyond or through, sham geezer, shaman gazer

another bar, more beer, the trip is steadying itself now, more manageable - a stone cold harbour, this tavern – in the sooty, grimed toilets staggery Goths pee over the ridge of their leather studded belts in slick streams of yellow-green – *E9 through fuzz pedal* - & through the cracked grid of a wiry window frosted, ANTI is seen daubed on an Etam boutique next to the Sharp's Burger & Chicken house – always against, always anti-everything – Degory laughs & The Punk Troubadour groans as veteran hippies hijack the jukebox & rally in musky, saffron ranks – they nod their snarled hair as strains of the Ozark Mountain Daredevils waft through the bar making the anarchist rebels in the snug yell – apocalypse approaching, keep your head low for there are horsemen in the sky – in the real world far-flung miners huddle over braziers & flying pickets charge – *acapella, four part, repeated practising of scales* - bags of used consumer goods form bleak ridged ranges in the ghost-torn roads – lights flash, sirens & dim cries are heard, thud of pigbag rock on papa's shield – Albion Civil War, these steamy ghosts, yes, wisping their way to heaven through the burst ribcages of the tatty confederate dead

The Union Troubadour he flashes once more to last Friday's beery afternoon at Dean St. & Romilly - a Soho-soaked, bullish Degory Priest was dreamily reminiscing of his time in Amsterdam – a small church behind a secret wall - & he told of the mystical old figure he had met out by the dockside – he passed an address & phone number – the day was full of diamond light, enriching the already flamboyant colours of the street

The Troubadour had ignored him but something in the tale stuck because he thought of it now, how the figure that he had spoken of had reminded him of his old childhood dream – the hat, cloak, face unseen – he pondered the collective unconscious as they escaped the threat of the bar, the priest with half a pint of Guinness sneaked under his topcoat

outside it is chaos, the cops have started a charge to stop a phalanx of stragglers from going up a side-street & there are ugly cries & yelps as the mood shifts & the reds tangle with the blue line as it collapses - but Degory now - look at him go! - thieving the baton of a stunned police man –

breaking his panda-car window & handing it to a small boy who bursts out laughing & runs off with it waving above his head the copper in pursuit like the scene was ripped straight out of a comic

& Degory just smiles as he jogs through hurricanes of musical debris up the crossfire main-street of stones & rolling hubcaps & black burning tyres stacked & melting – smog flowers

The Troubadour Of Revolt spies the Pubcorner Wizard as he sits in a filthy beer garden - deep in his cups - calling out priest-ward a litany, bait & hook

"...a holy man running! – Christ but heaven must be ablaze! - or there's a good fuckin' bet to be placed...Father, join me for a trickle of joy-juice...we only have ourselves to blame after all..."

The Lost Troubadour, who has at last given up chasing the priest's coat-tails, sits in an alley & takes out his notebook

& how many more dry days of a broken April? – will spring make it to summer? – how many houses, hotels, bedsits will shuffle by in consecrated night? – an acrid snare & pungent bass pounds the ears of our anti-hero– a lifetime of song can be buried in one deep note – still, young – an Apache of the plain shadows, low moan of Marvin Jr. – three-stepping through dangers, through these pauses in time – a caesura of hushed oaths – you are time's thief, tired of the red noise - now wanting white & quiet, a quiet of his own

& finally they both meet up somehow at the gate of The Grand Gig In The Park & the wretched hejira inevitably crashes & burns at this, the final field of dreams – Red Jimmy is there already, standing on a crate, he purses his lips at the churning soundcheck on the stage in middle-distance above a sea of spiky, lacquered & skinned heads – the hippies have slunk away to the back to dream of past rebellions in a tent made of patches & hope, odour of rancid sandalwood & lava-lamplit, lumpy mattress bygones - sham revolution '69 - the soft lips of punk girls black on powdery white - everyone craning necks to see the band, nudging & shambling, a hundred unnameable energies passing through the crowd like a current - leaflet paper-trails lead to busy, fast-talking militant stalls of dark badges & blood-tight literature - bleak pamphlets stamped in the typeface by a century of stern graduate schoolbooks - the prospect of Nevsky - deepest blood red the Proudhon, biblical black the Tolstoy - & Thoreau green as a pondered meadow - *a deftly plucked C maj7 on nylon guitar, straight staccato rhythm of tambourine* - what looks like, & may well be, dog-food smeared on bent paper plates is passed in a line down the communal chain -The Lonely Dog Troubadour takes a plate of yellow aromatic lumps speared by a plastic fork with two prongs of three missing - cud memory, ugly chunter of abomasum - crackle & spit of the hungry, bilious speakers - fed back, repressed pluck of detuned strings - wayward politics & staunch musical opinions swirl into the head & then out of the head into other heads that are busy talking to other heads that as a consequence begin a new strand & talk it out of their heads into heads who

Uroborus, the tasty tail of time - Jimmy Pursey yowls - aahyezalldooin?

a fat punk boy sits in pressed grass with a lunchbox consisting of two ham rolls & an apple - while his father argues Trotsky to a sallow woman in a grey shawl, quiet & nodding - a mantra from the MC of cars parked illegally - will the owner of - blue paper aeroplane thrown at yellow balloon bearing the legend 'PEAS' - it misses & the legend sails into heaven where it can pop against the barbed wire atop Old Pete's waiting gate

a biker jacket hung wearily on a rosebush, its own legend partially obscured - just the mysterious words 'Dr. River' remain visible - *descending horn scale in G*
"...& who is Doctor River?..."
asks Degory Priest much later, very stoned
"...for whom does the river doctor flow?..."
'...Jesus made the water wine but the devil is your barman...my head aches, my brain rebels...grant me a few moments solace as I void the old colon & peruse the daily rag for the wisest word...'
saith a passing cur
'...who gives a rat's fart about old philosophies...hot air long dispelled by the iceman from the mountain...thus speaketh I – Degory Zarathustra - hold a candle to history by all means but burn it at both ends...we walk in the walksteps of forefathers - these bastard peanuts are stale - ah, me...so dear old dreadlocked departed Bohemia crawls underground again...leaving markets sellin' tie-dye bloody shirts & brass bangles to ward of the existential dread...'
he farts
his wry face quizzical in demi-monde illuminations of a headlamp's glinting chrome – he examines the rogue packet of peanuts with suspicious eye
'...there, sell by June 5th...months old...four to be exact...what kind of fucker sells old nuts to a man of the cloth?...'
he shouts the question through the window of a startled security man's Vauxhall Viva van making him spill his coffee & use unholy epithets toward the holy head as it retreats – but the priest's mind is on the next jape & scampering across the Mary-popping rooftops of his drug-tangled landscape – *A minor to B minor*
scorched earth of music, year zero – these radio burns on the endless unfolding tapestry are the blemishes on the skin of time - back on the stage, red words like bruises

tumble from regiments of Marshall amplifiers highly stacked – an anaemic waif in a mud-spattered, grey army coat is shouting the wrong lyrics to 'Boredom' – the priest yells into his oblivious ear

'...say what comes to your heart, Brother Renegade – may you never get to live by the party line – give peas a chance & Lennon's on sale again – old princess Yoko can't get comfy – it's all for the buzz, cock - soul singers, poets burning out like blimps in foreign fields of Pathe news – O the duality! - act dumb, Brother, write out your poems to nowhere! – read your Berryman dreams & sing as you dive from the bridge of sighs – & for why? - because life, my friend, is boring but you must never admit it – listen to the wag that tells old jokes to your soul...'

told, succinctly & not unreasonably, to shut up & fuck off he does so with a deep bow – The Troubadour can hear a saxophone & presumes that X-Ray Spex are playing, the view of the stage a distant memory - & yes now Degory Priest is singing a made-up blues to some wizened old tune of the American Bardlands – a ripped heart from the breast of Pocahontas – as old pissed-up but still waving Berryman plummets to earth in league with Donny Hathaway's spectre from a Minneapolis parapet – just the two of them – good old JB hits the deck & knows no more his dreams & eulogies – his books in the college & his broken glasses in a museum – a wag dogs somewhere & The Troubadour is losing the trip's edge now & sips the priest's firewater from the shared, stolen Guinness glass – a trebly hum through his mind dissolves, the kick-drum bores holes in the shocked air above the crowd's baying – The Troubadour gazes up to the tree to see if any angelic vision is forthcoming *glissando strings of a harp descend through plangent minors* – a skinhead on a precarious branch is pissing on the head of an insensible biker - bore-dumb, very hum-drum – a thrashed chord & the last of the alcohol goes flying straight to hell

*

meanwhile, back in the permanently paused temporal wasteland of a billion smoky lunchtime pubs, The Grand Revolution Of The Proletariat stews in the juice of another insurgency postponed – the newspaper mastheads are blood red & blot out the sun, playing charades with the stars & mirrors - coffee hubble-bubbles in a stained pot on a camping stove on the faux-marble kitchen worktop – breed of bitters, grumbling saints – look now & behold a deflated trinity, Degory, Red Jimmy, Lonely Troubadour – they sit at a table with a chatty, wide-eyed girl who says she is from Jamaica – Grace, she calls herself – Red Jimmy mutters 'Amazing Grace' into the ear of Degory who raises a churchy eyebrow before allowing a gentle half smile to crease his cheek – she prattles like a rehearsing nun, a speed-bible, all secret tongues & glottal coughs, a waif that they seem inexplicably to have become adhered to along the way, permanent, like chewing-gum on a shoe – these heart-worn pilgrims that were so puffed with the rhythms of insurgency at the Last March's outset now order their tired beers, watery & shit-brown, in the auditory shadow of the last bell before the bomb drops - ring-a-ding-a-fucking-ding – in this anon palace, this dingy dump of dominoes dragged – the waif Grace, embarrassingly punk-aware, red daisy-booted chic, blushing at the thrill of it all – by way of preparation for the conversations ahead, silently, in his head, The Newsreel Troubadour cascades back through old footage of boxing fights, natural disasters, framed photos of stiff-jawed assassins in East-end saloons – *strum of G on Rickenbacker, hint of a slight chorus effect, phasing* – or an extravagant journey to the fatal motorcade, JFK turns, waves - who is he trying to arouse? – gunshot merciless, straight to nowhere, boys, knoll & depository, bushes & burnt books form the shadows taking aim – Jackie chasing his devastated mind across the boot – The Troubadour blows the smoke of his cigarette at the pearl-coloured light bulb & watches it swirl around it like ectoplasm - he drawls in a voice that his ageing heart does not entirely recognise

"...this is my modern mythology – the pentagrams of our age – witch burners & grave-diggers, the old news is bored so every now & then they haul another fable out to titillate - there's a conspiracy going around that Lee Harvey did it..."

the girl looks at him with faintly smiling lips, perhaps, & yet a frowning brow

& the implacable Captain Rehab looking back sees it all of course – hears the music play on, subliminal – Gil-Scott Heron, doleful hipster, & Howard Devoto, somnolent, wise monk – deepest street cool followed by Burroughs flim-flam lit by hand-me-down daylight

& yes, still locked together tightly Degory, Grace & The Lonely Troubadour have distanced themselves – they no longer need each other's words & are alone, safe within their own tacky B-movie – mandate my arse – the sewer's grace notes worming from the floorboards

& yes the moon is a dull, white ray-gun's flame frozen into the glacier of forever, a lens-shutter opening

& Pubcorner Wizard is there, has always been there, in his rattle of a flotsam stick chair – The Rattling Troubadour sits astride a somewhat sturdier stool opposite & waits – & sure enough the oracle bloviates

'...you look lost...am I right?...'

'...ha!...is it that obvious?...'

'...want my advice? – I'll give it ye anyways so do fuck off now if ye don't – set sail, follow anything, anywhere – it's all the bloody same – move on, rest a bit, move again...'

'...move for the sake of motion eh? – what's the point? – what's uh...my reward, so to speak?...'

362

'...a river clings to one true belief under brethren clouds & she rolls unquestioning – all else is loss & envy...'

'...so, I'm barely even a river then – not even that bloody much...'

'...see that rain out there? – well, once upon a time it was an endless ocean – only to be sucked up without so much as an annunciating angelus into useless heaven by some bloody interfering god or other – heaven, a dream-state, neither newborn or dying – then, without warning, dropped, splat, into a gutter, whisked hurtling down a drain, through a fetid sewer-pipe & out into the bloody flow & off we go again...'

'...re-incarnation...'

'...better than that...'

'...an atheist river – it has its possibilities...'

'...better still...'

'...can I get you a beer?...'

'...more filthy water, ha!...yeah, pint of Dictum's ta...'

The Troubadour, pondering, fetches two thinly-foamed jugs of dark ale to the bottle-crowded table

'...that thing you just said – about the rain – I'd like that to be the sole quote on the back of my biography – if my bloody life warrants such a depressing endeavour of course – let me write it down, do you mind? – it is perfect, just that quote, black background maybe, yeah, no colour...no distraction...'

'...everything's a fucking distraction – the big secret is to find out from what, exactly, are we being distracted...what, pray, will be the title of this esteemed biographical fiction.?...'

'...I don't know, a single word, something cryptic, arcane – or just leave it blank maybe – like an unfinished crossword answer – or a jigsaw with pieces missing – call it what you like – a blank slate, up to the reader...'

'...like a river...'

The Blank Troubadour winked at the slightest grin slow appearing on the old Pubcorner Wizard's unshaven face
'...better than a river...'
The Wizard stared at him until The Troubadour felt the sudden need to close his eyes – behind him at the bar two Americans talking loud of their nation's pithy history - brash Texan brogue - & how, inevitably, it was being mostly written by the winners – they are scattershot in their selective blueprints, randomly choosing events from their country's allocated pages of time & speculating as to their truth, their resonance – don't trust the printed word, they hinted, always read between the lines, they cautioned each other – they go together to the jukebox & push a roll of coins into the slot – chnk! k-chnk! – The Troubadour frowns, he fears the worst, but surprisingly the first bars of 'Rhythm Of Cruelty' ring out – The Troubadour, his face resting on his open palm, in a dreamy voice, without opening his eyes, mumbles
'Secondhand Daylight...I bought this last week...'
The Americans overhear – they give him a thumbs-up, grinning, unnerving, like Mormon twins hovering too long at a closing door
'...Love Devoto, man, great lyrics...' one says
'...better than Shelley?...' says the other
'...Pete or Percy?...' says The Poet Troubadour & after a pause the Mormon ghosts both laugh - hearty yank laughter
& behind The Troubadour's closed eyelids, The Wizard sees rattling magazines of snipering bullets hit the motorcade – repeats of old soap operas, correctly used in the service of distraction – Oswald twitches his finger & J.R. Ewing falls dead in a Dallas shower – & Martin Luther King is dead, long live Martin Luther – opening a can of worms – someone knocking at the door – bruise of faith, blemishes on the skin of the epoch – & later, later, as the night falls enough for them to no longer wonder where they are, the songs merge like bacterial gobbets - steel pulses throb in

kettledrum skulls – sickly Lebanese clouds & cartoony
bleeps & bloops – a lightshow, olden of style, hippy era -
brume of gloopy planet faces – blissful smiles of moomin-
headed anarchists – Vietnam chopper blades alternate with
the ceiling fan's hum – the devil is dreading the pompous
pilot at the controls & the last helicopter leaving Altamont –
105 & rising, going to be a White Xmas – *C major, heavy
strum, on cheap folk guitar through huge speaker distorted*
– testing, testing, one two, one two three what are we fighting
four? – & bless his soul, what's wrong with the fatty white
man in the Graceland palace? – he was on the toilet
midnight to six, man - first time he's ever opened his dumb
hill-bill mouth near a steely mic – all the way from Memphis
- Dillinger on the running-board in a needle-smart suit as he
takes aim & fires – the king's TV explodes - cool news - &
always the music, the music the bloody thread wriggling
through history to tag each memory with a few pretty notes,
a couple of verses

   & elsewhere, beyond this pub window that an ashamed
night has made opaque, the priest is drifting back through
different hours, with a different music, to the stoned park -
from the gates of David – his drug-strafed mind struggles to
discern real from otherwise, twisting the letters that make up
his thought, he is clueless, he has no solid answers to the
welling vagueness – a rumbling basement party throbs from
a pavement grill – he stands astride it, holy Marylin, mother
of god – coat teasing in the staccato waves – The Upsetter,
globular thump & mental rant – it slowly slides across the
fragrant air in stilted, echoic waves – an unsound system
saying nothing too much, saying it loud – he could fake his
hipster entrance, assimilate, bring them sinning to his fold -
many black ears here to plug with Soma, he thinks – but he
cannot pass for a native – priestly jackboot, nothing like the
real thing, sweet sweetback, cakewalk & bootblack

& all across the bubbling city the pulse reverberates - all
the crazed new sounds are beatifically integrated into the
soup - risen through time from the spicy bellies of a
hundred deafening basements - time was, his youth or some
such arcane whimsy, when this dubby thud underpinned the
bell-bottomed strut of a sun-baked pavement, he would
recoil into his white shell, don his paler mask & dance out
of time, conspicuous in his heartfelt arrhythmia – he would
shun the high-strung sibilance & pin sharp steps in bold suits
– ye really gotta hear The Four Tops on acid, man – try &
get some down-home feel in your bleachy bones – & the
underground days were all nights, back in the druggy vortex
of Mornington Crescent's lidded heavy windows – behind
unsmoked aspidistras - playing revolution all night with
white-bread Malcolm Xs marking the spot from stage right,
seeking the buried treasure in second-hand record stalls – or
further back yet, sad half-remembered melodies heard at
churchy parties – furtively pairing off with the most adherent
wallflower girls – all the love they lost in slow-dancing scout
huts & converted papal halls – late, last-dancing Martini
horses awaiting the gunshot's mercy – the pound of bass
from Philly, royal colonisation - cheesy & lyrical in blue/red
disco strobe & cold glitter-ball shrapnel – the sound of the
founding fathers, mother, father, sister, brother, O brother
there's too many of us dying so where the fuck art thou? –
meanwhile, at the dark end of a lonely street some cool,
angular hipster, some Jesse James Carr lookalike, spins a
gun & approaches the fizzing live microphone through veils
of reverb - from a drive-by Buick 6 William & Dan Penn
hold a pair of flick-knives to the trembling treble of his voice
   old-time throaty rebels rocking the cradled blues –
splintered dada beats – & punk flowers evolving, awakening,
stretching up - undertonic Eires to the throne
   the good old stiff-upper-trippy, lippy British army out
there with flowers in their guns & boot-polish in their hair -

fifteen hundred tons & what have you got? - not another day older & a socialist plot - white youth, no vinyl solution - black youth live outside the constitution & looking for Robin in da Hood - this park of dreamers, this park of fumes - a good place for a new picnic under the lightning rod of social change

all this & more the sad priest let fly in whispers from a silent mouth agape - it is late & the last march is over - the crew has shaken drunken, druggy Grace & he & The Lonely Troubadour have found themselves again - they are dry as a desert in a pub with no name

The Polar Bear, The Stagger Inn, The Pillars Of Mercury, The Dumb Waiter, The Bollocky Bawd, The Insipid Fox, The Queen's Arse, The Blind Beggar, The Fat Swiller, The Rampant Goose, The Shite & Onion, The Avant Guardian, The Bleak Itinerant, The Stout Librarian, The Bald Ventriloquist, The Duchess Of Infinity

they care not, as long as they are allowed to nurse their wounded ales & sit staring into a lifeless mirror behind the beautiful, rosy-cheeked barman, grinning like a toy soldier in red-coat & tie

& later still, from a different hell, back where it all began a million years ago, their circle unbroken, they stumble to the pavement up twisty stairs cracked & without Red Jimmy who has stayed to chat to another wizard in a different shadow - they sheepishly emerge, Laurel & Hardy, blinking & always astounded at the universe - they didn't even know they were kept underground - blinded by the neon scissors cutting the cloth of the shy, starry firmament - numbed by the incessant street's garish blink of slogans - neither of them the slightest bit concerned by the sad wail of sirens & grunts & shouts for help & mercy - oblivious, as a solemn-faced party dreg slithers by on ripped boots with a whisky bottle tightly gripped, hat askew - he shouts in their face that the niggers are coming - laughs like a flushed toilet full of bottle-tops & pukes into a damp pile of yesterday's newspapers

"...car for Mr. Hitler!..." - Degory cries

he gets in & of course it is crawling with snails – he exhales a sigh, sweetened by cognac & tired lies - the last white man in the city of oily night - still heavily panting like a chased dog – still roaming the old atheist boulevards with his Ginsberg bald-spot - forever looking for a broken, holy gun to angrily fix – the priest halloos the dumb night

'...ye who seek to meet faces! – shall only meet thyself! – you Kerouac elegiacs! – you Bull Lee bullies! You howling black lakes! Ye Eliot messes! Ye cracked dawn chanticleers & chroniclers of night! - I shall serenade y'all with equal measures of shite from the papal bull...let the devil be my megaphone...'

"...three a.m. is the hour of conspirators...'

says a woozy voice from the awful doorway of a blind pig bar just closing - *D slid up from one fret down*

this confidant has new information, a tale to tell - Elvis alive on the moon – Loch Ness chock full of giant lizards & the Roswell crash-site in the desert thick with the wreckage of other, further worlds – out on the unfold of strobing highways & rural routes deaf vampire televisions are drawing blood from the teary blues of sharecroppers

& the suits & ties are pouring lemon-floated piss into the enamel carafes of wine bar urinals – furred lemony square adrift on a hot, buttery river – time passeth slow & lo, The Terrible Priest gathers himself, raises his febrile voice one last time

"...this city's like the plug pulled out of a dirty bath – I'm sick of trying to get saved – from now on let's get lost - taxi-man, sail on brother...sail me to my mother moon or a land of milky honey – save my sorry Hancock arse with a last trip around the big city sprawl..."

& he bows deep, waves a shaky hand, pale as a threadbare glove of cheap silk, & falls sideways into a clatter of bins spilling out the rotting fruit, grease-rags & ugly, ashen, beery dregs all over the cursed pavement – ah, fuck it, he'll sleep where he fell, he thinks & sticks a defiant middle-digit up, past the traffic lights, in the general direction of the great sleeping almighty

*

Red Jimmy & Low-Fi Troubadour, implacable both, dutifully free-smoking in chains, café table, Chinatown morning early – Jimmy, he is pregnant with pause but presses play & says mournfully

'...he's got plans y'know, The Priest, for you, I mean...'

'...oh yes? – maybe I have plans for him...'

'...I smell the shit on the wheels, pal – he don't stick to plans exactly, if y'follow me? – don't mean he doesn't have them though...he's totally fucking mad, of course he is, but he figures that the world is mad too & it kind of evens out – like everyone is following a map of Prague but they're actually in Paris, y'know? – or tryin' to solve a puzzle with yesterday's clues...'

'...I like a puzzle...ask me a question, a riddle...do ye know any?..."

'...uh, yeah, here ye go - what is there more of in the universe, hens or boats?...'

'...uh...I...what do...uh?...'

'...too late, time's up – you gotta go with the first thought – first response, best answer, always...'

'...ko-ans – is that what...'

'...better, more like the quicksilver babble of a speed-freak – old Degory tutored me in the art – he has his uses – see how disarming my spiel can be?...'

'...I like you despite myself ha! – that's true...you're not one for small talk...'

'...small talk is for small ideas, pal – even babies can point to the fuckin' sky & make up shit about the weather – hone it down, I learned that on the railways...'

'...you were a bloody union rep, so Degory told me, that right?...'

'...yeah, back in the days of the militant underground – back in the good times - not now though, too much shit involved – I'm just a drone again now, prefer it – y'see both sides of the coin though, running the union stuff - bosses, plebs – trust neither of the cunts – all want their turn of the screw, y'know?...'

'...more anarchist than socialist then?...'

'...who cares? – really I mean? – I cry for night, it falls, now cry in darkness – Beckett, you read him?...'

The Troubadour nodded though he hadn't

'...yeah, thought so, you look the type – good old Sam, Endgame gotta be the best, then Krapp & let no fucker tell ye different – stay out of the stressful, the old bloody rows – apolitical, a-bloody-everything for that matter – sages, proper ones, true wizards, y'know? – they don't ever deal in platitudes, ephemera – only give ye hard-boiled sweets you can really suck on – it keeps its flavour, y'know? - all the rest of their guff is nowt but fuckin' sherbet, pal, gone before ye tasted it...'

they moved on to Soho & found another little café, medium-greased, English as tattered bunting, poster of Bobby Moore holding the world cup aloft – in plain sight it rotted, hidden, never seen before in all Jimmy's time a wandering –he sat dumbfounded for a minute staring about him, astonished by its enigmatic existence

the owner was called Ash – he had ash on his blue trousers, his face ashen, he dwelled in the ashtray of his truncated appellation forever – he stubbed his cigarette butt on the drainpipe by the door & watched the last spark fly upward 'til all that remained was his name

The Troubadour flicked his own ash a few inches beyond the ashtray &, whilst nobody watched, hastily smeared it into the myriad blemishes of the off-white tablecover – Red Jimmy shook himself free of his reverie

'...never seen this place, love it – perfect dissolution, the café of memory - this is where you should bring a woman on your first date – get her a fry-up & sit reading the Daily fuckin' Mirror while she pushes the bubble & squeak around tryin' to make eye contact – fuckin' great place this – beyond the intelligentsia's ken, y'know? – or misty-eyed girls at bus-stops, moony fuckin' barmaids drunk on a barfly's fumes – I suppose you want to write the great English novel, or some epic metaphysical fuckin' poem explainin' the obvious to dullards? – or some bloody double-album of prog-rock bollocks is it? – well, don't put a woman at the heart of it – you can bet they'll mess it up, make it all sticky & leave their fuckin' pubes on the toilet seat or cook posh food when you're craving egg & chips – to them you're a distraction, at best, trust me – pleasant or otherwise, y'know? – they absorb you like black holes – drained of anger & light – switch off the light & you're left with blind anger – this coffee is foul, want another one.?...'

'...you ever been in love Jim?...'

Jimmy paused & sniffed the coffee mug – thick aroma of carbonised ink, trace of bacon, washing-up liquid

'...love? – once – rub a dog's nose in its shit & it learns soon enough – I'm romantic though, don't get me wrong – capital R – you read any Gurdjieff? - love without knowledge is demonic – you'd like all that crap – words with smoke in 'em – natural as a lungful of Old Holborn & about as fuckin' good for ye – words don't work unless they're hooks – leave some cool tough-guy scars, y'know? – women, ha! –

may as well get requited love from a fuckin' rock – you want another coffee or what?...'

he gestured toward Ash who was piling the empty cups & plates from an adjacent table – his cigarette dangling precariously from his lower lip – ash fell on his apron – the next cigarette waited behind his hairy ear for a kiss of flame – the burgeoning sun caused him to squint through his own smoke – he glanced at them briefly, thinking, just more café talk, they'll forget tomorrow everything they've said & start again – he cleared up morsels of a million conversations – he wiped his hands on an eggy napkin – the sunshine warmer, the embers, the lost dreams, ash of past love

across the nondescript road a young girl clad in ballerina attire, no more than twelve, pirouettes & coupés in the red gaze of a one-legged tramp slumped in a doorway of The Admiral Duncan – a pool of lagery piss blossoming beneath his wrecked suit-trousers – the tableau is unflawed, the sick poignancy laden with an ignoble & unsustainable dramatic tension - a pushy starling tries & fails to pick up a burger bap blackened at its apex due to injudicious toasting by a tired vendor – the girl spins & spins, the old tramp stares & coughs – icy grace of matador, pathos of wounded bull

the sorrowful, blue road for miles stretching long

the confetti of time, the fractured ephemeral happenings unravel – the indiscriminate events drop randomly through the warp of a speeding windscreen's rectangle – the endless, spooling, road-hard news & tomorrow the party starts at noon

The Hipster Troubadour & Red Jimmy got a case of dynamite-strength homemade hooch – Jimmy's soul is still haemorrhaging romance but his snarly mouth just wants to brawl – he vows that he shall catch the last train homeward – though it is not home, not his anyway – he sets out his neat, machine-rolled, prison-thin cigarettes in a foolish chain,

looping in an infinite pattern that never returns to its origin –
he stammers his little mumbly story – every syllable a threat

'...they say it's so hard to kill a dream but believe me this
is as easy as it gets - got loose wires in my heart, pal – got an
absurd rhinoceros outside my door at night, no cure for that
– my supposed meta-life is just stray theatre - don't make me
over when you go, old chum - time is racing fast, for sure,
but my healing bones are dawdling – wish I was in Bantry
again back there with me old mum - or at Tilbury Riverside,
yeah...back on the barges – bunking the late-shift under a
disgusted moon, way down there at the dockside staring at
the crane's black profile against the ever-changing clouds –
the weeks are getting mighty astral again - ah, fuck it - the
only woman worth remembering is the one I can't forget...'

& with that Red Jimmy's head is long gone – way out on
the cracked streets – with his pack of stolen Luckies & Van
Morrison albums – ah but the Astral Troubadour still plays
the wired passenger spouting out all the wrong directions –
chiseller hobo – his spartan heart blustery in green swirl of
rag-shirt – pioneer spirit, seventy-proof, would that we could
follow - he is encountered again by Jimmy & the priest in
tow, from nowhere, as they all decline with the hour &
slither in a pool of ruined time – the good old back & forth
– back on the Islington drag - all the same old new - the
priest has been daubing a few grainy portraits of late - used
to be at Slade, he said – Red Jimmy thought that he had said
he had been in Slade &, as a fan of their early stuff, had
been impressed – he dabbles now, but still does a bit of
likeness to keep the old shaky hand in – he turns to sad Jim

"...are ye still wanting the painting lad? - I've not quite
perfected your self-portrait yet - it's in the boot of my old car
but it's up on bricks getting the chassis welded now – looks
fuck all like you so you'll probably love it..."

Red Jimmy nodded twice and made a square with his
hands & squinted through it at his inquisitors who posed

theatrically & the priest tweaked his waxen, wiry 'tache –
grown from nowhere – Troubadour & Priest framed in his
finger lens, both of them fake demure, coquettishly playful,
voxish, winking

"...I only like old music now – fuck art..."

Red Jimmy raised his bushy eyebrows as if at the child-
like absurdity of his own statement

"...jazz too - there's a club, underground - it is uh...kind
of out there on the edge of things – a buggy little place – it
lives beneath the river y'know? - my kind of world –
underground or under-river, all the same to me - I'll show
you if you like..."

so on & on through the wary streets, arm in arm, all
three blundering – the Majestic Father Thames sleeps down
by the Embankment bridge – they lurked awhile among the
sweet, homeless kings & queens under the arch of damp
brickwork - & passed around an unlabelled bottle of sour
whisky mash – a drear figure that appeared to be made of
drenched wool & hessian sporting a ruined bowler hat gave
them a swig of clear liquid from a small vial – it tasted of
grenadine & was viscous, clinging to the throat – a smell of
sweating patchouli brought a tear to the breeze - suddenly,
after scrounging his fourth cigarette from a passer-by, Red
Jimmy, eyes bright, hair wild, gesticulated conspiratorially &
gracefully ducked into a previously unnoticed archway that
led to a dimmer alley utterly concealed from the street's
view – downward the path sloped in near darkness, distant
music, vaguely classical, chamber quartet – from a rusted
vent there was a sickly reek of warm bread & urine - the
poor light hung with dancing insects & swirls of burnt paper
– the unnerving sense of a vast weight of green water
hanging overhead – & through the swim of cigarette smoke
the peeling roof of the tunnel seemed paper-thin, it was like
drowning in air knowing that vast water was perilously
suspended above – & yes the distant homeless waved from

the tunnel, from way on back there in the shallow light of the entrance & smiled, nodding approval

"...here..."

a small opening in the wall, the pipes & electrical wires that ran the length of the tunnel roughly draped around it, the red & yellow wires tied loosely with rope – a small, tin sign – The Isis Club - & below in red italics *vox malus ac tenebras* – Red Jimmy disappeared into the gloomy interior - peering through the dimmest doorway, The Lonely Wary Troubadour & the intrigued, circumspect priest ventured slowly after him – a gentle path slopes downward – dripping sour water from rusted pipes, the smell of patchouli stronger now, tingling in the throat

after a few hesitant seconds of doubt they stepped out a little more confidently, their bleary eyes gradually making out more of the surroundings – a moose head, a set of horse brasses, silver topped canes in a wooden rack, coats hung on hooks – arcane graffiti, beautifully written in a longhand of antiquity – a message in thick ink on white plaster-board

hark, the choking sob of city
confluence of time & song
established 2nd September 1666
ignis super - musica inferius

they increased their pace, Red Jimmy becoming invisible in the slow-curved obscurity ahead – they came to a door of dark, panelled wood & the priest tentatively pushed it open - any show of braggadocio they planned to affect was sharply arrested by an extraordinary vision – a large space, surreal after the claustrophobic path they had so far been used to – their eyes were drawn upward to a high ceiling hung with the faint red lights of a tinkling chandelier - out of the murkiness of the huge arched & vaulted chamber looming before them they gradually made out a small wooden stage – six high-backed chairs evenly spaced out – each had instruments leaning against or resting on them – violin, cello, clarinet, trumpet, saxophone & flute – behind, to stage left, an upright piano with, perched on the top, a bottle of rum & an empty glass – there were big cushions scattered over the concrete floor, low tables with ashtrays – high on the magnolia walls hung old reproductions of impressionist masterpieces - the gaudy hues softened by cigarette smoke and light from a single sallow bulb that dangled, shadeless, above each one – Red Jimmy appeared again, from a narrow doorway, with a tray full of drinks & placed it on one of the tiny tables - the priest & Troubadour took their place on two cushions next to him – craning his neck, the priest saw a barman leaning across a counter smoking – bright optics & glasses hung behind him under a neon sign

'ISIS'

slowly, on the stage, the floor lights glowed into life - there was a small cough from the wings & a bald, hunched conductor in a long tailcoat & bow-tie wandered on & bowed solemnly – he about-turned in a military fashion & stood with baton raised – one by one the musicians – all in identical red jackets & black trousers - ambled into view & solemnly took their places' - two swift gestures with a baton set the music in uneasy motion – like a door long unopened, rusty, blurred strains, quavering high creaking notes & low drones that somehow fell together & clotted awkwardly into lethargic blocks of dense, blue sound
The Troubadour sipped at his dark wine & narrowed his gaze from under his limp beret – the casual priest lit a cigar from a selection of smokes laid out on the tray & grasped tight the flaccid, damp hand of Red Jimmy - as if it were the throat of a sworn enemy – woozy tributaries of eerie, longing strings – flute trills burgeoned – the subdued

brass breathing slippery hints of thriving evil in the musty, suspicious air

The Troubadour relaxed pleasantly into the odd music's myriad twists & turns & grew, if not to like, to expect the seemingly random key shifts - Jimmy handed him a programme

CLUB ISIS PRESENTS
Soul Music From The Delta
by
The Cryptic Carthorse Sextet

another modal shift - a new sonic conundrum - a different circle of questions that hung in echoes from the sodden walls - not problems they needed to solve - Old Captain Rehab, speed-eyed, startled as a sprung daisy, staggered uneasily from a hidden cubby-hole, fresh with the knowledge of the future times, brandy bottle in his fist, swaying blissfully to the swelling cadences - & at the dead centre of the floor, swathed in greeny smoke, The Lonely Troubadour sat, cross-legged, unseen & unseeing - other figures now emerged from the bar doorway - that tall, achingly sombre chap in a green-floral shirt & wrap-around shades - was it old Miles Ducat? - sky basement DJ of the old new-town? - why was he here? - & the bundle of denim & paisley asleep on a stack of corkboard partitions with the New Musical Express over his face, dull snores emitting? - he was familiar too - but the Troubadour was not sure - some revenant brought by The Captain from future times, perhaps - maybe himself looking back at the sad nostalgia of his youth diminishing

a dwarf waiter strolled past carrying a stacked pile of empty glasses - he wore Bermuda shorts, bright blue & red that, due to his size, were turned up just above the ankles - he wore a grey T-shirt adorned with the legend

'THE CHANGELING MUSCAT LIED!'

who the fuck is Muscat? – the priest was up dancing with an invisible dream-girl – his black gown & vivid red dog-collar floating in the smoky chiaroscuro – he thought to himself
    '...*I must select two songs for the day and then construct my sermon - god is elsewhere...time is ripe...*'
from beneath his cassock he produces a small tape machine - he pushes the record button and the cassette jerks alive – he watches, mesmerised, as the tiny hubs begin circling clockwise – in his mind's eye he clambers over the heads of the growing crowd & mounts the stair to a pulpit – slamming his fist on the ebony lectern, he fixes a stare above the upturned faces to an inverted cross on the far dark wall between a stencilled flyer that reads

LIVE MUSIC
In Residency All Next Week
'THE DUCAL MITES'
Launch party for their new album
'Civitas Crystallini'

& a torn bullfighting poster, feathered arrows protrude from the snorting beast's arched back – The Hipster Priest, his inner voice, at first hesitant, rises angered in his swollen imagination on waves of soulless music, reaching, slowly a calm authority & plateau
    he blends his thought at a meeting point, a confluence of anger & light – junction of weird & edgy
    & through a widening delta of cool, differing waters – his head-voices descending through misty, softer intonations, riding the low music, until it once more flourishes, ending in trembling timbres of a feverish, consecrated zeal & now, as

his swimming head surfaces for air, the priest hears his own voice cut through the dense wad of shaky hullabaloo

"...gotta get down to it, children - back, back to me, alone, remembering some fabulous time in the terrible past when I stole Dylan Thomas books from the holy library - words on pages started to merge & imply other things – messages to me alone – perhaps unintended by the author, driven by an automatic spirit-hand down through the eras – blue & white words that gave off odours instead of icons – Neil Young I was & cheesy in my beans - but these quixotic recipes leapt at me from the blank spaces to astound my pulpy head & baptise me deeper in a cool water of beautiful confusions – entering in trepidation - like the first rush of holy amyl-nitrate - the big people's world where everything rhymed – endings & deep internals, fused across the page in delicious diagonals – let the assonance ride the dissonance – join the phrases, let integration run mad – rhyme anything with everything - lassoing mantarays & Saturdays, blending vixens & moccasins, raisins & thousands, mercies & curfews, dogs & gods - until new streams trickled away from the river's run & irrigated that arid land with a new green poetry – beached mantarays found on a Saturday by vixens in moccasins eating raisins by the thousand despite the paltry mercies allowed by the curfew – this world of wonders, it was mine & now words became inmates of a library rather than a bookshop – free to every blasted mind – get your ticket & take the ride - no spiritual monies required – thieve all you need from this blood-spattered Kafka castle of wild literary uproars, drink deep of vodka's paramount oceans & let the bad voices of a long gone time flood in..."

sweat poured from his brow, the saxophonist, matching his mood, launched into a frenzied solo, golden arpeggios bounced off the walls into his brain - & then, just as the music quietened again to a burble of querulous flute & char-grilled strings, The Silently Mouthing Priest appeared to hesitate, framed as he was, renaissance-hued, spittle-flecked lips, saintly in the dismal yellow light – tapping at the ghostly cracked pulpit & listening to the imagined congregation murmuring along with the lop-sided lurch of the music's drowsy flight – then with a solemn, raised hand he halted the grumbling & the sextet sank to an almost inaudible trembling – & Degory Priest saw in his mind's eye a great ship, triple-masted, dissolving in mist & he allows a rehearsed lukewarm tear to fall – the stricken priest takes a greedy bite from a chicken leg he had craftily procured from the dwarf waiter – pausing to savour the succulent, white flesh - he then opened a large, red book - on the cover of which was etched in silver leaf

OF DULCET AIMS
An exiled prophet Speaks

he looked up at another point in far space, possibly a star imploding, & began reading into the gently whirring tape machine he held close to his lips

"...let the sermon flow as it will – for if sentences form from nowhere then god has his reasons – not all language serves reason - may it worry heaven, this moribund tale - a tale of the rebellious, anarchic unconscious – set fast against all blithe authority – this is your unfolding history that cannot end well - the memories, perhaps, of one calumny among many, memories that grip the soul & mutate - a concordat of incongruencies – an alloy forged by the forces of light & anger within us – it will take greater hearts than mine to achieve such heights, such peaks of clarity – I train my disciples in this dying art of thoughtless rambling, our malevolent wandering – yet nevertheless it befalls my lowly person to charm the insecure snakes of epiphany out of each of our sublime baskets without getting bitten by your venomous tongues! – a new kind of prayer, a hymnal to rip ye from your wombs! - a holy severance! - the welcoming surgeon cuts the umbilical cord! - slaps the mewler's arse! - that shock of a new cry - freeing a silence inhaled in the womb - a voice that resonates beneath the frequencies that hurtle across a million roadside pylons - a road guiding you through the scum & dross of an unwanted existence - you have lost track of the river, for she is gone away, that Mother Of Rationality - be sure she will not be back again to reel ye in - there will be no secrets I shall keep from ye, she says, other than my identity - all else it must tell - hear me well, my people, my flock, homeless beneath a thousand, million arches, crumpled in a billion doorways - these aching, tattered sacks of human debris that cruise the breakers of life's ocean

& yes they must be reborn, completely rehabilitated & instructed in the ways of wisdom begun in the first light of knowledge - an inaugurated brotherhood of the broken cleaving madly to an unstoppable desire to achieve a final consummation, an anarchistic harmony, if you will allow - & because the ruling classes will not relinquish their power - because their sovereignty is inert without their subtle use of boredom, this revolution will be televised - my drunk, beautiful army, seeking an emancipation of the music in our hearts..."

a fat pause - the flute traces a delicate arabesque over ascending shivers of the chocolate-rich cello - he mops his soaking forehead with a black napkin stained with stale wine & chicken juices

" ...a parable - please indulge me good people - now I ask you to hold fast in your head a bedsitting room of low quality - see clearly this room before you now - a solitary un-curtained window - beyond that, an awful, bitumen-dark night - all outside has fallen to chaos - yet some buildings still remain - there's always a church somewhere among the wreckage every time a bomb has fallen - & if, as the smoke clears & fire recedes, if you look up at any of these bomb-blasted structures – any godless ruin that survived – there will be, without fail, something true written on the wall that endures - the plaster may peel and fade but the encrypted message is pure rebellion, always – moods that outlive the moody – soon the lights go up again - happy hour is here – feel joy rising in you, feel the shape of such an hour – bending with the slow pleasure that passing years have dripped upon the soul - &, with a quavering voice, offer your gasped supplications to a neglected god - for freedom's sake – in the here & now of the world, the sky & horizon a far wall, unattainable – for my parable has a far wall also – so I ask you to visualise now on the far wall of my parable, next to the light switch, under a monochrome photograph of your mother & father - carefully depicted in needlepoint, there is a framed quotation that reads

'...to be loosed
by my devilry
from earthly dirt
is all I ask
of haunted heaven...'

& see that there is also, besides the illuminated aquarium full of tiny golden fish, a hamster cage containing a stuffed toy frog & next to that a birdcage with no bird - the bird was never in the cage so I have no need to set it free - seen and yet unseen – the duality of imprisoned thought –
• the old grand design unseen - unseen, too, through the same murky window at evening's fall, the houses of no-god – perhaps even old Blake's Nobodaddy - that rise motionless into a sky the colour of watermelon - they morph, according to desires, from twisty-cloaked sentinels that comfort with their duty of impregnable protection toward vulture-priests such as I – such as I have become - with my ludicrous, stern

face up here in this underwater club of night, fuelled by this mixture of grape, grain & alchemy, commanding with my rhetoric your awestruck silence – to present to you pure religion in her bondage mask, for you alone my heathen friends - a new kind of music will follow my sermon & listen to this music well, for it is not casually chosen – it is to become part of your free will, a symphony of days – rich & mysterious, as is the very oath of the mind's natural autonomy – a singular music set on the tidal drift – it has no lifeboat – it contains a multitude of voices – lose yourself to their sound & in the laughing air you will discover that they are indistinguishable from the beauty of silence..."

Red Jimmy threw an empty wine bottle that crashed against the pulpit sending shards of red light tumbling across The Troubadour's wearying gaze – just as sleep descended & weighed down his eyes, each fragment of the bottle seemed caught in its own pirouetting dance as the flute notes flittered all around them & soprano horn lines, muted, shimmering, traced their brilliant, diamond arcs all the way to paradise

*

elsewhere & where else, the Lonely Troubadour busks in a subway by the yawning early market - rotating four or five songs to a cycle of faces & tossed coins of myriad value and origin - he hallucinates a woman, gothic, sleek, serpentine – her name preceded her - Closer To God Like The Moon – a danger sweetly approaching – an opaque, preternatural lure who, descending from the library steps, that eternal fairyland of words, plants a coin into his upturned hat & drifts on clouds of dewberry perfume into the massed, sweating hordes clamouring to be served at the fruit stall - market pavement, early – he accosts her with a

cry - he now has coin enough for two - a drink later? - she
promises to return - never does

*

the first gleam of daylight, in its gossamer cape, can
often seem weak & tenuous - yet it is the night, concealed in
her modest veneer of velvet robes, that shrouds a far more
uneasy heart - for night is sickly, she breathes like a drugged
patient, releasing the minutes like long sighs as each dawn
slowly nears, silently lipping the emerging horizon - it is
quiet beneath the moon's eye, voiceless - a knowing, smug
silence that lusts to paw the sun - it is wringing out the
dishcloth sky to an insipid grey - the statue of dusk - a
memorial to the death of dreaming - see her marble breasts
- morning's leech-light cannot kiss them - Punch moon &
Judy sun, disputing the firmament - creeping up on each
other as a tired world spins - waiting to bleed all traces of
compassion from the waking, puffy, curtained eyes of
morning - sackcloth-lidded, tumoured in draining alcoholic
jungles of shivering memory - sticky eyes popping open - a
taunt of light mockingly skips from the gilded rooftops,
tugging at the silver wires of a clouded, muscular sleep - the
bleed of first noises, the anguished punctuation of gulls -
last night's storms and disputed, hallucinatory bloodlines all
forgotten - & behind the sleeping sea an ocean made of dust
- the closed down world where every line written is an
epitaph, every note sung a church bell moaning for the leash
rope to be loosened on love - god curse those gulls! - in
spreading skies they circle & swoop - angels waiting for the
fall - the great negative print behind the eyes, black on white
- in astonished seconds held & frozen, looping in the
hospital sky - safe as the last ward where nothing is breathing
- where all operations failed - silent in the blue beyond the
post-mortem - nature ends quietly reflective in shallow

thought – his first daydream is of Blake, his book open on the bedside cabinet - this poetry will not stand, he thinks – without the balm of sound this careful symmetry is not beautiful - beware of the tigers

return, then, if you will - once more to the city of sleep – but be sure to leave the door of sentience ajar – the night poet stalks the dark avenues, feel your breath quicken to the rhythms of his speech – it is an expressionless mask, tribal, unpainted, speaking a cowering dog of language – an ugly nocturnal flower of evil - & yet with a teasing, lucid stem, strong, replete with a virile sap – sink back on pillows of sweat, the ship of dreams will find form around you – find harbour in that warm, blanketed morning where, stretching deliciously, nothing wakes – he feels his heart lift anchor & slip away from the fading uproar – putting trust in that night author &, in the last tidal washes, it is his solitary, whirlpool voice that is heard – tune the dial easy across the airwaves – frequencies in the crushed static - the radio of the earth's core – the click of the radio alarm & the DJ's surefooted vernacular - *maestro, music please!*

*

small mirror in a Travelodge – two days of drinking, why is he in a Travelodge? – vagueness & fear – splash the face with cold water from the tap – a gig in a pub, it was very late – last tube train gone, cheap room – the buzzing fluorescent strips of light & cakes of soap disintegrating in the bath like butter in the sun – last night, a dream of a fairground, wherein a murder would take place - but elsewhere, far on the other edge – a murder he knew was happening but he found it hard to concentrate with the fairground's lights & faces & congealed music – there were stalls of candy floss – confused speakers full of arguing genres - Philadelphia pushed a horny hand up the skirt of shy Tamla – powder-blue suits, the trippy lights were mayflies - there were gypsies sweeping up ticket-stubs, cigarette packets & crisp bags – percussion & treble folded into one another to make a scuttling beat underpinning everything – horn sections set free by these huge, overflowing speakers hung above the Waltzer – the muddy grass, the deafening sensurround – the love I lost t'was a sweet love - giant tea-cups revolve the squashed families & they screech as they spin, sucking The Terrified Breath Of Ghosts into their lungs & retching up a panicked wail - he finds a gate behind the tollbooth & clambers over into a dark field – he lights a sparkler as the sun rises

it is not any longer any kind of dream he recognises, no ship, no sea, no river – like that moment of waking when a voice he thinks is still part of the dream is really mother rousing him to breakfast – eyes open, eyes tight shut - & in-between those two universes a dark matter expands, undetected, essential - the barked, hubristic words of the fairground crowd turn to birdsong, as a poem in a flame turns to ash

a theoretical murder, a homicidal act, at once mysterious & beautiful is happening, he knows, but cannot prevent it – Jewish heart-line, Talmud, sunshine tomorrow, Tanqueray - he could not remember her name – she wrote her name on the pub window in black lipstick – she adjusted her red stockings shamelessly, a jukebox in the pub, the loud band sprouting black punk flowers, her shiny boots faultless in the strip-light's deviant glow from the hallway & always, always her black lipstick name - he couldn't remember

*

it is the faltering hour, the hour preceding happy hour – a turgid wash of regulars in the Intrepid Fox & carefully, The Pubcorner Wizard, by the light of a moon-slice, cuts strings of paper girls from the daily news – his Walkman on, the evangelical drone of Son House filling his head – Red Jimmy moulders in wet jeans by the hearth with hippy ghosts of sad jasmine puffing heavenward from his drying headband – he dreams of rodeos, gangster's molls & locomotives – becoming lost in a nocturnal circus of western flashbacks – feeling a sense of release as old acid squeezes his spongiform memory like the wringing out of a rainy neckerchief – his battle with whisky long lost & he has no mind to begin kicking over its statues – he slides his shot glass two feet along the bar

"...double Bell's...hey..." - he motions with his crooked finger to The Wizard – "...you want?"

The Lonely Troubadour spins & calls from the jukebox
"I'll have his...he owes me..."

a long day – they all got to the pub at opening time – something did not feel right about the world – as if there was a low pulse of sorrow beneath the surface, thick grey weather outside, the door slamming periodically in the wind – the re-telling of old jokes, no laughter

The Troubadour decided that what was missing was a bit of The Fall – he sifted the coins in his pocket & pressed the button on the jukebox - the low irritant stutter of Psykick Dancehall swills around the familiar nooks & hollows – mohair guitars strangling a slug of bass – Jimmy Red slides the whisky toward The Troubadour but it catches on a stuck beer mat & tips over the bar top – with a justifiable oath The Troubadour licks up the rolling juices causing a fit of smoky laughter to gurgle around the room – Jimmy Red slapped the table

"...that boy'd suck the morphine from an amputee's lips if he had a thirst on..."

The Careless Troubadour ordered another in a brusque, cavalier manner that clearly annoyed the barmaid – her eyes lowered & her lipstick, thick, shiny black lipstick, turned firmly down at the corners - he downed the drink in one &, with an expansive gesture of open arms, fell backwards from his chair into a mop & pail that clattered over, spilling foul water in rank pools beneath his head

in the ensuing laughter & confusion they were asked to leave & Pubcorner Wizard had manhandled The Bleary Troubadour into a taxi & sent it homeward – accompanying him all the way to his door, upon which he threw up & could not open with his tangle of bent keys – The Wizard pointed out the problem, his door-key was upside down – finally a loud entrance was achieved & though it was only half-nine The Troubadour crashed into bed & immediately began sending vibrant snores to the sick ceiling - The Wizard helped himself to a coffee before leaving & stole The Sleeping Troubadour's last three cigarettes

& sleep was becoming pure mercy – the shocking first crack of light falls on scampering visions – the slow, awful instigation of memory – the inner yelp of dismay that comes with almost remembering the previous day's dreadful scenes - The Troubadour felt the message was being made clear to him – as if he had written it across his own eyes in floating blood – & sure as caffeine scraped the rust from the hubcaps of the wheel of becoming, he was destined to be alone in the coming struggle – he was free to describe any part of the vast, elephantine universe he chose, in any which way - people he had known for a long time now, friends & foes alike, were changing irrevocably – daily they had worried him, they bled through voiceless streets past shuttered cafes & pointless refurbishments, catching themselves, their mistrusting glances gazing back from deep shop-window mirrors bisected by closure notices - flap of dog-eared posters with their shouted promises of bright, angry music

the change was gradual, it had settled on his mind like a touch of frost – a breathless film of hazards

yet still a new world beckoned from elsewhere, quiet &
diffuse as dust – what was he waiting for? – the word of a
prophet? – a sign?

or maybe a flash of wild romance would lead him astray
– because that was it, that was the conundrum, for all his
self-will, his professed no-shit-given attitude, he needed to be
inspired by other voices to kick off from the shore, make
the break – he knew it was too comfortable to stay, yet that
very comfort made it so easy a decision to postpone the
exile – his record collection was full of teasing prophesies –
exhortations to flight, they poured from the radio every
night – words of will to power – the migrant urges daily filled
his dreams with distant birds

a clatter & clack - letterbox

for who dreams of prophets now? – the drag of decade
falling into decade – the seventies become the eighties at a
single toll of Big Ben – betwixt a falling leaf & a tap of
varnished nail on checkout till?

the question, with a thousand others, pressed him to
speak again to this strange, lessening man he daily
encountered, unshaven, in the dour mirrors of hungover
mornings, to hear again the allegories declaimed by that
ignoble voice but ah! – raising his head to speak, of what
exactly he knew not, he saw nothing except layers of the
flimsy night trailed across a dim, bulging moon – short-term
recall is the detritus, the damage after a storm has blown
through – just residual sketchy familiarities of a town – he
addresses his face unflinchingly, blurry eye to jaundiced,
bloodshot eye

the manila envelope on the doormat – he picks it up –
something bulky, solid – he rips the seal with his biro nib

a cassette
with a scribbled note
The Priest

you fell asleep
my sermon continued through your snores
here is what you missed
love & light, Degory

he absently wandered, with the unlabelled cassette in hand, to the player in the front room, slid it in & clicked the play-button

"...life's spent waiting for a catastrophe, son...we're just fuckin' snooker balls, ricocheting about at random – one day you're surrounded by others – all these...all of the bright colours - & they're all whizzin' around as bloody mad as you...then boom! - there's a hole, a net...I'm at the peak of my powers, pal...that's what terrifies me ha! – I know the weight of history behind me, the decline towards the past & up ahead the decline toward the fuckin' future – you think I don't feel that? – you think you're the only one that dreams of escape yet craves the drugged routine? – past, future, one & the same – all the words in the world to use & all we can do is moan like fucking drains – tune in to the commuter mumbling on a platform on the way to drudgery, listen to those cunts..."

he switched it off & clicked on the kitchen radio – he had it tuned permanently to Caroline but mysteriously it was now Radio 1 that assailed him – he searched his pocket & found a stub, the tobacco falling from the bent, squashed papers – he gestured angrily with his ruined cigarette toward the radio as it bleated the chart rundown from the echoing kitchen – he swore at the dial & clicked it off – he pressed the priest's tape on again

"...cheery farts...they study all the intricacies, all the myriad ins & outs of the music, practice for years to master
• their craft & for what? – the old-time jazzers in the Sunday pub – playing East-St Louis Toodle-o & Georgia to nine

390

cunts reading the Observer & scoffing the free roasties off the bar – cheery farts...to most people trad jazz sounds like cheery farts...it is a little-known truth that we are fed on literary morsels & drenched in music's stale slops & what a fuckin' industrial-strength tragedy it is!...Shakespeare don't come close, let me tell ye brethren...every tubercular, shite trumpeter that is out there wallowing in Sunday lunchtime hell is a potential fuckin' Lear out on the heath, pal – give us Down By The Riverside! – play that When The Saints Go Marchin' In! –aah, go jump in the fuckin' river & march those whiny saints in after ye – may merciful Jehosophat save their burping arses - but everything & anything can happen given time – no looking backward once that river is crossed – all bridges collapse behind ye, all of 'em! – all the bastard politicians resign in disgrace & anonymity, god fuck 'em all & as for us lot, as for we mere ghosts of vicars, wittering shells of priests...Christ on a Vespa, wouldn't give ye the froth off me snot for an ounce of 'em..."

The Shell-shocked Troubadour returned to the cracked bathroom mirror to shave as the priest rambled on – always the mirror, always returning to that inescapable, over-familiar, slow-changing face - he thought back to his childhood, his dreams – did he really have dreams? – maybe he dreamt of having dreams – maybe this was a... - no none of that old horseshit – no dream within a fucking dream excuses – he recalled, dimly, how sleep used to be a thing to fight off, to resist rather than welcome – mum I don't want to – read me a story – just another half hour – I'm just finishing my game – only got to stick these cards in the scrapbook, only got to push this bus around the road-mat to the depot – just ten minutes – I'm not even tired – then cajoled to bed & off goes the light & he slips away – away to the great dream ship

he saw himself now, his eyes closed so that the mirror cannot see, standing by the rail above its stern, the poet prodigal, the reluctant returner – all behind him lost, devastated history, his vocation in floating tatters on the mushrooming surf - & suddenly he is sifting through a box of old cars, toys – they run through his mind like an endless sad Whitman list of white-bearded remembrance - a one-legged Action-Man parachutist lay prone atop these myriad childhood relics – the box is growing heavy – & abruptly, on a whim, he hurls it in the air – begone! - farewell to this fraudulent box of youth! - & in this glorious waking dream the hundreds of tiny cars, the farmyard beasts, the train tracks & heavy replica diesel engines & Pullman carriages, signal boxes, tunnels & bridges, the playing cards, the dice, the Ludo board with draughts squares on its reverse side, the Monopoly set pieces, tin car, thimble, flat-iron, dog, boot, top-hat & battleship, down it all falls, do not pass go or collect two hundred pounds, the fluttery fake money, fivers, tenners, hundreds & thousands that that counterfeit millionaire had amassed, begone!

the Subbuteo footballers, tumbling, welded forever into their half-moon bases like the concrete boots of mafia narks, the tiny goals & nets, the marbles, the snakes & ladders, the tiddlywinks, the Meccano girders & screws, the fading, creased football cards that came free with unwanted bubble-gum, the comics, Beano annuals, the jamboree bags, sherbet-dabs, liquorice allsorts, chocolate tools, wagon wheels & flying saucers, the Batman car with ejector-seat & tiny red plastic flame pulsing from its exhaust, the battered spinning top with a gaudy clown's face, the Christmas tinsel & baubles, the ping-pong balls & matted, stippled bats, the Scalextric track & racing cars of many colours, the orange, plastic Hot-Wheels loop-the-loop, the play-dough & plasticene, all cellophane-wrapped neatly in corrugated strips – all of the glorious trappings of childhood plummeting to the dream ship's wake – all except the stone-faced, implacable Action-Man, perfectly caught by a random gust of wind that blows obligingly across the estuary tides, coming in off the dockside, buoying up the billowing plastic parachute – it had never worked in real life, the hundreds of times he had dropped it from his bedroom window or hurled it upward from the tree by the swings – but now, freed by the caprices of the dream-state, the other toys long drowned, he saw it float serenely, evenly downward – the last leaf of a child's autumn – an ageless parachutist – twisting one last time in the river wind before hitting the frothing wake & disappearing like a doomed poet to its eternal, watery tomb

& The Ageless Troubadour opened his eyes, the mirror faithfully showed his grown-up face, stubbly, smeared with shaving-foam – a halo failed to manifest itself above his matted hair – & he knew that he truly grasped the city then, he knew her message – as he picked up the dull razor from the hooped cup, he saw the past receding, falling, drowning in the sea of his widening gaze - from the kitchen a holy voice filtered into his reverie, a slithering voice – dark as a monk's cowl-shadowed head – sliding into the subliminal spaces between waking & slumber – confessional, church-morbid & hollow

"...may it worry heaven – our blind pilgrim's progression - stay tight to the world ye grew up in, my brothers – tend to the blemishes in your Eden - water your weeds with the piss of your ancestors, feed your roots with the bloody shite of those dead old borrowed dreams – the path to Arcadia is a narrow one – shaky rope-bridges & overgrown cinder trails - the transition from child to man is but a ritual of discarded games – a new set of games ushered in – the stakes higher & the skills required for success more intricate & demanding – travel light across the heavy miles

& yes then the move from town to city, then to another city beyond, a yet stranger city - & tell me how long does it take for a place to become too familiar? - for the thrill of

393

discovery to turn to a debilitating, low-grade ennui, having passed through the sickly-sweet realm of comfort...let this declaration of intent be your fabled intent – amen, brothers, a-fucking-men..."

the tape clicked to silence – birds chirruped at the window, dead flies crumbling to dust on the sill - he dragged the blunted razor across his cheek leaving the pink ravine of his stung, new-born skin visible, his eyes watching his eyes watching his eyes – the scraped foam fallen - a fresh, swept pathway to follow blind – a path to which his trembling finger pointed – skin-soft, razor-dug through thick, treacherous snow

he sloshed the cool water across his cheeks revealing his tingling, blotchy face & gasped at the rush of it like a deep-sea diver surfacing – something had changed, taken root in a fertile soil – there were bodies of water shifting like tides in the fever of his mind – can he speak to it, this tide? – can he harness its wisdom as a guide? – speak to me, he silently implores, eyes closed

*

here I am

*

& finally, after a dead day of psychotic geography via rover ticket on bus & tube train, he found himself, through the beckoning of the subconscious guide, at the airport – a novel, unexpected sense of agoraphobic thrill after the tight humanity of the tube journey – an intimation of ultimate escape made his spine shiver & his head go mildly dizzy – the heavens await at the purchase of a ticket – he would not go today but the possibility remained tantalising - the feeling he got standing on a high diving board when a child– the steps behind him full of impatient swimmers – the water pristine below awaiting his plunge

no reason to be elsewhere right now, he thought - & he watched the family of Germans chat among themselves pleasantly as the smallest of the five children whirled about with a toy aeroplane – the gentle, transcontinental politics of families, mild admonishments & rehearsed glances, chronic gestures & expressions – he found them oddly peaceful in a way he could not quite fathom - it was a pregnant kind of tranquillity enhanced by the muffled sound of the aircraft whining from behind the glass

outside the enormous window he watched a bored man of an oriental persuasion with a large broom listlessly push dust, leaves & varied debris that he was fashioning into small triangular piles that collapsed & dispersed almost as fast as they were constructed – the man watched the journey of a disturbed feather that his gentle sweeping had set to flight rise before him & paused his task to smile at it, remove his cap & try to catch it – only to waft it higher out of reach – the man was unaware of the fact that he was the object of attention, he wiped his brow, leaning on his broom in jaunty fashion with crossed leg in the air behind him – it was a mime, a dumb show set to the industrial wheeze of the constant aircraft noise & conspiratorial mutterings in German from the family group

the man had made the Troubadour think of a Japanese girl he had spoken to briefly on the platform at South Tottenham station a month or so ago – she had a nervous, almost comic, way of looking from side to side, never making eye contact unless she felt that her point was not being understood fully – she had told him he reminded her of a drunken bargeman that she almost married in Amsterdam & proceeded to relate a sorry tale of abuse & degrading circumstances that led to her flight to London three years ago – he had no idea of how to respond to this

&, feeling slightly awkward, had asked her what book she was reading – she stared above his head, across the wet roofs of north London, shiny & dense in bleary evening drizzle, & answered 'What Am I Doing Here...' which he took to be an existential *non sequitur* until she held the book aloft & he read the title – What Am I Doing Here by Bruce Chatwin – just then a train pulled into the station & she suddenly kissed him on the cheek & said '...I like you, thank you..' then turned & skipped behind the silver sliding door & sat next to a tall man in a grey macintosh & trilby hat

The Likeable Troubadour suddenly & unexpectedly felt a loss akin to that of a death of a distant relative, one that had never been close yet had always sent birthday cards – he raised his hand to wave but stopped short & remained there in dull rain - a perfect rain, heavier now but not quite unpleasant - motionless standing with one finger tracing an empty gesture in the space between them – but she was already deep in her book & she never glanced once at him as the carriage pulled away forever

the oriental, feather-chasing cleaner was darker of skin, possibly Indonesian, than she had been – still, he had hung the memory on a hook for him to try on & he felt a kind of warmth toward him - & then, before realising he was actually doing it, he found that he was tracing the upward path of the feather as it was carried on the various eddies of the jet engine's expelled air - at times he thought he'd lost sight of it only for it to reappear, dancing this way & that against the dim sky, until it passed before a lighter patch of cloud & vanished

*

no question mark, he thought – what am I doing here – it wasn't interrogative, it was just five words – he tried saying them to himself without a questioning lilt & found it impossible to do with any real satisfaction

a flight to Stuttgart was announced with Nazi stridency from the tannoy & the family hurriedly gathered their clutch of cases & bags - & The German Father smiled strangely at him as they all moved toward the departure lounge

PART 3

FAST FORWARD

"To forget is the secret of eternal youth. One grows old only through memory. There's much too little forgetting."

Erich Maria Remarque

"I'll affect you slowly as if you were having a picnic in a dream. There will be no ants. It won't rain."

Richard Brautigan

🖇pring gouache, summer pastel, autumn acrylic, winter charcoal – & he'll never grow so old again – two strummed guitars & a campfire roaring with folk songs in the head – blue running into green – the sound of syncopated mystics – dynamite & river run - & dream rolling on – gotta go, go find somewhere to stay – somewhere to lay my weary head – just for a few days - just forever, sugar baby – under the street's neon ignitions suffused with Christmas rain – from the city of smoke & mirrors to a city of diamond soul - & a new year peeking at the Troubadour through the barges sliding under the footbridge at the end of the Panamakade – perspiration of raw gin blossoming – the slate sky low, swallowing the tips of cranes – the mordant drag of a bad year's end – tonight the fireworks, tonight the streets of lit faces sparkler bright – tomorrow the fallen sticks of beat rockets, frightened pigeons & scorched grass by the canal – days of a new city, he made his move - lapping cat of time – cleansing lick, he hoped

a storm was coming, the pilot had said

*

the memory warehouse is, or is not, to be found on a dusty road in a remote location to the east of the dockland region of the city of Amsterdam – a badly overgrown path of motley cinders & wood-shavings leads to a heavy door of roughly painted, brown metal that hangs partly off its hinges – close inspection reveals the work of a burglar – tell-tale chips in the paint, scratches, gouges near the bolt-holes – once inside you are given a bouquet of yellow jonquils by a frowning butler in full dress costume – he has no hat & is bald except for shiny black islands of hair above both ears – he gestures you down the aisle of sheet metal shelves full of shoeboxes crammed with scraps of paper, empty bottles, photographs etc. - after you have failed to find, indeed have forgotten, that which brought you reluctantly here, you emerge with your butler in tow from the fluorescent shallows of the building blinking into a warm lake of sunlight which, though pleasant, you find curiously dispiriting - you finish the half-bottle of rum in your top pocket & toss it behind you carelessly - the butler solemnly picks it up & - tying a manila label to its neck - retreats into the warehouse again - all day you are aware of birds, louder than usual, singing on the telegraph wires, the cold statues in Dam Square, the truncated awnings of the red light district, on the undulating barges of the blown canals, the red tiled sill of your hotel window - the motorboats are silent, tethered, trams & cars are - you think - moving slower, as if following a cortege - as if they have forgotten temporarily where they are going - always prone to melancholy & a vivid sense of justice, despite your sins, you will grow fond, in later life, of 'true crime' police TV shows - you think of the endless police TV shows you watched back in Camden with Red Jimmy - how the young criminals felt indestructible, uncatchable - the fugitive urge - to push the risk - go mad, make a mistake, the fire of youth - one rush of bloodshed & a whole future erased for victim & perpetrator - you think of them in their cells, walking solemnly in cold exercise yards - as the slaughtered bystander sleeps six feet deep in cloying, syrupy earth - you will feel now a guilty empathy with them both - the time cut off, the possibilities wasted - the auld triangle jingle jangling - hear it, that sound - romance of the old lag stories - whittling woodcraft, darning socks, imprint of key in soft soap, the desuetude of mind - there are the occasional mildly uplifting moments, of course - unexpected sunlight, starched, fresh linen, a sweet sadness visiting in the guise of birdsong by a barred window - the careful hoarding of tobacco dust in matchboxes - a death row deferred for a yet more enduring melancholy - it was the maudlin weight of newsprint – gossip of the carefree, cares of the unknowing, all headed for different nooses, all bothered by dreams of electricity – & finally you are released from the prison, imagine - & when out walking alone at night you are suddenly inexplicably nervous, a strange terror growing in your head & stomach – each street you approach could be the one from which the nameless monster will leap – finally it pounces & you catch a brief glimpse of its magnitude & horror that, later, your ageing memory fails to recover

The Horrified Troubadour startles awake as the robotically cheerful announcement from the pilot tells him to fasten his seat belt

*

Schipol airport from the air looked like a series of beige crosses dimmed by a slow rain as the plane descended part blind, drifting in & out of scudding clouds – the hectic terminal hummed with dusky foreign murmurs – Jack Definitive met him at the bookshop as arranged – tall, mobile features alive with Nordic urgency – his body seemed primed to ambush - a slight frame, a boxer's tautness of limb – the sly implication of power, the strength of wet iron bridges – his trousers were creased, loose linen despite the cold - his faded green biker's t-shirt stained with cranberry juice under a brown, faux-suede jacket – whilst they walked to the car The Immigrant Troubadour checked his pocket – a few boiled sweets, the cap of a biro, a rover bus ticket – now where was...? - ah, there - Ursula Major's address scribbled in pencil on a torn beermat

*

he put his rucksack on a guitar case in the back seat of Jack's blue Fiat & was driven to his hotel in a dense fug of marijuana from their shared joint - Hotel Rokin was a tall thin building - in the typical Dutch style of quiet, stoned elegance – on a street off Dam Square sufficiently bustling & energetic enough to keep the vital blood of a new city pumping in the veins

the ride had been achieved in near silence save for a few chatty bouts of cool nonsense & the low jazz from a scratchy radio station – Jack seemed distant, wary, as if slighted by some calumny of which The Troubadour was unaware – he was glad he had booked a hotel room & not, as the priest had suggested, stayed with this strange, serious, vaguely menacing man - roads, buildings blurred agreeably past the smeared window – a faint hint of orange peel in the air from the vent in the dashboard, the joint's smoke sulking behind it with heavy-lidded eyes of a sham guru

The Troubadour was already slightly stoned as he checked in & took his heavy pear-shaped keyring up the thick, brown-carpeted steps to the top floor – the bed was firm, the bathroom neat & small, a view of the street from the window, trams, tourists, snakes of slow beeping cars – he was no longer in England – another country - already the day had taken on an indolent air of unreality that was perfect for his inner mood of nebulous, dissolute thoughts

he had a plan, of sorts – he would spend his time in the city investigating streets that tourists shied from – sit in cafes with notebook & pen, observe, observe – slowly let the chemistry take hold - modifying his train of thought to the rhythms of the city & emptying his crowded skull on to a journal page at day's end – if indeed the days ended at all – the writing should be as automatic as possible, he thought - he would sort the mess of words out when he returned, if he returned, to London

Degory had bought the journal for him - a grey ledger, finely ruled - & the priest had written in red crayon on the inner leaf

'MIRACLE OF AMSTERDAM'

the pages waiting quietly in line behind the title for orders - he was as alone as he'd ever wanted to be - he would write at night - the night was to be his suitor, his spirit guide - the words secreted in dark corners where devils of vivid memory were crouching, shrouded

he put on a fresh t-shirt & his shabby, blue suit jacket & strode out into this promised hell with a cheery wave to the desk boy, Robin, his new best friend in the universe - alive! - the air was crisp with joy - the clean streets jangled with conflicting music from fat car horns & tram bells - he closed his eyes & began to restate his mission - to not return home unchanged - he was no tourist, no dilettante - he must give in to all experiences totally - remain determined to disturb the staid old electricity of his heartwire, to alter his life forever, somehow, or set a better course to the possibility of renewal - first new rule was to keep to the plan - a vague plan that had been ambiguously nurtured by a million boredoms & lost stratagems - he wanted to become a part, a turning cog - feel the vivid machinery of the universe churn around him - to know his potency in relation to the unseen grand design - he wanted to rid himself of the inner shore, find his open sea & dissolve like sugar in the convections of its warm trade currents - root himself in new earth, become conscious & grounded - hold fast his newly-opening mind reborn as the ancient Englander's *gemynd* -a function of purest memory

*

Theo, known as 'sailor' for his ubiquitous hooped t-shirt & neckerchief, read from *Le Surmâle* with burning eyes – his third coffee gone cold & ash from his cigarette speckling his dark green trousers – he had suffered The Hungover Troubadour to sit with him as the cafe was unusually busy for the early hour & they now both exchanged brief smiles of acknowledgement across the Gingham tablecloth – The Troubadour ordered a brandy with his pastry & Theo called the waiter back to order one for himself

"...livens the morning, y'know?..." – looking up from the stained pages Theo smiled wider but said nothing – after a while the two brandies were delivered & they performed a solemn mock clinking of glasses

"...here's to mornings..." the Troubadour said

"...why? - because they are the first step to the possibility of another evening?...coffee is just a spirit guide – the way pointed out – are you tourist or native?..." - slight accent, German possibly – touch of the Crowley in this jack tar – sea of loneliness he sails – me too, though – sip of brandy, golden section – that's the finest rotgut – these brawny cafes full of empty poetry – dark blights of the soul – cod-eastern fuckery & occultist gobbledygook masquerading as spiritual acumen – a sham world between the shite & god's arse – still, always nice to pass the hours blathering – always nice to prolong the always – always is as always does - *die welt als wut und licht - die welt als abstossung - die welt als Glaube - sich erinnern heißt existieren*

they got a little drunk, hired two bicycles, they chatted warily for an hour - Schopenhauer, Lennon, Braque, Brel & Tin Tin - & agreed to rendezvous at The Bulldog that evening – Theo promised to bring some of his sketches – bloody dauber, might have guessed – all skulls & glib fairy women, no doubt – crucifix & raven – everyone has a *shtick*, a contrived way to fail at something bigger than themselves – the biggest, most harmless lie unperturbed, tranquil, The Raven Troubadour felt full of the bright morning brandy sun & in total charge as he strode forth, for the first time in ages, of his slowly strengthening body – begone, omens & farewell to fear – the gnawing of his mind by worrisome devils shall cease – nevermore!

his ungnawed mind however was not now entirely his own - who goes there? – Newtown Baby, Troubadour, Old Captain Rehab & the invading dream world

in the first late bar he found he sits head in hands as – on his cassette Walkman headphones - old Degory, the beastly priest, weasels words on the tide of who knows what stolen, cheapskate hallucinogen or devil-tainted juice – list!...for he witters onward

'...do ye think it is special? – this or that pulse? – ye tell me that you find soul music spiritual, that ye feel lifted by it somehow - will it change your life? – hell, man! - you know it will! - your life ain't worth shit & is easy to change, like a baby's nappy - ye are looking for change so hard that almost any alternative will do – once, I'll wager, you gazed upon houses & fields, pubs & cafés, without any thought of their impermanence – gazed dumb at picture books of resilient old heroes of the blues, guitars in tall cotton unpicked - as a pimply white cipher like myself, you've been in awe of strong black men down through history – now, ye have borrowed a halfway beat, a rhythm of dust that will suit your awkward, shuffling feet & a black man speed-talking shit over it dressed like a spaceman crossed with a fucking pimp - you're in liberal limbo - where is your mind? – blue rain dripping slow from a rusted brown gutter – you're like a defrocked clergyman, rigid in your suit of desired certainties but stuck with the flitters of a poorly delineated doubt – feeding off the energy of a faith beyond your words – sick-drunk's teat-bottles supped in train stations, threatening passers-by with your evil muttering about truth & honesty –

swing a fist, a glass, a cane – stab them in the neck with your keys – executioner, handle puller, runner of finger beneath the practised guillotine – cancer will show no mercy such as this when one fine hour it leaps up & gnaws at your empathies...'

& turning off the cassette the groggy Troubadour glugs his god-knows-what grog & to a woman unhappily adjacent bellows the name of the song throbbing above their heads – when she merely smiles & wanders to the toilet he decides to christen her Madame Erst – she will be his first muse of the odyssey

& he takes out his blank journal & unleashes the full, warped subconscious nature of his cracked biro – the ink talking, not letting reason interrupt the gush of interconnected ideas - the anagrammatic balloons floating upward to nowhere – the bitching itch scratched - scrawling & crawling through a lost prose of loosened tethers - primordial the only word he held lovingly close to mind

"...Madam Erst ye have but one life!! – do not spend it, like myself, in riddle solving – I am no riddle, there are no answers – I can speak in cryptic code if you would prefer – now this drugged night has stroked our brows with feverish fingers – very well. Madam, rest your strange head on the pillow of night & let my words disengage from reason & float before you in novel forms – new language from old – that is the necromancy of the historian – your intellect deciphering messages from the long dead poetry – writing & rewriting out the stanzas until the very letters become indistinct & begin to once more assume their pictorial characteristics – Madame, as this night progresses, let us likewise dissolve & digress – say what you will & it will immediately be unsaid – untied bundles of words set free to reassemble as they might – let the dogs of language run wild - let the only drama stem from dramas met in fake moonlight – come now, ye are a smart dame made smarter by the art of deception & that lost

art of remaining incognito – your name, Madame Erst, is. I fear, losing its grip already - so, in this pristine, diamantine metropolis, keep your head low & ride the trams, dame of disguise – in a city that made trams - past the Bulldog Bar & beneath the Rizla ad - stammer out sentences that make yourself out to be some mad master of ceremonies in life's mad stream – O Madam, your times of wanderlust now faded – Sultans in Doha encountered, gurus in Madras met on the sly – I have encountered well-travelled women, Rosie, The Duchess Of Infinity, I have sat, rammed, furious & uncomfortable, on hot buses eating bad sandwiches & blindly reading Joyce because it makes me feel smarter than the shit-heads burning their city money on a pyre of lust – I have pondered clues, constructed Edam cheese in a pickle – unpicking mad streams of consciousness - or Beckett - if you dare to dream all Sam dreamt – sail the seven oceans of lust on gunboats – bring new order to your city's name - stowed away with the master of arms - powerful with tattoo & ancient of ship – three-masted, arm twisted around your waist – the rutting sailors rough as rams tamed by your charm – you venture through desire, in love with gods of war & the sea – Neptune your slave - as Mars mated deviantly with your pliant mortal flesh – Mars himself tamed, broken, by whisky consumed by the dram, meats cooked via recipes of all nations – then back from this verminous port to the City you love to finally write your tales, read the letters sent wild, but they seem arbitrary, confused in time - an MS dreamt out of sequence – mere fables told to all the sailor boys on leave - & you wander, aimless until you find this island within the city – until here, in a corner of the Bulldog Bar one day, sat Mr Mead – as I now shall pretend to be - & a reawakened love dared to touch the core of your satin-wrapped soul – satin from your dear old Mammy - for curiously your old Mam's trade was the humble haberdasher's – your wan words are Mr. Mead's *waking wonder – they are our children, no less – out they run under the distorted night sky crying out 'I'm a sun driven insane by the moon...look ye upon this – a mad star, me....transformed!' – we must let them be free else forever be by rationality caged – & then where will their own dreams be, eh? – fucked for all tempis by the bird that fugit – listen, Madame – this old song playing now – bird of snow-light, brighter for the darkness through which it fell – dark as that shady man's hat, familiar, that hat? – he is rain, made of rain – I christen him thus & henceforth he shall be thusly known – inexpressibly & unaccountably sad beyond words – the one I love forever is untrue – that song – forever – bird in snow – untrue...ah!...wings of lust, feathery desire..."*

he underlines the last resigned exclamation, puffs out his reddening cheeks & rests his pen – at a nearby solitary table, overcome by fumes from the relentless day of whisky drams & evanescent as steam torn asunder by the harbour winds, sat sad, tame, eponymous Mr. Raine – watching without being watched The Anonymous Troubadour closely as he furiously writes the whole mess into his journal & lets his brain drift & liquefy into clues & half-answers, baited & hooked by riddles & tricks – Mr. Raine, not his true identity, has a hat pulled low, cigarette smoke curling up around the brim, swarthy face obscured but keenly observing The Oblivious Troubadour's gaze as it flicks from the journal to the erstwhile Madame Erst, following her shape with his pleading laser eye, as he becomes the resting dust after her explosion, her one unanswered puzzle, the vanishing tail to her meteor

*

the following lunchtime, vodkas at a canal cafe – in her strange nether-land, away-from-hometown they bask – still wrapped in the previous night's allure – several potent

408

machine-rolled cigarettes still lay like thin spectres in her silver case – a flask of warm brandy they covertly shared beneath the sun-beamed table - oasis of odd intimacy – ice & lemon in a mid-day tonic – bubbles are flashbacks - tiny dim codas to the night's fading symphony – undertow of changeling – the laconic metamorphosis from devil to angel - a tad coy, surprised in mid-change – his old addiction, change – the moon that had ruled with her solemn lunacy now an icy dim dot, lost in dawn-light

Madame Erst has metamorphosed, she now heralds the pale light of day under her true guise, Ursula Major, great she-bear, coy, devastating & captivating, she lights her joint with the first wincing flare of the struck match, glimmers from which hold for a brief asterism in the shade of her form – she has several spent old boxes of dead matches in her cavernous pockets – theosophic, a messenger heaven-sent from the Galactic Logos to the Seven Stars of the Great Bear - phillumeny & the search for ancient wisdom, for sacred illumination, the one true flicker

across the street she spies a familiar old character wafting the damp sidewalks – approaching his home after a night of wild pursuits – his red door & old tin nameplate - a shy knock on rust, weary - he's in – she considers him a disobedient son, regales his stuck memory in her head with wayward words - white tails smelt from ways away – old mystic's white tail smelt odd, she muses - but these watery words have already been poured forth over the rocks in The Troubadour's skull & not without flushing out some nervy scuttlers from the nooks & tributaries

all night he had been plagued by incubuses, threats of violation to his clandestine female side, tempted by hints of the old Amsterdam that had never been stalked, where the riotous sailors dragged disinterred cadavers for doctor's meat, where witches strafed the sky & ghosts of all his childhood cartoons blending in the murk – rock bottom &

hollowed out - down among the soon-dead where seafront scarves of fog & sad bunting are drooping - where all is other & he is another

& Ursula senses it at once & taps him lightly on the temple to set free the linear from the circular, saying in a sensuous, low whisper

'...O my sweet Captain - go now - put on your old ranters hat again - be lucky & spew it all out...tell me your everythings...tell me these cartoon people, exorcism & rebirth...free your animated furies...'

& Captain Baby Trouhab, from high 'pon the fo'c'sle proud, opens up his wide, unwise old cakehole, his snide, rewired, fake porthole, & tells it like it isn't, just so - straight from the up-all-nightmare journal - his Septuagint, his Gita, his Pentateuch, his briny, shiny new priestbook proud - in the beginning was the endless wordplay & so it will be forever more without boundary or failure - harken to him

"...may it worry heaven, I remember that sexy old skunk - lascivious Monsieur Pepe Lepew - *mephitidae amoureuse* - permanently *a la recherché de la femme fatale* - Fifi La Fume *peut-etre* ?- yes, I remember now - the old skunk's fumes descending the staircase of the Bulldog Bar last night as my star ascended in this miraculous City Of Diamonds - he moved - *bien sûr* - in an elegantly animated fashion as we gradually breathed his heady perfume - & Old Spike the grumpy Bulldog bouncer, moves in on him, claps his back in an overly aggressive manner & barks a suspicious hello that reverberates all around in comic reverb - he then barks again, at Thomas, the desperate old mouser, who is crouched & hissing idle, catty threats at little Gerald - *la souris souriante* - from the door at the top of the stairwell - then barks again for good measure as Thomas scampers up the road - anyway, Pepe saunters to the bar & orders a beer & Martini chaser & requests a look at the - ahem -'special' menu - now, Bugsy Lapin, the wisecracking bartender, wrinkles up his perceptive nose disapprovingly as Pepe's piquant aftershave drifts across the stacked glasses & empty bottles – the whole bar sniffing & sneering by now – '...we've only got the house ale today Pep...pint of Dictum's?...' – he nods his assent & the dark bottle is slid along the bar top – finding himself so far back in time once more here in old hamster jam, & unused to the local potencies of ale & leaf, Pepe focuses with difficulty – & his cutesy button eye almost pops from his head at a busking elderly jazz band with a rinky-dink old piano on castors – so damn *square*! – ah but is it not so that my dreams are like old time jazz? - he twists mad librettos in his head until every last meaning can be squeezed from the pith – gesticulations & genuflections of word, garlands of a wild linguistic animation illustrate his every utterance - like the jazzman wrenches notes from the gripped brass – that bony septet of the damned square will ever be blurting their spilled inversions – notes on gelid air dart & hang – suddenly they break into 'NYC's No Lark' by Bill Evans – slow, vain, fattened bells of a distant church – Pepe thinks of his childhood, his tormented puberty – cavalcades & carnivals, where unctuous red lamps of vigorous churning light were suspended on long poles – the skunk village of N'est-ce Pas, its little cornershops, dim, pachydermal postboxes – the shuffly, skunky kids waiting by the lugubrious teenage outposts, for example Le Moko, a sad club of dark smoke & Le Chat Noir, a puppet theatre & salon of dubious repute – the graveyard of skunk writers, all who hope to be a poet lie there in unmarked tombs – or else are tied to the dirty street tables dedicating yet unwritten quatrains & alexandrines unto their own pussycats - stench of bardflesh - sty of Orwell - poesy pigs with their ink-wet metatheses – the police state of all nations in flux – the brain squirms, that time-lapsed maggoty churn – he saw it once, now in which film was it? – Boo knew it well, little darling – but now it is unrecallable out here beyond the authority of that safe-house, that warden world – blue meanies, blues & bennies, Dexedrine runners – they close the gendarme net around both lazy *flaneur* & deep topographer alike - letting no gentleman meander whither he please – hauled before the courts where some fake-maned regent lionises the lofty law & swipes a paw to send him down to the cages - real truth raw & roaring - now, Madame, Ursula - as you very well know those Bulldog lights are a low cherry-blossom red - & after a shot or two - & a little something extra, winkety-wink – yes, I began to sense a grim & shivery menace - a low, fuzzy, stoned danger began to manifest & hang like a demolition ball in the fetid air – an old foe in a dark suit, smoking under his big boy hat spied on me all night, now what do ye make of that! - & what's more, at a table, centre bar, bold as ye please, a Times crossword was being picked at by a suspicious, salubrious soul in a shiny snakeskin suit– sometimes soundly saluted as Sydney, not seen in these sordid spaces for centuries – & softly he sings out the sham solutions & salient sentences to himself in his sonorous, subtly persuasive & sinuous lisping style

"...6 down, lunatic heals deranged mind, eleven letterssss..."

he slyly serenades to the hushed customers – yet nobody even so much as looks up! - a damned snake! - egad! – in the shadowy nook by the smouldering fireplace Richard, an intimidating dark-cloaked figure, truly dastardly expression, sips his Dictum's Ale & pats his scrawny, motley, asthmatic dog & whispering the answer to himself unheard, sniggers into his sleeve – Old Pepe, meanwhile, selects something aromatic from the menu – perky hot pig? – ooh, dat rabbit looks tempting! - & settles at the table between the silent poles of Richard & Sydney, spreading the tail of his evening coat out across the back of the chair

enter Bugsy's friend Dylan with Jack Definitive, my airport feather long flown - to bless this scene with troubled lines of oceanic changes – now, good old Jack, a peculiar sort & no mistake, orders a German ale & holds up a canvas on which five child's pictures of a rhinoceros are crudely drawn & labelled A to E – now, Dylan puts down his glass of *Wortelsap* & lazily points them out with a stick & asks the multitudes

"...which creature is your favourite?..."

this query intoned, of course, in his languid, chewing drawl – once again nobody even looks up - except the Dastardly Richard, who again mutters darkly & sniggers to himself – this time Old Pepe overhears Richard mumble the phrase

"...the answer is rhino E..."

but he could have been mistaken

"...next question!..."

yelps Dylan, one ear folded down - & Jack Definitive, a little tired now, duly initiates a curious dance sequence of pecking motions & flapping arms – the clientele smile but offer no answers – then yet again from behind his hand Dastardly Richard muffles a snide, albeit measured, critique - "...poor pheasant mime...though strangely, man, I empathise..."

his dog wheezing beneath the table in unison with his master's dry cackle – anyway, old Pepe is puzzled by this tangled wordplay & grumpily downs his drinks & picks at his plate of rabbit – having long grown bored of both the food & clientele, he stands up & yawns - & with a practised air of aloofness, clambers up the stairs where little Gerald sits nervously – Pepe sees him there on the stair – right there

"...well..." - he declares - "..nice shoes, Gerald old chap...a bit noisy on the marble, I'd wager, but they suit you well!..."

& with a courtly bow he is gone – striding out into the early evening he emerges & pauses to soak in the brittle late-autumn air – he listens, silently – far distant but vivid as truth he hears a voice – the voice of Captain Rehab, echoing down the rosy streets – the animus, the sole true voice of this cartoon generation – still in the mind's watery eye he steers his hellish ferryboat from the past - into a quieted, roosting harbour it steals uncaptained - her foghorn long & misunderstood, as all moans of sadness are misunderstood – & in his heart the bone-dry sun is going down but everything else is rising slow – warily, night treads the eggshell shadows forming – the cartoon protagonists hunker in deft silences as cagily, strong, dry ciders wreak alcoholic havoc on the nerves of these willing dependants – in the cups of hundreds of time's victims everything softens in washes of impressionist light – maddened dogs tied to fuzzy lampposts, bicycles, a rigid black shape now shifting across the land that is memory's shadow – the accumulated ancient energies coagulate & flatten to an acidic erg - the battery of suspicion fuses, setting fires in hearts, in the interwoven argot of lovers - poets are useless here, lost for words, lost because of words – soon they moon & spoon in June's balloon - sly as a brown fox quickly jumping a lazy god – so, ultimately, all powers are levelled – on the street hobos beg in spongy voices –beyond their poverty a figure clad in a long cloak of shimmery black slips vaporously into an alley's slim twilight – & buskers are wailing of lost love & found anger – their torched songs of the raped earth make even the homeless old cadgers icily draw money from their empathetic pockets – a world condensed to a single reason, a silvery, wintering reason, frost on the cognition – a world of icy girls promenading with a proactive curled lip – the gluey handbills stuck on trees, spread out across the miles of damp plasterboard - every poster a poem &, with its cagey lyric, sets the agenda by which inspiration's indelicacy rigs the rules – yet ordinary life endures - from bright, aromatic windows vendors selling spicy meats – aromatic garlics, dicey pork strips – a saintly streetlamp glows by the tiny church he never enters – where the experimental nature of an acid-driven clergyman is even now rewriting parallel religious histories – & that rogue there - floundering in the wake of my imagined wraiths - why if it isn't the Right Reverend Degory Priest Defrocked & Mocked Esquire - resplendent in tall topper hat, well made, expensive, a full beard & sideburns – he seems contented, sated - as a ghost he's made god pay at last, perhaps – manna built these new castles in the air, the old city has withdrawn – he rants & rails on the sad stone church steps – lost to a billion antiquities of his own fashioning, years spent studying palms, tea-leaves & the drift of phantoms across the moon's unblinking eye – he has decided that he died at this time, this very hour, on new year's day in 1621 – he memorialises & eulogises his own dust – O hear him preach a sermon still, though long swimming in writhing, eely terrain

"...truth is a beautiful cage! - all truth is coded & buried underground in cavernous vaults hewn from holy words - I scarcely dig a few inches & there it is..."

ah, let him intone & atone for *quid est veritas?* - *est vir qui adest* – this is my tale, my journal, Ursula, so I put what words I wilt into his garlicky gob – Hear now, as I make him say

"...we lend words to each other only to see if their weight changes in another's hands – alchemist! - pour the leaden poetry! - all that glisters into the mortar & grind thy pestle! – the granules that make up my soul not applicable..."

& so I say saith the man who was always & never there – advocating crimes before escaping once more – reeling back through the pages of magical history, searching the cocaine wars for his Charlie peace, though it ends at the end of a swinging rope – before he sleeps the sleep of the unjust & crawls back inside his truth pen reading his sleuth's pages behind his eyelids - drily denouncing the dirty, distant world – as he is, in this present incarnation, with a bright red carnation in his topmost buttonhole, as Diggory old Degory he gaily goes – shovelling the same old compost, spouting the same old floral lies – trowelled from the gritty bible-trough at which he nightly snuffles – all the burned bridges, the devastated villages, that litter his derelict domain - & he is untouchable now - of such a man there is nothing more to be said – so I'll say nothing more, for now, Madame...Dear Ursula..."

Madame Ursula Major eventually smiled as she stubbed the joint out in the small, hexagonal ashtray – the day was afloat now – buoyant on a tide of prospects – she could hear strains of eager music dreamily rolling back through the centuries – a punk flower nailed to the prow of a three-master - starlings saluting the airy nothings on prosaic ledges above creamy, gurning Bob Todd gargoyles - the spiralling music of the independents swirled – pillaged songs of fallen supermen– half-all too human, half Christ-wafer – leering at the lost kingdom of bourbon – she hears 'Waiting For The Man' sneeringly smear the air from a funky radio sat high on a windowsill – digging the here come the ace of spades lyrics, digging how they bleat through the fog in a field of riffing staccato grasses – lakes of laconic chill where lacy ice grids the mud flats – driving music for endless trips on perfect roads - heading north to the revolution, twenty four dollars left - the vinyl grooves, devout autobahns on which icy cars of styli glide like priestly swans, impervious to the undulating tracks – searching down the new hero, sleek, avuncular & twinkle-eyed – their nature serene & rapt with the lure of the long-gone – underground, shiny-booted, whip-crack & slow strum - scratch of viola, tubs thumped, two guitars electrified with the inevitable explosions of youth – going deeper into the darkling wood - with Lou's bleak mercy the thin thread leading through the forest back home

*

all his heroes were malleable & fattened by gluttony now – their skins tighten around them, closing in like prison walls – wild animals that took on the likeness of the pelts that they wore – the writhing criminal bulge under all cities – low people with supposed high minds have taken over these proud streets, receptacles for the waste of a bloated, rich society - *peau de chagrin* - & other such balls-ache

The Bloated, Balls-aching Troubadour wandered from a low bar on the blustery quayside, blew his nose & that sonorous parp set the key for a thousand sea songs in his head – his voice obese & pliant, not putty exactly, but nonetheless subject to the teasing fancies of melody's fingers – ah, melodies, he pondered, ineffable in their progressions, yet always desirous of change – desirous, too, of conquest – & these were well-travelled songs - songs dragged out of beaten tribes as last breaths – seafarer's blues yodels - the croak of an ebony poet straddles the staves – he lets his voice strut through their reactionary lines - the quayside shimmered in splintered moonlight – the dockside always drew him in, always changing & forever the same, no matter the city - here where he sees blue girls on a green tandem imitate the joys of adolescence & wallow in an unimagined freedom – he listened to their tumbling giggles as they mocked the aged sailors & rehearsed their half-forgotten rounds of skipping rhymes & bojangling, tambourine-tapping rhythms – the old men become more wistful in their earshot - old women, always a little teary but more resolute – nostalgia feeds happiest on the fatter sentiment – & even old seadogs grind their gears to the dolorous, eerie chants The Troubadour offers, shanties from every harbour - hear them as they cut through the superfluous blub of the girl's playground voices

'Charlie Chaplin went to France

To teach the ladies how to dance.
First the heel, then the toe,
Then the splits, & around you go!
Salute to the Captain,
Bow to the Queen,
& turn your back on the Nazi submarine!'

& he is once more back aboard the westering ship in Old Rehab's mind & again the obedient ghosts they hop, skip & jump-jive talk – girls scurry up the dockside steps, boys lay flat by drainpipe corners beneath to see what they wear underneath – look at them looking, hear their urchin's snicker, wide-eyes upturned, reddening cheeks flat on cool flagstone yet flushing hot vermillion

'I see London, I see France,
I see Becky's underpants.
Are they blue? Are they pink?
I don't know but they sure stink!
Teacher, teacher, I declare
I see Becky's bottom's bare!!'

Captain Rehab closes his fist on the heavy wheel as he recalls them - stops his ears with wax to unhear The Shanty Troubadour bellowing now

'Christopher Columbus
Was a very brave man.
He sailed the ocean
In an old tin can.
& the waves went higher and higher and over
1,2,3...'

& benevolent sleep would refuse him even the respite of dreams & all through these stowaway reveries the great ship

418

of remembrance resolutely sailed – the Captain grown stout, sea- syrupy old Rehab, watching from the great prow as the crew, gathering amidships, fill up their hearts & lungs with five fathoms of his fatherly lies – his blubber warms his coral skeleton & shivers to the sea-songs' pulse – pearls, that once were his eyes, he makes thereof a bracelet, both warden & talisman, against each mortal part of him that doth fade with those sweet old tunes from the briny past – along the flat, curve of coastal roads, suspended on telegraph rungs, time's tablature, the magical tadpoles are dancing her staves – sip the Dandelion Wine & clear the decks for something opulent, weird & wondrous this way wends - & from a blunted shore through fog a priest halloos – waves a vulture-tipped cane & then contributes a stanza

> *'A sailor went to sea, sea, sea.*
> *To see what he could see, see, see.*
> *But all that he could see, see, see.*
> *Was the bottom...'*

neither in dream or undreamt these images freed from time, blown soundings, blotches from either the booze or the skunk danced before the Troubadours gaze as he sat himself helplessly on a freezing bollard fat with ragged rope twined tight

The Dream Ship is in full voice now, the stowaways & crew filling three sails with the wind of song

> *'Now when I was a little boy*
> *And so me mother told me*
> *That if I didn't kiss the girls*
> *Me lips would all grow mouldy...way haul away...'*

Newtown Baby rocked in his hammock & The Lonely Troubadour fetched a lute from his cabin joining him in cutlass-sharp harmony only slightly flattened with a belch of grog

'...whiskey-o...Johnny-o
John rise her up from down below
Whiskey, whiskey, whiskey-o...'

phlegmy notes of frogspawn groping up the mast of the melody - the harpy sail-ropes plucked by Old Boreas himself who throws in a refrain

'...up aloft this yard must go
John rise her up from down below...'

& they will sing long into the night & the rum will drip its last sorry drop, plip, from an upturned cask into their last gawping gasp - & under a drooping moon thrown splat against a creosoted fence of oaken sky – mad old Rehab has to be talked down from turning the ship right 'round right then & there, by Christ & all his fist of silver, just ye watch me, boys

' ...we're going away to leave you now
Good bye, fare thee well
Good bye, fare thee well...'

& as Aurai blows kisses to cool the brows of these fiery travellers & as the bilious ship contemplated, with a graceful nodding, Hespereides priming the canvas – the spring of melodies became licked incessantly by the salted tongue of a coming winter

& yes eventually, though the strains & caterwauling still occasionally reached a groggy crescendo, a distant land-mass gradually sought counterpoint between tree & mast –

with the ness of reclaimed grasses poking tongues, the tousled oaks bowing deep to Dryads in grove and glen – & though somewhere still stirred the minor voicings - just before the sleep sucked them under – above the lessening din an unholy, unmistakable yammering, barely the priest's voice at all, more a babel of all voices – drenched in good or contrarywise

*'We're going away to leave you now
Hoorah, me boys, we're homeward bound...'*

& the river cries constantly but ushers its tears ever forward so that they may resolve like a great harmonious chording in a strength renewed by the ocean's current – resurrection, resurgence, recall - the trinity of dragons that chart these dreams of a determined river – grinding the pearl to dust, eating away at the terrified shore - roll forward & live forever - else turn the corpse's gaze once more, eastward, to the broadening delta's spectacular gape – hear its messaging, return in turn & turn again, it murmurs – there are sentinels waiting at the estuary's mouth – time to lace your boots & smuggle your offended soul homeward once & for all

*

home?

*

The Disenfranchised Troubadour has lost his great bear Madame Ursula, his muse, somewhere in the weaving back roads & has found himself once more easy by the gentle surge of the dawdling canal

dawn broken, & even the ramshackle voicings of this bush-bearded, swashbuckling port of meaty Amstel's ham is

unlidding the beige blinds from her rouged windows –
leaving, imprinted on the lacy retina of hastily dragged net
curtains, a dark woodcut of the street that begins, slowly, to
come down from a luxurious trip

still a few straggling flashbacks wander to & fro - on the
bank opposite, Pepe LePew, slipping out of character now
as the crepuscular dissolutions waver & sway – & emergent
in the gently softening half-light he reels once & vanishes
back through the cathode rays to poetic childhood – as the
morning tourists, tanned, impossibly awake, merge with the
workaday locals until at last he could no longer tell which
was which – pig to pig & gargoyles leering at the night ladies
hitching up petticoats for the last flirt

the big world, the outside world, sleepy, unreal & only
slowly coming to - & he notices the shift of inner voice from
cartoonish to mock-sermonic - the witchy words still sweetly
mingle to riddle & anagram in his cryptic, crypt-kicked head
– all the nonsense he read to Ursula, all the barely-legible
sprawl of his psychedelic blarney that now filled page after
page of his journal – he stares at nothing & everything, eyes
agape, wide as tulip fields, ephemeral as the clouds - & the
clouds mirror his nothingness, mere weals licked across the
night by dawn – spirals of beard-smoke huffing & puffing
high above the looming Scheepvaartmuseum

suddenly, still on the outskirts of the dream, he spots a
figure crossing the bridge up ahead slowly but not slowly –
hat pulled low, quickly stepping now to the far shore – he
rubbed his face, the acidic lexes still blottering across his
sky, hazed by a forgiving light of frosted glass, still yet made
him unsure of all he had unsaid with his own eyes &
unheard with his own mouth – his words were crossed,
snarled in the act of thought itself – the more he tried to
think the less he thought – words just happened to him

he could just make the figure out - hermaphrodite in
framed gothic, which colour was mooted? - what gender

meant? – dwarfed by the closing houses the figure yawps as blinds are drawn – tall houses, narrow windows – was it his own voice calling out the ever-cryptic question to the first balm of light?

'...egad! - men rent these steepling hives?...'

& the unleashed world was now reduced to a pile of unfinished crosswords & his mind a mass of thin, burnished crossed swords, the moot points of which bring forth clichéd squeals from the city's residents – the shacks creak with decay, the stacked rooms freeze in winter & steam in summer as psyched lice crawl the floorboards of their lofty hovels like junkies in search of illusion's crack

what was his mind? – whose? – from where did these unsinkable boats of language set sail? – these black, fuzzy spiders of hindsight – the cold air before him was etched with the graffiti of repressed memory – he tried, in vain, to read their clues between the blobs & squibs & O how Baby Rehabadour inwardly prays now to put a full stop astern of these cleaving sentences? – but at each furrowed circus of concentration there were yet more puzzling hoops to jump through - heart palpitations, sweat – or was it rain – beetling down his neck beneath his shirt – no longer a cartoon now Rehabadour began to re-embody, to slip back into his old crawling skin-sack – his ruined brain emerging in rain from a sunny day – parts of his head still spoke in furred tongues – he found that his wilder thoughts were now becoming more orderly – he sensed that Degory's spirit had left him – left him in both mind & body

stabilised momentarily & curiously, but not unpleasantly floating a few inches above the paving, he walked the cool, rain-wet streets – his pant of nervous breath calmer now – the bicycles swooped in brief excitement through glowing oily puddles that threw the reflected sky drunkenly into a host of gleaming prisms – he absent-mindedly put the lost priest's cassette into his Walkman

"...while the rich post their typed-up copy in dying magazines on how the ropy cops itch to bring them to their padded knees – ye will notice how rolling water in the canal is once more reflecting the waterside houses whose windows in turn reflect water in which houses are reflecting – your head swims in water's house – read your poems through water – buy a new notebook to copy scripture, water-bible – oh but look, The Poor Troubadour can no longer write due to a frightened mind full of scattering birds! – fat farm-birds waddling out in a fan-shape – fat farmy words – sentences like chickens running headless amok – catch that hen & make a boat of it – ye can't throw any thought away – the ideas are flowing but they stack up at the dam – malevolent no-god – your precious city mapped by fools, the sky ripped by constellations, the psychic graph paper of the river's mad plans – spikes & plateaus show how you are faring in your wayfaring - mirrored signs in shop windows reveal new signs - deep orthographies to study deep & in which to drown..."

*

back at the hotel he feels suddenly sick & hurries to the bathroom - how long does a bloody trip last in this city? – until you get there, sir – that's it, mumble away to yourself, answer your own questions, get it all out in a treacly heave into the morning light's bleachy, porcelain bowl

& now the helter-skelter slide is complete – the earth is sky & the heavens solid – trees kiss each other & embrace clumsily in light winds, birds' faces melt to wicked sidelong glares – posters are portals to worlds of wiry words – old diamante city, my old mother, The Crazy Troubadour is liberated by the returning normality & now shall fling you a ragged tune from his old sailor's almanac - pilchard juice in his effervescent beard – with a touch of the blind hobo's recalcitrant charm – clueless eyes closed under the riddle of a starry night sky - the soul must agree to be eager until all is assumed, all is considered – always remember the moon – remember the ghosts - remember you saw Old Rummy Rimbaud last night, Chaplinesque with swinging cane – or was it poor Crane with his gin blossom friction – ghosts from fiction & past realities, ghosts from cartoon infancy - you saw it all, you saw the maddened symbols shift in sunlight & reveal many brighter symbols thrice renewed – silent, listen – listen to silent goodness & see no evil as you float merrily aloft with gargoyle birds – dangle your lithe tridactyl limbs in a steep angled drag as a drugged wind from Nirvana raises your supplicant arms to the firmament as the fresh, brutal sun arises – he wanders now, unreal, unmoored, he buys relics from a street auction there in the Grachtengordel - but show caution to the vendor's wiles – he is a charlatan of the tidal wrench – the vendor babbles as if reading the troubled mind before him like a script – he is looking for Jim Morrison who is dead, dead, dead - but he saw him, he said, outside the Melkweg one wretched night when the heroin had exploded softly in his heart – don't listen, pass by quickly with his hot sticky breath breathing bad poems on your neck - for you are stoned, inarticulate at the creaking open door of perception

he sees Old Maudit, in the back seat of a beaten-up Cadillac, checking his hair & combing it back in the rear-view mirror as it cruises like a black death-barge through the graveyard – he tries to pull reason from a stony path, the excavation of diamond thought – he stares at the jewels in a shop window display - perfect against velvet draped – a box of unfathomed brilliances – cool as a mint kiss from a julep whore-mouth under a railway bridge in heaven – quell this tumbling head, this eager acrobatic mind, take it walking like a leashed lobster through the nervous streets of pestilence – note, in the jewelled window, your aged face, the glinting portholes of your crusted eyes - take every fist of be-suited laughter as a badge of honour – interpret that song that the forest has passed all the way down to the thin white trees on the avenues by the canals – listen, the trees are singing - *ville de diamants, ma triste vieille mère*

back to the stable hotel room - from the Rokin window, high – birds below, as you soar, the street of changes, skin over the throbbing bowel flowing – evil drug-runners on the road slide by on frozen urine – he feels trapped, not safe, & hurries out again leaving the fat key with a bemused Robin at the desk – he goes to a bar & drinks three frothy beers & a whisky – in the alley where the locked toilet resides Our Heroic Troubadour pisses himself - too tired to unzip & too hip to try – he wobbles to the street, it is crazed, speeding, the trams sizzle like bacon on the damp tracks – girls giggle behind their cupped hands at his damp-spreading crotch, a slow-widening carnation softly affirming, from a limp root, the drying sun

"...let cool wee I let freely trickle never be dammed..."

good to be back unsafe again at the hotel - he removes his stained trousers & sits on the bed laughing – maybe the trip has finally pushed him through that fearful last portal to madness – is it that old game? – yes, perhaps this is the only reality now – a hesitant blob of frazzled now tinged with an uneasy aura of disbelief, a shifting, constant suspension of credence – he made a mental note to highlight his planned biography in haphazard places, shadows behind the lies

he thought of poor Theo & how he had spoken of his 'collapse into atheism' – a nihilism that pushed open any door - & how he had likened it to the pataphysics of Jarry & the early Dada crew – he thought they had diluted the purity of their primal urges but he had vowed to resurrect their cause, to live the curious life, walk the strange walk

& yes to Theo, life was not viewed as a random set of clues – it was just a realm that existed beyond metaphysical inquiry – beyond the nature of inquiry – gaseous, amoebic, passing through any barriers of doubt – the strange was the norm & vice-versa

but as much as the Troubadour had wanted to follow this woozy philosophy he always had the nag of reason at his ear – like a huge balloon's flight halted by a forgotten guy-rope, his ascent into pure derangement would always be tugged back to earth

The Pataphysical Troubadour settled his mind & pulled on a creased pair of red denim jeans over delightfully fresh underwear, he then gleefully sloshed his grubby, astonished face with a handful of tap water & decided to visit the famed Melkweg & see what the poultice of music could do to help soothe his descending heart

*

& on & on sails the sorry saddened ship – trance-wrapt in cracked-wafer winds – The Ageless Lonely Troubadour & Captain Rehab rehearsing a music-hall shuffling dance & swopping their beautiful Pierrot & Columbine masks at the helm - guided by invocations & bad maps, tethered to the devil's timetables - past stations & symbols – lovers, acquaintances, familial flesh – cinematic backdrops hurtle by – tall waves loom, hillsides lost in thick fog, volcanoes dormant & thunderous – this ship of last hope, bound for despair – they both know this now, how could they not? – an anger bubbling under their reason fed by livid red coals over which the wise have walked with fire as a bride – they read through histories of pain - centuries flayed as slave-skin, deep welts of guilt – they sail past glowing fields of summer young & old, out of which the occasional memory will come running to wave as they pass – but it is the times of his mysterious youth that play out most often – old meadows like smeared windows –bed-smell, linen-hinted, mum bringing toast from downstairs as you wake - dad going to work, his bike-bell – klingring - at the doorstep's drop – the shout of summer gone & a new term strikes lightning in a fist of guts – rain first, rain spits – pin-prick rain, slippery rain – its falling a recurrence in the dream cycle - always the grey pavement slowly rained upon - uneven cracks & broccoli forests of sour weeds in the cool, cool rain - piercing the chalk of fading hopscotch smudges - the caravanserai of slugs & snails, silvering pioneers, head beetling, antler radar – all under ever downward thin lines of blurring rain

a memory of Boo, why now? - a picnic, a tablecloth, she had a little basket of sandwiches, no rain that afternoon - he had promised to bring a bottle of wine, not beer – the insects disturb her, he brushes them from the cloth, they hold hands & wonder at the day sky, laughing, hiding her planets - & the more she stares the more she sees, like night stars - but the day is happy, a success, he thinks – why? – there are no revaluations, no compensations akin to that long walk home, he had thought – he must hold these moments in his heart, he had thought – yet only now, hungover in a rattling tram in a foreign city, it is allowed to come back – brutal, graphic, unblemished by melancholia or remorse – a sweet & sour slice of cherry life

*

& then the daydreams of Rimbaud started – dreams that staggered open highways in indeterminate countries & rolled onward past dusk, night over night – his meandering through the lesser-known regions of the city, friendly forward motion - falling, moving forward, faster still – the spinning tape recorder cogs skittery, mice laughter, cartoonish – time will constantly turn the cassette over & replay – print a new obsession on its virgin reel – he found a book on the history of Paris & learned that Rimbaud &

428

Verlaine lived in the Rue De Cassette – no-god up to his sniggering tricks

& The Tricky Troubadour mused on how the days & nights were darker in Old Smokytown London – yes, here, everything shines with an eerie inner candescence, as if a heart was shining at its core ready to burst

he passed an old woman selling a morose & suspiciously motionless goldfish in a barely translucent plastic bag – dead fish, no vibrancy in his bleary oval – transient wriggler gone, his gold stolen - ochrefish - remnant

& later in The Bulldog basement, there goes old master Rumboat – sliding under the green table to kiss the boot of an echo - hey! Artie! Hey! Ram-Bow! - do that old song, the old routine! – remember Mornington's crescent moon? - your flame of mocking laughter pushed a pram full of fairytales past my flowering window – your open road more fiery than Whitman's – O mordant balladeer, sticky corpse-rat, idolatrous sodomite, amputated scab-meat, rainbow-damned gunrunner, a Distant Cousin Troubadour, no sentimentalist ye - closing down every heart-breaking song with a smug curse or symbolist yelp – those hallucinatory visions – that sensory derangement, but for what purpose?

The Troubadour downs his rum & hurries up the steps on Rimbaud's winged feet – his hellish seasons in his pocket next to the journal, as if they were being introduced to each other as potential mates - & before him now, in the street, a little man in a smart green jacket – why, he appeared from nowhere like a jack in the box! - fire wizard, Zebulon

The Lonely Troubadour, sensing that this creature somehow (how?) possessed the power to quash the trip that still sputtered & embered in the grate of his brain, welcomed him into his ever-expanding cast of oddities with a grin – at last, the final character, the referee of this cartoon universe from which he is slowly recovering – one to announce the show is over, to bring down the last curtain, albeit in a roundabout fashion – perhaps with his intervention he may finally be rid of these spectral animations once & for ever amen – the figure stands stock still in the glare of his gaze – the last hallucinatory shadow flickers & the creature, mounted on a single bedspring, apropos of nothing, suddenly announces with a Teutonic, disciplinary air

"...zeit zu bett gehen! ..."

so The Lonely Troubadour sighed a resigned sigh & in the receding suffusion of waking dreams, yet still free from any earthbound laws, he sleepily headed homeward toward the hyperreal hotel – though he had doubts even now - & as the sun skulked over the gauzy rooftops to a cavernous sky, he fetched the heavy slab of key from Robin the smiling, sentinel receptionist & - with a sigh for every step - climbed up the spinning staircase – safer now, the night rendered witchless but still spellbound - the mother of all clocks began to tick once again in his skull – he clumsily undressed in shrouded streaks of borrowed lamplight – no thoughts any more, each word holy, zen-twisted, as if they were all grey monks, drifting toward eschatological horizons

for time, even perverted time, must someday end or be perceived to have ended – & the television, grown tired of childish things, is for the big people once more, picture books blur to heavier tomes, the real poets, the cabal of mystics who innately understand all you barely dream of

yes, up the apples & pears, little sleepyhead – say goodnight once more, to your funny little heroes, they will be back tomorrow & tomorrow – cue the music – the dying refrain & let all the credits roll 'til the moving hand writes – a preachy prayer & a fierce war-cry - Hosanna & Barbarous! – for that, *volken*, is all

*

Ursula Major, pilot light glowing, kindred star, sharing from her flask of *saki,* refusing to be diminished by the flower market's fragrant bouquets of violent symmetry

& she speaks softly to herself, reading from her little diary then extemporising, but if you crane your neck & cup your ear then her tales will get told – tales of harsher wintering - pass them on

"...I'm a winter baby, moon-wary, lucid – you do not fret me with your rugged wooing – your words are useless in my ears – I have the ghosts on my side, primed, ready to spook the air around your heart & all of your abandoned dreams – walk with me a while, I shall not buy you a guitar & you, in turn, must not buy me flowers..."

she plucks a withered leaf from one of the stems & turns it in her fingers as if it were a precious stone – this way & that, she tests its pliancy with firm pinches - he could watch her perform this finger-ballet for hours, his eyes mist like a mirror held to a poet's last breath – she continues, his ears reaching to grip every word

"...& take a snapshot of my corpse should I die & send it as a postcard to my past lovers – think of me as a great river – between rocks my dreams pooling to still water – light of my winter stirred in rainbow creeks -above this river, a daylight so sharp it stings the eye with a touch of snow – the starlings unchained – they are swimming in pockets of purged air – aiming their excitable beaks at the disappearing moon...'

she breaks off her litany & turns to face The Attentive Troubadour

'...there is a singer I want to see at the show tonight – he is on at seven I believe – we can leave before the main act if you prefer – they are very loud – my heart is not easy with loudness – see, this flower is the best flower – see how it has begun to die a little? - it has lost its ego & can be praised – we all need a little death to keep us humble..."

they walked by the way of the red-light district through guilty tourist huddles – she fed him the skunk-joint at intervals, tubes of mist from beneath the Jamaican flag - watching his juddery inhalations like a nurse watching a heart-line blip – this was the old part of the city, 14th century morality & mores, *de wallen,* closing in on the night - paid in cash for services rendered, the oldest profession, the city compliant & trusting the trade – the swooning ladies in the plush red windows - a fat Canadian's camera fails, he is frustrated – no ghost images taken, no souls allowed to be stolen here – he leers over a Japanese woman lazily smoking beside a lavish curtain – The Troubadour permits via a tasteless blotter a curious slither of acid to slip the net of his psyche – it blooms, devils & grotesques crawl indistinct behind her black spidery hair, Heironymous mon amour, the oriental girl's brief kiss, I like you, the airport feather rising – in his mixer gut the nagging *Saki* detonates – the lady changes her pose, she makes her modernist shapes fracture in the half-dusk

The Skunk Saki Troubadour grins through a toothy smile & she is the orange sunburst of a deep red Stratocaster - & the Canadian is Old Hebert, Ubuing his wobbly rhythms in a jerking dance – stinking life, godshit on his military boot-heel – *lese majeste* for the puppet king – tall trees wave their wands over the rippling canal & he is the wraith of old Mr. Josephs, old physics prattler – teaching his own tainted chemistry to the seeds that drop like the beginnings of a snowstorm from the wild blossom tree of a lactating cosmos – or maybe they are the motes of his dusted chalk equations finally finding their route earthward

the tourists are tiring of the no show - & as they take their grumbling leave the curtain closes - The Troubadour takes Ursula by her long, cool, soft arm & looks back at the figure of the helpless Canuck as, spitting into a tissue, he staggers sideways into sidereal unconsciousness - he hits the pavement like a coal-sack & is devoured instantly by a passing swarm of insatiable goblin poets – their teeth sharp as needles & the type of black eyes that reflect only sorrow

it seems the acid lingered yet & the brief affair with weird chemistry was still glowing, forever perhaps – but no it was merely the defiant fizz of the thrill cigar before it is finally stubbed beneath a bored boot-sole

The Poetic Troubadour smiles wanly into her smile & he knows he is lessened by the exchange - Ursula Major & Troubadour Minor – knows in one flashing instant that both of them know the final everything - like figures blasted by a tear of lightning, a moment remembered forever for no sane reason, only the tethering ropes of a heavy connection – he is frozen in that sudden fractal of self-awareness, a period of transition – consumed by an ardour that transcends the net of hours – he knows this day is radiant & that it will all stay rooted in him – he knows that his veins, if so polluted, will carry doubt through their tributaries to the open heart – she stood illumined, the image flared in that grip of streetlight - like a raindrop frozen by chance photography – he smiles wider, as if the smile was all she could see - she laughs & becomes a jewel

*

The Melkweg is eternal & within its walls real-time avails not – it is always someway rooted in the shift of years – for it came from the rich, ancient, hemp-aromatic underground of music, redolent of all the haughty amphitheatres of an age in decline – an empire where a propped-up corpse of music could play out its throes - dragged flight-cases, well-stacked, spicy vans with lank-haired graduates running down the tired minor scales of a dying era

it was once an old dairy, before being occupied by the retreating hippie army in the 70s – thud of drum check –

one-two one-check – a pungent nest of vile roadies cup their claws around a soggy joint – a thousand, thousand damaged ears dulled, distractedly tuned to a faint spectre of pleasure on the outskirts of listening

in the smaller rooms angry experimentalists atone & detune on weekday stretches - the hissy hi-hat, elastic bass & eerie saxophonic squeals all underpinned with gravel-booted snare & the rhythmic click of a wayward rail – above murky stages hung lidded constellations of clotted starlight – a place where Captain Rehab would go to relive past debauch – the Melkweg's unhealthy structure was, after a fashion, kin to his olden mode of transport - a dead sailor's ship adrift toward uncertain destinies, a stalwart vessel out of luck, in constant fear of change, helpless to defend itself as crazed horsemen ride pale through its drug-blooded doorway

in every room the unremitting stench of heavy grass, like dung coated in honey left in a baking field - the eternal third encore's final chord is left ringing above a crushed prairie of dandruff & patchouli – shanties of electric hellfire blared out to a melting ship of fools - four souls mill about, snaking the causeways & eddies to the cheapest bar – where the dream ship becomes a train & back again - train and rail, ship & sail in rain & hail – a hydra lashing – the rags of blues that polish the country pearl – unison, amity, a perfect sonic weld that tenuously married tradition's bulkhead to a driven wheel, summer heat to wild winter wine – all of musical time riding the surf & sailing the sleepered track in turn

& now it is the beginning of the newest decade & the old ship lumbers onward, stuck in its recurring dream-state – the dead crew gratefully cling to the mast – but its post-punk pistons churn until the mainsail billows, black flower wilting on the prow – then sails fade to machinery, the sky gorged by steam gushing from the funnel & taunting the blackened, dissolving rigging – ripped old drug pirates scuttle its beery decks & yell forth an icy black mass from the crow's nest – a joke-shop eyepiece held up to a black-eyed face – a thrice-stoned bedlamite somewhere on high shouts 'all aboard!' or 'land ahoy!' & urgently shovels another rattle of base coal on the lurching flames - or cranks open the sail-sheet to balloon in the sway of trade winds – safe, Europeans, home at last - Westward Ho! – put your trust in the ship of changes & let our destiny be tutored by its bawdy, irreligious drag

Troubadour & Ursula Major blinking at the swirling weed-smoke - in the small hall, they curled like cat-nipped felines at the stage's feet, made unearthly in the shade from ranks of interrogatory spotlights – then, unannounced, a tall thin, unsmiling man of indeterminate age - The Troubadour had estimated mid-fifties - stepped briskly out to the solitary vocal mic glinting under a pale blue light wreathed in grey smoky spirals

he picked up a cherry red Washburn electric guitar & expressionless, strummed a soft but resolute G minor to F minor alternation – plectrum clicking like a quiet buzz of electric razor under the skin of each changeling chord

'How Do You Know It's A River'

he said & then, without a breath's pause, he sang in a madrigal baritone of skeletal honey – the slow, mournful verses evolved, punctuated by the subtle emphasised pluck of a flat-picked figure that gently filled each space between the lines – the plectrum discarded, his damp head in the spotlight now seemingly made of smoke & vivid steel

entranced, the Reverent Troubadour scribbled the lyric in a stoned shorthand on the last blank flyleaf of his journal

our dream house is small
& the weather's
left to chance
the past stretches
beyond
our moony

backward glance
O tell me
how do you know it's a river?
how do you know it's a river?

yes & earlier that very day, elsewhere, in the vacillations of the busy city morning, lost in a quiet, old-fashioned cafe on the gently indifferent Wolvenstraat, he had watched small boxes lifted from a van & passed to a serious man in a peaked cap, he had passed them in turn to a waitress who stows them in the red-brick alley to the darkened storeroom at the back

in need of a sit down, a civil refreshment, a pastry maybe – & so The Civil Troubadour enters, squeezing past the last careful transference of boxes – he quickly smiles, excuses himself - *welkom meneer, ga zitten* – the waitress gestures him to a table at the back of the cafe in a small alcove – a solitary tulip in a glass, no tablecloth but four little doilies stacked neatly & held down by a large red wooden pepper mill, by the counter he sees three bulbous Buddhas shyly from a metal flowerpot peeking – a miniature picket fence of cool powder blue encircling a table of wooden idols of the East – on a low shelf stout, old tins of exotic teas, their names long fallen victim to a gentle rust

this was clearly not The Rusting Troubadour's universe but it was certainly a welcome rest from too much here & now – like dipping his journeyed, blistered feet in an arctic stream, washing the sand from the toes

the waitress patiently awaiting her orders, black apron, white, starchy shirt, heavy pendant of opal set in silver – a character from an old dream of waiting-room magazines & tea-rooms, she held in the orbs of her gaze old movie-reels whirring the grainy action of dead years inexorably onward, the audience's dumbfounded faces gazing up – he instantly felt a creeping deja-vu – knowing it was her world window

436

showing the already seen, his journal displaying the already written, the slow, silent past teases through any window nudged open - he could stay here forever but will leave soon

& he wondered why the dreams in Amsterdam are unrelenting in their stoic fixation upon the past – though somewhere, back in the future, the ship rolls onward to the estuary's mouth & out into the possibilities of a terrifying ocean - & at the wheel remains a vain Captain that sees its vast, unruly span only as a mirror in which the old comforts are reflected & looped

*

one night, long gone, in an icy sweat, the cold image of the dreamt sea still vivid, The Romantic Newtown Baby was approaching a street on the town's outskirts, new buildings, anonymous shops, people scuttling head down going about the daily chores, when strangely a section of the street mists over, as if cigarette smoke had been blown across it, & an old cinema now loomed where moments ago the newsagent had stood & the details of it were far clearer than the here & now that had easily drifted into a peripheral blur

& yes, the sign above it read Radion Cinema, clear as day, there were birds on the roof, there were two people entering the front door, himself & Boo, in an alley to the right there lurked a familiar tall figure, he stood casually reading a defunct newspaper, his down-turned head causing the brim of his dark hat to obscure his features

The Newtown Baby was not frightened, it all felt natural - & in his bones, he felt an overwhelming sense of still being a living part of this olden time, its images by far more real than the brash modernity of that false life that he had so abruptly & easily departed - a fear not of being stuck in that circling loop of hours, entering & watching the same old film over & over forever, but rather a fear of having to one day return, to leave the security of the corny old film's escapism & be hauled forward to the hotel room, the sound of traffic, the drip of the bath's leaking tap

so vivid was this fear that on waking his first feeling was that of disappointment, such as may be felt on coming back from a beautiful holiday & returning to work – he stood up, naked, at the window & lit a cigarette looking out at the tall Dutch buildings, the bland tourists & pallid commuters in their garish modern clothes, the impatient motorists in their futuristic cars & such a wash of sadness came over him that he unscrewed the top of the wine bottle & took a vicious swig to quell the disappointment & steady his resolve

the tram rattled into view from behind the curtain's border & its antique charm, its dysfunctional beauty, hit him in the pit of his gut like a photograph of a dead pet – he felt calm, the tap dripped, his cigarette consumed itself where he had rested it on the sill, he let out a purgative sigh as the pigeons took flight from the pavement & a long, disconsolate hoot blew from a stuck lorry, sounding like his saxophone soul had offered up the first bar of a lowing lament to his isolation

he thought of the train whistles in old westerns, the ships signalling through fog off the wharves by East-India Dock, he thought of the streets of Soho, blue Sunday rain & most of all, running beneath it all, the tumbling, insistent laughter of the river

*

Theo The Sailor sat on the chuntering tram as it snaked along the busy streets, criss-crossing through compliant traffic, tinkling its warning bell as it approached junctions as if to say 'old world coming through, make way, make way' – the tourists smiled at it, the way people smile at photographs of bi-planes & horses pulling carriages down rutted streets –

they were triggers, grandparents of reassurance, bloodlines leading back to the easy dead

The Troubadour broke the sailor's daydreaming

'...wheels spinning, Theo?...'

'...I was just thinking about how every city becomes one great city in your head after a while...I been all over, boy...& it all merges into one pile of bricks I'm tellin' you – these shops, those lines of trees, could be New York or Milan or the fuckin' moon...'

'...you been to the moon lately?...'

'...we have all been to the moon in our dreams – used to be a jazz club called Moon & Stars around here back in the sixties...a real dive, prostitutes & bad speed ha! – red lights, I remember a row of deep red bulbs all along the top of the bar, the bar was stone, rough top that you couldn't stand drinks on properly, had to find a flat bit – they had a parrot in a big cage that used to swear in German, fucking hilarious – seemed to pick on the German clientele too, must've been goaded by the accent or something – the red bulbs...yeah, it's weird though, I remember the rest of it being in black & white? – like old films, or sepia, like photos – what do you dream of? – beer I expect!...'

'...I used to dream of a ship, funny, you being a sailor after all...I think there's colour in mine, hard to tell, dreamt it a lot - but now I can't remember most of them – or don't want to ha!...most of the waking hours are like a bloody dream these days...I go to sleep for some reality ha!...'

the tram rattles & rocks & of course he does remember everything, he remembers it well & then remembers all over again – & he wonders was it a dream dreamt last night or centuries ago? – with Captain Rehab & Boo playing chess at a table outside the Cafe Boheme in Soho - light rain – a soft dusk – cosy, genial mumble of traffic

he

'...men are more likely to kill themselves...'

439

she

'...but women try more often...'

he

'...your knight is vulnerable...careful...'

she

'...I was always a little careless when on horseback Captain...'

dissolve image in crystal - soft laughter - petals & cat tongues lapping - Boo continues shyly, looking away at the road

'...I tend to speak these days without my old voice, the voice I had for him - I speak mostly of will...of little else, truth be told...all we are doing is rebirthing - I talk about salmon striving to spawn & oft times the tide is daunting...oft times...'

he

'...the Troubadour - & I refer here, of course, to my former self - who seems to me to be far more immature than I recall - sometimes perhaps evenlike a small petulant child -.I imagine his name spoken in his mother's voice - shrill...in admonishment...'

she

'...a child...maybe, yes...'

he

'...& blind...blind & poor...poor blind Troubadour ha! - so the villagers say in vicious whispers by the threatened church...'

laughter nervous, secretive - conspiratorial - a traffic-smeared pause then the Captain again

'...I suppose we shall be consequences of his failings - do we even exist outside his twisted mind? - I mean, are we following him in his blind faith or merely sniggering by the church?...'

& The Insouciant Dream jump-cuts to the small Santa Claus church high above the new town - the sun is out after freshening rain – the wet stone & tamped grasses between the headstones - the leaves muddy in piles by the tool shed swept – for the old gardener is the grave-tender & digger too – he rests on his old broom & slyly watches as Boo & The Captain wander silently, hesitantly up the steps from the road – he glares at their vacillation as if it is a gainsaying of his creed – stares as if to dare them to defy death – he holds his broom before him – a weak sentinel's defiant last stand - The Captain shivers & his voice as he breeches the quietude is brittle, tentative

'...let us pass...'

jump-cut back to the chess café, the Soho traffic – there is Boo, her smile blooming slow, like the weeds stretching for light through cracks in concrete – & yes she is answering his questioning absent-mindedly whilst closely regarding his face looming swollen in the teaspoon's fisheye

'...haven't seen you on your bike recently...the red one..?'

'...it's broken - I fell – it's ok though – damage not too bad but needs a little love...'

he

'...it really suits you, I love to watch you ride - how you used to race down Clay Hill Road..! – back in the new town, I mean...'

she, reading from her notebook

'...urged by the wildness in my heart...the weather parting...'

he

'...a cycling Moses descending with tablets of truth for the barstool disciples...'

she, raising her coffee cup

'...here's to The Basement In The Sky - & to a town in the grip of fever - bereft of promise...long bereft...'

he

'...we will be there when it closes...'

she
'...to drink & toast old times...'
he
'...old times...pah! - may the vengeful god destroy them
- I am sick of old times, I who have to live in the present! -
may we remain blissful in our anticipations whilst retaining
that cool, exquisite doubt - for it is only in doubt that truth
can flower - remember the loves that we have loved - they
are branches of the same tree of doubt - some bright with
leaves, others barren, stark..."
then Boo, softly, to herself
"... damage not too bad but needs a little love - old
loves...may sweet Jehovah grenade them..."
& the reverie breaks, the caustic city cracks through
time's mirror - the streets hove into view & it is the shock of
the ever-present now
& the tram forever rattled & rocked & pulled away with
Theo waving from the window - the day was still, air serene
as a reflective sigh - a grey cat sleeked through two green
walking sticks leant against the wall of a rugged stone wall
surrounding two small potted bushes - his mouth was dry,
first place best place, new part of the city - no beer yet, stay
with it a little longer - nice aura of the past about this part of
the city, he felt warmed as if lit from within - keep the faith,
faith in the present
& here & now, in an Amsterdam café, he stared at a
solitary tulip in a glass of clear water & realised he was broke
- his mood darkened, the quaint became threatening, the
austere became chilled & morbid - he stared in horror at
little spoons cupping the brown cubes of sugar, the tinge of
green to the one high bulb, had he been in here before? -
he gazed around the café as if he had been transported
there that instant from his far London home- it was like
watching a theatre, a sideshow of marionettes, automata - it
was not a house of worship or a bar but it was, he mused,

442

merely another palace of devotions, a church of stimulants, the tannin hit & the rush of peace – a cathedral of tea-leaves, mouldering souls with bitter mouthfuls, each sip a purse of disdain, her cracked lips barely wetted – why the persistence of memory? – he had never visited this area

the blissful, grey cat from the street plays sphinx in a red fur basket tossed under the plain kitchen chair by the bright window – the grey hair of the old ladies, the grey hair of the motionless cat, the grey eyes of the waitress as she bends to leave his change in a gold-plated tray

he thinks of his bewitched Chinatown & the good, thick Turkish coffee, the plastic tablecloths wiped with a sweeping cloth, once, twice, back & forth, a new ashtray, done – he looks up, as if to god, & sees the cadmium ceiling plaster paling, no hint of any nicotine wash – the plump bulb dead centre, like a remorseless sun in a desert sky, the queer light diffused, soft at the spongy flood of outer shadings

the tree taps against the window, hey, it's windy out here, it says – he could stay here for ever but will leave soon – the waitress polishing the scratched glass clock-face & she winds the key forcefully, three quick, harsh revolutions, set the hour, one, two, three

the old ladies glance at the invisible wind through the pleading branches – the greeny-yellow bulb, the paling sun, the cadmium glow, the desert – otherwise no colour, shades of monochrome gliding against the furniture in breathless patches – the coffee in Chinatown, a million miles distant, the mind cannot hold such distances – hey, it's windy out here, the tapping branches, the tight lips, pursed sips, boxes of aromatic new teas stacked up in the hallway, the giggling Buddhas peeking, the drab cat, pallid – clock ticks

he will stay here forever but will leave soon

*

443

& from the Rokin's window, early morning, the light slinking above wet rooftops, The Troubadour feels as if there is a mad creature that stalks the city's inner nucleus – its cat-eyes peer out, as stars peer from the night sky's forest – from low-slung, mascara-rimmed cloud slides the sun's true, cyclopean stare – yes & under that gaze the eternal somebody has emptied a rubbish bin (of course, of course) & the grisly contents are all strewn across the tram-track, or maybe it is an urban fox's work, sneaking away to the bestial ground beneath the old city with its plunder from the plastic world – back to where the sailors sleep off their drunk in glorious rolling dreams, down by the wharves alive with the scampering current of rats – there are hearts to every city – the pumping core that will not be thwarted, the veils upon veils of history that their metal & glass cannot erase - & The Heartfelt Troubadour raises his teary eyes to level with the outward gaze of the Hotel & realises that water has won the last battle – the city was now submerged & adherent to the laws of underwater physics – robotic cars subtly dispersing the currents as weightless people swim the dirty pavements, noiselessly entering the towering bulk of glass buildings as deep-divers investigate sunken galleons - & he thinks of poor Grace, the erstwhile mad woman they could not quite shake back in dear Soho – how she was planning to drift through Amsterdam next, having at last exhausted the patience of London – & was she out there now? – a part of the hub, the sleeping worm in the Mescal? – he could almost smell the Sandalwood in her wake, dreamcatcher Grace, Duchess Of Infinity, another lost someone somewhereing in the great anywhere searching for something, anything

& glowering out at the stagnant street, as the mornings & evenings merge to one essence, kiss at their edges & flow together, the way sky meets the sea on days of low fog, he stares & asks himself a moot question - had he come all this way just to look backwards? – it was a question that had felt rhetorical even as his reluctant mind was conceiving it – was the adventure, his prized miracle, little more than the testing of a hopefully greener grass? – he put his trust in this city & he hoped its' fire would eventually redeem him, bring forth his truer self, undiminished by the old disbeliefs

an alternative London, unlondon, lower case, he wrote it this way in his journal – a city newly painted, without those foul nooks & pissy crannies wherein lurked the many furies plotting his downfall - or maybe even an unessex, drained of familiars & loaded with better weed & ornamented by tulips - it was as if he had sought a yet flatter vista upon which his molehill thoughts could seem mountainous – the relentless, uniformity of Essex mudflats morphing seamlessly to canals, polders & flood plains

& he lit a cigarette, three left, enough – window shut & locked, nothing to do but just stare & stare until the veil drops – unamsterdam, unlondon, both under the spell of rain that deceives their denizens into believing that they live ashore – he raises his tired eyes, above the panoramic view that the hotel enjoyed, to the lightening sky - & there, with a gasp, at the dead centre of the waking heaven, he saw the bottom of the dream-ship's hull, noiselessly edging through the grey-blue mass, he saw a thousand tiny fish swooping in the banished surf from the vast stern - & he knew, right then, that he had the explanation, the answer – the crew were all no doubt still aboard, singing, rigging sails or sleeping off the grog, but that was all past & future – he knew now that he himself was the present, the focus, the full stop, the pause - & he resided not aboard the safe ship of dreaming, that secure, unsinkable vessel out of time, but deep within the ancient secret of the very ocean she sailed – the amphetamine rush was slow, the acid rush was dreamy, all the reliable booze swam around his head – he had been underwater in his daydream all along – the cats were

gleaming sea-lions, the dog-walruses bark – the songs had all
been sung with a choir of drowned ghosts

The Drowned Troubadour's apparition extinguished
the cigarette on the red sill & lay back on the unmade bed –
he flicked on the tiny radio attached to the wall & fiddled
with the tuner until civilisation loomed through the static
jungle – an incoming message from another planet, foreign
DJ bantering, bits of the shipping forecast in dry, reassuring
English, sprinkle in some faked laughter, the cadences that
exist in every morning wireless – a song begins – Joni – & it
is coming on Christmas – he shuts his eyes & counts off the
bars of the melody & tries to see her fingers on the keys,
tries to see the reindeer, the skater's escape

& he thinks of the city, submarine, hushed, outside the
window that, should he choose to fling it open, would surely
let the massive, unstoppable weight of ocean roar into his
world – & maybe that was inevitable, maybe that is what he
wanted right then, a new concern – but for now he heard the
fresh solaces that encircled his skull & was happily floating
free of worry - the soft car-horns, a quaint tram's tinkling
chime, the deep buzzing of the reception bell – a wordless
winter choir, songs of joy & peace – to sail away on

*

& Jack Definitive walks, early morning, the first joint
always heady, always a rush, nausea rising with the weight of
a late night slice of pizza – the birds are too loud & the cats
too silent in waiting – he has no purpose, at least none that
springs to mind, & The Troubadour's visit hangs heavy in
his heart – a favour to that mad old priest, a duty of care –
well, enough of that – he has seen too many of the holy
man's recommendations – he only wants his simple life to
endure – any pain, such as it is, slowly nulled by the sweet
smoke, memories fogging pleasingly at night – his record

446

player & kettle working, the camping stove sufficient to boil anything he drags back from the shops, the mayonnaise & chips & pizza & good German sausage all readily available in his locale

walking is free, thinking is optional, regret an obligation – he no longer considers the past, it has outlived its use – the future is a forest inhabited by tame animals – the here & now is a warm second-hand overcoat that he has borrowed to ward off the snow – he listens to jazz, the more atonal the better, the uneasy marriage of textures & mis-shapen melodies – he has soundproofed his apartment with egg boxes – he cranks up the volume late as the clock slows to morning – Cecil Taylor, Archie Shepp, Albert Ayler – these are his deities, his tether to the spinning earth – chemical infusions, blood spirits, no words to bully the meaning, no picture painted to suggest or mislead – forward motion, no nostalgia

*

The Nostalgic Troubadour, still occasionally graced with chemical vestiges but anchored in spirit, strolls - with a head full of red stained glass & yellow bicycles – ghostly, alongside the dull waters of the spooky Zwanenburgwal – his cane prodding the canal pathway, on past the old woman selling books from her barrow – he had made a pact with her to purchase a little something every time he was passing

he perused the worn spines on display for a while & chose a book of Alfred Jarry's Ubu plays – he had felt an empathy, a sense that his own world was becoming more pataphysical daily – he purchased Spinoza's Ethics, worn copy, well-thumbed – a work probably a long way beyond his levels of concentration but he liked the local connection & his phrase - *'if you want the present to be different from the past, study the past'* - a *bon mot* that he had come across somewhere back in London was it? – yes, probably via the priest - & lastly a selection of intriguing poems by Hendrik Marsman in Dutch with thankfully a corresponding English translation set out on the opposite page – he quickly read one poem as a taster & it ended with the simple line - 'the sun is yellow' – the honesty of which took his fancy for a reason he could not quite, at least at that moment, explain to himself - the melancholy, haggard old bookseller woman, who had little English but knew just enough to be cordial, smiled at his choices & hastily put the money in a battered tin cigar-box that served as her cash register

he felt, as he wandered aimlessly on, that little by little the underwater city was reclaiming his mood, every detail sharpening its focus to reveal new nuances – the low clouds were shifting their demons in the unhurried wavelets of the canal – a ginger cat, blissfully asleep beside a black, growling Alsatian on a partially-sunken barge – it was all so clear, he sensed that a kind of purity, a liberty, albeit weakened by his lysergic experimentations, had permanently suffused his every thought & was presaging a slowly burgeoning augury of knowledge, a necessarily closer examination of his life, as well as a liminal meditation upon its dark, traditional sister, death

another potential slapstick man, his body a sequence of ridged folds akin to a tardigrade, swathed in a ridiculous chequered suit & topped with the absurdist cherry of a bright red flat cap, waddled from a doorway up ahead, snuffling & squinting at the day like a surfacing mole – his shirt a size too small & his shoes a size too big – upon his gaudy yellow tie a thick red spiral – absurd! - & he is speaking to Theo in an admonishing, supercilious tone, the effrontery! – The Effronted Troubadour approaches them – Theo cowed, his sailor's cap at his feet, as the fat man lectures him on servitude, the obnoxious ways of the lower classes – just as The Troubadour was about to intervene

448

Ursula magically appeared from a doorway & strolled over to complete the scene – she seemed to know the fat man & spoke in the wake of a rare silence

'...hello Mr. Hebert, hello Mr. Gluck, hello Troubadour – what seems to be the problem here?...'

The Troubadour thought, Gluck, so that's Theo's name, German, as I suspected – the fat man explained that Theo had assailed him with a lot of old nonsense about the upper classes lording it over the swine & he had taught the impudent fool a lesson by knocking his hat off & giving him the benefit of his opinion in full measure – Ursula turns to The Troubadour & smiles, saying gently

'...none of us are god – we can all talk about how one is best, the other worst, but there is always a tomorrow & tomorrows change things – it may feel like the same old tomorrow to us but there will be differences, little things that we don't quite understand as well as we did yesterday & still the fact remains, we are all here because of the almighty, whether he exists or not, whether we believe or not...'

The Fat Man coughed, frowned & began to speak but The Troubadour interjected

'...I dreamt last night that this city was disappearing, my home city too, underwater, the whole thing adrift - & in a sense they are vanishing, from brick to glass, the walls either transparent or a mirror – it is an illusion of water, the water's dream in which we live – perhaps in the future there will be one solid centre to all cities wherein live the troubled of heart, the poets, painters, craftsmen, sailors, old soldiers, pawnbrokers, tobacconists, churches, brothels, anyone or thing that has been traduced & abused over time will move inward, walled off with real, opaque bricks & mortar, to live their strange lives in as much peace as they can tolerate, outside of time's flow, undisturbed by events that do not concern them, too low to be tugged by currents, each entity its own anchor...'

'...I like that...' – she picked up Theo Gluck's cap & put it on his head – he immediately did a little fake hornpipe jig & said

'...the cities want to be sinister again – sinister, we have that word too, yes?...'

he glanced at Ursula who bowed her head – he turned, smiling, to The Fat Man

'...we have no quarrel, sir – I should not have babbled on at you like I did – I have been without sleep for too long & I humbly apologise – tomorrow, I will be silent by way of repentance, forgive me...'

& Theo Gluck The Sailor comically took off his cap & bowed, leaving with a polite wave at his little crowd of actors, quickly followed in a bluster by The Fat Man, who trailed after him as if he were a dog on a leash, over the bridge & out into the waiting city

The Waiting Troubadour & Ursula, left in awkward silence, in hushed tones they briefly discussed the storm that had been threatening for days, ever since The Troubadour's arrival in fact

'...*ein reisiger sturm*... - they say it'll be the worst in years – maybe tonight it will come – there was a little boy I met when I was out cycling early this morning who said that it may come as soon as tomorrow – he seemed unsure – I'd best be going, I have to meet somebody...'

'...me too...' – The Troubadour lied

two fallen leaves on the canal-side walkway, waiting for the wind, neither of them stirred

*

all he had to meet was his past, truth be told – a few brandy schooners full of the past duly ordered at a lazy little bar just off the square - yes & somewhere back there & whenever it ever was - good old Boo & the hapless Eternal

Troubadour Ghost ride alone through grey-pigeon showers of a cool august - the train roof luminous with sunbeams the balmy glow to feed - a sharp, knifing memory that's killing the present joy of just living in this parcel of time - a time that was lost in dreams as careless love was saved in song - & Boo, how back then we drank up every teardrop in the eternal dusk of the Liberty Belle! - a human, existential pub it was - ah, but alas they will have changed your name, a paint job, stained old patchouli jukebox gone, the local pissed-up saints withdrawn to bring in the holy grail of families - but you still open at 10a.m. in our hearts - as Captain Rehab sipped at his brandy soda in the corner now, its own Pubcorner Wizard, Old Micky Blue Eyes, never failing to preach a variation on his bitter gangster creed - kiss the darts you fat deceiver & be loyal to your squad as your bitch wife necks a brandy in the dream kitchen - The Sagging Captain puts his head on his folded arms & feels the table vibrate to the first chosen tune of the long day - spinning all the way from a motor city far - & at another Table, The Troubadour, having spent all day wandering around heart in hand waiting to give, glances at Boo at the bar lifting the two ciders carefully spilling, & wonders, could it be? - The Captain knows, of course, the answer & much more but is silent as the anthem drones sweetly & his chest begins to swell

& yes, yes urgently that devious old Captain Rehab wants to tell you so much - to call you suddenly by telephone from a different morning an ocean of stars away - O my love these things you ought to know! - dig that telephonic hole & throw in the sluggish, drunken slur of crippled words

& leaving a pub in a night of castles, juice of tangerine & a world stuck in a web of wires stretched over pylons elegant, majestic across the night-swallowed fields - he hears them in bubbles of a quieter air buzzing like a nest of bees -

somewhere above his head the conduits of broken sentences pour & pour
"...everything is a river when one stands still in space..." someone said right then, right there – a tall dark figure, the chooser of song, by the jukebox smoking, the wisps curling around the wide brim

*

all is movement & you're a proud stone slowly pounded & licked small by the tide of changes - & what if you saw Old Rehab, your future self, washed up & lost out on the street tonight, Young Troubadour? - what then? – or if in a dream, even, if you saw him stranded somewhere far out at sea? - why then, could you make a reed boat big enough to sail him home? - from distant harbours where he blew in & blew out, steam-headed & bent on his wildcat bliss – sending you telepathic messages, or a postcard from a lost friend in a sick city – they tell you bad news - I'm here in the port of Amsterdam & I'm tired of all these red tram traumas, mama, he wrote – & each night I see old tandems of ruby red, they appear in dreams leaning on bright primrose walls
& these messages will feel either faithfully authentic or obnoxiously intrusive, depending on your waking brain's mood today here in this foreign city, depending on your hands pushing the window wide & your nostrils smelling the astringent burst of a forbidden supper loose on the diamond breezes – suddenly remembering when a swarm of mind-wasps drove you into the Haarlemmerdijk & you bought a faded denim jacket with torn leather trim lining the breast pocket from which you hung two daisies & a bead necklace - you needn't give up the ghosts of your future – breathe the wet air, fat with bacon & marijuana – the inevitable crash - & when the sun was upward wending then down the Rokin steps you swept - into Dam Square with a wide hat & bluster

of pirate – then up Damrak - along with The Unreal Thing,
a crusted goth, who reads you interminable extracts from
the life of Cortez - of the songs of that river dog – Amstel &
froth, brandy that swills in huge bowls that fit two cupped
hands like a crystal ball

*

& later, much later, Theo the Sailor, frozen to the spot
where a link was forged across the river – it is 1270 – do you
remember? - it had gates which held back the watercourse
at particular times in order to circumvent flooding - working
girls were banned & forced to bait their hooks underground
– a region, a sliver, a crumb of the world rotting forgotten in
memory's molar, eating through the enamel to the nerve
    the tension of the timeline then tightens a notch - down
through many lost eras – & yes time becomes an island of
dead souls rearing heavenward from the darkling seas – no
maps, no compass – residing somewhere off the coast of the
everyday humdrum dependencies - & seeping into the soft
land to quietly seed – & instinct tells you it is a mothering
soul that writhes in such earth - for in memory time is a
guardian, desiring only to be a kind of blithe comforter to
your complaints - for nobody wants to believe in full & this
spectral haven is the one last safe harbour to doubt
    & so the timeslip shivered - the buildings, warehouses,
walletjes - & the red-light district, all sneaked through the
cracks in the little canal-side white-brick walls cupping the
deft water as it flowed - from late medieval times all the
dealings & weighty traffic of the dockside falls away – it was a
blasphemous time & priests were outlawed - the bold, brassy
Madam and her sultry nest of girls would venture out at
night visiting pubs & inns to pick up their clients from rows
of cold-hearted bars with glottal names, de Houttuinen,
Zeedijk - resounding with clinked glasses & forced cries –

echoes of lust borne high on the yawning quay's quieted zephyrs & eddies

& yes out there, in the moon-cursed night, a sailor sings of squalid nightmarish hallucinations that he transports from the wearying fathoms of his oceanic mind

O red wine of Hamsterjam, there on the bar – where? – right there – well, we declare - while the Germanic-scarved little *fraus* still plod on through the seedy, van-coughing, sunflowered backroads – squeaking their cryptic small talk in domestic mouse-houses – but the city it sleeps while the canal's margins blub – it has a belly full of baguettes & beer – sly visitations of the trinity – leaving the bliss-spouting Troubadour all alone & out on the rat again

& yes, as the Still-Lonely Troubadour sadly walks these puzzle-paved, clog-struck, hoof-streets with his crazed gaggle of ghosts & occasional comrades, he hollers to the roasting hot bar full of Bulldog vanity with his arms open wide

'...barkeep! - bring me extra beer & pitch it down my throat, parched by time & your fragrant resins & graced with the indecent scent of finest marijuana freshly procured from the landlubbered barges of the Thames mud! - & free me up to partake in that cake of crumbly devilry lurking in its nicotine underbrush – light up my sacred old pipe of war packed tight so no joy can escape...'

he casts his sceptical nose to the firmament - he contemplates pissing up a bollard outside as Ursula she weeps for his vain, adulterous disgust with all things mortal - & yes he wants so to disprove the universe but alack he's too damned, too plump with self-importance, to take a crack at oratory & so he stands up, jokingly hoot-snorts his way to the Dickensian toilet bowl with no seat & cracked enamel bowl - he unzips his snagging fly & can see rumba, tango & taps dancing across the black, dog-eared mirror, a parade of sneering faces misted, easily visible, reflected over both his heaving shoulders – he offers up warm burps, base-poetry of the tired stomach's eruptions – the transvestites crapping their pants as the yank tourists leer – the nervous mince of man-women by the door perforated by dagger wounds, they press their white thighs together & overhang the green sinks adjusting roughly rouged lips & horsehair wigs – clowns of androgyny - they've gone to heaven in a little row boat & mouldering clap fizzes in their harbouring loins - the pitch & bitumen voice of the off-duty barfly-maid – she is assailed by low lechery & whiskey-tones – long heart-sick of their tall tales whimpered & swung canes gashing the feathery illuminations – the sailors spike their ribald dialectic with the snarl of blue gag & cheap stunt – the good old bad boys revolve, boogie, fall about laughing with the furies, bereft of a single dream's yearning – squashing their hearts with rum to sour the echoes of a wounded guitar – Brel-bursts & Charles has no voice - with the dry, gasp of torched modesty in their wheezy, accordion lungs – & they tumble out into the sweetmeat morning with a dead sky turning – dwindling women slung under hat-lamps – she drinks, O she drinks & he drinks too, ah yes he drinks anew - to the vigour of the whore-hearted spirit of the inner city blue, to golden Amstel damned

*

& elsewhat & elsewhy - Theo, who, with grace & good cheer, dies here barely thirty years hence 'neath an old sentimental willow tree by the water flowing, yes, he will lie serene & unsatisfied by a smashed streetlight in the wake of a melancholy brawl – but now is the past & he's born-again, yawn-again, beastly & priestly – touch of Degory's piss & salted Tequila about him as he dances - sweltering & pulsing he burgeons in the flapping throng - the genesis of love, no less – a Columbus of the desires – Cortez begat Degory as, via the wet tongue of Dictum's Ale, he related aphorisms of eternity – fearless Theo Gluck, he asks lonely men for their poems & they are shyly read to him by pub-light – he absorbs each line, they sicken yet take root in the turned sod of his skull's mud – in doped, so-hopeless, bo-homeless, boo-hoo blind pigs, where the jacks all meet their queens, flushed & rummy & by music dealt too cruel a hand - The Helpless Troubadour saves a piece of him in his journal

roll ye out again, crank the handle, shake the chain - for in a witchy world a spell is never far - priest of anguish, he writes, *you are a pedagogue although never so ordained - such & such is much too much beneath the stars*

killing the pages, killing the time with longing & smoke-tossed coins of chance - heads & tails of the client-trawled coryphées - Theo bawls to the bored bar-staff

'...I don't get it, why ever should ye want to choose another way to live? - ye surely don't want to know that small world out there! – come with me my lovelies & I'll show you a good old-fashioned bad time...'

Theo disdainfully scours this den of souring intellects that have long putrefied in advance of their final internment – & he is a searcher for stowaways now, a walking tongue-twister, a Mickey Finn in the gin shrewdly slipped – before they know it they are all aboard, lug up the ramp & put out to the wild seas under throaty sails that can gulp the grog & bleat the catchy music of the spheres – O Captain! Captain! - rehabilitate your soul! - here in this nebulous district! – dear dear Dumpsterham – rummage their stinking bins of love for to pick out the bits to which flesh still clings

a flash of mad Degory Priest at the pub window, sudden appearing, as was his wont - clutching a hammer & a bottle of whisky half gone – The Troubadour knows well that he is elsewhere & unreal but is charged with the desire to render him manifest with a choice volley of oaths – the phantom priest spies him first, though, & smashes the pane & berates him thusways

"...ahoy there! - Theo! - ye bloody old faker! - you're no more a bloody sailor boy than I'm a fuckin' chimpanzee, man! - sure ye used to make us all green with your pink silk ties & all those bloody crumpled corduroy suits - fuckin' ridiculous ye were! - I tell ye now ye never got the shit-kicking ye deserved - & Jesus woodworkin' Christos your women! - God's balls! - the fuckin' women he had! - eye for the ladies they call it...did they have eyes, old chum? - or did ye blind 'em with science & your bitter old blarney?..."

The Triple-Masted Troubadour heaved to & ordered two more full schooners of rum & watched amused as Theo The Landlocked Unsailor shut his eyes to the onslaught of the holy ghost & sank, like a defeated armada, into the churn & grift of the swift-perishing night's giddy swell

*

& after hours - way after the dance, listen - a virulent music is pounding in his aching slumber - a thousand years back from this street, this hour, this country, Old/Young Newtown Baby stands nervously on the step of the girl's parent's house & blinks like a deer into her hazel eyes - he ponders the wondrous truth that somehow all his ambition is now fulfilled by the mere walking of this heavenly animal back from their night of carousing in the Basement In The Sky - all centuries of love converging to this point - regaling her doubting ears with the immutable old hearsay of poorly-wrought poetry, rare humours & easy politics - she is an ocean before his shore, yet still he rails knowing well all argument is sinking, the cause, for tonight, inexplicably lost, presumed drowned, in too many pale sweet draughts of flowering ale & sharp needles of burnt rum to mention

& he dreams in guttered dozing - a trip in a plane to sun-washed shorelines offering the promise of affluence beyond imagination, he painted a pretty picture for her to devour -

the later the hour, the more explicit the fantasy, all promised
to her in a taxi's back-seat clasping the vinegary paper cone
of still-warm chips that unhurriedly drips a vile grease on to
his torn jeans

*

ecce homo - The Auld Lang Priest Of Pain, balmed by
his latest holy tirade, cocks his fizzy head to one side at the
window like a dog listening to helicopters & whispers
"...sun melted the road to heaven, old boy - eye of toad
it hubbles & croaks anew - remember that old tune on the
jukebox when we caroused back there in the buried bar? -
you sang I am a linesman for Notts County & I ride a large
toad - the witchy tar is fine, man! - god's last fuck but I need
a drink!..."
a maniac cackle & swish of cloak & he's off to sleep
aboard the last train through hell
& yes indubitably he will get off in the old fisherman's
town & surely go blustering by the fishy old cockle-sheds
where he will no doubt menacingly hum the theme to On
The Waterfront, his burnt-out Brando heart savouring the
monochrome violence - Steiger on a meat-hook slumped
back in the Amsterdam of his contentious mind

*

two frogs by a lily pad awaiting a tram
"..ils appellent ça la ville du diamant, monsieur..."
"...c'est trop cher pour nous, je crois..."

*

& though by now his mind was spiralling he clung to the
scrawly words with which he filled his journal & trusted that

458

they would be translatable in the event of his demise or, should he survive, be reworked in order to give voice to his voyages in these dark regions

& though a possible return to his old city, or indeed a homecoming of any kind, seemed unfathomable, there was – still yet remaining in his perceptions - a thin thread of his old reality patiently waiting to be followed - & perhaps it would lead out of the forest, perhaps not –time will tell – or if time, as he now understood it, still applied then it would, in theory, tell

a single blade of grass, plucked from the cracked street, revolved in his teeth – the music, flute music, weaving from a high window, like everything, disturbed him – the beautiful rendered sinister, tarnished – he looked at his reflection in a shop window – his head transparent, the tree behind him creating the all-too-plausible illusion that his mind was a tangle of bare branches – he sighed, an overwhelming rush of desire gripped him – it was a desire for rebirth & the song that billowed in his dry throat was a song of springtime

*

& just me now, alone at last – voices, faces, all gone to earth - a fleeting sliver of the dream left with its accompanying questions

what fills the gap behind departed conversation? - are there more hens than boats? - which is worse, failing or never trying? - do you feel like you've lived this day a hundred times before? - whither the sledging hill? – & should I follow Antigone or Creon up that cursed hill? – am I disgusted with the promise of routine happiness? – pray tell, who has the more difficult task: the stern governess who dutifully reprimands her meek pupils concerning their most solemn errors or the renegade pupil lagging behind his

459

classmates with an inky satchel full of bad homework & leaking biros?

& yes what tunes does the devil own? – & who judges their luring melodies outside of god's court? - or the artful apprentice who illegally deposits stolen money in a foreign account & later (when the hoo-ha has subsided) puts it to use building orphanages in Rwanda? – was his initial crime wrong when such benefits ensued?

don't hang up, honey, I know it is so late but please hold the line – you've heard this dream a million times but I beg you just once more – tell me, who am I (essentially)? - what is my authentic fundamental nature? – I'm dreaming of my accidents & drunken escapades though I failed to be there when they happened – where did I lose my leather jacket? – these days it seems the losses come in riddles – clean house, wash the rugs, where is that Muscatel I'd spilled? - what is my true personality? - what's the speed of dark? - what is my greater purpose? – how, when required, should I end my life? - who is Mr. Death? – Mr. Raine? – Who was that fat man in the spiral tie? - why is deism a cult? - what happens to all the sweet, sweet hope when we merely exist & hold no aspirations to immortality? - why does x stand for a kiss? - is there a god, and, if so, what, pray, is her disposition, natural history & general humour? – oh & yes, what exactly is time's fucking problem?

& yes he, once upon that time, saw, in the green spume of the Amsterdam canal, a dead leaf trapped by an iron buoy chain – the eddies produced thereby created the illusion of the leaf moving backward, flapping like a spawning salmon against natural currents, in a desperate last lunge to the old tree from which it fell

you can't go home again, the Troubadour thought & sighed, closing his journal – you can't even telephone – that old telegraph pole has fallen to the axe, lines severed, not even the gossip of wraiths skitter down the cables now – no sweet song to sing to love, just the relentless morse code of the maddened crickets – farmland to wasteland & return – most of humanity's hours are spent dredging their sleep for fat fish only to reel in another bicycle wheel or rusty tin can – listening close to the tin can, it is a conch of fake memory, beery once, like your good self, like the tin can & string telephones of the olden summers, long-distance, metallic voices, messages from Mars – the astronauts speak like that, he thought – it was a beautiful time, when even wars were temporary & everyone obeyed the tea-time truce – was it beautiful? – yes, he supposed, it was – tearfully he reopened the journal

& hear us no-god, in heaven thy dwelling-place, though you feign sleep now you can still fake a dream tomorrow - or are we never awake? - write these answers in the wrinkled notebook of your astonishingly vivid, ruined imagination you bloody old fraud – never give us answers, or even clues – keep the whole caboodle in the scabby folds of your phenomenological, telekinetic cerebrum & - in a quiet blue moment of your own sweet black dream – for just once in your life pick up the god-damned phone if it's ringing

*

yes &one more hungover morning, long ago & far away, back in the new-town, he thought he spied, peripherally, a dead fox in the dry fountain - but it was only a lost woollen jumper
yes & one other hungover morning, longer ago & further away, he thought he spied, peripherally, a woollen jumper in the dry fountain - but it was only a dead fox

*

461

in legend, no less, it is told that he once upon a time saw, in London, an artist vomit on a blue, blank canvas – & legend declares that it had made his inquiring mind scurry back to the safety of the memory hole, the calmative words, back to his established, though haunted, fountain of familiar words – no paint from that day on, just plucked ripe notes, a storm of language – the catgut & wood

& now, in The Hotel Rokin, how he longed to be able to smile back at these surly, dislocated memories of old Boo & the dead fox, woollen jumper – & at last to mourn them equally, for which is sadder? – mourn, yes indeed, but it was more important to write it down, way down – suck the meaning 'til it swells like a snake-bite - & once & for all let you go home, angel, & lick the wounds of a four-string guitar until it heals you a tune - & then watch as you - primed to sing - point your two sweet red lips to that old yellow heaven & moan

*

a stranger day - positive/negative – weird day - anything can happen today kind of day – the afternoon is a blank page scrolled into an old typewriter awaiting the punch of the ink - clear head for the first time in days - pile the diary pages against the door to exclude the draught of memory – each new page a sea of adventures yet to be plundered - the aftershave he put on this morning is cheap as his hat – tang of gin, dry old woman's flavourless choke - two glasses of white wine & a bow from a Japanese girl at the flower market – she liked his hat – The Troubadour in his new, cheap, felt fedora, gangster faking the slinky walk – black as death with a leather band in russet-brown – he hummed a repetitive riff that nagged his brain, what was it? – sharp mind, clear, gets it instantly - spelling out the energy produced when two rough surfaces are rubbed together –

F.R.I.C.T.I.O.N – guitars that suggest a police siren – straight into the Venus De Milo's ghostly clutches – his clear, cheap-hat head was full of cut-up phrases leaking through from dim days long past – he leafed a book in a dusty bookshop – quick leaf, too much nervous energy to browse at length - a sepia photograph of a zeppelin above the pyramids, a woman's back, she gazes upward – or is it a man? – there are certainly two other figures in there also but she/he is the punctum

today has an urgency to it, he felt, an awareness of an unknown purpose that had been missing from his visit so far - he feels that he is in tune with the whole city, the real inner core that he had spoken of, feeling its newness & antiquity in equal measure – the way atonal music whittles at your prejudices until you pick out a cooler melody, the way faces appear in rose-patterned rugs if you stare long enough – he almost skips, smiling at the black cat that scowls yellow eyed beneath a delivery van – breathing deep, allowing the ache of the past to enter his skin

& London felt much further than an expanse of water away now – back there, the streets still held their breath as time slipped by & the implacable rolling Thames cast nary a sideways glance at the sad, slow declining of the dockside wharves & quays – the interminable docks, who said that? – easy, it was himself talking to the priest – back in the days of staggering about after a hard morning session in some godforsaken illegal boozer's den – the old quare couple, *drole de menage*

he cocked a music-hall, theatrical ear at another peal of baroque piano music from a different high window in the Browersgracht – no, a harpsichord it was, not piano – that mechanical, evocative, staccato-tight march of metallic notes – possibly a girl rehearsing, female touch, frightened scales – nervy arpeggios under thin fingers – soft perfume risen from the nape of her neck – so many windows, which one? - that one, the open one – a tall building full of secret music – tower of champagne song, sweetening the stark, clean rooms that go a long way to describe the soul of this squat, antiseptic country

he takes a beer & a cheese baguette at an open-air café – to just listen awhile, the music still there, though its faint now – somebody left their paper, English, The Telegraph – Tory shit-rag, he thinks immediately – Pavlov politic – the busy street, no not too busy - the bicycles stacked against a red door – that old man there, smoking a pipe fixing the chain on one of them – those bright yellow primroses in that muddied terracotta window-box above him – the old bike-fixer, his gnarled, greasy hands leave a mark on the light-brown bowl of the puffing Meerschaum – he wipes it with a fresh rag – his dog asleep next to him on the round cobblestones, stirring chases in its slumber as an old canal boat is docking, amiably bumping against the hog-tied buoys

The Troubadour holds his breath, eyes narrowed, as the whole scene fixes in his heart - shimmering peace & distant music – the beer is beautiful, golden as a sun – he sweeps the baguette crumbs to the gobbling pigeons – one clue left – there's always one they can't get – 8 across, 6 letters - '...not a land rover...' – car pun? - the canal boat owner secures the thick rope to the bollard with deft fingers – the music stops, leaving a space in the air like a sudden bereavement – did Rimbaud stay in this city? - what made him think of that?

& he is receiving a dream song from way back when – he welcomes it this time, closes his eyes to make it as real as possible – he is there now - down in the new-town park of fumes - it is chill & deepest night – once more he is that bright-souled Newtown Baby, compelled by romantic urges - he crosses the bridge over the silent dual-carriageway and descends into the shadows - on a bench by the lake - rain or snow avails not - a lamp burns behind his eyes, brighter than a million suns, it warms his expanding heart - so tired he was back then, so early to be disillusioned & bereft of answers to all his ill-formed questions, now he turns them over to the wisdom of poets long dead, he laughed at the thought – come all ye ancient bards & troubadours & I'll tell ye of my loves & hates – get the words right, cart precedes horse, at least in the dictionary - questions, like answers, must be earned - must these backward glances endure even in day-mares? – yes, for there Newtown Baby sits on a bench by the glassy, moon-stained pond - where, clad in rough blue bib-overalls, he used to wash down the ploughs & tractors & random farm machinery for the museum in the park of fumes - the smell of the diesel still wafts from the exercise book full of scrawled bad poetry on his knees – diesel-flavoured requiems, right now, here to be twisted and shaped, set into permanence - every bauble of shiny truth he had thus far stolen from the old books or tales badly told of his nocturnal debaucheries – every traduced opponent safely interred in the shallow, forgetful dirt of words - buried treasures

he thinks of the priest – yesterday he had received a barely-legible letter addressed to his room at the Rokin – he had 'gone sane' as he put it

am now roaming the south coast of Emerald Ireland in search of rebellious fire & Patrick Kavanagh's bones - in the nicotine snug of a Bantry Bay pub watching Bugs Bunny's drawl being callously gunned down by the lisping, stuttering Elmer Fudd - drizzly night down in the engine house, catnappin' just as motionless as a mouse & a man come along an' he chased them out in the rain - was that Fudd? – or woodpeckin' Guthrie - or mayhap the world-weary, wily coyote still constantly being compacted under that Sisyphian whistling, plummeting rock & I'm now wondering if we are in fact made weirdly immortal in this real world thanks to the constant sacrifices of those childhood animated martyrs, sump'n to fink about, boy

& the priest he wrote of Liam, the idle barman, locked in an eternal cycle of slow Guinness poured & lazy glasses squeaky dried with a blue tea-towel – the letter ignored all sequence & order, much like his speech

up to Dublin fairly gritty, where the girls are all titty, in search of folly alone – before rejoicing with labourers, my kith – or walking & perhaps contemplating by the municipal gallery under a ashy sun, feeding off the energy of the river's surprises - the fairy-lit, mysterious glints & swells of her tumbling dreams rolling into mine eyes as I walks in a nonchalant breeze along the banks of the bottle-green Liffey

& The Troubadour wonders if Ireland could be a lost home – he thinks of the word home & what home is to him as, lurking in the yin of the daydream's yang, Paddy Captain Rehab watches the gallivanting holy fool from Dublin's Essex bridge in a stained naval coat & thinks too of his many false homes, still out there, swilling in the liquid past

but The Troubadour finds home wherever he swings a cat - & he thinks of poor Jimmy Red, that cracked Liberty Belle from that same weary isle - poor Degory Priest too - & whither Boo & her soulful, patched-denim intricacies of mind? – walk on, don't let the good times roll away

he found a haven for day-drinkers & in this throwaway, chipper pub he duly drinks from a golden grail – thinking how this would be Boo's favourite pub in the whole of Dutchland &, letting thought follow thought, recalling how once, down in the park of fumes, they had integrated body & soul, surreptitiously, among the dragonflies & earwigs – under a shock-mouth moon amazed & almost convex with recoil – O coy moon, brightling button stuck on blueblack suede, the buttons of her blouse tapped out the beat of their beatnik lust – she bore no grudging fruit & he spurned her flagging heart

but maybe Auld Dublin Town would have suited them both well – look Boo, a dark pool, they could dive in &

merge with the cheery departed – & there's the prodigal himself Old Tom Maher, poeticising his part-prose, part-prattle all over the swashbuckling bloody place – better than here, these damned squares & rectangles, tulips & bicycles, not geometry for curvy old Boo, tulips & bikes, she'd eat one & fall off the other – good mood today, clear head, don't have too many too quick – Dublin, yes, an old soldier with a new mask, beardy pubs out in the sticks, cow-dung flops & the bus-driver delivers the eggs – hauntings leak through winding streets, bright balloons of music swim upward, yanked to stillness by the weight of words, swirling fogs of carcinogenic breath carry lilting lies through twilight realms of stone & peat-hearths - & in every jacket pocket a crumpled manuscript festers unpublished – yet still the townsfolk search, year on fabled year, for dull jewellery in the compacted, sodden mud, Lestrygonian wharves squeeze the river 'til it gasps for air & the last choke from a swung scythe will be its echoed eulogy – ivy rooms, brief encounters, Belacquas & Blooms - & always, always the snowy dead

*

the leaves of ivy drumming their fingers querulously on the wall – waiting for to get to heaven but alas there's only sky, only sky - & with a sigh Mythic Madame Erst, in real life Ursula Major, cycled determinedly against an east wind through Dam Square toward the Rokin hotel – the low, rude blues of much cooler seasons engulfing her & finding within her soul, if not a mirror, then a pellucid tarn in which to peer & hopefully catch a glimpse of the many tumbling magic charms of late autumn – her taut skin exuded the odours of dried-fruit, in her eyes the soft, still pools of unshed tears, in shelter from the winter winds, are seen to briefly shine & ripple – as she approaches the hotel The

467

Tearful Troubadour stares down through the harsh wind throwing specks of rain around in galvanic circles & tosses his cigarette butt to its thrall – it flies upward, the arc distressed by an updraft, whirling excitedly westward suddenly on the whim of nature & then he loses sight of it as his focus melts to a dim rainbow newly forming, glowing fuzzily in an intermittent distance above the slabs of black, wet rooftops – Ursula, he burns with the poetry of her rhythmic name – the shaving foam still smeared on his half-shaven cheek – a raindrop stings his eye as she ties her bicycle to the metal pole – a heart full of many faces, a road disappearing to the flat horizon, consumed by the jaws of sky & earth

Ursula Major - big bear of a woman - take it from me – to know her like the sparks in the sky at meteor time - solid German stock, she said – tales of her mad old family home, blue windows sealed with tinfoil in the winter - two rabbits loose in her bedroom – where she sang arias in a scout-hut choir, dreaming of that distant home as she pedals the wet Amsterdam streets with three huge, smiling sunflower heads in her handlebar basket

she frequented dark cafes alone with her darker moods, yet emerged from these coffee-scented shadows crying out with her sense of wilfulness & poise restored

"...*ein fluch, seufzer, dann versuchen, versuchen wieder...*"

The Troubadour, hazy with a vague alcoholic amnesia, will continue forever to pretend to recall her ample legs in oxblood corduroy, the scent of patchouli and mint rising from her hair – how she would brassily holler as she freewheeled past

"...hey! schmerzlich! - get this!..."

& she would throw both legs wide & with one hand raise the grey-blue hat & cackle the cackle the cackle - cackle, yeah

"...es ist meine stimme..."

& with nobody on the dockland shore to hear them. the gulls, who he knows all secretly pity him, have infested the squares & flea-markets - & yes he now stares bleakly out at the disquieting city with freshly jaundiced vision – hark at them, bleating and cawing in sarcastic indignation! – Old excommunicated Bishop of Ebb-Tides! – struck-off Quack Doctor River! – the patient, he's remembering again! – fetch his earmuffs! - Captain! – cease all shore leave & fire up the ship's engine! - for it seems his eternal nemesis Moriarty is once more at the gates! – forget nothing! - we can live on memories after all, good or bad!

ah, but in her mind the huge, grey, bloated bombers are growling over Dresden's fragile crockery & her father died in its wreckage - O Fondest Ursula!! - *als verschwand die freude?* - did the past dry up? –do your memory's river-beds of cracked, arid clay give off their vegetable stench still? - as if the torrid watercourses never once freely flowed or in winter months froze, trapping your secrets in a measured ballet of ice – yes & as if, left alone by said river many years ago, The Fledgling Troubadour never smoked six Marlboro lights & watched his casually flicked cigarette ash burrow deeper into the fizzing snow – the waters run through it all

you watch the flooding of memory island from your solitary lookout with no regrets - & this king of darkness must not reign - these fallow hours require at least a taper-worth of illumination – then by my green candle I declare let it be seen!

back in London The Troubadour had smelt old sadness on every breeze, he had the mind of an assassin in the heart of that deep-rooted city – but in Amsterdam even the sleaziest dockside bars were clean & the older streets, when vacated, rarely reached the heights of melancholy that his heart truly craved, that delicious gloom that tallied with his paling worldview for here, the diamond is king & Ursula its insubordinate queen – she could be a kind of a purgative, perhaps, that will serve to cleanse him of all his futile, mooning thoughts – somebody to drive in the dagger hard, twist out the heart, leave him factory numb, without nostalgia or poetry as cure or palliative – a sea-spirit running riot through his delusions, his old dream crew now urged to desert the ship like rats, in what was after all, the darkest hour of the voyage so far

O Ursula! – if only it had been you back there moaning on the sofa on that mudded estuary bed way back when, when – sweaty & suffused with love's fervours – gorged by narcotic charms of poesy, from which there are no known means of escape - The Muddy Troubadour had wrestled in lust with a punk mermaid, drunk barmaid, junk comrade – no matter! - we were castaways, no ship sees us nor wants to – & The Troubadour, set free upon a cliff edge, balks at the contemplation of the abyss

& Hamlet yawns – the day dribbles like the incessant rain that creeps like lava across the Rokin's molten window – he must not yet give in to returning - no train, boat or plane to haul his duffel-bag of pity back to London – he has no means to get to the station other than walking & his wiry, skunk-induced paranoia is high & the acid still trembles in his eyes – he looks to the empty grey sky for stability, eyes full of the hot iron filings of failed tears – he is momentarily glad there are no evil cawing gulls above him now to mock his imagined imprisonment in this cage made of air – he daydreamed up a blimp, greyer than the clouds – he picked up his pen & notebook

a corpulent ship of the winter wind – seems so under... unrestrained by the tethers of...so anchored by the weights of...it puts all paradise in a fog of temper

cross it out, tear out the page - to hell with prose! – flee, muses! – go screw yourself you bitches!! - fuck you all!!! – let them creep like a vampire out to the forest with their crow's feet & mascara – go haunt the basement juke-joints where the decrepit alkies drag death from their smokes & the stars grow dimmer with each swig of rum - reel ye in the harvest of sin & find a shitty rhyme within! – he thinks of the punk mermaid again, feeling at home back there now – live there, he could – build a shack out of driftwood, old barges – cosy enough when the sofa is not damp - & when it is, why then, walk hand in hand by the serpentine water with her broken pink umbrella & pick the fleas from your grey army coat! – more lines to unravel, more sputtering farts of poetry - hell's bitches, I need words like a bullet through my name

Ursula, whispering

"...it's best if you wash in the rain, do you remember? - *kalt...ein licht von einem Stern das uber dieser hauptstadt ausstrahlt...*"

for time is a lonely train, a ship of revenge - hear her in dreams of seas, calling you her captain - calling failed, sea-weedy Ishmaels & Queequegs drown – their rags dragged down through a fog of rowdy seasons - & they are calling ye too, O Lonely Troubadour, like once she was - but that ship is long gone – there's nobody on the sands, never was - just plant your weary old feet in the red mud one after the other – there is a slight pain but it will soon stop one bright day – that's the way - onward to the holy might-have-been - or an acceptable semblance thereof

gone too, that sweet princess of silences - met fair only once as they passed in the street - firework night it was & ye watched her walk toward ye & asked if she was lost – you mumbled, even smiled just a little, maybe you had chosen to have said something at an opportune second & she said...something – lost now, lost - & then you watched her walk away down the street again as the rockets punched the sky - all around her morsels of burnt paper falling from a bonfire in a garden – do you remember? - ye passed a princess, yes, in a glow-worm street - two hasty, pungent hearts out pillaging the dissident world under gunpowder skies - she was searching past ye & ye thought yourself beyond her - but she owned the real magic of it whole - the lure of the white witch that shrieks on the hill

& you know that Ursula owns it deeper - what sustains this half-life you inhabit? - wishes & fairytales? - eyeing this constant stranger as though ye knew her - as if she were a sister to the devil himself - they told you never to look back, no never look back - but how is that even possible when the sneaky past surrounds you always? - forward is backward - suns rise & fall at all points of your spinning compass - plod ever onward & choose your favourite slice of the clock - the summers were tropical then, way back, gilded by trust, by fond ruminations - the floors sweating, the windows white, Ursula breathing, catching your nervous face in her compact mirror - yet her brief glance was cold as a scalpel - she was an executioner in another time, perhaps? - a demon nurse, potions, fables and placebo pills to dispense - plink plink fizz by the hospital bed, slippery drift to coma - & you are nobody special, nothing to recall, just another anonymous upturned old paleface in a bustling ward - tubes & needles - the antiseptic reek - ah, where did you go? - nobody knows

& Ursula cycles toward your memory lane now - maybe you will see her again - a little later, when her star aligns with your regret, at the end of this bloody procession - a little later, yes - the twelfth of whenever - then maybe the once brilliant light will choose to glimmer anew - or some other phantom may substitute her - Amandine, waitress, Bohemia unexplored - why now do ye recall the name-tag on the soft even swell of her breast? - she gave back a glance, yes, but 'twas shyly returned - now do you remember? - she passed you by, made you over, because she had to be anywhere, somewhere - perhaps with someone? - or did you dream it? - time enough for ye to fish for her with your late, ghosty words - memories are the worm on the hook

Ursula knows in her bedsit eyes – she dreams of a room in Paris with her paint-by-numbers but soon-to-be expensive daubs hung askew on a frowsy wall – she knows a rose is a rose is a rose – she can drink clammy ales in dank saloons, pray in wet churches as the birds in the eaves coo & blether – she will lustily curse out her past lovers before the next bomb of a climactic yes

yes, a brief episode is all, The Sad Troubadour mused – brief as dandelion spores in dream-flight – Germanic, Insomniac, Nordic, Mythic & intense – the sugary madness of Ursula - rangy in the shape of her shadow then, in lilting gait down that sad, light street – out of the CCTV glower of the bar they strode – he had puffed out his Troubadour chest - prouder than he should be – Ursula Major smirked beside him - & he held a hand carved from exquisite marble – dank, sudden whiff of the ocean from her straying hair - the old dockside was always beckoning in this sailor's city – yet he knew how this would end – a farewell wave before the wave eternal – he was lost & knew, that where drowned men meet the rough sea's bed, there his heart dwelled – mother, lunar – The Captain knew it, funky in his seafront bar, meeting the sticky mermaids with a sorrowful smile – be that woman from the deep blue sea, for me, for me! - a solitary ray ascending the beach of shiny stones – pearl mother, fresh from the depths to his shore, gull-wild & riding blind the avian rodeo of invisible eddies, let it be – daughter of love, Aphrodite, her mother estranged – you will go to Paris, Ursula, he thinks – but until these moments are taken from him he will whisper London's grubby, scratched pearls into her shell-like

& he slows his step & allows her to slink on ahead – lets her beautiful lips prattle on, her cryptic grist to his effable mill – it is the purpose in her stride that makes men follow – unpretentious, grace of antelope - & he is hearing, already, in the slow-roughening wind, the last slam of a door & a key turning – he could almost hear the scratch of his biro across the snowy page

let her go!
she was too erstwhile, too other
with her tightly plaited hair
& magnificent sarcasm –
searching vaguely for something
but never lusting for anything - let her go!
wary, wired & beleaguered
may ye e'er remain –
breathing too madly too late

his cloak of dank music draped over the stars – feasting on his crackling headphones, he now rarely switched them off, blocking out the moonlight in his brain – he became an unwitting ghost of the auld blighted triumvirate – he became I – all seeing I - Baby Troubadour & Bastard Rehab – & surely destined soon to begat Old Mouldy Maudit, out on the island of the solitary tree – just Maudit – rhyming twee with endless twee - the anger & light – just Maudit – he

*

there he is

*

& how did she haunt his houses? – in sleep over prayer – layer on layer - his thick grey hair tied back – that leathery diary of doctrinal secrecies tucked in his worker's belt – old Dutch church, low – hard faith gave him the spiritual nudge – so he wakes early to the thump of a dropped bible at arm's length – trust the flinty glare of chance - the random nature of the resulting open page forming the theme of the day's research – rumours emerge in her letters - she is engaged to a belly-dancer in Paris - she went mad on benzedrine & Cuervo Gold – saw maddened *djinns* whirling in the back alleys off the Quai Louis-Blériot – she got put in a clinic & the swine belly-dancer fled to Amsterdam

    & yes by day he loses himself in the old music – Tallis & Mundy – The Gregorian Throb - his inner radio retuned to a quietude that fell with the curtain of eventide – speechless stations & half-stations of the radiophonic cross wheedle & whine bringing forth nuances in the sounds only his fine ear could discern – no longer young, if indeed he ever was – no matter, he had no wish for posterity - his pocket-exercise books pile up next to his unchanged hotel bed, fused tangles of bad handwriting awaiting to be decanted into the grave of the journal – each stained page a *grimoir* of diurnal notations, choice seasons from a vacation in hell – an attic portrait, his profound yet unfound, unfinished masterwork, two more leaves full of dread should ruin it if he's careful

    meanwhile, 'twas there in the house of retreat, in the castle of annihilated dreams, that the authorities found her - she nightly left the bedroom window wide open to storms both real & imaginary - the resulting mildew on the wooden frame of the cracked fanlight was finally the straw that resulted in getting her tired, broken body evicted – ten polythene bags of pills & a deadly blooded needle under the rags in the cupboard under the sink - O Ursula

    & did you cry out for mercy on her behalf? – did you once quail? – it's all fine, all good history now, Old Maudit – I know you will wait – I too am stuck in the past but you are still the once & future king of nothing – still sailing – on

*

Jack Definitive, alone in the lunchtime cafe – he had spent a morning trying to think of how to get out of showing the local sights to The Troubadour – he had not invited him to this city – he was no spirit guide to wastrels – The Troubadour could not take his smoke because he had been weaned on the piss-weak Soho grass – this stuff was Rasta-blessed, wholegrain, elemental fire – burn slow & breathe deep – he needed distance from such over-excitable wanderers as this Troubadour Of Sorrow, this would-be Rimbaud – all his bleary, antic perambulations – this constant obvious gathering of tired books to his heart – his hats, scarves & alcoholic indulgences – his fatuous opinions & dumb poetry

he looked at his watch, Janus-faced with tiny date in an oblong recess, yin-yang symbol – glass of hours – half-past two in the theatre of cruelty – there is a Balinese dance troupe at the Melkweg tonight – he was going to ask the Troubadour to come with him but the thought of the subsequent conversation rumbled in his gut like approaching thunder – he quashes the idea with his Marlboro into the dregs of a rainy ashtray & swigs his Cinzano & Lemonade to cleanse his pallet of all guilt – he needed the dance to himself – vivid masks, fluid motion of dark limbs – & above all the drums booming through the shivering hall

Jacks – he is all – Ironfoot, Ripper

he shivers too – he has never felt so disillusioned by the prospect of an acquaintance – it is as if The Troubadour was here to murder his pleasure & invade his state of grace via skunk, so long in preparation & so beautifully achieved – he had given him his number – fuck him, fuck him if he can't find his own hell in a new city - & with the last bravado swig of Cinzano he, there & then, vowed to not return his calls

*

476

The Troubadour swore at the cupped receiver – he heard the ring vibrating through the line – fuck him, ten rings & hang up – 8, 9, 10 click – fuck him – he vows that he shall give the night full reign & dance with every smiling waitress that doesn't slap his face – he spent the last coin for the unmade phone call on a box of matches to light his slim cigar – he pondered his state of body & mind among the bustle of bicycle & purr of tram – the tall buildings, gabled & ominous, stare down from above – a city built on wild wood from the Schwarzenwald – rooted, like Ursula, in Teutonic mulch – the cosmopolitan chatter around him from the busy café tables somehow reminded him of listening to foreign radio stations as a child – it was as if the tram-wires carried the old blarney through the streets after him

he left, striding out purposefully without any purpose other than to appear purposeful – the quickly quaffed beer quickened his step – good mood again, finally shaken the acid fog – he watched the urgent shadows thrown across the pavement by hurrying tourists – they looked up, around, everywhere but down, pointing their madly clicking cameras at each other – he would point his pen – write a bible of a book to unexplain it all on ripped, unravelling pages – find a title to cherry the cake on the journey home – home, his heart balked at the nauseous word – hell had given him his punishment, the rock is balanced at the top of the hill now, time to take a breath &, when the last chapters are done, feel free to dip into whichever page at will & see if it rolls to the foot once more – that is how memory works after all, he thought, & this trip will be nothing if not the swansong of memory

he found his father's ghost in a cool doorway smoking – his father resembled a defeated Clark Gable – he had cycled to work every day rain or shine – & like this Doorway Angel he smoked thin, bruised roll-ups of cheap tobacco – staid jackets & tight neckties – plain stiff collar & crooked, wiry

477

lips – The Doorway Angel mumbled abstractions in low zen asides – Clark Gable was a hell of an actor

later in The Troubadour's future he would see Harry Dean Stanton in a film at some hipster London cinema – by that time The Troubadour would of course be changing again, emerging from his new cocoon as The Butterfly Captain – he would drawl to his latest waitress that the handsome actor she so admired, up yonder on that there silver-screen, resembled his father in later years – & yes she would laugh & think it charming – he would wave a hand in casual dismissal & flick open his father's cigarette-case to offer her a Lucky Strike – or a Chesterfield, yes he would smoke Chesterfields by then

beneath a café table by an unexplored canal he finds a postcard of a painting – Sisyphus by Titian – stained by coffee-cup rings & spattered with mud from a passing bicycle – art endures all manner of slings & arrows, he mused, & picked it up & put it in the inside pocket of his jacket next to his notebook & his aching heart of gold – he too, he thought to himself, carried many schemes in his soul – he was under curse & was brim-full of betrayal & rivers

a motorbike noisily pulls away from the lights, its blackened exhaust-pipes un-baffled or destroyed by chronic misuse – for a few seconds the ensuing silence is lucid, terrified – as if the rasp has rent a tear in the fabric of contemplation – it is almost a whole minute before the astonished birds resume singing – the still air is filled with the kind of gulping wonder that follows news of a suicide, a fragmentary illusion that had somehow leaked into this corporate carnival, this pastiche of a metropolitan rush-hour

The Troubadour consulted his half-read philosophical back pages & decided to adopt a sarcastic, belligerent mood to while away the windy walk to nowhere - *Hey! You Failed Goalie Dreamer! – yeah you in your old mac & slicked hair brushed back! – you were wrong, boyo – a man is mostly*

prey to lies about himself – Titian's labourer held the guilty
burden on his back – muscly god give me strength!

he relaxed his bitter jaws & puffed grey smoke through
unclenching teeth – but it was no good, he could not be
bothered to prolong the game - the freefall of fun is over

& yes, the rock is back at the foot of the hill once more
– awaiting any slapstick worthy – any old Jack or Jill, Romeo
or Juliet, Laurel or Hardy - to begin the tediously drawn-out,
tragicomic shoving once more – it is all for nothing, angel, &
everything is akin to a dream if you forget half the story to
begin with

he looked up ahead & saw that The Doorway Angel had
limped to a bar to which he was being refused entry – The
Respectable Troubadour inwardly saw himself twice, in both
his lost father's ghost & the hobo's pitiable, refuted pride –
he would once & for all banish the omen, he determined, by
drinking, by way of a tribute to the ejected protagonist, from
that very bar – banishing omens, he thought - it was one of a
million daily superstitions that wormed at his nervous id

the bar owner pushed the The Doorway Angel lightly in
his chest & he staggered away swearing in doubled Dutch –
& yes The Sobered Hobo Troubadour staggered with him
for a short while in a grim, futuristic reel – for in this wretch
he foresaw himself as a papa paternal, long failed in joy, lost
to the vehement world of drunken song, a cowardly pilot
found drowned in the rotgut behind his drunken propeller

yes & many, many years hence, the toothless Captain is
crooning lullabies as Old Maudit cups his ear to hear – the
icy draught of time's breeze – shut that window & pull the
blind – mute the hasty road

& the hobo lurches away again & shouts a cheery fuck
you, in English, to the indifferent street – The Troubadour
is pretend-shocked by such base, vicious language from so
distinguished a thespian - frankly, my dear, right now he
doesn't give an Amstel damn for linguistics

& O dearie dearie, my oh my, the day is turning once more to dry dust - its gilded cogs creaking to life in a morsel of peeking sun – & from a future ship's bridge a Captain reflects on the manifold flaws of his ancestors – with Dylan warbling on his Walkman singing girly blues of Brownsville & a lifetime's bad poetry is congealing in his veins – so he tweaks a prickly burr from his wind-troubled, matted beard of barbed wire – & through his eyeglass he spies the pier-head that signals the estuary's last heaving tilt toward sea – it grows formless from a fold of diaphanous haze in leisurely distance, The Pier-Watchman's trousers rolled up, thin legs cooling in the motionless water - tableau

& yes, O yes, The Old Seadog sighs, re-possessed by the insubstantial world of language & thereby in essence staking his urgent claim to remain forever young – he smells fire on the wind, wheels burning, wheels of prayer - & thinks - that Harry Dean Stanton, he's one hell of an actor

*

"...I met myself travelling from the mad past before descending in feathered, red pain to this pampered hell & I told myself of my conquests there – bragged how the wild crowds had swarmed & put up notices - & in a trance on the dockside in high winds under the swinging, silent cranes - I know not whether I was in London or Amsterdam but it was certainly one of the two - I had a statue erected & to my past dedicated - until days shortened, the glory slowed & mere baubles & plaudits were no longer tossed at my throne - & lo, a new conflict swelled in thickening air - while at first the jabs were playful, testing the new permissions, the last blow was subtle & the final sad fall barely felt – ah, me! - the great people of this kingdom once proud were now like patients - patients chewing the limp food & sipping at milky tea in spill-proof beakers, half-sunken in the crush of pillow -

detonated faces shrouded in blue linen - a heartsick
expression belies their once stiff resolve & stoic grimaces -
around my tawdry throne my wordly gathered scraps - all I
had left to hand were a few clothes, books, a tape recorder-
filthy clothing scattered around that desert bed - reading
only the most melancholic prose - fashioning sermons for
blasted rocks & crash of tide - all dreams emptied out - yet
of my words & tempests little is seen...mrstqqqllvp...slypp...ft
fft..."

The Troubadour clicked stop & pulled the cassette from
the machine - the red tape tangled, unspooling - taking a
bookie's pencil from his breast pocket he wound it back,
carefully smoothing the creases until it was contained once
more without too much serious damage - he proceeded on
his way without the priest's scripture for a while - a good
thing - clear the head of influences - a chance to re-invent
the day

after wandering a while without thought or distraction he
came to his senses again via the sound of water flowing - he
scanned the bric-a-brac, pseudo-antiques & bad jewellery of
a hippy stall down by the canal - a young couple were
reading on a black iron bench - the bored girl looked up
from her book & smiled a smile that recalled in him
something indefinably tender & protective - an episodic
warmth - he frowned at his own sentimentality - bah! -
hippocampus, hippy campus - begone, kindly associations
of a progressive nature! - he needed salvation like a chord
building from the root, the home key - Theo had plans for
The Remorseless Troubadour's Salvation, tomorrow he
would take him to meet a friend - friend - of his? - or
mine?, he thought

on a whim he purchased a bracelet of fool's silver with a
small blue gem set awkwardly in a rough recess linked in
clumsily to the chain - the bad workmanship - did she? -
the bauble's laughable crudity appealed to his unstructured

mood – the world offering another little absurdity to distract from the trials & torment - he read the label with its tiny, neat, handwritten description

Tanzanite, birthstone of the new year's eve – dark blue, used in amulets & talismans of antiquity – wards of evil spirits – bad omens, desperate voices – it brings the wearer strength through sensitivity – a more profound, far deeper connection to the spirit

blah & blah again – the marketing department of the cosmic unknowable, he thought – cheap though, something to remember his trip by – as if he – the hippy girl who ran the stall in a fog of incense smiled, as indeed it seemed everyone smiled a needless smile on this smiling day - & she placed it on his wrist with thin, dextrous fingers that brushed his skin like a moth testing a candle flame – that's what I'll remember, he thought – the stone was already just an *aide-memoire* – the brush of skin was all – a dusting of cells exchanged, strength through sensitivity – hippy silver, foolish

*

The Troubadour had met Theo The Sailor early & they had got a tram to the outer canal ring – quaint villages & suburban scenery, tree-lined avenues, lawnmower buzz, cars in driveways, gently wafted by – Theo had brought his 'medicine chest' along & half a bottle of warm tequila – on disembarking the tram, sluggishly, imperceptibly, they fell into a kind of shallow trance state as they walked - smoking & talking about many differing subjects that, if not deep, were certainly broad

the night offered up new avenues of chance by way of their gaseous leaks of idle chatter that grew tendrils & clawed upward – the issues that were only vaguely broached & poorly blessed with varying degrees of insight included Stockhausen (brave/inconclusive), the odd art of Mr. Austin

Osman Spare (occult, intriguing – but they reserved opinion until a reliable biography could be read) & lastly the knottier, if admittedly more mundane, problem of how to mend a badly broken watch (Theo had somehow managed to seriously damage his precious Heuer Skipper, it had told the perfect time since the day he'd won it a year ago in a game of Faro in Istanbul) – everything is believable & all is possible in an impossible universe

it was during this latter rambling discourse that the sailor had finally mentioned the purpose of their trip out of the city, meeting The Radio Repairman

"...ah, man you got to meet The Radio Repairman – his workshop is out next to the Memory Warehouse – if he is receiving today, that is - & if you are high enough, then he will see you – it's ok, he talks while he works – you watch, he will carefully lay out his little transistors, wires & coils in such a way that from your elevated position it will look like a map of the universe – he is a strange cat, Dutch but with a German dad I think – he used to be a merchant sailor, I said I wasn't really a sailor but he told me that I was – I just didn't know it – that's why I got a few jobs on the merchant ships - he sort of drinks in the same clubs as me so we are bar brethren – he speaks like an oracle – real riddler talk – but if you are in the right uh...frame of mind, he will for sure enlighten you – he's wavy gravy for sure – but I always go to him at least once a week – better than paying the fuckin' shrinks y'know...?"

they had, without The Troubadour noticing, ventured some distance out to the hinterlands - the spiritual edge of the city – regions that are generally elusive when maps are consulted but will be found by happy accident if suitably bewildered – the buildings here were older & much more spaced out – there were grubby, snuffling farm animals kept in dumpy gardens, greenhouses, strawberries sold from shed windows & the tram tracks had dwindled in number – all of this landscape slowly dissolved to a few featureless storage hangars & silos with painted red names

NERGENS - DROOMSCHIP - VERVLOEKING

The Troubadour scribbled the heavy words in his notebook – in the misted distance The Troubadour thought that he could almost make out the menacing bulk of The Memory Warehouse's ominous façade – it must have been a week since he had stumbled across it on his first day of exploring – he had fallen asleep on a tram & got off at the last stop – he could see the tram stop now, rusty, patient, deserted in the haze – it had only been a week, he thought, though it had seemed more like a century's drag – the nights bleeding into days so indistinct & ethereal they could have been a child's dream

just then, out of nowhere, a rugged, small house came into view – almost dwarfed at the corner of a block of empty apartments at the end of a row of shuttered shops, covered in scaffolding & huge dust sheets – it was very old, the newer apartments had been grafted onto this curious remnant – new brickwork surrounding it like a protective mother – the quaint little shopfronts seemed simultaneously demeaned & invincible, tucked tight in the embrace of modernity - the brickwork showing the dutiful, easy care of its maker – loose grey tiling above the lone window, painted with a strange old lettering, an illuminated manuscript in ceramic form, fine marginilia & border work – the letters & figures danced in the lessening light of late afternoon - a handsome, hand-painted sign in the entrance porch, English

ELECTRICAL REPAIRS
ALL WORK CONSIDERED

the door was partly open & a dim staircase led up into a gloomy hallway lit by a single dusty bulb of low, spectral wattage –at the far end of the passage was a bright red door with a larger sign

DE RADIODOKTER

Theo knocked gently & a deep voice bade them enter – a man of middle-age, at a desk piled with electrical equipment of all sorts & vintage, looked up half-smiling through a greying beard, heavy-set green eyes peering over half-moon glasses

"...Theo! – long time no see my friend..."

"...yeah man, I couldn't come last week...had some uh, important stuff to sort out y'know...? – this is my friend, he's from Old England – been on a bit of a pilgrimage from what he tells me – he has a troubling recurring dream – I said that you can fix that ha! – like you got rid of my old curse – the crazy Budapest gypsy remember...?"

"...indeed, 'twas a most powerful malediction that she was throwing your way, I believe it was an *ala* & it brought you bad weather on many of your voyages – so, my English Pilgrim, what is the nature of this dream?..."

The Troubadour quickly looked at Theo who nodded encouragingly & - with a strange smile - strolled back out of the room saying that he would be in the library – Theo sat down in a tall throne-like chair directly opposite The Radio Repairman who fiddled with a large screwdriver & showed no impatience at his long hesitation

"...it's hard to describe...I just fancied a talk, really..."

"...first we have to have a conversation – then we can talk..."

"...ok, right – is this really uh...I'm not sure why I'm here...how you can help..."

"...I fix radios..."

"...yes, I see that – have you always been into that kind of...electrical stuff..."

"...careful, we're getting lost here – let me ask you something – what are there more of in the world do you think, hens or boats?..."

"...what?...oh, well...hens – let me think – yeah, got to be more hens – there must be millions of..."

"...we are governed by impulses – the passing world isn't always there – you are aware, I trust, that it is through our dreams that the universe reveals its possibilities – listen to the rain in a field & you will hear each drop, you will hear snakes, you will hear the quiet electricity of the big bang reverberating through the wired grass & trees – & if you look closely, you see the leaves act, in storms, as if they were transistors – rain distorts the light into abstractions – it gives up vital new interpretations of the world – it suggests that not everything you perceive is complete – like lightning reveals a flash of summer in a night sky – animals sense a coming storm – well, some people do too – via the outer reaches of psychometry, there are books in the library down the hall, choose some that speak to you & return them whenever you like – learn how to latch on to objects long disappeared from your life & once more feel their force – relate them to both your waking & dream states – become a magus – again there are books in my library, Old Persian texts, magic that dreams of itself – from the root, be able to grasp – life offers us puzzles, riddles – it lures us into believing that every clue can be solved, that it is all a game that we can win if we just work out the exact answers – if you follow that road then the chaos will alas engulf you – it will be locust day, the crowds maddened by a growing inner rage – old testament anger, blood lusting & apocalyptic – unstoppable exodus of souls - these are the burning grounds of our vast inchoate mistrust – the ceremonies of industry, politics, lay churches, art, film, music & sport all have diluted chaos for their own ends –

this is the high magic beyond ritual, complex & arrogant –
then there are the peasant's spells & incantations that touch
only the primal, cheap lusts of a newly stretching brain – like
Theo's so-called curse, I lied, it was nothing, the *ala* barely
wounded him – you see it is easy to curse the willing
believer, mandrake & eldritch, a road lined by dark trees,
the kind of psychic talk that echoes around mausoleums –
stay clear of such distractions & focus solely on the rain – I
once studied a sad pigeon that stood motionless on a rainy
rooftop for twenty minutes – it seemed like twenty seconds,
it seemed the earth stopped spinning & I even missed my
tram! – you see, the bird had been utterly entranced by the
rain spirits & had entranced me in turn – falling rain itself is
silent, but when it strikes the earth you hear the spirit hiss as
it unburdens itself into the world – now then, you dream of
water, I am right, yes? – no don't speak yet, I see by your
face that it is so – there are reasons why the spirits of water
are trying to connect with you, that is what you must
discover – meditate upon the coming storm, it will be huge,
extensive flooding & much damage – find somewhere, a
place to be safe, & think about the sounds you hear – your
thoughts should be like chocolate resting unbitten on the
tongue, savour the melting, the discovery – the rain came
from our mother, the ocean – it brings messages from the
shades of our oldest ancestors - the rain delivers these
messages then rushes through the conduits, the waterways,
back to the great grey mother's open arms – these spirits
return constantly & will continue to return until we
understand them – fear not, it is not mysterious, there are
no unsolvable mysteries, merely events as yet unchartered,
all is clear in time – water, to most uninitiated people, seems
to be a shifting mass, much the same thing over & over,
repeated until the shore or horizon cuts it off – but a map of
a desert will appear to be blank & yet the desert has many
houses – push the divining stick further down until water

rises – I am interested in the countless things, the immeasurable mathematics of infinity – the lemniscates of micro-biology, the division of cells, things becoming smaller to grow more plentiful – it has echoes in eastern myths, of course – the wheel spun for prayer, the wooden carved idol, humility of gods not venerated, a mere reminder, an *aide-memoire* - here's something for you to think about – close your eyes - now, picture in your mind a desert – in this vast space now visualise one charred black tree & a red house with four windows, three lit with a yellow light, one closed off by a blue Venetian blind – can you see it?..."

"...hold on...yes, yes I see it..."

"...good – now, hold that image tightly in your head & slowly count down, from ten to zero, never losing your concentration on the image, careful now, don't allow any tiny aspect of it to fade - & when you reach zero I want you to open your eyes wide suddenly & say the first word that comes into your head – don't think about it until you mentally say the word 'zero' to yourself & then blurt it out, ok...?"

the Troubadour nodded, eyes tight shut

"...right...ready, go!..."

ten, nine, eight, seven, six, five, four, red house, burnt tree, three, yellow, blue Venetian, two, one, zero

"...river..."

eyes wide open – the Radio Repairman's face, smiling, staring, closer, a few inches from his own – garlic & a hint of blackcurrant breath - he could hear church bells through the open skylight, sparrow song & the falsetto voice of an opera singer faintly weaving in & out of the breeze

The Troubadour felt very tired suddenly, heavy of limb & his breath slowing – he closed his eyes again - he thought of the bluebird shirt he had bought just before leaving home – he thought of the rainy day he had spent – where? - among gravestones, a hill, somebody riding by on a bicycle –

he thought of the singer Nick Drake, he is strumming a blue guitar, solemn, a solemn song – he had never cared for much of his work but there were a couple of tunes...a sewing machine, an umbrella – Rembrandt, his face both young & old – he'll wear the shirt tomorrow, the last day in Amsterdam – a good day to wear a bluebird shirt – he felt full of golden light yet submerged, as if partially buried in soil, his puffy body a sack full of treasure resting below a layer of mud

The Radio Repairman then tapped him lightly with the handle of his screwdriver on his nose & spoke

"...wake up, Sleepy – Grumpy's makin' breakfast..."

& the spell broke & The Radio Repairman was suddenly laughing uproariously, madly

& then he, just as abruptly, stopped laughing & leaned luxuriously back in his chair

"...look, I've fixed this fuckin' radio whilst you all been dreamin' – listen..."

he clicked the knob – it was an old machine, beautiful brass motifs & a glowing arched dial with ornate fake marble inlays – the beautiful rush of static fizzed & crackled awhile – The Radio Repairman twiddled the second knob until gradually from the distortion the bones of a song emerged – it was familiar, definitely familiar, but somehow he couldn't quite...then it disappeared into the hiss forever

The Troubadour stared at the radio on the table before him – the back panel was still off & the Radio Repairman was twiddling with something in there, one eye squinting, tongue out, like a child threading a needle

"...so, am I just another radio that needs fixing? – is that it?..."

The Repairman looked up, smiled

"...nope – we ain't nowhere near as important as radios, brother – don't go getting on your high horse, my English Pilgrim – only a few rules matter - there is anger & light in us all – in everything – the sudden glance of a wary fox – the drumbeat of striped shop awnings in a hailstorm – a nun's genuflection as she passes a graffiti-strewn icon – a swinging pub sign in autumn – a magician stubbing a cigar butt into a tin ashtray still damp with spilled beer – tired ostrich feathers glued together to frame a painting of dogs & cats playing billiards – always pick up any feather you find, by the way, they are no accident & their symmetry is part of the psychic disturbance transmitted from Blake's lost tomb – ivy exploring the wall of a timeless pawnshop – bunting after a carnival, limp & unreadable in the storm drain's grill – the unstoppable cancer of rust on an abandoned car – I notice you staring at the radio when it talks - as if it could stare back at you – I breathe poetry to these diodes & wires – I can be heard on any frequency – or in-between stations, AM or FM – my voice lives in the creases of an unspooled tape, in folded silences – I am every misunderstood line of poetry – a blistered codex in a forgotten language – the salty scroll's dense intuitions – cave art kissed by children – anger, light, you see? – O my English Wayfarer, have you noticed how the sunlight is confused by frosted glass? – I often observed this phenomenon when pissing in public toilets – the sunlight thus distracted is like how your memory is triggered out of the blue by a long-neglected symbol – the play of sunlight is not inconsequential, it illuminates found objects in such a way so as to bring to life a part of your history that may be healing, have healing properties, or need healing itself – a Madeleine doorway to a dream's source, read any Proust? – he got it – had his cake & ate it, you could say – but dreams, that's why you came here, am I right? – all dreams are like oceans – hiding currents of anger, teasing your eyes with the light bouncing off each wave – you watch this unfold from the prow of your ship – yes I know all about your little ship full of your past & future selves, I'm a radio repairman, of course I know - eventually you begin to

understand that it is the anger beneath the beauty that gives
the sea its power over you, that carries the ship forward –
the light is only there to make the contemplation of anger
bearable – once this is known the ship will have fulfilled its
function & you will be at one with both angry sea &
distracting light – both birdsong & the jack-hammer are
music, both can be notated & recreated, Messiaen
attempted it I believe – you see, both Jayhawk & jack-
hammer are born of the same orchestra – an orchestra is
but a bewildered carthorse, lugging its crotchets & quavers
through pagan, philistine streets – make the apt connections,
My English Detective – solve mystery before it has the
chance to deepen – I see that you have walked with Ursula
Major, yes, I know that too - I saw you buying books at
Oudemanspoort market – she is silver, she has the weight of
old Germany in her – Lohengrin, her spirit, he is long
mixed up in her Wagnerian heart – her head is Faustus but
her soul, her soul is a veritable Bayreuth for charlatans &
old demons – tell me, have you read of the doctors Faustroll
& Faustus? – she is the apostrophe before the former & the
Neitzsche to the latter – she whispers her enigmas like dry
leaves into your ear - Gotteramsterdammerung – & just like
that you become part of her angry sea, watching the light
play upon her like a kitten following the spots thrown by a
glitter ball – you will be unaware of how much you have
learned from her, believe me – learning is a jigsaw puzzle –
you spend most of your life collecting pieces & only at the
end do you begin to put them together – puzzles depicting
only sea & sky are much harder because all the pieces look
the same – but they are not the same, as the parts of the sea
are not the same – radios leave a mark on the tapestry of
existence – the air is full up of dead speech – pixies & elves
giggling in the ether – wise people get quieter as they age –
they start off life like a babbling mass of circling seagulls &
finally end up as a solitary rook on a disused railway line – a

weathervane rusting on an old library roof, not knowing that all life is beneath them, unread - still they creak & spin slowly, trying to tell which way the wind blows - the wind doesn't give a shit - the wind is fucking with their minds, it channels its laughter through the autumn trees - absurdist theatre, the gestures of clowns - they tumble & fart, blow their raspberries & honk horns as fat psychiatrists puff cigars at them in brown, book-lined studies - the legion of the unknowing, blind arbiters of sanity, they all sit expensively & doodle automatic lizards & blinking pyramids on their jotting pads - your repressed confessions are soaked into those pages that form your journal, your prison - a red bicycle passes, a yellow wall crumbles to the hopscotch pavement - yes I know about that too - a sack full of dead memories, sack full of found feathers - they fall at the same pace..."

The Radio Repairman paused & pulled a thick book from a shelf just above his head - the cover was blue with green lettering

'GREAT WESTERN PHILOSOPHERS'

it was fake, the insides hollowed out - & from its secret compartment he smilingly produced a half bottle of Mezcal - the squat bottle had a beautiful red, yellow & gold label comprising of eagles, snakes & gothic, old Mexican lettering - he poured two casual, heavy measures into two glasses he conjured from beneath the desk - it was clear liquid but not quite the way water is clear - it looked the way water would look if it had unexpectedly gone insane

"...Nahuatl...see that language on the label? - sniff it, it has the whiff of death about it - death, *muerte*, those strange words we give to nature - the taste of this is the taste of the wind found in shadows thrown by dormant volcanoes - try a little, take it slow ..."

cool flame, throat tightening

"...well now, it's been my pleasure talking with you again, *mi peregrino Ingles* – feel free to peruse my library, third door on the left as you leave...'

The Pilgrim Troubadour finished his glass &, with a fire in his head, took his unsteady leave & weaved a little as he walked past all of the doors & out into the dead street - the sun was busy falling past the tall cranes & crystalline buildings shimmering on the horizon, dragging its melting tail slow across the land

he decided to find a tram & finish this strange day in the city, among solid people – this outskirts' hinterland had got too far beneath his skin – now really he desired the wash of insignificant others – a bit of cheap, small conversation, to purge what was, he felt, a growing nihilism within him – the birds sang, too loud, too cheerful

& he found that as he walked he held virtually everything & nothing in his mind – he was ready for anything & nothing mattered, except for the steps in front of him as yet untaken

the Repairman's strange sentences rolled around his brain licked by the fiery alcoholic cocktail of the Mezcal & the ill-advised earlier tequila – what had he meant? - red house, was it? – yellow light? – or bike? – his walking had slowed & at the threshold of a kerb he stopped suddenly at a telegraph-pole-perching crow's raucous caw – & slowly a small detail from The Repairman's eulogy loomed from the swirling pool of words in his head – hang on a minute...

"...pleasure to talk with me *again?*..."

*

he got on any tram heading anywhere – Theo had long gone, he had just been the delivery boy, he supposed

later, sitting on a hard bench by the bickering waters of the Herengracht, he nodded to sleep, becoming as one with the distanced traffic filtering through the lap of waves against the barges & sporadic gull's yawp – his nap was brief but intense – he twitched in REM state & dreamt abundantly – it was, even for him, an uncommonly lucid vision of a stay in a hospital – presager, a glimmer of future shivering through, an unsettling yet potent episode of psychic foretelling – he is in bed, a small discomfort, left side, in from the left now – the hospital receptionist notes in her reports an influx of 26 new arrivals with the usual myriad grievances – kids fallen from trees, hands glued together, girls nursing broken bones after falling from bicycles – the bright waiting area rings with their la-la singsong complaints – leaves blown high, some greenery maybe he saw – was it from a window? – perhaps on the way here? - slivers of fluttery nature are always loose in the wind, waving somewhere at something, or nothing – hospitals disturb us, yet we seek our due benevolence as we arrive bewildered – patients sleeping by day so we see them wave at us in the night, the dull, sick ones, their tranquillized faces – we gaze on them in wonderment, they hang there in half-light & their awful pinched, moribund features can be determined dimly by the late-shift nurses through the walls of sweeping gauze – wrapped in bedclothes, they are many & vary only in tonal subtleties – bleak Easter Island wedges of unrelenting dismay – The Dismayed Troubadour shook his head to clear it of this morbid foresight

the wary priest had talked a little of his hospital hours – before the tape unspooled – is he talking to me now? – what brought this mordant dream on? – yes, we all end up bound in those prim, starched sheets but are rarely vouchsafed a presentiment of it – there, only painkillers & hallucinogens are my friends - & when reality is a screen, a screen that is more curtain than wall, then that is fertile ground for mortal auguries - the nurse's faces almost smiled - so, the place has energy then! – which in itself is benevolence of a kind – doctors, surgeons, physiotherapists, this parade of helpers drifting by his upturned feet like grave visitors – tomb tourists – day & night the servicers glide by in shades of milky blue & dispense pills, suck his blood into measured phials - adjusting beds & refilling jugs – almost smiling by day - a little more serious after the pallid yellow strip-lights flicker on & the awful threat of an abandoned darkness fills the far window - & so the night rolls down her heavy rocks of Sisyphean blinds – a fall to music, as ever - a *te deum* by Arvo Part perhaps - Estonian choral calmatives, or an eerie wind whistling gently through hung headphones – the menu says the main stations are free but TV is too dear to view – in his healthier hours the voices are a background irritant – here, in the deep night, they try & console with their odd, rumbling steadfastness – voices haunted by the whistle & chilling fizz of other frequencies – somewhere out there in the frenetic ward, beyond the headphones, piping choral triplets burst from lapsed I.V. machines - a lone alien's communication signal – merciless gloss of surfaces

why these presentiments now? – is there not horror enough to come?

they say that god has dark sides to her heart - a yank of the rope to twist the attention back to pain - this after all, after the intervals & conversations, is why you are here - laughter is encouraged - grins – death maws split the faces of the angular heaps of terminal crones piled against stacked cushions in the pissy day room - in morphine delusions there are clowns at the institute - the clients spread the word - clicking tongues behind the menus, pamphlets - pause of spoon to mouth - was that the flop of an outsize shoe? - a bicycle bell amid the blips & echoes? - clowns that own the worst parts of the mind's darkness - the only contact must be by secret request, signals, winks, but participation is on the whole encouraged - they are here for the children, a light distraction, so they say - anachronistic perhaps in a world of chirruping electric toys - but the clowns are a gesture the

495

parents smile at, if nervously - look at them, pumped with a stodgy fake grandeur - mocking any escalation of tragedy, unreasonable hopes - a tense tableau waiting for a slapstick fate & the inevitable bathos of the face-slapped pie of no-god – the wards fill up daily, yet the new influx want to explore, they have no patience - they ply their fresh limbs through the airless corridors - still immodest in paisley dressing gowns - they glance at us in our ward as if we are their wild past thrown back at them, mute comedians in an antique farce – bad actors wasting the nuances of the craft, the subtle timing of the banana-skin slip – Adam's fall was a pratfall, a belly laugh chill to the heart – in the flaky dream he winces in his musty bedsheet at the elegant, resigned shrug of the doctor – a weary entropy drifting through their godless eyes - we are a roadblock to their journey home – to their safe world of slippery violence & home sweet home comforts – little they know of our desire to throw off our gowns & let loose a wave of profanity - & because we do not, the cruel, repressed explosions are hoarded in a mush of brain-rot – dearest doctors, we are the chestnut graveyards in your sunlight thoughts – yet we were once as you were – the hospital radio plays old music - this is the age of the silicon chip – the patients are wallowing in stale electricity, weary spirits, they are not immune to the frequencies - they are not heathens – the dream rolled on, no ship in sight - the long trek to the canteen for exercise – rubber legs unsteady - an egg & cress sandwich swaddled in cling-film beneath a cracked plexiglas incubator - nature, her bountiful gifts she doth bestow

but all that not now, no, not now, no – that all still yet to come, yes – prologue to an untold end, yes – the forever dilemma of how to end? – & moot pointed horns thereof

yes that's when they will flourish, these croaking dustbags in their starched sheets across miles of wards – they will finally give full range to their one finale, their last turbulent

expression – dredging the river of time for one last blub –
the visiting hour over – the ward empties, in the home sweet
home the crosses hang on magnolia walls with the sepia
photos of the dead & the bad art - visitors awkward with
their oh-dears & mumbly how-are-yous - every concerned
face bloated with good intent – just before he snapped
awake to the chill of Amsterdam's stark colours, they loom
above his sweating bedclothes like mourners watching the
casket descending – a temporary resurrection - he is the
visited & they patiently await his decision

*

here I am - or

*

or another vision of a future deferred – he is Maudit,
old & now I am Maldoror in the prime of youth - the quiet
shoreline bent to invisibility – the stacks & shapeless piles of
the refinery trying their utmost to exist in a distant rain – he
plugged the earpieces in & the CD was sticking so he
squinted at the tiny controls embossed on the side of the
Walkman & pressed FFW for a little bit, which sometimes
seemed to urge a little more life from the fading batteries –
the five real ales clinked happily in his shoulder bag – head
full of old rubbish but nothing mattered in this sickly kind of
weather – no bad memory invaded the pastel green pasture
of this hour – sea & shingle, the nodding buoys &
sometimes there was a man fishing, always men, always
alone – the limp thread dangling from an ill-fashioned rod
of poor wood – sometimes he saw mermaids, ghosts, they
would thrust their bent backs at the shore as they drank in
the whims of the ugly, mutant sea's grey weight – that
remorseless slug of remorse, sliding her fingers back & forth

across the stones as if comforting them – there, it's not so bad, there, it's all for the best – the world a globe of immense, watery sorrow, a giant's sad shifting tear – terror in the soul - the terror of falling or missing a secret rendezvous – it festers, gripping his gut with acidic vices – always trusting to a vacant sky while knowing it will be the sea that brings the news, the stone-cold, indubitable missive of great import, the final prayer – it will soon come to him, on that glorious day, yes, now he knew - it was simply a matter of pre-arrangement

& Maudit will wait, his last incarnation, as far out on the estuary lone gulls hang like lanterns in a slithering mist - & beyond them, he knows, there is that grand dream-ship of his childhood smoothly drifting with the steering tides – now & then a glimpse, a half-heard song, an ancient tar's cry, then silence, as the curtains of fog are drawn once again across its sweeping sails – in mute expanses of shroud the old pier stands on its barnacled legs of sodden wood – waiting for the circle to be unbroken – waiting & listening for the tell-tale slurp of a differing wash – sentient, knowing the new disturbances in the habitual flow – waiting for another night to crawl away from the seeping dawn – & waiting for The Prodigal Troubadour to find himself at the pier head, strumming the first few chords of an old tune under blotches of decembering cloud – knowing too that his ship is soon to become the sea again, his voices soon to fade & join the choral tug & ebb – may it worry heaven to learn his weeping hymnal – gut-string, root & madrigal wires - & yes, somewhere out there - on an abandoned ship thick with bombs waiting for the whole shebang to blow - & where a maddened holy man swings a claw-hammer to beat out the final bell's song – tolling of the grinning horizon, timpani of end times

*

in that formless steam that has always haunted the docks of every port in the known world - & seemed to emanate like old Banquo's spectre from beyond the everywhere & nowhere - The Lost Troubadour stretched his shoulders in gentle clicking flexes - he opened the newspaper, read a headline

'ELIZABETH JORDAN CARR
FIRST TEST-TUBE BABY
BORN IN NORFOLK, VIRGINIA'

left my home in - California on my mind - the pages catching in the wind - he stretched the broadsheet & closed it again with a long sigh so theatrical in its nature it made him chuckle to himself - his boots were leaking, his eyes held an aching deep at their root - he saw the crossword on the back page - one clue left - 7 across, 8 letters - 'confused, I drop old-fashioned young lady for one who returns' - second letter R, fifth letter I - the rain has smudged most of his answers - he noticed with dismay his yellow fingernails & that his thumbs are wrinkled & smeared with ink from his leaky pen - Degory Priest had told him to trust in the past, not any old dream of how things may be & he wanted to somehow believe this advice unquestioningly - but part of him - & the current nautical environs reinforced this notion - cleaved to the dim hope that his childhood ship of dreams would roll nightly forward forever - perhaps out there in the dirty fog above the stark cranes & winches of these Ports Of Amsterdam - were there any wise phantoms in the low fog? - will they show him the way to the next whisky bar, show him the way to go home? - the whole, bleary view was a collapsing house of cards in slow-motion - Jack Of Diamonds high - new Amsterdam falling & London calling - Jack - he didn't answer - never called - why?

499

he closed his eyes – or maybe he didn't, maybe it was real - & saw the tall figure leaning against a huge cable drum by the gangplank of a large ship that hovered in a swirl of condensation & puffed smoke from his reeking clay pipe

The Dreamy Troubadour quickly pulled a sheet from his notebook & composed the sketch of his message in his head, mouthing the words like a child reading – he read it several times &, once satisfied that it conveyed his heart's truest wish, slowly approached the figure that no longer fired any trepidation or doubt in him

he approached confidently, somehow knowing that this time he would not beckon him & retreat – this time he was truly ready

& he was a mere few feet away when, without looking up & with his secreted face still shadowed by the familiar broad hat brim, the figure held out a white-gloved hand & took the message silently with the briefest nod of assent, he offered a momentary glimpse of a cold white eye, sightless

& yes, he then took out a children's book, primary-coloured, the cover of which he quickly held to his chest, thus obscuring the title & then he slipped the folded note between its yellowing pages at about half-way through

The Troubadour slowly opened his eyes & was momentarily disoriented by the fact he was still prone on the dock, he knew he had approached the figure? How was he still lying there? – he checked his notebook & the page with his message was torn out – so he did give it to him! – he looked across the wharf to where he had just walked – the figure had gone

& where in the world can he live, he thought, if there can be no dividing border betwixt the vivid dreamworld & this drugged reality? – he will live in a land called 'here' – a zombie isle of the gently numbed half-dead – awaiting the inevitable unfolding of tragic events with an accepting smile – gnawing at the clues until something vital gives way – learn, perhaps, to solve the past before it gradually deepens to an unknowable darkness

The Weary Troubadour stood up slowly, ditched his newspaper in a cold barrel of rainwater & wandered forever the long miles to his hotel bed – tomorrow was his last day – he had a plan, a bad plan, but a plan nevertheless

*

on returning the following day to the haunted warehouse of bad memory he discovered, to his chagrin, that it had been newly-painted a disturbingly deep red - & instead of the calm, courteous butler awaiting his knock, the door was already wide open & a heavily bearded man was seated on a log outside partially blocking the entrance,– ancient, with a wrinkled face palest brown, milk chocolate & grime-specked – & yes he wore a long *djelleba* of pale yellow with two red pockets at either side & hung around his scrawny neck a vulture skull necklace in tarnished bronze & in his drooping earlobe an earring of silver, with a tiny mirror hanging from it, glinting even in the pale light – he sat below a wooden sign hung over the door bearing the legend

TEMPLE OF MAUDIT
KING OF THE RAIN

scholar of the science of ultimates, rod, root & flower – yet this Old Maudit he now moves in less enchanting circles – the slime beneath the altar – mistresses & veils - a doctrine of bad faith uttered by low monastery voices – who?

he is all our dim endings congealed - half moon & star in his greying god-beard – eschewing any school or method, he remains standing after all others have departed - a describer of conclusions – vowing to purge the dry intellect & detect the instant, the momentary shudder of reason – explorer in the unreality of all things, architect of all our good & bad dreams, our vague ideas & impressions

once he dwelled on the Essex marshes – thick-rooted himself in dank clay – but now he is everywhere – invading every conflicted mind's most doubtful realm – instinctively The Rooted Troubadour knew that he was now staring at memory incarnate – the embodiment of everything that endured of his past, yet also a gleam from a possible future – what memories did he deal in? - the child's harbour at sunset, bright rowboats tethered & nodding by a jetty, scuzzy daubs of leaves above a boulevard of rain-damp tables – a yellow bicycle against a bright red wall

there he stood, this ancient of days & nights, with one resolute hand outstretched, solemnly forbidding entry at the warehouse door – The Troubadour tried to ask him why it was that he was being excluded but his words were just seeds blown to silence on the elastic wind – it was now the time for silence – no questions for fear of their answers – time to return with the experiences fresh in his mind – an attempt to be the embodiment of beautiful things encountered – time, at last, to go home - though you can't, really, ever again

& the old man spoke at last, his voice was soft thunder over far-off mountains, the cold hand remained raised, a sad refusal, a reluctant forbidding

'...before you enter you must leave – before you go back you must stay where you are – before you look forward you must look back – this warehouse holds everything you are & have been – everything outside is what you are not - only you can be what you will be – the past is a fallen apple, the present is the tree, the future is the new bud on the branch – listen to the rain, listen deeply, as if you are holding the sky like a conch shell to your ear – then listen to the voice of that rain, listen as if you *were* that shell...'

he watched, helpless & bursting for a few more clues no matter how bizarre, but before he could speak he saw Old

Maudit, vision of his own legacy, fading, slowly at first like a television screen detuning, then his whole being just utterly drifted to atoms before the huge red wall of the warehouse

it wasn't a dream, this was the dream

so once more, it seemed, The Drifter Troubadour was not able to get the chance to understand himself, at least not through the sage thoughts of another, & so he bowed his head in defeat & walked the pilgrim path to the tram-stop where Theo stood waiting, whistling an old Beatles tune – he recognised it immediately & gladly joined his comrade & whistled along in a queasy harmony - *tres bien ensemble*

the small newspaper stand sold postcards – he bought one depicting an endless field of yellow tulips against a red sky – shepherd's delight, he thought – poor, Boo

*

Last Sacred Morning - something loved, in the ribbon of light across the bed – Ursula had slept while The Sacred Troubadour Of Spent Lust scraped carbon from obligatory layers of dark, aromatic, thick-buttered toast but had slipped away as he took a shower - & of course the infuriated wireless in the other room chatters to nobody about the possibility of bad weather - let it rain, what harm is there in water?

*

on the bedside shelf the notebook, soiled & stained, lay open to a pressed page

yes & on the torn inner-back cover of her book of T.S. Eliot's Collected Verse a song they had written last night, somewhere, now unwritten, now gone – a vanished melody they had both tunelessly wailed & bleated to a drowsy harbour dawn

we were bound together
while you were here
my last night
our last...

their performance of the half-written duet rings in his
ears above the hard blues suddenly riffing from the
unstoppable radio – the blues will fade, he thought, the old
love song always returns, endures - he had built his shaky
house in its tangled branches – & though it may fall from
grace, from sweet concord to atonal cacophony – it is still a
song no matter how badly it is sung - & it is still about love

his heart was beating too fast for the unfolding hours of
late morning & he is already thinking of a last walk in the
Westerpark – stillness of cool water, the leafy drip of dew

she woke in her dream still dreaming – she woke from
her dream undreamt - dressed quickly in coy shadows &
departed still dreamless without a word – all had been
spoken

& yes of course they had shared valedictory exchanges
via nuance of soul – stammered brief warming gobbets of
old poetry in their intoxicated fervour – their singing &
laughter seemingly eternal in their raging cups, filling the
bars, it almost convinced them that the dream would endure

& yet already the birdsong has replaced her voice, it has
signalled the final act & it duly begins, the drawn-out
catastrophe of this ultimately useless passion play is written

his gut registers that indigestible cramp of loss – his
memory of her, hauling anchor across the sea-bed's silt –
the crunch of his bitten toast

a flickering light through a disturbance of curtain &
without even the sinking finality as the door clicks behind
her, yes without even that punctuation

a hush, beyond it a wasteland

eyes closed, he lets the moment fester – he tries to picture her dressing, he tries to picture her singing, cycling, dancing, crying

he tries to picture her at all – he cannot

skeletal December dead now, the crueller month – nothing stirs, the world is denuded - & yes, fare-thee-well old Madame Erst, Ursula Of The Canals, Inconnu & Valkyrie, chooser of the slain – may you find the freedom of old Paris walkways & let holy words of the saints reach deeper down into her pulsating heart

bon voyage, ladies, bon voyage

*

to whom it doesn't concern,

weather is here wish you were beautiful blah blah - a week & a half is enough for me – been to museum & saw a cowboy – walked the canals & bought books – found a memory warehouse & met the curator, mad, egotistical, you'd get on well – met Jack D. at airport, never saw him again – the acid is weaker but weirder, the skunk is insane – my mind (it turns out) is a bin-liner full of cartoons - met incomprehensible Ursula, mystic, soul-mate, I haven't said goodbye & probably won't – met a part-time sailor (Theo) & with his advice will (by hook or more likely crook) stow away on ship homeward 3pm tomorrow – see you at the Boheme & I'll tell you all I know which is not much – wave at me from the pier, I won't wave back – pretty card eh? – tulips good, three lips better

yours in hope, Anon

p.s. the answer is boats, I think

*

the air felt thin, as if he had been suddenly transported during his slumber to a mountain top – he breathed deeply but his oxygen level was not right – hypoxic illusions – small creatures at the peripheral - blotches haunting his sight – a tall ship out on the water, the Nordzeekanaal, tea from East India – dockers from across the centuries swarm the ageless quays – foreign shouts of conflicting directives, the same, age-old sailor's curse & jibe – the warm gusts of the rich, warm air exhausted from the galley's vents, tinged with fish, hot beef & a faint bleachy tang of detergent - sleep had eventually found him on a rotting pile of old hessian sacking in the gap between two warehouses – a pale cat, almost white, stared mournfully down from an oil barrel at him mouthing silent meows as he made eye contact – cats, he thought, are French & are always questioning everything - *y a-t-il plus de poules que de bateaux, monsieur?* – scowling, meowling it snaked behind a rainbarrel to skulk – Dutch cats are still french but have learned to speak Dutch – skinnyfish - *moge het de hemel zorgen baren...*

he had stumbled, he remembered – tumbled into the useless glow of a dying lamp – he had drunk long & deep in the harbour bar – purloined a full bottle of cheap white wine somehow from a neighbouring table – arguments, ejection, shouts that the police were on their way – he had ran into the tremulous night toward the docks - he had fallen deep into the flagstones of the puddle-bright wharf – his cheese & pickle sandwich squashed in his coat pocket stippled with the crumbs of a forgotten roll-up – after hours, after the book of hours, eight cigarettes left, nowhere to buy more – he stared at the sky, black & inviting between the dripping clouds – he could just make out the looming dinosaur cranes & bulky, squat shapes of containers, the ships' huge, grey hulls hung beyond, silent, waiting, another kind of night - the rain from below looked like ants & he closed his eyes imagining them falling on his cold forehead, tickling as they trickled over his sodden collars, scrambling inside the bluebird shirt that stuck like cold toffee to his cold skin – & he pictured the tiny creatures carrying away pieces of his thrown sandwich above their heads – the drumming of the drops on a stretched canvas mimicked the military, cartoon tattoo as they walked – eyes shut, listen, picture the picture, gingham tablecloth, sandwiches, cups, spoons, fruit & cakes walking – trrrrum-trum-trum-trum, trrrrum-trum-trum-trum – who's picnic? – he saw himself caricatured, double-taking the slow marching food, the parading cutlery

he felt as if he could wake from this world any moment, as if he was now in control of how much strangeness he was being subjected to – wake to warm rolls & honey, soft radio inanities burbling by the turbulent kettle promising tea – close his eyes once then re-open, that's all it would take & it would all disappear – wet shirt, ants, cranes, drumbeat, old picnics, Amsterdam – how much was real anyway? – & if it disappeared then what would be there in its place?

homeward, the nostalgic thought gripped him though he was unsure of such a thing as home – what was back there welcoming him? – the new town's call? – London's roar that he had felt so eager to escape? – a mad priest raving on the pier? – he needed a spirit guide, a last throw of the dice

*

the coast was clear & the gangplank down & unguarded – SS Maiblume, Theo had said – & given its apparent easy access he had made a wise choice – & yes The Troubadour scurried up quickly & dived through a metal door into the boat's interior – metallic air strummed the wires that dangled from the ship's walls – swollen, cello resonances – lament of a despondent, far-off bellow that hung in the mind – for the first time in what felt like days he caught his breath escaping in rapid, staccato bursts – stowaway – the thrill of illegality was too enticing - there appeared to be nobody aboard at all at first but as he made his way down iron steps into the belly of the ship he heard voices, German & relaxed, laughter & glasses clinking - he took a swig from his stolen bottle - it was coming from the only door in the passageway, beyond it there appeared to be storerooms, small cubbyholes - the door to the conversation was left slightly open - he listened - the voices were convivial, the chatter of people playing cards, or around a bar table after hours

'...es wird schlimm...'

'...das schlimmste seit einem jahrzehnt...'

'...eine achterbahnfahrt...'

The Troubadour used their laughter to sneak past the slightly ajar door & selecting a warm cubby-hole under two huge lagged pipes he settled down - he had been very tired throughout the evening, the rigours of his dissolute times catching up with him - no sooner had he swigged a little more from the bottle & checked his journal was secure in his inside jacket pocket, he laid his head down on a heap of oily rags & collapsed to an unusually dreamless sleep - as if dreams had no more time for him

*

metal ship - how does she float?

clouds gathering - the air getting thicker, heavier - every corridor the same as the last, uninhabited, otherworldly - grey pipes, gunmetal swaddled in lagging - the old refinery - they would pass it - a break in the monotony of grey, a plaque, no - a manifest! - a cork noticeboard, handwritten list of names - ships sink, hens float - a list of the crew perhaps or some older crew - dead crew, he meant - the names are odd, not German, no - English but strange, old-fashioned - he would adopt one for his new life, maybe - pick a name from the manifest as an alias - start a new journal, yes, yes – & no more heartsore Troubadour - let's see, whichever name takes my fancy – like picking nags at the bookies - Gilbert Winslow? – that has a certain charm, what else? – Humility Cooper! - that's on the short-list for sure

O tell me does the moon drag a storm? – pray, which spirit is to blame? – & does that falling ghost of sea release a thousand drowning sailor's prayers that will whisper in the walls of the city's cosy houses? – wrath of no-god – blimps they sent up to catch the fire – Hindenburg, the fire from within, Germanic crash & burn – fork of lightning touching a far shore, blasted tree, leaves incinerated in the inferno – leaf-dust, cauterized oak – & yes Joan Of Arc was struck by the cruel flames of god's madness – & it is impossible to conceive a stormcloud on a summer's day – in the thrall of a deluge the sun is but a drifting memory – all weathers cancel each other out – keep listening to the rain until the touch of sunlight silences the voices – spirits, vampires, dissolving at the first streak of dawn

ok, stop reading the journal, focus now, get back to the old passenger list, ok, what other names here? – Remember Allerton, ha! - his first name is perfect, who names their son Remember? – I think there may be a better second name somewhere though, combine two maybe? – Desire Minter, good one, minter of desire, that's a trade worth learning, who else? – Myles Standish, hmm, kind of like that, put it in a song maybe – next – oh fuck, what the...

he stared in disbelief – the name seemed to burn in sharp relief, in fiery red letters on the yellowing paper – Degory Priest – a chill strafed his spine & weaved a churning knot in the pit of his stomach – Christ, that old seadog, old no-god sailor, ship's chaplain? - surely not – what terror did he install in some poor crew's hearts, some poor believers, did he genuflect over their sweating foreheads as demented stormwinds tossed their cabins? – did he reel off a guilt-

tripping sermon after a murderous fight? – the crucifixion
didn't just happen on Calvary – poor Kayo bleeding at his
feet – the storm winds are weighted by auguries, they plough
the furrows of land & ocean for the seed of spirits – where
the storm meets the sea, my dream-ship rolling, capsizing,
all souls lost – my overarching mythology, my spirit voice in
water, my heart

*

he awoke from the staring eyes of sainted Karl Malden
to the true dream – the creaks & cries, gush of salty waves –
foreign tripping tongues berating their betraying gods – the
ship heaved & lurched madly - he put his stolen wine in his
shoulder bag, nervously lit a cigarette, shook the sleep away
& ventured out into the dull, metallic corridor air – he was
unsteady, damp head pounding, his heart patting his chest
like a doctor searching for a faltering pulse beat

& as soon as he had woozily climbed the rusting iron
steps leading to the deck he realised that something was very
wrong – he saw two bearded men in boiler suits, one older
man with a white flowing beard, the other around forty, with
intense dark eyes like burning pellets, they were wrestling
with the ropes & pulleys of a lifeboat, swearing viciously

he clung to the freezing rail for dear life – he stared at
the raging sea as if he alone was witnessing the birth of a
further, undiscovered universe or recalling another planet
far away, then as the ship pitched to the other side he saw
the furious sky full of darkness, flashes of sheet-light
intermittently describing its mordant contours – there were
more of the crew on deck now, being hurled this way & that,
crashing into pipes & rails, babbling unheard orders,
instructions – a poetic gesture rears its head

like Crane I'll leap – sea thirsty
vaulting the handrail with a wave

510

& yes he eked & edged his way along inch by terrified inch carefully clutching & unclutching his grip on the rail, through the confused yelling masses, to the midmost point of the huge swaying vessel – & he was frozen, clandestine amongst the waves of fear, nobody paid him any attention, all too involved with the imminent catastrophe to wonder at his unsuitable clothing & unfamiliar face, he was just another enigma in the nightmare that was unfolding

& yes through the swarm of yelping bodies he suddenly, astonishingly, saw Theo, desperately trying to operate the jammed winch of a hung lifeboat – dear god! - had he been aboard all this time? – was that, he wondered, how he himself had gained such easy access?

gladdened by the sight of his face, a face that among these unknown ghosts shone as if lit by a brotherly light, he hoarsely called out to him & was frantically beckoned – the lifeboat was smaller than the others, bright green, with a number & name etched on the prow – *5-1597 Chancewell* - The Troubadour clambered in, expecting to somehow have to explain himself to an uncomprehending group of sailors, outline his reasons for occupying a space, blag a passage to safety, but the vessel was empty – six rows of empty wooden benches – the waves crashed into the violently rocking boat soaking him down to the chilled bone – high above him Theo yelled something & waved frantically & began slowly lowering the wildly swinging boat seaward - & yes as the Troubadour looked up, narrowing his stinging eyes against the lash of rain, a heavy black bag thudded down on to the lifeboat's sodden floor beside him – he fell backward as another cruel wave hauled the vessel lurching to leeward viciously – he clung to the bag & wedged his feet under the nearest bench – he was resigned to fate, ready to die in this nightmare or else wake to a better world – but he felt that his destiny was to go down, down with the drunken dead of the dying past whose spirits revelled in the lost, silty depths among the freakish fish & silent shells, & whose voices now lashed the groaning timbers either side of his head – the waves were so vast & engrossing that he felt as if he were underwater already, spiralling, reeling in a mad breathable impossibility of hurtling water - bedknobs & broomsticks came to his mind & he laughed, gulps of salt & brine making him gag & choke, his shins lacerating as they chafed the wooden seat - all is phantom now, all mist, he thought, the motion has no longer any meaning, it is incomprehensible, close your eyes, be stillborn in the aspect of sleep, face the worrisome water spirits with humility, open-hearted, aquine – & yes The Troubadour tried to imagine himself on land, in a warm dockside pub, a new round of whisky & beer on a tin tray, fire in the hearth – the water quelled to a whisper, the rocking & groaning soon subsided to a gentle pitching, an easy, soporific sway – like a cradle being gently swung, he felt calm as a baby drifting to darkness – bear called bear, Boo, Ursula, Degory & Red Jimmy, Theo disappearing under the vast swell of unconsciousness – he was waving goodbye now, in-between dreams, a delicate, susceptible place, where one's actions require no explanation or motive – where the numbered questions are innocent, undemanding & where the first answers are always the most heartfelt

*

Red Jimmy sat rolling his carefully built cigarettes & placing each one in the silver tin – each one its own answer to the question – 'shall I smoke a cigarette?' - & each time the tin emptied, one by one by one until all the answers were correct – he swigged down the last of his pale ale & hurried the few yards to the barrier

Degory Priest was there waiting, as arranged, prickly & thoughtful, slumped in the first seat of the last carriage

512

'...Jimmy my dearest lad – are we all set? - is the boat ready? - engine fully petroled-up? - you have sustenance for the voyage, I trust?...& ye took the little gift I gave ye, yes? – an hour ago, as arranged?...'

to each of these inquiries Jimmy nodded solemnly like a relieved sinner receiving a blessing – he eyed the priest, the book hanging out of his pocket – title visible in case anyone saw – the casual pretension an art in itself – no sense of the oncoming strangeness yet – did the old bastard slip him a placebo? – he wants to get all the epiphanies & god-damn everyone else – Christ alive, for sure I'm not going out to the bloody middle of the river stone-cold fucking straight! – if he's given me a fuckin' dud I'll - no, he'd peeled it from the same roll, remember now, yes – he trusted him after all – had to, really – a small, potent stain on blotter, deep in the gut, spreading wings in the skull juice - the benign wafer of forgiveness

'...good, good man – I feared ye were too down in the mouth last night to make it today – all that talk of clues & omens – what are omens, lad? - the first fruit of adventure! – here, I have the rascal's postcard to hand – he'll be sailing into the estuary at...uh...four-thirty or thereabouts, all the unforeseeable anomalies of the voyage allowing, of course, but no earlier certainly...plenty of time, lad, plenty...'

'...we could've met him in London tomorrow – don't see the point of this fuckin' rigmarole...'

'...nonsense, our little prodigal deserves a welcome fit for his newfound standing – something ceremonial with a hint of the apocalyptic...did ye bring sandwiches?...'

'...yeah I did them last night – nice & simple, whatever was in the larder really - two corned beef, two cheese & pickle...& some nuts & raisins...a bag of cheese & onion crisps & the pork scratchings you nicked...'

'...excellent choice, I have myself purloined the required liquid refreshment – a good choice of sustenance though,

sir, solid fare - beef, cheese, pickle, nuts - recipe of angels –
right then, here we go...'

the train at last slithered groaning out of Fenchurch
Street station & - after a sudden wash of blackness, starless
as purest night - exhaled from the shadows of the tunnel into
a ticking, sleepy half-light – a gentle trickle of yellowy brick
facades, occasional blinks of red roads stroked by rolling
cars, the cauterized stunned face of an elegant old church,
surrounded by the unsolvable, vindictive black glass of the
office blocks

they sat silently, each seeing through the smeary window
his own poetics - face to face they sat, on torn, ash-coloured
seats, long denuded of their pattern by a million arses - as
the outskirts of London & the devious looming threat of the
approaching Essex fields streamed past the carriage window,
all sense of their mode of transport beginning to dissolve –
train, plane, car, ship – it availed not - for no matter the
manner of vehicle it was the hidden motion of water that
surely accelerated their souls

a river untenanted, time in fluid impatience plunging
them back to whence they came, all the way back, though
the path had long disappeared beneath the tides – hypnotic,
these unsure colours whirling by, as if escaping the future,
shapes tumbling hurriedly away from wherever it was they
were now headed – a flashing image between tall buildings,
an omen, the black rugged cross on a warped church, both
militant & evangelical – serious Degory 'Priest absorbed in
his book-reading & nervous Red Jimmy chewing a handful
of peanuts

a holy if queasy silence had descended, even the
chudda-chudda-click of the train rendered subliminal, not
even background music, a clock forgotten in a hushed
waiting room – the ship of fools swayed on waterlogged rails
- & as it slowed to each corner's curve, some of the passing
shapes took on a clearer form – stacks of pallets, tufted

grass, wiry dead twigs & pebbles on weak, rusty swathes of scarred hinterland dust – huge rusting rolls of never-to-be-used chicken-wire resting against a hellish fragment of an undemolished wall

Degory Priest silently re-read the postcard from The Distant Troubadour, smiled, & replaced it in his book – the Café Boheme be buggered, he thought

he prodded Red Jimmy who had almost nodded to a hallucinatory slumber with the lullaby chunter of the wheels

"...wake! - damn your arse! - there'll be time enough to doze when we're dead, dearest boy!...ye need some stimulus 'til the old blotter gets a grip – now then, this book I have here – tell me, have you read any Cioran? – you really bloody should you know Jimmy boy...no punches pulled there - & better than that thin gruel of old soupy Beckett & the brutal slabs of bloody union history you stuff in your mouldy brains...god's teeth..."

"...yeah, tried him once - can't get on with it – too dense & too fuckin' miserable – fuckin' relentless – at least old Sam has a laugh now & then..."

"...he's a drunk shouting on a street corner – funny by accident, his act would be pitiable if he didn't occasionally pull up his existential trousers...no, this guy Emil is real, the kind of real that we shy away from – I tell thee, if nihilism is to thrive as a viable philosophy - & I humbly believe it must – we shall require a bible that undermines the last frayed threads that support all our scrawny old gods – when you blathered last night, in your cups, about Gurdjieff, that pot-bellied fake, smoking fine cigars & talking seven shades of gobshite among his stinking rugs & Eastern tat – he bloody well killed Katherine Mansfield you know? – probably got her digging his holes to Hades out at the *Prieuré* – she should've stuck with her cello or else stuck it up the fat fraud's arse – hang with the musical universe, find bliss in a few bars of Mahler – in thrall, she was, to that bogus bumpkin – intolerable bloody oaf, scribbling shorthand muddy conversations with those boring shits & dim halfwits that he pretended to meet – unremarkable bloody men, all of them – no, to lock yourself away in a Paris apartment & skive off from the University job, free meals in the canteen – now there's anarchy..."

"...I still prefer the Irish approach – it's easier to recognise futility when you're smiling – or old Chaplin, Buster Keaton, Laurel & Hardy – sadness dripping off them while you're pissin' yourself – the hardest guffaw brings tears too - just like the old pathos does – it's the same fucking water from the same eye – dab it on a sleeve & it dries to nothing – give me a good old belly-laugh & the day's set fair for all misery..."

"...hark, the slapstick sadist speaks! – laughing hard at a condemned man's fart as the bloody hangman's trapdoor opens – ah, we forgive many sins in the name of humour – a good thing I suppose – anyhow, to the task at hand – is the boat primed & readied?..."

"...yes, yes, I've told you - beneath the pier...the motor's fine – the sea is calm – if it all goes wrong it's down to you – I've done my share of the bargain – how long are we going to be freezing our tits off out there?..."

"...as long as necessary Jimmy lad – The Troub says in the postcard his boat should arrive at the estuary mouth any time after five on Sunday – what time is it now?..."

"...three-o-five..."

"...good – we'll have time enough to get out to the wreck & no problem – he is returning, methinks, a sadder but much wiser man, Jimmy boy – drained of useless ambition, last remnants of pride fading, health nicely compromised, I have great hopes for him – no, our welcoming gesture must befit the occasion's weight – the bloody fool says he wants us to wave from the bloody pier, how quaint & suburban! – how like the gauche dilettante! - no, my boyo, there must be

516

danger, there must be the chance of spectacle, fireworks –
the day is young & that bloody old wreck is full of pretty
explosives – what better way to greet a ruined prodigal than
with the threat of apocalypse...."

"...& you're sure it won't blow us all to fuck & back?..."

"...it's been a sleeping beauty for years Jimmy boy –
much like your good self – fear not, I'm only going to stand
up on its protruding...whatever it is...prow? - arse? – I'm
afraid the correct nautical term eludes me – I'll stand
thereabouts anyhow & we shall fittingly salute the glorious
returning wanderer, declare his homecoming in a fashion
that suits his newfound transformation of heart – I believe
he will recognise the import of it, he will appreciate the apt
symbolism – it is almost perfect, the returning journeyman
hailed from the wreckage of a dormant bomb ship by his
holy spirit guide! – tell me now how can it not impress? – he
would expect no less, I'm sure..."

"...that thing's got to blow someday – it'll take out the
fuckin' refinery they say – go down in history – Richard what
was it?..."

"...S.S. Richard Montgomery & bless all who failed in
her – aye, blow us to holy hell it would – still, *que sera* & all
that be-bop, old bean - there are worse ways out of all this –
now, crack the rum – I believe I feel the gorge of the lysergic
gods a-rising - let's get into the mystic, Jimmy me beauty..."

*

in his weak, youthful imagination The Troubadour was
an edge walker, a border drifter, somebody who dwelled on
liminal ground, detached from the tethers, set to break the
boundary & fly if required – he was adrift now for real – his
lifeboat was the only border he knew right now, between
himself & the rest of the universe which as far as he knew
consisted of light years of unbroken ocean – & the once pig-

headed certainty that was the sky had proved itself to be a fiction & the earth merely withering memories dressed in the guise of solid stone – the blithe, irreplaceable sea, for now his only real truth, yawned before him as he lay on his front with both arms resting on the prow – a somnolent, grey expanse of indefinite vacancy, an infinite procession of meaningless, teasing glimmers

he rolled over & sat up, aching back against the slatted bench & swigged from his dwindling bottle of wine – over half emptied now - his eyes sharpened to the horizon, the only focus of interest, the last line of demarcation in this new vacuous cosmos – the wine was dry & cold & welcome – a purity in its cleanliness, the startling tang of a preacher's sudden guilt – to drink of a good wine is to confess, in a sense to resurface, he thought – & yes the miserable old sea became more like salty wine with each swallow – between the slurp of wave on wood he saw half-faces in the resulting foam – grimacing, drowned skulls, seaweedy hair, hinting at souls lost thousands deep – another swig of wine – skull's clarity, ideas, plans & schemes to be locked tight in bone – drinking felt innocent & necessary here – there was nothing to be charmed by, nothing consequential or romantic - just the wide, strange zoo of heaven looking down on a dawdling ocean – '...god's pub...' – he said to himself then wrote it down, underlined twice, in his damp notebook – his hair had grown matted & straggly, the longest it had been since his early teens – it swung like kelp in the ebb of north winds

"...the sea...me..." - he whispered to nothing

the simple rhyme amused him & he wrote it down just beneath the previous written entry – god's pub/the sea/me – done, a poem called 'God's Pub' – he considered a second line but nothing came to him that didn't detract fatally from its appealing artlessness – it meant a lot to him & made him laugh each time he glanced at it – childish, or child-like – why is there a difference? – he didn't know – he closed the notebook & swigged again - he felt like a fugitive from a prison - suddenly freed after years of wasted rotting in a half-remembered cell - cruel torture, bad food, tinny water - the days chalked off in marks scratched in brickwork - he was undetectable now, a tiny renegade speck on this great, unmappable plain - sufficiently buoyant & as excusable as all of nature's debris taken up by this swirling, elemental brew - he lit his last, amazingly still dry, cigarette & gently welcomed the cool, urban smoke into his chest, a memory of brick-dust, earthy colours, leaf-mulch - he thought of London - it seemed centuries had passed since he left - he breathed the clean air deeply between swigs & puffs, the trusted drunkard's alchemy working its spell on his mood - the tobacco & briny air tinged with cucumber, mint - a strange anomaly, so far from any fertile shore - he thought of his little craft sailing beneath Embankment Bridge, himself hailing the cheering crowds gazing down from above - throwing flowers, confetti, laurels of daisies - cucumber & mint - maybe it was a waft from a submarine garden rising, a perfume of uncharted fathoms, released in puffs to the skim of tidal breezes - he saw emerging in the surface cumulus fine tapestries, weaving lines & figurines, a madman's vision, the finality of the fairy feller's masterstroke

perhaps, he mused, he had gone mad - this would be a perfect time & place should that be so - better here than in bedlam - Bethlehem was that from? - he stared hard at the impenetrable sea - the grimy pictographs desperately trying their glyphic twists in a futile stab at communication, ripples feeding on each other like parasitic languages, cloaked autobiographical nests of rolling dirty foam - all her sunken unwritten ghost stories untold, lost except in that eddying, temporary calligraphy of flux

& yes it is a fact that no sane man stares too long at the open sea - for terrible truths gather here, The Troubadour thought - & yet he still heard the sea's voice scumbled into his every sentence, moistening these gossamer layers of dust, a blindly searching babble of patois trying to break surface, the subcutaneous blarney of a billion sailor's yarns, all of it cleaving tight to a dense conformity that sought to lend it a tale, give it credence - & yes, yes after all these years heading toward self-determination, toward chaos, it was ironic that it should be this huge mass of stoic orthodoxy that may claim his last breath - though the sea, in truth, is merely an anarchy that has been unwillingly enchained - & when a body falls prey to the sly failings of age it is the sea's aches & agonies that it finally echoes - a poor man's moan, baleful, anchored in a bed of guilt, immemorial

he stared up at the clouds massing above the thin belt of the horizon - blue wedding cakes frosted with silvery-orange icing - the storm now burning itself away, a sour, yellow sun impudently warming the fleetest of the clumps of belligerent tumbleweed that had so recently pitilessly wrecked the S.S. Maiblume - did she capsize? - did she endure?

'...poor Theo...Jesus...'

a light veil of pale greeny-gold draped across the rusting ocean of crushed roses - the sea it seemed to him had never looked so endless, so incalculable, mystery thick as algebra - it was a giant wounded beast harbouring a million grudges behind its one unblinking eye, with all beginnings & endings writhing in its grasp - yet it has no beginning or end - only human endings - a wash of rainy spectres, all those trapped voices bubbling

Theo's now too

& if the dream he now sought dwelled anywhere then surely it was out there within her cruel, godless regions - to be sure for a while he could skim these friendly tides like a thrown pebble - but it is always the sea that survives us - & everything is underwater in the end, home at last

he lay back, head on the soft, wet wood, & relaxed into a calm, untroubled sleep - waiting for the next guiding voice -

& trusting more than ever before in his dream-ship to guide him home

*

& yes the dream dreams the dreamy dreamer – the judgement comes swift, the last call enduring – & a minute in our dream-states can carry the immense weight of all known time in its heart – remember now, try to recall – but the dream ship kills all words that are surplus to its needs – for the sea's poetry is miserly, it is only in times of acute sorrow that the briefest phrases disentangle & float idly by – watch them disappearing in the awkward turbulence past the stern, listen to the narrative blubbering as it sinks to nowhere, only to resurface anew for a different salty sailor centuries hence – or unsaved words that wash up on a beach dead as time, messages escaped from bottles

The Captain sighs & relights his pipe – before his steady eye the pier dissolving to steamy fragments – behind him, he knows, the most part of this mock-heroic old vessel has also offered itself up to oblivion – the trance has at last reached its pivot & hereon a new phase identifies itself, a phase that is requiring finer, stronger means of travel

from the East-end all the way down to the mouth of the feverish Thames, these are the meagre points that his life's voyage have duly joined – the clear mission now, to venture onward – past where the infinite waves are opening to wider stretches of yet more zealous water, ah but this is an argosy mapped out for much braver adventurers than the elderly Captain – true he has achieved grand things, come this far, suffered not a little, & the debt, surely, is now paid in full

he puts his binoculars up to his eyes & saw at first only grey, oily smeared outlines, rubbed-out ghosts unfurling – but, on narrowing his gaze a little, he could make out the yellow buoys of the old sunken bomb ship's graveyard & he smiled at the happy sight of a small boat puttering toward that doomed, lucky islet with a dark figure standing, a squat navigator steering - & training his gradually focusing gaze yet further he could make out a speck, another craft? - a loose morsel of driftwood? - unable to make it out he dropped the binoculars to his chest & briskly rubbed his hands together to stave off the sudden chill & then folded them in hopeful supplication - though he knew the old deities had abandoned him long ago - prayers were duties nonetheless & he mumbled his heartfelt thanks for his safe passage to whichever risen wraith was in earshot - & right on cue the great ship's wheel imperceptibly fades to vapour beneath his resting forearms, the huge sail too now becoming more indistinct, caught somewhere inbetween a yawning nowhere & the bitter sky

& as The Captain cupped his ear to hear the massed gulls' eulogy, the ship's bell offered a last, throaty clarion song as it chose hush, misted soft & was lost

*

it was time at last, time for the dead to return to their silt beds & starfish pillows - it was time to begin the real work, time to wake up

he trudged the few steps down to his sanctuary cabin as it began to fade & locked the door despite knowing that there was not a soul left now to disturb him - he opened the huge leather-bound ship's log to the first page & dipped his quill into a freshly opened pot of ink - poised for a while, he glanced up at the pictures he had amassed down through the long strange years, so many mementos, the bounty of a life's procession - a sepia polaroid of à bear called bear, Boo, grinning in Trafalgar Square smothered in frozen flapping pigeons, Miles Ducat behind his decks of vinyl, ugly smoke caught belching from his cheap cigar, a surreptitious

snapshot of a waitress taken from across the road from The
Café Boheme, mad Degory & Red Jimmy dancing outside a
pub they had been surely thrown out of, Theo tripping, eyes
wide, shiny as two dinner-plates, in the Bulldog bar & finally,
Ursula, stony-faced, soft-focus hair caught in a gust of wild
wind, casually waving from a bridge over a misted canal
    how to begin at the ending, he thought – how to make
the serpent swallow its tail? – a blob of ink from his shaky
quill dropped on to the exact point of the first ruled line &
so, taking that as a sign, he fashioned a passable letter M
from its suggestive, but accidental, shape – My Stories? –
My Voyage? - Meanderings Of An Old Seadog? – Mystical
Traveller? – perhaps his old idea for a biographical novel
'Mercenary Thoughts Of A Lush'? – none of these took a
firm hold in his enthusiasms – no matter, the title can wait –
to begin – a religious quote perhaps, set a pious tone then
slowly unravel the niceties? – yes, that satisfied his quest for
veracity, his secular leanings – he smiled, of course, he had
just the phrase! – a slight paraphrase of the first line of a
book he had adored a long time ago – in its time a most
scandalous & unusual tome! – yes, a little subtle reference to
that work of bizarre, dark genius would be a most
appropriate way to start – thank you dear Isadore! – Bless
you O imperious Comte! – now, before this dream ends, let
the tall tale be told

*

    The Troubadour, blinking against the gargantuan watery
slur before his eyes, tried to focus his heart upon both
sound & vision – he thought of Ursula, that far-off
afternoon, a mere week ago – a week! – how she had
danced, waltzing nobody but the Matilda on her broad back,
floral dress spinning gently against her twirling frame like a
whirlpool defying the currents of the breeze from the canal

& how she sang her folk songs to herself alone, how she strummed an imaginary mandolin, blew kisses across an invisible flute & how, leaning close to his ear in a passing swoop, breathed those strange syllables in her ragged tongue

the canal had tinkled between the cars humming, the moon, crested by a puff of smoke, wizened by the scars of evening - the piercing shape of a crow fattening a branch in shadows against the white bricks of the bridge – a red bike gently leaned against a yellow wall, the tourist postcards neatly stacked on the display in the closed shop doorway - views of the tulip fields, the canals, the windmills, the agonized sunflowers, the gaudy umbrellas, the old painter's face slyly peeking from a mirror, the neon signs of bars & clubs, the lurid rouge of the beckoning windows like pouting lips offering kisses, the memory of kisses, her pouting lips like a hatchet-wound cleaving the darkness

yet all of these petrified images were somehow contained within that hushed phrase, that passing haziness of her exhalation, that had carried her souring perfume with its drift as she whispered into his ear a confusing farewell

& though he did not comprehend it he had nevertheless remained silent, accepting - & he had closed his eyes & had known, then & there, that he hungered to go home

*

the motor started first time & soon they were chugging out past the pier exchanging swigs from a soon-emptying bottle – Red Jimmy muttering against the bite of the gathering sea wind & pulling his collar up whilst, with his other hand, tweaking the shuddering tiller to keep them in line with the dim hulk up ahead in the distant murk

the priest wobbled at the prow, headphones on, the dark strings of Rachmaninov swilling through his fiery brain – his face a nest of illusions squirming

& there is an island in his mind, still as night, tall cliffs sheer as glass either side of a dense swathe of cypress trees, trees of mourning, weeping as the silence rings out through the lap of broken waves – *Gräberinsel, Toteninsel* – a woman's voice, deeper still than the impenetrable dark, it whispers imprecations to a lost love just beyond the last exhausted frays of song – the heave of orchestral minors shift – the priest, maddened, lets out a yelp – he raises his cane as the motor is cut & they glide gently between two yellow buoys to the blackened, barnacled hull – the woman's voice, again – the priest cups his ear & bids hush to the waves – there, there it is, clearer now – *er wird gerichtet!* – the swirl of fog & phantoms, any one of which could be hers

The Delusional Priest got out & clambered atop the freezing metal hull – he peered through a pair of silver battered opera glasses toward the clueless estuary's rippling mouth, kicking at the trembling hulk of the partly-sunken bomb ship beneath him – the SS Richard Montgomery, a wartime ship loaded with tons of explosives that had been a deadly relic threatening the estuary mouth for decades – it was said that it could blow at any hour & cause unthinkable destruction – yet there, unsteady on her promise of doom, the mad priest raved, kicking & stomping, occasionally striking the hull with his vulture-topped cane – his gargling, rummy baritone drifted across the plastic swelling surf – the old ship's protruding wreckage his new pulpit, goading the threat, coaxing an Armageddon from her tired fusions of wood, metal & rain

"...Lo! Bredren! – 'tis late here in Elysium & we are no longer stirred deeply by joys – no longer dragged by tired old seasons or shifting moon-blown sands – all Olde England's woods denuded & autumn cheeks in blush – go forth & cheerily disturb, disturb these signs of summer's rout & the guilty, bedraggled aquiescent moulder it heralds –

no & no again in unison sayeth this trinity of time - hear ye pale horsemen! - if this be the autumn of our lives, why then we shall wrap up in scarves & mohair bundles & let the good lord's messenger know that we know this much - that we're here only for the wink of a mayfly's eye!...'

from the adjacent moored motor boat Red Jimmy cranked up the tape of Rachmaninoff's Isle Of The Dead & munched on the last corned beef sandwich, huddling his donkey-jacket closer in a vain attempt to offset the hypothermia he felt would finish him - he yelled up at the crazed priest, mostly unheard

'...we must have missed the fucker, there's nothing out there! - just the bloody ocean & she ain't listenin' - give it up man for god's sake! - I'm fucking freezing my poxy, Irish arse off here...'

the priest barely broke stride, his oratory peaking, his voice more resonant than ever for the brief respite

'...let the bollocky bells declare that we are not afraid of winter! - nay, we are glad to be here & while we're here we are gladdened yet more not to have to depart - for as sure as shit sticks to a sandy shovel - there's salt in the morning's air needing a taste - & the old childhood yard is as open as a doomsday tomb & shrinking by the day - you swooning flop of disciples can subside to Jesus & his Daddi-o if you must - but forgive me if I just abstain awhile & - disapproving glances of the laity notwithstandin' - sneak out in aforesaid childhood yard & kiss my former self demurely goodbye upon an abashed arse-cheek - for yea I saw the awful neat lawn & the Christ-forsaken trimmed hedges & prepared myself at heart for the battles to come - it is time, brothers, sisters - let this old bulge of bombs blow my bollocks to Bow if I'm wrong - I believe in you, Troubadour! - I'll tell ye 'til I'm hoarse - until my last gasp's spent to shout for joy - come home, my brother, to a last shot at planting seeds to grow memories! - come now to your last chance! - grasp the bloody nettle with your old faithful Degory! – for 'tis a last chance to trespass on the flags of the suburban, neutered grass, running full pelt across their immaculate patios, with a bellow, a crescendo of affirmation rising from our throat - & for one last unsullied, glorious time, run as fast as your ageing bones can stand & take a good hearty drunkard's kick at that insolent bloody pile of motherfucking leaves..."

*

the tiny speck of the lifeboat bobbed in blind obedience to wake & surf, against the current, thanks to an ancient, mystic, favourable wind, imperceptibly toward the estuary mouth – no Pequod this nor Orizaba doomed, no romance – just his little HMS Speedwell, blundering each lilt of wave without any suggestive nudge of time or exalted hint of recall registered beyond that bilious lurching
    then, a pause for musing, invisible engine at idle, just her murmured complaints at the cleaving of the water & her lazy patterns – the boat rose & fell more steadily now & The Stowaway Troubadour's time-cooked brain had somehow made the necessary calculus & allowed only the sound of his breathing interspersed with distant squawks of gulls to bother the joyous quiet – he took in the auditory shifts, the liquid movements – if he closed his eyes he was back in his old gratifying childhood dream – on opening his eyes once more he was confronted by the illusions of the sea's ancient mind - he saw wreckage, hulks of old vessels, harpoons rusting on a broken deck of bleached bones
    if a pattern is not sought for yet still is revealed by a commingling of the sensations then one ultimately becomes an innocent slave to their design
    & so it was that he had the curious feeling of being, himself, a single wave among a shifting, countless number he sensed that he had never been so real, so close to the

pith of the natural world & his huge, yearning tiredness allowed the hallucination free reign

he felt assured that his destination was predetermined & his whole essence relaxed into trusting to this journey – wherever one sails shall be wherever one lands – ultimately disembarking wheresoever sea meets shore & making your best home there or else perish in transit – tell your tallest tale to the scrub of promontory sand & the story shall be neither affirmation nor denial – it can try, perhaps, to describe the miles of travel but it is finally left silenced, motionless on the cold page, webbed in pockets of time, simultaneously lost & found, hopelessly broken, mended, only to be broken again

yes & looking back with satisfaction, knowing that nothing of the ensuing journal could ever again be altered, find a deep resolve, a wish to press forward – past love receding, for it held no weight in historical time, it crushed no butterfly that changed the fate of the universe, it is far beyond the grasp of change, beyond fact & fiction, believing only in itself whilst understanding that the self has no definitive substance or moral root – as if the meaning of trust was a simple, peasant belief – the way a river believes in the sea & is guided only by the fast-eroding banks – mutable, seeking all directions at once, yet ruthless & self-restoring – it searches for nothing, this old seadog's yarn – it merely observes the storyteller vainly searching his scriptures for a hint of cohesion, of meanings within the discovered meaning

The Meaningless Troubadour flicked through his wet notebook, looking for clues, reasons – all is either forgotten or misunderstood – the inky texts are salt-encrusted, damp & bleary, merging questions with solutions – he only knows that a journey is ending somewhere & that his imaginary ship has served its purpose – ferrying his past selves to this crossroads, this point of confluence – henceforth his tale will grow taller & wave like wheat-fields in the grip of new storms – the last train's sad song is sung, its rhythms declining, an ultimate, harrowing *rallentando* toward the soft cymbal crash of the terminus

& will someone perhaps be waiting there, waving? – mouthing a hello? – a goodbye?

& he drifted back, a seemingly antediluvian drift, to a submerged vision of the diamond city – he saw in his mind's eye the outskirts, the indistinct edifices, the pale, planetary glow of the sky – that strange day that he had wandered from The Memory Warehouse in a daze, got on the tram with Theo, dozed for a while, been shaken awake & alighted in a district unknown to him – he had then lost Theo at a market stall that was selling old cassette tapes from which he had bought Mahler's *Kindertotenlieder* & a slightly unspooled & battered copy of Tonight's The Night by Neil Young – he had reeled the crinkled tape tight with his biro & put it in his shoulder bag – he then placed the Mahler tape into his Walkman & fiddled the tiny headphones into the cup of his ear – low strings, a woman's restrained, awkward hysteria rising & falling – entranced, & with the already hyper-real townscape misting around him, he began walking with no direction in mind – the peculiar, tall buildings quivered &, in his peripheral vision, streets fell back like playing cards

after walking in this semi-stupor for several minutes through a gap in some cypress trees he saw dim & unusual shapes rearing against the orange, dusking sky – as he drew closer he saw that it was the remains of a fairground – skeletons of marquees, muddied, dirty merry-go-rounds & a hesitant Ferris-wheel rocking back & forth, its cradles singing in the gathering winds above the trees – he sat on the edge of the carousel & lay back, above him the semi-circle of dead, coloured bulbs & the looming face of the gaudily-painted horse, faded & chipped now but still its red eye stared out eternally waiting for the circle to turn again – light fading, dusk played a weary violin but the night had its own orchestra, trees swaying, the constant phantom moan between pylons, the birds ticking like wristwatches, blood through distant arteries coursing – sleep came, though he was not tired – it came like autumn – that nip of chill stinging through late summer twilight – no dreams – just a brief blackness, a tunnel with no train

The Troubadour woke suddenly & the light had almost gone – he made out the ridge of trees black on a dark purple cloud, he rolled over & the headphones fell to the ground – the dropped white wires lay strewn across a thick earthworm crawling, glistening, silvery & purposeful, across the grey mud beneath the carousel steps – the air was still, the wind dropped – he looked down again at his feet & the worm had transformed itself into a tiny amphisbaena that was busy moving back & forth across his muddied boot – it paused, looked up at him briefly, then vanished leaving a silvery loop of slime on the cracked leather – he spoke to its absence in a phlegmy, fractured voice he barely recognised

'...fellow cryptid...'

The Troubadour coughed, dragging himself up & stretching in a comic, noisy yawn – how sad, the strains of slowing fairground music – how much sadder still a fairground fallen silent – he thought about the seafront back on the English coast in winter – shuttered arcades, ghost trains covered in tarpaulins kicking up their skirts in the fiery wind off the sea – how he had often stared down the short jetty to the colourless heave of water, breathed in the sickly brew of seaweed, stale bread, metallic streams of thin air, the reek of oil, candyfloss – the grinning clowns behind the coconut shy, the tall imported palms incongruous in-between the inverted Ls of the streetlamps – at night, under those lamps, he remembered their thick, creamy light pouring down, illuminating the sinister, predatory lines of cars, the Rossi's ice-cream parlour, the green slopes up to the promenade

& he saw himself & the deserted fairground as if from a satellite, as a miniscule dot, a co-ordinate pinpointed in a tiny dark field clinging fast to a Dutch city's border, the English coast was not far, just a thumb's width on the map, the mouth of the Thames grinning, the tiny splinter of the pier – the stringy wake of a small boat hung like a hair stuck in its teeth

a vision of a past vouchsafed or a future unwritten – how big he was sometimes & sometimes how pathetically small

he looked at his wrist for the time – he had never owned a watch – he stared at his wrist, the whiter skin where his bangle had stopped the sun

he rubbed his eyes, they ached terribly, but he found the pressure pleasant - he put his headphones on, changed the cassette & pressed play – maybe tonight was the night he would begin to walk with no purpose only to cease when he felt as if he had arrived – guitars, strangled & distorted by the tape's kinks, veered through the changes as he reached the road & raised a ready thumb, lining it up so that its blistered bulb blotted out the moon

*

& yes the streets are our memories – they curve away, joining others in an endless circular tease – promising vague destinations with their winking signs – peopled by the undead, travelling sideshows to entertain, distract – blue are the streets of memory, tinted with that unpaintable blue of a dusk that follows a day of solid drinking – the wearisome walk to home or wherever a tenable bed may be – the old clock too tired to chime, the hour unimpressed by your indignation – it is these holy hours that fuel the regret that sours any ambition – up all night typing poems, like toy rockets fired at doomed stars – the sky alive with them, fleas on a gothic mattress – how did that field, that stream, those thick, lush summer trees suddenly simply disappear? – the city multiplies, breeds a lust for other cities & there are stones in your mind, the cheap chemicals cannot erode them

yet between your weakening flesh & a false, longed-for Brigadoon lies an ocean that has been there since the first ignition of time – it will let you rest a while, soothing your bones with maternal undulations, ripples of compassion – then it will spit your salted carcass out on a pebbly beach – go back, the road awaits you there, back on that timeworn path past the solitary tree – a desperate landscape souring your gnarled heart – you tread warily, heavy of breath, black of mind – the animals you encounter speak of the circus they escaped – they are free but own no joy for it – the limitations of love & the performer's hankering for exhibitionism still draws them back to the ring

& yes everything we escape we soon crave anew – greener grass over the fence, that garden you once tended, bored, longing for change – know now that nothing changes but the perception of the past – & the past is a dark soul selling trinkets at the fair, yes, the past is a clown rebuilding his forever collapsing car while the audience howls – the past is where memory ekes out its death throes – a solitary monster, forbidden river

& it was toward such a river that The Troubadour now drifted, a speckle, a fraction,, a confluence of latitude & longitude - the salmon that fights the tide that flees from the genesis - shifting like an untracked pinpoint on the liminal radar of time

& he let out a cry, involuntarily, for the first time in his life, maybe to the sea, *for* the sea perhaps – a bawl to the ear of the stony-deaf old flop of ocean, to that cloth-eared old mother of this repugnant mewling brood into which he had, unwillingly, been initiated – a cry like the tree falling in a forest unheard

yet it was not a cry born of pain, not at all - this cry was for everything & anyone – for redemption, for forgiveness, for no god-dog gone, for a home where the heart is not, for the past & future, for the here & vibrant now, for the price of a pint found in an old jacket, for liberty, fraternity & the eternally bewildered rebellious cause, for love's lost the love that loses love, for the sake of the song, for art & her pretty illusions, for a brotherhood as yet unfound in a widening desert, for Boo, Amandine & all the mystic waitresses of the sweet old night's hurrying realm, for the delicate, damp wood of shunned churches, for Faust's caustic payback, for the bitter eulogies spat in granite subsiding in the graveyard earth, for Crane's drunken leap into eternity, for Joyce's Hellenic blarney, for the wildcat bliss & Berryman's plunge from the bridge of sighs, for the beaten beats & the blind cult of rolling shadows, for the silent T in beret, for the mystics, the transients, the seekers of grails & fleeces Golden & Veedon, for a harbour dawn & her necklace of cafe pearls, for the ghost railways melting to their points of vanishing & for unimaginable cryptids & cool magic, for the motorpsychogeographical nightmares of the souls sick of their subterranean home, for Babes Of The Newtown, Troubadours & Captains of the disappearing dreamy ships fading from glory into the misty delta dusk, for fatty chips wrapped in greasy paper at the edge of the stoic wharf, for the bells hung on Christmas air, for the warehouses full of forgotten reminiscence on the edgelands of every unvisited city, for the falling of man & the men of The Fall, for Whitman's slippery road to everywhere, for the miraculous & subtle curses, for old mouldy prophets dragging their wriggling sacks of news to the mountain of unpublished literature, for Tom Maher, poet, & his whisky fire & songs sung with eyes shut tight in smoky bars, for Hallelujahs &

Hosannahs, for seasons in hell & slum poetry, for the blazing cross of our murderous litanies, for Degory, Red Jimmy & their charlatan monastery of nihilistic resignation, for the gaudy fairgrounds, for the Park Of Fumes & the contemplative benches of a cider starlight, for crab-scuttle rockpools under a barnacled pier, for toy cars pushed through dirt highways, toy trains whistling, for the boy's face close to the carpet to watch them grow real, for the tamped bass strings of crusted bluesmen, for the street holler & the One-Armed Bandit's stutter & prize, for cello sadness, for the entropic sluice of twilight & sunburned sorrow, for the Buddha quietude of stagnant waters, for the indefatigable rolling rivers slurring their psalm of sailors seaward, for memory & forgetting, for anger, light & joyful tears & heartbreakers, crestfallen, & pillow-wet, for Rosie & Old Santiago, for the dead, for circling birds at dusk & the mad warbling dawn, for the hobo dignity of ragged blankets & stolen milk, for fallen leaves blown to the suck of tides, for the wise fable & dishonest torch song, for the tenuous connections, the sinuous communications, encryptions & synchronizations of the leitmotif-strewn currents shuddering through time, for Ursula lost to those currents, for the blare of a jazz horn & pluck of borrowed guitar, for a red bicycle against a yellow wall, for Mackay & the sledging hill of snowy mud, for the ice-cream chiming headaches & creamy soda floats, for cropped lawns & silvered autumn trees, for the clink of fisherman's sails at rest, for the purest babble in the mouths of babies, for the gently rocking hammock in the empty ship's cabin, for the corroded iron temples of the frosted refinery, for the mislaid Folkmares of a psycho-pastoral Albion, for fever-dreaming commuters shackled to their desolate minds, for trimmed cricket squares & lemon tea, for dark rum & fairy-light dancing through a snug window, for the factories cooking themselves in death-smoke, for The Basement In The Sky & all who sailed in her, for Miles Ducat, DJ to the universal starry nightclub, for the secret doors & alleyways of trippy London's necropolis, for Sunday roasts & the sleepy purr of television, for hopscotch & skipping rhymes of tambourine delicacy, for a city viewed from a hill, for the park-bench memorial plaques & car-crash floral tributes, for the blood's river song, for Narcissus trembling at the shore of adoration, for the ripe fruit of the sinner, for an ashtray stuck to an unwiped table, for the gash of hate across the eyes of a weary, broken people, for the white whale of lust, for across the sea a poem looms unfinished, for whom the last bell tolls in tired pubs, for virtue undermined, for the tortoise not the hare, for the clown wiping a pancake smile from his downturned mouth with the resigned melancholy of a tethered dog, for the cobwebs in museums & the shameless mausoleums, for the spastic ballet of a crazy cranefly's jig, for father's firm hand engulfing a mug of hot chocolate & for oxtail broth staining his virgin bread, for this rescue-boat of life in which he is heading to no home, from which these cries sound out, for nothing really, for nothing but the unstoppable & all too human need to just finally cry out loud

*

& ye ancient no-gods, hear the sailor boy's prayer – O Lord & when I am finally safe, home, no not home, but safe somewhere, not this everywhere, this fat nothing pretending to be everything, only then & after years of sleep shall I turn my head again to the north star, free myself from the sinking sun, a-drooping so prettily there in the west - the glut of moons that rise to signal another shaking night, only then, in cover of pirate shadows, the new dream ship can start its engine, only then will I step frivolously on a firm path with the brilliance & terror of your fake starlight blinding – a new world, yes, for an old song to sing – find the song in the web of muses – the rules we bend to squeeze the last heartache from the singing railway's blues – it may still live in the throat of a found shell – it may sail twinned with a somnolent zephyr, kissing the beach with toffee-apple breath – there is no use in trying to hear it – it is not your song – it is like trust, or perhaps the forgiveness of a spurned love – it must be earned - amen

*

so – here we all are – the bad voices – black nor white, Baby nor Troubadour nor Captain – Jimmy Red nor pitiable priest – nothing surprises us, you & I, I'm nobody, everyone, everywhich - nowhere special but everywhere at once – Gog, Magog, Maldoror, Malatesta, Miles Ducat, Macintosh, Moriarty – heroic Theo, Ursula, perhaps even Old Maudit soon, what will his story be?

falsifier, unflinching stauncher of verity

& the madness always offering many voices but you hear just one – encounters with many men & women & mashing their personas to a pulp so as to best deal out the measured shots – a blended suicide malt, just add myself – ah, enough now, no more clues

low mass of a fallen church – holy ash of burned pulpit – tombstone mind, graveyard head, nobody to love – if we lied then it was our necessity – nothing happened the way we said, it is twisted, cloaked in sea mist – red bicycle against a yellow wall, black crows over dull ochre corn, amber grain, Albion's security blanket – it doesn't matter if anything really happened or not, just let the weary denouement commence – sorry if we implied a truthfulness – it is a curate's egg, this life of stardust, a Moebius strip, an onion of gradual recall – no insight until the crying's over & it is peeled right down to the flesh, until the Rizla hoodlum heart is exposed, naked, white, one leaf left nearing journal's end, epilogue, elegiac epitaph for an elephantine eulogy – the eponymous water's song obscured – & now I am St. Euclid, debased, *sans* pronoun personal – no more clues – wobbling up here on the taut line, below me the crowd whisper 'fall, fall' – but I make it ok, I'm alive, they applaud, I solemnly bow

& don't cry because boys don't – what use? - tears mean nothing to the sea – words are tears, let them flood & hide the heart in the deluge – words are old rain

& no of course I am not really out there adrift on a speck of lifeboat bobbing toward London town - & yet there I am – & no there was no storm, no memory warehouse or dockside visions, no message to the past, yet there they all are, preserved, exhibited

& yes of course there was no grand dream boat, ah but still, for a while at least, onward she sails – disintegration, returning to water - that much true enough

& I am not writing this but I will

& yes I will not listen to this song again & will not change a word because all is believable, all has the snag of faith - so say it out loud & proud the good old word-stuff, the best old whinges & excuses – say the words that get in the way of the story, rocks in a river eroding, leaving the flow unhindered – & what, pray tell, is the answer when we haven't a clue?

& meanwhile here's a parting glass, a welcoming gesture, a glimpse into the future – he sits at a table, unknown cafe, weak February sunlight, traffic agreeably purring – the book on the table blows open to a page, he reads it bored, plucks lines out of the morass – more poetry, then – he never learns – a dead poet witters afresh about putrid things, rotten rooms, wallpaper, shadows, an angel with open eyes, death, the same old compost

next time, he thinks, next time it will stop at the ending, next time the beginning will be the end – until then, he thinks, here's a last question to leave unanswered, a teaser,

537

he thinks – here at long last something to bring closure, to slam a heavy door – a blurt of silence, a muting, terminal catastrophic punctuation, an ending to begin with

*

& yes, somewhere beyond the elegant dissolution of the estuary's drab parade of forms, there a raging, choleric priest curses, pauses, curses again - then cups an ear to the swerve of tide – as if tuning his radar to the maddening serenity of Poseidon's sermon - & good old Red Jimmy swigs the last dreg & belches, cursing in turn this old pointless preacher's witchy, water-borne hollering – silhouetted on the ticking prow, spray salting his dark hair white, frantic gestures & runic utterances, symbol heavy, dolorous

the mist was deeper now, that Wagnerian, noisome fug that oozes from a thousand pin-pricks of nowhere whene'er a tragic finale beckons

ship sirens, gulls, the traffic & fairground bluster & bells are all muted here, the arcade's call to arms a dim reveille on a battered toy horn – major triad, nothing roused – but still always a wayward wind, with nothing else to do despite, strums the eager wave to loosen a tune

hear it as a lazy cello's counterpoint, feel the melodic ooze, tangled in a choir of drowning sailor's bawdy limerick – or else hear it as an anguished motif of creaks & screeches recurring in her complex symphonic machinery – listen close & long – for a great love has halted here

& when this tiresome epoch is blanketed at last in forgetful dust & when all our precious baubles & toys are rendered as futile as flint tools, quaint ephemera to future archaeologists, then & only then shall the tomb's curse be enacted – then we shall have our revenge from beyond the nameless paved-over sepulchres – a lone curse fired by the murderous history of our heart's toiling – let it shatter their peaceful wonder, let it be so, no more useless words, only a beery sigh

*

& with his determined little boat nearing the estuary mouth The Becalmed Troubadour is attentive & still, eyes closed, calmer now, almost resigned – he finds peace in a distant tap of wood on metal, new strange words jumbling in the crossed wires of the night's telegraph – & he dreams a resolution in the dominant sea's chordal shift & as his little splinter of boat slowly enters the river's understanding, he is entranced – for what?

for the sea, always the returning sea

& she is becoming river beneath him once more - & he can sense it, a sublime phasing, a motion akin to the drift from puberty to sadness – adding warp & woof to threadbare, irreclaimable, long-gone times – his hope acquiring substance & gravity, as if the beautiful past was waning by the second

& now, in that perfect light of the golden hour, the water is anything he wants her to be – it moves the boat forward, faster, revolving, spooling with the ebb – he looks over the side & he sees in her temperate sheen a familiar old face mirrored, somewhat older, somewhat kinder, gawping from her weightless yearning deeps, bearded by the gathered kelp & curdling spume in her dark pools

*

& again a far-off moony voice is heard - again? - perhaps, though it is definitely audible - & yes it is hard to discern amid the easy gulls' maturing cries - but he wants it to be there, within that sad old song, he needs to hear it now more than ever – deep in the oceanic retreat & pulse, urging his returning ghost ship onward

yes & listen, it *is* there, he is certain now - grumbling its abundance of madrigals in sweet disillusionment for all time – or until the lamenting river's final crescendo falls to the ocean's welcoming hug

he hears it sing yet feels no urge to share, for it will be heard by all in time, may it worry heaven

launching soft, now swollen, growing ever louder, that ancient clandestine sea voice so long hidden way behind her concluding innermost mystery, that post-script, that intimate & ultimately unsolvable clue - that unbroken siren chanting of her cryptic delta music

- end -

Basildon, Southend, London, Amsterdam (1978 - 2021)